ROSIE
HER INTIMATE DIARIES
Volume One
Volume Two: Young, Wild and Willing
Volume Three: Reckless Raptures

Available from New English Library

The Pearl volume 1
The Pearl volume 2
The Pearl volume 3
The Pearl omnibus
The Oyster volume 1
The Oyster volume 2
The Oyster volume 3
The Oyster volume 4
The Oyster volume 5
The Oyster omnibus
Rosie – Her Intimate Diaries volume 1
Rosie – Her Intimate Diaries volume 2
Rosie – Her Intimate Diaries volume 3
Rosie – Her Intimate Diaries volume 4

Rosie
Her Intimate Diaries

Volumes One, Two and Three

NEW ENGLISH LIBRARY
Hodder and Stoughton

Rosie 1 copyright © 1991 by
Glenthorne Historical Research Associates
Rosie 2 copyright © 1992 by
Glenthorne Historical Research Associates
Rosie 3 copyright © 1993 by
Glenthorne Historical Research Associates

Rosie 1 first published in Great Britain in 1991
by New English Library Paperbacks
Rosie 2 first published in Great Britain in 1993
by New English Library Paperbacks
Rosie 3 first published in Great Britain in 1993
by New English Library Paperbacks

This collected volume first published in Great Britain in 1994
by Hodder and Stoughton
a division of Hodder Headline PLC

A New English Library paperback

10 9 8 7 6 5 4 3 2 1

British Library C.I.P.
A C.I.P. catalogue record for this title is available
from the British Library

ISBN 0 340 62330 6

Printed and bound in Great Britain by
Cox & Wyman Ltd, Reading, Berks.

Hodder and Stoughton
A division of Hodder Headline PLC
338 Euston Road
London NW1 3BH

VOLUME ONE

Rosie
Her Intimate Diaries

Introduction

The Intimate Diary of Rosie D'Argosse is an authentic,
uncensored erotic odyssey of an Edwardian young lady. The
narrative may well shock and surprise the modern reader
for it uses frank and uninhibited language to tell of a
fascinating variety of sexual adventures which were
obviously greatly enjoyed by the writer of this hitherto secret
diary — for we do not readily associate these times with the
present day idea that sex can be fun. As many social
historians have noted, our picture of the age is one of
demure, downcast eyes, of maidenly tinkerings at the piano;
of portly, bewhiskered men of business standing solemnly
beside them; or perhaps of pale young curates delivering
lectures on the perils of the Sins of the Flesh to the humble
and ever-respectful lower classes.

But in reality there existed a gleeful alternative to the
ostentatious display of high-buttoned, waistcoated
worthiness and underground magazines from the 1890s and
early years of the twentieth century such as *Cremorne
Gardens* and *The Oyster* — known to the Edwardians as
'horn books' — reveal a totally different social world of
high-spirited, energetic sexual fulfilment peopled by
consenting adults that flourished behind the façade of public
respectability.

What is most certainly true is that the prudish and
hypocritical morality that prevailed during these stuffy times
ensured that no mention was ever made in print of any free-
and-easy attitudes to sexuality. For it has always been the
self-imposed duty of the upper and middle classes to protect

the lower orders from their own base instincts, and even as late as the 1920s, volunteers from the National Vigilance Association offered their services to the police to assist the all-important task of stamping out any kissing and cuddling in public parks and other 'zones of móral danger'! Perhaps even more extraordinary were the activities of the Social Purity and Hygiene Movement which promoted the notion of utmost sexual restraint amongst youngsters of the lower orders and actually set up night-time patrols to combat 'immoral behaviour' and report any unlucky courting couples to their parents or even the police!

Books like the script composed by Rosie D'Argosse provided a platform of fierce resistance to the guilt-ridden climate in which they first appeared. They also provided a much needed source of knowledge about sexuality at a time when probably even the majority of young people were ill-equipped to cope with masturbation, the universal first sexual experience of adolescence. For as unbelievable as it may now appear, as late as 1911 the Australian Dr John Clarke, an internationally recognised medical authority, could write of masturbation as 'the scourge of mankind' and clergymen and teachers would warn against the dire perils of self-abuse by assuring teenagers that the practise would undoubtedly lead to epilepsy, blindness and insanity.

Although written as a novel, Rosie's story is largely genuine and comprises true-life incidents in the lives of two radical 'wild women' whose heretical views such as their support for female suffrage and rejection of the stifling social conventions of the era horrified members of the ruling Establishment.

The idea that young women could actually lead independent lives and take their pleasures in the same way as their male counterparts scandalised even other women whose conditioning perhaps led them to accept their role as second-class human beings. In Rosie's story, Mrs Ogden, the headmistress at St Hilda's Academy, launches into a tirade against the philosophy of a new freedom for women, telling her girls that in marriage 'the normal relationship

6

between husband and wife must be of control and decision on the husband's side and deference and submission on that of the wife'. Sexuality, too, must be repressed at all times, adds Mrs Ogden, and during the unfortunate necessity of sexual intercourse, well-bred ladies are best advised 'to lie back and think of England'.

Such ideas were anathema to Geraldine Newman and Anna Barnes-Cooney, the two scribes who penned Rosie D'Argosse's adventures which was first published in Britain by a still anonymous group, 'The Friends of Venus and Priapus', in the summer of 1907.

But what do we actually know of our two writers? Without doubt, in her personal life, Geraldine was an unashamed libertine who enjoyed a great number of amorous liaisons. Many of these were with members of the notoriously 'fast' South Hampstead set, most notably with one of the leaders of the group, Sir Lionel Trapes, a wealthy connoisseur of gallant literature who introduced Geraldine to the delights of orgiastic club parties at his mansion in the fashionable North West London area of St John's Wood. Sir Lionel, incidentally, contributed regularly to the spectacularly rude illicit bi-monthly magazine *The Oyster* in the 1890s and may well have suggested a writing career to her.

Other men in Geraldine's life included the well-known Society *roué* Colonel Leon Goldstone of the Second West Oxfordshire Fusiliers; Lord Bresslaw, a member of the charmed circle of friends of the Prince of Wales (later King Edward VII); and the financier Sir Ronnie Dunn whose erotic escapades feature heavily in the popular 'Jenny Everleigh' series of saucy novels which were co-authored by Geraldine and her friends, the suffragette agitators Belinda Francine Kirkup and Heather O'Fluffert.

Anna Barnes-Cooney, whose finishing-school experiences mirror the story unfolded in the novel, led a quieter life. The daughter of an Indian Army officer, she spent her earliest years in New Delhi before being sent over to England to begin her education. And although the St Hilda's

7

Academy school in the text is a purely fictional establishment, Anna was fortunate enough to attend a genuinely progressive boarding-school in Sussex so there is every reason to suppose that many of the events described by her in the novel are based upon events to which she took part.

School stories were especially widely read during the Edwardian era — the exploits of Billy Bunter at Greyfriars made *The Magnet* one of the most popular boys' comics before the First World War and there were many schoolgirl tales too — though hardly penned in such delightfully bawdy terms as presented here.

Another point of interest is that when Rosie meets some of the swashbuckling young men of leisure, members of the *jeunesse dorée* who lounged their sybaritic way through lazy days and exciting nights, our authors introduce real people who must surely have given permission for their names to be used. Included amongst these are the insouciant Sir Andrew Stuck, an immensely rich young baronet whose wild weekend parties were the talk of fashionable London; the Marquis de Soveral, Portuguese Minister at the Court of St James and English Society's favourite diplomat; and the enterprising entrepreneur David Nash whose prescient decision to invest in the burgeoning cinematic industry made him a millionaire by 1921. Her erotic escapades with these gentlemen are carefully noted in book two of these intimate diaries which will be published towards the end of 1993.

This may well indicate that readers of Rosie D'Argosse believed themselves to be part of a loosely organised, like-minded group and that ordinary members of the general public would always be excluded from this close, private fraternity. It is true that the circulation of this illegally published novel was probably so exclusive that the use of real names became a daring indulgence, a kind of curious in-joke amongst the *cognoscenti*.

As Phyllida Barstow commented in her interesting book on a very important part of late Victorian and Edwardian social scene, *The English Country House Party*: 'Gorgeous

8

as butterflies, carefree and conscienceless, they gorged and gambled, rode and revelled, flirted and fornicated as they pleased. A hundred years later, knowing how completely that privileged world would vanish, only the dourest of killjoys could grudge them their half-century of fun.'

Harry Barr
Venice
November, 1991

9

When one burns one's bridges, what a nice fire
it makes.

Molly Farquhar

Foreword

Why should I not publish my diaries? In its pages there dwell far more interesting anecdotes about noted personages from across the entire social spectrum than appear in the censored, restrained recollections and apologies of our best-known and respected men of letters — though when I informed my greatest friend, Sir David Nash, the infamous Mayfair rake, of my intention 'to publish and be damned', his cheeky comment was that most of the letters in my manuscript would be French!

But I firmly believe that the truth should be told and I have not succumbed to the mealy-mouthed hypocrisy of the age by bowdlerising events. If I may be allowed to quote from a critique by Captain Philip Pelham, who has kindly reviewed this volume for that jolly little magazine, *The Oyster*: 'Rosie D'Argosse has charted her erotic career for the delectation of all lovers of gallant literature. Her lusty narrative, as liberal as her sensual appetite, is as joyous and unfettered as the forbidden fruits she so lovingly nurtures. As she eloquently recalls her graphic, undraped stories of licking and lapping, fucking and sucking, she takes the reader on a delicious and voluptuous voyage of endless arousal, a journey enhanced by the sweet, stirring sensations of Rosie's pulsating prose.'

One final word — some may be surprised that I have not hesitated to name those ladies and gentlemen with whom I have enjoyed the noble art of *l'arte de faire l'amour* during the last four years. Let me assure any concerned reader that all who have been named have given me their express permission to mention their roles in my intimate experiences. Perhaps surprisingly, none have flinched from what some may feel is scandalous exposure and, indeed, even my dear old uncle Lord Gordon MacChesney has been eager to refresh my memory about certain rather recherché events that took place down at Argosse Towers down in the heart of the Sussex countryside.

Rosie D'Argosse

1

Early Days

I had the greatest of good fortune in growing up in our family seat in the heart of the South Down country of West Sussex. Argosse Towers is an imposing mansion that stands in delightful surrounds some three miles from the sleepy little market town of Midhurst.

The characteristic Downland landscape is a perfect panorama of moulded promontories and ample spaces. Gracefully rounded hills run into each other in gently curving lines, and in the distance the far horizon is shut out by vague blue hills, and across to the east lies the Wealden plain, divided by dark hedges and brightened by the red and grey roofs of the villages, the greenery of wide woods and fields, the purple of plough-lands and the yellow acres of corn.

There is little I need to say of my life up to the day of my sixteenth birthday, which took place on the twenty-second of June, in the year nineteen hundred and five. I was happy enough, to be sure, for my Papa and Mama were the kindest parents one could wish for, but I did not see them as frequently as I really wanted. You see, dear reader, Papa enjoyed a most successful career as Permanent Second Secretary in the Foreign Office. This meant that he had to spend weekdays in London and frequently Mama would journey up to our London house in Belgrave Square and accompany him to important Government receptions for visiting dignitaries and the like.

Mama also travelled with Papa when he felt it necessary to go abroad to spend time on delicate diplomatic business. During these more prolonged parental leaves of absence, my younger brother Jonathan and myself were left in the charge of my Mama's bachelor brother, Lord Gordon MacChesney, who supervised the running of our house — a task he relished for (though it was not until shortly after my sixteenth birthday that I knew it) my nice Uncle Gordon loved to fuck Sarah and Alice, the prettiest of our maidservants and to have his cock sucked by young Polly, the daughter of the local blacksmith.

More of Uncle Gordon shortly; for the moment let me state that my education was first at the famous Trippett College For Young Ladies in Chichester, but my final schooldays, before I left Sussex for finishing-school in Switzerland (and I write of these uninhibited days later), were spent at St Hilda's Academy for Young Ladies in Devon. My brother Jonathan, I should add, had followed my father's footsteps and had gone to Eton after attending a private preparatory school near our home.

And indeed Jonathan figures in the first incident of intimacy that I ever witnessed at first hand which took place on a glorious afternoon just a few days after this all-important sixteenth birthday.

I had decided to take myself off for a walk to Letchmore Woods. The weather was perfect for such an activity. Although it was one of the hottest days so far of a glorious summer, the air of the Downs is always fresh and pure. It has a quality which elevates the spirits and even on the warmest day you will almost always find a soft, sighing zephyr to cool the mopping brow.

So I ambled across the springy turf, idly considering what games we might play at my birthday tea, which was being postponed to the following weekend in order to allow Papa and Mama to attend for they had been in London since Tuesday. I had invited five of my best friends, Sheena, Katie, Gillian, Mary and Susie to the feast and I was looking forward eagerly to the party.

16

All was peaceful and serene as I made my way to the top of a knoll and I had decided to lie down on the dry grass and study a chapter of *Great Expectations* by Charles Dickens, for Miss Caughey, my English teacher, had set this book for us to peruse during the summer holidays and we would be tested on our knowledge of it when we returned to St Hilda's in the autumn. It should have been a perfect place to read Mr Dickens for no noise comes from the plain but the occasional lowing of cattle from Farmer Massey's fields or the musical tinkle of a sheep-bell as the flock moves along a slope.

But this afternoon this rural tranquillity was broken by what appeared to be sounds of some kind of human activity from behind a large bush that grew half way down the small hill on the opposite side to that which I had just climbed. From my position I imagined that I could hear three young, boyish voices and, as I was curious to discover what they were doing behind the bush, I scrambled up and walked quietly down the hillock to find out exactly what was going on.

The voices were now becoming clearer and the first voice I recognised belonged to Alfred, our page-boy, who was six months younger than me. Then I made out the dulcet tones of my brother Jonathan who himself would soon be fifteen. But as I drew nearer I realised that the third voice was in fact that of a girl — and unless I was gravely mistaken it was young Sarah, the prettiest of our maidservants, who was at least a year, if not more, older than me, who was larking about with the boys behind the bush.

Now I could clearly make out the words which were interspersed with a great deal of excited giggling. 'Look at my willie, Sarah, it's swelled up so big,' I heard my brother say excitedly. 'Won't you play with it like you did with Alfred's?'

'Why, Master Jonathan, you naughty boy, how rude you are,' scolded Sarah in a tone of mock severity, 'though I must admit you've got a very thick prick for so young a lad.'

17

'It's not so big as mine though, is it?' claimed Alfred. 'And I bet he can't spurt out as much spunk as I can.'

'No, probably not, but let's have a little contest to make sure. Come over here, Alfred, and stand next to Jonathan and I'll see what I can do,' said the lewd girl.

I was shocked by this bawdy talk for though I had secretly read copies of *The Oyster* which Papa kept locked in his private cabinet, I had never actually heard, let alone seen, anything like this! So you may well imagine that I was fairly trembling with excitement as I dropped to my knees behind the trio and peered round to see what Sarah had in mind.

Well now, I had surmised that I might see something I had never seen before, but I was shocked by the lewd scene which began to unfold before my very eyes.

Alfred and Jonathan had taken off their shirts and trousers and were standing naked as Sarah pulled off her clothes and (to her credit) busied herself folding them into a neat little pile, though naturally my gaze was turned immediately towards the two boys whose tools had grown into enormous flesh poles, hard and stiff and topped off at the end by uncapped ruby-coloured helmets. You must remember, of course, that this was the first time I had seen an erect prick in all its manly glory. I noted that neither Alfred nor Jonathan had more than a light covering of hair around the root of their cocks, but when I turned my head round to look at Sarah, a sharp intake of breath escaped my lips. For her love mound was covered by a veritable thatch of curly black hair, far thicker than the silky covering of down which lay between my own legs. I looked on in breathless excitement as the lusty girl stepped forward towards the boys and grasped their rampant shafts in her hands.

She proceeded to rub their staffs up until they stood like two bursting truncheons high against their bellies. 'Dear me,' she laughed, 'it's very hard to judge these fine specimens. Your prick is longer all right, Alfred, but I do think Master Jonathan's is just a little bit thicker. Now let's see how much cream I can coax out of you two beauties.'

18

I watched entranced as Sarah grasped the two red-helmeted cocks and continued to frig them vigorously as the boys yelped like two puppies with the sheer pleasure of being tossed off by this uninhibited girl, who appeared to be equally aroused from the gleam I saw shining in her eyes. Within a very short time the young scamps began to spend and the first spurtings of white juice shot out of their pricks like miniature fountains. Both boys produced substantial streams of sperm but I was proud to see that my young brother's emission was just as copious as that of his older companion.

'Oh, that was really super,' sighed Alfred, as he looked down to see his staff slowly subsiding into limpness, 'but I would so love to experience the real thing which I bet is even nicer.'

'So would I,' chipped in Jonathan eagerly. 'Please let me fuck you, Sarah. You can see that I'm quite capable of it.'

Sarah burst out laughing. 'I've seen that you both are, Master Jonathan, and I'm equally sure that I'd enjoy it too. But I haven't got time today and anyhow you've both just spent by yourselves.

'Well, with just a little help from me,' she added modestly. 'Don't be greedy, boys. After all, you've both been tossed off and you've had a good look at my titties and my bum. That will have to suffice you for the present. Come on now, we'd better get dressed because if we don't get back soon, Alfred and I will be missed at the house.'

The boys looked very disappointed but obeyed her and slowly began to pull on their clothes. 'It's a jolly shame for you that girls can't toss themselves off like boys,' remarked Alfred.

Sarah looked at him with a grin. 'What do you mean? Why, don't you know that we can enjoy ourselves without anyone else just like you?'

'Gosh, can girls spend by themselves too? I didn't know that,' confessed Jonathan shyly.

'Of course we can, you silly boy. Shall I tell you how I like to play with myself?'

'Yes, please,' they chorused, and I could feel my face turn

19

scarlet as I felt embarrassed that anyone, let alone my young brother, should know of my secret pleasure. However, eavesdroppers seldom hear any good of themselves, as the old saying has it, and besides, this would constitute a sufficient punishment for my admittedly inadvertent spying upon this randy scene.

'Well now,' Sarah said, with a wicked smile playing around her lips. 'My favourite is at night just after I've had a nice warm bath. I then stand in front of the bathroom mirror and slowly dry myself with a towel. I close my eyes and imagine that in fact there's a handsome young man running the towel over my breasts and between my legs, making my body shine with a silken glow.

'Then I open my eyes and I look at my dark, thick cunney hair which curls round my crack. I let my hand slide down and let my fingers move lovingly around there and play around my moist pussey. When I'm ready I part my pale pink cunney lips with the tip of one finger and begin to rub myself off which makes me feel good all over.

'When I find my clitty stiffening up I scuttle into my bedroom and lie on my bed with my hand mirror and ladies' comforter (*a dildo − Editor*) which cost me four shillings (*twenty pence! − Editor*) at Dr Bucknall's Surgical Stores in Chichester last year. By setting up the mirror between my legs I can see myself playing with my pussey. Then I separate my cunney lips and can see right inside my juicy damp cunt. I'm getting really excited now and all my juices are flowing as I push two and then three fingers in and wiggle them about to get myself really wet. It's time now for Dr Bucknall's imitation cock which I pick up and rub up and down my slit which tingles now with anticipation of a good fucking.

'After a few moments I push the dildo inside my cunt and then gently take almost all of it out. Oooh, just thinking about how lovely it feels is making my knickers wet!'

Truth to tell, this racy narrative was also making my pussey damp and I just couldn't stop my hand from diving down to start stroking myself as Sarah continued: 'I play

20

like this for a while and gradually pick up speed, twiddling my titties with one hand as I push my dildo in and out faster and faster, deeper and deeper until wooosh! A lovely feeling explodes in my pussey and sends lovely waves all over me as my love juice now flows out of my sopping crack. I used to do this quite a lot but since Lord Gordon's been here I don't need a dildo because I've got his big thick tool ready and waiting whenever we feel like a little fuck. He's already told me to come to his bedroom this evening so I know that I won't be getting much sleep tonight.'

'Isn't Lord Gordon too old to have hard-ons?' asked Alfred, to which Sarah gave an immediate answer. 'Not at all, young Alfred, that's something else you and Jonathan should know. People aren't past it by the time they've reached forty. Why, Lord Gordon's sixty-five and he can still fuck like a rattlesnake.'

By now they had all finished dressing, but I could see that Sarah's story had excited Alfred and Jonathan so much that their cocks were fairly bursting out of their trousers. Sarah giggled as she too saw the huge bulges in front of the lads' trousers and she reached across to pat them. 'I can see that you were certainly hanging on to every word,' she chuckled, 'and that you can't wait to have me finish you off. Well, let's get back to the house and I'll see what I can do after tea. Be in your room at five o'clock, Master Jonathan, and I'll come to you just as soon as I can.'

'That's not fair, I won't be able to join in,' protested Alfred, heatedly.

'Don't worry, I'll see to you after supper,' Sarah promised, as they walked down the hill towards our house, leaving me feeling extraordinarily frustrated as I scrambled up to my feet, flushed with all the exciting images which were spinning through my brain.

When I followed them back a half hour later, I could hardly contain the strong feeling of pleasurable anticipation which seeped throughout my entire body. What was so especially exciting was the fact that Uncle Gordon's bedroom was next door to my own, and, unknown to him, when I was younger, Papa had a hidden peephole fashioned into the adjoining wall between the two rooms. This work was carried out so that the nurse who slept next door could keep an eye on her charge without disturbing me, for as a child I was a very light sleeper. Tonight though, this secret peephole would afford me my first view – and a grandstand one at that – of sexual copulation and I could hardly wait until ten o'clock which was the earliest time I could go to bed without arousing any suspicion of feeling unwell or getting into mischief of some sort or another.

At dinner I could hardly take my eyes off Jonathan, who looked terribly pleased with himself and I wondered enviously whether Sarah had helped him to make his first journey across the Rubicon just a couple of hours before. You lucky boy, I thought, there is no man I really want at Argosse Towers to rid me of my tiresome virginity. If only Jimmy lived with us instead of in London. I should explain here that Jimmy was the Honourable James Harold Fortescue Horobin, second son of Viscount and Viscountess Sevenoaks, who were amongst my parents' oldest friends. Jimmy was eighteen and had just gained a place at Cambridge University to read English although his father had hoped that Jimmy would follow his footsteps and take up a commission in the Grenadier Guards. More of Jimmy shortly, dear reader, for very soon he enters this story.

To return to my tale, Jonathan had gone to bed at half past nine and at the stroke of ten, I put down the book I was reading and walked across to my uncle who was engrossed in his copy of the *Sporting Life*.

'Good night, Uncle, I am feeling a little tired so I shall go to bed now.'

'Are you m'dear? Well, have an early night and you'll feel fully refreshed tomorrow,' he replied, and he gave me a chaste goodnight peck on my cheek as I moved away from his chair.

Now, Uncle Gordon rarely retired before midnight. But as I fully expected, on this occasion I heard him climb the stairs and enter his bedroom not more than a quarter of an

22

hour later! Five minutes after I heard the door close, I glued my eye to the peephole and was very soon rewarded. Uncle Gordon had taken off all his clothes except his vest and undershorts and he was sitting on the bed looking impatiently at his door.

Neither of us had long to wait for very soon I heard a knocking on his door and Uncle Gordon sprang up and rushed across the room to open the door. In popped Sarah, clad in a dressing-gown and slippers and as soon as Uncle had whisked her in he bolted the door behind her. 'No one saw you, did they?' he asked, anxiously. 'No, of course not,' she said. 'And even if they did, it's none of their business 'cos it's more than their job's worth to peach on us. After all, who would Lady D'Argosse believe if such a story were told to her? The tittle-tattle of servants of Lord MacChesney, her own blood brother?'

'Don't bank on it,' said Uncle Gordon, gloomily, 'because whatever else she maybe, my sister Cynthia is nobody's fool and she would probably believe a servant's tale rather than any explanation from me in such circumstances. Mind, it would be me who would get into hot water rather than you if we were found out as she would insist that I seduced you.'

Sarah giggled and replied: 'And so you did, Lord Gordon. I was a good little girl till I met you.'

'Go on with you, m'dear, you have had more pricks in your pussey than I've backed winners at Sandown Park races,' said Uncle, joining in her laughter.

'I must almost be a virgin then because your bookmaker sends you a box of cigars every month and he wouldn't do that if you were a lucky punter!'

'Ha, ha, ha! No, I don't suppose he would, just like I wouldn't give you a five pound note every week if your clever little cunney didn't tease my old cockie so deliciously, you naughty miss.'

This teasing badinage continued as Sarah and Uncle began to kiss and fondle each other on the bed. Sarah slipped off her dressing-gown to reveal that she wore only a thin nightdress underneath it. She rolled up Uncle Gordon's vest and pulled it over his head whilst he repaid the compliment by doing the same to her nightdress. The happy couple then dissolved into a loving embrace and my uncle's hand cupped one of her firm, full bosoms as they freely exchanged a most passionate kiss. My little titties began to tingle as I saw him squeeze Sarah's white globes, first one and then the other, and I rubbed my own nipples up to little red stalks as Uncle Gordon's lips broke away from Sarah's to move downwards to suck on the rosy red stalks that topped her sinuously ripe breasts.

Sarah's right hand now strayed to Uncle Gordon's lap and her fingers dived into the slit in his drawers to release his naked prick from its uncomfortable prison. Beforehand I could see the outline of a great bulge straining against the material of his pants, but I must confess that I was absolutely staggered by the tremendous size of my uncle's todger.

Though till this afternoon the only male organs I had seen had been limp and soft; compared even to the stiffstanders of Jonathan and Alfred I had viewed only hours before, the upstanding length and girth of Uncle Gordon's erect penis astonished and frankly frightened me. I judged its veiny thickness to be five inches in circumference whilst I estimated the veiny staff which Sarah was stroking with such eager relish to be at least nine inches long. There was no way that such a monster could be accommodated in my tiny crack and surely Sarah would be unable to take in this huge staff in her cunney even if she had already stretched her slit from previous fuckings?

I watched with fascination as Sarah leaned backwards and my uncle clambered over her. But he did not lay upon her but knelt down with his knees pressing the sides of her beautiful body. He then moved himself forward so that his prick, which still stood up as high as a flagpole, was positioned just an inch away from Sarah's mouth. This puzzled me until Sarah grasped hold of the veiny shaft with one hand and cupped his hairy pink ballsack with the other and I wondered as to what on earth was she planning to do with his throbbing prick.

In just a few seconds my question was answered for Sarah licked her lips and encircled the purple helmet of Uncle Gordon's cock with her tongue, jamming down his foreskin before taking the smooth knob between her lips. She sucked hard, taking at least a third of his rigid rod into her mouth while her hands played with his dangling balls. I could hear the sound of her tongue slurping round his pulsating pole before letting it out of her mouth. She then began to lick the swollen staff, drawing her tongue from the base right up to the gleaming knob. He clutched at her hair and shuddered violently as the lewd minx circled her tongue all round the fleshy red dome, washing his knob so sensuously that a hoarse groan of sheer delight escaped from my uncle's throat.

'Suck me off, Sarah! My balls are bursting with spunk!' he grunted, a request which she seemed happy with which to comply, for she took hold of his thick prick and with a sharp intake of breath somehow managed to cram all but the last inch or two of his enormous shaft into her mouth. She held his huge cock, lightly in her hands as he moved his hips backwards and forwards, releasing much of his rigid rod from her mouth before pushing it back in again. Sarah sucked away vigorously, keeping her lips taut on his length, kissing, suckling, licking and lapping as she took him into her mouth in long rolling sucks.

She continued to suck until with a cry of 'Here it comes!' he sent a stream of jism down Sarah's throat and she gulped down as much as she could of his copious emission. Despite all her efforts, however, Uncle Gordon pumped so much love juice into her mouth that some of his jism spilled out from between her lips and onto her chin. Sarah obviously enjoyed the taste of his libation for she rubbed his twitching shaft furiously to coax out every last drain of love juice from it.

'Oh my word, Sarah,' panted my uncle, as he removed her hand from his now deflated tool: 'I do believe that you are truly the finest fellatrix outside London.'

Sarah looked at him with a puzzled expression. 'Fellatrix?

What's that when it's at home? There's no need to go calling me names just because I'm a simple country girl and not one of your high and mighty ladies in society.'

'No, no, m'dear, you misunderstand me,' said my uncle, hastily. 'I assure you that I paid you a compliment. Fellatio is the posh name for oral sexual intercourse and a fellatrix is a girl who performs the noble art.'

'Fellatio, you say? Well, that may be how you say it in London but down here people simply call it good old-fashioned cocksucking.'

'Good enough, my girl, why don't you show me again just how well you do it?'

'All right then,' she agreed and kissed the tip of his tool and drawing back the foreskin to uncover his smooth round knob. But despite taking it into her mouth and licking it all over, my uncle's prick obstinately refused to swell up even when Sarah took the limp shaft between her lips and nibbled away with her white little teeth.

She took the soft tube of flesh out of her mouth and said: 'Oh dear, oh dear, Lord Gordon, I really thought you wanted to fuck me.'

'I do, my dear, of course I do. I just can't raise a cockstand just now,' he replied, gloomily.

Her face brightened. 'Don't worry, darling, I'll stick some hot mustard up your arse. That's the cure for a drooping prick we use round these parts.' Not surprisingly, my uncle blanched at even the mention of this famous old Sussex remedy. [*Whilst not endorsing this unusual and rather drastic recipe for treating impotence, modern sex therapists such as Professor Zwaig note that such an application as mentioned here can certainly do no harm to the patient – Editor*]. 'That's very kind of you, Sarah,' said my uncle, faintly, 'but I think I know an easier way for you to make my poor old prick rise up again.'

'What do I have to do?' she asked.

'Smack my arse with your slipper,' he instructed. 'A good whacking rarely fails to give me a hard-on.'

Sarah shrugged and picked up her slipper as my uncle

26

turned over onto his tummy and stuck out his dimpled bum cheeks, opening his legs slightly so that both Sarah and I had a god view of his hanging ballsack. Sarah passed her hand lightly along his bare bottom and then lifted her arm. Thwack, thwack, thwack! She laid into him with a will and I could see his posterior change its hue to a warm, pinky tint. Watching her chastise his wriggling backside made me tingle with arousal. An awakening interest crept into my loins and I closed my eyes for a moment to allow a blissful familiar feeling radiate out from my dampening pussey to my titties and then all over my entire body.

At this point Sarah dropped the slipper and began slapping Uncle Gordon's arse with the palm of her hand. This obviously excited him for he gasped: 'Yes, yes, crack away, Sarah! A-h-r-e! How invigorating! Cut away, my girl!' Obediently she struck a few more blows with quite a considerable force. Then she passed her arm around his waist to see whether her hard work had achieved the desired result. He moved across the bed and lo and behold, what a difference Sarah's spanking had made to his previously flaccid penis! It was now standing up stiffly to attention in a rampant state of erection. He drew back his foreskin himself making its purple helmet swell and bound in his hand.

Sarah looked lasciviously at his gigantic stiffstander and murmured, 'Go on, Gordon, stuff that big donger in my juicy cunney.' He needed no second bidding as she lay on her back, her legs slightly apart — in a trice he was on top of her, his hands roving over those lovely alabaster-white breasts, moving his hands over the large pink aureoles and raised red nipples. He gently squeezed these succulent little cherries up to perfection as Sarah's body arched like a sleek cat as my uncle kissed her knees, her calves and her inner thighs, his hands all the while massaging those divinely full breasts.

She now parted her legs further, exposing her luxuriant crisp bush and for a moment I could see her protruding cunney lips before his head buried itself between her legs

27

and I could hear (though not actually see) him licking and lapping around her open crack.

My own cunt cried out with unfulfilled desire as Uncle Gordon continued to suck and play with Sarah's slit and my mound was on fire as he now lifted himself over the trembling girl and mounted her, guiding his enormous ramrod inside her squelchy cunt. Directing every last inch of his shaft snugly inside her cunney, Sarah now closed her thighs so that his cock was well and truly trapped in her nookie. Uncle Gordon could hardly pump in and out because Sarah's strong cunney muscles were gripping him so tightly, but he had no complaint as she started to grind her hips round, which massaged his prick quite exquisitely. I could imagine his hard pulsating penis throbbing powerfully inside her love channel and when he clutched Sarah's plump bum cheeks and smack his lips over one of her engorged stalky nipples, my pussey became wetter and wetter as I wriggled my hand between my legs and rubbed my pussey as hard as possible.

Now Sarah shifted her thighs and as the pressure around his pole eased, he began to drive wildly in and out of her delicious slit, fucking at such speed that I marvelled at his athleticism. 'Oooh, Gordon, you fat-cocked fucker, you've made me spend already — Oooh! I'm going off again! — Oooh! Oooh! Oooh! AAAH! What a glorious spend! Come on, darling, fill my cunney with spunk!' she panted as she writhed in ecstasies of delight — for the lucky Sarah was being brought off time and again and she worked herself off to a huge orgasm as the fierce momentum of my uncle's fucking sent her cunt into new paroxysms of pleasure.

For the grand finale, she brought her legs up against the small of his back, humping the lower half of her body upwards to meet the violent strokes of his raging member which shafted in and out, in rhythm with the ever-quickening jerks of her hips. The contraction of her sopping pussey now sent Uncle Gordon to the brink and with one final thrust he melted into her as he reached his climax, spilling spasm after spasm of love juice into her vitals as she herself

28

shuddered into an explosive spend and even my own now saturated pussey sent out delicious waves of pleasure crackling throughout my entire body.

Sarah and Uncle Gordon were equally happy with the result of their exertions. 'What a splendid old cock you have there, my lord,' said Sarah, her bosoms rising and falling as she lay gasping for breath. 'My God, you filled me up completely which is more than most young chaps can do, that's for sure, with that big old cock. It's as they say, the old fiddles play the best tunes.'

'Thank you very much, m'dear, but I always say that it's not the age of the ship that counts, it's the way the captain steers his ship,' he replied modestly, 'and let me add that you have an absolutely divine love channel, Sarah. It must be the prettiest little cunt I have ever fucked. I just love the way my cock slides against its wet, velvety walls. Truly it must have been a cunt such as yours that the Scots poet David Taylor had in mind when he wrote:

> How oft I've sworn to my true love
> The world no sight can show,
> To match her locks, her lips divine,
> Her bosoms hills of snow.
> But yet I find myself forsworn,
> Two lips I have beheld;
> Still lovelier on this happy morn,
> A mount that hose excelled!
> Her bosom boasts no swell so fair
> No tints that these eclipse;
> Her head had no such jet black hair,
> Nor such enchanting lips!

'Thank you, Gordon, that's really lovely. Would you write that down for me please?' said Sarah, snuggling up beside him. 'Now, I suppose that another little fuck is out of the question?'

' 'Fraid so, my love, my old soldier won't stand up again for another couple of hours at least, not even if you tried

29

out your peculiar idea about shoving mustard up my arse, which in any case sounds jolly uncomfortable, if you don't mind my saying so. Look, you can stay here all night, can't you?'

'Yes, of course I can, only we won't be able to have a lie-in. I must be up early to begin my work. If I'm not downstairs by half past six, Mrs Callaghan the housekeeper will come into my room and see that I've spent the night elsewhere,' she warned.

'Gad, that would never do. But don't worry, I'll set the alarm on my bedside clock for six a.m. I don't mind waking up so early, especially because my prick will be standing up nice and stiff again by the morning.'

'Then you had better set the alarm for half past five,' said Sarah, with an infectious giggle which set Uncle Gordon laughing and at this juncture I leaned back from the peephole. This erotic encounter had been most pleasurable to watch but I positively ached for a stiff prick of mine to slide into my cunney. Then suddenly I had a brainwave — whilst it would take too long for a letter to reach my boyfriend Jimmy Horobin in London, and in any case I would be terrified of my *billet-doux* being seen by someone else, I could always contact him first thing in the morning, for last year Papa had a telephone installed. Hurrah for Mr Alexander Graham Bell! I rejoiced as I settled down in my bed to dream of what sensual joys Jimmy Horobin could offer me.

2

My First Fuck

I was too excited to sleep well and I was only in a doze when I was fully woken by the shrill sound of Uncle Gordon's alarm clock. I heaved myself up to look at my watch — for dawn had already broken — and saw that it was only just after half past five, far too early of course to telephone Jimmy! But were my uncle and Sarah already engaged in a further bout of copulation? I went over to the peephole and fastened my eyes upon the couple who were entwined together in what was to me a new fashion.

Sarah was standing naked on the floor but leaning over the bed with her elbows on the mattress. The rounded contours of her backside jutted out and waggled invitingly as Uncle Gordon, who was also quite nude, suavely smoothed his hands over the quivering springy globes of her lovely derriére. He then took hold of these delicious rondeurs and parted them as he carefully positioned the stiff shaft of his penis between her two lovely bottom cheeks until the tip of his knob was touching the crinkled little entrance of her bum-hole.

'H-a-r!' grunted Sarah. 'I think your pego is a bit too big for bottom-fucking, darling, unless you can grease it well with some pomade.' (*This was a perfume oil used to make the hair smooth and shiny — Editor*).

'No problem, my dear, I have a bottle to hand. You must forgive me, for I should not have to be reminded to oil my

31

tool before buggering you,' he cried, as he rushed over to the dressing-table and proceeded to lubricate his shaft until it fairly glistened in the sunlight that now poured into the room.

He repositioned himself behind her and sure enough this time his cock slid freely inside her, quickly enveloping itself between the in-rolling cheeks of Sarah's mouth-watering arse. I noticed that Uncle Gordon pushed in slowly at first and he considerately asked Sarah is she could take more of his thick staff. 'Oh yes, yes, don't stop now!' she gasped and so he worked his shaft in and out of her uninhibitedly, pushing his whole body forwards and backwards, making her delicious buttocks smack loudly against his belly as he heaved away.

'My cock's right up your bottom, Sarah!' he cried out as he leaned over her to fondle and weigh her lush breasts and to diddle her juicy pussey. She turned her head round to meet his lips with her own and as they kissed I could see from the provocative wiggling of her posterior there was no doubt how much she was enjoying his thick prick pounding in and out of her gorgeous backside.

'This is too wonderful, oh, keep rotating your arse, Sarah and I'll shoot my spunk into you,' my uncle groaned, as the aroused girl mashed her bum-cheeks against his belly. 'Now, Gordon, give it to me!' she commanded, and he needed little effort to obey, for within seconds, with a tremendous jerk of his hips, he flooded her rear dimple with such vibrant thrusts that I could almost see the ripples of orgasmic delight that ran down Sarah's spine as she achieved a superb climax. As she artfully pushed her bottom back and forth, spout after spout of creamy spunk lathered her puckered little orifice as Uncle Gordon pumped his jism he groaned with joy.

He withdrew his still-stiff staff from her arse with an audible 'pop' and Sarah turned round to grasp his rammer which glistened wetly from his own copious emission. 'You know, I think there is still some life in your old cock,' she said, thoughtfully, rubbing the shaft between her palms until it stood up almost as proudly as before it entered her nether regions. 'Why, it looks good enough to eat, don't you think?'

'Suck it and see,' said my uncle, hoarsely, as Sarah knelt down in front of him and began to lick the spunk off his cock. She gave his prick a loving squeeze and uncapped the mushroom shaped crown which she greedily gobbled into her mouth. Uncle Gordon eased in a further three inches or so between her lips and Sarah sucked noisily upon her sweetmeat. I noticed with interest how she varied her sucking with long lingering licks along the underside of his now fully erect penis, a technique I had only read about in the pages of *The Oyster* (*perhaps the most spectacularly rude underground magazine of these times written by members of the notorious South Hampstead set and only recently republished in five volumes by the New English Library, London and Carroll and Graf, New York — Editor*). But now I could see the technique actually performed and in great style as Sarah switched to nibbling the rosy dome of Uncle Gordon's throbbing prick with her teeth. Then she circled the base of his shaft as she sucked in almost all of his twitching tool and this brought Uncle Gordon to the brink of ecstasy. An aching cry of release escaped from his throat as, arching his back, he jetted spurt after spurt of sticky semen into Sarah's waiting mouth as she sucked and swallowed again and again until the last drops of his manly essence had been discharged.

'Oh, I did enjoy that,' said Sarah, as she kissed Uncle Gordon's gleaming shaft which was now losing its hardness and had visibly shrunk back into its normal flaccid state. 'I must say that your sperm has a really tasty salty flavour to it. Now then, what would you say to a little fuck?'

'Hello, little fuck,' he said, wittily. 'And that's just about all I could say, Sarah, you wicked minx, it'll take me all day to recover as it is.'

'You can always try the mustard-up-the-arse treatment,' she giggled, and for a reply he smacked her lovely bum-cheeks in mock anger. 'I don't think so, my girl. Anyhow, you'd better get back to your room before Mrs Callaghan comes storming upstairs to find out why you're not already at work.'

'Gosh, you're right, I'd better go,' said Sarah, slipping on her dressing-gown and slippers. I was later to discover that Uncle Gordon was also fucking our housekeeper every Tuesday and Thursday evenings which was another reason he wanted to keep secret his tryst with Sarah — but that is another story which will have to be told at another time.

As the stimulating show next door was obviously ended, I rushed back to my bed, threw up my nightgown and plunged my fingers into my fur-lined little pussey which was already wet through with excitement. I only had to jerk my fingers in and out for a few seconds before my girlish cunney juices gushed down my thighs as I brought myself off.

After my morning bath I joined Jonathan and Uncle Gordon at the breakfast table. I only required a simple meal of orange juice followed by tea and toast. Jonathan, too, ate sparingly, for he was going to play tennis at the Nettletons' with his school-friend Frederick and some other young fellows. We were fortunate enough to have Colonel and Mrs Nettleton as neighbours for their son Charles was an excellent player who won the All-England Championship at Wimbledon last year and he was kind enough to coach the local lads who expressed an interest in this game which is fast growing in popularity. (Why I take the time to mention this fact will become clear shortly.)

In contrast, through, my uncle Lord Gordon MacChesney munched his way through porridge, a generous plate of kedgeree (*a favourite Edwardian dish of rice, cooked flaked fish and hard-boiled eggs — Editor*) together with lashings of buttered toast plastered with Mrs Callaghan's admittedly delicious home-made strawberry jam. Obviously, my randy relative needed to refresh himself after all the indoor exercise he had taken and indeed I was soon to learn that the devotions at the altar of Venus and Priapus can be most tiring and the body should always be revived by good food

34

and drink after an enervating stint of sucking and fucking.

It was time now to telephone Jimmy who was hopefully in London. To secure total privacy I went to my parents' bedroom and locked the door behind me. I recognised the voice of Miss Maggs, our local telephonist, when she told me that she would try to make the long distance connection stràightaway, and I hoped that, unlike many country operators, she did not listen in to people's conversations. However, Miss Maggs achieved the link with London without any trouble and I prayed that Jimmy would be at home as I gave my name to the servant who answered the telephone at the other end. I asked to speak to Jimmy and I almost jumped for joy when he asked me to hold the line for just one moment.

'Hello Rosie, what a lovely surprise to hear from you,' said Jimmy, cheerfully, when he came to the phone. 'How are you all down in the country?'

'I'm very well, Jimmy, but I am not ashamed to admit that I am very lonely. Papa and Mama are away, Jonathan is out playing tennis and Uncle Gordon is not much company for me. Would it be possible for you to come and visit me? We could spend lots of time together, just the two of us.' I was tempted to add a remark of perhaps a more intimate nature but who knows who might be listening in either here or at Jimmy's house — nevertheless, I added: 'I would love to take a walk in the woods with you and have a picnic lunch. The weather is wonderful today, blue skies and lots of golden sunshine.'

'It's very tempting,' he said, with an eagerness that broke through the distance between us. 'I was going to watch the cricket match between Eton and Harrow this afternoon (*a great Society event — Editor*) but as luck would have it my parents are also away so I'm just going to skip the cricket and take the first train down to Midhurst.'

I squealed with delight. 'Oh, how marvellous! I'll have the coachman meet you at the station. You'll manage to get the eleven o'clock train from Victoria, won't you?'

'I'll be on it, never fear,' Jimmy promised, and after a

35

short pause he added somewhat shyly: 'Er, should I bring an overnight bag?'

'You can stay overnight, Jimmy? I'm so pleased — perhaps you can stay for a few days. I'm sure we can find plenty to do all day.'

'And what about at night?' he asked teasingly.

I was so happy that I became reckless and caring not whether Miss Maggs or anyone else was listening to us, I replied: 'Ah, that will be our special time. I have some secret plan for the warm summer evenings which I know you will enjoy even more than taking outdoor exercise during the daylight hours.'

'It sounds spiffing, Rosie. Let's say goodbye now as I must get Goulthorp to pack a bag for me. Should I bring my man along, Rosie, or will you spoil me as usual so that I can leave my servant at home?'

Jimmy might have guessed that I had planned some hi-jinks when I told him to leave Goulthorp in London as the staff at Argosse Towers hardly had enough to do in the absence of my parents. After blowing a kiss to each other down the line we said *au revoir* and I replaced the receiver with a blissful smile on my face.

The sun was now shining fiercely and as I entered the drawing room Uncle Gordon looked up from his armchair and the sheaf of papers he was studying and said: 'Rosie, my dear girl, I hope you won't be going out for too long in this weather because I don't want you over-tiring yourself — but if you must venture outdoors, do remember to take your parasol for too much sun will affect your lovely complexion.'

I informed him that I was only going to Midhurst Station in the carriage to meet Jimmy Horobin who would be staying a night or two with us. My uncle frowned. 'Really, Rosie, you should have told me beforehand that you were expecting a guest. I shall have to tell Mrs Callaghan to prepare a room for young Horobin. Is his man coming too?'

'No, he is coming alone as it is only a short informal visit. I'm sorry I forgot to mention the matter before but I have only just confirmed the arrangements with Jimmy on the telephone.'

Uncle Gordon sighed. 'Very well, Rosie, but could you have not simply written a letter instead? A telephone call to London costs at least five shillings (*twenty-five pence or about forty-five cents! – Editor*). I won't sneak on you this time, though your Mama will accuse me of needless extravagance, for she has it in her head that I use the telephone constantly to speak to my London friends when the truth is that I come down here to get away from the noise and bustle of the city.'

And to fuck our prettiest servant girls, I added silently, and live off the fat of the land. Still, Uncle Gordon was a nice old stick really and he and Sarah had just afforded me a most educational and entertaining diversion, so I meekly accepted his rebuke which, after all, was not unfairly given.

'I am going out myself shortly to Mr Andrew Bennett's house over at East Lavington and I don't expect to be back till around six o'clock because you remember my interest in folk songs? Well, Mr Bennett has purchased the latest recording equipment and we hope to get some villagers to sing into the machine and preserve these old ditties for posterity. (*Alas, these priceless recordings, made on shellac cylinders to be played on acoustic gramophones driven by clockwork and amplified by a large horn, were lost during a fire at Lord MacChesney's London home in 1921 – Editor*). You and young Horobin are welcome to join us this afternoon if you are interested.

'Than you, uncle, but I think we have already made other plans,' I said, with genuine regret, for I have always derived great enjoyment from all kinds of music. 'Do send me a set of the recordings when they have been finished. Are those sheets on your lap some of the songs you will be recording?'

'Yes, we'll try and get through as many as we can. Look, here is one of my favourites. Would you like to hear it? It's called 'Rosebuds In June':

Here the rosebuds in June, and the violets are blooming;
The small birds they warble from ev'ry green bough,
Here's the pink and the lily,
And the daffydowndilly,
To adorn and perfume the sweet meadows in June.
'Tis all before the plough the fat oxen go slow
And the lads and the lasses to the sheep-shearing go.

A pleasant, simple melody, don't you agree? Farmer Massey is giving his labourers an afternoon off to come and sing for us and Mr Bennett is providing a barrel of beer to loosen their throats. I'm sure we'll have a most rewarding day.'

Not as rewarding as the day I hoped to have, I said to myself as I pulled the cord to summon Sayers the butler and inform him of the day's arrangements and of the impending arrival of our guest. I also suggested a luncheon menu he should ask Mrs Moser, our cook, to prepare for Jimmy and myself.

I could scarcely wait until just before noon when Haines came to the drawing room to inform me that the carriage awaited me. Haines the coachman had brought out a very smart landaulet (*a small four-wheel carriage with a top in two parts so that it could be closed or thrown half or entirely open — Editor*) and in no time at all we were at the station. The London train was as punctual as ever and my spirits soared as I saw Jimmy leap down from his compartment. He had already pulled out his two cases by the time I reached him (I could not be too forward in front of Haines) and offered only my hand in greeting.

'Welcome to Sussex, Jimmy! It was so good of you to drop everything at a moment's notice for me.' I said, brightly, as Jimmy clasped my hand and kissed my cheek. 'How could I spurn such an urgent invitation,' he smiled. 'I can hardly wait to find out what surprises you have in store for me.'

'You won't be disappointed,' I promised, as we walked to the carriage. I told Haines to lower the roof so that Jimmy and I could talk privately and as we pulled away from the station Jimmy whispered: 'You know, I may have the tiniest inkling of what is in your mind, Rosie. I just pray that I've guessed correctly because I'll be overjoyed if I am on the right track.'

I pondered my reply as I looked at my handsome hero. Jimmy was so good-looking, being blessed with a slim figure, a fresh-complexioned face with sparkling blue eyes and a trim moustache as fair as the hair on his head which he wore always slightly on the long side, which I am sure he knew pleased the ladies but irritated his father, Viscount Sevenoaks, who was an old-fashioned 'short-back-and-sides' individual. I decided to act boldly. 'Did you have in mind something like this?' I said softly, and without further ado kissed him firmly on the lips. He responded by taking me in his arms and returned my advance by embracing me as our mouths mashed together and I could feel his cock rise against my tummy.

This was as far as we had ever journeyed on our voyage to paradise although I had let Jimmy feel my breasts through the silk of my ballgown as we canoodled together in a quiet corner during the dancing at his eighteenth birthday party back in March and I had often wondered about his hard, bulging manhood which had so often pressed against me.

I fought to keep control as Jimmy's tongue entered my mouth and we french-kissed with a burning passion. But his hands were roaming freely across my body and my nipples hardened as he fondled my firm young breasts. My own fingers were dangerously near the big bulge between his legs and it took only a little gentle pressure from his elbow to force my hand lower and stroke the hard pole I could feel straining against the soft flannel material of his trousers. Our tongues were now moving madly in each other's mouths as Jimmy unbuttoned my blouse and slipped his hand inside to ease down the straps of my chemise over my shoulders. He now squeezed and rubbed my bared breasts which made my pussey dampen perceptively. With his left hand he somehow managed to tear open the first buttons of his flies — but just as I was about to handle a naked cock for the very first time, the landaulet suddenly jerked to a halt and we almost found ourselves sprawled out on the floor.

'I'm terribly sorry, Miss Rosie,' called out Haines. 'We're at the railway level-crossing and the bloody keeper's rushed out of his cottage to close the gates on us, stupid bleeder. Oh, beg your pardon, miss.'

Somehow we managed to stifle our laughter as we heard our driver shout out: 'Why the hell couldn't you let us through, Mr Tong? There's not a train in sight, you silly old bugger!'

'Don't you talk to me like that, coachman, I've got to shut the gate at twelve eighteen, train or no train. Be patient and you'll live longer,' said the offended Mr Tong.

Haines lapsed into an angry mutter but I took the opportunity of delivering a little smack on Jimmy's wrist. 'Take your hands off my titties, we'll be home in ten minutes. After luncheon we'll be able to find somewhere private and we'll have all the time in the world for spooning without any interruptions.'

Of course Jimmy was as frustrated as me at the unwarranted intrusion on our petting but his face brightened as he buttoned his trousers and I readjusted my chemise and did up my blouse. 'Gosh, that sounds great — a romp in the sun with Rosie. What more could a chap ask?'

'Well, how about a decent lunch for starters?' I said, and we snuggled up side by side as we waited for the twelve twenty-two train to Chichester to chug through and we moved forward again as Haines snarled a final imprecation at Mr Tong.

'That old fool really is what my housemaster would call a "jobsworth",' said Jimmy lightly.

'What's a "jobsworth", Jimmy?'

'Oh, one of these people with tiny authority who never deviate from the rules even when it is pointed out how silly the regulation might be. Ask them to be flexible and they always say: "I'm sorry, sir, but it's more than my job's worth to do that." '

I smiled at his shrewd comment but felt it necessary to say that Mr Tong was not entirely in the wrong. 'Suppose the twelve twenty-two express had been a couple of minutes early? We would have been sent to kingdom come if for some reason our wheels had become jammed in the railway track and in a panic we were unable to alight quickly.

'On second thoughts, you are absolutely right. Haines was simply in far too much of a hurry to get home for his lunch,' he agreed.

'He was more likely in too much of a hurry to get his hands on Alice, the chambermaid who will be making up your bed tonight. I've seen them cuddling in the servants' quarters before now and I once heard Alice tell Sarah, who looks after my room and Uncle Gordon's suite, that Haines has got the fattest prick she had ever seen.'

'Isn't she a lucky girl, then?' Jimmy chuckled, as we reached Argosse Towers and I saw Sayers waiting at the steps to open the door of the landaulet for us. With him was young Alfred, the page-boy who would take care of Jimmy's luggage and I hurriedly whispered to Jimmy that Alfred was also well-endowed for a lad of his age. 'How on earth do you know that?' grinned Jimmy. 'It must be this fresh country air.' 'No, no, I just happened to come across Alfred and my brother comparing the size of their cocks.' I explained hastily, deciding to leave Sarah out of the story in case Jimmy got any naughty ideas about her!

'I'm sure you'd like to change before luncheon,' I said, as we strode inside. 'Would a simple meal of vegetable soup, red mullet and salad with Mrs Moser's famous apple pie and cream to finish off with be enough for you? We will dine fully tonight when my Uncle Gordon returns.'

'Sounds absolutely scrumptious — can you give me half an hour to unpack and wash my hands?'

I have a sneaking suspicion that Mrs Moser and all those downstairs knew that Jimmy was a very special friend of mine. Certainly, Sayers and Sarah (who deputised for

Dennison the footman who Uncle Gordon had taken to Mr Bennett's) waited upon us at luncheon in fine style and could hardly have been more attentive than if His Majesty King Edward VII had been sitting in Jimmy's chair! And afterwards, just before we were about to retire next door to the comfort of the superb Blue Room to enjoy coffee and petit fours, Mrs Moser herself appeared in the doorway — a rare sight indeed, for she was rarely seen outside of the kitchen.

'Excuse me, Miss Rosie, Mr Horobin, I hope you will forgive me coming in but I do hope that you enjoyed your lunch.'

'I'll say we did, Mrs Moser,' said Jimmy, heartily. 'I wish you would come and work for us in London. Since we lost Mrs Bickler's services to Lady Arkley, Mama has found it impossible to find a really first-class cook.'

Mrs Moser was really pleased. 'Thank you, sir, that's very kind. But I'm very happy here and I've been to London twice already and it's a nice place to visit but I wouldn't like to live there.'

'Well, I don't think I'd disagree with you. But before I leave, I must especially compliment you on your apple pie — it was absolutely delicious and just a little bit different. What's your secret, Mrs Moser?'

'I don't really know, sir, except that in the filling I use the rind of a small lemon and two tablespoons of lemon juice with a pinch of mixed sweet spices in the filling.'

I think Sarah was a little jealous of the praise Jimmy was lavishing upon the cook for I was sure I heard her mutter something about a dab of mustard! So somehow managing not to giggle, I said: 'And the meal was served quite splendidly too, wasn't it, Jimmy?'

He turned and gave Sarah a dazzling smile. 'Oh yes, Sayers was as efficient as ever and Sarah, you were quite splendid — and much prettier than Dennison!'

Sarah returned his smile and bobbed a curtsy. 'Thank you, sir, it was a pleasure to serve you.'

Now it was my turn to feel an irritable twitch of jealousy.

'Good, now let's have coffee in the Blue Room, Jimmy. Then we'll go for a walk, alright?'

'Yes, yes,' he said, but I noticed he was still looking at Sarah who I could have sworn had provocatively licked her upper lip at Jimmy as he turned away to follow me out of the dining-room. Nevertheless, I put the incident out of my mind as we relaxed together on the new Chesterfield Papa had purchased at Harrods a few months before. (*A Chesterfield was a large, tightly stuffed sofa, usually upholstered in leather — Editor*). But soon after we had taken a few sips of coffee, Jimmy put his arms around me and murmured softly: 'Dash it, Rosie, it's jolly hot outside, why don't we take a short walk to my bedroom?'

'What a splendid idea,' I replied. 'Only we must be careful and ensure that we are not observed. All it needs is one servant to discover us and you can be sure that the gossip will spread not only all over the county but even back in Society circles.'

'Damn Society, I despise it,' he grinned.

'Don't say that, Jimmy. As Mama says, only people who cannot get into it take that attitude.'

'Fair enough, Rosie, but I do so want you to come with me. Can't I persuade you?' he asked, with a roguish smile.

Jimmy held out his hand and pulled me to my feet. To be honest, I needed little or no persuading for frankly I wanted to fuck just as much as Jimmy but it would have been unladylike of course to have admitted it at this stage. So as we made our way carefully to his bedroom I pretended to chide him saying how naughty he was to drag me upstairs and how we would be far better off taking a gentle afternoon stroll round the estate — which was actually all very silly because I would have been extremely angry if he had taken note of my protestations and actually turned back! Mind, if I had genuinely not wanted to be fucked, I would have disengaged my hand from his and simply stalked off into the drawing-room. Just as I have never believed in prick-teasing, as the vernacular succinctly describes the practice, I demand to be respected when I decline an invitation to

43

have sexual intercourse. Not that Jimmy would ever have tried to force me to do anything against my will — and let me say here and now, woe betide any man who would attempt such a contemptuous course. Fortunately I have only ever had to knee one over-persistent man in the groin and that was Sheik Yormonai from Mesopotamia at a soirée given by Papa's friends at the Foreign Office.

But on this never-to-be-forgotten afternoon there was an unspoken yet telepathic desire for sexual congress between this handsome youth and myself, a desire of such power that nothing could prevent or deny its fulfilment. I do not believe that even if, for instance Uncle Gordon had returned unexpectedly, we would have just passed him by with a hurried greeting and continued our way up to Jimmy's bedroom without interruption.

As it turned out, to the best of my knowledge we managed to reach our haven without being seen. Once we were safely inside, Jimmy wisely locked the door behind us and held me in his arms. 'Rosie,' he began, but I put my finger to his lips for at this moment no words were necessary. Our bodies crushed together as we held each other tightly, kissing and cuddling with great fervour as we staggered as if intoxicated by the emotion of the moment until we fell in an untidy heap upon the bed.

If anything, this total tangling of our limbs intensified our passion — our lips were still locked together and our tongues continued to make darting journeys of exploration inside each other's wet mouths. I shuddered with excitement as I felt Jimmy's hand move slowly, lingeringly over my shoulder and down towards the valley of my breasts, moulding the silk of my blouse against the skin. This sent shivers throughout my body and I smiled dreamily at Jimmy as I heard him catch his breath when he deftly undid all the buttons of my blouse. For as I shrugged off the garment he saw that I had taken off my chemise whilst he had unpacked his bags and my swelling breasts now stood out proudly in glorious nudity. He let his quivering hands cup my rounded bosoms and then his mouth moved from mine and he kissed me all over my neck and throat before his lips reached my already erected little titties. He took each nipple in turn between his lips whilst I unbuttoned my skirt and wriggled out of it as Jimmy sucked eagerly on my red, tingling titties.

I was now engulfed in frenzied waves of ecstasy and I raised my bottom upwards to let Jimmy pull down my nickers. His hands then moved from my breasts across my flat stomach to the golden triangle of crisp blonde hair that nestled between my thighs. His fingers began to caress and stroke and probe until my pussey was wet through with love juices. Carefully, he gently inserted the tip of his finger in my sopping slit and I cried out with the almost unbearable sensual pleasure of this new joy.

I closed my eyes and let the erotic electricity of his frigging send sparks of fire throughout every nerve and fibre. And then he parted my thighs and dipped his head between them and with his tongue licked and lapped at my cunney which nearly brought me off then and there. Not surprisingly, when he forced his tongue between my cunt lips, my clitty swelled up to greet him, popping out of its hood and he playfully nibbled at it with his teeth, nipping and sucking, which sent me quite mad with desire. 'Take me, Jimmy, take me!' I begged, a heartfelt cry that was answered just as soon as he somehow managed to tear off his clothes whilst continuing this divine oral cuntal stimulation.

When he was finally naked he raised his head from my drenched pussey and lifted his wiry frame over me. I was aching for the feel of his prick which I grasped in my hand. It was as smooth as silk to my touch, as big and firm as a polished wood baton and I slowly rubbed the hot pulsing pole which made him sigh with a fresh lust. 'Rosie darling, I want to fuck you,' he breathed softly. 'Are you ready for me?'

'Oh yes, Jimmy, yes, please fuck me,' I whispered back, still stroking his lovely swollen shaft. 'I want your darling penis inside me as I have never wanted anything in my life!'

Our mouths pressed together and my arms clasped about

his shoulders as I opened my legs and wrapped them around his waist. Jimmy cupped the two cheeks of my bum in his hands to raise them to greet the uncapped purple dome of his majestic tool which nudged its way between my cunney lips. He hovered for an instant and then I thrilled with rapture as he plunged his prick inside my pussey and I crossed the Rubicon into womanhood! There was no pain whatsoever (riding my pony Billy had happily broken my hymen at least a year before) and I shall never forget the joy as Jimmy lay over me and rove his bone-hard cock between those welcoming cunney lips into my yearning pudenda.

Oh, the gorgeous feelings that swept from my pussey all over my body as Jimmy's hard, stiff prick slid in and out of my juicy crack, each inward thrust making his knob kiss the furthest reaches of my insatiable cunney, each vigorous poke rousing a new sensation within me. My juices were now flowing like water from a breached dam, keeping the pathway well lubricated for this marvellous prick which pistoned so beautifully in and out of my eager cunt. He gradually began to pump faster and faster, his big balls banging against my bum cheeks as he thrust into me again and again. My pussey pulsated deliciously around his juice-coated cock and there was so much moisture pouring out of me that I could feel it running down my legs.

At first slowly, and then with quickening pace, I felt the first stirrings of orgasm speed through me. Within seconds our fucking reached a crescendo of mutual excitement and, as I sucked in my breath, I felt the first waves of a fierce, shuddering spend fan out from between my trembling legs as I twisted my cunney around Jimmy's splendid tool. He in turn began to heave and buck with increasing rapidity as I took off to that unique journey to paradise. 'Fuck me, Jimmy, fuck me!' I screamed without restraint, mindless that a passing servant would have heard my lewd words. And Jimmy willingly obliged as he shot stream after stream of warm, sticky spunk deep into my saturated cunt. My own spend occurred simultaneously and I revelled in the glorious

46

climax as his strong young cock pumped merrily away until his ejaculations of sperm subsided. He withdrew his deflated shaft which was now just semi-erect as he rolled off me and lay on his back gasping with exhaustion — and perhaps a little pride for, to the best of my knowledge, this had been the first ever fuck not just for me but also for my dear boyfriend.

But my sexual desires had still not been full assuaged. I took hold of Jimmy's cock in my hand and gave the shaft, which was still wet from all my spendings, a good rub up and down which certainly caused him to wake out of the post-fuck stupor that effects all men. May I take this opportunity to note that now, being well schooled in *l'arte de faire l'amour*, I do realise just how violent an exercise a good fucking can be for a man. Even liberated ladies such as myself who do not simply lie back supinely to receive our spermy injections do not use up as much frantic energy as our male partners, and I trust that this will be noted by all female readers of my memoir.

Be that as it may, Jimmy was now fully *compos mentis* and the naughty boy caressed the back of my head and gently but insistently lowered my mop of golden curls downwards so that his huge throbbing tool was only inches from my face. My heart beat faster as the mushroom-shaped crown of his cock neared my lips. It was obvious what Jimmy wanted me to do but in all honesty I was genuinely concerned — for surely I would not be able to accommodate all of that giant shaft in my tiny little mouth.

'Oh, Jimmy, I don't know whether I can do it,' I said, falteringly, as I continued to stroke his pulsing prick. 'Of course you can,' he replied encouragingly. 'Just begin by licking my knob and then let nature take its course.'

Well, I could only try, I reasoned, so I kissed the purple uncapped dome and let my tongue run over the smooth skin. I lapped up the remaining drops of spunk around the 'eye' of his helmet and it was highly erotic to think that this fleshy lollipop had only minutes before been pounding in and out of my pussey. I opened my mouth and began gobbling the ruby knob with relish, slurping and sucking it as my hands jerked up and down the thick shaft. I then jammed down his foreskin and sucked away in earnest while Jimmy jerked his hips backwards and forwards, thrusting ever more of his big cock into my willing mouth. He tried to push every inch of his prick between my lips but I simply could not take it all in and I gagged, upon which the sweet boy hastily withdrew until I had recovered. But I sucked lustily upon as much of this yummy sweetmeat as I could cram into my mouth until Jimmy's cock twitched violently and with a hoarse groan he cried out: 'Start swallowing, Rosie, I'm going to spunk, yes, yes, A-h-r-e!' And what a mighty spend of sperm Jimmy sent spurting into my mouth. I gulped down as much of the pleasantly tangy liquid as I was able but my mouth was already filled with his palpitating prick, so some of his jism spilled out between my lips and ran down my chin. How lewd! How exciting! I so enjoyed sucking and swallowing his creamy emission that I was quite disappointed when his cock, now milked dry by my palating, began to lose its stiffness.

A gleam of pleasure animated Jimmy's face as for the second time he lay back *hors de combat*. 'I don't know why you are so tired, Jimmy Horobin. This time around I was doing most of the hard work,' I said, in mock indignation.

'True enough,' he admitted, with a cheeky grin, 'but honestly, Rosie, you sucked my dick so expertly that I am feeling quite drained.'

I was flattered by his words. 'Did I really, Jimmy? Did you know that was the first time I had ever sucked a cock? And of course I have never been fucked before either.'

'You darling! Damn, we should have had some champagne on ice to toast the end of your virginity. Mind, I do hope that you don't regret losing your maidenhead to me,' he said, with a note of anxiety in his voice.

'No, of course not, Jimmy, especially as my monthlies finished only two days ago so there's no worry about unwanted aftereffects! Was it the first time for you as well?'

'Yes, and fucking was every bit as nice as I had always

imagined it would be. I'm sure that no girl can fuck better than you, Rosie. Also, to be frank with you, I have been sucked off just one before this afternoon, and though I'm not saying I didn't enjoy the experience, having you do it was even nicer.'

So Jimmy had been sucked off by another woman! A twinge of jealousy passed through me and I said reproachfully: 'Oh, Jimmy, I would have loved to have been the first girl to have kissed your cock. Do I know my rival? I'll scratch her face, the rotten cat!'

'You silly little goose,' he laughed. 'I assure you that there is no rival around with whom to do battle. No, it's, er, a little embarrassing really, though I'll tell you what happened if you really want to know.'

I urged him to tell me all and he blushed. 'I wish I hadn't been so honest, but you'll keep this to yourself, won't you? Very well then, I'll confess all though come to think about it, I can't truthfully say that I've any regrets about the matter!

'It actually occurred when I came home at half term in late February. I kept myself in good physical trim because I had just been chosen to play football for the school team. So every afternoon before tea I would go out for a brisk three-mile run round Hyde Park. Well, one day the weather was quite beastly with rain coming down in a howling wind and to cap it all I slipped in some very fresh evidence of horses so I came back home looking (and smelling!) like a tramp. I rushed upstairs to my bathroom and could hardly wait to sponge myself down in hot soapy water. I enjoyed a luxurious soak and then climbed out and dried myself in front of the full-length mirror. As I dried myself I lightly brushed the edge of the towel against my dangling prick which began to stiffen slowly as the soft material tickled it. I looked in the mirror and saw myself take hold of the swelling shaft. As I lightly rubbed my cock it sprang to life, swelling up to its fullest height and girth.

'Like Narcissus I stood there admiring my meaty shaft which over the last year had developed into a weapon of formidable proportions. Well, you can guess what I did next! Carefully I rolled back the foreskin from my knob and I manipulated my cock up and down in my cupped hand. I closed my eyes and thought that nice though this was, how much nicer it would be if my prick was actually sliding into a wet, welcoming cunney! But this reverie was suddenly interrupted by the sound of a soft gurgle behind me. I opened my eyes and to my horror saw in the mirror that I was not alone! Tessa, a young chambermaid we had only recently engaged, had quietly entered the bathroom and was staring with interest at my nakedness.

'Naturally, I was so shocked that I let go my swiftly shrivelling member. "Tessa, what on earth are you doing here?" I gasped. "I'm sorry, sir, but Goulthorp, your valet, told me to change the towels and I didn't know you were in here. Please don't report me, sir, or I'll get the sack," she implored, with tears in her pretty brown eyes.

' "Now, now, don't fret, I won't say anything. Worse things happen at sea, you know," I replied cheerfully. She clasped her hands together and said: "Oh Mr James, you are kind! Thank you so much, I'm so grateful. Yes, I'm sure I know what you'd really enjoy. If you'd like to stand still and close your eyes for a moment, we'll both find out.'

'I was genuinely puzzled — what could Tessa mean? Still, it might be fun so I obediently closed my eyes and whilst I waited I heard a rustling sound. "You can open your eyes now," she said, and when I did so I took in a sharp intake of breath. For Tessa had taken off her white maid's blouse and untied the straps of her chemise.'

Jimmy paused and moistened his lips before continuing his confession. 'With a sensual smile she pulled down the garment and for the first time in my life I saw the beautiful breasts of a lovely young girl in proud, unfettered nakedness. Her bosoms were firm and rounded and I noticed how each tapered in delightful curves until they came to rich crimson nipples surrounded by pink circles. She said shyly: "Mr James, you can feel my titties if you like." With my mouth open with surprise and my prick now quickly returning to its former erect state, I stumbled across and her taut titties acted as magnets to my hands that desperately desired to squeeze those succulent white globes. How I marvelled at the way her hard, pouting nipples pushed against my fingers, as I pressed those gorgeous mounds of flesh against my palms.

'She kissed me and immediately her tongue was in my mouth which made my prick stand up to its fullest height up against my tummy, throbbing in expectation of delights to come. Tessa took hold of my quivering cock and knelt down in front of me saying: "What a whopper, Mr James! You are well developed — why, it's even bigger than my boyfriend's and he is at least six years older than you." She took my swollen shaft in her soft hand and cupped my balls with the other whilst she let her fingers run across the underside of my quivering cock. I uttered a little moan of pure pleasure and she whispered: "Does that feel good, Mr James?" All I could do was to nod my head for I was almost swooning with delight as she added: "You do like my tickling your tool? M'm, I think you do — well now, just see what you make of this then," she crooned as she leaned forward and to my joy took my now-throbbing tool and proceeded to suck it into her hot, wet mouth. Her darting tongue moved to and fro along my shaft and as she licked the tip of my knob, my ballsack tightened. I thrust my prick frenziedly between her lips, almost choking her. I knew that I could not hold back from spunking even though she had only been sucking me for less than half a minute. Tessa must have sensed my urgency for she lapped furiously at my engorged dick whilst lightly squeezing my balls. This sent the sperm rushing through my stem and the creamy white juice rushed out of my cock which jerked away madly whilst this copious emission filled her mouth. She swallowed every drop of jism and when the ejaculation had finally subsided she gently kissed my now semi-erect penis which I withdrew from her mouth.

' "My, you *do* have a fine tadger there," she said admiringly. "And your sperm has a lovely salty flavour. I stood there dazed as Tessa slipped back the straps of her chemise and put on her blouse. "Damn," she added, "I'm sopping wet down below." She lifted her skirt and pulled down her knickers to reveal a huge wet patch on them. This blunt but naughty act made my shaft harden up again and without sounding too conceited, I think Tessa would have been willing to fuck but we heard someone coming up the stairs. There was a knock on the bathroom door and unfortunately it was my man Goulthorp who had come up to enquire whether there was anything I required. When I told him that all was well and that his services were not required he then asked if I had seen Tessa. "Tessa? Is she the new chambermaid?" I asked, motioning Tessa to stay silent.

'Tessa hid behind the door as I called out to Goulthorp that Tessa had probably gone downstairs. "Very good, sir, I'll look for her there if you do not require my services," replied my valet. As soon as the coast was clear, Tessa gave me a quick farewell kiss, pulling my prick one more time "for good luck" as she put it, and, well, that was that, I never had the opportunity to have any further fun with her.'

'Oh, come now, Jimmy, you needn't be bashful with me,' I said, struggling to keep any note of reproach out of my voice for, to be fair, Jimmy had freely confessed all and, as Jimmy later remarked, any man would have been tempted by a seventeen-year-old seductress who stripped half-naked in front of you and proceeded to lick your prick.

'No, that's true, Rosie,' Jimmy said earnestly. 'I will admit that every night for at least a week afterwards before falling asleep, I tossed myself off thinking about how Tessa had sucked me off and how delicious it would be to fuck her. But the pretty young minx left our service only a fortnight later in I suppose rather amusing circumstances.

'Mama had pressed Tessa into service one evening shortly after the events I have just described to take charge of guests' coats at an important reception. My parents were giving a party for the famous Italian opera singer Majora, as Queen Alexandra had expressed a keen interest to meet the great

Signora Majora and Papa felt it his duty to oblige Her Majesty. Well, Rosie, the lovely Tessa caught the eye of Sir Peter Lucas who was escorting Her Majesty in the absence of the King who was doubtless carousing elsewhere with Mrs Keppel (*one of the most famous mistresses of the jolly King Edward VII – Editor*). Anyhow, the next day Goulthorp told me that Sir Peter had fallen madly in love with Tessa and had actually offered her his hand in marriage which naturally enough Tessa had accepted! His family went berserk when they heard the news and before the announcement of their engagement could be put in *The Times*, Sir Peter's father Lord Eastmidlands offered Tessa £1,000 to return the ring Sir Peter had already purchased from Smolasks (*a famous Edwardian Bond Street jewellers much patronised by the upper classes – Editor*)'

'Gosh, what a tale – and did she accept the offer?'

Jimmy laughed. 'Yes – but not until the noble Lord had raised his offer to £8,000 and the diamond ring which she sold back to Smolasks for at least £500! The last I heard from Goulthorp about Tessa was that she had set herself up in a nice little house on the Kings Road, Chelsea and was supplementing her not inconsiderable income by posing nude for the society painter Frederick Newman.'

'So all's well that ends well,' I said brightly.

'Y-e-s, I suppose so,' he said guardedly.

His reticence puzzled me. 'Well, what in heaven's name can be wrong in your scenario? Everyone came out of it well enough – Tessa has enough money to set her up for life, you and Sir Peter Lucas tasted the forbidden fruit whilst Lord Eastmidlands, who has pots and pots of money, can be satisfied that he assisted the rise of a poor member of the working class.'

'Ah, you've almost come to the point, Rosie. As far as my story is concerned, the only fly in the ointment concerns the sorry state of a poor member, who may not be of the working class but is still in urgent need of assistance,' he said with a grin, lifting up his limp prick for my inspection.

'Oh dear,' I said, taking his flaccid cockshaft in my hand.

'I'll do what I can to aid Mr John Thomas. perhaps this will do the trick.'

And I leaned forward and planted a huge wet kiss on the ripe red plum of his helmet. I juiced his now stiffening shaft with saliva and slipped my hand underneath to feel his hairy ballsack. Lovingly, I went down on him and gave Jimmy's big penis a thorough, leisurely suck. His shaft grew and grew until I found it difficult to keep it in my mouth, so I switched to his balls and began licking and lapping at his sweet nuts. He gurgled happily as I paid my homage to his most private parts — especially that so sensitive area between his balls and arsehole — and this prolonged salivating soon had the desired effect.

I had just had the time to once more work over his bare knob and to flick my tongue over its slitted end when his balls began to pulsate as the spunk started its journey upwards. As I gave one last slurp, a stream of warm love juice spurted into my mouth and Jimmy's prick throbbed wildly as I held it lightly between my teeth. I sucked and swallowed his sticky white emission that poured out of his magnificent penis until I felt the spongy textured crown soften. I rolled my lips around it and nibbled away at the round bulb of his knob until his shaft shrivelled into its previous limpness.

To be frank, my pussey was now discharging juices too and I would have loved Jimmy to have given me a final good fucking but he could not be fairly expected to oblige and I bade him rest as I snuggled into his arms for a nice little snooze. After all, there would be time enough later that evening for more fun and games to which we could both look forward to with gleeful anticipation!

I smuggled myself out of Jimmy's room without difficulty and as I bathed and changed for dinner I reflected on how much I had enjoyed making love. Can there be a more pleasurable activity in the whole wide world? I thought not then and I remain steadfast in this belief after four years in which I have experienced (as readers of my diaries will agree) the thrills of fucking in many forms with an equally wide variety of partners both male and female — and sometimes both together! However, back to this all-important day when for the very first time a thick stiff cock pushed its way through my love-channel. As previously arranged, Jimmy came to my room at half past seven to escort me down to dinner. I wore an evening dress of light blue, simply but exquisitely cut by Mama's dressmaker, Monsieur Aspis of Jermyn Street and Jimmy had changed into his evening dress and very fine he looked indeed in his sparkling-white dinner shirt and silk-lapelled black jacket.

'Your Papa told me recently that Americans call evening dress a tuxedo,' he remarked. 'An unusual word, isn't it?'

'Sure is, as the Yankees say, but actually I know the etymology of the word. It is derived from the exclusive Tuxedo club in New York,' I said, as we made our way downstairs. 'No, I'm not especially good at general knowledge, it's just that Uncle Gordon, who visits America often, was asked to join the Tuxedo. He is a country member.'

'Yes, I remember!' said Jimmy, which made us both laugh out loud as we entered the drawing room where Uncle Gordon awaited us. He rose from his chair and I was surprised to see that he had changed into the undress uniform of the Third Lancashire Rifles, a volunteer regiment of which he was a lieutenant colonel. (*Although too old for active service during World War One, Lord MacChesney played an important Intelligence role whilst serving as Military Intelligence at the British Embassy in Portugal between 1914 and 1917 — Editor.*)

'Ah, here come the young people,' beamed Uncle Gordon, shaking hands with Jimmy. 'James, good to see you again, my boy. Now I would like you and Rosie to meet an unexpected guest who is dining with us tonight, Mr Andrew Bennett. Rosie, you know Mr Bennett, of course. Andy, may I introduce the Honourable James Horobin; James this is Mr Andrew Bennett who is a friend and neighbour of the family. His good lady wife has unfortunately been called

55

to the bedside of a sick relative so naturally I invited him to break bread with us this evening.'

Mr Bennett was a pleasant gentleman, somewhat younger than Uncle Gordon, and as neither he nor Jimmy were shy, we all got along famously. Sayers poured out drinks for us but whilst the men downed Bucks Fizz (*champagne and orange juice — Editor*) I preferred to sip mineral water. Of course the conversation turned to the recordings Uncle Gordon and Mr Bennett had made that afternoon of rustic folk songs and apparently an unfortunate incident had marred the proceedings.

As we strolled into the dining-room, And (as the genial Mr Bennett insisted we called him) told us of the afternoon's happenings at his home. Whilst we tucked into Mrs Moser's delicious Continental *hors d'oeuvres* — chopped eggs and onions mixed with a small amount of boiled potato — Andy entertained us with the following anecdote: 'The recordings of Sussex folk song started well enough although at first the yokels were somewhat in awe of the apparatus and as we had thought, they needed to loosen up. So your uncle and I decided to have a barrel of beer brought in and we invited the singers to help themselves. Well, my word, I've never seen drinking like it — not even at the annual dinner we give the farmworkers at the harvest festival.'

'And still they gazed and still the wonder grew, that such small frames could carry so much brew!' misquoted Uncle Gordon with a short laugh, though this criticism did not prevent him motioning Sayers to refill our glasses with more champagne. 'But we certainly got the lads to sing though I hardly think we can release the results for public consumption.'

'Why not, Lord MacChesney?' asked Jimmy. 'Did the drink make their rustic dialect unintelligible?'

'Far from it — the words were all too clear! To give you an example, I heard choruses from "The Jolly Three Ladies of Huxham" that I could hardly repeat even in front of the most liberally minded audience.'

Perhaps it was Mrs Moser's tasty food which kept Sayers

busy refilling our glasses but when I excused myself before
our main course to wash my hands, it obviously had taken
only a few minutes coaxing from Jimmy to persuade Andy
Bennett to give a rendition of the rather rude verses. I opened
the door slightly and saw him stand up and sing:

> 'The jolly three ladies of Huxham,
> Whenever we meets 'em we fucks 'em,
> And when that game grows stale
> We sits on a rail
> And pulls out our pricks and they sucks 'em.
>
> Now the poor little vicar of Huxham,
> Had a cock which though thick was a short 'un,
> He made up for his loss,
> By having balls like a horse,
> And he never spent less than a quartern.
>
> But those three jolly girls from old Huxham,
> This is the true story about 'em.
> They lifted the frock
> And tickled the cock
> Of the vicar about to confirm 'em!
>
> Then out spoke a young girl out of the blue,
> Who said, as the churchman withdrew,
> "My vicar is quicker
> And slicker and thicker
> And longer and stronger than you." '

Jimmy roared with laughter and said: 'I do hope you
recorded that fine song for posterity, Andy, I have several
friends that would be delighted to purchase copies though
I dare say it might be difficult to find a store that would
put the record on general sale.'

'You could always sell copies through the columns of *The
Oyster*,' Jimmy suggested. 'I think you would coin it in.'

Uncle Gordon nodded. 'That would be a good idea if we

needed to make some money but thank goodness I couldn't spend all I have even if I live to be a hundred.'

'Fair enough, Lord MacChesney, but that reminds me of the story of Sir Charles and Lady Farnesbarnes — do either of you know it? No, well, it appears that one day Sir Charles came home and said to his lady wife: 'My dear, I'm afraid I have lost a great deal of money in unwise speculation and we must immediately make drastic cuts in our household expenditure. To begin with I suggest for a start that we dismiss the cook and you learn to prepare our meals yourself.'

' ''Very well,'' said Lady Farnesbarnes, ''but only on the condition that you sack the chauffeur and learn how to fuck!'' '

This jest was much appreciated by the other two gentlemen but when Uncle Gordon saw me enter the room he hastily changed the course of the conversation to far less interesting matters such as the state of the weather and the health of Mrs Bennett's sick aunt. Nevertheless I thoroughly enjoyed the splendid repast and after we had finished Jimmy and I decided to go out for a short stroll in the warm evening air.

'Uncle Gordon and Andy Bennett are two game old boys, aren't they?' said Jimmy lightly, as we made our way towards the new garage Papa had built last September for our new Mercedes motor vehicles he had bought on a trip to Berlin. When we neared the garage, however, I noticed that the doors were unlocked and I whispered to Jimmy: 'Should we raise an alarm? We may have found burglars on the job.'

'On the job maybe,' I said carefully. 'But I'll wager that we have not been troubled by intruders. Listen to that noise carefully, can you not distinguish the sounds of breaking and entering from the whimpers and liquid sounds of a couple engaged in making love?'

Jimmy cupped an ear and listened intently and then turned to me with a grin. 'By George, you're right, Rosie! The only breaking and entering going on in there is that of a cock sliding into a juicy pussey!'

I suppose that we really should not have eavesdropped but as Jimmy said at the time, it was just possible that we may have been mistaken and that someone was trying to steal our lovely new motor car. So we crept up quietly and Jimmy opened the door very slightly and a flood of light spilled out. It only took a swift glance round the door to confirm my original theory — the strapping young footman Jack Dennison had sneaked away from the house with Kathie, the bouncy little kitchenmaid and together the pair were writhing half-naked on a couple of blankets filched no doubt from the housekeeper's stores. Jimmy was about to speak but I put my finger to his lips. 'Now, you wouldn't like to be interrupted at such a time, would you darling?' I whispered.

So we watched with mounting interest as the pretty girl slipped out of Dennison's embrace to lay on her back and pull down her chemise. The material fell away from her large milky-white breasts which she touched lightly, her fingers brushing the nipples softly and then passing upwards to run through her hair. This movement of the girl's arms made her breasts lift with the flushed pink circle which ran around each nipple heightening its colour, framing the erect little teat at its centre. The two lovely orbs of her ripe young breasts gently bumped together as Kathie lowered her arms again. She then wriggled out of her knickers and ran her hand through the curly brown triangle of pussey hair that covered her cunt.

'Well, Jack, all the goodies are on display — do you want to buy or would you rather send them back to the factory?' she giggled.

With a low growl, the footman rolled over to cover her body with his own — though not before I had time to admire his athletic physique and massive tool which was now pressing against Kathie's belly as he slid his hands under her legs to fondle and caress the bare globes of her bottom. He pressed his lips to the inviting red titties, kissing, sucking and nipping at the delightful little pink paps. He then released his hands from her bum-cheeks and pressed them

59

against the tuft of brown hair between her legs before lowering his head and kissing her pussey whilst his hands sped upward, tweaking and rubbing her engorged titties with his fingers.

Despite his youth, Jack Dennison was obviously an expert muff-diver because Kathie was soon yelping with pleasure as the footman's tongue ran along the edges of her pussey lips before flicking inside to lash itself around her clitty which made the buxom lass shiver with desire. Then he heaved himself up and was about to plunge his rampant thick prick into her sopping wet cunney when the little minx grasped his veiny shaft and said: 'Oh Jack, let's be really rude. Let me suck your darling cock before you fuck me. There is no one here to see.'

With difficulty Jimmy and I suppressed a gurgle of laughter. Of course, we had no desire to spoil their fun and I suppose we should have moved away but though the spirit was willing, the flesh was weak and Jimmy and I simply stayed rooted to the spot enjoying this stimulating feast of erotic entertainment.

So we continued to watch intently as Kathie slid down a little, still somehow managing to keep herself curled up for Jack Dennison to tease her sopping slit. As the young man felt the wet warmth of Kathie's soft lips around his uncapped knob, his back arched in ecstasy. She kissed his bare helmet as she played with his prick — coyly at first, sliding her hand up and down the sturdy shaft before tightening her hold as she opened her mouth wide to suck in the smooth-skinned crown of his big cock.

Kathie sucked hard as she drew its soft fleshiness against her tongue and she gradually slid her hand down to the base of the shaft to make more room for her mouth. Down and down went her head as she crammed in more and more of the throbbing pole until she felt it pulsing furiously at the back of her throat. She gagged for a moment and was forced to ease a couple of inches of his immensely thick penis out of her mouth — for Dennison's prick was simply too big for her to suck from top to base. The clever lad quickly observed this and I noticed that he was careful not to push too deeply as he began to slide his enormous rod in and out, fucking her mouth delightfully as the so-sensitive crown of his cock disappeared between Kathie's wide-stretched lips.

Feeling those soft lips caress his cock made Dennison's back arch in ecstasy. 'Yes, yes, suck my prick, Kathie!' he panted as she licked and lapped at his glistening shaft — not that Kathie needed any urging to suck lustily on his fat tool until with one last slurping lick she threw herself down on her back and opened her legs wide, exposing her puffy, tender cunney lips that protruded from the brown curly triangular bush of crisp pubic hair.

'Now it is your turn, Jack. Come now, satisfy me and put it in!' she ordered. His stiff staff waggling out like a flagpole, Dennison answered her call and clambered upon her rich, ample curves. A moan from them both signalled that he had found the target immediately and their lips met in the sweetest of kisses as Kathie jerked her lovely bum-cheeks up and down in order to absorb as much of his cock as quickly as possible. In a trice and with a choking cry his shaft was lodged fully inside her willing cunney and their pubic hairs mingled as I distinctly hear his balls bang against her bottom.

I slipped my hand down to Jimmy's crotch and was hardly surprised to find that his cock was rock hard and straining uncomfortably in the confines of his trousers. I could hardly blame him, for I was excited myself. Dennison was a handsome young man and the girl was a perfect little Venus, sweet seventeen with large breasts as white as snow, capped with distended red nips. I deftly unbuttoned Jimmy's trousers and pulled out his naked prick, rubbing and squeezing the hot shaft which made my lover sigh with pleasure.

Meanwhile the saucy maid was also swimming in pleasure, uttering little cries that she no longer wished to conceal. 'Oh, Jack, what a nice, thick prick you have. Ooh! Oooh! Fuck me harder you bigcocked boy! Crack away now!' she muttered fiercely.

Dennison did as he was told and I could see that her crack had received all of his cock and he was clenching it tightly as she rotated her hips sinuously, moving her cunney lips up and down his pulsating shaft as the willing lad vigorously heaved his buttocks and her bum answered his thrusts with little jerks of her own. 'I shall come in a minute, go faster, faster!' she howled. 'Right, here we go,' he panted in reply as his balls smacked against her bum with every long thrust. His body tensed and then he shuddered violently as he impelled the first gush of sperm inside her. 'Aaah! Aaah! That's lovely, I'm coming too!' she screamed out. 'Do more, more, more!' as she clawed at his back and crossed her legs wildly as the virile young fellow pumped spurt after spurt of creamy spray into her welcoming cunt.

This excited me so much that almost unconsciously I rubbed Jimmy's prick so hard and fast that he had only time to gasp 'Look out, Rosie!' before a little white fountain of spunk jetted out from his prick, mostly splattering against the garage door but a substantial amount shot over my dress.

'Oh dear, I am sorry,' he mumbled shamefacedly.

'Not to worry, darling, it wasn't your fault,' I assured him. 'We'll go back to the house and I'll change. Sarah will surely know how to clean sperm stains though I suppose it will be rather embarrassing to ask her!'

Jimmy grinned. 'You don't have to ask Sarah, sweetheart. Just pop into the chemist and ask for a bottle of carbon tetrachloride. It's the best cleaning fluid there is. All the boys at school keep bottles handy to clean their pyjamas up after a good night's wanking.'

'My, the things one learns.' I murmured as we took one last fleeting glimpse of Dennison and Kathie who were now lying down in each other's arms, quite exhausted after their passionate exhibition of *l'arte de faire l'amour*. Of course, we were both feeling terribly randy and when Jimmy followed me into my bedroom I was not displeased when he began tearing off his clothes.

'What on earth are you doing, Jimmy, there are no spunk stains on your trousers?' I asked sweetly.

'No, but there will be unless Mr Pego kisses Miss Quim,' he replied grimly, as he sat on my bed, pulling off his shoes and socks.

A moment later he was naked and the sight of his supple, muscular body aroused me even more, especially when I saw his cock rise up in salute as I lifted my dress in both hands and lifted it over my head. It took only a few moments more and then I too was naked and we embraced lovingly as I sat down besides him. Jimmy's fingers lightly brushed my breasts and my titties immediately jumped to attention.

'Do you like my nipples, Jimmy? They're not as big as Kathie's, are they?' I whispered.

'It's quality, not quantity which counts,' he said gallantly as his mouth came down to meet the soft flesh, his hands gently pushing my two globes together as his tongue came forward to circle around my engorged nipples. Then his mouth opened and drew in the red little soldiers, his tongue constantly moving, sending delicious vibrations throughout my entire body. Then I guided his hand down over my white belly to my hairy pussey and I let his long, tapering fingers caress my blonde pubic bush.

I gurgled happily as my cunney fairly throbbed from his probing, my juices beginning to pulse from me in a warm, sticky wetness. His mouth was on my titties again, his tongue reaching out to slide deliciously round my nipples as his hand moved purposefully in and out of my now thoroughly wet cunt until he was sliding his thumb around my pulsating clitty, pressing it and releasing it in a dangerously exciting way. My juices flowed freely as he inserted first one, then two and then finally three fingers up into my raging cunney.

Like myself, Jimmy may have been a novice at fucking but the dear boy had me squirming in ecstasy as his skilful fingers slithered over my clitty, sending me into deliriums of pure joy. I reciprocated by grabbing hold of his stiff shaft and moved forward to bring my lips down to the mushroom-shaped dome of his knob. Insouciantly, I let my tongue run the full length of the shaft, running back to the crown to catch a sticky drip of come that had formed at the 'eye' of his helmet. I ran my lips around the tip and then opened my mouth to accept its entrance.

By now Jimmy was so excited that immediately he forced at least three inches of his swollen todger between my lips and my body jerked instinctively away from the utter force of it. He retracted slightly so that his tool lay motionless for a moment, throbbing gently on my tongue. I closed my lips around the warm shaft and moved my tongue slowly across its substantial width. I sucked greedily on Jimmy's gorgeous big cock and twisted his head down so that his face was pushed into my own sopping groin. Jimmy realised what I wanted and my body fairly shook with delight as he removed his fingers from my crack and began circling his tongue around my dripping slit.

I felt his mouth flick across the grooves of my cunt which sent off fresh waves of pleasure crashing through me. I just had to have his lovely cock inside me now so I gently raised his head from my pussey and lifted my own from his throbbing tool.

'Jimmy, I'm ready for you now,' I said, and he needed no further words as he rolled on top of me as I spread my legs as wide as possible, keeping my hand on his prick to guide his knob between my yearning cunney lips. Dear Lord, his thick cock felt quite incredible as he pounded into me with exciting speed and power. 'Slow up for a moment,' I advised, and when every last fraction of Jimmy's prick was inside me and our pubic hairs were entwined together, I closed my thighs, making my handsome boy open his legs and lie astride me with his cock trapped sweetly inside my love-channel. He could not move his prick forwards or backwards as the muscles of my cunt were gripping him so tightly.

'Got you!' I giggled triumphantly.

'I'm more than happy to be your prisoner,' he countered, 'and I think that I deserve a sentence of not less than twenty-five years hard labour licking out your pussey.'

My reply was to grind my hips around, massaging his shaft as it throbbed merrily away inside my cunney which was by now dripping its love juices all down my thighs.

He grasped my bum-cheeks, which I absolutely adore, and I eased the pressure around his cock so that he was able to fuck me again. Jimmy responded by driving his pulsating pole back at terrific speed in and out of my cunt. Every last nerve in my body thrilled with exquisite rapture as I heaved up to meet his wild thrusts and I wound my legs around him so that his heavy hairy ballsack banged against my bottom as he buried that massive cock in to the very root. We rolled, we screamed together as we fucked happily away. From the insistent throbbing of his shaft I knew that Jimmy would soon be spurting his spunk inside me and sure enough, my cunney clamped down in a final burst of ecstasy as his stiff, jerking tool shot a tremendous wad of hot love-cream deep inside me. I pushed my pussey up against him, burying his cock even deeper to let all that wonderful milky froth bathe the inner walls of my cunt until my whole body glowed with lust.

We lay still for a minute until Jimmy slowly pulled out and sat up, his chest heaving as he gasped: 'Never mind Kathie or any other girl, Rosie. I just cannot believe that any girl could hold a candle to you when it comes to fucking.'

This was a kind thought but I felt it was right to say something of importance to us both. 'Jimmy,' I said gently. 'I do appreciate the compliment and I assure you that I feel the same way. But well, frankly, neither of us has enough experience to know whether what you have just said is true.'

Jimmy looked puzzled. 'Rosie, I don't think I quite understand you,' he said anxiously.

'Well,' I replied carefully, 'don't think for a moment that I haven't enjoyed our fucking tremendously because I have — but we both need to broaden our horizons. Not only must there be other ways of making love for us to explore but by only fucking with other partners will we know whether we have truly touched the heights.'

He bit his lip and looked extremely crestfallen. 'Yes, I see now what you are trying to tell me. But, oh, Rosie, I will miss you horribly!'

'You silly boy!' I cried. 'There is nor reason at all why we should not continue enjoying ourselves — all that I am saying is that if you want to fuck Kathie, I won't mind at all. Similarly, if I encourage Dennison to stick his shaft between my legs, you must try not to take umbrage either.'

Jimmy brightened up at these words. 'Perhaps we could do that together. What did Sir David Nash call his *fête à quatre* in that letter he wrote in the last edition of *The Oyster*, oh yes, a whoresome foursome,' he mused, his eyes gleaming at the thought of such lewd rudery.

Well as the old Sussex saying puts it, if you brood over your troubles, you'll have a perfect hatch. Jimmy looked on the bright side and as it turned out, he was to take part in a whoresome foursome far sooner than he could have possibly imagined.

Although I urged Jimmy to follow the Latin poet's advice to *carpe diem, quam minimum credula postero (seize the day, trusting the morrow as little as you can — Quintus Horatius Flaccus, c. 65 B.C. — Editor)*, I had no idea that later that very evening I would be encouraging him to slew his proud prick in and out of the love box of pretty Polly Potterley, the daughter of our village blacksmith. Readers blessed with retentive memory will recall her name for I mentioned her at the start of this narrative as the girl who sucked off Lord Gordon MacChesney whenever my randy old uncle could find the time and the place to be alone together with her.

I promised to keep a truthful record so I must unblushingly recount how Jimmy's initiation (and my own!) into partaking of the joys of forbidden fruit, i.e. making love with more than one partner. The facts of the matter are as follows: Jimmy waited for me to change and we decided to make our way to the music room. Jimmy was an accomplished pianist and I had accepted his offer to play for me whilst we rested from our previous erotic labours. On our way we met dear Uncle Gordon and Sarah who were just entering his bedroom. He looked terribly embarrassed and coloured up a bright red when I said sweetly: 'Good evening, Uncle, are you having an early night?' 'No, no, no,' he said hastily. 'I'm just going to instruct Sarah about my, ah, my, ah —'

'Bedclothes, perhaps?' said Jimmy helpfully.

'Ah, yes, thank you, young Horobin,' said Uncle gratefully. 'That's quite right, I'm just going to show her how I like my sheets and blankets to be arranged. Come, Sarah, this won't take long.' And with that he pushed the giggling girl into his room, and following her in smartly, closed the door and locked it behind them.

'Good old Uncle Gordon, I said he was a game old boy,' said Jimmy cheerfully, as we made our way to the music room. Our entire family play the beautiful Bechstein piano Papa purchased in Prague five years ago, whilst Jonathan (of whom I have neglected to mention was staying the night with the Nettletons who lived a mile or so on the other side of the village) and Mama were both talented violinists and were always in demand to perform at musical *soirées* given by Lady Judy Cole and other Society hostesses in London.

On reflection, I simply cannot offer an explanation as to why that night, almost without exception every inhabitant of Argosse Towers, resident and guest alike, all seemed to be engaged in some form or other of sensual play. Perhaps it was one of the herbs Mrs Moser used to achieve the superb piquancy of her *Poulet a l'Indienne* or some succubal grape used to make the '98 white Bordeaux Uncle Gordon had taken up from the cellar during the afternoon. But whatever the reason, quite unbelievably for the second time on this extraordinary evening, Jimmy and I stumbled across a second scene of sexual intercourse!

Perhaps prologue rather than scene would be a fairer description — for sitting on the piano stool with his trousers and underpants around his ankles was our dinner companion Mr Andrew Bennett, and kneeling between his legs was none other than pretty Polly Potterley, gently masturbating his thick semi-erect prick.

Here she was, holding Mr Bennett's substantial stiffstander in her hands, lightly kissing his hairy balls; truly,

67

when one does what likes and gets paid for it (and I am sure Polly was receiving more than grateful thanks from Uncle Gordon), one found one's niche in life. And Polly certainly enjoyed her work and was to find fame and fortune only a few short years afterwards. (*Polly Potterley went to London in 1907 and after meeting Sir Lionel Trapes became involved with several members of the ultra-fast South Hampstead set. After several adventures she married Derek, the simple-minded son of General Bedford Dunton-Green in 1911 and was left a small fortune and a country house in Kent when her husband was killed at Vichy Ridge during the First World War — Editor.*)

Now, we were able to view Dennison and Kathie's coupling in the garage without being noticed but here there was no hiding place to hand, although I must record that neither Mr Bennett nor Polly seemed unduly bothered by what I would have thought to be an unwelcome intrusion. 'Hello there,' called out Mr Bennett hospitably. 'Do come in but lock the door behind you if you don't mind. Polly's going to suck my cock, aren't you, my dear, and I would prefer not to have any further interruptions.'

'Good evening, Polly,' I said, trying hard to keep my *sang froid*. 'What a surprise to see you here. Actually, when you're here I rather thought that you might be engaged with my uncle.'

The pretty young jade smiled sweetly back at me. 'Good evening to you, Miss Rosie. Yes, usually I'd be sucking off Lord MacChesney by now but tonight he wants to fuck my friend Sarah, your chambermaid, so he kindly introduced Andrew to me so making sure that neither of us would feel lonely this evening. Lord MacChesney is so considerate, isn't he? But who is the handsome young gentleman next to you, Miss Rosie? I'm sure I've seen his face before somewhere, it looks very familiar to me.'

'I hardly think so, Polly,' I said stiffly. 'This gentleman happens to be the Honourable James Horobin. Jimmy, this young woman is Miss Polly Potterley.' Jimmy reached out to shake hands with the little minx who released one paw from Andrew Bennett's erect prick to smooth her fingers over Jimmy's knuckles.

'I know where I've seen your face before,' she exclaimed. 'I saw your photograph last week in the *Tatler*. Lord Gordon gives me the society magazines every week after he has finished with them and I've read about you, haven't I? You play football for Eton, and you scored the winning goal against Charterhouse for the Trewin Trophy last March, if I'm not mistaken. Oooh, how exciting to meet you, sir, what an honour!'

Jimmy licked his lips and though I could hardly complain if he acted upon the advice I had proffered less than an hour ago, it did strike me that words of simpering admiration from a pretty girl is a blandishment few red-blooded men can resist. Mind, from the look of Jimmy's face and the stirring movement noticeable in the front of his trousers, I could see that he was not even making an effort to counter the charms of this brazen young hussey. 'Don't call me sir, my friends call me Jimmy,' he smirked, as he and Polly exchanged a meaningful glance which they did not even try to conceal.

'Hold on a minute, you two,' cried Mr Bennett, who had also witnessed the mutual attraction between the randy pair. 'Now then, Polly, I don't want to sound troublesome but that's my old fellow you've got between your fingers and I thought you were going to give him a good seeing-to.'

'Oh, but I will, Andrew,' Polly promised him, although she looked straight at Jimmy as she added: 'I just love sucking pricks. I do so enjoy caressing a knob with my lips and sucking out the first blob of juice which I spread around the crown with my tongue. It feels so good licking and lapping a stiff shaft and taking it into my mouth. I like nothing better than when the man squirts out his sperm too, it is so exciting when it shoots down my throat that I always spend myself. There's nothing that tastes so fine and clean as spunk. Indeed, I could suck on cock for hours but none of the men can hold back for more than five minutes at best. It really is very unfair, don't you think, Miss Rosie?'

'I'm afraid I haven't given the matter much thought, Polly,' I said coolly, but Jimmy quickly took her part. 'It *is* unfair, Polly,' he agreed. 'However, I would very much like to offer my prick for your delectation.'

'Ooh, that would be lovely,' she replied with a saucy smile, before hastily adding: 'But first let me attend to Andrew who has been very patient.' The merry girl was pretty enough, her chin being charmingly dimpled with full and pouting lips which, slightly open, gave a glimpse of two even rows of ivory-white teeth set in the deep rosy flesh of her small mouth. Her nose was of the Roman cast, though not large, and her eyes were a sparkling, lustrous brown which matched her hair which she let down so that it hung loose down to her shoulders. She was wearing an emerald-green dress, low cut with a long skirt which I later discovered to be a birthday gift from Uncle Gordon, and when she leaned forward we were treated to a show of her full, white breasts and the dress was cut so low that her nipples were only just concealed by the fabric.

Polly began to manipulate Andrew Bennett's cock, taking hold of his substantial shaft with both hands, but suddenly she stopped and said: 'You know, Andrew, you have been such a good sport, I'm going to give you an extra treat. Would you like to see me without my clothes on?' Well, you can imagine the answer which burst forth simultaneously from the throats of both Andrew and Jimmy! So Polly shucked off her dress and peeled of her chemise and drawers to stand in glorious nudity before us.

I was forced to admire her rich, dark brown hair that clustered in ringlets over her neck and shoulders which contrasted in singular fashion with the dazzling whiteness of her skin. Her breasts were luxuriantly large, proudly jutting out and tipped with small but pointed nipples of a deep pink colour and which I now understand denotes strong sexual urgings in the character of the possessor. Her waist was graceful and her belly flat and covered right at the bottom by a generous growth of nut-brown hair; and from between the silky locks that grew over her love mount, I could perceive a delicious looking little slit with two rosy lips. Polly Potterley, I grudgingly admitted, was as luscious a sight of feminine pulchritude as ever I had seen and I must confess that her body awoke a sensual desire within my own body.

But Polly was now ready to send Andrew Bennett on a trip to paradise. She hopped down on her knees, and opening her luscious little mouth she enclosed his helmet with her lips, working on the sensitive tip with her tongue. She eased her lips, taking in a little more of his shaft as her hand circled the base of his cock. She worked the loose skin up and down the shaft as she began to bob her head up and down and Andrew Bennett's hands now went to the back of her head, pushing her mouth even further down upon his swollen cock. Somehow, Polly managed to swallow almost all of his hard rod and she was obviously enjoying herself as she sucked happily away on his thick prick, an activity that was accompanied by a most arousing and stimulating squelching sound as his stiff penis slid wetly in and out of her mouth.

Polly was well schooled in the art of sucking, for Mr Bennett was soon gasping as her little tongue flicked out and lapped lusciously on his throbbing stalk and when her teeth scraped the tender cockflesh when she drew his knob into her mouth, the poor man simply could no longer contain himself and he thrust his hips upwards and discharged a copious emission of sperm down her throat. Polly squirmed with pleasure as she swallowed as much of his creamy love-juice as possible gobbling the nectar spilling from the swollen sweetmeat pulsating between her lips.

Nevertheless, some of the precious white froth did drip from her mouth on to the beige Chinese carpet, something that Jimmy noticed and he muttered: 'Those smears will take some explaining away, Rosie. You'd better get that carbon tetrachloride first thing in the morning.'

Polly must have heard this aside for she looked up and wiping her lips of the last traces of spunk with the tip of her tongue and said: 'Oh, don't worry about the carpet, Mr

Jimmy. Sarah always keeps a bottle of Dr Humphrey Price's Famous Elixir handy. It's a really wonderful compound that removes stains from any material, whilst Mr Reynolds the gardener says a weekly dose has worked wonders for his roses.'

'I'm glad to hear it,' grunted Mr Bennett. 'I'm sorry I came so quickly, my dear, but your sweet suction finished me off far quicker than either of us really wanted. But my old John Thomas won't take long to recover if you're game for another go.'

'Surely, but first let me sample Mr Jimmy's prick,' cooed Polly. 'Why don't you two gentlemen get undressed, by the way, it's much more comfortable to fuck in the nude.'

Jimmy was the first to disrobe, and he and Polly looked a fine sight as they stood together with the voluptuous girl smoothing her hands over his slim yet muscular body. Their mouths slowly came together and as their eyes closed their lips met in the most passionate of kisses and their bodies too came together and their pubic muffs rubbed roughly against each other. Polly broke the embrace by sliding her lips down Jimmy's body as she slowly sank to her knees. He writhed and gasped with delight as her mouth reached his navel and when the strands of her silky brown hair brushed against his rising prick, he groaned out loud with barely suppressed excitement. Polly pressed his throbbing truncheon against her cheek as she lovingly weighed his heavy balls in the palms of her hands.

She now began to lick his balls, flicking her hot little tongue all around the hairy pink sack. Then she opened her mouth wide and took in both of his nuts, somehow managing to get both of them inside her mouth. As Jimmy moaned with pleasure she grabbed his huge stiff cock with both hands and, releasing his balls, began to nibble the uncapped mushroom dome of his knob. She then stuffed the purple helmet inside her mouth and began to bob her head back and forth, her lips working furiously to capture as much of Jimmy's cock as possible until she had gradually eased almost all of his giant whopper into her mouth.

Jimmy bucked and heaved, thrusting his tool in and out of her mouth in an ever-quickening rhythm and Polly guessed that she would have to stop sucking or Jimmy's proud young cock would spurt its spunk as quickly as Andrew Bennett's, which would never do. So she placed her hands on his shoulders as she lifted her lips reluctantly away from his pulsating prick. She pulled Jimmy down so that he lay flat on his back with his stiff cock pointing rampantly upwards. She climbed over him and pulled open her cunney lips with her fingers and started to rub her pussey to and fro across the end of his bulbous knob.

She then moved downwards a little to let his glistening helmet enter her yearning crack and she gently eased herself upon it so that every last fraction of his sizeable shaft was embedded inside her. She held him in place by cleverly tightening the walls of her cunney and paused for a brief moment, like a rider testing a new mount, before clamping her vaginal muscles on his engorged cock. Then Polly began to rock to and fro on her steed whilst Jimmy arched his body upwards in time with her rhythm, filling her pussey to the limit with his surging, pistoning prick. She pumped her tight little buttocks furiously up and down, digging her fingernails into his shoulders as she held on to her bucking bronco. Each luscious shove was accompanied by wails of ecstasy from the two of them. Jimmy grabbed her pert breasts and athletically moving his head upwards, sucked Polly's rosy nipples and she cried out: 'Oh that's lovely, that's delicious, you've made me come, you lovely fucker!'

Polly was as good as her word and Jimmy helped her in her ride to Elysium, pushing her up and letting her drop hard on his rock-hard penis. She shivered as she began to spend, trembling violently as she reached the apex and she pulled him tightly as she entered the throes of orgasm. This set Jimmy's sperm boiling up in his balls and they peaked together, his hot white love-juice creaming Polly's cunt as she shuddered into a magnificent climax.

'What a lovely fuck,' breathed Polly. 'You scored a bullseye with the very first dart. And my God, your cock's still hard — are you game for another go?'

'I am if you're ready — but what about letting Rosie and Andrew join in?' suggested Jimmy. By all means, I thought, for my blood was now fired by seeing this delicious girl suck and fuck my boyfriend's prick, so I hastily undressed whilst Andrew Bennett took himself in hand and violently friggs his cock so that it stood up proudly again, ready for the fray.

Frankly, I was uncertain as to how to enter the game but fortunately Polly decided to take charge of proceedings. 'I think you and I should start things off, Miss Rosie, so as to let the boys really relax and get their cocks as hard as possible. Don't you agree?'

'That sounds like a good idea,' I said carefully. 'What shall we do?'

'Well, why don't you lie down on the carpet and let me give you a massage,' she replied. I lay down obediently and Polly knelt in front of me, massaging the insides of my thighs. It was most pleasant and I made no objection when her hands dipped between my legs so that her fingertips lightly grazed the pouting lips of my pussey. My heart began to pound as she suddenly switched her attention to my breasts, lightly cupping the white, rounded globes saying: 'What lovely titties you have, Miss Rosie, I'm sure they are much bigger than mine.' I smiled my appreciation of the compliment as her fingers continued to squeeze and knead my breasts until she let her right hand trail down over my tummy and through my blonde bush. The she whispered: 'Spread your legs wider and I'll give you and extra-special treat!' The combination of flattery and the intense tingling feeling that was spreading all over me made it impossible to do more than murmur a quiet word of thanks.

I shuddered with pleasure as I felt her wicked fingers pirouette around the folds of my cunney but I was so heated now that as her fingers slid into my moistening honeypot and started to tickle my clitty that I achieved a little spend almost at once and I could see that Polly was now also becoming very excited.

Now we lost all pretence of restraint and Polly kissed me with fiery passion. She got on top of me and as our mouths met our breasts rubbed together and I could feel her thick brown bush brush against my own silkier blonde as she positioned herself so that our clitties touched each time she pushed her hips forward.

Like nipples, like clitty, the old saying goes and certainly Polly proved the role, as I could feel her stiff clitty protruding out of her pussey. Indeed, her clitty became so big when she was excited that she was able to direct the stiff little soldier to my own juicy passage. She then stuffed it, lips and all in my own affair and closed my cunt lips upon it, holding them tightly together with her hand. It is difficult for me to express how novel and delightful this unusual conjunction was to me. We were both so heated as our love-juices trickled down and mingled as we reached new heights of erotic joy. Without separating for a second, Polly rubbed and pushed inside me, the lips and hair of her cunney titillating my own cunt in a most thrilling fashion. We swam in a veritable sea of lubricity as we both spent mightily, feeling the strength of our orgasms course through our soft bodies.

But still this insatiable girl was not satisfied! She readjusted her position, turning across me so that she sat on her knees with her facing away from me. Then she seductively wiggled her tight little backside backwards so that her dark pussey passage was directly over my face whilst she leaned forward and spread my pussey lips with her tongue, sliding through them with ease as we both began to lick and lap along the slits of each other's dripping cunnies, exploring, tasting, tickling and sucking.

This picture of female saturnalia so excited Andrew Bennett that his trusty right hand flew to his upstanding thick cock and as Polly and I spent for a second time, Mr Bennett sent spurt after spurt of sticky white love-juice all over us, coating our bodies with jism as we screamed our delight at reaching again the summits of the mountain of love.

We stayed in this position as Jimmy now brought his strong young cock into the game. He knelt behind my head and positioned himself so that the tip of his unhooded weapon was pressed between Polly's bum-cheeks with his balls hanging down almost touching my mouth.

'Ah, Mr Jimmy,' gasped Polly. 'Would you do me the pleasure of fucking my bottom whilst suck off Mr Andrew again? Miss Rosie, would you kindly wet his tool with spittle to help him on his way?'

'My pleasure,' I replied gaily, and after moistening Jimmy's thick tool, I raised Polly's beautiful buttocks and pulled them apart so that her tiny, wrinkled little bum-hole was exposed to Jimmy's attack. He shoved in steadily but not too quickly as she wriggled and twisted until he had managed to insert almost all of his cock in her bottom as I licked and lapped at his nice big balls. this lecherous tableau so affected Mr Bennett that his prick swelled up very shortly to a good hard stiffness and he scrambled down in front of Polly so she could suck his cock whilst Jimmy bent over to fondle her dangling breasts as he jerked his twitching tool in and out of her arse.

Jimmy was first to spend, sending a shower of sperm into Polly's juicy bottom just before Andrew Bennett jetted his jism into her mouth. This double libation of love-juice sent Polly off again but though I enjoyed sucking Jimmy's balls, no one finished me off and I ruefully complained about this unhappy fact to my friends.

'I'm terribly sorry, Rosie, but it will take a while for my prick to perk up again,' apologised Mr Bennett.

'I'm afraid to say that goes for me too,' added Jimmy regretfully. 'Can you wait a while for us to recover?'

I remembered Sarah's advice to Uncle Gordon. 'Polly, you don't happen to have some mustard about the place by any chance?' She giggled and replied: 'Oh, you know about our old country remedy of dabbing a bit up their arses, Miss Rosie? It's a bit drastic, that — I've another idea, why don't you suck my pussey instead. I'll wager that will stiffen up their shafts soon enough.'

'Oh, I do so agree with you, Polly,' said Mr Bennett hastily. 'That's a far better suggestion. I'm sure that Jimmy and I would much prefer to see you suck Polly's pussey which would give us both much pleasure.'

The idea certainly did not displease me, especially when Polly stretched herself languidly down on the carpet, her legs apart and her hands jiggling her firm, uptilted breasts in a most inviting display of sensuality. I lay down besides her and leaning over, kissed her upright little nipples, twirling my tongue around them. I flicked them up to a fine state of erection and then let my mouth travel slowly along her soft, trembling flesh downwards to her groin. As I caressed her wonderful jiggling bum cheeks with my hands I let my own nipples, now hard with desire for this delicious girl, tracked down the length of her as I let my hips rest just inches away from the mossy brown bush between her legs.

Instinctively she cradled my head in her hands and gently moved it towards her wet, swollen cunney lips. I paused for a moment to take in the musky aroma before kissing the pink crack, making Polly shudder with anticipatory delight. Lovingly I began to feast upon her pussey, forcing my questing tongue deep inside her juicy gash, sliding up and down her slit. The quivering girl gasped with excitement as the tip of my tongue probed between her cunney lips, allowing it slide through her smooth passageway to find her erect clitty that was fairly pulsating with passion and I let it roll between my lips, sucking wildly on the chewy little morsel. Polly now gurgled her thanks as she twisted this way and that, throwing herself all over the place as she began to rub herself off against my mouth.

Jimmy and Andrew were both watching intently with their pricks in their hands and surprisingly perhaps it was the older man whose staff was the first to swell up. I had no desire for Andrew Bennett to waste his upright stiffstander so I pulled my lips away from the folds of Polly's pussey just long enough to urge him to place his prick in my cunt from behind.

'There can be no command that I would be more willing to obey,' said Andrew Bennett as he knelt behind me and raised by backside in the air, opening my legs slightly so that he could insert the tip of his plum crown between my cunney lips. I wriggled around so that he could push in his prick right up — but alas, despite Mr Bennett's frantic urgings, his tingling tool began to deflate and even though Polly took his shaft in her mouth and valiantly attempted to suck it up back to stiffness, his penis obstinately refused to harden and he was forced to retreat, making profuse apologies for the poor performance of his limp limb.

Nevertheless, this little piece of theatre did not stop me from tonguing Polly's pretty pussey and as Mr Bennett made his crestfallen way back to his seat, the lovely girl poured out her love-juice all over my tongue. It was extremely palatable to my taste, with a less salty flavour perhaps than Jimmy's sperm.

Meanwhile, however, I remained unsatisfied! 'My cock's still *hors de combat* but let me see if I can bring you off in a different way,' said Jimmy, jumping up from his chair and placing himself in front of me as Polly rolled herself to Andrew Bennett and commenced to play with his prick in the hope of encouraging a more permanent erection. I lay on my back, stroking my thighs sensuously and I noticed how the sunlight was playing across my body, highlighting the golden hairs of my bush as Jimmy's hand snaked between my legs and rose into the soft cleft of my cunt.

I grabbed his head and pushed his handsome face into my crotch and he nuzzled his lips against my cunney lips, kissing and sucking uninhibitedly, not like a novice at the art of cunnilingus (which he was), but as an experienced pussey eater of the calibre of my dear friend Sir David Nash (*more of this gentleman in the next volume of Rosie's memoirs — Editor*) who is surely one of the world champions of this noble art.

'A-h-r-e, A-h-r-e,' I panted, as his palating sent shivers

of desire exploding in my cunt. 'Who taught you to pleasure pussey like that?'

'It's just a natural gift, I suppose,' he said modestly, as he slid his hand inside my cunt to juice me up even more. Oh how his fingers twisted and turned inside my pussey and it felt as though an electric current had been passed through me and I could feel my cunney juice fairly dripping down my thighs. He then proceeded to lick out my love box until my stimulated slit was almost aching for a real fucking.

Jimmy somehow sensed how I felt for he rose up and straddled my body. I looked up and saw that his penis had now revived and was swelling up before my eyes to its previous delicious hardness. 'Assh, your lovely prick is back in business, please fuck me now, darling,' I breathed.

Nothing loath, Jimmy mounted me, guiding the tip of his knob between my pouting cunney lips. 'More, more — ram your tadger in to the limit!' I cried, as I raised my hips sharply to meet him, forcing in more of his rampant smooth shaft which alas slid out as I fell back. On stiffened arms, he teased my pussey by keeping his cock from entry until I tickled him under the arms and then with an almighty groan he drove down and I took in the whole of Jimmy's cock from tip to root. As our pubic hairs enjoined I wrapped my legs around his waist as Polly temporarily gave up frigging Andrew Bennett's recalcitrant cock to kindly slip a cushion under my arse to increase the delightful pressure of his prick against my cunt. Oh, the divine joy of possessing a hot, stiff shaft in one's cunney! Can there be anything in the whole wide world to even approach the pleasure of fucking with a powerful yet considerate lover who knows how to use his thick, upstanding cock? As Jimmy's stroke became more and more insistent I spent again and again. Then I felt Jimmy go rigid and hold his breath and it was his turn to climax as he ejaculated with a final great shudder and a hoarse cry which rattled out of his throat, he sent his semen squirting inside me, drenching my cunney walls as I squeezed his balls, releasing a further gorgeous sensuous spend that burst forth from deep within me.

This set off Polly again for she insisted on squeezing Andrew Bennett's ballsack and sucking his twitching tool until at last it stood up again, as fine and stiff as a flagpole. She then threw herself astride his hips and with a single downwards motion slid her hungry cunney up and down the quivering length of his staff. She crooned with glee as his glistening pole slid in and out of her sopping nest and they came off together in a grand finale of frenetic fucking.

As time passed we amused ourselves in a variety of postures until the two men pleaded for the proceedings to be brought to an end. 'My goodness, and they call themselves the stronger sex. I am sure that Miss Rosie and I could continue screwing at least till midnight but just look at the state of this little prick,' teased Polly, flipping Jimmy's limp shaft in a gesture of derision.

'Good God, what you need is a stable of studs!' snorted Mr Bennett, who took umbrage at her remark. 'Few men could have fucked as well or as often as young Jimmy and I did tonight.

'Surely you girls are not complaining?' he added plaintively.

I felt rather sorry for them, so I said: 'No, no, not at all, I think both of your cocks deserve ten out of ten for their efforts. Why, just look at the love-juice stains on the carpet! They'll prove quite a test for Dr Price's Famous Elixir! Don't be hurt, it's just that we girls still feel frisky.'

'You will just have to play with yourselves then,' groaned Jimmy as with a great sigh he turned on his side and in an instant fell fast asleep. Mr Bennett followed suit so Polly and I dressed ourselves and for a joke, gathered up the boys' clothes and hid Jimmy's togs in my bedroom and Andrew Bennett's in Polly's — in fact, though Polly and I could have carried on playing in this whoresome foursome, we were really quite exhausted too and after we kissed each other good-night, we both retired to our own rooms to await our lovers.

In fairness, I must record that Polly and I did not have too long to wait for our beaux. When they woke to discover that not only Polly and myself but their clothes were missing they guessed where both their girls and their clobber might be found. Jimmy managed to reach my bedroom and climb into bed without being seen but Mr Bennett's bare bottom was seen by Sayers on the stairs as the butler prepared to close up the house for the night. However, as our old retainer has always been the soul of discretion I cannot believe that he will report the incident to my Papa when my parents return home next week!

Finally, although Jimmy and I fucked and sucked each other the next morning *ad infinitum*, alas, a telegram arrived from Goulthorp, Jimmy's valet to inform him that he must return home immediately as his parents were due back in London the very next day.

3

Off to School

The next day I waved a fond farewell to Jimmy as he boarded the 8.45 a.m. train back to town. The only comfort was that we would meet again next Thursday at Lady Macdougall's annual charity ball in aid of indigent members of the bookselling trade. With luck we would be able to slip away far from the madding crowd and enjoy each other's bodies in one of the several guest bedrooms in her ladyship's mansion in the leafy village of Barnes on the southern bank of the River Thames near the London suburb of Hammersmith.

Life was far duller without Jimmy — and poor Uncle Gordon fretted similarly from the lack of a bed-partner as he was unable to fuck Sarah for the following three days. For much against his will, he was pressed into service by Colonel Nettleton to sit on the bench whilst the local magistrate dealt with the latest crop of miscreants. The only amusing anecdote I can record about this event was that one of David Pickering, a poacher, was apprehended by Maddocks, one of the good Colonel's gamekeepers, after Pickering had bagged a couple of rabbits for the pot from our neighbour's land. He would have escaped scot free if in the woods he had not come across the gamekeeper's wife on her knees lustily sucking the pricks of two of the potboys who work at the village inn. Naturally, this stirring sight caused Pickering to cease his flight and as he watched entranced by this stimulating spectacle, he was pounced upon by Maddocks. Even then, he could have escaped but when he saw Maddocks burst out from the brush and threaten to blow the boys' balls to kingdom come with buckshot from his shotgun, the plucky poacher broke cover and wrestled the gun away from the raging gamekeeper.

'Colonel Nettleton is so down on poachers that he wanted to give the poor fellow three months' hard labour, but I said Pickering deserved a commendation from preventing serious injury or even worse,' I heard Uncle Gordon tell Sayers, as he played snooker with our butler that evening.

'Did you manage to change his mind, My Lord?' enquired Sayers.

'Eventually,' replied my dear old Uncle. 'I wanted to reward Pickering with five pounds from the court funds for his bravery but the Colonel would have none of it so in the end we compromised and bound both men over to keep the peace.'

'A fair compromise, My Lord,' commented the butler, as he dextrously manoeuvred the remaining red ball between two of the other colours still on the table.

'Good shot, Sayers,' said Uncle Gordon generously, complimenting our old retainer on his fine play. 'Mind, you've given me the sporting gentleman's favourite choice — should I go for the pink or the brown? Mind, one had to feel sorry for Maddocks, it must have been a great shock for him to find his wife in such an indelicate position.'

Sayers shook his head. 'Not really so, My Lord, the woman in question is well known round the area for her predilection in seducing young men and her husband's rage was in my opinion mostly simulated. Maddocks is not unaware of the matter and indeed I have heard that on many Saturday nights they jointly invite a lad to join them in bed after Mr Stockman closes the tavern.'

'Stockman, Stockman, now isn't he the chap with extraordinary big bollocks?'

'So it is rumoured, though no doubt Sarah and Kathie would know better than I as to whether this is true.'

I left them to their game, musing that despite the thunderings from the Reverend Boms in the pulpit and the leaflets warning against the perils of the Sins Of The Flesh distributed to villagers by the Misses Allendaler, three crabbed old sisters who lived in the Old Rectory. As Oscar Wilde told Papa when my father dined with the disgraced wit in Paris shortly before he died: 'The Europeans have sex lives, the English have hot water bottles!'

Be that as it may, I asked Mrs Moser to prepare a slap-up tea for my best girlfriends, who, you may recall, dear reader, I had invited for my birthday celebration on the afternoon of my parents' return. As it turned out, Mama and Papa were delayed for twenty-four hours but I decided that there was no need to postpone my little party. Katie, Gillian, Mary and Susie were all able to come but poor Sheena Waleshaw was unable to leave her bed as she contracted a nasty chill after dancing the night away at her cousin Deborah's coming-out party a few nights before.

'How is poor Sheena? I hope that at least she enjoyed Deborah's dance,' I said to my friends.

'Don't worry about Sheena,' laughed Katie. 'She was the belle of the ball. Why, she had George de Souza, Sir Andrew Stuck and even the Marquis de Soveral fighting to place their names on her card. (*Until the 1930s, girls were issued with dance cards at such upper-crust functions and before the music began, gentlemen would ask for their names to be filled in for The Lancers, the Military Two Step and – the highest prize of all – the Last Waltz! – Editor*).

'Sheena always attracts the best men,' added Katie with a sigh. 'I bet she doesn't take a blind bit of notice of what old Ma Ogden was blathering about to the sixth-form girls last term – not that you can blame her for that,' she sighed.

Here I must explain that Ma Ogden, or Miss Edwina Margaret Ogden M.A. (Cantab) to be exact, is the revered headmistress of St Hilda's Academy For The Daughters Of Gentlefolk in sunny Devon where we all received our secondary education. 'Why, what did she have to say?' I asked. I had missed the last two days of the previous term, for during his Spring vacation Papa had taken Mama, Jonathan and myself on a most enjoyable holiday in Italy.

'Oh, she decided to call in several of her young ladies, as she calls us, for a private discussion on personal and private matters,' said Susie, with a cheeky giggle. 'I think Miss Ogden believes that we know nothing about what happens between husbands and wives in bed.'

'What about men and mistresses?' smiled Katie.

'Or between ladies like Miss Throng the games teacher and Miss Bulle?' I added, and we all pealed with laughter. It transpired that Miss Ogden, no doubt under the orders of the school governors, had attempted to teach the facts of life to the girls — most of whom probably had already as much if not more experience in *amour* than poor Miss O. who was not the most sensual of ladies and who had devoted her life to the instruction of mathematics and geography to young ladies between the ages of fourteen and sixteen, few of whom cared a jot for anything except enjoying themselves out of the classroom.

'Honestly, Rosie, you would hardly credit it,' said Susie. 'She began by saying how terrible were these wild women who demanded the vote. "This clamour for political rights is woman's confession of sexual enmity. Always remember, girls, that unless we are prepared to make of marriage a mere civil partnership, dissolvable at will, the correct relationship between husband and wife is one of control and decision on the part of the husband and deference and submission on that of the wife's. Never forget, girls, that where two ride on a horse, one must needs ride behind." I just don't know how we all kept a straight face!'

'Did she talk about you-know-what?' I wondered.

'Gosh yes, and the poor old thing was frightfully embarrassed by it all,' Alice chipped in. 'She gave us all a leaflet written by Sister Elizabeth Thomson which explains all about how penises swell up when men cannot control themselves and that married ladies have the unfortunate duty to let their husbands place their members in their vaginas. "If ever any of girls get married," said Miss Ogden, "you will have to let your husbands lie on top of you during their baser moments. I suggest that the best thing you can do is lie back and think of England for it is intercourse, when all is said and done, that causes babies to be born." '

Well, at least no one could argue with that latter observation. Mind, it set me thinking that I had better visit Dr Bucknall's Surgical Stores in Chichester as soon as possible for a douche, as although I had taken only a very, very small chance of becoming *enceinte* through my romps with Jimmy Horobin, in future I should prepare myself better for fucking and let the boys know that their purchase of French letters would be welcomed.

Meanwhile, the girls regaled me about their latest encounters with the boys from St Trippett's College who attended our school debates every term and – under the strictest of supervision – the school's Spring, Summer and Christmas country-dancing parties.

Katie was first to tell us of what occurred between her and Robert Bacon, the handsome captain of cricket at St Trippett's. She said: 'Girls, you mustn't tell a soul because you know what my Papa is like – if he ever found out what happened, he would take his horse-whip to dear Robert.'

'Robert and I had both managed to arrange absence of leave one afternoon – we met secretly and wandered through the woods together, holding hands and chatting away like the close friends we were fast becoming. I should tell you that I was wearing my tennis outfit (for I had told Miss Ogden that I had been asked to play with the curate of Little Bristow) and that the previous evening I had taken the scissors to the neckline of the blouse to give the garment a plunging *décolettée* finish that revealed the full, firm swell of my breasts to satisfying effect.

'My efforts were much appreciated by Robert for as we rested on a grassy knoll we were soon kissing and cuddling in fine old style. Oh, Robert is such a well-informed boy and I did feel so frisky that when he moved his hands from my back to rove over my scantily covered breasts, I made no attempt to arrest their progress. Of course, he was soon passing his lips over my naked nipples, kissing and sucking the titties like a real lover.

'I had never allowed him to go even as far as this before, but my blood was up and when he placed his hand on my knee and toyed with my thigh I knew what was to follow but again I made no move to stop him. So soon his hand was working its way up my leg and I even let him slip his fingers into the lacy knickers I was wearing and toy with my curly little bush.

'I know I should have put an end to it then and there but his fingers made me feel so good as they toyed with my trembling pussey lips that it was only when he attempted to lift my dress and press his face against my cunney that I called a halt and then only because I had already felt my pussey was already moist from a nice spend. Luckily, Robert behaved like a true gentleman and even offered to put his quivering bar penis back in his trousers (for he had unbuttoned whilst we were petting).

'To his everlasting credit, Robert Bacon did not attempt to force me to carry on further than I wished to go but we carried on canoodling and I will readily confess that I did take his lovely big prick in my hand. And oh! What a tremendous size it was! Whilst this was not the first time I had seen a stiff cockshaft, the upstanding girth and length of this one was beyond all my previous experience. I judged its length to be not less than ten inches and a full five inches in girth. Robert guided my unresisting fingers towards it and shyly I grasped this smooth fleshy pole with my hand, unable of course to fully circle it with my fingers. Though this was the first time I had ever touched a stiff manly organ, I knew what to do and I rubbed it up and down until it spurted a huge amount of foamy white spunk. We both so enjoyed the afternoon that next time I might let Robert proceed further down the path of love and allow him to play with my pussey whilst I lick his prick. I've always wanted to try that though I must say that his tool looks so big that I'm sure I'll never be able to cram it all in my mouth let alone swallow all that jism.'

Katie paused and said: 'Well, that's all that's happened so far, but Robert and I have planned an assignation for the first week of next term and I can't tell you how much I am looking forward to it immensely.'

Alas, *tempus fugit*, friendly reader and I must leave matters here for the moment, except to mention that the very next day my dear parents returned and after we had made our joyful reunion, Papa and Mama told me the most exciting news — if I was agreeable to the idea, I could leave St Hilda's immediately and in the Autumn take up a place at Madame Dupont's exclusive finishing school in Switzerland. Like Papa, I have always wanted to travel and I was thrilled to hear that he had managed to secure me a place in one of the most sought-after establishments of its kind in all of Europe.

Of one thing I was certain — Madame Dupont's would offer me the opportunity to put into practise the idea of obtaining a variety of sensual experiences. Jimmy Horobin had seized upon my words and acted upon them at the first available opportunity with Polly. Now it was to be my turn!

I stretched my toes catlike towards the roaring log fire and contemplated my first week in Switzerland at Madame Dupont's Academy for Young Ladies on the beautiful banks of Lake Lucerne.

The school building itself was divinely elegant with a sweeping gravel drive, lined with conifers, leading up to a tall, carved wooden door set between majestic stone pillars. In the centre of the tidily clipped lawn was a tiny fountain set about with stone nymphs, and the beds bordering the drive were filled to bursting with fragrant spring flowers.

My days at the Academy were filled with the kind of studies designed to turn myself and my fellow students — a motley collection of girls from all over the world — into elegant and accomplished young ladies of breeding. Mornings were filled with lessons in French, cookery, geography and history, while the afternoons were set aside for music, drawing and painting, needlepoint and long, leisurely strolls on the banks of the lake, collecting wild flowers and interesting pebbles from the water's edge.

Although it was spring and the weather was beginning to turn a little warmer, the log fire in the girls' drawing room where I sat was necessary to take the chill from the air. Indeed, I felt my cheeks flush with warmth as I surveyed the room with its floor to ceiling windows with their breathtaking views, walls filled with books and pictures and its comfortably worn chintz sofas and Chesterfields.

Since I was alone, I kicked off my shoes and removed my stockings, drawing my long skirt to above my shapely knees, the better to feel the sensual warmth from the fire against my long, smooth legs.

With a secret smile of pleasure and stretching languorously, I took the letter from darling Simon, my brother Thomas's best friend, from inside the bodice of my undergarment where it had nestled, undetected, in the cleft between my warm, snowy breasts. From time to time during the day I'd remembered its presence and felt a thrill of anticipation as I counted the hours until I could steal away from the other girls and devour its contents.

I began to read:

My darling Rosie,

Since you left this morning for Switzerland, my mind and senses have been filled with you and memories of our last, sweet congress. So wonderful and delightfully erotic was it that my only desire at present is to put pen to paper and write about it in full, for our mutual delectation. I wish to describe each delicious nuance, that we might both, in our different countries and with the wide sea dividing us, relive the drama of those magical hours when time stood still and I was putty in your tender lily-white hands.

Do you recall how I stood behind you and gently ran my fingers through your soft blonde hair, then firmly massaged your neck and shoulders until I felt you shudder with pleasure. Still rubbing and caressing your back and sides, my strong hands moved round and discovered the full swell of your breasts. I slowly undid the buttons of your dress and, beneath it, your chemise, which fell open to reveal your gorgeous breasts, warm and naked beneath my cool hands.

At my touch, at first as light as a feather, I felt them tremble with delicious anticipation and your nipples swell and jut proudly against my palms. I tweaked them mischievously, making you squeal with delight, and lightly ran my fingernails across the ample, rounded undersides of your glorious titties. My naughty tickling caused you to gasp and your breathing to increase in rapidity, making your tits jiggle and bounce in my hands.

Moving ever downwards and stroking your soft ribcage, at the same time peeling down your dress and chemise to below your flat belly, my fingers snaked inside your frilly white drawers, twisting and rustling your crinkly pubic hair which is as soft and blonde as the hair on your beautiful head.

Suddenly, giggling with pleasure, you escaped from my grasp and, cheeks flushed and tits bouncing, ran to the other side of the room, losing most of your clothes on the way except for your silky stockings and lacy garters. From this position you commenced a display of the utmost lewdness, the memory of which has had me frigging myself dry every hour on the hour from the time of our parting.

At first, placing a delicate finger between your soft, pouting lips and sucking it provocatively, your huge blue eyes looked sulkily at me from beneath your sweeping, black lashes. Then, slowly undulating your slim, sexy hips and gazing downwards, you clasped your large, firm white breasts in both hands and squeezed them together so that your jutting strawberry nipples almost touched, creating a long, shadowy cleft between them.

With a slow, sexy smile you turned your back on me, gracefully parted your long, stockinged legs and flopped *over like a rag doll, naughtily wiggling your round, tight arse high in the air and showing your silky blonde cunt hair and your pink pussey lips to me, as well as your little wrinkled anus.*

Unable to control my lust any longer I pounced on you, breathing furiously and nuzzling your hair, at the same time fumbling with your fleshy tits with one hand and lowering my trousers and undergarments with the other.

Dropping to your hands and knees, tits dangling, legs spread wide and arse proudly displayed in all its glory, you presented a spectacular image with your soft skin sheened with sweat and your cunt gleaming hot and pink. Panting with excitement and firmly grasping your hips, I sank my huge, engorged prick between the cheeks of your bum and into your welcoming cunt, the walls of which hugged me tight like a long-lost friend.

Slowly at first, then faster and faster, I fucked your tight pussey, grunting with the exertion of it, until I heard your little screams of pleasure and I knew orgasm was near. Only when I was certain you'd reached your climax did I thrust my cock into you one final, stupendous time and issue forth my jets of salty spunk.

Sinking to the floor next to you and taking your naked body, slippery and fragrant with sweat, in my arms, I kissed and fondled you and swore you'd always be mine. Please say you will, my darling Rosie!

I'll love you always and find myself weak with anticipation of your letter back to me. Make it soon, my angel.

Your own,

Simon.

With a deep sigh of pleasure and a secret, sensual smile, I stretched full-length on the sofa where I'd been sitting and threw my arms, with gay abandon, above my head to lose myself in a delicious erotic reverie.

Quite unaware of how long I'd lain like that, I started

with surprise when the door opened and Nicole entered. Nicole, born and raised within an extremely well-connected family of French wine growers from the Bordeaux region, was extraordinarily beautiful with waist-length, liquorice-black hair and ice-blue eyes, an aristocratic, aquiline nose and full, sensuous lips. She and I had become friends almost as soon as we'd met, recognising a shared sense of humour and a taste for adventure not immediately apparent in our fellow students who, for the most part, appeared to be rather a prim, stuck-up collection of young ladies.

Standing in the doorway, hands on hips and looking at me in a highly amused manner, she began, laughingly, to castigate me in her impeccable English — which was, I'm ashamed to say, infinitely superior to my command of the French language. Alas, we English are frightfully lazy when it comes to mastering foreign tongues, but I was soon to play my part in setting the record straight by mastering a foreign tongue of my own — and an extremely mobile and pretty one it was, too!

Looking slightly abashed, I raised myself on my elbow, bit my lip and blushed fetchingly, which precipitated a gale of girlish giggles from the gorgeous Nicole.

'What have you been up to, *ma cherie*? I've never seen you looking so guilty or, how you say, embarrassed! It's as if you might have a little secret you might wish to keep from me, no? But surely, *ma chère*, you wouldn't want to keep secrets from your little Nicole, eh?'

Smiling broadly and showing her even, white teeth, she advanced sinuously and with evil intent towards the sofa where I lay. Squealing with mock horror I swiftly scaled the back of the sofa — a tricky exercise bearing in mind the length and fullness of my skirt — and dropped, rather indecorously, to the floor below where I lay for a moment or two, panting with excitement, before getting to my feet and standing to face the laughing Nicole on the other side.

Moments later, glancing floorwards, Nicole spotted Simon's by-now crumpled letter and immediately ducked to retrieve it and then, despite my cries of indignation, began to read it aloud in her prettily accented English.

Unable to stand the impertinence of the girl a moment longer, I reached across as far as I could and attempted to grab the letter from her grasp. Anticipating my action, she slowly backed away, clicking her tongue in disapproval and dangling the letter between thumb and forefinger, just out of my reach.

By now my blood was up and the thrill of the chase was upon me. Growling like a cat, eyes glittering, I freed myself from the confines of the sofa and pursued the naughty young mademoiselle round the room, both of us shrieking with laughter as we circumnavigated tables, chairs, bookcases and anything which came between me and my mischievous quarry.

At long last, with a cry of delight, I caught Nicole by the arm and swung her round to face me where we stood grinning at each other like a pair of Cheshire cats, breathing heavily after our exertions and with shining eyes and flushed cheeks.

Slowly our grins melted away and I found myself gazing, searchingly, at this beautiful girl's face while she studied me with a look of pure wonder in her eyes.

Not since I'd entered this delightful country had I made love to another woman — indeed, nothing had been further from my mind — and so I was surprised and shocked to recognise the first, sweet sensations of sexual desire rise in my belly as I watched the delicious Nicole while she, in turn, watched me.

Raising a slim finger to her pouting lips she bade me be quiet and then, winking suggestively, she led me to the thick, wolfskin rug which lay in front of the glowing fire. As we stood, facing each other in the warmth, she nimbly undid the fastenings of my bodice, pulled it gently from my shoulders and sighed with pleasure as my large, firm breasts spilled forth. Running her wet, pink tongue over her lips in anticipation she gently took one of my breasts in each hand and, looking into my eyes all the while, lowered her beautiful face to my by-now erect strawberry nipples.

I leaned back slightly, arching my tits towards her questing lips as she took first one and then the other jutting nipple into her mouth, nipping gently with her teeth, sucking lustily and rolling them around her tongue until the feminine warmth and wetness between my thighs suffused me with such longing that I desired only to caress this gorgeous creature in just the way she was caressing me.

As though she read my thoughts Nicole raised her head, full lips glossy and pouting, and proudly bared her slim, lithe torso to my view. Like a young cat she stood preening before me, throwing back her shoulders to display her olive-skinned, pointed breasts with their Bordeaux-wine nipples.

Taking a stray lock of blue-black hair in her fingers, she softly stroked a nipple with it and we both watched, transfixed, as it rose and hardened like a ripe grape. Anxious that her other, sweet nipple should not feel neglected, I leaned forward and took it between my lips, my luscious tits dangling and lightly brushing Nicole's flat, olive belly.

Feeling her nipple swell tantalisingly in my mouth, I raised my lips to hers and, taking her in my arms, kissed her fully and passionately, our tongues entwining and exploring each other's mouths. The sensation of her naked, sweat-sheened tits pressing against my own, heightened my desire still further and when our nipples touched, a spasm of electric desire passed from my breasts to my throbbing, wet pussey.

Smiling conspiratorially we stripped naked and then fell upon each other, kissing deeply and rubbing our tits and cunts together in complete abandon.

'Darling Nicole, how I've longed to feel your naked skin against mine,' I murmured huskily. 'At night in my room I've driven myself almost mad with desire at the thought of my tongue exploring the dark, secret places of your body. Angel, will you let me lick the honey from your cunt?'

'*Mais oui, Chérie*,' whispered Nicole. 'I thought you'd never ask!' Then, slowly and gracefully she spread her slim, brown legs and stood, feet apart, hands on hips and pelvis thrust forward, sinuously undulating so that with each circle of her arse, her delicious pink pussey was fully displayed to my gaze in the rosy firelight.

Dropping to my hands and knees, tits dangling and bum thrust high in the air, I extended my wicked tongue and licked her swollen cunt, nibbling and kissing its shadowy folds and dark recesses and drinking her musky juice while my soft hands clasped her tight, boyish arse.

After I'd spent a minute or two at this glorious pursuit, I felt Nicole tremble and her body tense with the onset of her climax. Between groans of pleasure her breathing was laboured and uneven, and her body ran with fragrant sweat which I tasted on my lips and the scent of which filled my nostrils.

Moments later I felt her body relax and her breathing become more even. Sitting back on my haunches, I looked up into her face and saw there an expression of pure joy and mischief.

'And now for you, sweet Rosie,' she said, dropping to her hands and knees and gently pushing me back on to the thick, soft rug beneath us.

Tits rubbing against me, she licked the salty sweat from my belly while her tender fingers stroked and tickled my pussey, making me squirm and giggle with delight as she found my swollen clitoris and softly massaged it so that I thought I'd explode with ecstasy.

With the swiftness and grace of a gazelle, she straddled my body, her heels under my bottom to raise and display my cunt, and lowered her own pussey on to mine.

We moved together in perfect unison, our pubic hair mingling in a delicious cocktail of baby blonde and jet black, wet with our love-juices. Once again she reached down and found my clitoris, rubbing and massaging until I, too, reached my longed-for climax and sighed deeply with contentment.

Oblivious to everything but each other, we lay in each other's arms in the warmth from the fire and fell into a light but refreshing sleep.

* * *

I awoke the following morning with an inexplicable sense of mounting excitement. Inexplicable until I stretched my limbs under the crisp, white bedclothes and opened my eyes to greet the warm spring sun which suffused the room with golden light.

Smiling to myself I pushed the sheets away and lay there naked, bathed in a brilliant shaft of sunlight which pierced a narrow gap between the flowered drapes at my window.

As the warmth enveloped my body and the sun glinted on my golden pubic hair like light dancing on the surface of the lake outside, I began to feel those familiar sensations of longing creep from the tips of my toes to the roots of my hair. With quickening pulse I felt my tingling nipples rise and harden and the deepest recesses of my belly and pussey throb with a warm dampness as I imagined my darling Simon stroking my body, tawny in the sunlight, and pushing the blunt, swollen head of his cock against the opening of my womanhood.

I squeezed my nipples between the thumb and forefinger of each gentle hand, breathing deeply and feeling the twin peaks of my generously rounded breasts rise and fall in voluptuous rhythm.

My entire body tingled with erotic pleasure as I ran a delicate fingernail from the cleft between my breasts, down the length of my slim torso, over my flat belly to the tangled mass of soft blonde hair at its base.

Twining the silky strands around my fingers for a moment or two, I reached down and insinuated a warm finger between the lips of my pussey. As I found and began to gently massage my swollen clitoris, shockwaves of pure, unadulterated eroticism coursed through me and I began to feel weak with desire and suffused with a longing to be filled with a man's erect prick.

I gracefully parted my long legs, raising my knees and then, overcome with lust, thrust two, then three fingers into my throbbing cunt, moaning with pleasure and writhing in ecstasy on the rumpled sheets.

Flowing with the sensations of my swollen breasts and

clitoris, sexy bottom rubbing against cool white linen and cunt filled with mobile, questing fingers I climaxed with a rush of passion and warm, liquid honey which spilled forth onto my soft inner thighs.

Relaxing my body I allowed my breathing to become regular and even, smiling inwardly as I anticipated my next sexual encounter. 'I wonder who the lucky man will be?' I whispered to myself, little knowing how quickly I was to find out . . .

Later that day, lessons at an end, I felt compelled by the burgeoning freshness of the warm spring afternoon to explore the extensive gardens belonging to Madame Dupont's Academy for Young Ladies.

These gardens, which were beautifully maintained by an upright German gentleman of advanced years by the name of Franzmann, ran right down to a small private beach at the water's edge where we young ladies were frequently to be found in the warm weather, unbeknown to the stern Madame Dupont, dipping our bare toes in the clear water and giggling delightedly as the little waves splashed our legs.

A small wooden pier jutted out into the lake, to which was tied a gaily painted rowing boat belonging to Madame Dupont's son, Michel, whom none of us had met because of his being away at school, but who was the subject of a great deal of girlish speculation and more than a few romantic daydreams.

On this particular afternoon, there being a hint of a chill in the air, I made my way to the tall, heated glasshouse which lay at the very heart of the garden and which contained Madame Dupont's vast collection of exquisite orchids from all over the world. This glasshouse was one of the largest and most beautiful I'd seen, its clear panes glinting like a million diamonds in the sunlight, and its interior as green and scented as a tropical paradise.

Madame Dupont was often to be found in her moments off, aproned and with sleeves rolled up, a gentle expression softening her normally stern features, tenderly ministering to one delicate bloom or another, a tiny pair of scissors kept expressly for the purpose in her hand and a plant spray containing the finest spring water money could buy at her feet.

Franzmann, who shared Madame Dupont's love of orchids, carried out the more menial tasks involved in their cultivation, digging and planting alongside the great lady as she glided majestically from row to row, lovingly sniffing a scented bloom here and snipping away a dead leaf there.

It had been intimated amongst us girls that Franzmann who, to the best of our knowledge, was unmarried, shared more with Madame than a passion for exotic flowers. It was said that they shared pleasures of a far more intimate nature in each other's company, a fact borne out by my friend and fellow student Lisa who, when strolling through the gardens one balmy evening, heard the sounds of mature adult voices speaking in hushed, low tones, followed by much joyful chuckling and the rustling of headmistressy bombazine.

Swiftly crouching down in order to ascertain the true nature of what she was witnessing, Lisa clearly heard the voice of our revered Madame, exclaiming to her obviously male assailant: 'Franz, you naughty boy, I wish you'd stop tickling and find the time to free me from these dastardly stays. A moment longer in their confines and I swear I'll explode!'

There followed a quantity of male and female giggling, a hearty slap of manly hand against ample female flesh and a pink, whalebone corset sailed through the air and landed at Lisa's feet, whereupon she stifled the screams of laughter which threatened to divulge her presence and ran swiftly back to the school in order to regale the rest of us with the story of her horticultural experience, adding a great deal of speculative and lascivious detail for good measure!

I happened to know that on this particular afternoon Madame Dupont was engaged in marking French essays in her study, so I was a little surprised to hear the sound of a melodic tune being hummed within the sultry, scented depths of the glasshouse. I guessed the sweet music did not issue from the lips of the straight-backed, teutonic Franzmann, but it was clearly of male origin. Who could it possibly be?

Rounding a corner I chanced upon a glorious sight, the like of which I'd never before experienced, and haven't since. There, poised among the foliage and the delicately scented blooms was the most delicious male arse I'd ever had the pleasure to observe, clothed in charcoal-grey serge which clung provocatively to the tightly muscled masculine contours, leaving very little to my fevered female imagination.

Suddenly the whistling stopped and the young man to whom the arse belonged straightened and turned towards me with an amused and enquiring look.

'*Bonjour, Mademoiselle*,' he said, gazing levelly at me with eyes of melting chocolate. 'May I be of some assistance to you?'

'I'm sure I can think of a little something you can do for me, monsieur,' I murmured to myself, smiling.

'*Párdon, Mademoiselle?*'

'I said, I'm sure there's nothing you can do for me, monsieur. I'm merely out for a relaxing stroll before supper, and the glasshouse is one of my favourite destinations. By the way, my name is Rosie D'Argosse and I am a pupil at Madame Dupont's Academy for Young Ladies.'

'And I, Mademoiselle Rosie, am Michel Dupont, Madame Dupont's devoted son. I arrived here this afternoon *en vacance* from my college in Paris. I, too, had it in mind to explore the grounds before going to meet some friends in town this evening. The gardens are very beautiful, *non*? Maman and her friend, Herr Franzmann, like nothing better than to spend time together here, tending the flowers, and other things I have no doubt . . .'

His eyes met mine and a ghost of a smile played about his lips as he said this but then, swiftly changing the subject, he offered to introduce me to some of his favourite varieties of orchid.

Taking my slim arm in his, rather solicitously I thought,

gleefully, he proceeded to lead me towards the very centre of the glasshouse, stopping now and then on the way to show me a particular variety or other which caught his eye.

As we drew closer to the very heart of this fragrant heaven, the atmosphere appeared to become warmer and more humid, and the foliage was so thick and luxuriant that a great deal of the light from outside was obscured, creating a lush green glow, heady with the scent of some of the rarest and most costly blooms to be found anywhere on earth.

By now quite drunk from this intoxicating place, and more than ever aware of Michel's arm, which had been lowered at some point during our stroll and was now circling my waist, I was surprised and delighted when we came upon a little pool of crystal-clear water, surrounded by smooth, flat stones and with a small fountain playing at its centre.

'How utterly enchanting,' I whispered, turning to Michel with sparkling eyes.

'But not half as enchanting as you, Rosie. A girl with your beauty and sensitivity deserves an orchid which will echo those qualities, which is why I've brought you here . . .' With that, he reached out and plucked a deliciously scented bloom from a nearly plant, its blush-pink petals as heavy and as sweet as honey.

Carefully tucking the flower behind my ear, he gently stroked my cheek whilst gazing longingly into my blue eyes.

Now I'd heard that the French are a romantic race, but never before had I been seduced in so romantic a manner. By now fully prepared to accept my fate at the hands (and cock, I hoped!) of this handsome young Frenchman, I smiled saucily up at him, snaked my arms around his neck and pulled his face to within an inch of my own.

Closing my eyes, I slowly extended my little pink tongue and licked Michel's lips. After a second or two, Michel found my tongue with his own and we stood, lips not touching, tongues lasciviously snaking around each other. Then, lunging towards me, Michel pressed his lips against mine, thrusting his tongue into my mouth and there commenced the most delicious French kiss I'd ever experienced. All the more appropriate, of course, since it was delivered by a Frenchman!

Urgently opening my bodice with one hand and fondling my luscious breasts, he reached down with the other and lifted my skirts, then stroked my firm, rounded bottom through the thin cotton of my semi-transparent drawers before yanking them down to my knees.

Throbbing cock straining against the grey fabric of his trousers, he pressed hard against my by-now naked pussey and kissed me so passionately I felt I was being eaten alive. Parting my legs as far as my dropped panties would allow, I rubbed my glistening cunt against his stiff, serge-clad prick, leaving a damp, fragrant trail on the rough cloth. I felt for all the world like a randy female cat, leaving her scent on a favourite mate. A little something for him to remember me by, I thought to myself with a naughty grin.

Then, deftly unbuttoning his fly, I pulled his yearning cock free and caressed it for a moment or two, feeling it hot, dry and pulsing with life in my hand, before transferring the little drop of pre-ejaculatory cum from its tip to my finger, and from there to my tongue.

Smiling appreciatively as I savoured the salty taste in my mouth, I placed his eager prick at the entrance to my cunt, clasped his boyish arse in both hands, squeezing and massaging the taut, manly cheeks, and wriggled around a little so that the tip of his cock, wet with my love-juice, found my erect clitoris which jutted out like a tiny, miniature penis.

This was more than the poor boy could stand and, with a low moan of pleasure, he thrust his cock into me like a dervish, feverishly squeezing my sweat-sheened tits and pumping back and forth as though his life depended on it.

Should we have been discovered at that moment by some unsuspecting browser, what a picture we would have presented! Me with hair awry and breasts naked and free as nature intended, my dress pulled high around my waist and panties and stockings at half-mast around my knees. Michel, panting with exertion and quite red in the face, fucking my cunt with the enthusiasm of a man left starving in the desert having chanced upon a cool oasis with running water to slake his thirst and abundant date palms to satisfy his hunger. It occurred to me that I was most probably the first girl he'd fucked since he'd last been home from school. How utterly inhumane, I thought, to deny these young and virile flowers of manhood — many of them at the very peak of their sexual prowess — the opportunity of fucking pretty young ladies of a similar persuasion. Were I to be put in charge of the education of these sexy young tigers with their rampant cocks, I'd see to it that they received frequent visits from naughty girls such as myself, well versed in the art of de-spunking.

After what seemed like several minutes of glorious abandonment, I felt my orgasm approach like a tide of warm treacle through my loins. Then, with a tingling thrill of intense pleasure my senses exploded, at the same time as Michel, with a cry of delight and cock pulsating, shot jet after jet of warm spunk into my eager pussey.

We hugged each other tight for a moment or two then pulled away and smiled, wordlessly, into each other's eyes. As we straightened our clothing, Michel gazed into my eyes and said:

'Rosie, *chére*, that was one of the most glorious fucks I've enjoyed in many weeks. (My fears were confirmed.) 'Thank you, darling . . .' With that he kissed me on the nose, took me by the arm and led me back to the entrance of the glasshouse. As we parted to go our separate ways he said: 'Rosie, I have a little boat moored on the beach below and I'd planned to take my friend, Antoine, for a row on the lake next Saturday afternoon. Would you and one of your delightful friends care to join us? If the weather's good perhaps we could take a picnic, no? I'll arrange for our finest local shopkeeper, Pierre Bassinet, to prepare us a hamper, and I'll tell him to include a bottle or two of champagne.'

As he mentioned the champagne, I noticed a very definite twinkle in Michel's eye. Could it be that his plans included more than a simple row on the lake followed by a delicious but modest *déjeuner sur l'herbe*? Would my 'friend' and I be expected to perform in some as yet unspecified way? I certainly hoped so!

'Please say you'll come, Rosie,' pleaded Michel.

'But of course,' I said. 'We'll meet you at the pier at midday on Saturday. Meanwhile, *au revoir*, Michel . . . *You scheming scoundrel*,' I whispered to myself, giggling wickedly in anticipation of the forthcoming weekend's frolics.

Saturday morning dawned. Sleepily I opened my eyes and gave them a little rub. Brushing a stray, pale blonde curl from my cheek — which was still baby-warm and slightly damp from my recent slumbers — I gave a long, low whistle, parted my blushing lips in a sexy smile and began to giggle in a decidedly wicked manner, the sound emanating from deep within my throat.

I immediately recognised this particular expression of humour as similar to that which habitually issued forth from the full lips of the delicious Dora, a saucy and voluptuously popular lady of the night who for many years frequented the inns and taverns of London's Highgate.

Dora was notorious for her brashly extravagant and wantonly revealing ballgowns, worn day and night whatever the weather or the occasion, the necklines of which were cut so incredibly low that her big round breasts were all but completely displayed in their full, naked glory. Her modesty, if any, was preserved by a tiny strip of fabric which barely covered her succulent, and frequently well-sucked, red nipples, the generous contours of which were plainly evident under the lush material of her gown.

Men of all ages and from all backgrounds and walks of life had been known to pay vast sums of money for the voluptuous thrill of burying their faces between Dora's warm, white-fleshed tits and suck at her big, erect nipples. As a result, the fortunate Dora never found herself without a roof over her head or the price of a nip of brandy or a plate of oysters. More than a few gentlemen of means had offered to set her up in furnished rooms in a smart part of town if only she'd save her heavenly breasts and wicked favours for them alone, but Dora was by nature a woman of the street and while she still had her strength and her looks, on the street she'd stay.

The younger street girls would follow her, catcalling and rudely mimicking her swagger as she made her daily round of the taverns, gaming houses and licensed betting establishments, searching for handsome, horny men of discernment who were aching for a fuck with a woman of experience, and were willing to be parted from their hard-earned cash for a rummage in her drawers and a squeeze of her ample bosoms.

But I digress. The cause of my good humour on this particular morning was the delightful memory of a wickedly sexy dream I'd had before waking. I'd dreamt I was a young and beautiful concubine belonging to the king of Ancient Egypt.

I spent my days in the luxurious splendour of the royal harem, partially clothed or completely naked for the most part, bathing in warm scented water, rich with costly oils and essences, dining on wild honey and extravagant sweetmeats, or swapping wild stories and saucy anecdotes with the other women.

The older, more experienced concubines would delight in schooling us younger ones in the gentle, feminine art of pleasing men. In language of a most explicit nature and amid much hilarity, they'd teach us how to seduce, cajole and tempt a man on the one hand, while reducing him to a quivering mass of red-hot lust on the other with skilful displays of stroking, sucking and fucking to please even the most jade of male palates.

From these women we discovered the secret of nocturnal success in the royal sleeping chambers, and how to maintain the king's favour and keep him hungry for more of our bodily delights. We pure, gentle doves were trained to become ravening, sexy she-cats at the switch of a shapely hip or the wink of a glittering, black-lashed eye.

In my dream I was summoned by the king's personal bodyguard who told me that I'd been spotted by His Majesty in the royal gardens and, pleased and excited by what he'd seen, the king had demanded my presence in his private chambers that evening. Weak with anticipation and excitement (the king was potent in the extreme — a huge, well-muscled bear of a man with flashing eyes and a thick, glossy black beard), I set about the task of preparing my mind and body for a liaison with my master.

Aided and abetted by my friends and companions in the royal harem, I bathed, powdered, oiled and scented my smooth young skin, then applied kohl to my lids in the ancient manner, a mere hint of rouge to my already-flushed cheeks and a slick of fragrant beeswax to my full, pouting lips giving them a lusciously pampered sheen. Smiling with pleasure, I eased my long, lithe legs into a minute pair of satin panties, so brief they barely concealed my blonde pubic hair, which gleamed with aromatic oil, and plainly showed the little shadowy cleft at the top of my shapely bottom. I wriggled suggestively, causing my tits to jiggle in a delightful manner, as I adjusted the fit of these outrageously sexy briefs.

Next I insinuated my ample breasts into the matching upper garment, which was just about the smallest brassière I'd ever seriously considered as bodily adornment. Thickly encrusted with sequin and dangling jewels which glittered and shook as I moved, this exotic creation cupped my peachy breasts, barely covering my big rosy nipples which even now were stiffly erect and unbelievably sensitive in delicious anticipation of my forthcoming sexual encounter with Egypt's all-powerful ruler, who would hopefully, overnight, become permanently enslaved to my charms.

Gazing downwards, thrilled with this unfamiliar image of myself in sexily revealing clothes (I was used to spending my days in innocent nudity, clothed only in my smooth, warm skin), I ran my mobile fingers over the firm, glowing mounds of my captive bosoms, stroking the deep, dark cleavage between them in pure wonderment. Never before had my glorious breasts been thus uplifted and confined — previously they'd bounced naked and free as nature intended.

I then fastened a sheer, floaty garment around my lower hips, stepped into a pair of gold kid mules and brushed my long blonde hair until it glowed and shone as though illuminated from within.

Prepared at last, eyes shining, I was finally ready to receive the king's bodyguard who was to present me to the great man himself. Gazing at me solicitously, his eyes devouring my body lustfully, this servant of the king handed me a small leather pouch containing precious jewels — gifts from his master — and bade me adorn myself with them while he averted his eyes.

Peering inside the bag, amid excited giggles and squeals from my friends, I found rings, bangles and bracelets for my hands, wrists and ankles, a round, smooth opal for my forehead and large, glittering ruby for my flat, tawny belly.

Finally, semi-naked, ravishingly beautiful and burning with desire for sexual fulfilment, I proceeded towards the king's chambers amid low whistles and sharp intakes of breath from all those, young or old, who lined the route.

Arriving at last at a pair of vast double doors, fashioned from fragrant sandalwood and sumptuously carved with scenes of men and women in virtually every permutation of sexual congress, the bodyguard threw them open and, with a small clap of his hands and a lewd wink, indicated to me that I should enter. I quickly went in, averting my eyes from those of my master, and prostrated my young body on the floor, just inside the doors. As I crouched, quivering in anticipation of what was to come, I heard the doors quietly swing shut, leaving me to face the rest of the night alone with this great and powerful man.

After a moment or two a measured, deep voice said: 'Please rise, my little flower. Do not be afraid — I mean you no harm. I spied you this morning in the orange grove, inhaling the scent of a perfect white blossom while the sun illuminated your perfect beauty, and I immediately felt compelled to request the pleasure of your company this evening. Tell me, precious one, have you resided long at the palace?'

Slowly rising to my feet, as steadily as I could and with breasts rising and falling in my flimsy garment like the breast of a small, captive bird, I stood and faced the powerful being who had addressed me − a ruler so mighty he could crush and destroy whole empires on a momentary whim − and found before me a tall, gentle man of immense physical beauty and presence. Deeply suntanned, bearded, with compelling but compassionate black eyes and a deep scar across one cheek, this living legend was, plainly, a man first with a man's needs and desires.

Recognising this fact I began slowly to relax, replying to his questions as best I could in my low, musical voice. 'I was born in the palace, Sire. My mother was a concubine belonging to your father. After many years in his intimate service, because she had pleased him greatly and afforded him so much pleasure, she was graciously permitted to marry his most trusted personal servant, and I was the result of their union. When I was fourteen I, too, joined the royal harem, just as my mother had done before me, and here I am at your request − a faithful and humble girl willing to please you, My Lord, in whatever way you desire . . .' Lowering my lashes, I raised my hands from my sides and joined them, reverently, before my swelling, bejewelled breasts.

'Your mother must have been an exceptionally beautiful woman to have produced a vision such as yourself,' the king said huskily, his eyes roaming from my sumptuous golden hair to my full, voluptuous breasts, my shapely hips and long, coltish legs, then back again. 'But first,' he said briskly, regaining his composure, 'let us eat!'

He clapped his hands together sharply and four serving girls entered on swift, silent feet, carrying trays of exotic delicacies high on their heads. On reaching the dining area, which was surrounded by soft, bright cushions, they arranged the beaten silver platters containing succulent, spiced meats, fragrant, aromatic rice and ripe fruits in the centre on a profusion of richly embroidered mats. Lighting a number of tall beeswax candles in gleaming pewter candelabrum and pouring measures of heady red wine into two engraved silver goblets, they departed as silently as they'd arrived. As she left the chamber, the last girl turned to me in the wink of an eye and gave me the benefit of a wide but fleeting grin.

'Come,' said the king, taking my slender arm in his large, strong hand and leading me solicitously towards the delicious repast, then bidding me recline on the swansdown-filled cushions before eating and drinking my fill.

As we ate, the king spoke animatedly of his childhood and his father, his friends and enemies, his stately responsibilities and future plans for his great and glorious kingdom. I listened in polite but rapt silence, my eyes taking in the earthy opulence of the chamber with its costly hangings, gleaming treasures and sumptuous animal skins, the whole scented with the smoke from a jewelled incense burner and softly lit by the still, small flames of a thousand candles and the low, orange sun which was setting low in the west and casting a golden glow over all in its path.

Almost swooning with the scent from the incense burner and the effect of the heavy, blood-red wine on my senses, I turned my heavy-lidded eyes towards the man at my side and, momentarily forgetting my servile position within his household, felt an engulfing flood of womanly desire, like treacle, suffuse my gracefully reclining limbs an the base of my warm, golden belly.

Like a big cat, sensing the urgency of my emotions, the king stopped talking and turned towards me, drinking in my musky, erotically charged beauty with his eyes and nostrils, an amused smile playing about his strong, masculine lips. 'Do my eyes deceive me or is it true that I am having such a desirable effect on you, my little dove? My heart tells me you may be ripe for the plucking but first, I desire that you dance for me!'

The king clapped his hands a second time and musician

entered the chamber, seating himself on a pile of goat skins in the shadow at the far corner of the chamber. As the sweet, reedy music commenced I rose gracefully to my feet and made my way swiftly to centre-stage where I gazed levelly at the king with shining, lust-filled eyes and soft, parted lips.

Abandonedly tossing my luxuriant mane of blonde hair, I threw back my suntanned shoulders and proudly thrust forward my big, firm breasts, shaking them lewdly and making them jiggle and jounce, causing the sequins and jewels which adorned them to jingle and glitter in the candlelight. The monarch's eyes darkened with desire and he settled back against his pile of cushions, licking his sensuous lips in anticipation of the erotic display to follow.

Never once taking my bold, blue eyes from the master's face I moved my body to the music with sinuous grace, swaying and undulating my lithe torso, shaking my high, spangled bosoms and rotating my slim, womanly hips, causing the glowing, blood-red ruby in my belly to glitter and sparkle.

As the music quickened in pace and became more urgent, I threw off my golden mules and danced with increased passion and abandon, wriggling and gyrating my by now sweat-sheened body and shaking my damp, lustrous hair this way and that so that it whipped about my face like a tangle of shiny serpents.

Suddenly, without any warning, the music came to an end and I collapsed to the floor, my heart pounding and shoulders heaving with the excitement and the exertion of this dance of desire. The king clapped loud and long in appreciation of my display, chuckling low in his throat before saying in a voice shaking with desire: 'I am filled with joy by your dancing abilities, my blonde beauty. Come, experience for yourself the extent to which you have pleased me . . .'

I raised my bowed head and pushed aside the curtain of damp, pale blonde hair from my glowing cheeks, gazing at him through narrowed, lust-filled eyes streaked with kohl, and licking my generous parted lips in a lascivious manner.

In this fashion and on hands and knees I advanced towards the object of my desire, rivulets of sweat snaking between my big breasts which hung suspended like lush, sexy fruits, threatening to burst forth from their flimsy covering with each movement of my body.

Reaching the king, I gazed into his eyes and softly stroked the scar on his cheek and his thick, black beard, making him smile with amusement, before lowering my playful hands to his nether garments, nimbly unfastening them and pulling them open to reveal his erect, throbbing penis to my gaze. Never before had I seen a cock of such immense length and girth. It was truly a prick fit for a king and the sight of it excited me greatly, causing me to tremble and bite my lower lip in wonder, like a little lost girl at her first grown-up party.

'Please don't be afraid, little one,' said the king gently. 'You may take as little or as much of me as you desire. There is no joy for me in forcing myself upon you like a ravening beast. I wish only to please you as you have pleased me with your voluptuous body and the look of longing in your eyes. Why not find out for yourself how gentle is the giant between my legs?'

I needed no further encouragement. Lowering my hand to this mighty tool set in its bed of crisp black hair, I softly ran a fingernail from the thick base to the throbbing tip, causing it to convulse momentarily with a life of its own. Smiling delightedly and by now fully immersed in the task in hand, I deftly undid the clasp of my spangled bra, shrugged out of it and flung it aside, proudly displaying to the king the heaving, ample contours of my big, naked breasts with their stiffly erect nipples. Cupping them lewdly I squeezed them together and leaned forward to brush my wayward nipples against the king's bare chest, at the same time brushing my lips against his cheek and playfully wriggling my arse so that my tiny panties slipped down a little further, revealing the topmost wisps of my soft pubic hair and even more of my delicious, dimpled bottom.

Then, gently lowering my upper body so that my almost-bare arse was raised high in the air and my gorgeous tits were suspended directly above the king's massive prick, I rubbed my sensitive nipples back and forth along its full length, sighing with pleasure as sparks of eroticism flashed through my sexually charged body, before swooping down and imprisoning the entire shaft in soft, warm, womanly flesh.

This delightful pose left me in the perfect position to extend my wicked pink tongue and lick and lap at the king's muscular, hairy belly before, at last, falling hungrily upon his magisterial cock. Taking it, inch by inch, into my mouth and snaking my mobile, salivating tongue around its girth, paying particular attention to the gleaming crown, I held it in a firm grip between my lips and rhythmically raised and lowered my tousled head, causing the king to grunt and moan with pure, unalloyed delight. 'Stop, stop!' he cried, trembling with excitement. 'If you carry on in this manner I will shoot my sperm too soon, and that would never do, my shapely princess. Strip naked for me, right now, and I will fuck you as you have never been fucked before!'

With a petulant pout and a lithe whimper of disappointment – I'd so enjoyed the sensation of this wonderful, erect prick in my mouth – I let go of the king's manhood and slowly, sinuously rose to my feet. Cupping my beautiful, gleaming breasts in my delicate hands and absently tweaking my stiff, rosy nipples, my pout quickly turned into a sexy smile which within moments became a naughty giggle of pleasure.

Leaving the rondeurs of my bosoms, my hands slowly travelled the length of my golden body as I lifted my ribcage to further display my tits, and sensually swayed my arse from side to side in time to the sweet music which had once more begun to issue from the shadows in the corner.

Taking hold of my tiny, tight panties, I slowly lowered them over my curvy hips, wriggling my bottom to ease their descent, and let them drop to the floor where I daintily stepped out of them.

Suggestively sucking a delicate finger, I parted my long,

111

coltish legs and insinuated it between the soft folds of my aching womanhood, gently massaging my erect clitoris before sinking it into my warm, dark cunt.

The king could endure this erotic display no longer. Rising to his feet like a giant, horny bear with his prick sticking out in front of him like a veritable flagpole, he ordered me in a trembling whisper to sink to my hands and knees and spread my legs for him.

I quickly did as I was told, opening my legs a far as I could and thrusting my arse into the air, thereby displaying to him my little wrinkled anus and the pink, fleshy lips of my throbbing pussey.

With a cry of delight he threw himself onto his knees behind me and took my hips in his giant, masculine hands before burying his handsome face in my grateful cunt, nuzzling, sniffing and licking whilst issuing a series of soft, satisfied grunts like a veritable beast of the field. Almost swooning with pleasure, I thrilled to the sensation of his big, wet tongue lapping and probing at my sex, hunting out my hot, swollen clitoris and nibbling it gently and insistently until I felt myself about to enter that deep, dark chasm of climactic sexual joy.

Sensing the imminence of my orgasm, the king raised his head, urgently straddled my body and thrust his huge, veiny cock into my welcoming crack. Panting and moaning he pumped his giant prick in and out of my tight, hot cunt, his balls slapping against my naked bum, before filling me with jet upon jet of warm, salty spunk as I, too, reached my longed-for orgasm.

Climax over, his breathing slowed and became more regular and he gratefully lowered his warm, manly lips to kiss the glowing, velvet skin of my back and shoulders. 'Lie down, my darling, and I will stroke you to sleep. Maybe in a while, when we are sufficiently rested, we can make love some more, eh?'

The idea of another bout of abandoned fucking with this beautiful, tender man and his stately cock sent little shivers of anticipation through me all over again. Sleepy and thankful, I stretch my lithe, naked body on the tigerskin rug beneath me, closed my heavy-lidded eyes and gave myself up to his smooth caresses and soothing words of love . . .

It was at that moment that I woke up. On the point of falling into a delicious slumber in my dream, I awoke in my bed at the Academy to greet a glorious spring morning, filled with birdsong, the scent of fresh flowers and the promise of a myriad earthly pleasures — this time for real!

I snaked my arms above my head in a long stretch, thinking excitedly of Michel and his friend Antoine, and wondering what frolicsome little plans the darling boys had hatched for our mutual delectation, before kicking off the bedclothes and springing to my feet. As naked as the day I was born and baby-pink with sleep — I *never* wear anything in bed, whether alone or accompanied by a lover — I padded over o the window and threw open the curtains to present my luscious young body to the beautiful spring morning.

As I gazed delightedly at the flower-filled garden, a smile illuminating my countenance as surely as the sun shone on the warm grass, my hand strayed in an absent manner to the blonde curls at the base of my belly. Twisting the golden strands around my fingers and gently stroking the soft thatch, I heard a sharp intake of breath and suddenly became aware that someone or something was crouching amongst the foliage in the flower bed beneath my window.

Was it man or beast? Whichever, it was most certainly a voyeur of the lowest and most despicable nature, intent on feasting his eyes (for surely it must be male) on my innocent morning nakedness.

Blushing hotly with embarrassment and surprise I fully raised the sash of my already partly opened window and leaned out, feeling the cool air tease my rosy nipples into little erect buds.

Glancing down, who should I spy but young Pieter the under-gardener, knees firmly planted in the soft earth and sparkling eyes eagerly raised to meet my own. He was flushed and panting with excitement, his stiff throbbing cock straining against the rough fabric of his trousers as he knelt amongst the colourful blooms like a randy young satyr about to pounce on some poor, unsuspecting nymph.

'Why Pieter, it's you!' I whispered loud enough for him to hear but not so loud as to wake the occupants of the adjoining bedchambers. 'How long have you been there, staring upon my nudity in such a brazen manner! I should have you horse-whipped for this, you filthy-minded young cur!'

'Oh please, *mademoiselle*, have pity on a poor, wretched gardener with a ravening beast between his legs masquerading as an instrument of pleasure! I couldn't help myself, I swear it. When you opened your curtains and I saw you standing there in the window like a beautiful blonde goddess, I knew I ought to avert my eyes and leave immediately, but I was transfixed and my legs turned to jelly so I couldn't move, even had I wanted to . . . which I didn't! Oh, make a feeble, weak-willed peasant happy and allow me to feast my eyes on you a moment or two longer!'

Pieter! Up to his naughty tricks again, I thought to myself. That boy ought to be an actor. His thespian talents would surely be sufficient to gain him access to even the most prestigious stages of Europe — not to mention the warm, welcoming thighs of bevies of young, panting females.

Of less than average height and slightly but athletically built, the puckish Pieter had flashed his mischievous eyes at any number of my young contemporaries at the Academy. Charmed beyond measure by his honeyed tongue and lithe, bronzed limbs, they'd willingly conceded to him the very flower of their girlish maidenheads. There wasn't a bush or a tree in the whole of this sizable garden which hadn't witnessed scenes of urgent juvenile lust at Pieter's hands, or rung with giggles and shrieks of sweet, wanton pleasure.

I, on the other hand, was only too aware that on this occasion the tables were turned. Pieter of the mobile tongue and ever-open trousers was finally where he deserved to be and should have been from the day he discovered the hungry and feckless serpent at his groin — in the thrall of a beautiful girl who was more than a match for him in terms of lascivious wickedness. Me!

Tossing back my shimmering curls and running my naughty pink tongue over my pouting lips, I gave Pieter a knowing smile and a wink of complicity. Let's see how he deals with this particular little lady, I thought to myself, and immediately began to apply myself to the task of avenging those poor, bleeding hearts of my young friends and colleagues.

Arching my supple spine, I sucked in my breath and thrust out my big, luscious breasts so that they practically dangled from the window, allowing Pieter an excellent view of their generous creamy contours and the deep, secret cleft between them. Taking my juicy raspberry nipples between my fingers, I stroked, tweaked and tickled them until they blushed a deep rose pink and grew stiffly erect.

The warm, liquid honey which, as a result of my ministrations, began to flow through my body from the very tips of my nipples to the seat of my womanhood made me tremble with excitement and my breath quicken. Eyes narrowed with desire and sighing and moaning with pleasure I began to squeeze and knead my firm, fleshy orbs and then, seeing the effect this was having on the unfortunate youth outside, I withdrew my hands from my breasts, planted them on my hips and shook my tits at him through the window in an energetic and thoroughly lewd manner, giggling mischievously at his obvious discomfiture.

Used to lighting fires in the bellies of innocent, unsuspecting young girls before ruthlessly snatching their virtue, Pieter was totally amazed and nonplussed by my blatantly sexy shenanigans at the open window. Unable to control his emotions he'd ripped open his trousers and pulled out his hot, throbbing truncheon, the ruby dome of which was even now bobbing gaily in the morning breeze as, saucer-eyed and panting, he frigged himself frenziedly.

Slowly turning my back to him with a suggestion of demure coyness which little matched my mood, I glanced sexily over my smooth shoulder, winked at him again and blew him a little kiss before flopping forward like some bizarre, erotic toy and rudely waggled my naked arse at him through the window.

Grinning at him between my slim legs, hair like a gleaming blonde curtain which swept the floor at my feet, I saw him become momentarily motionless and his eyes widen still further, before grasping his prick with renewed vigour and pumping it back and forth with his flying fist until I felt sure the pressure within would cause it to explode.

Red-faced and sweating, he begged me in a trembling whisper to descend from my window and relieve him of his misery. But I had other ideas . . .

Slowly curling upwards with the sinuous grace of a ballerina I was once more upright, though still with my back to him, and I gazed over my shoulder and gave him by best and sexiest smile. Then, parting my long, slender legs and sticking out my delicious arse a little, I was able to afford poor Pieter an even more tantalizing view of my firm, gleaming bum-cheeks and a glimpse of the warm hairy heaven between them which, even as he watched, began to swell darkly and drip with my thick, scented love-juice.

Crouching miserably in the undergrowth with his naked cock hot and throbbing for want of a good, horny fuck with the object of his desire, Pieter began to whimper and whine at this latest rude display.

I suddenly found myself feeling sorry for the poor, helpless youth and was within an Ace of inviting him in through the open window to fuck my cunt in the way nature intended and he so obviously craved but, in order to dispel such philanthropic thoughts, I quickly brought to mind the pitiful looks on the faces of the lovelorn young girls who'd lost their innocence and their hearts to this thoughtless Lothario with his smooth tongue and wayward prick. My expression hardened once more at the thought, but not for long . . .

Insinuating a slim finger between the outer folds of my swollen pussey, I found my little pink clitoris and began to

116

gently stroke and massage it until, swaying sensually from side to side and moaning and panting with pleasure, I nearly swooned with delight at the liquid fire which swept through my sex-flushed body.

Oblivious now to the voyeur beneath my window, I plunged three eager fingers deep into the dark recesses of my cunt, stroking and tickling the smooth, velvet walls as I simultaneously rubbed my erect clitoris, giving myself up to the intense orgasmic spasms which wracked my smooth young torso.

Moments later, pleased and triumphant at having reached my orgasm in so pleasing a manner, I turned to face my audience of one and was a little dismayed (though secretly as pleased as Punch) at the sight which eventually greeted me. It took me a second or two to locate Pieter, so silent and motionless was he as he lay prone amongst the primulas, a little last dribble of spunk oozing from the tip of his limp, lifeless tool.

'Why Pieter,' I hissed through the open window, 'I've never seen you in such a pickle. So dejected and woebegone and full of remorse. Just wait until I tell the other girls! Now, straighten your clothing and be off with you before I scream and wake the whole house. And don't let me catch you peeping at me in such a despicable manner again. Or any other girl for that matter!

Jumping to his feet and stuffing his soft little dick into his trousers, Pieter barely looked at me as, red-faced and ashamed, he muttered an unintelligible apology before shuffling off in a crab-like fashion to another part of the garden in order to reflect on his misdemeanours, past, present and future.

As soon as the wretched youth was out of sight I clapped my hands together in delight and laughed until the tears ran down my cheeks. 'Well, that took the wind out of the young rascal's sails,' I said to myself. 'It's about time boys learned that we girls don't always need stiff pricks to play with in order to have fun. Naughty thoughts and even naughtier fingers will do very nicely, thank you, when a girl feels that

117

familiar little tingle in her pussey and has a mind to tickle her fancy!'

With that, I crossed swiftly to the closet in order to choose a suitable outfit for this day of days, filled as it was with erotic promise of the most exciting and compelling kind. I must choose quickly and with care, for this was the morning of my picnic with Michel Dupont and his companion, and I had not a moment to lose for it was already 8.45 a.m., I had agreed to meet the boys at 12.00 noon, and I had two hours of history prep to catch up on before I could escape to the little pier where he kept his boat, fresh-faced and pussied, sweetly perfumed and ready for fun!

Impatiently pulling the gowns this way and that in my search, a little frown of concentration creasing my pretty brow, I secretly thrilled to the sensual feel of slippery satin, petal-soft silk and crisp white lace beneath my fingers.

Then, with a sigh of relief and pleasure, I found the ideal garment in which to enjoy a companionable lunch in the open air amongst friends, followed by fun and frolics in the afternoon sunshine — a floor-length fine-cotton gown of cornflower blue, trimmed with wide, creamy lace and topped with a tightly fitted, lowcut bodice which revealed a daring quantity of peachy bosom and my tiny, cinched-in waist which was the envy of all but a few of the other girls as well as a good many of the tutors.

Pulling it from its hanger and tossing it on the bed, I first of all slipped into my snowy-white undergarments — a semi-transparent camisole fashioned from the softest and sheerest Swiss lawn, trimmed with lace and blue satin bows, through which the generous contours of my big breasts with their luscious nipples were plainly visible; a pair of little matching panties which, cut from the same sheer fabric as the camisole, showed my curvy bottom and the soft blonde triangle of my pussey hair and finally a pair of silky white stockings held up by frilly blue satin garters.

Checking my reflection in the looking-glass and turning this way and that, it occurred to me what a great pity it was that I was forced to conceal this delightful confection by wearing a dress over the top of it all. Wouldn't the boys just love it if I were to trip gaily down to the beach clad only in soft lace and sexy stockings, tits bouncing and bottom jiggling for all to see! But no matter, I felt sure that within a matter of an hour or so I'd be forced by the heat of the day, the situation and my emotions to remove my outer garments for the mutual delectation of the assembled group, and anyone else who may be around at the time.

Thus comforted, I swiftly donned my cornflower dress, wriggling a little and adjusting my full breasts in their tight bodice in order to show off my cleavage to its best advantage. Brushing my long hair a hundred times to make it shine like golden silk, I quickly ran downstairs for breakfast in the girls' dining-room before gathering up my history prep and heading for the library for a morning spent in the dubious company of Thomas Robespierre and the French Revolution.

And there I stayed until, at 12.00 sharp, I heard the big grandfather clock in the hall chime the hour and realised with a little thrill of panic that Nicole (for it was she who would be accompanying me and completing the happy foursome) and I were most likely going to be a little late for our liaison. But it is, I thought to myself, always has been and always will be a girl's prerogative to keep a man waiting. And, what's more, I felt sure their annoyance would be short-lived when they finally caught sight of the two of us girls, blonde and brunette, excited and eager and pretty as pictures in our summery clothes.

Nicole and I had agreed to meet by the front door of the Academy so, having quickly returned my books and papers to my room and, bright-eyed with anticipation, checked my appearance once again in the mirror above my dressing table, licking my lips to make them gleam and gently tugging down my bodice still further to show even more of my generous curves, I hurried to the designated spot and almost ran straight into her in my haste.

'*Mon Dieu!*' she cried in alarm, 'Where have you been,

you naughty girl? Did you not notice the time? I've been waiting here for you for at least ten minutes . . . with a rumbling tummy and damp pussey!' she added under her breath with a salacious grin, so I knew she wasn't as angry as I'd first thought.

'Have patience, Nicole. The longer they wait the more the boys will appreciate us when we arrive. They'll be altogether keener and their appetites sharper if they're left to cool their heels for a minute or two, don't you think? Anyway, what are you afraid of? Do you think they'll leave without us?'

'*Mais oui chérie*, of course you're right as always. Come, let's go before we waste any more time!'

Grabbing my hand in hers Nicole raced me down the steps and, picking up our skirts, we ran together across the garden until we arrived at the little beach and the jetty with the pretty boat moored alongside.

And there they stood waiting for us, Michel and Antoine, two of the handsomest boys we could care to spend this beautiful afternoon with, and neither of them in the least bit annoyed at our lateness. Michel advanced towards me and gallantly raised my hand to his lips, his eyes straying from my hair, to my lips, to my heaving, sexily exposed breasts, where they lingered wickedly before settling once more on my face and returning my warm smile. I noticed that Nicole and Antoine were exchanging greetings in a similar manner, Antoine's amused grey eyes showing every sign of enjoying the sight of the raven-haired, blue-eyed beauty who stood before him.

As well he might. Seldom had I seem my Gallic friend looking quite so alluring or, indeed, quite so openly provocative as she did this day. Dressed in rose-pink silk, which beautifully complemented her warm olive complexion, her long straight hair hung like a heavy, gleaming, blue-black curtain over her shoulders and down her back, almost to her bottom. Her perfect, finely chiselled features possessed an aristocratic, slightly haughty but undeniably voluptuous grace and her sensual, curvy lips were lush and inviting. She was studying Antoine approvingly, her blue eyes twinkling and the tawny half-moons of her semi-revealed breasts rising and falling in a most exciting and stimulating manner.

Or so the aforementioned youth obviously thought, for when I glanced at his crotch (a little habit of mine — I invariably find my eyes wandering to that most appealing of bulges whenever I'm lucky enough to be introduced to a man or boy not previously of my acquaintance), I was delighted to observe that it was swelling and becoming increasingly turgid before my interested gaze.

Nicole had noticed, too (she was a girl who obviously shared my predilection for cock-watching), and I saw her stifle a little giggle of merriment behind her hand before gazing once more in a thoroughly knowing fashion into the already infatuated young man's eyes.

The afternoon is looking promising, I thought to myself as I witnessed these events. Very, very promising indeed . . .

Michel took my slender arm in his and Antoine took Nicole's, then together we sauntered slowly and companionably towards the little boat.

'Rosie, *chérie*, I am so glad you were able to join us today for our little picnic, especially accompanied as you are by such a delightful companion — *très, très jolie* . . .' Michel glanced longingly at Nicole for a moment or two over his shoulder, and I was forced to give his arm a little tug in order to remind him of whom he'd first invited to join him for lunch.

Not that I really minded in the least. I'd already exchanged a burning, conspiratorial glance or two with the sexy Antoine, and my fevered feminine imagination was already toying with the notion of entertaining his randy prick in one way or another, possibly with the help of the luscious Nicole, or maybe Michel, or even both together . . . The possibilities were endless, but I swiftly returned my thoughts to the present and began once more to concentrate on making the very most of the here and now — yet another, even more appealing habit of mine!

121

'May I say how very glad I am to meet you, *Mademoiselle* Rosie,' said the supremely courteous Antoine in a low, heavily accented and decidedly appealing voice. I am sure we are to become close friends, *non*?' I certainly hoped so. The closer the better!

When we reached the boat, the boys helped us climb and made sure we were settled in our seats before Michel untied the rope, casting us off from the jetty, took hold of the oars and began to row with strong, even strokes. Very soon, settling myself against the pile of soft cushions which Michel had thoughtfully provided for our comfort, I felt my eyelids droop and was aware only of the soft, rhythmic splash of the oars, the golden sparks of sunlight which tipped each tiny ripple on the water, and the low murmur of voices, punctuated by gentle laughter as Nicole, Michel and Antoine became better acquainted.

I must finally have been lulled to sleep by the gentle rocking of the boat — fatigued, no doubt, by the machinations of Thomas Robespierre and his ilk which had filled my thoughts and my notebook that morning in the library — for I was suddenly aware of a soft hand shaking my arm and an insistent voice forcing me into wakefulness.

'What is it? Where are we?'

'Rosie, wake up! You've been asleep for over an hour, you lazy creature! We're back at the beach and the boys are preparing our picnic. Come, let's not keep them waiting. I'm famished and besides, I have a little plan. Listen, I'll tell you about it . . .'

I slowly sat up, yawning and stretching, and leaned closer to my friend in order to hear whatever scheme it was she'd concocted as entertainment for our hosts and ourselves.

When she'd finished, a little look of expectation on her face as though anxious for my reaction, I sat quite still, bolt upright and face expressionless, watching her anxiety turn to disappointment and her soft lips turn down at the corners in a petulant pout. Then I flopped back against my pile of cushions and grinned wickedly, pleased by my little joke and

122

delighted at the prospect of turning Nicole's deliciously saucy scheme into reality.

Nicole grinned back at me and gave a little sigh of exasperation, before urging me to my feet and insisting that I pull myself together so that we might join our Gallic hosts and avail ourselves forthwith of the sumptuous outdoor feast provided for our benefit — to be followed, no doubt, by sensual delights of a very different but no less appealing kind.

What a splendid sight greeted us when we reached the warm, sun-dappled spot where our new friends had chosen to share their feast with us. Smoked ham, a whole cooked lobster, potted meats, aromatic cheeses, succulent spring vegetables and freshly baked crusty bread, accompanied by a bottle or two (or three!) of excellent Bordeaux. But first, Champagne!

Michel took four tall glasses from the basket beside him and filled them to the brim with the cool, sparkling, pale-gold nectar which bubbled and flashed in the sunlight. Handing us a glass each he leant back on the soft rug and took a well-deserved sip, peering at me through narrowed, appraising eyes.

Gazing back at him I too raised a flashing glass to my lips and took a long, cool draught of the energising drink, giggling gently as the fizzy bubbles tickled my lips and nose, and thrilled by the warm, sensual languor which quickly suffused my shapely limbs.

Before long I noticed that Nicole, too, was in a state of effervescence as a direct result of the sparkling wine, and it was merely a matter of moments before she winked at me wickedly, thus indicating that we should carry out the first part of our plan.

Flicking her shiny, liquorice hair back over her shoulders she turned to face the boys, at the same time delivering a knowing grin in my direction, and swiftly undid the front of her silk bodice. Michel's and Antoine's startled eyes nearly popped out of their heads as Nicole's pretty, olive-skinned tits popped out of her dress, jiggling sexily. The memory of these darling, girlish breasts with their large, port-wine nipples immediately came flooding back into my consciousness, and I felt my horny pussey dampen as I recalled the feel of her hard berry nipples between my full lips and against my eager tongue.

With a theatrical flourish, chin held high with pride, the beautiful young mademoiselle stood up and, as she did so, her dress fell to her dainty feet with a seductive rustle of heavy silk. Completely and utterly naked, body gleaming in the sunlight, the slim, sexy creature turned this way and that, posing for us like a randy mannequin and displaying her smooth brown legs, pert boyish bottom, slender waist and high, pointed breasts from every angle for all to see.

Amid excited gasps and low whistles of approval from the boys, Nicole laughed and grabbed my hand, pulling me to my feet and rapidly undoing the fastenings on my own, cornflower-blue bodice. As my dress fell to the ground, revealing my voluptuous body dressed in semi-transparent, beribboned undergarments and silky stockings, big creamy breasts and curvy bottom all but completely visible, Antoine fell back against the rug beneath him, staring at us both, saucer-eyed, and exclaimed in a choked whisper: '*Mon Dieu!* What's happening to me? Have I died and gone to heaven? Tell me this is not a dream and that it's really happening. Please . . .'

Thrilled by the boys' delighted and positive response to our little erotic entertainment, I slowly and sensually stripped naked for them, baring my big, peachy tits and luscious arse and pussey to the world, loving the feel of the gentle breeze against my nude skin and breathing in the wonderful, undeniable odour of arousal which surrounded all four of us, suffusing this warm afternoon with sexual magic.

Kissing my friend lightly on the tip of her aristocratic nose, I ran with her, hand in hand, to the water's edge where we laughed and chattered, dancing like happy children in the clear sparkling lake, totally oblivious to everything but our own sense of innocent fun and wonder at this beautiful, God-given day.

Silent, wide-eyed and utterly shell-shocked, Michel and Antoine watched us from their vantage point on the plaid rug — like two hunting stoats, fascinated by a pair of alluring, frolicsome rabbits.

After ten or fifteen minutes in the water, Nicole and I made our way back to the rug, pink-cheeked, sparkling-eyed and thoroughly ravenous after our exertions. A million jewel-clear drops clung to our lithe, naked bodies and we shook ourselves like naughty puppies all over the reclining young men, eliciting howls of laughter and mock protest, before flopping down on the rug and rubbing our wet hair with the fluffy white towels which had thoughtfully been provided by our hosts — no doubt in the event of a possible unexpected tumble in the lake whilst out rowing, or maybe a quick, post-prandial dip.

By now the spell had been broken and all four of us were laughing and joking with infectious animation, enjoying the delicious food with vim and gusto and steadily polishing off first one, then two bottles of the soft but deceptively powerful red wine.

All the while, despite our noisy alacrity and high spirits, Nicole and I were more than ever aware of our voluptuous nakedness in the presence of these two, horny young men with their burning eyes and stiff, lusty pricks. Never once did their eyes leave our bodies and, once or twice, cool male fingers chanced to brush against our warm, sun-burnished skin, causing little ripples and thrills of pleasure and anticipation to pulse through our soft breasts and warm thighs.

'And now, my darlings,' said the handsome Michel, rising to his feet and lazily unfastening a shirt cuff, 'I feel it is we men who should return the delightful compliment you have paid us by shedding your clothes and displaying your beautiful nakedness for our delectation. Come, Antoine, let us disrobe . . .'

Transfixed, Nicole and I watched as these two gorgeous boys in the very prime of life and positively oozing male potency and sexuality, elegantly and with great aplomb divested themselves of their restrictive manly garb until they finally stood naked before us, side by side like a pair of randy stallions with erect, purple-domed cocks standing high and proud against their flat, muscular bellies.

Purring with sensual pleasure, Nicole and I smiled at each other and advanced together on all fours towards our delicious, succulent quarry. When we reached the boys we each in our own special way and with our own individual and inimitable style, began to gently stroke and caress the pulsing pricks of our respective partners — Nicole had chosen to pleasure Michel and I, Antoine.

The boys gently cajoled and encouraged us as we acquainted ourselves with their beautiful cocks and then, at a sign from Nicole, we both lowered our pretty faces, clasped hold of the boys' bare bums for support, parted our lips and took their majestic tools in our mouths. We licked and sucked and nibbled until we tasted the first few drops of pre-ejaculatory spend on our tongues — a flavoursome experience I can thoroughly and wholeheartedly recommend — then we swiftly swapped partners and I sucked Michel's prick and Nicole sucked Antoine's.

The darling boys were delighted by our little change-around and they shouted and moaned with erotic pleasure, becoming more than ever agitated and dangerously close, I felt, to shooting their salty sperm into our mouths instead of into our hot and yearning cunts — which of course would never do!

So in order to avoid the aforementioned — which would be premature in the extreme and guaranteed to leave us girls high and dry in so far as sexual gratification was concerned — we quickly uncocked.

Turning to face each other, Nicole and I slowly and gracefully fell into each other's arms, softly stroking and nuzzling and cooing little endearments and words of love, pressing our tits together and rubbing our stiff nipples against the other's warm, receptive flesh.

As our lips met and opened and we lost ourselves in deep, passionate kisses, our tongues entwining and probing the

126

deepest recesses of each other's mouths, my fingers reached out and stroked and tickled Nicole's warm pussey.

Nicole, in turn, began to manipulate my yeaning womanhood, her gentle finger running back and forth along the length of my juicy slit, softly massaging my little pink clitoris until I felt I'd die from the pleasure of it. And then I felt my climax approach and gave myself up to wave upon wave of erotic abandonment, panting and tossing my blonde head this way and that in ecstasy.

Temporarily sated, I gently pushed the smiling Nicole back on to the rug, parted her incredibly long legs and buried my golden head into her raven-haired muff, which was hot and fragrant with her musky love-juice. As I lapped and sucked at her aromatic cunt I felt her sigh and tremble, her breath catching in little ragged gasps of pleasure.

And then I became aware that events were taking another, not altogether unexpected, turn. Strong male hands took hold of my womanly, upraised hips and a rampant, throbbing prick nudged urgently at the opening of my swollen cunt — which must have been enticingly visible for quite some time with my legs parted and my arse thrust proudly in the air as it was.

Suddenly, as if convinced of his directorial accuracy, Michel or Antoine — for I did not as yet know to whom the cock belonged — gave a tremendous thrust and sheathed himself fully in my tight pussey, before holding tight to my bum and pumping back and forth with enviable speed and athleticism, and no small amount of panting and moaning.

Simultaneously, on opening her mouth to take a breath, Nicole became the proud recipient of another, no less desperate weapon, and found herself licking and sucking anew on this big, manly cock which began to fuck her mouth with passion, but also with great sensitivity in order not to overcome the poor girl with its splendid length and girth.

This glorious quadruple fuck drove all four of us to the very pinnacles of earthly delight and we all — Nicole, Michel, Antoine and myself — reached our respective climaxes within seconds of each other, shooting and oozing our sex emissions into each other's welcoming mouths and cunts.

After a while we all four collapsed in a warm, satisfied, lazy heap on the sandy rug and were in danger of dropping off to sleep, until the two boys yawned, stretched and jumped up, pulling us with them, and we all rushed headlong into the sparkling water where, in the manner of lusty young people everywhere, we laughed, swam, splashed each other's naked bodies and sported like a family of happy seals.

Some time later, companionably dripping, we returned to the rug and stretched out in the sun in order to dry ourselves before getting dressed and returning to the Academy. It was as I lay there in that wonderful state that lies between sleep and wakefulness, as naked as the day I was born and more than ever aware of the feel of God's fertile earth beneath me and the sensation of the sun and the water against my skin, my mind began to wander and I found myself recalling a delightful and rustic experience I'd enjoyed a few years previously.

Convinced that my friends would take pleasure in sharing with me my delicious reverie, I began to tell them of it.

'I had been staying on my uncle's farm in Dorsetshire,' I said. 'It was harvest-time, and all the able hands from miles around were busy at work in the fields. Each day my cousin Primrose and I would stroll about the countryside, and we would often pause to watch the time-honoured rituals of harvesting, threshing and haymaking.

'At this time of year, the labourers' whole families would come out to the fields to work alongside their menfolk. Even little children of five or six could be seen, busily carrying a few handfuls of hay to the stacks, an expression of earnestness about their angelic little faces.

'Primrose introduced me to some of the families that she knew from the village. There was Old Mother Moule, famed far and wide for her skills at mending. Her gnarled old fingers were now busily engaged with baling twine, and it was extraordinary to see how deftly she could gather up a sheaf of straw and tie it round. Then there was Mrs Knight, the laundrywoman, who had exchanged the old brass boiler of her daily trade for the scythe, while her children scampered and squabbled about her feet.

'In another field that day we met young Nick, the son of old Cave the farrier. He was a fine young man of sixteen or seventeen, tall for his years and with rich dark eyes. It was the dinner-hour, and he rose to greet us from the shade of an old blackthorn where he lay sheltering from the noonday heat of the sun.

' " 'Tis fine weather for the harvest indeed," he said in answer to our polite observations.

' "Is it going well this year?" asked Primrose.

' "Very well indeed, so as I gather."

' "And will you be looking forward to the harvest supper?" I asked, knowing that this was as great a highlight in the countryman's calendar as was Christmas in our own.

'Before Nick could reply, Primrose clapped a guilty hand to her mouth.

' "My goodness," she exclaimed, anxiety strong in her voice. "I had quite forgotten! I was supposed to go with mother to make arrangements with the minister about the flowers for the harvest festival. What time is it, Rosie?"

'I took my watch from my bosom. It was nearly twenty minutes after twelve.

' "Then I must fly," cried Primrose. "The Reverend Stitchum is a most punctilious man, and mother will be most annoyed."

'I rose to my feet, but Primrose demurred.

' "No need for you to come, my dear friend," she averred. "I'll go by the long pasture here, which will take me to the church gate by half-past. You can walk back to the house the way we came. Even half an hour in the company of the Reverend Stitchum," she whispered to me, "is a penance to deter the most wicked sinner. It is a punishment I could scarcely wish on my dearest cousin. Better that you shall linger awhile with young Nick here." And with that she tripped away across the field.

'Nick looked discomfited, perhaps embarrassed at being

alone in the company of a young lady, but I quickly put the farrier's son at his ease. We talked of this and that, of life in the village and his hopes that he might in time make his way in the horse-trade for, though so young, he had already shown considerable acumen in that respect. He had found two splendid Clydesdales going cheaply at a farm some ten miles away which Uncle had subsequently purchased, his recommendation being rewarded by two equally handsome sovereigns.

'Like many countrymen, Nick showed great facility with animals. But while many of his contemporaries were interested solely in those which they might trap or hunt, he loved them for their own sake.

'I was about to be going, but Nick said he would show me something. "It's only over here, behind old Moss's barn," he said. "The lane takes you out past the big house in any case."

'We walked through the copse and I noticed how firm and strong his hand was as he helped me over the little tinkling stream that ran through it.

' "Here," he said, as we approached the old barn. He pointed to a rusty piece of farm machinery, long disused and partly covered with a tarpaulin.

' "How interesting," I murmured, wondering what he possibly thought I would find so fascinating about Messrs Ransome and Rapier's Patented "Ipswich" Seed Drill.

'He must have noticed my momentarily quizzical expression, for he laughed and drew me closer. Again I noticed the firmness of his hand on my arm.

' "No, underneath," he said, speaking in a husky whisper which I found by no means unattractive.

'I peered past his pointing finger and there, in the gloomy cavern revealed by pulling back the tarpaulin, I saw what he had brought me to see. A fine tabby cat, around whom four delightful kittens were happily playing.

' "Oh how sweet!" I exclaimed. "Look at the little black one, with his white feet. And the ginger one — I bet he grows into a real bruiser!"

' "This one's my favourite," said Nick, and picked up a tabby that was the image of her mother. He stroked her gently while the mother looked on anxiously. "Don't you worry, Mrs Tibbles," he said. "Young Rosie here won't come to no harm."

' "Rosie?" I cried. "Why, that's my name! What a coincidence!"

'Nick laughed. "Not really," he said. "I named her for you. I found the cat had had kittens here the day you came to stay with your uncle. I heard you was called Miss Rosie, see. Hope you don't mind me being so familiar as to borrow your name, Miss Rosie. Only it strikes me as such a pretty one."

'I laughed, not minding at all, and stroked the kitten that had become my namesake. Mrs Tibbles began to show signs of annoyance, so we quickly restored her brood to full muster and quietly made our retreat.

' "Why name her after me?" I murmured as Nick replaced the tarpaulin.

'Nick blushed hotly. "Well," he stumbled, " 'cause I thought you were a real lady and she was too. And she's a bonny little thing, and so are you, if you don't mind me saying."

' "Of course not!" I tinkled. "Every woman likes to be flattered, especially by a handsome young man like yourself, Nick."

'I don't know quite how it happened, but we had been standing there for some moments, not knowing quite what to say, and then all of a sudden we were in each other's arms. Our lips met in a long, smouldering kiss.

'As my tongue probed his I felt strong, sensitive hands grasping my bottom cheeks. I pressed myself hard against him, feeling the steady stirring of his manhood through my summer dress.

'We broke for breath, and then once more we embraced passionately. I nibbled his ear, his neck. His hands seemed everywhere at once, caressing my arms, my thighs, my breasts.

131

' "Oh sir," I exclaimed, more for form's sake than from any genuine desire that he should desist.

' "Oh how I've loved you," cried Nick, his voice passionate with entreaty. "Right from the first moment I saw you I've felt drawn to you. And yet you always seemed so remote, so untouchable. You being from such a grand family an' all."

' "Oh fiddlesticks," I retorted. 'My father was an ordinary farmer, not half so grand as my uncle. His family held no higher social station than your own, my dear Nick. And not half the gentlemen I've met since then in society have had half your sensitivity."

'I kissed him again, full on the lips this time.

' "Come," he said pushing me towards the open door of old Moss's barn. Our lips were firmly glued together, and I surrendered to his judgement implicitly, as though he were my partner leading me backwards across a crowded ballroom.

'There was a squawk — he had unknowingly trodden on Mrs Tiddles' tail — and we toppled over backwards on to a bed of fresh straw, laughing.

'I felt his hand busy with the buttons at the front of my dress, and I did nothing to stop him. My naked titties were quickly exposed to view. He pulled back to look at them, and I heard him gasp.

' "Why, them's a wondrous pair," he gulped at last. "Ain't 'em just."

' "You like my bosoms then?" I asked coyly from beneath fluttering eyelashes.

' " 'Em's lovely," he said, and he buried his face in the deep cleft between my bosom. My nipples, as I could see, had perked up like organ-stops, and they seemed to fascinate him. I caressed them playfully.

' "Lick them, Nick," I whispered on impulse.

' "Lick 'em?"

' "That's right. Lick them.'

' "What?" he said, his eyes wide with wonder. "You're asking me to lick your nippy ends?"

' "That's right."

' "Lumme! Ain't you a dirty girl then! I never heard a girl ask me to do anythin' like that."

'Such a sweet, innocent boy! But he sucked my titties as well as any man I have known, and then I stood up, and shed my dress, and he pulled of his trousers, and I could see he had a most wonderful winkie there, straight as a ramrod and seemingly bursting with youthful vigour. Instantly I took a letch to have it in my mouth there and then.

' "Come on, Nick," I said, dropping to my knees. "Give me a taste of what's in store!"

'He seemed scarcely to know what I had in mind. But when I knelt there before him, and took hold of that fine manly cock of his, and licked around the purple tip, and then took it deep within my mouth, I could hear him audibly gasp out his pleasure.

' "Ah! Oho!" I heard him cry. " 'Tis too much. No one never done that to me before."

'I rolled my tongue around his cock, and tasted the sweet salt taste, and sucked him hard and deep. When I could sense that soon he would be able to hold back no longer, I ceased my lecherous labours.

' "Did you like that?" I asked breathily.

' "I love it," he cried, almost jumping up and down in his excitement. "That's what they say the French whores do, but I never thought afore now that folks really do it."

' "Oh yes they do, Nick. Lots of nice ladies do it, and they greatly enjoy doing it too."

' "Then I'll show you what I can do," he cried, and pushed me over backwards on to the straw. We both fumbled with my underskirts and then master Priapus was knocking at the door of my temple, begging for admission. I was in no mood to refuse him entry!

'In a trice his fine youthful cock was buried in me up to the hilt. Oh! How he fucked me that hot summer afternoon. In and out went his rampant charger, and how my bottom bounded up to meet his every thrust. His prick seemed to grow bigger by the second, until I seemed entirely filled by it, and about to burst.

'For one so young he was a lover of remarkable skill and tenderness. His spunk burst into me exactly at the instant I spent myself, and we rolled over and over in the hay until he uncunted.

'For several minutes we lay there in each other's arms, moist with the exertion and panting for breath. Suddenly from the distant fields came a whistle.

' "Stap me!" he cried. ' "What time is it? They're ready to start up again after dinner."

'I fumbled for my watch.

' "It's nearly one, Nick," I said.

' "Then I must be gone. Sorry, my dear, 'tis hardly fair to leave you like this. How I wish with all my heart I could stay with you all the afternoon long. But I have work to do, and I'll be getting in trouble if I let the others down."

'I laughed. "Not at all, dear Nick. I do understand, and I would fain be the one to get you into trouble. Here, give me a kiss, and then begone."

'He kissed me one last time, long and deep.

' "Shall I see you again, dear Rosie?" he said.

' "Yes indeed," said I. "I shall be here again tomorrow. We shall pay our compliments to Mrs Tiddles and her little pussies, and you can pay your compliments to mine."

'I swear that, as he went, he blushed quite scarlet at my words. Country girls, as he told me later, do not speak so, nor are they much advanced in the ways of making love. Lads neither, he added ruefully. I assured him that that was not how I judged him but, before the week was out and it was time for me to return to the bosom of my family, he had become a true carnal gourmet. In old Moss's barn, every dinner-time, we were transported for an hour into an altogether new realm of the senses. He fucked me from on top, from behind, with me sitting astride him. I sucked his prick and took his libation in my mouth I taught him how to lick my cunt and bring me to a spend with his tongue. Once, when we were feeling particularly randy, I took his

134

prick in my bottom-hole. But all good things must come to an end, and it was with parting's sweet sorrow that we finally took our leave of each other, with many murmured endearments and the promise that, at Christmastide, I would be back a my uncle's farm, and with me would bring a very special present for us both to share. But that, my dear friends, must be another story.'

'Bravo!' cheered Michel. 'That was, indeed, a charming story. How I wish there were time for us to practise some of those naughty tricks you demonstrated for that fortunate young boy! But now I fear it is getting late and we must return to the Academy at once, for I promised Maman I would take tea with her this afternoon.

Madame Dupont was undeniably fond of indulging in this peculiarly English habit and did so on the slightest pretext. I believed, secretly, that it was the hot buttered toast and delicious, sugary confections that went with it rather than the beverage itself which appealed to her expansive and expanding nature!

'Come, dear ladies, Antoine and I will be delighted to help you back into your gowns as soon as we are dressed ourselves.'

Michel was as good as his word and within a few minutes the four of us, arm in arm, were strolling back through the garden with the mid-afternoon sun slanting down on us through the trees and making dappled patterns on the soft, springy grass.

As we parted company from our new friends, smiling warmly and kissing each glowing cheek in turn in true French fashion, we promised to meet again soon in order to renew our relationship and share a further hour or two of companionable eroticism in the open air.

A day or two later, on entering the senior girls' study I was assailed by much excited laughter punctuated by a quantity of low, throaty, though undeniably feminine guffaws. What could have precipitated such earthy hilarity in this, a traditionally serene and tranquil chamber?

135

In the centre of the room, seated comfortably on a low, brocade sofa, sat an attractive and buxom lady of advancing years with twinkling brown eyes and an obviously merry disposition. She wore a peacock-blue gown of shot silk, generously boned and corseted in order to tame and hold at bay her ample bosom and rounded, womanly curves, and an elegant little hat with a long, black ostrich feather set at a jaunty angle atop her golden-blonde curls.

She was surrounded by ten or twelve of my classmates who, seated on adjoining chairs, on the floor or on each other's laps, were gazing at her delightedly with the sort of rapt attention rarely afforded to the Academy's more formal tutors.

As I entered the room she looked up and gave me a warm, inviting smile, gesturing for me to sit down. 'Good afternoon, my dear. I expect you're wondering who on earth I am — this middle-aged thorn between so many beautiful roses! Well, let me explain. I am Mrs Horwill, mother of Jane Horwill who I am sure you must know since she has been a student here at the Academy for over a year now.'

Indeed, I did know Jane Horwill, but I'd scarcely been tempted to further our acquaintance since she seemed to me to be the plainest, most unenviably tedious creature to whom I'd ever had the misfortune to be introduced. That this voluptuous, twinkling creature was her mother was almost beyond my comprehension, although it is a commonly held belief, and I certainly believe it to be true, that sparkling, elegant mothers have a habit of overshadowing their poor, unfortunate offspring — most especially the female offspring — imbuing them with a dowdiness made even more apparent when parent and child are viewed simultaneously. However, I digress.

'I have taken the opportunity of accompanying my dear husband, who has business here in Switzerland, in order to visit my daughter's school. Alas, poor little Jane is at present employed in a period of extra French with Mademoiselle Cartier, so I am entertaining some of your friends here with a few little stories and anecdotes. I do hope we won't be disturbing you. Do please join us if you have a minute or two to spare.'

With that, Mrs Horwill settled back against the firmly stuffed sofa and arranged her equally firmly stuffed gown around her knees, raising it up slightly in the front in order to facilitate the crossing of her surprisingly slim ankles and displaying her dainty little feet in their fashionable black button-boots.

Unable to resist the promise of a story (hopefully a naughty one, I thought wickedly!), I seated myself on a little footstool beside the sofa and prepared to listen. I was not, you'll be delighted to learn, in the least bit disappointed by what I heard.

Mrs Horwill cleared her throat and began:

'I had been invited to send a few days at the Somerset estate of Lord Somerville,' said Mrs Horwill at length. 'Of course, I had quite a shrewd idea of what that might entail. Lord Somerville was famous for the recherché eroticisms which formed a daily part of the amusements for those lucky enough to be entertained at his country seat. There were games, competitions, activities *outré* enough to enliven even the most jaded palate. In particular, I was anxious to see the famous "Nuditorium" which he had established there, and whose splendid facilities were, I gather, the talk of every gentleman's club the length of Pall Mall. My husband had frequently spoken of it — indeed, he had even suggested that, were his extensive shareholdings in the Bolivian tin-mining industry ever to bear as rich a fruit in dividends as he hoped he might realise from them, he might very well care to consider something of the sort at our own Yorkshire home.

'We arrived at the house in the late part of as splendid a summer's afternoon as one could have wished for. The house was perhaps slightly more modern than I had expected — built no later than the middle of the last century, according to his Lordship — but it was nevertheless a fine and foursquare edifice in the local stone, with some sixteen bedrooms and no less than two bathrooms. Downstairs, as well as a magnificent dining room and a ballroom that entirely equalled it in splendour, was the former salon that Lord Somerville had, with commendable speed, converted into his "Nuditorium" almost as soon as he had succeeded to the title. We were soon to enjoy its facilities.

'So hot was the afternoon that, as soon as we were shown to our room, I felt obliged to remove most of my clothing. I lay down on the bed in my drawers alone, practically panting from the heat, sipping occasionally from a glass of iced water. A cooling breeze blew in from the window, fanning the curtains that stirred lazily in the warm gusts. Idly I ran the frosted glass from which I drank against my bared bosom, and anointed my pert rose-bud nipples with drops of cool crystal. They sprang up immediately as if in salute.

'At this point my husband returned from the lavatory. "Now there's a sight to give a chap a bump in his trousers the size and shape of a Howitzer!" he exclaimed at once.

' "You still enjoy the sight of my bosoms, even after all these years?" I enquired of him, playfully cupping and squeezing my breasts and rolling my head from side to side, my tongue flicking my lips. "Come then, you must suck them for me. Take off your trousers so I can play with that fine cock of yours as you do so!"

'In a trice he was at my side, and his head buried between my smooth ivory mounds. He licked playfully at each nipple in turn, and then sucked deeply. Next, as I rubbed his cock, he drew in a mouthful of the firm flesh, and then another, until I felt he might actually swallow an entire breast.

' "Shall I spend over your titties, my dear?" he enquired of me, polite but urgent. "Though last night I swear you all but emptied me of a month's reserve of spunk, our long journey seems to have been a most wonderful restorative. Perhaps it was the jerking and lurching of the carriage. As it is, already my balls fairly ache with the lewd urgings of love."

' "Of course, my darling. I am always willing and eager to minister to your physical needs. Besides, nature knows

138

no finer lotion than spunk to keep skin smooth and supple, especially when it is of such delicacy as a ladies' bosoms.''

'I rolled over on to my side, and clasped that great ivory rod of his. I frigged him up and down a few times, and then pressed the bulging purple head between my titties.

' ''See how the firm flesh enfolds your cock,'' I exclaimed as he sensually rubbed his cock against my bosoms.

'He paused for a moment and looked down. ''See how I rub its tip against your exquisite nipples,'' he pointed out in turn.

' ''Shall I frig your cock until your spunk shoots all over them?''

' ''Of course, my sweet. Let my spunk gush all over those sweet strawberries.''

' ''It is such a perfect summer's afternoon,'' I purred, ''that strawberries and cream would be an equally perfect complement. How I do like to see a rich, creamy spend at such a time. I am sure, my dear husband, you have more spunk in you than any man I have ever known.''

' ''And you have known many men?'' he asked rhetorically.

' ''Many men. Many, many, many men. And many women too, but not nearly so many as all those many men. But not any of them could cover my titties with spunk the way you do.''

'I seized his cock and almost instantly was rewarded with a great gushing jet of cum that shot right across my bosoms. Five, six, seven times, that great spunker of his pulsed and discharged its precious fluid against my person, as I writhed and squealed in pleasure, for I had been playing with my pussey through the open gusset of my drawers all the while and now could feel my own spend upon me as the great heavy drops rained down.

' ''Aha!'' cried my husband, so loud that I am sure half the household might hear us.

' ''Aha!'' I cried in return, not caring a jot as we writhed together in the throes of our mutual spending.

'And then, almost in an instant, it was over — at least

for the time being. We lay back against the pillows in the breeze from the window, the rivulets of spunk already cooling, even as our ardour in turn diminished. With womanly acumen I rubbed the sweet fluid into my skin, not merely to prevent it running on to the exquisitely embroidered counterpane and spoiling it but also to gain the benefit of its wonderful properties of nutrition. A good thick jet of spunk, as I have said countless times to ladies and gentlemen of my acquaintance, is as fine a food for the skin as any of the costly preparations sold in jars by even the finest chemists of Jermyn Street. And then, for a moment or two, we drowsed together in each other's arms.

'Later we adjourned to the drawing-room for tea. We found that the company, as well as Lord and Lady Somerville, consisted of Captain Turvey and his delightful wife Annabel, and a Mr and Mrs Middleton, of Saffron Walden. After an excellent early evening meal of rice soup, rolled loin of mutton, curried veal and gooseberry fool, washed down with liberal supplies of a fine white Burgundy, we all took a turn on the terrace. Here glasses of champagne were served. Heated, perhaps, by the wine and the warm summer's evening, conversation gradually assumed a form and character that might have been eschewed in more polite society. Not lewd, exactly, but certainly a good deal more intimate than the polite and studied tone which so frequently characterises post-prandial intercourse.

'I am sure that Lord Somerville had read everyone's mind, for after our third or fourth glass he stood up and addressed the party.

' "Now that the evening is becoming somewhat cooler," he began, "I think it would be a fine thing, would it not, if we were to repair indoors and to show you something of that architectural indulgence for which, I gather, Somerville House has become celebrated in sporting circles. I refer, of course, to the Nuditorium my wife and I have established here in our ancestral home."

'There was a general murmur of consent. I am sure that both the Turveys and the Middletons were as keen as

Humphrey and myself to see it. Accordingly we took our glasses and, led by our host and hostess, strolled through the splendid reception rooms of Somerville House until we came to a fine carved door of English oak.

'Lord Somerville produced a key from his waistcoat pocket. "I prefer to keep the suite locked," he explained. "There are many valuable items kept here. And besides, we not infrequently are obliged to entertain guests — mostly serious men of politics, and from the world of commerce, and such dull company whose general humour would not, I am afraid, be much improved were they to pass through this particular door. But I am sure our present company will find nothing whatever to offend them within — indeed, it is the fervent hope of myself and my dear wife that you will find a very great deal to amuse you here."

'He stood aside, and we were ushered into a room richly furnished in the oriental style then much in vogue. Further apartments in turn led of this.

' "Let me show you some of the best features," said a voice, and we turned to see our hostess, Lady Somerville, emerging from one of the side-chambers. She was quite naked.

' "Yes indeed," cried her husband, not in the least perturbed by his wife's appearance in a state of paradisiacal innocence before his guests. "But first we too must disrobe. There is no point in having a Nuditorium without nudity, after all!"

'He quickly suited deed to word. I glanced at Humphrey — he seemed mesmerised by the radiant and entirely naked beauty of our hostess — and nodded my eager assent. In a second we, too, had undressed, and stood sipping our champagne in the unclothed company of our fellow guests. I was taken particularly by the splendour of Captain Turvey's cock, which was already showing signs of rapid and considerable tumescence. My husband murmured his appreciation of the size and firmness of his hostess's bosoms, and vowed to have the better of them before the evening was out. I too took quite a letch

141

to suck the tits of an English lady, and told him so, *sotto voce*.

'Leaving our clothes piled on the floor where we had stepped out of them, we made a tour of inspection of the apartments. Lord Somerville pointed out some of the features of interest — the ingenious system of mirrors whereby a watch could be kept on activities in the bedchambers directly adjacent; the large bed in the centre of the room surrounded by armchairs and divans, so that ladies and gentlemen might sit comfortably and enjoy a drink or a fine cigar while they watched others of their company disporting themselves on the sheets and pillows; the marble bath; the Italian piano; the countless fine prints and paintings showing scenes that would satisfy every conceivable erotic whim. It was, in truth, a veritable temple of Venus, and we loudly proclaimed our wholehearted approval to our ingenious host and hostess.

' "Of course," said Lord Somerville, "one always takes great care to choose one's guests with taste and discretion, so that future friendships — not necessarily of a purely amatory nature — may have the chance to blossom here. Many a useful connection in the City or the House — or, dare I say it, at Court — has been forged here.'

'He pulled aside a curtain, and drew out a device not dissimilar to a magic-lantern, mounted on a wheeled trolley.

' "Guests who stay at Somerville House are, of course, cordially invited to sign the visitor's book. It is a source of no small gratification to my wife and I to look back over those pages from time to time on the long and lonely winter evenings, and to read once more the names of those brilliant and distinguished friends who have graced our humble home with their presence. As you will see, we also have an interesting record of the guests who have whiled away an hour or two in the Nuditorium."

'He struck a vespa, and a searing beam of light lit up the room. Then a photograph, much enlarged, was projected on the wall directly opposite his Lordship's magic lantern.

' "Count von Buhlen, of Danzig, fucking the wife of one

142

of our most distinguished portrait painters. And another —
Sir Egbert Claughton, our ambassador to the King of Spain
— proudly showing what is unquestionably the longest prick
my wife has ever had the pleasure of enjoying. Now we see
Sophie and Emma, the twin daughters of General Hapgood,
licking the cunt of the splendid Lady Erinmore. See, here
is Lady Erinmore again, with my own prick in her mouth
while she is fucked from the rear by the Maharaja of
Filthistan, a potentate with the finest collection of erotica
in the whole of India. What exotic bout we ran that night,
I can tell you! Here is my wife again, playing the fellatrix
with the Bishop of Bath and Wells — what a pair of balls
he has on him, to be sure! And now Mrs Neaverson and
Mrs Dugdale — deadly rivals their husbands may be at
Westminster, but here are their wives busy dildoing each
other in fine style, while Her Majesty's Sergeant-at-Arms
masturbates vigorously in the background.''

'I could not resist giving my husband Humphrey's cock
a sly squeeze, and noted with pleasure that it was already
as stiff as a regimental flagpole. Indeed, others had been
similarly impressed with the photographs, for Mrs
Middleton was sitting with her legs apart while her husband
played skilfully with her pussey. After we had seen the last
lantern slide — a remarkable study of the operatic diva La
Ciccone being fucked by Sir Constantine Learie, the
sportsman and politician, while simultaneously being
enculed in rear by the pianist Horobin — we all
spontaneously burst into applause.

'Lord Somerville modestly acknowledged our tributes.
"Something slightly more energetic now, perhaps!" he
called, and his wife sat down at the piano. "My dear lady,"
he beseeched me, "would you do me the pleasure?"

'I half expected to be pushed backwards on to a sofa there
and then, but instead of this he led me off in a delightful
waltz around the room while Lady Somerville accompanied
us on the piano, exhibiting no small accomplishment at the
musical arts. The others quickly joined us, Captain Turvey
with Mrs Middleton and his own wife, Annabel, in the arms

143

of Hugh Middleton. My dear Humphrey was profitably employed in turning the music for his hostess.

'We were all, it should be remembered, entirely naked. Though I have experienced many sensations in a life largely devoted to the pleasures of the flesh, I had never encountered any that was quite so novel, or as titillating, as that of dancing closely together in *flagrante delecto*. There is always the delight, when dancing fully clothed, of knowing that the press of one's bosom against a manly chest is discreetly acknowledged and appreciated, and similarly of feeling the insistent stirrings of one's partner's prick against a gartered thigh. But this was an entirely different proposition.

' "And how do you like my Nuditorium?" asked his Lordship when we had completed the second circuit of the room.

' "I think it is excellent," I replied, lightly rubbing my Mound of Venus against him. He lightly squeezed my bottom-cheeks in acknowledgment. "My husband speaks of installing something similar at our own home. On a more modest scale, of course, for our means are perhaps not quite so limitless as your own."

'Lord Somerville laughed gaily. "Nonsense, my dear girl! From what I hear at my club, old Humphrey is one of the richest men in all England. I am sure he can quite outdo me in that respect. My wife too has long admired his acumen."

'We both burst into laughter at this wordplay, and glanced over at where our respective partners were seated at the piano. Lady Somerville's fingers flickered lightly over the keys, while Humphrey was leaning across and cupping her fine breasts as he had so often caressed my own. From time to time, they would exchange knowing looks.

'Presently we sank on to a divan, and watched the others as they progressed from waltz to polonaise to mazurka. Lord Somerville poured me a glass of champagne. Despite my nakedness, I was quite panting with the exertion of the dance, and welcomed the libation. Almost unconsciously, I lay closer to Lord Somerville and casually stroked his fine chest. He in turn drew his long, aristocratic fingers up and down my spine in a way that quite made me tingle with longing. In a second we were kissing deeply and passionately, our tongues flicking each other's.

'Fired by a fierce longing, I whispered lewd imaginings in Lord Somerville's ears. It was as though I had ignited gunpowder. He pushed me backwards, covering my body with savage kisses, his hands seemingly everywhere at once. The music resounded around the room, yet louder still seemed the rush of blood through my ears. I lay back on the cushions and within seconds he had mounted me, his questing cock probing deep within me as a voluptuous thrill coursed through my loins.

' "Ah! I die" I cried, as he thrust hard against me, his great lordly ball-sack seeming to slap against my bum-cheeks in time to his powerful movements. In and out went that splendid cock, splashing in the lubricious secretions of my pussey like a dog splashing happily in a river.

' "My God, dear lady!" he exclaimed, as I slapped his bum hard and urged him to still greater exertions. "It is too much! I can hold back no longer." And with that his great tool shook me like an earthquake from within, and I could feel great pulsing gobs of spunk shoot into me as I squealed with my own spending and bit him sharply on the neck.

' "I never knew a cunt that was so tight and yet so wet at the same time," he said when he had recovered his breath and uncunted.

' "But were you not once *in amorata* of Miss Langtry, the actress?" I ventured. "They do say that, for powers of nip and squeeze, her pussey could clamp a man's cock down as hard as if it were in a vice on a bench."

' "In comparison with having the pleasure of your own dear pussey,' he murmured, 'fucking Miss Lillie Langtry was like lobbing a jug of cream down Regent Street."

'We both roared with laughter to such an extent that the music came to an abrupt halt. The others had, it seemed, been so carried away by their own intrigues that they had scarcely begun to realise what had passed between Lord

145

Somerville and myself. However, soon there were other combatants in the lists of love. lady Somerville was busy sucking Humphrey's cock as he stood by her at the piano, while Rachel Middleton and Captain Turvey were playing a delightful game of ''sixty-nine'' on a Kashmiri rug by the fireplace. Hugh Middleton, in turn, was busy rodding Annabel Turvey from behind. I could see the fine shaft of his love-staff as it thrust in and out of her, and I pointed this out to Lord Somerville.

' ''Aye, he has a fine cock, it is true. And see how her titties swing as she kneels before him! Mrs Middleton has a fine pair of bosoms, does she not? Come, my dear, what say you that I shall suck one of them while you suck the other?''

'So saying, he practically pulled me to my feet and led me across the room. He lay down beneath Rachel and his tongue began to lick and flick at her nipples with commensurate skill. In a trice I had lain down beside him, and my mischievous tongue began its saucy work.

' ''Oh, what rapture! exclaimed the object of our ardour. ''How I love to take on several partners at once!''

' ''And how I like to see a woman making love to another woman,' cried Lord Somerville.

'The sight of myself lying, legs apart, beneath Rachel Middleton must have driven Captain Turvey to a frenzy of lust. His eyes rolled, and I could feel his body shuddering as he shot his load into her. He uncunted and fell back on to the rug, but Mrs Middleton's ardour seemed unassuaged.

' ''Quick, my Lord, put your own cock up my cunt,'' she breathed. ''I am sure I can't be satisfied till I have two men's spendings in me. And Henrietta, let me lick your cunt even as his Lordship fucks me from behind, and let us all three spend together.''

'I lay down before her, and parted my legs. For the second time inside ten minutes, Lord Somerville unsheathed his great sword and plunged it in her right up to the hilt, even as Rachel buried her face in my muff and licked greedily.

'A nice cock in the pussey is a splendid sensation, but

146

surely there is little in the realm of the senses that quite equals the exquisite pleasure of woman cunt-licking woman. How Rachel's probing tongue found my every recess, how she lapped and nipped with consummate skill! I spent once, twice and had very nearly reached my third climax before Lord Somerville's shouts betokened his imminent spending.

'After this the party retired to the marble bathing-hall where, purified and refreshed by further generous bumpers of champagne, we laid plans for further lewdness.

'Our next bouts were handsome Hugh Middleton up my cunt while I sucked my dear husband's prick; Lord Somerville fucking Annabel Turvey in front while her husband enculed her from the rear (she, it had been admitted as we bathed together, being rather fond of this double insertion); Lady Somerville and Rachel Middleton dexterously dildoing each other while studying their reflection in one of the fine chemise glasses that were placed to good advantage around the room.

'After that, I took on Captain Turvey while his wife licked both my cunt and his cock, on which I was spitted; my husband fucked Rachel Middleton kneeling down while Hugh came all over her tits; and Lord and Lady Somerville enjoyed a splendid and entirely orthodox fuck in each other's arms.

'A little before midnight, our heads fairly spinning from the champagne and our strenuous exertions, we made our separate ways unsteadily to bed. My darling husband, bless him, still had sufficient spunk in him to pay a final tribute to my charms, before we fell into deep and undisturbed slumber.

'The following morning we all breakfasted together. Such was the discretion of the company that, before the servants, there was not the slightest hint of the improprieties of the night before. The titled lady who, not twelve hours before, had taken my husband's cock in her bum now decorously assured him it would be no trouble to send to the kitchen for more bacon. I, meanwhile, demurely passed the sugar to the man whose spunk I had earlier so greedily swallowed,

147

while Lord Somerville politely discussed local matters with his two other lady guests, despite my having seen with my own eyes them taking turns to suck his cock and lick his wife's quim. And then, myself perhaps slightly sore and my husband complaining in private of the odd twinge here and there, we made an affectionate farewell to the party, and so took our leave of Somerville Hall and the remarkable pleasure of its Nuditorium.'

Mrs Horwill gave a deep sigh of satisfaction at a story well told and, for a brief moment or two, stared off into space with a little grin and a twinkling eye. The atmosphere in the senior girls' study could be cut with a knife. No one spoke for a full five minutes as, to a girl, we sat motionless, fighting to commit each delicious nuance and saucy twist of Mrs Horwill's reminiscences to memory.

Suddenly someone giggled, then before you could say 'hot furry fannies' the whole room was laughing and joking and chatting in a thoroughly enlightened and animated style.

Mrs Horwill was delighted at the effect her lustful little tale had had on us. She sat in our midst, four-square and smiling, like a proud bitch with her litter of squirming, mischievous puppies.

For myself, I was still finding it almost totally impossible to believe that this was the mother of plain Jane Horwill, a girl I'd scarcely glanced at, let alone shared confidences with, since my arrival at the Academy some weeks before. I decided then and there to make a mental note to find out more about her in the days and weeks that followed her charming mother's visit to our illustrious establishment. Maybe there was more to our Jane than met the eye. We would see . . .

'*Do* tell us another story, Madame,' begged Lucille, a pretty little blonde with shiny ringlets and a dusting of freckles on her retrousse nose.

'My dears!' laughed Mrs Horwill,' I swear I shall lose my voice once and for all if I agree to recount any more of my exploits, and that would never do. My dear husband and myself have been invited to dine this evening at the British

148

Embassy in Lucerne, so I must preserve my energy and my vocal chords or there'll be hell to pay.

'The Ambassador himself is a dear, sweet man — a gentleman and a scholar — but, alas, he lost his loving wife to whom he was totally devoted in a boating accident some months ago, and is still reeling from the shock of his loss. Indeed, so deep is his sorrow that from time to time he loses all sense of reason and finds himself saying things and acting in ways hitherto unthought of, which would make his dear departed wife turn in her grave.

'Why, only the other day my husband and I were indulging in a spot of Whist with the Ambassador in the drawing room at the Embassy. Darling Humphrey was droning on, as he is wont to do, about the fine architectural heritage of the town in general and the Embassy building in particular, waxing lyrical about the giant porticos, the stately colonnades and the delicate cornicing to be found within.

'The Ambassador and I were hardly listening, disrespectful though it may be to admit such a thing, and when Humphrey left the room for a minute or two in order to answer a call of nature, the illustrious gentleman leant across, planted his hand firmly on my upper thigh and, looking me full in the eyes, made me promise to make my excuses this evening after dinner (I decided in a trice that I could complain of a headache or somesuch) and slip away from the assembled gathering so that we might meet in his chambers for a post-prandial glass or two of brandy, and maybe a spot of spontaneous entertainment of our own invention if the time was right and our hearts felt mutually inflamed by the idea.

'I have to admit, my dears, that the very thought of an hour or two spent alone in the company of the great man elicits within me emotions of a thoroughly unladylike nature. Indeed, I feel quite lightheaded at the notion.'

With this, Mrs Horwill leant back and rested her ample frame against the elegant brocade back of the sofa, breathing rather too rapidly for comfort and frantically fanning her flushed cheeks with a small, painted silk fan which had previously been concealed about her voluptuous person.

'Tell me, my sweet,' she said breathlessly, looking expectantly at a sultry brunette by the name of Mariette, 'would it be possible to partake of a little glass of something to soothe my nerves? Maybe a small brandy, or even a soupçon of Schnapps?'

'*Mais non Madame!*' exclaimed Mariette with mock horror (the twinkle in her big brown eyes gave a clue to the fact that she was quite obviously highly amused, despite the severity of her tone). 'Alcohol is strictly forbidden at the Academy (but not within its grounds, I thought with glee as I remembered my sensual little *déjeuner sur l'herbe* with Nicole, Michel and Antoine a few days earlier, and how our randy foursome had polished off several generous measures of champagne and red wine on that lazy, hazy, sexy afternoon), but if you will permit me, I'd love to share with you a letter I received this morning from my dear brother, Jamie.

'He and I are twins and, as you might expect, we share more than our looks! He tells me absolutely everything and always has done, and since he's a very naughty boy indeed with a quite spectacular passion for pretty young girls, his letters to me are often of a thoroughly explicit nature. Indeed, the one I'm about to read you made me blush to the very roots of my hair when I first saw it. Anyway, here goes!'

Mariette's sparkling eyes and eager demeanour gave a lie to and quite overshadowed her modest protestations of embarrassment. Tossing back her bonny brown curls, withdrawing two or three crumpled, well-read sheets from the bodice of her dress and clearing her throat in readiness, she began:

' "My darling sister, Mariette, I am aching to recount to you a randy little anecdote told to me the other day by dear old Bertie. He and I had been enjoying a glass or two of beer in the open air with some friends of ours, when suddenly he came out with a tale to make your hair curl and put roses in your cheeks! The circumstances were rather as follows:

' " 'It looks like it's going to rain,' observed Cristabel, who had been studying the clouds over the distant mountains.

' " 'They say that if you can see the Eisberg clearly from here before 10 in the morning, then it will rain before luncheon,' said Antoinette.

' " 'And if you can't see it, then it must be raining already,' added Monsieur la Rochelle, with his customary dry sense of humour.

' " 'What's all this?' asked Bertie, who had evidently been dozing underneath the laurel tree and had just now awoken with a start.

' " 'I said it looks like rain.' said Cristabel.

' "Bertie picked up his half-drunk glass of beer, and held it up against the sky.

' " 'My word, you're right,' he said at length, after studying the pale fluid intently for some while. 'It certainly does look like rain. With, I might add, just the very faintest flavour of hops.'

' "We all laughed uproariously at this gem of Bertie's wit. Another bottle of champagne was broached, and again we drank deeply. Bertie, however, topped up his glass with beer. He came from a long-established line of brewers in Wiltshire, and I was touched by his devotion to the beverage that made their name.

' " 'I say, Portland, old chap!' he called at length. 'Let me pose you a question. Why is this glass of beer — of whose quality I am distinctly not enamoured — like making love in a punt? Let's see if a Cambridge man can answer that one, eh? Let's put a fiver on it to make things more interesting.'

' "Lord Portland, not the brightest spark of Edwardian England's manhood, looked puzzled. But the natural instincts of the sportsman rendered him incapable of refusing a challenge.

' " 'Have a swig yourself, my dear fellow,' urged Bertie.

'It might get the old grey matter ticking over. Though not as well, I might add, as if you were drinking our very own Celebration Ale, which we brewed especially to mark the Coronation of our present King. That sir, was a beer as fine as any that I have ever tasted.'

' "Lord Portland took the proffered glass and sipped reflectively. 'Why is this beer like making love in a punt? Hmmmm, let me see now. It's dry, to be sure. Could that be it, I wonder? Wet and dry? No, surely not. It has a faintly nutty taste, though. Because only a fool would consider making love in a punt? No, it can't be.'

' "His brows furrowed again.

' " 'Why is this beer like making love in a punt? Hmmmmm. Hmmmmm.' I thought I could almost hear the cog-wheels whirring around inside my head, but then he gave me the most outrageous wink.

' " 'Why is this beer like making love in a punt, you ask?' He paused, and took a deep draught of the amber nectar. 'I'll tell you why, Bertie,' he said in a quiet undertone. 'Because it's fucking near water that's why! Eh? That's a good 'un, what? Thought you'd got me there, didn't you? Fucking near water, that's the answer to your riddle! Come on now, old boy, cough up! Let's see the colour of your money!'

' "Bertie paid up in great good humour as befits a gentleman. 'Actually,' he began, 'my question does put me in mind of another little riddle of my own, that actually took place some few years ago, when I was in Venice. I had been staying with the Powells — excellent people, who had come originally from Bicester — and one evening we went, as one might, for a gondola cruise on the canals.

' " 'Venice, is, as you will know, a most delightful place, especially when the softer light of early autumn adds its own special qualities. The evening was made even more delightful because I was seated at the rear of our gondola, squeezed in between the two Powell daughters, Rebecca and Suzanna, twin sisters of some seventeen years.

' " 'For over an hour we passed along the canals and

lagoons, admiring the splendours of the buildings as they were lit up by the setting sun. It grew chilly, and at length rugs were passed out by Mrs Powell. I was given a particularly large and thick one which I spread loosely over the laps of the two girls and myself, and we resumed our journey tucked up in perfect snugness within its capacious folds.

' " 'After a while I became conscious of a movement on my leg. At first it was no more than an animal might make, as when a cat brushes herself against you. Then I was aware that it was moving gradually up my thigh. Thinking there might be some insect crawling about beneath the rug, I wriggled slightly to try and shake it off, but was hampered both by my being closely hemmed in by the Powell girls and my wish not to alarm them. You can imagine the panic that would have been caused had I said I suspected there was a spider under the rug.

' " 'My wriggling proved ineffectual. To distract myself, I began talking instead in an animated fashion, drawing attention to this church or that tower, without really knowing what I said. The Powell girls listened politely and added observations of their own, obviously quite unaware – or seemingly so – of my discomfort.

' " 'The movement was now around my groin. Then I became aware that soft fingers were caressing the bulge at the front of my trousers, kneading and squeezing it until my cock was inflamed with longing. The strange nature of my position made my arousal even more exquisitely unbearable. Though it was obvious that either Rebecca or Suzanna was responsible, each girl showed an almost complete detachment from the business in hand. Rebecca was talking to her father, who was seated in front of us, and Suzanna was telling me something of the history of St Mark's church. Their expressions alone betokened complete innocence.

' " 'So this state of affairs went on for some little while, and then the mysterious hand quickly unbuttoned me and took hold of my prick. I looked at one sister, and the other, and then back at the first again. They acknowledged my glances with a smile or a casual nod, as one would on momentarily catching a friend's eye. There was not the slightest suggestion that one of them — and I could not for the life of me tell which — was quietly playing with my cock beneath the rug.

' " 'The situation was unspeakably erotic. I longed to pull back the rug, to take a sister in my arms — it didn't matter which, for they were both exquisitely beautiful — and plunge my burning cock into her there and then. This, however, would have been quite out of the question. At the very least, it would have horrified her parents, who were sitting only a few feet away. It might even have capsized the boat, and sent us all to Davy Jones's locker.

' " 'So I simply sat there, seething with lust, while that expertly skilled hand worked up and down my cock with firm, discreet strokes. Light fingers fluttered elegantly against my blazing prepuce, and yet not a ripple of movement showed on the surface of the rug.

' " 'Soon, inevitably, I spent — all over her hand, the rug and my trousers. I was powerless to stop it, even had I wanted to. My laboured breathing must have caught Mrs Powell's ear, for she turned to glance at me for a moment. Through a whirl of bawdy feelings I was aware of Rebecca casually discussing plans for tomorrow's excursions with her father, while Suzanna was exchanging playful banter with her young brother, Tom, standing in the bow of the boat. For my part, I felt like subsiding into a heap.

' " 'In time, but my mind still quite aflame, we returned to our moorings, close to the Powells' apartment. I had the presence of mind to quickly button myself as we gathered up the rug and stepped out of the boat. Thanks to the darkness and a discreet readjustment of my jacket I was, I think, successful in concealing the very obvious marks that were evident on the front of my white trousers.

' " 'We spoke for some little time on the shore before our party broke up and I returned with the Powells to their home. Not a single sign did I detect from either of the sisters that

154

they had been in any way involved in what had happened on the boat. And yet the bare fact of the matter was that one of them — a girl I had neither made overtures to, nor even spoken to much during the course of my stay with them — had quite unashamedly tossed me off earlier that evening, not merely under a rug, but under her very parents' noses.

' " 'Their mother, I now think, might well have suspected that something was afoot. From that point on, at any rate, we spent quite a bit of time together, touring the many museums and antiquities of Venice. This culminated, as such things will, in a most enchanting afternoon spent at the Excelsior Hotel — it being quite out of the question that such adulteries could be carried out under her own roof. But that, of course, is another story. For the moment, I rather fear that the heavens are about to burst, and unless we can get back to our lodgings within a few minutes we will, I am afraid, be in for a drenching.'

' "Well, Mariette, as you might imagine, Bertie's tale fired the collective imagination of the assembled gathering in no uncertain manner! Emboldened by the alcohol we had consumed and flushed with heroic fervour by Bertie's story, it was as much as we could do to keep our hands off each other until we met again that evening, after dinner, for a glorious romp in my chamber!

' "I might as well tell you that Cristabel and I have been meeting in private, for similar such entertainment, ever since. I will let you know when next I write how the affair progresses.

' "Meanwhile, take care of yourself at that school of yours in Switzerland and be good, and if you can't be good, be careful!

' "With very much love, Jamie." '

Coughing slightly, Mariette refolded the letter and replaced it in the soft little nest from whence it came — inside her bodice, between her warm breasts — and the rest of us burst into a round of spontaneous applause, accompanied by assorted whistles and cat-calls from some of my bolder, less decorous classmates.

155

By now thoroughly enjoying myself — our little gathering had turned into quite a party, thanks to Mrs Horwill and Mariette and their saucy stories — I was quite crestfallen when the door to the study swung open and there on the threshold, stood Mademoiselle Cartier and the unfortunate Jane. The tutor stood there open-mouthed, like a fish out of water, and was obviously totally taken aback by the almost tangible aura of jollity which assailed her.

Jane, on the other hand, was red-faced and obviously highly embarrassed at what she perceived, quite rightly, to be yet another example of her mother's habitual impropriety.

'Darling!' boomed Mrs Horwill to her unfortunate daughter. 'How wonderful to see you, and looking so . . . so . . . healthy, too.' She could hardly have said 'attractive' or 'becoming' I thought, meanly, and giggled behind my hand.

'Come, I've been simply dying to see your room — and to meet your tutors, of course (this with a deferential but not entirely convincing nod in the direction of Mademoiselle Cartier, who was by now quite white in the face with shock.)

'As you can see, I've already made myself known to some of your young friends,' she informed her daughter, turning to we girls and giving us an enormous, conspiratorial wink, eliciting a veritable barrage of juvenile titters and giggles from our little group. 'Now then, show me the way if you please.'

With a flourish of peacock silk, trailing an aromatic cloud of expensive French cologne, Mrs Horwill left the study. Her daughter Jane, blushing hotly and with eyes raised heavenwards, fiddled with an imaginary rosary and followed resignedly. Mademoiselle Cartier, ashen-faced, brought up the rear.

As the study door softly closed behind them, those of us that were left exchanged glances before collapsing into uproarious laughter, vowing to somehow engineer a further meeting with the delightfully entertaining Mrs Horwill before she finally departed for England.

* * *

156

Some weeks before I'd joined Madame Dupont's Academy for Young Ladies, the esteemed principal had decided, working on the advice given by some of the college's governors, to allow us senior girls, in twos and threes, to visit the town from time to time in order to avail ourselves of some of the fine museums and galleries to be found there.

One sunny spring morning, shortly after I'd completed my toilet and consumed a hearty breakfast of crusty rolls with Morello cherry jam and a large, steaming cup of aromatic black coffee, I was called to Madame's study together with a fellow classmate, Justine.

'*Mademoiselles D'Argosse et Villeneuve,*' she said. 'I see by my diary that it is the turn of you both to visit the town. After lunch, I'll send my carriage to the front door of the Academy and the driver will wait for you there until 2.00 p.m., at which time I expect you to be correctly attired — don't be fooled by the weather; it's not as warm as it looks — and ready to embark on your trip.

'The mistress who under normal circumstances undertakes to accompany young ladies on these expeditions into town, Mademoiselle Bernard, is currently indisposed, so I'm relying on you girls to act with the decorum expected of your class, and to conduct yourselves with the grace and bearing necessary in order to bring credit to yourselves and your school.

'Please instruct the driver as to the places of learning you wish to visit. He will drive you to them and wait outside each one until you feel you've absorbed enough, at which time he will return you to the Academy in time for supper. You will have taken tea — an English custom, I believe — at one of the hotels in the centre of town. May I recommend L'Hotel Royale in the Rue Fontaine. Now all that remains is for me to wish you both *bon voyage.*'

With that she made a small gesture of dismissal and turned her attention to the papers on her desk.

Justine and I curtsied politely and left the room. Once outside the door and on our way to our classroom for a lesson in Geography, which I always found tedious in the extreme, we looked at each other and grinned conspiratorially.

'How kind of Madame to allow us an afternoon on the town,' I said, a wicked gleam in my eye.

'And just at the right time,' agreed Justine. 'My boyfriend is in town at the moment, spending part of his annual leave. He's a Professor of Humanities at the Sorbonne in Paris. I received a letter from him the other day outlining his plans, where he pleaded with me to try and meet him for an hour or two during his visit.

'The dear boy obviously misses me dreadfully. Maybe I could arrange it so that I just happened to be walking past his hotel when I discovered a pressing need for some light refreshment. I believe the hotel where he's staying, L'Hotel Candide, has a reputation for baking the best pastries in town, and utterly delicious they are, too — as light as swansdown and filled with fresh fruit and cream.

'Wait! He happened to mention that he would be accompanied by a friend from Paris — Maurice DeClerc, a Professor of Fine Art. Rosie, your luck's in! Maybe you, too, could discover a similar need for coffee and pastries!'

'But what about Madame's driver?' I asked with curiosity. Maybe Justine knew something I didn't — she had been a student at the Academy for a term or two longer than me — but I failed to see how we could evade the eagle eye of the wily Gruber. He'd been in Madame's employ for a number of years and must by now have become well versed in the girlish pranks and tricks of her young students.

'And anyway,' I continued, 'Maurice is probably five feet tall and built like an ape. I certainly shouldn't like him if that were the case. I do have certain standards to maintain regarding my male acquaintances, you know.'

'Not a bit of it,' replied Justine, who must obviously have met the gentleman in question, 'he's six feet tall and built like a Greek god. And as for Gruber it's well known that one only has to grease his palm with a franc or two to ensure his total compliance. Indeed, he welcomes his free time in

158

the town. It's been rumoured he has a lady friend there whom he visits whenever the opportunity arises. So, this afternoon for him holds the promise of an hour or two's lovemaking as well as some extra cash to bolster his income. I might even find it in my heart to do him a little favour . . .' she added mysteriously. 'I owe him one from my last trip into town. What more could the old reprobate want? Come we must hurry to our class. We're five minutes late already and we don't want to fall prey to the sharp side of Mademoiselle Phillipe's forked tongue — the old dragon!'

Hurrying along at Justine's side, I couldn't for the life of me imagine what she'd meant about owing Gruber a favour. I wasn't allowed the opportunity to discover the reason, however — just as I opened my mouth to ask we arrived at our classroom and Justine pressed her finger to her lips and bade me be silent. I needn't have worried, though — I had oodles of fun finding out!

A few hours later, morning lessons and lunch over, Justine and I descended the steps of the Academy looking for all the world like two respectable young ladies of breeding about to embark on a mission of mind-expansion. But it was to be more than just our minds which were expanded on that glorious afternoon.

Glancing at each other with little smiles of complicity, we alighted the steps of the carriage and seated ourselves comfortably within — side by side, ankles crossed, dainty gloved hands in laps and jackets tightly buttoned.

No sooner had we commenced our journey into town than the carriage stopped, Gruber jumped down from his driving seat and came round to the door of the carriage, opening it and peering in at us with a look of expectation on his face.

I marvelled at Justine's bare-facedness as she smiled sweetly and handed him a small, sealed envelope. Obviously she's been through this procedure before, I thought to myself. Then, mouth open in surprise, I watched as she carefully removed her gloves and slowly undid the buttons of her jacket, and then her high-necked white lace blouse.

Pushing these items of clothing to one side and looking down her nose at the by-now sweating Gruber in a thoroughly patrician manner, she pushed her shoulders back, thrust out her chest and proudly displayed to him her nubile young breasts which were snow white, uplifted and rosebud tipped.

Having got over the initial shock of this brazen display I began to see the potential of the situation and, as I looked longingly at Justine's darling tits, a plan began to form in my mind.

Lasciviously running my pink tongue over my lips, pussey growing increasingly damp at the prospect of the fun to follow, I too undid my upper garments and, savouring every erotic moment, peeled them back to reveal my full, rounded breasts to Gruber's gaze.

The poor man was now quite red in the face and, fumbling with his fly buttons, issued a series of small, strangled cries.

At first gazing lovingly at my beautiful twin assets, I began to fondle them with my soft hands, following their full, snowy contours with my fingers and stroking the plump strawberry nipples until they grew firm and pointed.

Continuing in this way, I raised my big blue eyes and looked levelly into Gruber's, which by now were like organ stops. He'd pulled his cock free and was frigging himself like a man possessed, grunting and shuddering by turns.

Turning to face my pretty young friend I gently smiled and stroked her cheek with my finger. Then, placing my hands on her shoulders I pulled her towards me and we began to explore each other's faces with our parted lips before sinking into a deep, erotic kiss. Our girlish arms twined around each other and our tits pressed together, nipples touching and sending ripples of pleasure through us both.

At last, with a long-drawn-out groan, Gruber ejaculated into the handkerchief he had ready for the purpose then, swiftly and with a furtive glance around him, began to tuck his still-slightly erect cock back into his trousers. His task completed, he gave a couple of embarrassed coughs (not very convincingly), leered suggestively at us both and slammed the carriage door before climbing back into his driving seat at the front of the vehicle.

As the carriage began to move off again, Justine and I looked at each other for a moment or two before collapsing into fits of thoroughly unladylike laughter, shoulders shaking and naked breasts bouncing with mirth.

'Did you see his face?' I shrieked. 'I thought for a moment he was going to die from a heart attack when I showed him my tits!'

'And did you hear him whimper like a little lost dog when we began to kiss?' said Justine. 'My only regret is that he chose to spunk into his handkerchief. If he'd taken it upon himself to squirt it over our bosoms I'd have taken great pleasure in ordering him to lick it off them — first yours, then mine — so that not a sticky trace of it was left. Dear me! The very thought of his big, wet tongue lapping the salty cum from my nipples has made me incredibly horny.'

'You wicked girl, Justine. The very idea of it! You've made my pussey go all damp and hot again,' I said, more seriously this time and gazing longingly into Justine's mischievous face.

'Are you thinking what I'm thinking?' she whispered, all amusement gone from her voice. 'If so, I'd love it if you'd play with my nipples for a while before we get dressed again.'

Looking at me with her big, brown eyes she gave me a suggestive little wink then, tossing back her thick, waist-length strawberry-blonde hair, leaned back against the seat of the carriage in a thoroughly abandoned manner.

With a look of serenity on her face she closed her eyes, her pert little breasts rising and falling as she breathed, blush-pink nipples tantalisingly erect. With her cute, *retroussée* nose and generous, upturned lips she looked for all the world like a contented kitten waiting for its mother to commence preening.

Taking care not to touch her nipples, I softly stroked her adorable tits with the tips of my cool fingers while she

161

squirmed with delight. For a brief moment I almost thought I heard her begin to purr.

Turning my attention to her nipples I began to gently flick them, noticing at the same time the rapid thumping of her heart and the little goose-bumps rising on her sensitive white skin.

'Please suck them, Rosie,' she begged in a small, hesitant voice, a look of gentle pleading in her wide eyes. 'It may seem strange but it's a long time since I've had a girl make love to me. I need to remind myself of what it's like to feel the insistent pressure of soft, feminine lips around my nipples. Don't tease me, Rosie. Do it now!'

I hadn't the heart to keep the poor girl waiting so I moistened my full lips and lowered them to each of her trembling nipples in turn, nibbling the taut rosy flesh and sucking deeply.

Concentrating on the delicious task in hand I became aware of a tiny, stockinged foot, divested of its shoe, insinuating itself under my gown and between my shapely thighs as I knelt on the carriage floor. Obligingly parting my legs and feeling the damp fabric of my brief panties stretch, and the folds of my ever-willing cunt part and begin to throb in expectation, I sucked and lapped at Justine's nipples with an even greater diligence before asking in a low, seductive voice:

'Tell me, darling, do you plan to fuck me with your pretty little toes? I do hope so! No one's ever pleasured me that way before. Here, let me help you.'

With that I reached down, flung my full skirts over my back and pulled down my knickers, thereby displaying my upraised naked bottom to the bug-eyed occupants of a passing cab.

A moment or two later, hearing the muffled screech of brakes and a splintering crash, we guessed that the unfortunate vehicle must have somehow left the road. How strange, I thought to myself, that my lovely bum, for so long the source of endless pleasure for myself and countless others, should be the cause of so much needless damage.

Had the poor, deprived driver never seen a pretty girl's bare-cheeked arse before?

Attention drawn back to the growing need between my legs, I took a sharp intake of breath as Justine's wriggling toes in their silky stocking found my erect clitoris, rubbing and massaging in such an expert manner that I felt my orgasm rapidly approaching.

Sucking lustily on Justine's warm, naked tits and wriggling my bare bum in the cool air of the carriage, I felt my wet cunt shudder with a series of tiny contractions as my climax arrived. Justine reached her orgasm at the same time and the carriage was filled with the sweet sound of soft, feminine moans and sighs of satisfaction.

Silently now, I pulled up my damp, lacy panties and straightened my stockings and skirts before planting a lingering kiss on Justine's smiling lips.

'Let's consider that little bout as a kind of rehearsal,' she said after a moment or two, a sexy plan forming in her mind. 'I'm sure my boyfriend, Pierre, and his handsome friend would be only too delighted to watch us enjoying each other's company in such a manner. What do you say, Rosie? Do you think we should lay on a little entertainment for the dear boys?'

'I can think of nothing nicer than a spot of naughty theatricals,' I agreed. 'Especially if we include some of the Candide's fresh cream pastries as props, and even more especially if we invite our audience of two to join in the frolics after a while. It's quite astonishing where on one's body one manages to disperse dollops of cream when one's having fun!'

Giggling wickedly, we discussed our plans for the afternoon's entertainments as our carriage grew ever nearer to our destination.

After what seemed to us to be a lifetime of waiting (so anxious were we for the fun to begin!), our carriage finally entered the outskirts of the town. Peering out of the windows of the vehicle, wide-eyed like two little girls on their first foray into the grown-up world — which we most certainly were not! — we saw tall, gaunt, slab-sided warehouses, a grubby-looking railway siding and numerous mean-looking dwellings with washing hanging outside and smoke curling from the chimneys.

Men, women and children thronged the streets, laughing, arguing and calling out to each other as they went about their daily business. A cheeky-faced young boy on a coster-monger's bicycle which seemed to be several sizes too large for him, caught sight of the two of us in our carriage like a couple of prim china dolls and grinned widely, removed both hands from the handlebars in a lewd gesture, then favoured us with a loud wolf-whistle before continuing on his brazen way.

Justine and I exchanged glances of indignation before breaking into amused smiles and eagerly returning our attention to the hurly-burly world outside our carriage window.

A swarthy, bewhiskered young man operating a barrel organ, on top of which danced a small, chattering monkey dressed in a suit of miniature clothes, stood on a street corner. Leaning back in a lazy, leisurely manner against his music machine, he was slowly inhaling the smoke from his long clay pipe whilst gazing with heavy lids at his companion — an exotic street girl with heavy, garish make-up and big, melon-like breasts which shook and wobbled as she moved.

She was engaged in loud and animated conversation with the man, eyes rolling and expressive painted lips moving nineteen to the dozen when all of a sudden, anecdote at an end, she slapped her thigh and erupted in a gale of side-splitting laughter.

As we passed the colourful pair the man caught sight of us, winking and gesturing to the young whore, who turned and faced us before raising her gaudy skirts between thumbs and forefingers of both hands and dropping down in an exaggerated, mocking curtsey, facial expression fixed in an attitude of imperious dignity, made all the more ridiculous by her clown-like, painted features.

Favouring her with warm smiles to show we appreciated

164

her little joke and were not in the least offended, the saucy young wench grinned and blew us a theatrical kiss before turning her back to us and, quick as a flash, raising her skirts to above her waist, bending over and wriggling her voluptuous, bare arse at us.

Speechless and red-cheeked with shock and embarrassment we fell back into the gloom of the carriage and pressed our heads against the seat-backs for fear that the cheeky young strumpet would see our discomfiture and exact still further revenge for what I could now see was our over-privileged, patronising manner towards her.

As we rumbled into the more salubrious, central part of town our pinched embarrassment faded and turned into beatific pleasure as we contemplated our plans for the afternoon.

Rounding a corner into one of the main streets, Justine recognised our destination, L'Hotel Candide, about halfway down on the right hand side. Gesturing to Gruber to stop the carriage by rapping smartly on the roof with her knuckles, we both set about the task of straightening our gowns, checking our appearance in the useful little mirror set just above my seat in the padded interior fabric of the vehicle, and prepared to alight.

Gruber drew the carriage to a halt a hundred yards or so away from our destination, lumbered down from his drivers' seat and ambled round to help us climb down to the pavement. Opening the carriage door he took each of our hands in turn and, eyes gleaming lasciviously, was rather too solicitous, I thought, in aiding our descent. When it was Justine's turn to alight she gave him a merry little wink and displayed for his benefit several inches of shapely, stockinged ankle and calf — an unnecessary expedient, I thought, since the poor man was already damp with perspiration and quite flushed with fresh excitement.

Before setting off towards the hotel Justine blew the unfortunate Gruber, who was by now putty in her naughty hands, a pretty little kiss and made him promise to meet us in the same place in three hours.

Amid much spluttering and coughing Gruber agreed to her request and climbed back on to his drivers' seat, rather painfully I fancied since his erection was the size and shape of a small Howitzer, before hurtling off down the street in the direction of his innocently unsuspecting mistress.

I hope she's ready for him, I thought with a grin. If the poor man doesn't spunk inside a warm cunt within the space of five minutes I swear his balls will explode with the build-up of pressure from within!

We entered L'Hotel Candide through a pair of heavy swing-doors fashioned from smooth, glowing mahogany and thick panes of crystal glass, and found ourselves in a totally different world from the one we'd left outside. A world of silent, deep-piled carpets, subdued lighting, polished wood, fresh flowers, hushed voices and the delicious aroma of freshly brewed coffee.

Glancing around I noticed a small, elegant desk behind which sat an efficient-looking young lady with a striped blouse, spectacles and a rather prim, severe-looking hairstyle. She was peering at us over the top of her glasses in rather a pointed manner.

'That must be the receptionist,' I hissed. 'Come on, Justine, you'd better explain what we're here for . . . On the other hand,' I giggled, immediately visualising the likely furore cased by a true revelation of our intent, 'perhaps your explanation had better be a little less inflammatory!'

Clearing her throat and linking her arm in mine, she marched purposefully with me to the receptionist's exceptionally tidy desk and, chin held high in the manner of one who is used to being obeyed, began to speak.

'Bonjour, Mademoiselle,' she said in clear, even tones.

'Bonjour, Ma . . . Mademoiselle,' replied the slightly discomfited receptionist after first scanning Justine's hand for signs of a wedding ring. 'How can I help you?'

'My sister and I have arranged to meet my brother and his friend here this afternoon for coffee. Messieurs Renoir *et* DeClerc. I believe they are staying at L'Hotel Candide, *non*?'

'*Mais oui*, Mademoiselle. The two gentlemen to whom you refer left the hotel ten minutes ago in order to go for a little stroll in the park. Monsieur DeClerc assured me they would return within half an hour. Indeed, the gentleman did mention something about being sorely in need of a cup of strong coffee and one of our pastries.' Glancing around her to make sure no one was listening, she whispered, 'I've heard tell that one of them was fortunate enough to make a killing at the Roulette wheel yesterday evening, and they both spent the rest of the night at La Moulin Rouge, spending it!' She giggled irreverently until, embarrassed by her little outburst, she bit her lip, eyes downcast, and continued.

'Would you be willing to wait in the salon until they return? It is just at the end of that corridor over there. I will be sure to tell them you are here, waiting for them, when they return from their walk . . .'

'*Merci*, Mademoiselle. We will wait for them in the salon.'

As we left the desk, the young lady's expression softened a little and her mouth curved into a wistful little smile. She gave a small sigh and, with an absent look, followed or progress towards our *place d'assignation*.

In those few seconds I realised that she couldn't be any further advanced in years than Justine and myself. Had she guessed the truth behind our little fabrication? Did she yearn in her heart of hearts to join our little party for an afternoon of frivolity, fun and flirtation − possibly followed by fanciful frolics − with a pair of devilishly handsome young men, which I felt sure was the delicious fate awaiting my friend and I?

Settling ourselves on a small settee in the salon to wait for Pierre and Maurice, Justine and I attempted to attract the attention of the young waitress who dodged backwards and forwards between the kitchen and the salon with trays of coffee and cakes for her clients − a mainly elderly collection of ladies and gentlemen, and most certainly highly demanding of her attention to their gastronomical needs.

As my eyes followed those of the waitress, hoping in vain

to attract her over to us so that we might place our order, my attention was caught by a solid, rather heavy-looking gentleman sitting in the far corner. Grey-haired and whiskered with a ruddy complexion and a pronounced pot belly, he had been gazing at us over the top of his newspaper with considerable interest since we'd entered some five minutes previously.

As my eyes met his, the randy old gentleman gave me a big, suggestive wink, then coughed in a self-conscious sort of way and pretended to return to his newspaper, glancing up at regular intervals to check my reaction to his rather forward gesture.

What an excellent manner in which to pass the time until our young men arrive, I thought to myself. A saucy little dalliance with a horny old duffer who, by the look of him, is old enough to be our grandfather!

Edging closer to Justine on the little settee, I gently nudged her with my elbow and, with a whispered explanation and a little series of gestures, alerted her to the comic, as well as the erotic, potential of the situation we now found ourselves in.

'Maybe he thinks we're a couple of working girls,' Justine hissed at me under her breath.

'Then we'll not disillusion the old boy,' I replied. 'Come, let's make his day and have some fun into the bargain!'

The next time my eyes met his I, too, winked suggestively and indicated with a little tilt of my head for him to join us at our table.

Eyes widening with surprise and delight he swiftly folded his newspaper and did as he was bid, pausing for a moment to instruct the waitress in hushed tones (continually glancing across at us all the while for fear we might disappear in a puff of smoke) to bring a fresh pot of coffee — for three — and a plate of Florentines.

Justine and I once again exchanged knowing glances, primping and preening, moistening lips and adjusting our posture in order to enhance the jut of our breasts for the satisfaction of our new 'friend'.

'Good afternoon, ladies,' he said to us in impeccable

English as he sat down, rather heavily, in a chair facing us on the other side of the small, rococo table. 'Allow me to introduce myself. My name is David Hostridge I hope you will not be offended but I noticed from where I was sitting that you were experiencing a little difficulty in attracting the attention of the waitress, so I've taken the liberty of ordering coffee and Florentines for us all, if that meets with your approval?'

He gave an obsequious little smile which served to irritate me intensely, reinforcing my desire to teach this rather patronising gentleman a lesson.

I smiled sweetly at him. 'Why, sir, how extremely kind and generous of you to favour us with your presence in this way,' I simpered at him from behind my fan, coyly fluttering my long eyelashes, before dropping the dainty confection of ivory and lace to the floor beneath the table.

'Allow *me*, Mademoiselle,' he said with a flourish.

'No, sir, allow *me*!'

With these words I dived under the table and, totally ignoring the dropped fan, began to tickle and fondle the portly gentleman's ankles and calves through the smooth fabric of his trousers. (Fortunately, my exploits were completely obscured by the heavy damask cloth which draped to the floor on all four side of the table, shielding me from the possible gaze of interested parties.

I felt the gentleman in question stiffen slightly with surprise, then commence a rather false-sounding and slightly falsetto conversation with Justine who, judging by the somewhat quavering tone of her voice and the way her toes were curled inside her shoes and her legs under the table were pressed tightly together in the tense attitude of one desperate to hold something in, was finding the whole situation amusing in the extreme.

Ignoring the deceptively bright conversation going on above my head, I deftly removed the shoe and sock from Mr Hostridge's right foot and quickly popped his big toe into my mouth, sucking sweetly and exploring its contours with my wicked tongue.

169

As I did so I unbuttoned the front of my bodice and pulled aside my chemise so that my big, creamy breasts flopped out and hung suspended, luscious and naked and the perfect place to rest a man's bare foot, which I held in both hands and rubbed over my warm, yielding flesh.

When I tickled the soft, sensitive underside of his foot with my large, firm nipples which were by now like organ-stops, I felt him tremble with excitement and his voice reach an even higher register as he struggled to keep mind and body on an even keel and maintain an element of sense in his conversation with Justine.

By now, of course, the subject of their discourse was completely lost on me, so filled was I with lustful and erotic imaginings.

Letting go of his foot and snaking my hands upwards to his crotch, I quickly undid the buttons of his fly with great difficulty, I might add, since the fabric of his trousers was stretched almost to breaking point over his fat, pendulous belly and the enormous erect prick which lay beneath it like a thick, coiled serpent.

At last I managed to free the big, throbbing cock from its confines, stroking and squeezing it and pressing it against my firm white tits, and feeling it tremble and pulse in my tender hands as though with a life of its own.

When, finally, I lowered my head and took David Hostridge's huge, veiny member between my moist, pouting lips, nipping lightly but insistently with my even, pearly teeth, I felt a tremendous shudder and a huge surge of emotion course through his body.

At that moment, mouth crammed full of hot, engorged prick, I became aware that two more individuals — men — had joined in the conversation.

'Justine! What a wonderful surprise! How glad I am to see you, *ma chérie*. I'd almost given up hope. Maurice and I travel back to Paris tomorrow and I feared we'd leave Lucerne without having had the opportunity to spend some time with you. You've met my friend, Maurice, I believe?'

170

'Indeed we have met, Pierre,' agreed an attractively distinctive male voice. 'Mademoiselle, I am delighted to have this opportunity of renewing our acquaintance.' Maurice politely kissed Justine's proffered hand in the charming French manner. 'But I do hope we haven't interrupted your conversation with this gentleman. Monsieur, I don't believe I've had the pleasure . . .'

Maurice, it is true, may not previously have had the pleasure, but the gentleman referred to was at that precise moment enjoying pleasure of the most intense and exquisite kind, and showing every sign of inadvertently proclaiming his joy to the entire salon.

'Ahhh . . . No, no, I don't believe we have . . . Ooh, ooh, ooh!'

'Forgive me, sir, but are you entirely well?' asked Pierre, placing a solicitous hand on the older man's arm.

'Why, yes! Perfectly well, thank you . . . aargh, aargh, aargh! Just a spot of indigestion, I fear. Must have been those Florentines. Poor old insides can't stand the strain of too much rich food these days. Ha, ha, ha . . . AARGH!'

With that, the lecherous old devil shot his salty spunk into my busy mouth, as I continued to suck lustily on his game old tool, milking it dry and smacking my lips with libidinous pleasure.

Red-faced with shock and embarrassment, and thoroughly chastened by the experience of spunking before an audience, Mr Hostridge stuffed his rapidly deflating cock back into his trousers, rose unsteadily to his feet and muttered an unlikely excuse about a prior engagement with a colleague on the other side of town, whereupon he shuffled away, hunched over in an effort to disguise the damp stain at the front of his semi-unfastened nether garments.

Wordlessly, Pierre and Maurice watched him go with looks of amused puzzlement, while I rose from beneath the damask tablecloth like Venus from the waves, glowing with triumph and satisfaction at the knowledge of a job well done.

'I don't believe you've met my friend,' smiled Justine.

'Rosie D'Argosse, absolutely the wickedest, naughtiest girl at Madame Dupont's Academy for Young Ladies!'

The two young men stood speechless for a moment or two, eyes and mouths wide in amazement, before the truth finally dawned and the comedy of the situation prompted them to laugh out loud.

Pulling themselves together and remembering their manners, they took one of my hands each, planting gentle kisses thereon by way of introduction, all the while gazing into my eyes with delight and anticipation. They, too, it would seem had caught a glimpse of the sensual pleasures to follow.

An hour later, Pierre, Maurice, Justine and myself found ourselves comfortably settled and delightfully engaged in the luxury, two-bedroomed suite which the two young men were sharing at L'Hotel Candide.

The long drapes at the windows were modestly drawn in Maurice's bedroom, bathing everything and everyone in a warm, peachy glow but, to be frank, that was all that was modest about the voluptuous scene within.

All four of us were sitting or lying, as naked as the days we were born, on Maurice's large double bed. Two empty bottles of champagne lay, discarded, on the floor beside us. The warm atmosphere in the room lay heavily on our senses like a richly scented, sexual-charged cloud. A tray of assorted cream confections beckoned us, temptingly, from the bedside table.

Languidly, Maurice raised himself up from his prone position on the crumpled, musky sheets and lazily leaned on one elbow. 'Well, my beauties, which of you is going to volunteer to offer me one of those delicious cakes in a way I can't refuse? A prize for the girl who dares!' Raising his eyebrows in an attitude of enquiry and sexily narrowing his eyes, he glanced from one to the other of us, expectantly, his gaze eventually falling on me alone with a look of smouldering passion.

Long, lean and lightly muscled with dark, curly hair and a close-cropped beard, Maurice was everything I'd hoped he'd be — and more. He was all the things I looked for in a man, and the moment I'd set eyes on him my heart had skipped a beat.

Now, with the memory of our recent stimulating conversation fresh in my mind (which had shown that we had a great deal more in common than a fancy for each other's bodies), and at the sight of his magnificent, long prick which was slowly rising against his belly, pulsing with life and a need to possess, I desired only to give myself to him — totally, absolutely and irrevocably.

Never before had I felt this way about a man and, goodness knows, I'd known men aplenty, despite my tender years. Used always to being in full control of my amorous relationships, this particular man had reduced me to so much putty in his hands, wanting only to be shaped and moulded into a thing of beauty and life and passionate feeling between those sensitive, artistic fingers. Could I, for the first time in my life, have fallen in love?

Gazing back at him, heavy lidded and gently inhaling the heady, male scent of his body, I reached across and plucked a cream cake from the table beside the bed. Teasingly I took a delicious bite, then licked the cream from my lips like a naughty kitten before gracefully reclining on the crumpled bed.

Scooping two dollops of thick cream from the centre of the rich confection, I tenderly deposited them on the very tips of my engorged strawberry nipples which, already, were aching to be licked and sucked by the man of my dreams who lay before me, transfixed and softly panting with mounting excitement.

Taking another scoop of cream, I lay back fully on the bed, spread my long legs with the grace of a dancer and sensually anointed my hot, aching pussey which throbbed in unison with my love-sick heart and longed like never before to be filled to bursting with my wondrous new lover's prick.

Thus garnished I turned my sexy blonde head to face Maurice, eyes burning with lust and as yet unrequited love.

Then, as if by magic, I found that we had been granted the entire bed to ourselves. Pierre and Justine, no doubt inflamed by my erotic display with the whipped cream and Maurice's obvious complicity in the warm, highly sexual gastronomic scene which would surely follow, had tactfully retired to Pierre's room and were, even now, engaged in eroticisms of their own.

Alone at last with my lover, I spread my gentle arms and my long, slim legs as far as they would go, willing Maurice to enter me and make me his with a ferocity I'd never previously known.

And I am glad to say that Maurice did not disappoint me. With a low groan he fell upon my breasts and my nipples topped with whipped cream, sucking and feeding upon them like a hungry babe until tears of joy pricked my eyes and, with a sob, I begged him to attend to the sultry haven between my legs.

Lowering his dark, tousled head he licked the rich cream from my dark, throbbing cunt, rubbing his nose and stubbly chin against my unbelievably sensitive clitoris and making me cry out with exquisite pleasure.

Unable to bear the sweet pain of his tongue a moment longer and desperate to be filled with his big, throbbing cock I took hold of his broad suntanned shoulders and pulled, his face up to meet mine.

At the same time as he thrust his eager tongue between my welcoming lips, exploring the deepest recesses of my mouth, his erect cock entered my hot cunt, pushing and thrusting with vitality and vigour until, with mutual passion, we cried out with joy at our simultaneous orgasm.

Moments later we tenderly kissed and our bodies entwined. From the next room we heard Pierre and Justine reach their passionate climax. Faces almost touching, Maurice and I smiled into each other's eyes. God was in his heaven and all was right with the world . . .

VOLUME TWO

Young, Wild and Willing

Introduction

The diaries of Rosie D'Argosse invite readers to step back into the golden Edwardian era which for the idle, well-heeled upper crust was a time when the strict standards of sexual behaviour which epitomised the manners and *mores* of the Victorian age were crumbling fast.

Whilst lip service was still paid to the old, stern ideas, the Edwardian aristocracy enjoyed a secret world of sensuality, of illicit liaison and secret rendezvous, of Bohemian bawdiness in intimate circles where blissful hours were spent behind closed doors and the Eleventh Commandment — Thou Shalt Never Be Found Out — was deemed of far more importance that the sum of the other Ten.

Young members of this hedonistic society of the *jeunesse dorée* such as Rosie and her friends Lord Philip Pelham and David Nash were ready and eager for change from this stiff-necked, hypocritical morality and they pursued high-spirited, uninhibited lives in which free-wheeling sensual relationships played a major role in direct contrast to the stern dictates of the established doctrine propagated (if not actually upheld by those at the top of the social ladder) of sexual abstinence with only a minimum of the most basic bedroom activities even within marriage.

Although Rosie d'Argosse is a fictional character, the adventures described are undoubtedly based on true-life incidents in the lives of her creators, Geraldine Newman and Anna Barnes-Cooney. These two girls, who both hailed from rich and distinguished families, first met in the early 1900s at rallies of Emmeline Pankhurst's militant Women's Social

7

and Political Union which demanded immediate legislation to allow female suffrage.

As Professor Harry Barr noted in his foreword to the first book in this series, Geraldine and Anna's families were horrified at the girls' espousal of such heretical ideas as votes for women. Their rejection of the stifling social conventions and the grossly unfair distribution of wealth led to many thunderous confrontations with their scandalised parents, who fortunately never discovered that in addition to their radical ideas, their daughters cocked a further snook at the straight-laced Establishment by penning their lightly disguised sexual adventures in the often spectacularly rude illicit magazines of the period.

Most scholars of gallant literature would agree with Professor Barr who is of the opinion that the first book of Rosie's diaries was primarily composed by Anna Barnes-Cooney. Stylistic differences in this second volume would suggest that in that case Geraldine Newman must have written most of these perhaps even more explicit erotic encounters which were first printed *sub rosa* in twelve monthly magazine instalments by 'The Friends of Venus and Priapus' in 1908. Incidentally, none of the diaries were available in bound book form until 1911 when a shrewd Scottish entrepreneur, one Graeme Johnstone, published them in leather-bound editions with the brazen imprimateur of 'The Edinburgh University Press' on the title pages! The actual printer was in all probability Oswald Knuckleberry of Manchester who produced several illegal raunchy magazines such as *The Oyster* and *The Memoirs of Rupert Mountjoy* around this time.

The older of our two authors, Geraldine Newman began writing saucy stories after her first-ever love affair with one of the foremost connoisseurs of erotica, Sir Lionel Trapes, a high ranking Treasury official and friend of the then Prince of Wales, who contributed many pieces (including a spirited defence of his old friend Oscar Wilde) to *The Oyster* and *The Cremorne*, perhaps the most widely read privately published underground periodicals amongst the upper classes.

A feisty, outgoing girl, Geraldine often used in her recounting of Rosie d'Argosse's escapades the names of her real-life lovers such as the occasionally indiscreet Dr Jonathan Letchmore who must have been an invaluable source of gossip, Colonel Piers Rankin, David Nash and the insouciant, handsome young charmer Robert Bacon, a shameless dilettante with an irresistible attraction for the ladies.

When this book of fictionalised autobiography, totally uncensored and delightfully erotic, first appeared, it had to be written and published anonymously and then secretly distributed. However, in this second book of extracts from Rosie's diaries we see that beneath those swelling, high-buttoned bodices, under that waistcoated, upright, self-satisfied worthiness, the interest and appreciation of sexuality has always existed, however repressive the climate of 'respectable' opinion may be at any prevailing time.

Perhaps the majority of Edwardian ladies simply did lie back and think of redecorating their living-rooms whilst their husbands exercised their conjugal rights. But despite all the strenuous efforts made by the official culture to minimise the importance of female sensual desires, there were still girls like Geraldine Newman and Anna Barnes-Cooney who ridiculed the extraordinary idea that well-bred ladies were disinterested in the joys of sexual discovery and used the popular if illegal 'naughty' magazines to persistently question the many taboos and to express their desire to experiment with the mechanics of the copulatory act. It is now widely accepted that this enquiring attitude was important in leading to the more relaxed, self-understanding state which exists today, concomitant with the multiplicity of positions on sexual morality that currently exist as the twentieth century draws to its close.

Yet many of the old arguments are still with us and the content of the letter which Geraldine sent to her cousin Kate Radcliffe in defence of her work almost ninety years ago still has relevance today. Defending herself against a charge of vulgarity, she wrote: *'I believe that my memoirs will please every lover of voluptuous literature, all who wish to read of the burning desire for the embrace of a passionate lover and of the consuming need for the thrills of the flesh. I know that those of a liberal disposition will agree that there can be no great sin in enjoying to the utmost all those delicious sensations for which a beneficient Creator has so amply fitted both sexes.'*

Martin Wellend
Cairo
November, 1992

10

Impropriety is the soul of wit.
The Moon and Sixpence

W. Somerset Maugham
[1874—1965]

Foreword

Whilst Lord Philip Pelham, Lady Belinda Nayland, Lieutenant Peter Lucas of the Grenadier Guards and Miss Judy Cole-Leamington amongst others have warmly congratulated me on the recent publication of my earlier book of memoirs, it has been made known to me that there are others who have begun a whispering campaign in the salons of Belgravia and Mayfair and also in the best country houses in my home county of Sussex to denigrate the happenings recounted in my admittedly uncensored diary of recent events.

These ladies and gentlemen have expressed their disquiet as to whether it is seemly for a young lady to write a frank and uninhibited account of life in the upper echelons of Society. I would reply only that my hope is that many people from all walks of life will derive harmless pleasure and amusement from its publication and that future generations of readers will find this history of interest.

As before, I wish to reiterate the statement made in my first book that all those mentioned in this narrative have given me their express permission for their names to be used. Frankly, I thought such repetition unnecessary until my dear old friend David Nash insisted that without such a statement, the day after this second book is published the cross-Channel ships would be packed with certain members of the so-called upper classes who suddenly decided to take the Grand Tour or simply make any excuse they can think up for spending the next six months in France!

So let me reassure these silly folk that they need spend

no sleepless nights racked with uncertainty as to whether I shall expose secrets which could lead to these memoirs being perused with anguished care amongst the very highest in the land. I have no desire to make extra work for the legal profession and in any case, I would never in almost any circumstances divulge private matters appertaining to *l'arte de faire l'amour* – for do we not all clutch certain secrets close to our hearts?

Rosie d'Argosse

1

In Town Tonight

It was with a mounting sense of excitement that I woke up early on the morning of the first Monday of April, nineteen hundred and eight. My room was already enshrined by the sunlight, in marked contrast to the dreary wet weather we had suffered over the previous few days, and I fervently prayed that this bright spring sunlight heralded the end of the squally showers which yesterday had forced the cancellation of an afternoon's lawn tennis with my dear friends Kitty Bedford, Charles Nettleton and the village curate, Reverend Horace Bristow. I skipped out of bed and after pulling off my nightdress, padded across to the window where I looked out and gazed at the glistening green privet leaves and the white stitchwort in the arches of the still-drenched grass.

By all accounts it had been an unpleasantly bitter winter at Argosse Towers, which readers of my first book [*Rosie Vol One: The Intimate Diaries — Editor*] will recall is situated in the glorious countryside of West Sussex, though I had missed the worst of winter having only recently returned home after my happy stay at one of Europe's most famous finishing schools for girls, Madame Dupont's Academy For Young Ladies on the beautiful banks of Lake Lucerne. Of course, my dear parents were blissfully unaware that the first lesson learned by the frisky girls at this exclusive establishment was how best to translate their theoretical

15

lessons on human biology into practice with the aid of Michel, Madame Dupont's good-looking sixteen-year-old son. Michel suffered the boredom and frustration of attending a strictly run boarding school near Paris but his vacations were enlivened by many lascivious romps with the thirty or so female pupils who vied with each other to play with his virile young penis.

My hand stole to that magic place between my legs as my mind wandered back to that exciting afternoon when I had first seduced the handsome young lad. After a walk in Madame Dupont's extensive gardens we found ourselves in the glasshouse where the headmistress cultivated her exquisite collection of rare orchids from all over the world. How passionately we had kissed and how wonderful it had felt when at my whispered urging, Michel's trembling hands had roved across my heaving breasts. My fingers now pressed against my moistening pussy as I closed my eyes and recalled how his throbbing cock had strained against the grey serge fabric of his trousers and how after I had deftly unbuttoned his fly and pulled out his yearning prick, his bare shaft had bounded and pulsed in my palm.

By now my fingertip had found its way between my pouting cunney lips and I let out a little sigh of pleasure. But my lewd reverie was temporarily disturbed by the sound of voices coming from almost underneath my window. I was not alarmed, for although I was alone in the house except for the servants — Mama and Papa were spending a few days at Easton Lodge, Essex, home of the Countess of Warwick — at least one of the voices was familiar. Unless I was much mistaken, it belonged to our strapping young footman Jack Dennison who wielded, according to Elaine, my personal maid, a colossal nine-and-a-half-inch cock which was in much demand, not only by the randy village girls but also by the wife of General Hollingberry whilst her husband was away inspecting our gallant troops on the North West Frontier.

I opened my window, looked down and sure enough there was Dennison, his trousers already in a heap around his feet.

He had pinioned pretty Norma Radlett, the eighteen-year-old daughter of the village grocer and provisions merchant, up against the wall, though the unprotesting girl was obviously just as keen to enjoy a knee-trembler against the wall as my well-endowed young footman for she was now pulling down his underpants whilst his hands were busy opening her bodice and fondling her large, luscious breasts.

'Oh Jack, what a colossal cock!' she squealed as she grasped his tremendous tadger. 'It's so thick that I can hardly get my fingers round it. Do you mind if I make a closer inspection?'

Without waiting for an answer she slid down onto her knees and I craned my neck forward to see the saucy minx open her mouth wide and take his rounded, uncapped knob between her lips. She sucked some three inches of his shaft inside her soft mouth, her wet lips straining to encircle it before she began to tongue-fuck his huge rod, moving her head to and fro. Her auburn curls bobbed up and down as she slid his succulent shaft in and out of her mouth, as Jack bent forward to keep his hands round Norma's chubby, round bosoms.

Furiously, I began to frig my moistening cunney as Norma now released his twitching tool and tugged down her knickers. She stood up and turned round, her arms stretched out in front of her with her palms flat against the wall. Jack threw up her skirt to reveal her pert bottom which she wiggled sensuously as she turned her head to see him take hold of his pulsating pole and position it neatly between her bum cheeks.

Jack went to work with a will and her bottom responded to every shove as the sinewy young footman drove home, his pendulous balls banging against the backs of her thighs. He worked his sturdy cock in and out of her honeypot from behind in great style as she wriggled in delight, crying out: 'That's it, Jack! That's the way! Fuck me with your thick prick, you randy rascal!' He moved in and out of her juicy cunt with a steady grunting motion and my fingers mirrored the action of his cock as they slid faster and faster in and out of my now sopping love channel.

17

Perhaps because he realised that they were in grave danger of being discovered (little did he know that already they had been seen!), Jack now decided to bring Norma off as quickly as possible. He snaked his right hand round her waist to dive into her bush and massage her clitty as he pulled her towards him with every inward thrust and pushed her away with each outward movement so that Norma jerked back and forth on his rigid rod.

Suddenly she screamed out: 'Yes! Yes! I'm coming, shoot your spunk, you lovely big-cocked boy!' and with a great shudder she reached her climax just as Jack jetted his jism and creamed the walls of her womb with his copious emission. I held my breath as my fingers now raced in and out of my cunney until the first waves of a small but very pleasant spend radiated out from my groin all over my body. I stood panting with my head against the window frame as I heard Norma say: 'So I'll see you tonight at Sally's party, Jack. Isn't it grand, her parents being away and you having the night off!'

I chuckled as I quietly shut the window and went back to lie on my bed. All things being well, I would also this evening be in the arms of my new sweetheart, Lord Philip Pelham, for I had booked a seat on the early afternoon train to London where I would be staying at my Aunt Elizabeth's house for the rest of the week. My maid Elaine would accompany me for although the house in Chandos Street, off Cavendish Square, was fully staffed, Aunt Elizabeth and Uncle Sidney would also be, like my parents, guests of the Countess of Warwick for the next few days.

(For those of you who have already perused the earlier volume of my reminiscences, let me explain here that my previous beau Jimmy, or the Honourable James Harold Fortescue Horobin to give him his full nomenclature, was now studying at Cambridge University and we had jointly agreed that whilst wishing to remain good and true friends, it would be best for us both if we ended our intimate association.)

I lay back and hugged myself as I anticipated the joy of

making love with Philip this evening. With my parents' permission, my dashing young man-about-town was taking me to hear Edward Elgar's First Symphony at the Royal Albert Hall and then we would go on to supper at Zaines Café, the fashionable Jermyn Street haunt patronised by the fast young set of which Philip was a leading member, before returning to Chandos Street and making love with him for the rest of the night.

There was a knock on my door and I was so engrossed in my thoughts that I called 'Enter', quite forgetting that I was lying stark naked on top of my eiderdown with my legs wide apart and my hands gently caressing my luxuriant blonde-haired mound. Fortunately it was only Elaine, my attractive maid, at the door who had come to enquire whether I had chosen which outfit to wear for the journey to town.

'How about the new green jacket and skirt which you purchased just before you left Lucerne,' she suggested, apparently unconcerned by my state of nudity, though I had heard gossip that she partook of the joys of Lesbos in addition to enjoying the more normal procreative activities. As occasionally I enjoy the soft touch of feminine hands and lips upon the more private parts of my person I had no reason to be concerned with household rumours.

'The green outfit?' I said doubtfully. 'Are you sure?'

'Oh yes, Miss Rosie, the colour contrasts wonderfully with your light skin and blonde hair and the clothes fit you so beautifully.'

'They should fit beautifully considering how much I paid Monsieur Rubenstein,' I murmured thoughtfully, 'and yet I'm not absolutely convinced, Elaine. Run my bath, please, and I'll think it over.'

She went into the bathroom and turned on the hot water tap. I listened anxiously to the succession of sepulchral rumblings, for unlike our town house in Belgrave Square, the arrangements at Argosse Towers were somewhat primitive and indeed, not before time, workmen were due to come in the very next week to bring them up to modern

19

twentieth-century standards. But for now all appeared well and so I relaxed when I heard the roar of water cascading into the iron tank encased in mahogany which the previous owner of the house, Lady Scadgers, had installed in 1872.

Elaine came out of the bathroom and said: 'Miss Rosie, I've just thought how I can convince you to wear your Swiss outfit. We have identical measurements, don't we? Well, why don't I model the clothes for you and then you can see for yourself?'

'What a clever idea, Elaine, please go ahead,' I said and without further ado my maid began to undress. She took off her mob-cap and shook her long dark hair free until it reached her shoulders. Then she slipped off her blouse and skirt and stood clad only in a short chemise which she hiked up over her shoulders, showing off to best advantage her high, uplifted breasts which if slightly smaller than mine, looked just as rounded and soft as my own and were capped by rich rosebud nipples that pointed out cheekily from the centre of her large, red circled areoles.

I could not help but admire Elaine's supple, sensuous body as she wriggled out of her knickers and my gaze swept over her smooth, flat belly which was dimpled in the centre with a sweet little button, and the whiteness of her skin set off the mass of black curls which nestled between her thighs.

'Let me first turn off the water,' she said and I was convinced that she deliberately flaunted the jiggling cheeks of her exquisitely formed backside at me as I watched her walk slowly into the bathroom. When she returned she said: 'The water's rather hot, Miss Rosie, may I sit down until it's ready and then I can sponge you down.'

So I asked her if she would like to rest on the bed, and of course this was what the cunning little cat wanted and in a flash she was cuddling up beside me and placing her hand on my thigh. I must confess that I did not push her away and she moved even closer, brushing her pretty face up against mine as her other hand slid round my shoulder. Kissing my cheek softly, Elaine began to stroke her fingers inside my silky blonde bush and at first I pretended to ignore

20

the sensation as if I did not find it to my liking, though of course I thoroughly enjoyed it!

But when her fingertips began smoothing a passage along the edges of my cunney I heard myself sighing with pleasure, and then instead of lying there passively I put my arms around her, holding her deliciously soft body against me as her fingers continued to rub against my pouting pussy lips, shivers of sheer delight coursed through my entire frame. Elaine then began to fondle my naked breasts as our mouths crushed together and I found it impossible to deny her as her wet tongue slid into my mouth and lapped lubriciously against my own.

Now she tweaked my engorged, raised nipple between her thumb and forefinger and I lay back as with her other hand she glided her fingers into my sopping slit. Her thumb prodded against my clitty and I squirmed with the thrill of it and pressed my own hand against her dark, moist pubic thatch. She let out a throaty gasp as I slid two fingers between her cunney lips and, as I sank them in to the knuckle, Elaine pushed herself upwards, arching her back and wriggling her body as if to signal me to penetrate her love channel even deeper.

She thrust her three fingers in and out of my juicy cunney at a quickening pace, with her thumb rubbing inexorably at the erect little ball of my clitty. Then suddenly she moved her body down and my finger slipped out of her crack and she raised one of her legs and locked her thighs around my knee, writhing her sopping wet pussy back and forth as she buried her face between my legs. Her hands slid under my bum cheeks and she squeezed them firmly as her lips found my cunney lips and my senses reeled as my head fell back against the pillow and I moaned and panted as her teeth nibbled against my clitty. I pushed her head tighter against my tingling cunt and I purred with pleasure as her tongue slid between my pouting pussy lips. I came almost immediately and her clever tongue prodding through my pussy kept bringing me off in a series of exciting little spends.

After this marvellous oral fucking she lifted her head and

whispered: 'Please finish me off now, Miss Rosie.' An understandable and reasonable request with which I was more than happy to comply. Elaine straightened herself up and lay beside me and I eagerly pulled her long legs apart and nuzzled my lips around her hairy black curls, and now my hands clamped themselves around her gorgeous bum cheeks and my tongue flickered unerringly around her damp crack, which opened like the petals of a flower as she lifted her buttocks to enable me to slip my tongue through the dark pink cunney lips and lick between the grooves of her clitty in long, powerful strokes.

As I tongue-fucked the trembling girl her pussy gushed out her aromatic love juice which ran over my lips and dribbled down my chin. I felt her rubbery clitty stiffen, desperately wanting more and more to explode, and I rubbed harder and harder whilst I spread open her cunt to allow a finger inside her dripping slit even as I was tonguing her clitty. This extra stimulation worked like a magic charm and very soon Elaine's soft body was bucking and heaving as a tremendous shudder ran through her and she spent copiously, drenching my mouth with her love juices which I gulped down with real enjoyment.

We lay panting with a mixture of exhaustion and pleasure as we recovered our senses. 'You're all hot and bothered now, Elaine. You'd better come and join me in the bath,' I said. 'It's such a big old tub that there's plenty of room for us both.'

Well, we clambered in together but we simply could not keep our hands off each other and we dissolved into a passionate embrace, kissing rapturously and thrusting our tongues back into each other's mouths. Our hands were everywhere, grabbing and squeezing as our bodies writhed together, demanding release. I clasped Elaine firmly round the waist with my left arm whilst with the fingers of my right hand I frigged her hairy cunt. She opened her legs wider and displayed her stiff, fleshy clitty which projected from between her pussy lips and rubbed her own palm fiercely against my crotch and then stabbed her long, tapering fingers

22

in and out of my saturated slit with an intensity which caused me to cry out in ecstasy.

Suffice it to say that I spent far longer in the bath than I had meant to, but we both achieved more wonderful spends before Elaine threw a huge bath towel around me which I passed back to her after I had dried myself. As a special treat I opened a tin of Dr David Pickering's Fine Talcum Powder and dusted over Elaine's back and bottom with this excellent product. I thoroughly recommend a liberal application of this lightly perfumed powder to all my readers, both male and female, for though admittedly extremely expensive, it is used by most ladies in London Society including Her Gracious Majesty Queen Alexandra, as it always leaves the skin feeling soft and silky smooth.

'We'd better get dressed straightaway,' I said, giving Elaine's soft bottom a final pat. 'I don't think there's time for you to put on the green costume, but I'll take your advice and wear it today. Now, after breakfast I'll choose the clothes I want you to pack for me. Get Dennison to bring the cases down for you. Oh, and don't forget to pack a bag for yourself. You did realise you were coming to London with me, didn't you?'

She smiled cheekily and said: 'Yes, and I'm greatly looking forward to it, Miss Rosie, especially if I can come as nicely as I did just before!'

'Go away with you,' I chuckled. 'Remember, we're having an early lunch as we're booked on the two-fifteen train.'

I finished dressing and went down to the breakfast room where Sayers was waiting for me. 'Good morning, Miss Rosie,' said our faithful old butler, pulling out a chair for me to take my place at the head of the table.

'I suppose you will take your usual breakfast,' he sighed, shaking his head sorrowfully. I nodded my head and suppressed a smile as I saw him struggle to keep a look of disapproval from appearing on his face.

Sayers had served at Argosse Towers since I was three years old and I knew he was deeply suspicious about my refusal to partake of the enormous meals he was used to seeing prepared when my parents were at home. He was happier when my young brother Jonathan was living with us, for Jonathan eats like a horse and was always ready to tuck in to whatever was provided by our superb cook, Mrs Moser. Alas, last week Jonathan left Argosse Towers for the summer term at Eton and, try as he may, our poor butler could never interest me in more than a light breakfast which consisted of an apple or an orange after tea and toast with only very occasionally a bowl of porridge and cream or a small plate of scrambled eggs.

I considered this to be a healthy and nourishing diet but Sayers was genuinely concerned that I might harm my constitution by not having a 'proper' breakfast, especially those offered when we entertained guests for a country house weekend party. These gargantuan affairs began with porridge and cream, after which guests took their choice of poached, boiled or scrambled eggs, bacon, ham, devilled kidneys, haddock and other fish from a row of silver dishes kept hot by spirit lamps on the large sideboard. On another sideboard stood a selection of cold meats and a side table would be heaped with fruits of the season whilst of course there was always an abundance of toast and scones together with a selection of Mrs Moser's home-made jams.

'May I call up Mrs Moser from the kitchen so that you can give her the household orders for the day?' he asked as with a flourish he presented me with a copy of the morning newspaper on a silver salver.

'By all means, but I am sure you have not forgotten that I want to leave for the station not later than a quarter to two this afternoon,' I replied. 'I am not taking a vast amount of luggage so Haines can use the motor car for the journey.'

'Are you sure you wish to travel by motor, Miss Rosie,' said Sayers doubtfully. 'The landaulet has just been cleaned and polished.'

'No, thank you,' I said firmly. 'My father sent Haines to Tong's Garage in Brighton for a fortnight so that he could be instructed in driving and making simple repairs to motor vehicles. He'll never be able to take up a position as a chauffeur if we don't give him every opportunity to practise.'

Coincidentally, when I picked up *The Daily News*, my eye was caught by an interesting article on the arrival of motor cabs in London. In 1906 there were only ninety-six such cabs licensed but now there were almost two thousand plying for hire. It appeared that like our coachman Haines, the hansom-cab drivers were adapting to the change. The writer concluded: *'It is satisfactory to know that the displacement of the hansom does not mean, as a rule, that drivers are being thrown out of employment. The men who cease to drive horse-drawn cabs generally find themselves transformed into motor-men. The principal companies maintain staffs of instructors at the depots and there are daily classes in motor-cab driving at these places. A man who has had charge of a hansom becomes proficient in the art of controlling a motor cab very quickly. Even a novice can be trained to pass the severe examination of Scotland Yard in the course of six weeks or so.'*

What an exciting age to live in, I mused, as I read on about the new aeroplanes now being manufactured in Europe and in America which will soon transform the possibility of travel by aeroplane from city to city or even country to country into a reality.

Mrs Moser came in and I told her that I required an early luncheon and that I would not be returning to Argosse Towers until the weekend. 'Don't prepare anything too elaborate for luncheon, Mrs Moser,' I warned her, knowing that the cook shared Sayers' concern that I was slowly starving myself to death!

'Very good, Miss Rosie. What would you say to starting with vegetable soup followed by fillets of chicken in lemon sauce with new potatoes, grilled tomatoes and green beans and a fruit compôte as dessert.'

'It sounds absolutely delicious but it's far too much,' I told the disappointed cook. 'I'll just have the main course, which sounds delightful. Oh, and please ask Sayers to chill a bottle of the '03 white Bordeaux. I'll only have a glass or two with my meal but I'm sure that you and he will ensure the rest of the wine is not wasted.' I spent most of the morning choosing my clothes for the next few hectic days and nights. Aunt Elizabeth was happy for me to stay with her for as long as I liked, but I could not break my promise to Kitty Bedford to come back for her twentieth birthday ball on Saturday night.

Frankly, I would have preferred to take more frequent trips to our great Metropolis and would heartily agree with Dr Johnson who opined that 'the man who is tired of London is tired of life'. But though our family owns a town house in Belgrave Square, this year Papa has rented out our London home because he and Mama will be living abroad for the next six months, and when they return to England my parents prefer to spend as much time as possible far from the madding crowd here in the peaceful rural surroundings of West Sussex.

Sayers brought me the morning post whilst I was browsing among the newest acquisitions in the library. For several years now my parents have had an account with Blow's Bookstore in Charing Cross Road and even whilst they are away, Mr Blow makes a weekly choice of two new books to send to us. He is keenly aware of my parents' likes and dislikes and so rarely do they ever send books back to the shop. However, my own taste in literature is naturally different to that of my parents and I had not found a book I wished to take with me to read on the train when Sayers brought me my mail.

He also placed a plain large envelope on the stack of unopened parcels of books from Mr Blow before he left the room and I wondered what this could contain as I opened my solitary letter. However, I was pleased to see that my correspondent was none other than Jimmy Horobin from whom I had not heard for about a month. Jimmy writes a good, meaty letter and I settled down to read what he had to say.

I began to read:

26

My Dearest Rosie:

Spring's touch has come early to Cambridgeshire. Many more birds are singing now that the sun is at last breaking through the thick clouds which marred our days till last weekend. At dawn this morning I was wakened by the short, gabbled song of pied wagtails perched on a nearby roof and yesterday in Bearsden Wood I saw that the sparrow-hawks are back at their nesting sites, soaring high, gliding above the forest, surveying the prospects before dashing in pursuit of small birds along the woodland edge. The snowdrops opened late this year but have now flowered in broad white pools under trees and the first daffodils are now waving in the breeze.

I have palled up with a chap named Robert Bacon who I think you met when he was in the Upper Sixth at St Trippett's College in Chichester. You will probably remember that he was very close to your chum Katie Archer [see Rosie Vol One: The Intimate Diaries — *Editor] but like us, they decided to break off their relationship when she left St Hilda's Academy to study the history of art in Paris and he was offered a place at Trinity College to read politics, philosophy and economics.*

Perhaps we were drawn together because we have both been missing the jolly times we enjoyed with our sweethearts, Rob with Katie and me with you, darling Rosie. I am not ashamed to tell you that I miss our wonderful sessions of passionate love-making quite dreadfully and especially at nights when I retire to my room and lie alone in my narrow bed, I think of you constantly. Sometimes I dream about you and some of these dreams are really torrid — only last night I imagined we were back in your lovely big bed at Argosse Towers and that you had plumped your gorgeous naked bottom on my face and you opened your legs so that I could kiss and suck your sweet pussy!

At other times I have lain awake thinking of the soft, white globes of your breasts with their large strawberry nipples and of how my hands would traverse the flat, dimpled plain of your belly until they reached the silky mass of blonde curls and the pouting love lips which would open so readily at the arrival of my stalwart shaft.

Of course I then have to yield my swollen, rock-hard prick to the embrace of the five-fingered widow and with increasing rapidity I pull my hand up and down my twitching staff until with a sudden spurt, a fountain of sticky sperm shoots out from the little 'eye' on the top of my knob.

Now there is nothing wrong with a good wank despite the blatherings of the parsons. After all, if there were any truth in their dire warnings against tossing off, ninety-nine per cent of the male population would be either blind or insane by the time they had reached the age of forty! But tossing off is only a substitute for the genuine article and cannot be compared with the true joys of l'arte de faire l'amour, so do give my love to your lovely little cunt and tell her I think of her daily!

However, I would be less than honest if I did not tell you that I did find some consolation the other day after Rob and I had gone punting on the River Cam. As one would expect of such a bold and gregarious chap, Rob took little time to make himself known to some of the prettiest girls around town and he pulled away from the bank with a lovely Spanish girl named Maria in his boat. She was here to learn English and was rather lonely and homesick, for her present command of our language is limited, but unlike most Englishmen, Rob is fluent in both French and Spanish so as you can imagine, the two of them soon forged a close friendship, chatting away in Maria's native tongue.

Rosie, I must admit that I was jealous of his success but the glorious, exceptionally warm spring sunshine soon put me in a better humour and after some twenty minutes or so, I decided to to make for the shore and sit down for a short rest. Gloomily, I started to toss some stones into the water and later I discovered that it was the sound of splashing that brought my presence to the attention of Miss Louise Cumberland. At this point I must interpolate the fact that Louise is the matron of Walshaws, a preparatory boarding school for boys situated on the outskirts of the city, and that she had decided to spend her weekly free afternoon in taking a quiet walk by the river.

Unfortunately, the unlucky girl (she is older than me but is still only in her mid-twenties) tripped over a fallen branch and badly sprained her ankle. She was hobbling back to the road when she heard me chucking pebbles into the river and so she called out: 'Help! Is anyone there?'

I scrambled to my feet and walked briskly to the towpath where I saw her. 'Hello there, I wonder if you could assist me to somewhere I could sit down. I'm afraid I've twisted my ankle and it's rather difficult for me to walk just at the moment,' she said, her face contorted with pain as she limped painfully towards me. Without further ado I ran across the path and offered my shoulder for her to lean on.

'Here, do ease your weight onto me,' I said. 'Look, my boat is just down here. You can rest your ankle until we arrive and I can call you a cab to take you home.'

'Thank you, you're very kind,' she smiled as we slowly made our way to my punt. Louise found it rather awkward to manoeuvre herself into the boat, but with my help she was soon settled nicely in a seat. Before I clambered up behind her with the long pole required to push us off into the mainstream, we introduced ourselves and it was when I asked if she were a student, Louise told me about her employment at Walshaws School.

Although I have had little experience of the art of navigating a punt, within fifteen minutes I had steered us back without too much difficulty to the landing stage where I helped Louise out of the boat and suggested we sat down for a while in The Crown Inn which was only a hundred yards walk away. 'You should drink a little brandy, Miss Cumberland, for medicinal purposes if for no other reason. It will deaden the pain and refresh you,' I said. She hesitated at first but then with a warm smile thanked me and accepted my invitation. She was forced to lean heavily on me (an experience I did not find unpleasant) as we walked the short distance and soon we found ourselves sitting comfortably on a bench in the garden of the old hostelry.

I ordered brandies for us both and perhaps the smooth yet fiery spirits loosened our tongues for soon we were on first-name terms, and we chatted away like old friends over a second and then a third brandy. By then Louise was not shy about telling me some of the more amusing aspects of her work when I remarked that she must find her duties at Walshaws somewhat boring.

'Not really, Jimmy, for the principal, Dr Waller, is very kind and the pupils do not give me very much trouble. I have to cheer up many of the younger boys who are often very homesick, and I do think it strange that apparently loving parents will happily send their sons away from home at the tender age of eight to fend for themselves.'

'Boarding schools teach many good lessons, including self-sufficiency and an ability to mix sociably with one's fellows,' I remarked, 'but I do agree with you that eight is far too young an age to be bundled out of home into a strange new world.

'However, most of them learn to adapt to their new circumstances and I'll wager that some little boys become little terrors by the time they are ready to leave.'

Louise sighed and said: 'Very much so, Jimmy, and Walshaws being a boys' school, this occasionally precipitates some embarrassing moments for me. For instance, there are three young lads in the top form — Malcolm, Colin and Alan — who are all only thirteen years old but physically look far more mature than one would expect, and many people would judge them to be at least two or three years older than they actually are.

'Well, one evening last week after lights-out I was passing by the recreation room when I thought I heard the murmur of voices. No-one should have been in there at that time and so in case I had chanced upon some intruders, I opened the door very quietly and slowly. The room was dark but a small candelabra had been set up on a table standing by the far wall. By this light I could see these three boys who were standing in a semi-circle, their pyjama trousers round their feet, all handling and stroking their penises.

30

'Whilst I must say that I was not overshocked to see such a gathering, for it is only natural for young boys to play with themselves, what did surprise me was the size of their cocks. The three lads were slowly frigging pink, rigid tools which were standing stiffly up to attention and each prick seemed big enough to satisfy the most demanding pussy! "Right, let's see who can come first," Colin called out. "Are you ready, one, two, three, go!" They began handling their tools at a great rate of speed, rubbing their shafts, which in fact were not so small as one would expect at such a tender age. It could have been only a minute later that all three began to spend, the first spurtings of white cream shooting out of their pricks like miniature fountains.

'I was tempted to sweep in and put a halt to the proceedings, for the three of them should have been tucked up in bed at this hour, but then I thought that more harm would be done if I reported them to Dr Letchmore rather than let sleeping dogs lie. So I backed out of the door as carefully as I had entered and walked away down the corridor. Do you think I was right to do so?'

'Oh, undoubtedly you took the correct course, Louise,' I agreed. 'All their juvenile horseplay is designed not only to discover who can boast possession of the biggest penis, but also to revel in the joys of having a cock which can provide such pleasure! When the time comes for them to discover the joys of real love-making, such behaviour will cease of its own accord.'

Anyhow, I insisted on taking Louise back to Walshaws and she accepted my invitation to dine at De Souza's Chop House on her next free evening which would be on Friday night. I will not go into the details of what occurred that evening in this letter, for I have yet to finish an essay for Dr Macdougall, but suffice it to say that after dinner we went to a party thrown by young Ian Osborne and there we watched a performance of some very daring poses plastiques. (A late Victorian/Edwardian equivalent of modern strip-tease. Showgirls would pose in so-called scenes from the classics which gave the excuse for them to appear

31

scantily clad or even semi-nude — Editor.) My prick feels far more happy with life in Cambridge than it did before I met the charming Louise, whose sprained ankle, you will be glad to learn, is now completely healed.

Do write to me soon and tell me of all your adventures,

Love,

Jimmy

I took a deep breath and then slowly expelled the air by blowing out my cheeks. On the one hand I was genuinely pleased that Jimmy had found consolation in the arms of Miss Cumberland, but on the other I was left feeling curiously miffed that he was now pumping his lovely thick prick through the wet walls of a pussy other than my own tingling love channel, which had begun to moisten whilst I was reading his naughty letter and remained unfilled by anything except my own or Elaine's fingers.

Jealousy is an unworthy emotion, I told myself as I rose and looked down at the thick buff envelope Sayers had placed on top of the parcel of books from Blow's. It was addressed to my uncle, Lord Gordon MacChesney, and was marked *Strictly Confidential*, but I was almost certain that what lay inside was the latest edition of *The Oyster*, a secret, very naughty magazine which my randy relative had subscribed to for many years. Uncle Gordon was due to visit us next week and obviously he had given instructions for his next copy to be delivered here!

This would neatly solve my problem of what to read on the train, I thought, for I would be returning home before Uncle Gordon arrived and so could replace the magazine in its envelope without any harm being done. So I picked up the envelope and went upstairs to my room where Dennison was locking up my two valises. 'Good morning, Miss Rosie,' he said politely. 'May I wish you a very pleasant stay in London?'

Well, I found it impossible to refrain from making some barbed comment about what I had seen Dennison and Norma Radlett up to earlier in the morning! 'Thank you,'

I said as languidly as I could manage. 'I have an extremely busy time ahead of me. Indeed, I have so many people to see and so much to do that I shall find myself up against the wall if I attempt to cram everything in. Not that this is necessarily a bad position in which to be, of course.'

The footman gave me a sharp look but said nothing as he grasped hold of the handles of my cases and I opened the door for him and added: 'I find London such a noisy place these days. One is constantly being wakened by the rumblings of dustcarts or the bawlings of paper-boys. At least in the countryside it is usually possible to sleep undisturbed except for the singing of birds and other, sometimes rather unusual sounds which float up to one's bedroom window.'

Dennison had the grace to blush but wisely made no comment as he hauled the cases out of my bedroom. I grinned as I made a last-minute check to ensure that I had not forgotten to take anything, and then followed him downstairs to the hall where Sayers awaited me. 'Luncheon is served, Miss Rosie,' he intoned sonorously and Mrs Moser herself came bustling in to serve her delicious dish of chicken in lemon sauce. I ate my lunch under the eagle eyes of the cook and the butler and pronounced myself well satisfied with the fare provided.

'I hope that you and Mrs Moser will finish this bottle of wine,' I said to Sayers as he topped up my glass.

'Thank you, Miss Rosie, we'll do that, never fear,' said Mrs Moser. 'Now you've plenty of time to catch your train. Elaine is waiting for you in the motor and the luggage has been loaded, hasn't, it Mr Sayers?'

'Indeed it has,' said the butler, pulling my chair away from the table as I rose up to leave. 'May I wish you an enjoyable stay in town, Miss Rosie. If you can let me know the time of your train on Saturday, I will see that Haines meets you at the station.'

I said I would send a message before I left London and Haines opened the rear door of our new Mercedes automobile for me. Elaine was sitting in the front seat next to Haines and when our driver switched on the engine she turned round excitedly and said: 'Isn't this exciting! I've never ridden in a motor car before. I'd love to try and drive one.'

'So would I, it would be great fun to speed along at forty miles an hour, but even the best vehicles need a mechanic as they are still not totally reliable and we suffer a great deal from punctures on poor roads around here,' I warned her as Haines engaged the clutch and we moved off smartly to the railway station.

We arrived in good time and Haines accompanied us onto the platform with our luggage which he would place in the guard's van for us when the train arrived. I enjoy travelling by train, especially through the wonderful Sussex countryside. However, as I consulted my watch, which confirmed that the train was already three minutes late, my experience told me that as usual I would have to cope with the three classes of train which appeared to dominate this section of the Southern Railway — those that depart and never arrive, those that arrive and never depart and those that shoot through in transit, as if their wheels were running on the tracks of an unknown destiny with neither beginning nor end!

Nevertheless, the train finally arrived some eight minutes late and although I had reserved Elaine a first class seat next to me, I noticed her fidgeting as the train chugged out of Midhurst station.

'I assumed you would enjoy travelling first class for a change,' I said a trifle acidly to my maid, and her pretty face coloured a warm shade of red as she replied: 'It was very kind of you, Miss Rosie, but if it's all the same to you I'd like to go to the back and sit in a second class carriage.'

'What on earth for, Elaine? Is my company so dull that you do not wish to share a compartment with me?' I asked crossly, and she shook her head: 'Oh no, nothing like that at all. It's just that — well, between you and me, Miss Rosie, I saw Humphrey Allingham-Jones get on this train and he and I have had an understanding, so to speak, for some weeks now.'

'Humphrey? Our vicar's younger son? When did you meet him? I thought he was working as an articled clerk at a firm of solicitors in Worthing. Surely neither of you attend one of his father's Sunday schools?'

Elaine giggled and said: 'Oh no, we met at The Dog and Duck on my afternoon off. Humphrey's not a bible basher like his dad. He's become a Socialist since he started work and once he passes his examinations he wants to stand as the Member of Parliament for this area.'

'I hope he's not holding his breath,' I grunted, for it has been a constant source of irritation to my Papa, a staunch Liberal, that this constituency has always returned a Conservative to the House of Commons. 'Tell me though, Elaine, how does your Humphrey stand on the question of votes for women?'

'He's in favour of giving us the vote, Miss Rosie. Humphrey says that one day there'll be a female Prime Minister. I said that was a bit far-fetched but he didn't seem to think so. Anyhow, we don't talk all that much about politics but we do love to kiss and cuddle and we haven't had much of a chance to do much canoodling. The vicarage is out of bounds and I can hardly take him back to Argosse Towers, so we've had to use Lover's Lane, the little road that runs through the village green down to the football pitch.'

'That can't have been very comfortable lately with all this wet weather,' I said thoughtfully. 'Go on, you be off, Elaine, but it'll be crowded back in second class. You bring Humphrey here and I'll go out for a cup of tea in the refreshment car.'

Her eyes sparkled and she said: 'Oh, you are kind, Miss Rosie. I'll bring him along straightaway.'

Elaine returned with her handsome young follower and after we had exchanged greetings (for I had known Humphrey since his father became the local vicar some eight years ago) I stood up and announced that I would retire to the dining-car. After ordering a pot of tea, I settled down in my seat and as I saw the carriage was almost empty, I carefully pulled out Uncle Gordon's copy of *The Oyster*, which I had rolled up and popped into my handbag. To my surprise, as I glanced through the magazine, the name Mary Smyth flitted across my field of vision. Surely this could not be the Mary Smyth from the quaintly named Balls Pond Road in Canonbury, North London, who was a classmate of mine at Madame Dupont's? But yes, there was her name and address affixed to a letter in the *Ask Doctor Jonathan* section of the magazine.

My hands trembled slightly as I read Mary's query avidly. She related the fact that she had been lucky enough to bed Mr Peter Stockman of Mayfair who is generally accepted to be the proud owner of the biggest penis in London Society. What problems could this have posed, I wondered as I perused her little essay. For the sake of brevity I will précis her words [*Mary Smyth's letter can be found in the paperback book* The Oyster Vol 4, New English Library, 1989 — *Editor*]. She had informed Doctor Jonathan how, '*like so many girls before me, I gasped with wonderment when he pulled down his drawers and revealed his astonishingly thick cock which sprang upwards from the mass of black, curly hair at the bottom of his belly, and the tip of which reached high above his navel . . . I reached down to take hold of his enormous shaft which throbbed like hot velvet under my touch. I planted a kiss on his uncapped knob and Peter asked me whether he could have the pleasure of fucking me from behind. "Certainly you may," I replied, "but please do not go up my bum."*

I raised myself up on my knees and turned to face the bedstead and stuck out my bum as provocatively as I could. Peter leaned over me and I felt the crown of his monstrous cock nudge against my pussy lips. He slipped his cock inside me and gently moved in and out in slow, rhythmic thrusts. It was truly extraordinary how my poor little pussy managed to accommodate his mighty monster, but my juices eased his passage as he pushed in, withdrew, pushed in, withdrew as I shuddered in voluptuous ardour . . . Peter's prick felt wonderful, thick and hot, stretching my cunney channel and filling it deliciously. He used his cock expertly, varying his angle and speed, and his staying power was immense. We must have fucked for at least fifteen minutes before the wonderful performance ended as he shot thick wads of creamy jism into me, and I screamed with delight, for I too had spent almost instantaneously as the warm, frothy spunk spattered out inside my tingling pussy . . .

I thoroughly enjoyed being fucked from behind and my current beau, Mr George Lucas, has had me in various situations: standing up, me on top, sitting on a chair, etc. However, I honestly prefer the good old-fashioned way of lying on my back in a comfortable bed and letting the man do most of the work!

Am I missing out on hidden joys?

I turned the page to find out what the medical columnist [*Doctor Jonathan Arkley, who was* The Oyster*'s medical adviser, was a notorious turn of the century rake and a leading member of the ultra-fast South Hampstead set — Editor*] had replied to Mary's *cri de coeur*. I must say that I was in full agreement with Doctor Jonathan who had written: *The so-called 'missionary position', where the man lies on top of the woman whose legs are spread apart to accommodate him, is the commonest sexual position by far throughout Europe. It is so popular simply because it is, in my view, the most comfortable sexual position of them all! However, there can be many refinements which are detailed in* Fucking For Fun *by Professor James Ward and* A Lady of Quality *by Lady Elstree, which I would highly recommend to all readers. It may be purchased at Hotten's, Piccadilly and other shops for twelve shillings and sixpence and is worth every penny.*

Variety is the spice of life and experimentation will stave off boredom. I am sure you will find Dr Ward's book of great interest and you may well find that there are positions other than your own favourite prick/cuntal conjunction.

This was indeed wise advice from the famed medical counseller of *The Oyster*, and I resolved to send a copy of his advice, along with Dr Ward's book, as a present for my dear friend from nearby Eastbourne, Loretta Gibson, who only recently confided to me her deep disappointment that her lover, Edward, had been tiresomely unwilling to experiment with any alternative sexual games in or out of bed.

I rolled up my copy of the magazine and put it back in my handbag as I glanced up at the clock. I had given Elaine and Humphrey almost a quarter of an hour's privacy, but now I would have to return to the compartment because the guard would soon be coming round to check the tickets and I had Elaine's and mine in my bag whilst, of course, poor Humphrey would find himself banished back to the second class carriage at the rear of the train if I did not return before the tickets were collected.

Upon my return I noticed that the loving couple had been sensible enough to draw the window blinds so that they could not be seen by passengers walking through the corridor, but of course the door itself could not be locked and so I glanced round to ensure that no-one was approaching before I slid it open.

What a lascivious sight greeted my eyes! The randy young couple had discarded all their clothes and were engaged in fondling each other's naked gleaming bodies. I quickly shut the door behind me and sat down in the corner. 'Don't let me disturb you,' I murmured softly. 'I'll present the tickets should the guard knock on the door.'

'Thank you so much,' said Humphrey hoarsely as Elaine reached down and clasped her hand around his hard, stiff cock. She delicately fingered the large, bulbous crown before she leaned over him and extended her tongue to lick and lap all around the plum-coloured helmet. Then she circled her tongue around the domed knob and, without using her hands, sucked in almost all of his veiny shaft which twitched delightedly as she sucked his prick vigorously, her lips and tongue varying the pleasure in both speed and intensity which left the lad gasping out tiny cries of ecstasy.

Humphrey's eyes were now closed and he was breathing so heavily that his chest rose up and down in a jerky rhythm as Elaine took all but the hot, velvety knob out of her mouth. She looked up cheekily to his face and giggled as she returned to her sweet labours. She washed her tongue over his helmet with long, swirling licks and then plunged her mouth down again, giving the sensitive ridge round the knob a teasing brush with her teeth.

Her silky black hair bobbed up and down whilst she bobbed her head up and down his glistening penis until she had taken all of the pulsating staff deep inside her throat. She began to frig herself as she slid his rock-hard rod in and out of her mouth, rubbing her nipples lewdly against his groin, and it was little wonder that Humphrey's body soon went rigid as the sperm shot through his shaft and the sticky white jism cascaded out of his twitching truncheon. Elaine gulped down his creamy emission, milking every drain of jism from his jerking tool which now began to soften in her mouth, and she lifted her head up and smacked her lips.

'M'mm, that was nice,' she panted as she lay back in her seat. 'I do so love sucking cocks, don't you, Miss Rosie? I would like nothing better than to lick and kiss their pricks for a long time, but none of the men I've ever been with can hold back for more than five minutes. They all went wild as soon as I started to suck their cocks and each one spent too soon for my liking.'

'Present company excepted, Humphrey,' she added kindly to the exhausted young man who lay sprawled out beside her. 'We had to finish quickly just now because we might be interrupted at any moment by the ticket collector and come to think of it, we'd better get dressed right away, hadn't we?'

Elaine rose and slipped on her knickers as she continued: 'Yes, I do love letting my tongue caress the smooth, warm skin of a big, fat, juicy knob before popping the twitching, thick shaft in my mouth and sucking out the spunk. It's so exciting when the boy squirts out his jism and I like the clean, salty taste, too! I've always enjoyed sucking pricks ever since

I went into service and my first mistress showed me how to do it. I had inadvertently come into the drawing room where Mrs Jennifer Jarley was greedily gobbling down a blob of raspberry jam from her boyfriend's cock on the Chesterfield. [*A large, leather upholstered sofa with straight upholstered arms of the same height as the back — Editor*]

'You couldn't blame my mistress for being unfaithful to Mr Jarley, who rarely paid her much attention. She was only twenty-nine years old and had no more than a normal sensual appetite but her husband, who was almost twenty years her senior, seemed to be far more interested in hunting and shooting than taking up his conjugal rights. Mrs J. often complained to me that her husband only fucked her once a month at most, and then only up her bum which led her to the belief that he was at heart a secret devotee of Mr Oscar Wilde and the homosexuals. Anyhow, she kindly taught me how to suck a cock, beginning by holding it lightly and applying wet kisses to the knob. Then she advised taking the tip in the mouth and rocking it to and fro whilst licking it, just like you would with an ice cream cornet. That's all she had to tell me really, and I found it a very natural thing to do when she offered me her lover's prick to practise on.'

Humphrey was about to speak when we were interrupted by a knock on the door. 'Leave this to me, it must be the ticket collector,' I whispered to my fellow passengers. 'Just keep quite still and don't say a word.'

Slowly, I inched open the door and in my grandest voice said to the uniformed official: 'Yes, what do you want, my good man?'

'Your ticket, please, Miss.'

I rummaged in my bag and brought out our railway passes (how useful it was that Papa is a director of The Southern Railway!) and the man handed them back to me with a deferential air. 'I regret to say there has been a signals failure at Clapham Junction, and we'll be stuck in a queue of trains waiting to get into London.'

As if on cue, the train began to slow down and he added: 'I'm afraid we'll be about half an hour late, Miss.'

'It cannot be helped, these things do happen occasionally,' I said graciously. 'However, please see to it that my maid and I are not disturbed until we reach Victoria.'

With a smile I turned to Elaine and Humphrey and said: 'Did you hear what he said? We'll be delayed for thirty minutes. How fortunate for you! Don't mind me, do carry on with your love-making.'

The happy pair needed no further urging and in a trice they had torn off the clothes they had already put back on and were sliding, joyously naked, into each other's arms. I pulled out my copy of *The Oyster*, but I could not concentrate as the moans of the two young lovers reached fever pitch and so I glanced up to see how matters were progressing. I smiled as I saw that they had pulled down the arms of the adjoining chairs to make an impromptu mattress and that Humphrey and Elaine were now kneeling face to face on the long, unbroken seat.

Elaine's face glowed as she reached out and enclosed his swollen, stiff cock in her fist, gently frigging it just below the helmet. Except for the rhythmic movement of Elaine's hand they were still, their bodies pressed together, their tongues and lips engaged in sensual exploration of each other's mouths whilst his throbbing tool lay pressed against the softly accommodating pillow of her white tummy. Moving back slightly, Humphrey snaked his hand round her slender waist and grasped one of her rotund bum cheeks. Elaine responded by rotating her hips in slow, voluptuous circles, riding his intrusive wrist as they continued to kiss and cuddle.

It was time now for Humphrey to insert his sizeable member into Elaine's juicy cunney and as she lay back, she held firm on his pulsing hot shaft to guide his cock through the slippery gates of her pussy lips and into her yearning cunt. He scrambled to his knees and his blunt, fleshy knob hovered between her love lips before sinking gratefully between them and into her welcoming love channel. Elaine's hands slipped round to clamp themselves on the taut cheeks of his bottom and his arms went under her shoulders as she

41

lifted her hips to allow an easier passage for the thrusting penis which was now squelching merrily in and out of her sopping slit. Humphrey increased the speed of his fucking and fairly bounced up and down on the trembling girl who clawed at his jerking backside and heaved herself upwards at each stroke to draw his thick prick even further inside her.

To his credit, Humphrey rode my excited maid expertly, despite the lack of width on the seat and the fact that in her frenzy Elaine began to writhe and twist almost uncontrollably. But Humphrey ploughed on with this unexpected, frenetic fuck and I could hear the erotic noise of his penis sliding in and out of her juicy cunney and the slip slap sound of his balls banging against her arse.

'Aaah! Aaah! I'm there, I'm there! Fill me up with your love cream, you randy rascal! Y-e-s-s-s! Y-e-s-s-s! Y-e-s-s-s!' she yelled out in triumph as the force of her orgasm crackled through her body, and although I was concerned in case she should be overheard, naturally enough Elaine was oblivious to everything except for the flood of frothy white spunk which was now inundating her lubricated cunney, driving them to that blissful state of divinely beneficient happiness only to be achieved through such a magnificent copulatory conjunction.

'Aaah! What a wonderful fuck,' purred Elaine as she stretched her legs languidly along the seat. 'I do believe that I should like to spend the rest of my life with a stiff cock up my cunt.' And with that heartfelt valediction to Humphrey's shrinking penis, she lay back to recover from her frenzied bout of love-making.

Meanwhile, this stimulating sight had made me extremely damp between my legs and I assumed a reclining position in my corner whilst I swiftly unhooked my skirt and ripped off my panties. Shamelessly I opened my legs to display my silky blonde bush and ran my long fingers through my pussy hair and rubbed my moistening mound before slipping my hand between my opening thighs and brushing my fingertips along the pouting pussy lips.

'Would you like Humphrey to fuck you, Miss Rosie? I'm

42

sure he would be delighted to oblige and I'd be pleased to suck his prick up to attention — Humphrey, you'll oblige Miss Rosie, won't you?'

'With the greatest of pleasure,' said the good-looking young man gallantly. 'I would like nothing better than to fuck you, though I think you must allow me breathing space before we begin for I don't think my tadger will be ready for action for another few minutes.'

'Dear me, Humphrey, a young gentleman like you in prime condition should be good for one more cockstand,' chided Elaine, taking his flaccid cock in her hands and rubbing the soft tube of flesh between her palms, and I noted the brightness of her eyes, the flushed complexion and the slight breathlessness which accompanied her remark.

Without doubt, there is something about a train journey which sharpens the sensual senses and as I once inadvertently heard my Papa's friend Colonel Goldstone of the West Oxfordshire Rifles say to my Uncle Gordon when he thought they were alone: 'Did you visit the new Turner exhibition at the Tate, old boy? I went round last week with Mrs Mallin and pretty excited she became, I can tell you. She could hardly wait to get back to my place afterwards for a spot of rumpy-pumpy. It was that painting *Rain, Steam and Speed*, don't you know, that made her feel so fruity. Violent storms, thunder clouds, the glare of flame from the engine — and none of those long-haired nancy-boy critics have understood that the painting's all about the excitement of fucking in the train. The steady rhythmic motion of passing clickety clack over the rails helps induce a state of heightened sexual awareness and in my humble opinion, there's little that can beat an amorous adventure once you're safely tucked away in your compartment and the countryside is speeding by.'

Well, we were actually stationary but our carnal appetites had certainly been affected by the journey! After a minute or so, Elaine's manual manipulation of Humphrey's prick began to to have the desired effect and his shaft began to swell and harden in her hands. When his shaft was standing back at its fullest height, I eased back on the seat, opening my legs to stroke my damp pussy with my fingers. 'Go on, Humphrey, your cock is good and ready now,' said Elaine encouragingly and he heaved himself up to stand in front of me, his hands on his hips and his veiny, thick shaft protruding almost vertically like a flagpole from the mossy growth of dark pubic curls.

'This is a nice, meaty-looking cock that needs a good sucking,' I said roguishly as I lifted myself up onto my knees and opened my mouth to receive the rounded purple knob between my lips. Taking a firm grip of his pulsating prick, I sucked lustily on his throbbing tool, enjoying to the full the salty tang of the drops of pre-spend juice which were already leaking out of the tip.

In different circumstances I would have sucked him until he spent his tangy jism in my mouth, but the poor lad had already bestowed copious emissions inside Elaine, and I wanted to feel his hard thickness deep in my cunt which was now very wet indeed and flexing itself with unbridled anticipation. So I tongued his knob one last time before pulling my mouth away and lying back on the seat.

Humphrey knelt between my thighs and played with my breasts before lying over me and grinding the underside of his shaft along my crack. I gyrated my hips in a circular fashion and brought my pouting pussy lips into direct contact with the tip of his cock.

'Put it inside me, please,' I whispered in his ear, bracing myself for his onslaught. He slowly inserted his hot, smooth-skinned weapon and I sighed with pleasure as he rubbed my clitty with the ridge of his helmet as he eased himself forward. My cunney fairly throbbed, pulsing my juices from me in a warm, sticky wetness. Humphrey's mouth was now on my titties, his tongue reaching out to slither round my nipple whilst his rampant cock reamed its way into every nook and cranny of my saturated cunt.

I purred with delight as he slewed his wonderful prick to and fro at a steady rate of knots and then, as I gasped out the fact that I was approaching a spend, he changed up a gear, thrusting in and out at an ever-increasing speed, his hairy ballsack fairly banging against my bum with each attack as his engorged, twitching tool pounded away inside my ripe, juicy pussy with all the energy he could muster.

Just then, the engine driver must have been given the signal to proceed for the train now lurched forward and it was as well that the guard did not decide to return to our compartment because we were both well past the point of no return. Ah, what bliss I experienced as his pulsating penis plugged and stretched those innermost recesses of my cunt, his shaft moving in sharp, stabbing thrusts and my body thrilled with excitement as I felt the first waves of a marvellous spend course their way through me. He crushed me to him as with a hoarse cry, Humphrey also climaxed and we came together in a luscious, simultaneous climax as he spunked powerfully into my cunt, filling me to the brim with his copious ejaculation, his creamy sperm mingling with the gushes of love juice that were flowing freely from my sated cunney.

Humphrey collapsed on top of me and withdrew his limp, wet cock around which I made a fist with my fingers. 'No, no, much as I would love to continue, the spirit is willing but the flesh is weak, as my reverend father might say,' he groaned.

'Don't worry, Humphrey, even where fucking's concerned, enough is as good as a feast and I'm very well satisfied,' I assured the dear boy as I gave his soft, glistening shaft a loving squeeze. 'We came together which was an added bonus, was it not?'

'Yes, I wish that Elaine and I could come together more often,' he said, and I was about to tell him that this was not a matter about which he should be over-concerned when my maid chirped up: 'Oh, Miss Rosie, I do wish you would tell him not to be so silly and stop worrying about it. It really doesn't matter all that much.'

Elaine had thoughtfully pulled out a hand towel from her Gladstone bag [*a large piece of hand luggage consisting of two equal-sized hinged compartments — Editor*] and had

45

come over to dry my perspiring body for me. 'Honestly, Humphrey, I'm sure Miss Rosie will also tell you that coming together isn't the be-all and end-all of a good fuck.'

'Absolutely so,' I said, taking the towel to wipe away the moisture from Humphrey's hairy chest. 'There is no point at all in trying to time your spend to achieve such a situation. Holding back to wait for one's partner is often welcomed, but forcing forward just to come with your girl is quite unnecessary. One can become obsessed with timing and become so involved that everything else is forgotten.

'In any case, climaxing at different times can allow your lover to concentrate on exciting you in other ways which can be far more important,' I continued, and this advice did appear to put Humphrey's mind to rest as his brow cleared and we began to dress ourselves — not before time as we were now picking up speed and, outside, the open spaces of the countryside were giving way to the outer southern suburbs. When we had completed this task, Elaine and I kissed Humphrey good-bye. He was travelling to town for a lecture that evening at Lincoln's Inn by the famed jurist Professor Massey on certain intricate aspects of international commercial law.

'Where will you be staying the night?' I asked and Humphrey informed us that his firm had reserved a room for him at Wright's Private Hotel in Bedford Square.

'Can we offer you a lift there? My Aunt has arranged for her chauffeur to meet us at Victoria and I will gladly instruct him to take you there after he has dropped us at Chandos Street,' I said, but though thanking me for the offer, he declined for he informed us he was not journeying alone but with his employer's secretary, who had come to take notes of a meeting he had to attend at a barrister's chambers.

'We'll be hard-pressed to be punctual because of the delay, though I wouldn't have missed this glorious experience for the world,' he said with evident sincerity. 'But I must return to my carriage or Miss Murdoch will wonder what has become of me. However, if either of you are free later this evening . . .'

His voice tailed off and Elaine looked hopefully at me, 'Elaine could visit you later and indeed I will not be requiring her services after seven o'clock,' I said with a smile. 'As far as I am concerned, she can stay the night with you so long as you make sure she is back at number forty-seven Chandos Street by half past eight tomorrow morning.'

Elaine clapped her hands together in delight. 'Oh, you are kind, Miss Rosie! Could I stay with you tonight, Humphrey?'

'I don't see why not,' he beamed happily. 'Edwina Murdoch had booked a double bedroom and I see no reason why we cannot sign you in as the second occupant.'

'Good, that's settled then,' I said. 'And whilst it was a great pleasure being fucked by you, Humphrey, I trust I may count on your discretion in not mentioning what happened this afternoon to anyone.'

'You have my word, Miss d'Argosse,' he said formally, kissing my hand before he pulled up the blinds and let himself out of the compartment and into the corridor.

We arrived only twenty-five minutes later at Victoria and Randall, my aunt's chauffeur, was waiting for us on the platform with a porter in tow. After the luggage was all bundled into the new Rolls Royce Aunt Elizabeth had just purchased, Randall guided the motor through the crowded streets, through St James's Park and past Buckingham Palace on his way up to Hyde Park Corner where we were stalled in a monstrous mêlée of coaches, cabs and a variety of conveyances. It really is a disgrace that our admittedly under-manned police force cannot cope with keeping the ever-increasing number of vehicles which clog the streets of London on the move. As we forced our way through it occurred to me that what the city really required was a special force of traffic police whose duties were solely concerned with admonishing careless motorists and issuing summonses to both commercial and private drivers who park willy-nilly along the king's highway, causing grave obstruction to all and sundry.

Nevertheless, I was happy to be in town where spring's

touch seemed to be everywhere — in the air and on people's faces. The wonderful sense of all-pervading youth was astir, heightened perhaps by the delicious fucking I had just enjoyed. This good humour led me to tap upon the dividing window between Elaine and me and our driver and say: 'Randall, don't fret, I have no appointment pending until this evening.'

'Just as well, Miss,' replied the chauffeur glumly as he swung the car into the whirl of vehicles around Hyde Park Corner. 'Traffic's getting worse and worse these days.'

Nevertheless, we arrived safe and sound at Chandos Street and old Simpson, the butler and Mrs Beaconsfield, my aunt's cook-housekeeper, were on hand to welcome me. I informed them that I was expecting Lord Philip Pelham to call for me at seven-thirty that evening and that I would probably not be returning until the early hours. 'It isn't necessary for you to wait up for me, Simpson. If you give the front door key to Lord Philip, he will kindly open the door for me when we get back. I will take the responsibility of locking up after he has gone.'

'Are you sure, Miss Rosie?' said the old retainer doubtfully.

'Yes, I have in fact spoken to Lord Philip and he is more than pleased to take the keys with us,' I said briskly. 'And incidentally, I have given permission to Elaine here to go out this evening. However, she is staying overnight with her, er, brother Humphrey and will not return here until tomorrow morning.'

I went upstairs to my bedroom and in the absence of Walker the footman, our erstwhile chauffeur, Randall, brought up my cases a few minutes later. He was a handsome fellow of no more than thirty years of age, well-built with broad shoulders and I recalled Aunt Elizabeth bemoaning the fact that the female servants on her staff had all 'taken a shine' to the good-looking driver.

Elaine helped me unpack and at my request Patricia, the senior housemaid, brought up a pot of tea and a plate of delicious cucumber sandwiches along with the afternoon newspaper. I was surprisingly hungry though I have always found that there is nothing like a good fuck for stimulating even the most jaded of appetites. Be that as it may, I found myself yawning after munching my sandwiches and drinking two cups of the special tea which my aunt's sister-in-law, Lady Bailstone, regularly had delivered to the house from the family plantations in Ceylon [*Sri Lanka — Editor*].

There was time for a thirty-minute rest before I had to begin dressing for the evening, so I pulled out of my case a letter from my dear old friend David Nash which I had received the previous day, but which I had been saving to read for an appropriate time such as this when I could concentrate fully on his epistle. I must note here that David, despite his tender years, has already written extensively for *The Times* and other leading newspapers on various aspects of modern life, and last year was commissioned by no less a publisher than Messrs Dunton and Green to write a book on travelling in the United States. Coincidentally (after the usual salutations and enquiries after my health and that of friends and relatives) David began by recounting the joys of railway travel and, as his views will be of interest, I copy his words here:

It has a somewhat startling effect on the mind of the visitor from Europe when he hears from American railway officials that generally speaking, their passenger business does not pay. In almost every instance it is to the freight business that American railway companies look for their main revenue and they do all they can to attract passenger traffic for they believe that a man ships his merchandise by the line that he himself travels.

Competing companies vie with one another as to which can offer the travelling public the greatest comforts, conveniences and attractions and on such trains as 'The Pennsylvania Special' one finds comforts matching the grandest of our hotels. In addition to the ordinary arrangements of Pullman sleeping cars, there were available on my train a bathroom, a barber's shop and a library.

Besides the open sleeping cars there are drawing rooms and compartment cars where a greater degree of privacy may be obtained and for businessmen, there is a shorthand writer and typist who accompanies the train a good part of the distance, and anyone can make free use of her services so that travellers to New York or Chicago can carry on working just as if they were in their own offices. To this end, the closing stock market prices from New York and Philadelphia are received and posted up en route.

As for lady passengers, they are furnished with a lady's maid and the latest electric contrivances are provided upon which curling tongs may be heated. Also, the electric lights are so arranged that one will be directly over the passenger's shoulder whether he is sitting in a corner seat against the window or reclining in his berth.

Anyhow, I decided to relax for an hour or so in the private lounge provided for first class passengers by the East Coast company on the New York to Washington line. As is my usual practice, I peered out of the window as we chugged along at a steady fifty miles an hour, but rural scenery between these two cities is relatively commonplace, although American wooden farmhouses are always painted in bright, cheerful colours and add colour to an often hum-drum landscape. After a while I sat back and shuffled through the newspapers and books the conductor had left on a table. There was nothing there that I wanted to read and I was just settling down for a quiet nap when I noticed that someone had stuffed a magazine underneath the cushion of the seat opposite me. I pulled it out and in an instant realised why the journal had been furtively hidden away! The reader had either been disturbed and had secreted the publication away and would come back later to retrieve it, or he had left the train and decided not to take it home with him!

It was a 'horn' magazine simply entitled 'Estelle and Her Friends at the Seaside' and consisted of photographs of extremely attractive young ladies in various stages of undress. This was much more to my fancy and I pored over the photographs which began with the eponymous Estelle wearing only the skimpiest of costumes with the straps of the bathing suit hanging over her shoulders, followed by a photograph of the lovely girl without any covering over her firm, ripe young breasts. My cock began to harden, especially when I turned the page to view the cheeky miss stark naked with her back to the camera and sticking out her pert little rounded arse to the photographer's gaze.

I quickly leafed through the rest of the magazine and my prick bulged out from my lap as I scanned the pictures of Estelle and a group of her friends parading naked in front of my eyes. I tugged at my shaft which was now pushing fiercely against the material of my trousers and demanding to be exercised. One picture in particular of Estelle lying on her back completely nude with her legs apart engaged in fingering the lips of her pussy which were only partially hidden by a growth of light cunney hair had me panting with lust. However, my concentration was broken by a knock on the door.

'Come in,' I called, hastily crossing my legs and placing the magazine on the seat beside me. To my astonishment a perky blonde girl entered the compartment and her face was very familiar, but I couldn't quite place where I had seen her before. 'Good afternoon, sir,' she said brightly. 'I must apologise for disturbing you but I believe I may have left my magazine in here when I went back to the dining car for luncheon.'

In a flash I realised the extraordinary truth that this attractive young lady was none other than Estelle, the girl upon whose naked charms I had been slavering over the past few minutes! I was so taken by surprise that I sat tongue-tied, but Estelle's eyes swivelled down to where my hand was partially covering the title page of the journal concerned. 'Ah, I see you have found it for me, how kind. Do you find its contents pleasing? If you like, you may keep the booklet for a little longer before returning it to me,' she said kindly as she smiled down at me.

I cleared my throat and somewhat tardily raised myself up from my seat. Frankly, I was so flustered that I hardly knew what to say, but I did manage to blurt out the fact that I found the photographs most delightful and the sight of the voluptuous beauties displaying their proud young bodies had made the tedious journey quite memorable. She was very taken with my words and she accepted my invitation to partake of afternoon tea with me. The delicious girl informed me that her name was Estelle Woodway and that she had left her home town in the northern area of New York State to seek fame and fortune in the hustle and bustle of Manhattan. She worked in one of the big department stores on Fifth Avenue when she was spotted by Professor Alwoodley of the New York Academy of Arts, and was persuaded by him to pose in the nude for the advanced students' weekly life studies class.

A few months later a French photographer friend of Professor Alwoodley's, a Monsieur Eric, offered Estelle and the other models at the Academy fifty dollars each if they would allow him to photograph them au naturel at Coney Island. Naturally, several of them took up this generous offer and Estelle asked me if I agreed that Monsieur Eric had produced a most stimulating selection of photographs. I assured her that they were most delightfully erotic and I suggested that we drank to the photographer's health in something a little less prosaic than coffee. I pressed the bell for service and at my request the coloured attendant swiftly brought us a bottle of iced champagne.

Well, we toasted Monsieur Eric, ourselves and our two great countries and speedily consumed the full bottle of sparkling wine. Like other Californian wines, incidentally, the best American champagne compares very favourably with the original, being produced from transplanted French vines in the ideal West Coast climes. After the attendant had removed the empty bottle and the glasses, Estelle asked me to lock the door behind him. I obeyed but just as I was about to sit down, with a delicious little chuckle, Estelle reached out and pinched my bum!

'Ooh, that was naughty, wasn't it!' she whispered in my

ear. 'But I'm afraid that champagne always has the effect of making me terribly randy.'

'I say, steady on,' I stammered as her fingers stole down to rub themselves sinuously against my prick which immediately began to swell up in salute. 'Er, does this mean to say, um, that is, er, I mean — '

Estelle giggled and said: 'Oh very well, David, you're such a smooth-talking young man I can't possibly resist you! I hope you can fuck as well as you can speak.'

I deemed it unnecessary to reply to this last rhetorical remark and simply turned my face to hers. Our lips met and she stuck her tongue in my mouth whilst, showing commendable dexterity, unbuttoning my fly to release my erect, straining shaft from the confines of my trousers. Her delicate hand squeezed my throbbing cock and then this sparkling beauty undressed in front of my delighted eyes. I stood up, trembling with excitement as I shucked off my jacket, shirt and vest. Now, just for an hour or so after I had seen her nude body in a photograph, here she was in the flesh standing naked in front of me, her firm, uptilted breasts standing out magnificently as she looked saucily up at me. Out mouths met and my hands ran over her hard, engorged red nipples as her own hand encased my pulsating prick which bucked and jerked in her grasp. She pulled her face away as we staggered across to the sofa on the other side of the room and the train lurched just as we crashed down together, though fortuitously Estelle finished up on her back and I was on top of her, my head down between her legs.

My heartbeat began to quicken as I breathed in the unique, tangy, feminine aroma of a pussy anticipating the arrival of a stiff thick prick! Estelle was justly proud of her pussy for her creamy thighs were full and superbly chiselled out and the silky covering of light blonde fluff between them formed a perfect if transparent veil over her pouting cunney lips. I breathed deeply and then my tongue raked across her clitty, then slipped down to probe deeper inside her cunt. Almost of their own volition her legs splayed wider, bent at the knees, as she sought to open herself still more to my wicked, flickering tongue. I slurped lustily as I drew her cunney lips into my mouth, licking eagerly to suck more and more of her love juice which was now flowing freely. She gasped, jerking her hips upward as her stiff clitty was drawn further and further forward between my lips and her hands clutched at my head as her legs, folded across my shoulders, twitched convulsively with joy.

'David, I . . . I . . . I'm ready for you now,' she gasped and my head jerked up from between her thighs and, gently, I stretched up and positioned myself above her trembling soft body. She reached down and pulled my cock towards the slippery entrance to her cunt and my whole being tensed with excitement as the swollen dome of my knob teased its way between her cunney lips and plunged into her juicy, wet furrow. Slowly I edged my cock deeper and deeper inside her and wave after wave of exquisite pleasure rolled through every fibre of my being. I was tempted to ram my rigid rod in at speed, but I held back and instead of rushing in and out in a mad frenzy, I pumped my pulsating prick in and out of her clinging cunney at a reasonable pace, going all the way in and then withdrawing all but the very tip of my knob before plunging in again to the full.

I have found this method of fucking to be preferred by the vast majority of girls and it certainly had the desired effect on Estelle, whose bottom began to roll around as she arched her back, working her wet cunney back and forth against my thrusting tool. Estelle loved to fuck and she gasped: 'Come on now, big boy, I want that thick prick of yours to make my cunt tingle!' as she turned her head to watch us in action in the long mirror which had been set up against the wall.

Nothing loath, I sheathed my cock so fully inside her that my balls nestled against her bum cheeks. Then I began to stroke my prick in and out, faster and faster, building up to a spend and I shuddered with pleasure as I felt the moment of spending was near. I shot my spunk into her receptive love channel with a hoarse grunt, panting with pleasure as the muscles of her cunt tightened gloriously around my shaft as with a gigantic woosh! the squirts of sticky, white froth burst out from my knob, hot and seething into her nook. Gush after gush exploded out of my cock until the last faint dribblings oozed out of my excited penis, but I continued to drive my still-stiff shaft to and fro until Estelle cried out in joy as she, too, orgasmed and thrashed around in the glorious ecstasy of her shattering climax.

Her blood was up and after a few minutes' rest, we changed positions and I lay on my back and Estelle took hold of my cock and manipulated the soft shaft between her palms until it stood up again, stiff and hard as a rock and ready for another joust. 'Stay where you are, Mr Nash,' she cooed as she rubbed my shaft in the vale between her uptilted breasts with their deep red nipples. Then, kneeling before me, she slung my legs over her shoulders, and taking my shaft in her hands, began to tongue my palpitating ballsack. Then she moved up to embrace my helmet with her generous lips, opening her mouth and sucking in my prick until it almost touched her throat.

How wonderfully Estelle sucked me off! Up and down, up and down bobbed her pretty head until, with a low throaty growl, she changed the steady movements into an frenetic circling pattern until I could stand it no longer. I shouted: 'I'm going to spunk, I can't hold back — do you want it in your mouth or in your cunt?'

For reply, Estelle's adroit tongue continued to ply up and over my knob which made me squirm with pleasure and now she gobbled my twitching tool in earnest, slurping greedily as she felt my sperm pumping up the glistening stem ready to explode in her mouth. She craned forward and somehow managed to force the entire length of my prick into her mouth, her lips almost touching my balls. The sensations were unbelievably erotic as my cock pulsed under the stimulation of this lush tonguing, and I ejaculated a torrent of frothy white jism into her hot mouth as she cupped my balls in her hands as she milked my prick, swallowing every *last drop of salty essence which she gulped down with evident enjoyment.*

As we lay recovering from this fine joust, we heard the conductor calling out that we would arrive in Washington in twenty minutes' time. Hastily, we dressed ourselves and exchanged addresses. Estelle agreed to dine with me that evening at my hotel where we made up a foursome with Count Labovitch and a sensuous Russian girl named Sasha — but I would blush even to write of what occurred afterwards upstairs in my suite.

Give my love and best wishes to all.

I put down the letter and idly rubbed my warm, tingling cunney as I thought of all the naughty games David Nash, who is one of the sturdiest cocksmen it has been my pleasure to know, and his friends would have played in his bedroom in the smart Washington hotel. I wriggled my knickers down over my bum and began to frig myself, using my thumb to massage my clitty as I slipped my fingers in and out of my tingling crack which was already very wet. My hips jerked wildly as I spread my legs and then I came in a sudden release, clamping my legs about my hand, my inner thighs gleaming with my juices as I sank back on the pillow.

It was time now for a well-deserved nap, for unless Lord Philip Pelham had suddenly decided to take holy orders (which would have been a most unlikely change of heart by the pleasure-loving young rascal) I not only had a wonderful feast of music to look forward to but also a night of intimate intrigue and all the thrills of lustful delights. For Lord Philip (the son of Viscount Cheadle) never failed to drain to the very dregs the cup of physical pleasure, and I speculated that it would be many hours before I would see any other bed again except, of course, to engage in Lord Philip's and my own favourite activity!

2

If Music Be The Food Of Love

I was reading the afternoon newspaper when, at seven-fifteen precisely, the front doorbell rang and moments later old Simpson the butler opened the doors of the drawing room and announced the arrival of my beau, Lord Philip Pelham, and I must say that the handsome young scallywag looked even more dashing than ever in his evening dress and flowing silk cape which he had carelessly draped around his shoulders.

'Rosie, my dearest girl, how absolutely marvellous to see you again,' he beamed as he kissed my hand. 'And not only do you look as charming and as pretty as a picture, for I would have expected nothing less, but you are obviously ready to leave without delay. I so appreciate punctuality and my driver will be relieved that he will not have to race like the devil to make sure we are in our seats in time for the overture.'

'Punctuality is the politeness of kings, Philip. I hate to be kept waiting myself and so I do try not to waste the time of others, especially such friends as yourself who have much better things to do than wait around for me. Oh yes, and that reminds me, would you mind very much taking the keys of the house from Simpson — as we may be home very late I did not wish to keep him away from his bed just to lock up after I come home.'

'How thoughtful of you, my sweet girl, of course it will

57

be my pleasure,' he cried and then lowering his voice he added: 'It will also allow us some latitude after the concert, won't it?'

Simpson handed over the keys and wished us a pleasant evening. The evening air was brisk and I was glad to see that Philip had purchased one of the new Rolls Royce motors with these new adjustable windows which one can pull up or down according to the weather, and here I must digress for a moment to note the vast difference between the early motor cars with all their imperfections and the modern vehicles with their engines which start automatically and other vast improvements. What a difference there is between motoring as it is today and as it was only five years back.

Mellor, his new young driver, opened the door smartly for us and we climbed into the back. After he had adjusted a smart grey alpaca rug over our laps, Philip immediately snaked his hand around my waist. 'Ah, how wonderful to hold you in my arms again, Rosie, it's been far, far too long since we last made love,' he murmured softly, nibbling my ear as he squeezed me closer to him.

'Oh come now, Philip,' I teased, stroking his cheek with my fingers. 'It's only been three months and I hope you won't try to convince me that you have been living in a monastery since then. For a start, I saw your photograph in *The Tatler* not so long ago at Elspeth Didsbury's coming-out party at her parents' house in Bedford Square. If you didn't fuck Elspeth then I'm sure you speared some other girl with that naughty cock of yours. Come now, tell me the truth, I promise I won't be annoyed.'

'I didn't fuck Elspeth,' he protested with a chuckle. 'Though I must admit that it wasn't for lack of trying. Alas, she fell for the charms of Mark Adams, one of my friends from the Varsity, and I hardly saw her for the rest of the evening.'

I looked directly into his merry brown eyes and said: 'Phil, you're being somewhat economical with the truth, for you may not have fucked Elspeth but in that case, I would like

58

to know the name of the girl with whom you did spend the night.'

Philip sighed heavily and looked up to the roof of the car. 'Give a dog a bad name,' he said mournfully. 'Still, you're quite right, I did indeed poke one of Elspeth's guests, a cousin of hers, as it happened, from Warwickshire by the name of Belinda Kirkland.

'It all became rather embarrassing, actually, because we had commandeered a room in the servants' quarters at the very top of the house. Well, just as I had rolled off the little minx, and I must say that she fucks like a rattlesnake — though why we imagine that this small reptile has an interesting sex life is beyond my comprehension — and we had just finished a most satisfactory coupling when we heard some strange sounds from the adjoining room, rather as if someone were shifting a large sack of flour around in a confined space.

'I listened again and now I could make out voices and pick out some words which left little doubt as to what was taking place next door! Belinda pressed her ear to the wall and exclaimed: "The saucy devils! Do you know, I think I can hear my little cousin Cecilia — but who on earth is the gentleman in there with her? I should very much like to find out."

' "Perhaps we should see what is afoot," I suggested, noticing the pink flush of excitement upon Belinda's face, "just to make sure all is well."

' "Oh yes, Philip," she agreed instantly. "After all, Cecilia (or Sissy as we all call her) is only seventeen and I think it is my duty to ensure that she is not being forced into doing anything against her will."

'I murmured some words to the effect that I could not believe that there were any gentlemen present at the party who would be caddish enough to force their unwanted attentions upon Sissy, but that it would be as well to check matters out for ourselves. We slipped on our dressing-gowns and crept out of the room then, holding our breath, barely daring to make a sound lest it should reveal our presence,

59

I gently eased open the door and peered through into the darkened room. However, the light from the passageway and a small table light on the chest of drawers illuminated the scene well enough for us. Sitting on the bed was a gentleman we may well see at the concert this evening. You have met him before, Rosie, as I introduced him to you at the charity ball we went to last October in aid of the East End Winter Relief Fund, and in the circumstances you will probably recall his name.'

I looked at Philip with a puzzled expression and said: 'I was introduced to a great many people at that function. You'll have to give me a clue.'

Philip smiled and tweaked my nose. 'This will make it too easy for you, but after you had met him I whispered to you that he was reputed to be one of the most well-endowed young men in London.'

'Robert Bacon,' I exclaimed and Philip chuckled. 'Right in one, Rosie, I knew you'd remember him once I'd mentioned his claim to fame.'

'*Touché*, Philip, but do tell me more, for I have heard a story about Mr Bacon from another source. My friend Katie told me an interesting anecdote about some fine fun she had with Robert when he was captain of cricket at St Trippett's College, and she was in her last term at St Hilda's.' [*see* Rosie Vol One: Her Intimate Diaries – *Editor*]

'You must tell me about it, Rosie. I know one shouldn't pass on scandalous gossip but as I always say, what else can you do with it! Anyhow, to return to my own story, Belinda and I could see Robert Bacon sitting on the bed facing us, his trousers and drawers lying in a heap on the floor and his shirt drawn up around his waist. Kneeling in front of him, wearing only a frilly pair of French knickers, was the enchanting, slender form of Sissy Kirkland and she was slowly frigging in her hands the stoutest member I have ever seen in my life. The lascivious couple were so intent on their business that they continued, unaware that Belinda and I were watching them from the doorway. Sissy's lips were now kissing his helmet and her tongue began to wash round the huge pink dome.

' "I don't think I can take it all in," she said doubtfully, but Robert urged her to try. "Do the best you can, my dearest," he panted and the young girl took him at his word, opening her mouth to gobble in as much of his veiny, ivory staff as she could. This way and that she played with it in her mouth, now sucking deep, now licking only the very tip of his knob with her soft, velvet tongue. Robert ruffled her hair as she worked his monstrous member in and out between her lips and he gasped: "What a wonderful sucking-off, but you'd better stop now or I'll shoot too quickly."

'Sissy rose from her knees as Robert stood up and positioned himself behind her. She now leaned forward and placed her hands on the bed, with her legs apart, and Robert clasped each of her gorgeous, rounded bum cheeks and pulled them apart, exposing her pussy and rear dimple as he asked: "Where would you like it, Sissy? In your pussy or up your bottom?"

' "In my cunney, Robert, in my wet, warm cunt, slide your lovely big cock right into my cunt and spunk me as hard as you can, my dear fellow," she squealed and in a trice he was behind her and I could see her hand reach back and steer Robert's rigid tool between the cleft of her bum cheeks and into her waiting, welcoming love channel. He found the mark and began slewing his tremendous tadger to and fro, sliding in and out of Sissy's sheath and she called out: "Aaah, you dear boy, I'm so *full*!" throwing all caution to the winds as she bucked and swayed in time with his urgent thrusts. "Fuck me with that enormous thick prick, you randy boy . . ."

'Robert's arms were now wrapped around her and his hands were squeezing her firm, high breasts which sent her really wild, and she thrashed around like a being demented as, rocking backwards and forwards she began to climax, and Robert now shouted out that he too was coming and I could almost feel the spunk shoot out of his cock myself as Sissy screamed: "Aaaah! Aaaah! More, more!" as he

61

flooded her cunt with bursts of sticky white jism, pumping out his copious emission until he was drained.

'I glanced down to see that my own cock had swollen up at the sight of this lewd *tableau vivant* and was poking its head through my robe. I looked across at Belinda and saw that she, too, had been most excited by the lascivious spectacle of this young couple engaged in the throes of *l'arte de faire l'amour* and was unashamedly frigging herself, sliding her fingers in and out of her juicy cunt.

'Without a word, I took hold of her arm and gently pulled her out into the passageway. I closed the door quietly on the young couple and guided Belinda back to our bedroom where we stripped off our robes and fucked ourselves silly for the rest of the night.'

I sighed and Philip took hold of my hand under the rug and boldly transferred it to his naked stiff cock which was standing ready for action. I had been so engrossed in listening to his tale that I had not noticed his hand steal down and undo his fly buttons. I made a fist round his hot, smooth-skinned shaft, but only rubbed it up and down for a few moments because, as I muttered to Robert, the whole evening lay ahead of us and I certainly did not want to waste his love cream in such a pedestrian manner.

'Come on, button yourself up, you naughty boy, we're already in Exhibition Road, which might be an apt place to show off your tackle, but I'd rather you didn't, if you don't mind,' I added jocularly as Mellor dextrously drove through a gap in the traffic which was already blocking the area around the Albert Hall. We came to a smooth stop outside the main entrance where a flunkey opened the door for us. 'Be back here at ten o'clock sharp,' Philip called out to our driver as he slid across the seat to get out onto the pavement.

'Good evening, Lord Pelham,' said a girl's voice beside us as we walked through into the concert hall. Philip looked across and his eyes lit up. 'Miss Matthews, how delightful to see you again. Rosie, may I present Miss Laura Matthews. Miss Matthews, may I introduce Miss Rosie d'Argosse.' We smiled at each other and I must say that I was taken with the looks of this extremely attractive girl. Her soft-featured pretty face was set off by a mass of brown curls and she was wearing a most fetching off-the-shoulder blue gown and, although she wore a fur stole, she was obviously blessed with large breasts, the tops of which spilled out over her dress.

'Surely you have not come alone,' said Philip to this divine creature, who giggled and said with a cheeky grin: 'Now, now, Philip, you know I don't often have to do that! I am being escorted by Mr Robert Bacon. Perhaps you are acquainted with the gentleman?'

'Yes, of course I am. How coincidental, his name cropped up in conversation just a few moments ago, didn't it, Rosie?'

'Indeed it did, and I do hope that I shall be able to meet this remarkable gentleman,' I said lightly.

'Remarkable? There's nothing remarkable about Robert,' said Laura Matthews. 'He spends his mornings at his club, his afternoons playing cricket or tennis and his evenings dining out at the best houses in London.'

I was tempted to mention the reason why I thought Mr Bacon remarkable, but I held my tongue, though Laura Matthews then added some words which showed that she must have been a member of Philip's hedonistic 'fast' set of young people who revelled in the pleasures of the flesh. She said that Robert was also something of an aesthete, having had an essay published in *Blackwoods' Magazine*, and had written a short poem which had just appeared in the latest issue of *The Cremorne*.

'Has he now?' said Philip with interest. 'Perhaps you would care to recite it to us.' But Laura shook her head and said: 'There's Robert over to your left. He's coming towards us and you may hear his verses from his own fair lips.'

We turned our heads and saw Robert Bacon struggling through the chattering crowd and waited until he managed to make his way to us. He was a good-looking young man, tall and well-made though by no means plump, and he was as fair-haired as I am, with the blue eyes and light colouring one would expect of a man with Scandinavian blood on the maternal side of his family. When he reached us he held out his hand to Philip. 'Hello, Philip, how are you? You know Laura, of course, but whilst I think I have been introduced to this charming lady, I must throw myself on her mercy and beg forgiveness, for I don't recall her name.'

Well, I wasn't offended in the slightest by Robert's honest confession. We had only met fleetingly some months before and I certainly took no umbrage. In fact I liked the cut of Rob's jib and was delighted when, on behalf of Laura and himself, he accepted Philip's invitation to join us at Zaines Café after the concert.

And of the concert, what can I say? Mr Elgar's First Symphony gave the enraptured audience music which filled the hall with a glorious feast of sound which ravished the ear and captured the heart. Typically English in its rhythms and cadences, I am certain that future generations of music lovers will treasure the work, and Elgar's name will be synonymous with the best music composed during this exciting first decade of the twentieth century. [*Elgar's First Symphony was rapturously received by the critics, and even such popular newspapers as the* Daily Mail *devoted a whole column of its front page to it — Editor*] On the way back to Zaines (which is situated in a tiny street just off Berkeley Square) I mused about how music can rack the emotions, being able to move us so much more than language, literature or the colours on canvas.

'Music is continually fertile, loved, ingenious, inexhaustible and perhaps the most open and accessible of all the arts,' I said to Philip upon whose shoulder I was leaning as we threaded our way through the traffic along Piccadilly. We arrived before Robert and Laura, and Signor Luigi, the owner of the high-class yet slightly raffish establishment, greeted us in person.

'We have a special cabaret later tonight, Milord. Do you wish to reserve seats after you have dined?' he asked. A large grin spread over Philip's face as he pressed a sovereign into the restaurateur's hand. 'Mr Bacon and his guest will be dining with us, Luigi. Please make sure we have four front-row seats for the show,' said Philip and Signor Luigi bowed his thanks and showed us to our table. Whilst we waited for Laura and Robert I studied the faces of the other diners and I whispered to Philip that there seemed to be a number of faces present which I was sure I had seen in the weekly illustrated magazines.

'Oh, the cream of London Society patronises Zaines,' said Philip airily as he studied the menu. 'The food and service are first class and it is essential to reserve a table these days. And the restaurant's cabaret shows put on upstairs are really something special. However, not all customers are told about these performances which take place on Tuesdays and Saturdays up on the first floor before an audience consisting solely of diners who have been personally invited by Signor Luigi.'

'Why ever not? Is there a lack of space? I would have imagined that Signor Luigi engages the finest singers and dancers for his shows,' I remarked innocently, and Philip almost choked with laughter.

'Well, not exactly,' he replied, 'though the cabaret at Zaines is reckoned to be by far the best entertainment of its kind in Europe.' I looked puzzled at this remark and he added: 'You'll see what I mean later, Rosie. Ah, Robert and Laura have just arrived.'

We enjoyed a delicious dinner suggested by Signor Luigi himself. After a tasty *antipasto di Ortaggi*, a dish of truffles, mushrooms, artichokes, fennel, peppers, celery, pickles and dressing, we continued with *Risotto con peoci alla Veneta*, a plate of rice with fish stock, mussels and garlic, and for our main course we were served the house speciality of *Abbacchio alla Alicia*, a tender, soft, roasted leg of lamb with quince and sherry sauce, with baked potatoes and a selection of vegetables followed by a home-made sorbet with a fruit compôte and profiteroles. We drank an unfamiliar but very pleasant white wine named Trebbiano d'Abruzzo from Signor Luigi's native central-southern region of Italy bordering the Adriatic and the high mountainous part of the Apennines.

'May I suggest that we retire to the room where coffee and liqueurs will be served?' suggested Philip, rising to his feet. 'The ladies' room is also upstairs, if Rosie and Laura wish to refresh themselves.'

We went upstairs after Signor Luigi had nodded to a doorman standing at the foot of the staircase that he could unhook the plaited red rope from the bars to allow us through. Then Laura and I made our way to the ladies' cloakroom where, after using the spotlessly clean facilities, I watched Laura tease her curls with a comb. A beautiful Slavic girl dressed in an exquisite pink gown and an elegant diamond necklace passed behind us and I stared after her in undisguised admiration as she opened the door and went outside.

'Laura, who on earth was that girl? I've never seen her before, but wasn't she just stunning!' I said enviously, and Laura gave a tiny smile. 'Her name is Countess Marussia from Samarkand. She certainly is stunning, and did you see that necklace? I'm sure I saw it in Smolask's windows in Bond Street and it was priced at two thousand pounds.'

'She must also be very wealthy,' I commented, but Laura shook her head and said: 'I don't think she will ever need to worry where her next meal is coming from, but the odds are that Prince Adrian of the Netherlands bought her that necklace. Robert knows him from his university days and says that the Prince is besotted by her.'

I mulled over her reply as we also went out and joined our partners in the room where the cabaret would take place. There were tables and chairs set out throughout the large, lavishly decorated room where, on a raised dais by the window, a string quartet played on manfully, though they could hardly be heard above the chatter. In the centre of the room, however, there was a circular, uncarpeted gap and this was illuminated by a small bank of stage lights at the back. Signor Luigi had been as good as his word and a waiter showed us to our table which was at the very front of the stage. Philip had ordered a pot of coffee and a bottle of Courvoisier brandy which was promptly brought to us. Then, to a smattering of applause, two flunkeys now carried in a mattress on the base of a double-sized bed. The mattress was covered with a crisp, sparkling white linen sheet and two fluffy pillows were placed upon it.

'I have never seen such curious stage arrangements for an opening number,' I said in all innocence, and Philip gave me a wicked smile and whispered in my ear: 'There will be no changes of scenery and nor do the artistes change their costumes, but nevertheless I think you will find this a most colourful spectacle.'

What the blazes did Philip mean? Well, I would just have to wait and see, so I sat back in my chair and listened to the musicians who were playing a selection of popular overtures. Robert leaned over to me and murmured: 'These musicians were all in the orchestra we heard earlier at the Albert Hall, you know. They may well have been as thrilled to perform Elgar's First Symphony as we were to hear it, but they can relax and play simple light pieces here — and get very well paid for it into the bargain. See the leader, Mr Webb? How extraordinary it is that a man of such huge physique can delicately coax such wonderful sounds out of his instrument. I am sure that at times he must almost lose it in that great beard of his, and yet it is said that he has but few peers in Europe.'

A waiter sidled up and asked if we required any further refreshment, as the show would be beginning very shortly. 'We'll have some more coffee during the interval, and bring a plate of *petits fours* for the ladies,' said Philip. 'Very good, my lord,' said the waiter, and Laura asked me if this was the first time I had watched a cabaret at Zaines. She said that she hoped I was not easily shocked. Curiouser and curiouser! I could hardly wait for the show to start.

I did not have long to wait and soon the lights dimmed and, to a great cheer from the table behind us where my papa's old friend Colonel Goldstone of the West Oxfordshire Rifles was entertaining a party of brother officers, Signor Luigi took the stage. 'My lords, ladies and gentlemen, once again it's cabaret time at Zaines! And to begin our show, directly from Sadler's Wells, dancing to the second movement of Schubert's Quartet in D Minor, a very warm welcome please for Miss Jenny Thirkettle and the aptly named Miss Carola Bedwell!'

Signor Luigi led the applause for the dancers who came out through the tables into soft beams of white light which lit up the stage as the rest of the room was plunged into near darkness. The two girls, one brunette and the other blessed with long silky strands of light auburn hair, were both wearing vaguely Grecian wisps of white muslin, through which one could plainly see the rounded contours of their breasts and the dark patches of hair between their legs. To the slow cadences of Schubert's beautiful music, they draped themselves on the mattress and entwined their limbs together, their hands busily running all over each other's bodies, nipping, squeezing and rubbing in the most lecherous manner. Carola, the brunette, took the lead in the proceedings as she laid her trembling partner face down upon the mattress, pulling up her hips so that her dimpled round buttocks were directly facing our table. Jenny shyly raised her head from the pillow and smiled, upon which Carola raised up Jenny's skirt over her waist and the beautiful white spheres of her glorious bum cheeks were laid bare to us.

Carola started to stroke these deliciously soft globes, and then she slipped her hand between Jenny's slender thighs, and my pussy began to moisten as I saw the pretty girl quiver with delight as Carola's long, tapering fingers began to caress her pussy. She wriggled out of her skimpy costume and lay naked as Carola frigged her slit until she gracefully turned over to lie on her back. Carola tore off her own skimpy robe and, with her arms raised as she pulled off her top, displayed a pair of smallish but superbly proportioned breasts, proudly uptilted with large cherry nipples which all the men must have ached to suck.

Now they were both nude, Carola continued plunging her

fingers in and out of Jenny's auburn muff. I sighed with envy for there are few more pleasurable things in life than feeling an enquiring digit seeking out and playing with one's clitty, to be followed by having a head clamped between one's legs and a questing tongue probing delicately at one's notch, licking and lapping around the entrance to the juicy, wet honeypot.

Carola was now performing just this service upon the lucky girl and her bum was now wriggling lasciviously at us and, through her parted legs, I could see the outline of her cunney lips through the tangled strands of pussy hair. Jenny screamed with delight as Carola slipped a hand behind her and began to frig her little wrinkled bum hole as she sucked noisily on her sopping sheath. We sat back and watched with the fullest attention as the two tribades cleverly moved themselves into a *soixante-neuf* position, each tonguing the other's cunt, and I could see Jenny's juices dribbling like honey from her parted pussy lips as Carola flicked gently with her darting wet tongue at Jenny's erect, pink clitty. At the same time, Jenny was giving Carola's furry bush a thorough tonguing, soaking her curly hairs with saliva as she worked her tongue deeper and deeper into her soaking snatch.

The brunette certainly had a splendid cunt covered with glossy dark hair, and from the serrated vermilion lips of her pussy a stiff, fleshy clitty projected as big as a boy's cock. Jenny opened the lips further with her fingers and passed her tongue lewdly about it, playfully nipping it with her teeth. It was too much for Carola who cried out: 'A-h-r-e! A-h-r-e! I'm coming, darling!' and she spent profusely all over the other girl's mouth and chin.

Jenny then sank down and opened her legs to allow Carola to repay the pleasure she owed her. She raised herself above Jenny, who pulled open her own cunney so that Carola was able to direct her clitty inside it, and then closed her hand upon Jenny's mound, holding the love lips together with her hand until her partner spent with a shudder and slumped back with a happy beam on her face. This was an interesting

69

method of fucking I had not seen before, and I joined in the round of applause which spontaneously broke out from other spectators in the front seats who could see in detail this novel conjunction.

The girls scrambled off the bed and took a well-deserved bow, and the musicians changed from playing Schubert to a rousing chorus of a popular music hall ditty as Carola and Jenny snatched up their robes and walked briskly out of the spotlights back to their dressing room. Behind me I noticed Colonel Goldstone scribble a note on the back of a menu and pass it to a hovering waiter. Rob Bacon whispered to me: 'I'll wager a pound to a penny that the Colonel has asked those girls back to his rooms after the show. It'll cost him a pretty penny, too, as I know that Luigi advises them never to accept invitations from stage door johnnies for less than fifty guineas.'

I barely had time to digest this information when Signor Luigi was back on stage in his role as master of ceremonies. 'And now, ladies and gentlemen,' he cried, 'for the first time at Zaines, directly from New Orleans, we proudly present Amy and Lester in *A Black And White Odyssey*.'

The little band struck up *Way Down Upon The Swanee River* and a handsome young Negro came onto the stage. He was wearing only tight-fitting athletic shorts, and whilst his head was covered with frizzy curls, his features were finely chiselled and his skin was of a light chocolate hue which would suggest that he had at least one Caucasian amongst his grandparents. His physique was superb and when he took up an Atlas-style pose, the muscles fairly rippled down his bended arm and when he stood up, Laura said softly to me: 'What a magnificent specimen. Look at the width of his chest and how his torso narrows down to a flat stomach and narrow hips.'

He turned so that his back was facing the audience and he stretched out his arm to welcome his partner, Amy, onto the stage. She, too, was of mixed blood, her skin perhaps a shade lighter than Lester's, and she wore a low-cut white dress which accentuated both the lovely light brown colour

70

of her skin and the swell of her generous breasts. Amy's figure was Rubenesque in build, though she had a sensual oval face with dark fiery eyes.

With his broad back still facing us, Lester pulled down his shorts and I am sure that I was not the only lady to gasp with admiration at the sight of his lean, muscular flanks and then, as he turned around, at the sight of his heavy, dangling shaft which was of a meaty thickness one rarely encounters, and I must confess that the thought of sucking that enormous brown cock made my pussy tingle.

Amy stepped out of her dress and, as it fell to the ground, she stepped out quite nude like a dark Venus rising from the waves. Her breasts were large but firm, with big nipples set in rounded areolae, and as she moved across to embrace her partner, the lights gleamed on the shiny skin of the rounded cheeks of her bottom.

Seemingly quite oblivious to the presence of the sixty or so entranced spectators, Lester returned Amy's embraces and glued his mouth to hers in a long, passionate kiss. They fell down upon the bed and, as their bodies writhed around, one of his hands soon found her hard, cork-like nipples whilst the other pressed down upon the bushy tuft of black hair between her legs. Then, with surprising agility for such a big man, he effortlessly laid Amy down with one pillow behind her head and another under her backside, and his head was between her legs with his arms stretched up to allow his fingers to play with her engorged, elongated titties.

Lester was obviously skilled at cunnilingus because — unless she was putting on a show for those watching which I somehow doubt — Amy yelped with pleasure as his tongue ran along the edges of her pussy lips before flicking inside to lash itself around her clitty. He lifted up her hips and held her pussy against his mouth, which we could clearly see from our seats just a couple of yards away. She cried with joy as his pink tongue thrust into her cunney, stabbing in and out as his hands kneaded the chubby cheeks of her bum. Now he slurped harder in slow, rhythmic strokes, kissing and sucking her pussy, rubbing his large, moist lips

71

against her cunt, mingling his saliva with her love juice, and I sensed the waves of arousal which must have been coursing through Amy's body.

'Look at his prick,' said Laura softly. 'Have you ever seen such a monster cock before? Ah, the very idea of letting that monster slide into my nookie is making my knickers wet.'

Sensing perhaps that Amy was approaching the heights of ecstasy too soon, Lester abruptly pulled back his head and flipped the luscious girl over onto her tummy. Her hips and plump arse cheeks were raised high in the air as he moved between her thighs, nudging her knees further apart and taking his enormous cock in his hand, carefully guiding the huge, uncapped knob into her dripping pussy and starting to fuck her in a full, steady rhythm, burying his proud prick up to the hairs as his heavy, dangling ballsack banged against the backs of Amy's thighs. His arms slid round and cupped her breasts in his hands, holding them in a firm grip as he continued to pump in and out of her juicy cunt.

Her bum cheeks slapped sensuously against Lester's legs as she fitted into the rhythm he established as he pounded away, and we relished the sight of his gleaming brown cock see-sawing in and out of her cunney, above which the tiny rosebud of her bum-hole quivered and winked with each stroke. Reaching behind her, Amy caressed his big balls in her hand as she rocked to and fro, her head thrown back and her hair whipping from side to side. Amy was obviously spending as she yelled out her delight, and Lester now pumped faster and faster and several members of the audience were now on their feet, urging him on. At the very final stage he pulled out his gleaming, twitching tool and shot floods of creamy white seed spurting all over Amy's bum cheeks to an almost deafening roar of applause.

As Amy and Lester took their bows, behind me Colonel Goldstone was passing round a small bowl into which his brother officers were all chipping in silver coins. The gallant Colonel then rose and walked over to our table.

'I thought those two deserved a tangible expression of

appreciation. Care to chuck in a couple of sovs from your table, my lord?' he asked, and Philip immediately dived into his pocket and threw in a handful of coins. The Colonel also received a generous contribution from Prince Adrian and Countess Marussia before he walked onto the stage and presented the artistes with their unexpected gratuity.

He was rewarded by a kiss from Amy who was still standing naked and Lester, who had now pulled on his shorts, stood up at the front of the stage and made an announcement! 'Ladies and gentlemen, may we now offer you a speciality which we take part in at the Rising Sun *club privée* in Basin Street, New Orleans. Would any lady or gentleman here celebrating a birthday care to make themselves known by standing up.'

An excited buzz ran round the audience, but no-one rose to their feet. 'Well, we are looking for a lucky lady or gentleman who perhaps has an anniversary of some kind today,' suggested Lester in his deep, slightly accented voice (Philip later told me that he was a Creole from Louisiana and as I had suspected, there was a good deal of French blood in his family) and Robert Bacon murmured: 'I suppose that I have an anniversary to celebrate. It is five years to the day since my very first fuck.'

'Many congratulations,' said Philip jocularly. 'May I offer your cock my heartiest congratulations and best wishes for the future.'

'Thank you,' said Robert modestly. 'Come to think of it, today is also the fifth anniversary of my second and third fucks as well.'

'How extraordinary,' I said with great surprise. 'That really does sound far too complicated for me to take in.'

'Not really, Rosie,' he grinned. 'One day, three fucks, all one after the other with a trio of girls from our country estate near Sevenoaks in Kent.'

Philip stared at him with an open mouth and then with a mixture of admiration and jealousy in his voice, 'My goodness, Robert, you certainly started with a bang!' he commented.

Robert looked a trifle self-satisfied, so I decided to take up Lester's invitation on his behalf. I stood up and the spotlight played upon my face.

'Ah, ha, the lady over here has something to celebrate this evening!' cried out the big black man.

'No, I don't have,' I shouted back, throwing out my arm and pointing at Robert, 'but my friend over here has!' Laura and Philip entered into the spirit of things by rising to their feet and applauding Robert who, being a good sport, slowly rose to his feet.

'Come here, sir, don't be shy,' called Amy. 'Let me help you celebrate in style!'

With a shrug, Robert went over to her and she grabbed hold of him and whispered something softly into his ear. He looked nonplussed for a moment or two, but then gave a grin and this was the signal for Lester to wave to the band who struck up the haunting melody from Tchaikovsky's *Andante Cantabile*. The lights dimmed except for a blue spotlight which played upon Amy and Robert. She helped him to disrobe to a further round of applause from the audience, and I write unashamedly that the sight of Robert Bacon's superb, manly frame sent the blood coursing through my veins in a frenzy of sexual excitement.

His shoulders were so broad and his deep chest was lightly covered with fine, light brown hair and the swell of his dimpled buttocks raised my appetite for a fuck to fever pitch, especially when Amy proceeded to take hold of his thick prick which was rising majestically between his legs as he sat on the edge of the bed. It stood stiffly to attention, as erect as a guardsman on duty, throbbing rhythmically as Amy moved her hands round to stroke his swollen shaft. Robert gurgled with delight as she jerked her hand up and down his veiny staff and they kissed and embraced as if they wished to lose themselves completely within the other — to let their senses be pervaded by the touch of skin, the sensual aroma of aroused passion . . .

Their gentle caresses rapidly acquired an urgency as their naked bodies pressed together, and then Amy broke out of

74

their embrace and lay on her back, arching her body like a sleek black cat as Robert knelt between her legs. He started to kiss her feet, her ankles, her calves and her knees and then, as he began to lick her inner thighs, his hands all the while massaging her wonderfully full breasts, Amy opened her legs wide, fully exposing her luxuriant bush of curly cunney hair and her pouting, pink cunney lips between which jutted out a pert, stiff clitty.

Robert buried his head between her thighs and we could hear (if not see) him pay homage to her open cunt. I craned my head to one side and saw him flick his tongue in and out of her cunney lips and then his hand came down from her titties to roll the bursting little clitty between a thumb and forefinger.

Philip cleared his throat and said: 'Robert really loves pussy, doesn't he? Did you read his little couplet in *The Cremorne*:

Now cunt is a kingdom, and cock is its lord,
A whore is a slave and her mistress a bawd;
Her quim is her freehold which brings in her rent;
For you pay when you enter and leave when you've spent!'

As aforesaid, my whole body was racked by desire and now matters took a turn to show that I was not alone in being stimulated almost beyond endurance by this erotic tableau. To the muttered encouragement of Colonel Goldstone, a girl at an adjoining table stood up and began unbuttoning her dress. I tapped Laura and Philip's arms to attract their attention and Philip muttered: 'Well, well, Philippa Brimsdown's going to join in. This should be fun to watch.'

'She's one of the Leicestershire Brimsdowns,' explained Laura. 'Rather a feisty young lady whose voracious sexual appetite has enlivened many a gathering.'

'Very much so,' said Philip drily. 'There was that business at Ascot four years ago on Derby Day when she sucked off old Tum-Tum [*Society's semi-secret colloquial nick-name for King Edward VII, which fortunately never reached the ears of the King, who, though personally in many ways was a paternally minded hedonist, would never countenance the slightest irreverency regarding his own person or that of the monarchy — Editor]*

Urged on by Colonel Goldstone, Philippa now stood naked and ran on stage to a great burst of applause. She was a well-made girl with pert, uplifted breasts topped by luscious, big red nipples and her mound was covered with a thick profusion of rich auburn hair. She stood for a moment behind Robert, admiring no doubt his lean, masculine bum and then she slid her head under his parted knees — for he was still on all fours whilst he continued to suck vigorously on Amy's juicy cunt — so that her mouth was positioned just below his stiffstander. She grasped it in her hand and levered herself up so as to be able to kiss the shiny, uncapped knob, and then she opened her mouth and popped his helmet between her lips, eagerly licking this tasty morsel as she gently cupped his hairy ballsack in her hands.

Philippa now began to frig herself as she happily slurped away on Robert's throbbing tool, swirling her tongue around his wide, smooth-skinned helmet until short, convulsive jerks of his cock heralded an approaching spend and, sure enough, Robert squirted a frothy libation of sperm into Philippa's mouth, filling her mouth with gushing foam and she gulped it down with delight, sucking out every last milky drop of jism as she brought herself off with a great shudder and sank back sated on to the bed.

I stole a glance across to my companions and I saw that Laura's hand was down in her lap as her palm pressed against her tingling pussy, and not surprisingly I noted that a huge bulge had formed in Philip's trousers as he sat transfixed before the erotic spectacle which still had a further course to run. For Amy now wriggled round to kneel on all fours, thrusting her shiny, smooth bum in front of Robert's face. She turned her head round and said in a soft voice which nevertheless carried to where we were sitting:

'Mr Bacon, I've been fucked three times already this evening by Lester and Signor Luigi and my pussy's a little sore. So how would you like to fuck my bottom? I'd really prefer that, to be truthful.'

'By all means,' Robert replied politely and I was staggered to see his cock, which only just before had been so exhaustively milked by Philippa Brimsdown.

He took his now-fully-recovered hard, stiff rod in his hand and after greasing it with pomade from a jar provided by Lester who had stolen up beside the couple, positioned it between her bum cheeks. He drove forward towards the puckered little bum-hole which awaited his arrival, and Amy relaxed her buttocks as he drove forward, inserting his knob and about three inches of his shaft which she accommodated apparently without the slightest discomfort.

Indeed, she must have been pleased enough with this situation for she turned her head round again and said to him: 'Press on, Mr Bacon, press on! I want you to squirt a creamy wodge of spunk up my bum!'

Well, Robert did his best to please and Amy must have been blessed with an exquisitely tight back passage, for Robert's prick rose in and out of her arse at will whilst he passed his hand round to fondle her big, dark nipples and kissed the nape of her neck. His tool plunged to and fro out of her widened orifice, pumping and sucking like the thrust of an old railway engine, and Amy reached back with her hands and spread her cheeks even further apart as Robert quickened the pace of the fucking until he managed to ensheath almost all of his sturdy shaft inside her bum, corking her to the limit as her globular buttocks were drawn irresistibly tight against his pleasingly flat tummy.

Robert's arm now snaked round Amy's waist and his fingers dived into the curly bush of pussy hair and he slid his fingertips in and out of her juicy cunt and she worked her gleaming rump from side to side, wriggling lewdly until, with a throaty growl, Robert spunked inside her, shooting a flood of his creamy jism which must have warmed and lubricated her stretched rear dimple.

Instinctively I led the well-merited round of applause and Amy and Robert took a bow before she skipped off with Lester, and Signor Luigi came on stage with a blue towelling robe which he tossed to Robert, who slipped it on whilst he gathered up his discarded clothes. Signor Luigi announced that there would now be an interval of half an hour and, whilst we waited for Robert to return, a waiter came up to Philip and passed him a folded sheet of paper. 'A note from the table directly across the floor, my lord,' he said, and Philip quickly scanned its contents. He looked up and said to Laura: 'Here's some interesting news for you. No less a lady that Countess Marussia of Samarkand has invited us all to her house in Grosvenor Square for a late night party after the show.'

Countess Marussia! This was the exquisite lady I had asked Laura about in the cloakroom before we sat down to watch the cabaret. 'How marvellously exciting, I'd love to go,' I said eagerly, but Philip looked a mite anxious and he wagged a warning finger at me. 'Hold on a moment, Rosie, the Countess's parties can be pretty wild affairs, you know,' he said.

'Oh come on, Philip, don't be a wet blanket, we'll all have great fun there. Aren't we all known to be young, wild and willing?' declared Laura as Robert came back to the table, looking none the worse for his performance. She gave him a kiss on the cheek as he sat down and added: 'You're not too tired to go on to Countess Marussia's, are you? Or has that pretty coloured girl sapped all your strength?'

Robert grinned and said that he was game if we others were of a like mind, so Philip threw his hands up in surrender and said: 'Very well, on your own heads be it. Mind, as Prince Adrian of the Netherlands is with her, I dare say things won't get too outrageous, though with Marussia, you never know!'

Philip brought out the Waterman's fountain pen I had given him for his last birthday and hastily scrawled back a short reply accepting the kind invitation. He passed it to the waiter who crossed the floor and gave our affirmative reply back to the Countess who, after scanning Philip's answer, smiled broadly and waved to him. Philip ordered another pot of coffee and, whilst we were waiting, the Countess herself walked over to our table. Philip and Robert scrambled to their feet and Philip performed the introductions.

'Mr Bacon I have met before,' she said in an attractively husky, low voice. 'And after watching him in action tonight, I would like to get to know him more intimately. Miss Matthews and Miss d'Argosse, it is a pleasure to meet you both and I look forward to welcoming you to my house a little later this evening.' She paused for a moment and then said to me: 'Miss d'Argosse, your name is very familiar to me. Let me think for a moment . . . ah, yes, are you by any chance related to Lord Gordon MacChesney?'

'Yes, I am, Your Excellency. Uncle Gordon, that is to say, Lord MacChesney, is my mother's brother.'

'Very good,' she said with satisfaction. 'I rarely forget a name and yours came up in conversation when I met your uncle last summer.

'We were both guests at a weekend gathering at Count Gewirtz's villa in Tuscany,' she explained with a smile. 'Please give your uncle my kindest regards. He was a most stimulating dinner table companion, and I enjoyed his company as I am sure I will enjoy yours. Goodbye for now, Miss d'Argosse.'

The Countess, Prince Adrian and another couple left Zaines before the lights went down and the second half of the show began. The lights dimmed and Signor Luigi called out: 'Ladies and gentlemen, we present an historical sketch set two hundred and fifty years ago featuring Mr Stanley Wright of Drury Lane as the Merry Monarch, King Charles II and Miss Georgina Glenthorne, one of our leading young *ingénues* in the rôle of Nell Gwynne.'

Dressed in fine costumes which must have been hired from a leading theatrical costumier, the two thespians made their entrance. Mr Wright made a regal Charles II and Miss Glenthorne a particularly attractive Nell Gwynne, dressed in a simple, tight-fitting blouse and a short skirt, holding a basket of oranges. 'What is wrong with my oranges, sire? You have never complained about them before.'

'Whichever merchant you purchased them from deserves to be well whipped,' replied the king. 'The fruit is bitter with many pips and little juice. Nell, dearest, I regret that I must buy elsewhere.'

'Pray don't desert me, Your Majesty,' she pleaded, 'for how else am I to earn an honest living? Would you have me become a needlewoman and live by the prick of my fingers?'

The king paused and grinned lewdly at the audience, and he threw his hat down upon the bed. 'Perhaps that wouldn't be such a bad idea,' he commented as he sat down on the mattress.

Nell frowned and put down her basket on the floor. 'I have a much better idea, sire,' she said, and tearing open her blouse revealed the awesome beauty of her gorgeous bare breasts. They were soft and globular, each looking a little way from each other and tapering in lovely curves until they came to the two rich crimson points of her nipples. She shrugged off her blouse as she sat down next to King Charles and tweaked her large titties with her own fingers until they were as taut as two tiny red rocks, and then she cupped her bosoms in her hands and thrust them to within an inch of the king's nose!

'Here, Your Majesty,' she said sweetly, pressing her right nipple forward and proffering it to his lips. 'Try my fresh, ripe melons. I will guarantee that you will find them sweeter by far than the oranges. Taste them for yourself and see.'

He nodded his head sagely and started to nibble on her engorged tittie, and she moved across to take up a more comfortable position, unwrapping her skirt as she did so and, to no-one's surprise, she was wearing no drawers and so now sat totally naked on the king's lap. Naturally, the sight and feel of her nude body had the required effect upon the king's cock and she put her hand on his swelling shaft

80

and gave it a friendly rub through the shiny blue satin of his trousers.

'Let not a piece of fine cloth come between friends,' he declaimed as he unbuttoned himself and felt inside for his prick, which sprang out like a newly released metal coil. Their lips met and his hand strayed to her pussy and she twisted her legs over his hand as she lowered her head to kiss the mushroom dome of the royal cock. But after a quick lick she lifted her mouth away and said: 'Sire, we would enjoy this far more if you divested yourself of your clothes.'

'Another splendid idea, Mistress Nell, and I will readily heed your advice. Just allow me a few moments to throw off these wretched garments and I will be with you directly.'

He swiftly shed his clothes and I took good note of his squat, hard cock which stood up almost flat against his belly. Although not the biggest of weapons, it was of a very sizeable thickness which I rightly surmised would perform its function admirably. The naked couple now embraced and rolled over onto the bed and the king let his hands drop onto Nell's lusciously fleshy bum cheeks whilst he pressed her pussy against his iron-hard shaft which he rubbed against her.

Despite being watched by some sixty pairs of eyes, Nell looked as if she were really enjoying herself. She carefully opened her legs to give us all an excellent view as she spread open her cunney lips, revealing the glistening interior of her pink love channel. The king now knelt beside her and moved his hand across to her pussy. Slowly at first but then with increasing speed, he dipped one and then two fingers in her honeypot and Nell began to gasp and roll from side to side as he frigged her with great style, rubbing the tip of her clitty and taking the delicious girl to the very brink of spending.

'Would you like me to fuck you now, Nell?' he asked.

'Oh yes! yes! yes! Slam the regal rod right up my cunt!' Nell panted and slowly the king moved on top of her. She writhed in excitement, opening her legs wide and then clamping them round his waist so that her pretty feet drummed against his spine as he pressed his cock deep into her sopping slit. Straightaway she took up the rhythm of his thrusts and they rocked together in an immensely passionate fuck.

Nell's legs began to tremble and she arched her torso upwards to meet the fierce driving force of his surging strokes. Again and again he pounded in and out of her dripping crack and then to my surprise, quite suddenly — to give the spectators value for money, as he later explained — the king reared up over her. He gripped his twitching prick hard, gave it three or four long, hard rubs and sprayed Nell's breasts and belly with rivulets of sticky, white spunk. Then when he had finished, he brought her off with his hand as the band struck up *Rule Britannia* and the audience gave the two magnificent performers a hearty round of applause.

Signor Luigi announced there would be a further intermission, and Philip suggested that we should leave at this juncture if the company still wanted to go on to Countess Marussia's house.

'Quite right, Phil, watching all this splendid fucking is all very well, but it is somewhat like chewing gum which stimulates the desire without slaking it,' said Laura, rising to her feet.

'Very well, by all means let us make tracks. Perhaps the ladies would like to meet us in the reception area downstairs,' said Robert. 'Philip, you must let me put tonight's expenses on my account.'

'No, no, my dear chap, I insist on settling the bill,' Philip protested. I don't know who finally won this argument (I think in fact they took up Signor Luigi's suggestion that they split the cost of the evening squarely down the middle) but twenty minutes later, Mellor was pulling in Philip's lovely new Rolls Royce in front of number sixty-nine Grosvenor Square.

'Countess Marussia could not have chosen a more appropriate address,' said Philip wryly as Mellor jumped out of the car to open the door for me. As we were standing on the pavement, Robert Bacon's Mercedes-Benz saloon came smoothly to a halt behind our vehicle. His smart grey uniformed chauffeur opened the door for his passengers and Robert instructed him to wait outside. 'There's an all-night coffee stall in Mount Street, Topping. Here's a florin [*a two shilling piece (worth twenty-four 'old' pennies or ten pence in post 1971 currency) which was a generous gift as coffee or tea at one of these stalls would have only cost 2d (one p) at most − Editor*]. Go there and get yourself a hot drink and something to eat − and take Lord Pelham's man with you and treat him to whatever he wants,' he said kindly. 'I don't expect we'll be out for a good while yet, but I'd like you back here within the hour in case we decide not to stay.'

We walked up the steps to the front door and Philip pressed the electric bell. It was opened by a bearded servant dressed in a white Slavonic-style outfit of an open-necked blouson and baggy pantaloons.

'Milord Pelham, Mr Bacon? Come this way, if you please. The Countess is expecting you,' he said in good if heavily accented English. We followed him through the hallway to the drawing room. He knocked on one of the double doors and opened it. 'Your guests have arrived, Your Excellency,' he announced to his mistress, who was sitting on a sofa with Prince Adrian of the Netherlands. And who else should be there, standing with glasses of champagne in their hands, but Colonel Leon Goldstone together with Jenny Thirkettle and Carola Bedwell, the two pretty tribades whose charms, you will recall, dear diary, had so captivated the gallant Colonel that he had sent a note to them after their performance.

Countess Marussia made the necessary introductions and Prince Adrian, her amiable consort, poured out some champagne for us from a magnum sitting on a silver salver which was placed on a beautifully carved Louis XIV serving table upon which there was a buffet of platters of delicately cut smoked salmon, cucumber and other sandwiches along with plates of cold meats and devilled chicken, though how anyone could want to eat after our magnificent dinner was quite beyond my comprehension.

Perhaps my face showed my surprise at the sumptuous collation which had been prepared, for when I refused Prince Adrian's offer of food he said to me: 'Well, you may not want anything now, Miss d'Argosse, but after a little exercise it's surprising how hungry one gets.'

We all chatted gaily about the cabaret at Zaines — and naturally, all the guests complimented Jenny and Carola on their stirring performance earlier in the evening. Then at the Countess's invitation, Philip sat down at the Steinway grand piano and began to play a Chopin *étude*. I sat down in one of the soft, low armchairs and as I gazed upwards, my attention was drawn to the high, decorated ceiling, upon which I suddenly realised had been painted in light colours an extraordinary erotic fantasy.

The centrepiece was nothing less than an immense cunt from between the lips of which extended a large carved cock with balls attached from which hung a magnificent chandelier. Around this was a scene in a Parisian *thé-dansant* and depicted on a chair was a young nude couple, the girl seated on the lap of her lover. Between her voluptuous thighs, her pussy was shown to be delightfully stretched by his huge, stiffstanding prick and her arms were thrown around his neck and her smiling face was turned up towards him, beaming with the pleasure afforded by her well-filled love sheath. Around them danced a number of equally naked couples with their cocks and cunnies presented in the most exciting points of view. One man was pressing the soft buttocks of his partner, whilst she held his erect shaft in her loving grasp. Another fellow was shown squeezing the ripe breasts of his beloved whilst she cupped his pendulous ballsack in her hands.

'Do you like the mural?' enquired Prince Adrian as he sat down on the arm of my chair. 'It was designed and painted by the German artist Kneidel under Marussia's direction. When news of the idea was given to our friends, like myself many of them begged to be immortalised in the work. See, over there in the corner with his hands roving across the blonde girl's breasts is Count Gewirtz of Galicia, and on the left hand side is Lady Holingberry sucking the cock of Sergei Oskedufft, the famous violinist.'

'Where is your face shown?' I asked, and Prince Adrian sadly shook his head. 'Alas, no, for as you may imagine, it would have caused too many problems back home if my features had been depicted in such an uninhibited piece of erotic art. However, between ourselves, I can boast a minor part in the preparation of Kneidel's masterpiece. Do you see the rather splendid lady with green eyes on her knees next to Count Gewirtz? Well, that is my prick she is sucking. It was great fun modelling for the mural, even though Kneidel substituted the face of the winner of last year's Tour de France for mine in the finished picture!

'Ah, you must excuse me, our hostess is calling me over to her,' he concluded, but I was not left alone, for now Robert wandered over with Carola Bedwell just as Philip played the final notes of Chopin's melodic work and we joined in the applause. 'Your friend is a fine pianist, but I would like to hear something more lively,' said Carola and she called across the room to ask Philip if he would play a polonaise for her.

'Certainly,' he replied, and I wish I could have played with such verve and style. His mother, the Dowager Duchess of Didsbury, had made Philip take up the piano at an early age and he was by far the most talented musician in our circle of friends. His forté was light music and though his performance of the *Polonaise Militaire* possessed strength and exuberance, even with my limited critical abilities, I felt that he did not quite manage to catch the wistful gaiety, the slightly faded romance and nervous melancholy of Chopin's music.

Be that as it may, Philip none the less deserved our applause as he mopped his brow and rose from the piano stool. He strode over to us and said: 'I'm just going to wash my hands. If any of you wish to pair off whilst I'm gone, just let Prince Adrian know, he always acts as master of ceremonies at these little gatherings.'

'A little early for all that,' murmured Robert as someone

produced a banjo, and Jenny Thirkettle now sat down and strummed a chorus of an old music hall tune, although the words she sang would hardly have passed muster at the Holborn Empire! With a wicked glint in her eye she looked straight at Robert and in the manner of West Indian native troubadors, made up the lyrics of her song then and there:

At Zaines cabaret, oh, such a beezer,
Robert saw Laura's tits they were such a teaser,
And though she wore a dress to cover her front,
His cock swelled up when he felt her cunt.

We watched the fucking, such fine sport,
Lord Philip's prick bulged as he passed the port,
And happily he sang without a care,
I'll fuck my blonde beauty in Grosvenor Square!

I had the grace to blush and Carola slipped her fingers round my hand. 'It's getting a bit rowdy isn't it? I've been here before, you know. Countess Marussia has some wonderful paintings in the house. Would you like me to show some of them to you?'

'That would be very nice,' I replied and I followed the girl, who informed Prince Adrian as she passed him by that we could be found if wanted in the Blue Room, out into the wide corridor which led (as I later discovered) to the centre of the house and a marble staircase.

'Countess Marussia is a follower of the Impressionist Movement, and bought several pictures at the show brought over from France by Durand-Ruel two years ago,' Carola explained, and as I looked carefully at the pictures I recognised two paintings by Monet.

'All the others are by Cézanne, Matisse and Seurat,' Carola continued as we walked slowly, hand in hand, studying the colourful exhibition of magnificent paintings which adorned the wall. 'The Countess bought several pictures very cheaply at the show.' I nodded my head slowly as I remembered my Papa, who visited the exhibition brought over by Monsieur Durand-Ruel, saying that although it was well enough attended, relatively few paintings were actually bought. [*Any one of the paintings in Countess Marussia's collection would be worth millions today! – Editor*]

'Do you like them, Rosie, or are you one of those reactionaries who refuse to look at exciting foreign art and buy dull, unimaginative British pictures instead? Forgive my bluntness, my maternal grandparents were French immigrants, you see, and perhaps this is why I rail at the insular thinking of some of the people over here.'

'I love the work of the French Impressionists,' I said simply and Carola squeezed my hand. 'Though to be fair, it could be said that the manner and style did not have to be imported into England from France because they were already here in the later works of Turner and Constable. Many of our contemporary painters are impressionists though as my Papa, who is a keen collector, said to me recently, English painters such as Gilman and Bevan use a very different palette because of the need to capture the blurred London streets and houses and dark interiors.'

Carola opened a door on our right and said: 'Let's see the first and second floors later. It's so late and I'm feeling rather tired. Aren't you, Rosie?' As if on cue, I unsuccessfully attempted to stifle a yawn and Carola said: 'There, you see, I knew I was right. Let's go in here and lie down for a while. We won't be disturbed.

'Not for a while at any rate,' she added cryptically, which puzzled me at the time.

The room was richly furnished and was draped with the most expensive blue silk curtains, and in the middle stood an inviting four poster bed, also draped in the same pleasing shade of baby blue with silken sheets and soft, plump pillows.

'Through that far door is a bathroom,' said Carola, sitting on the bed and kicking off her shoes. 'Would you like to use the facilities whilst I undress?'

I took up the invitation and when I returned, Carola was

lying on the bed stark naked waiting for me. 'Throw off your clothes and come and have a cuddle, you beautiful creature,' she enjoined, holding out her arms towards me.

Now I have said before in these memoirs that whilst I do not believe the experience of a thick, hot cock in one's cunney can be bettered, I am not averse to an occasional sensuous joust with a member of my own sex. Girls are usually far gentler lovers, and few English boys can eat pussy as well as the female of the species. However, without wishing to sound disloyal to king and country, I must digress to note here that in my experience, the Italians as opposed to the French are the best pussy-sucking race in the whole wide world. I have always found out that to be licked out by a girl is a most pleasant experience, although unlike such out and out tribades as Lady Molly Gerfoyle-Smyth, I look upon a girls-only romp much as a keen golfer looks upon a game on the putting green — nice enough at the time but no substitute for the real thing!

So I had no qualms about disrobing until I was completely naked, and Carola complimented me upon the proud firmness of my breasts and the golden fluffy hair which fringed my pussy. I climbed into bed and we lay in each other's arms, saying little but kissing each other all over until Carola nibbled my ear and whispered: 'Rosie, what gorgeous breasts you have. I wish that mine were as rounded as yours with such fine, high-tipped nipples.'

'You have nice titties too, Carola,' I replied. 'They might be a wee bit smaller than mine but they are beautifully proportioned.'

'M'mm,' she replied, placing her fingers around my right nipple and rolling it around on her palm until, like its partner, it stiffened up like a miniature cock. She then let her hand stray down upon the fine, downy hair which covered my pussy lips and began to massage my thighs.

Carola's busy fingers made my heart quicken and my whole body tremble with desire. She threw off the coverlet and declared: 'Let us compare our pussies. I do love your pouting little slit, Rosie, and what a fine contrast we make between your golden blonde thatch and my black, curly moss. I'm going to kiss your cunney, darling, and then I will frig you until your cunt is all nice and juicy.'

I offered no resistance as she now started to squeeze the soft hillocks of my breasts which she cradled in her hands. I closed my eyes and relaxed as she continued this sensual exploration of my body, letting my head fall back as I felt Carola's lips close upon my nipple and begin to suck, tenderly at first and then more urgently as her hand moved between my legs and began a stroking action which was tender yet arousing as she let her fingers glide over my thighs, ever nearer towards my now moist muff. She slipped a long finger between the pouting pussy lips, moving them deliciously inside my cunt as the heel of her hand rubbed my clitty that was now as hard as a little walnut.

With a tiny sigh, I raised up my bottom to enjoy these delicious sensations to the very utmost, and Carola's lone forefinger was soon joined by a second and then a third as she finger-fucked me at an ever-increasing speed.

Carola now moved up over me and, still keeping her fingers embedded in my love channel, pressed our slippery bodies together and kissed me with such great passion on the mouth that I was now aroused to fever-point and I shuddered with desire, thrusting my breasts and my pussy against the lustful tribade. Her velvet tongue slithered between my lips as her fingers danced in and out of my now juicy cunt. 'Aaaah! Aaaah!' I panted with feline pleasure as the wicked girl moved her head downwards to the damp pleasure patch of silky blonde pussy hair and replaced her fingers with her tongue as she grasped my bum cheeks, one in each hand, and began to kiss my cunney, her mouth pressed against the wet, yielding flesh as she probed my crack gently with her tongue.

With a sudden dart, she then flashed the tip of her pointed tongue between my pussy lips and I revelled in the stimulation thus afforded as she licked, flicked and sucked my sopping sheath, her tongue delving deeply into the dark wet tunnel, and I opened my eyes for a moment to see that she had removed one hand from my arse to frig her own pussy, which was obviously as equally aroused as my own.

Carola's tongue now gave one final sweep of my dripping cunney walls and I began to spend, my hips bucking violently in a frenzied momentum as my excited pussy gushed out its aromatic emission which flooded Carola's mouth with tangy essence, as she brought us both to that delicious state of release which causes the very soul to dissolve in an ocean of lubricious bliss.

Soon we entwined ourselves together in a marvellous *soixante-neuf*. She straddled me with her knees on either side of my trembling body with her bum only inches from my face as she bent forward to bury her face a second time in my sweet snatch. As she did so, I wasted no time in wrenching apart her lovely bum cheeks, splaying them widely and making room for my lips to kiss all round the cleft between them. My tongue tickled its way round her wrinkled little rear dimple before moving down the crease to the lower opening of her cunt which opened immediately, the loose folds of the lips yielding instantly, and I gorged myself on the pungent wetness as my mouth filled with Carola's cuntal juices.

We sighed and moaned as we writhed away, tonguing each other up to new peaks of ecstatic delight, our white, naked bodies sliding across the sheets, our cries of passion half-smothered by the pressure of each other's pussies on our mouths. We sucked harder and harder, gulping down the love juice which was flowing freely from the pussies we were so vigorously reaming and neither of us would rest until we had extracted the last ounces of desire from our bodies.

I was tonguing deep inside Carola's cunney and her clitty had grown quite enormous as I nipped it playfully with my teeth, as she in turn sucked up the love juices which were pouring out from my pussy, gulping them down with great ardour.

'A-h-r-e! Please pull my clitty!' I groaned and, obediently, the gorgeous girl reluctantly wrenched her mouth from my sopping wet cunney and replaced it for a second time with her long, tapering fingers. Immediately she found my own swollen love-button and she caressed it expertly. Then I threshed around even more wildly as she slid a finger into my bum-hole and I thought I would swoon away with delight as spasms of fresh excitement thrilled through me, culminating in a gigantic spend of orgasmic lust.

It was now my turn to send Carola into the seventh heaven of erotic ecstasy and I pushed my mouth firmly up against her pouting pussy lips, moving my head back and forth as my tongue swirled around inside her cunt and I sucked upon her hard clitty, flicking my fluttering tongue all over her hairy quim, slurping the juices from her cunt which filled the room with the scent of raw sex.

I could feel Carola's climax building inside her and I worked my tongue even faster whilst at the same time inserting my finger between her yielding pussy lips. My tongue probed her secret recesses as I tasted the salty liquor of her sex; except for the earlier little romp with Elaine, which I described at the very start of these reminiscences, it had been some months since I had last licked a girl's cunt, but my tongue had lost none of its art.

Carola screamed with delight as she spent copiously and her juices washed over my lips and dribbled down my chin. 'Oh, Rosie, darling,' she moaned softly. 'You wonderful creature, you've sucked me dry! I just can't spend any more! Oooh, my cunt has been so beautifully sated that I don't think I could fuck again, not even for a thousand pounds.'

I rested my head against her thigh, well pleased that I had managed to bring her off so completely, when we almost jumped in the air with the shock of hearing a masculine voice say with evident amusement: 'Well, I'm sorry, Carola, but I can't agree to give you more than the hundred guineas fee we agreed on at Zaines, for you and Jenny Thirkettle to come here and perform after the show.'

Who was this uninvited visitor? I scrambled up to see none other than Prince Adrian himself standing at the door, gazing at our naked bodies, which were now glistening with perspiration, with a lustful gleam in his eye.

'Is this a game three can play?' he enquired, and when I replied in the affirmative he quickly stripped off his elegantly tailored evening clothes and joined us on the bed. Carola and I both grasped his substantial circumcised cock.

'My, that's quite a regal affair you have there, Your Royal Highness,' I said with genuine admiration as I slicked my fingers up and down the prince's penis which stood as high as a flagpole, but I could see that dear Carola appeared confused by the fact that there was no foreskin to pull back as she pulled her hand up and down his sinewy shaft.

'Have you not seen a prick such as this?' I asked Carola, planting a wet kiss on its smooth purple helmet.

'No,' she replied, looking very closely at the throbbing staff which she still held in her hand. 'I have never seen a truncheon without a covering for its knob, though I would imagine it must be pleasant to fuck or be sucked or tossed off without a foreskin to get in the way. For instance, I understand that Henry Blagerford, the general manager of our dance company, occasionally finds it difficult to snap back his foreskin when his cock swells up, and I am sure he would be pleased to lose his prepuce, though the thought of an operation scares him silly so he doesn't fuck very often.

'Not that that's any great loss to the girls as he's a nancy-boy,' she added absently, her fingers stroking Prince Adrian's palpitating prick whilst she spoke. 'So tell me, was it very painful for you to have a piece chopped off your love trunk?'

Prince Adrian shook his head. 'I couldn't really tell you as I was only two months old at the time. There was some slight malformation of the foreskin so my parents arranged for a Jewish doctor to circumcise me.'

'Why did they specifically want a Jewish doctor — oh, of course, silly me, Jewish baby boys undergo circumcision soon after birth, don't they, so your parents were wise to use the services of a man used to performing such a responsible task,' said Carola thoughtfully. 'Well, circumcision doesn't seem to affect sexual prowess, if the stories one hears about the famous theatrical impresario,

92

Sidney Cohen, are to be believed. Backstage gossip has it that he has fucked almost every chorus girl currently appearing on the London stage, and I've been told on good authority that the best way to get through an audition for one of his shows is to promise the randy old so-and-so a good gobble afterwards.'

'I envy the lucky chap! How marvellous to wallow in such cuntal cornucopia,' said Prince Adrian with a chuckle. 'Anyhow, thank goodness circumcision does not appear to have any adverse affect upon my sexual capabilities. O-o-o-h! O-o-o-h! O-o-o-h! Who is rubbing my cock so deliciously? Ah, it's you, Rosie, can you rub a little faster please and Carola, would you kindly cup your hands round my balls, yes, move your fingers around them, m'mm, that's truly wonderful.'

'Is that better?' I asked, jerking my hand up and down his thick ivory staff and he gasped: 'Yes, yes, even quicker please, I want to come now or my cock will burst!' I obliged him by rubbing at a faster rate and sure enough, with a sudden spurt, a great gush of sticky white spunk flooded out from the top of his knob. Unfortunately, he spent just as Carola leaned forward in order to take his cock in her mouth, which meant that her pretty face was too close for comfort when the Prince climaxed and his initial burst of jism jetted out unerringly straight into her right eye.

This brought the game to a somewhat inglorious end, although I managed to suppress my giggles as the Prince made fulsome apologies to Carola whilst we wiped ourselves down. Truthfully, I thought his copious ejaculation would end Prince Adrian's participation in any proposed *ménage á trois*, but I was mistaken — after only about five minutes he asked Carola if she would like to resume her attempt to suck his cock.

'With the greatest of pleasure,' she smiled and cupped his heavy, hairy ballsack in her hands as she bent down and lazily washed her tongue all over his uncovered helmet, lapping up some remaining blobs of his previous spend. But it took only a few seconds for Carola to suck his shaft up to its previous erect state and I added a lick or two of my own to his swollen, rock-hard shaft as Carola choked as she attempted to jam too much of his thick tool down her throat.

When she recovered, Prince Adrian then rolled Carola onto her back and slapped her bare bottom with his hand and, taking his meaty staff in his hand attempted to force a passage between her lovely rounded bum cheeks. 'Do you wish to take the tradesmen's entrance, Your Highness?' giggled Carola. 'I don't mind at all as I enjoy taking a cock up my arse, but for heaven's sake get Rosie to spread some cold cream on it first.'

By good fortune there was a conveniently placed jar of this cosmetic emulsion on the bedside table. I reached over for it and said: 'By all means, Carola, it will be my pleasure to anoint the Prince's prick for you.'

'Thank you so much, darling,' cooed Carola, planting a wet kiss on my nose. 'I adore a good bum-fuck, but a generous application of cold cream or pomade is always necessary before we begin.'

I opened the jar and smeared a liberal coating of the greasy liquid around the sides and then just inside Carola's back passage. Then I applied the same over the Prince's warm velvet-skinned shaft, which excited him so much that I was concerned he might spend in my hand. But such an unfortunate disaster was thankfully avoided and I again aided the happy couple by slipping a pillow under her tummy as she raised her bum high in the air, and I parted the delectable soft *rondeurs* of her buttocks to expose her tiny, wrinkled, brown bum-hole.

All was ready now for Prince Adrian to smooth a passage for his cock through to the edges of her puckered little rear dimple. He carefully positioned the smooth, purple knob and then slowly but surely buried his shaft up to the hilt, his balls flapping against her bum as Carola gasped with the force of this powerful sensation. 'Ooooh!' she gurgled as the Prince corn-holed her to the limit. He then slowly began to fuck the panting girl, attacking the tight sheath by shunting in and out of her arse vigorously as his right hand snaked around her waist to join mine in playing with her pussy. I now began to kiss Carola's wet muff and flicked my tongue in and out of her sopping cunt.

'Aaargh! Aaargh! Aaargh! Don't stop, don't stop, either of you! Shoot your spunk in my bum, Adrian, while Rosie brings me off with her tongue!' cried Carola as her hips juddered, her bottom squirmed and I was all but smothered by the squashing of her cunney lips against my face. She shuddered to her sublime peak of pleasure as the prince unleashed a torrent of sticky sperm inside her bum-hole, and there followed a full minute of the juicy sounds of our chorus of ecstatic sighs and squeals as we continued to pleasure ourselves to a state of exhaustion. With a 'pop', Prince Adrian uncorked his deflated shaft from Carola's well-lubricated arse and we lay sated from our erotic play.

Although I had enjoyed assisting the Prince and Carola, I had not yet achieved full satisfaction and my appetite had been whetted for a good old-fashioned fuck. So when I heard an apologetic cough from the doorway and looked up to see Philip standing there looking rather sheepish, I cried out: 'Come on, Phil, don't hang around miles away when I need you here. Take off your clothes and come and fuck me!'

He grinned and stripped off in record time before leaping forward and throwing himself in my arms. Alas, his foot caught Prince Adrian a glancing blow in the balls, which caused an anguished yell to burst forth from the royal throat. Poor Philip offered his sincere apologies, which were accepted through gritted teeth, but luckily the blow inflicted more shock than pain and very soon Philip and I could concentrate on the business in hand.

To begin with, he kissed me lightly on the lips and then our mouths meshed together and Philip's tongue was waggling in my mouth whilst his hands roamed all over my breasts and he rolled my hard, elongated titties up against his palms. 'M'mmm, that's very nice,' I said as I snuggled up against him as he descended below and reached my moist blonde bush, twirling his fingers through the silky blonde hairs until my pouting pussy lips fairly throbbed with anticipation. With his left hand he guided my head down to his lovely thick cock which was twitching wildly as I cupped my hands around it, my creamy, high-tipped breasts swinging over his face as he continued to finger-fuck me, dipping his fingertips in and out of my tingling, juicy honeypot.

Now I circled my own long fingers round his pulsing prick and I saw that a blob of milky pre-spend fluid had already formed around the 'eye' on his bared knob. My head swooped down and I lashed my tongue around his shaft, sucking up the salty cream before bending my head even lower and licking his hairy ballsack. Philip's lips had now found their way to my titties and I was concerned that he should not spend too soon, so I straightened up and lay on my back, borrowing the pillow I had slipped under Carola's tummy to stuff underneath my bottom.

Without further ado I opened my legs wide and, pulling open my pussy lips, commanded my noble lover to start our journey towards paradise. 'Fuck me, Phil,' I said breathlessly. 'I want to feel every inch of your dear cock in my cunney. Slide in your smooth shaft, you sweet boy.'

Philip obeyed me instantly and I felt his helmet nudge its way through my cunney lips and inside my cunt, which was so juiced up that he slid in his entire affair very easily as my own love juices dribbled down my thighs.

He began pumping into me with great pounding thrusts as my arse arched up and down to receive his wonderful penis, and his cock plunged deeper and deeper until my legs left the bed to wrap themselves around his back as my hands clutched his shoulders whilst his trusty tool squelched its way through the clinging walls of my love tunnel. A moan of exquisite pleasure escaped from my lips as waves of sheer bliss spread out from my cunt to every fibre of my being. Now Philip embedded himself inside me with a strong thrust which mashed my clitty against his pubic bone, and my pussy disgorged a further rivulet of love juice. He held us together, very still, smiling as my spasms came to an end, and I lay under him gasping for breath.

'Time to take the final ride,' he murmured and he started to stroke his cock in and out of my cunt, penetrating with lightning force and speed. This brought me to the very brink of orgasm — but then with a wicked grin he stopped still and held his position until the feeling subsided. He did this twice more until my body was screaming for release. Then with one final thrust he suddenly became rigid and I knew the end was near. I felt the throb of liquid fire as his climax juddered to boiling point and my cunt was flooded with his spunk as his creamy froth spurted and spurted inside me. This brought on my own final spend, which came in a sudden rush, and I cried out in ecstasy as my saturated clitty sent shudders of sheer delight coursing through my veins.

Philip lay quietly on top of me, careful to keep his still-swollen shaft inside my buzzing cunney as we slowly calmed down. Then he rolled off me and we cuddled up together whilst at Carola's behest, Prince Adrian called a servant on the internal telephone and ordered iced champagne and a selection of sandwiches and cakes to be delivered to us without delay. Despite our wonderful dinner at Zaines, I was now quite hungry and I recalled that when I had declined his earlier offer of refreshments, the Prince had remarked how exercise fuels the appetite. Certainly, it proved again to me the point that the worship of Venus and Priapus does make very real demands on our bodies. In my humble experience, I must admit that whilst sexual intercourse may be physically exhausting, without doubt it is most refreshing for the brain and I have almost without exception woken up feeling bright and breezy after a splendid night's fucking.

The bearded servant who had opened the front door for us when we entered the house now came into the bedroom wheeling a trolley groaning under the weight of two magnums of fizz and a fine assortment of food. We ate and drank for about half an hour and then Carola said: 'I say, where is everybody else? Are they all engaged in the same pursuit as ourselves? Let's go and seek them out.'

'What a super idea, that could be great fun,' said Philip eagerly. 'But I suppose we had better get dressed first.'

'No, no, quite unnecessary, it would be better to leave our clothes here, they will be quite safe. I am sure that everybody else will be in the nude by now, and we would all be embarrassed if we, too, aren't naked as nature intended,' insisted Prince Adrian as he stretched out his arms and swung his feet off the bed and on to the rich Persian carpet. 'Follow me, friends, I have a pretty good idea where they might be found.'

At his bidding we walked upstairs to Countess Marussia's bedroom. The door was slightly ajar and we crowded through to see our hostess, who was indeed stark naked, lying on pink satin sheets on her huge four poster bed, critically examining the stiff cockstand of Colonel Goldstone who was kneeling, equally bereft of clothing, beside her.

The Countess waved a friendly greeting to us and continued squeezing the Colonel's proud prick. 'Yes, Leon, your old organ seems in very good shape. I do think it might even have grown slightly since I last saw it behind the tea-tent at the Bishop of Hendon's garden-party last summer,' she said with evident pleasure as she sensually manipulated his veiny shaft in her hand.

One could not fault her judgement, for though older of course than Philip, Robert, or even Prince Adrian, Colonel Goldstone was still a fine figure of a man. His shoulders were as broad as Countess Marussia's were narrow and his powerful, masculine chest contrasted well with her graceful, creamy breasts which were crowned with ripe, swollen nipples, the size and colour of cherries which I am sure the entire company wanted to suck.

But it was the gallant Colonel whose lips found the Countess's pointed nipples as he took all the liberties one could desire with her lithe body, sucking her nipples, handling her bottom cheeks, frigging her clitty and rubbing his tadger, a vastly experienced if somewhat gnarled member which I was later told had fucked more than five hundred cunnies from all over the world, up against her pouting pussy

98

lips. They sank to the bed and she made the Colonel lie on his back as she clambered over him. Her sparkling white teeth flashed in a lustful smile as slowly she began to lower herself on to his squat, throbbing shaft which she held steady in her hand.

She slid right down on him, his prick disappearing straight and deep inside her cunt at the first attempt as their pubic hairs mingled together. She paused, like a rider testing a new mount, clamping her clinging cunney muscles round his cock as if testing him for size. Obviously all was well for she breathed a satisfied sigh as she now furiously pumped her tight, rounded bum cheeks up and down, digging her fingernails into his flesh as she held on to his body. Each lascivious shove was accompanied by a wail of ecstatic delight as the Colonel grabbed her breasts and brought them down to his mouth to nibble on her rosy nipples and trace little circles with the tip of his tongue around the rich, red titties.

Now he helped the Countess enjoy this erotic ride even more by pushing her up and letting her fall upon his glistening cock. She began to spend, shivering and trembling as she reached the apex and she pulled him in as tight as she could, her cunney gripping his cock even harder as she entered the throes of a lovely, big orgasm.

She slowed down and then came to rest, pushing herself off the Colonel's cock, and I could see that he had not yet climaxed. This must have also been noted by Jenny Thirkettle who had been frigging herself during the Countess's fuck with a black leather dildo of a substantial size. 'Would you mind holding this for a few minutes, please?' she asked me, and I took the godemiche from her as she joined the Countess on the bed.

They rolled over on their backs and both girls invitingly opened their legs for Colonel Goldstone's delectation. 'Who would you like to fuck first, Leon?' enquired the Countess with a merry laugh. 'Don't worry, whoever you choose, the other will not be offended, I promise you.'

In fact, the Colonel chose Jenny's juicy cunney for his

first port of call. He lay his handsome though thinning head of hair between her quivering thighs and worked his lips into the cleft which was only lightly covered with a downy covering of auburn curls. He sniffed appreciatively the delicate cuntal aroma of her moist pussy, and then slid his arm underneath her supple body and pulled up her fleshy bottom to provide further elevation as he placed his lips over her pouting crack and sucked it into his mouth, where doubtless the tip of his tongue began to wash it from all directions. The young dancer gave a sudden shriek which I assumed meant that he had found the base of her clitty and was twirling his tongue around the erect rosebud as she crossed her legs over his head, moaning her approval as he continued to work his tongue up and down, licking and lapping as she ground her cunt against his mouth.

In the meantime, so as not to disappoint the Countess, the clever old soldier let his arm run down to the curly thatch between her legs, and once he found her yielding love lips he rubbed them lewdly with the ball of his thumb before sliding two fingers into her damp slit. This caused her whole body to shake and vibrate as his naughty fingers tweaked her hardening clitty.

'Who will be the first to go off?' wondered Robert Bacon, but only a fool would wager which of the two girls would be first to be finished off by either the wet friction of the Colonel's tongue or the steady manual manipulation of his long fingers.

In fact the question was never to be answered because the Colonel now withdrew his hand from the Countess's cunt and he mounted Jenny's enchantingly nubile young body. She clasped his cock and pulled his knob into place between her aching love lips and he sank down upon her, wedging his substantial shaft snugly inside her love tunnel. Then she suddenly snapped her thighs together, making the Colonel open his own legs and lie astride her with his cock well and truly trapped inside her cunt. Carola leaned forward to obtain a closer view of the writhing pair. 'I find that position extremely satisfying myself,' she remarked. 'It is one of the variations during coupling which is good for both partners. You are comfortable enough, aren't you, Leon?'

'I have no complaints,' panted Colonel Goldstone, though he could hardly slide his cock to and fro because Jenny's cunney muscles were gripping him so tightly, but then, as she began to grind her hips, his prick was massaged quite exquisitely and I could almost feel it throb myself inside Jenny's sopping pussy which was now expelling its juices in miniature rivulets down her thighs where they seeped into the sheet.

He now inserted the tip of his forefinger into her arsehole which made her squeal and wriggle and she shifted her thighs which eased the pressure around the Colonel's cock. This allowed him to drive to and fro, his meaty staff sliding in and out of her squelchy slit in great style.

This thorough reaming of her cunt brought off Jenny time and time again as the fierce momentum of his fucking sent her into new paroxysms of delight. She brought her legs up against the small of the Colonel's broad back, humping the lower half of her body upwards to meet the violent strokes of his powerful prick. She squealed in delight as he pounded away, his thick prick slithering its way through her throbbing cunt, exciting her up to astounding new heights. The Colonel continued this magnificent fuck for at least three more minutes before he bore down upon her one more time, his lean torso gleaming with perspiration, and then he tensed his frame and with a cry his cock expelled spasm after spasm of sticky white spunk inside the velvety wet darkness of Jenny's cunney. Quickly, she squeezed her thighs together again and milked every last drop from his spurting length, refusing to release him until his shaft began to shrink, and he rolled off the happy girl and collapsed between Jenny and the Countess, panting hard to recover his breath.

This was a sturdy performance indeed by the gallant old soldier, and we insisted upon his telling us the secret of his amazing ability to hold back his spunking. 'Give me a few moments to recover and I'll spill the beans,' he gasped as

Prince Adrian thoughtfully handed him a glass of champagne from the silver salver which the Countess had brought in from the drawing room.

When he had regained his composure, we all sat around Colonel Goldstone on the bed and he cleared his throat and told us the following tale: 'Believe it or not, when I began fucking in earnest when my regiment was posted out to India, I did not possess any great staying power and, if anything, my eager young cock often let me down in that I reached my climax too quickly as far as both myself and my partner were concerned.

'At this time, of course, I was almost totally inexperienced in *l'arte de faire l'amour* and the only engagements in which my tool had found its way into a cunny had been those undertaken in a few hurried knee-tremblers with Florrie, our scullery-maid, as a sixteenth birthday present and as a going-away gift when I left home to join the Army, and an occasional conjunction with the girls of Madam Minnie's bawdy-house near Sandhurst.

'So when I started to fuck on a regular basis when stationed at Poona, at first I assumed that my spunking too swiftly was caused by my relative inexperience and over-eagerness to climb on top of Margot, General Block-Ruddle's wife, who regularly entertained the younger officers with manoeuvres of her own when duty called her husband away on some military exercise. Gad! What a rumbustious life we enjoyed when the General was away. I'll never forget the first time I fucked the lady in question — Margot had asked me to play a round of croquet with her. It was a very warm afternoon and when we finished our game she went into her house to change into fresh clothes whilst I sat in a deck-chair on the verandah, making friends with an iced ginger-beer.

'Then from behind me I heard Margot cry out: "Oh, Leon, would you come here please? I need your help." Naturally, I put down my drink and rushed inside. "I'm in my bedroom," she called out and so, after knocking

102

rather timidly on the closed door, I opened it and my jaw fell open with amazement.

'For there in front of me stood the General's wife, dressed only in a tight-fitting corset, at the top of which her splendid, creamy bosoms overflowed, and though her stays were still in place, she had managed to pull down her knickers and my eyes were transfixed by the dark, hairy mound between her legs. Somehow, I found the strength to tear my gaze away from her pussy, over which she artfully placed her hand as she said gaily: "Ah, Leon, there you are, I'm so pleased you stayed as you're just the chap I need. Shut the door behind you, my dear fellow — yes, that's the way. Now I must confess that I've been a very silly girl because I forgot you were coming round and I've gone and given all the servants the afternoon off. So I am in need of you to play the part of a ladies' maid as there are a couple of fastenings that I cannot easily reach by myself, and I would be obliged if you would kindly unhook them for me."

'She presented her back to me and, nervously, I fumbled with the remaining restraints and, under instruction, I pulled open the corset and let it fall to the floor as, now completely unclothed, she took a step forward and twirled around to show me her full, globular breasts in all their naked glory. "Give me your hands," she said softly and she took hold of my trembling fingers and placed them firmly on her lush, tawny titties.

'I was so dumbfounded by her wantonness that I stood stock still, but Margot eased the tension by saying lightly: "Now then, Leon, don't simply stand there like a waxwork at Madame Tussaud's exhibition. Wouldn't you like to massage my juicy berries, you lovely boy?"

'My fingers closed round her protruding, rubbery nipples which I felt harden under my touch. At the same time, Margot reached down and gently squeezed my stiffening prick as I continued to fondle her breasts. My shaft had now swollen up to its full height and was threatening to burst out of my trousers, and in her haste to undo my fly, Margot ripped off a couple of buttons as she pulled them and my

103

drawers to my ankles. I stepped out of them and as our lips met in a hot, passionate kiss, I tore off my shirt as Margot seized hold of my cock and pulled me over to the bed. Still holding my shaft tightly, she lay down and dragged me down over her, rubbing my member along the valley between her lively big bosoms, and I found this so exciting that I shot my load almost straightaway. Margot directed the flow from my twitching tadger over her titties, soaking her titties with my creamy emission. Then she made me rub my spunk all over her raised-up nips, a task I found most exciting, as I felt the swollen flesh push up against my fingers.

'But though I now desperately wanted to fuck Margot, my poor cock was lying limply against her large brown nipple, and the concern must have shown in my face because the kind woman gently pushed me off her and told me to lie back and relax, saying: "I'll stiffen your staff, Leon, have no fear. My, your soft sausage looks good enough to eat."

'Margot now picked up my shrunken staff between her fingers and she looked at me with a gleam in her dark brown eyes and said boldly: "I have a fancy to suck your cock — tell me honestly, dear boy, has any other girl been lucky enough to take this velvet-skinned tube between her lips?"

'Well, in the officers' mess we all boasted of the grand fuckings and suckings we had partaken of in former days, but I suspect that like my own, many such stories were culled from wishful imagination. But I resolved to be truthful and I told Margot that I had yet to enjoy the pleasure of being sucked off. "Oh, Leon," she said, clapping her hands with undisguised glee, "how spiffing! It will give me an extra thrill to know that I will be the first woman ever to tongue your knob!"

'She set to work with a will and, after giving a slight moistening lick to the crown of my cock, she proceeded to suck in the rest of my prick between her lips. Not surprisingly, perhaps, this did the trick as far as my flaccid penis was concerned, and my cock stiffened perceptively

104

inside her mouth almost at once. Margot was an extremely skilled exponent of the ancient art of fellatio and I lay back blissfully whilst her moist mouth worked up and down my ecstatic boner, licking and lapping at every inch of my pulsating length. Her hand gripped the base as she pumped her pretty head up and down, keeping her lips magically taut as with her free hand she gently played with my balls.

'Very soon Margot's swirling tongue collected the pre-come juices which began to ooze out from the 'eye' on my knob. She jammed her mouth over my helmet and slurped lustily on her penile sweetmeat. I almost fainted from sheer delight as powerful electric shocks of erotic warmth seeped through me, and with a hoarse cry I sent a fresh flood of gushing sperm down into her waiting throat. She sucked and swallowed every last drain of salty spunk until my cock stopped jerking and began to slowly deflate back to its normal, dangling size.

' "Aaah, how delicious," she said, smacking her lips. "Your spunk has such an invigorating taste! You will come round for dinner, won't you? We'll have a light meal, and then you can fuck me all night."

'I smiled my approval as we lay motionless for a while in the heavy afternoon heat. Then I got dressed and I left Margot temporarily to return to my quarters to bathe and change. I could hardly wait to go back to Margot and my youthful impatience must have shown on my face for Cootie Williams, a fellow subaltern and a damned good friend, pulled me aside just as I was on my way back to Margot's and said: "You going out to dine, Leon? Well, please do take care not to over-exert yourself. Don't forget you're playing in the cricket match tomorrow against the staff officers of the Punjab Rifles. And as captain, I'm looking to you for at least fifty runs, old boy, so I don't want you draining all your energy away on rumpy-pumpy tonight."

' "I haven't the faintest idea what you are talking about," I replied haughtily, but Cootie was not to be dissuaded. "Oh come on, my dear chap, I happened to be strolling past the

General's bungalow this afternoon and it didn't need Sherlock Holmes to deduce that Margot was fucking some lucky fella after I heard certain familiar sounds coming from the bedroom. Then I recalled that she'd asked you to play croquet this afternoon and I realised what was up."

'So my secret had been discovered! I was aghast and I replied anxiously: "You've really put me on the spot, Cootie. As a lady is involved here, you will not expect me to comment on your remarks. But I've listened to what you said and I'll keep myself in trim for tomorrow's game."

' "Quite right, Leon, neither a gentleman nor lady of quality should ever reveal the names of a conquest — unless of course one catches the clap from a lover and then it is one's bounden duty to inform all and sundry," he said seriously, but then my chum smiled and added softly: "Still, Margot is a wonderful fuck, isn't she? She takes a while to come, though, so you'll have to work hard to keep from spunking too quickly for her." I said nothing but a nod is as good as a wink and Cootie continued: "My advice would be to have a stiff drink before you start, though not too much or you'll have trouble getting the old John Thomas to stand to attention. If that doesn't relax you, whilst you're on the job, if you feel yourself coming too soon, try thinking about Mr Gladstone, railway engines or anything but fucking!

' "Or even better, old chum, come with me to my room and I'll give you a jar of an ointment Rajiv, my batman, gave me last month. Rub it on your prick just before you feel yourself spending, and you'll find that somehow it anaesthetises the desire to come."

'Well, I don't mind confessing to you that I was doubtful at first, but I took up Cootie's suggestion and damn me, the ointment worked like magic. It took ten minutes' solid shafting till she came, but I kept back from flooding her pussy till she was ready for me. We fucked till the early hours and I left her very well-satisfied with my performance.'

Colonel Goldstone paused for breath and I commented: 'So all ended happily for you,' but he shook his head. ' 'Fraid not, Miss d'Argosse, I don't know whether it was the effect of all the fucking, but in the cricket match the next day I was out for a duck. However, I partially redeemed myself by bowling out two of the Punjab team's best batsmen though, alas, we lost the game, much to Cootie Williams' annoyance!'

We sat in silence, mulling over this fascinating anecdote when Philip suddenly snapped his fingers and said: 'My God! I'm obliged to you, Leon. Your mentioning cricket has just reminded me that I'm supposed to go to Lords tomorrow and watch my cousin Quentin play for Oxford in the Varsity Match. Rosie, could you bear to come with me if the weather stays fine? I'll ask Fortnum's to prepare a picnic luncheon for us.'

'Yes, it could be good fun,' I said, 'and perhaps Robert and Laura would like to join us?'

'I'd love to — how about you, Laura?' said Robert Bacon, and then looked around him and clapped his hand over his mouth as we suddenly realised that a member of our party was missing. 'Oh, good grief, I'd forgotten that Laura said she was going to wash her hands before joining us up here. Where the deuce could she have gone?'

'I hope she has not been twiddling her thumbs waiting for us,' said Philip, but Countess Marussia waved away his fears. 'Of course she hasn't, you silly boy, I told Laura about the prowess of my young footman, Nikolai's, prick. He was a poor, uneducated youth from a village near Dnepropetrovsk and I took him into my service, more to help his parents who worked on one of our estates, but he has repaid me many times over.

'Many, many, times . . .' she said with a smile. 'Anyhow, I told Laura to seek him out if she found herself at a loose end so, if you want to talk to her, I suggest you go up to the second floor and take the third door on the left at the top of the stairs.'

We slipped on bath-robes and then Philip and I

accompanied Robert upstairs as directed, and when we came to Nikolai's room, Robert gave a peremptory knock and threw open the door. My eyes widened as we looked upon an erotic tableau — but not, dear reader, of Nikolai slewing his Russian rod inside Laura's hairy cunney. For although the handsome young lad was in the nude, we must have just missed seeing him pleasuring Laura's pussy because now he was slumped, looking totally exhausted, in a chair by the side of the bed, his cock dangling limply between his thighs. His thick penis was certainly of a substantial size even in a flaccid state, and I was struck by the large dimensions of his hairy ballsack which dangled low beneath his shaft.

'*Dobrey veyecher, vwi satitye, pojalsta,*' said Nikolai in a polite tone of voice.

'He's asking us in,' translated Robert who, unlike most Englishmen, had a good ear for languages and was fluent in French, German, Russian and Turkish. '*Spaseebo,*' replied Robert, and the three of us crowded in to take a closer look at the two soft, glistening nude bodies which were writhing on the bed.

One of these belonged to the missing Laura who was lying on her back, and between her spread thighs lay a pretty, chestnut-haired girl of no more than eighteen at most who, as Robert established from Nikolai, was named Tanya and was employed as Countess Marussia's personal maidservant. Tanya was positioned with her face up against Laura's hairy quim, carefully sliding a pink and green striped coloured china dildo in and out of her cunney lips, making sure that it rubbed firmly against her clitty at every stroke. She slowed the pace and then increased it and Laura's love lips were becoming flushed as all her energy concentrated on the clasping and unclasping of her cunney muscles around the china shaft, and her cries became more regular with the girl's steady plunging of the instrument inside her honeypot.

Laura lifted her legs, bringing them back so that her cunt was offered up to Tanya's loving rhythm of a series of short, rapid strokes alternating with deeper, slower ones as the dildo sank out of sight before reappearing, glistening with Laura's love juices. Then Tanya changed the pace again and I could almost feel Laura's approaching spend myself as her body began to tremble all over. She cried out: 'Yes! Yes! I'm there!' as her back arched in one last heave and Tanya pumped the dildo furiously in and out of her pussy.

'A-a-a-h! A-a-a-h! That's it! You've done it! Wonderful, wonderful!' cried out Laura, and her hands reached down to fondle the china shaft which was still embedded in her cunney.

In the meantime, the size of his huge bare cock poking out from the folds of his bath-robe showed that Lord Philip Pelham's attention had been irresistibly drawn to Tanya's lithe, gleaming body and especially the pouting, pink love lips which peeped redly out from the mass of profuse, raven-black hair which carpeted her mound. Philip shucked off his robe and knelt down on the bed, placing himself so that his thick, throbbing prick was directly in front of Tanya's face. Her eyes lit up and after a few rich, Slavic phrases, her tongue flicked out and teased round his purple, uncapped helmet which was already oozing tiny drops of jism.

The aroused pair had no need to break through the barrier of language for no words were necessary as the nubile young girl unknowingly, but in the most delightful way, made amends to the Pelham family for the loss of Philip's grandfather, a casualty of the famous Charge of the Light Brigade during the Crimean War. Instinctively she reached out and pulled his stiff penis towards her. Knowing beyond her tender years, Tanya understood his desperate needs and her tongue fluttered out, circling his knob, savouring the salty taste and I could see her even, white teeth scrape the tender flesh of his shaft between her lips, drawing hard as though she wanted to suck down to the very root. She sucked lustily and Philip responded by jerking his hips to and fro as he fucked her sweet mouth, driving his prick home until his knob reached the back of her throat. She gobbled greedily, salivating with her naughty tongue until with a groan, Philip's cock squirted out its frothy tribute and Tanya swallowed his spend joyfully.

After she had milked his prick dry she lifted her head and said something in Russian to Robert, whose face broke out in a wide grin as he said: 'Congratulations, Philip. Tanya said that your spunk tasted the creamiest of all she has ever tasted. Now, old chum, if you are up to it, she would be honoured if you would kindly fuck her. May I tell her that you will oblige?'

'Of course, but say I need just a few moments to recover from her glorious sucking-off,' panted Philip, for even a noted cocksman like my dear friend needs a short breather after spunking so copiously.

During this intermission I looked across to Nikolai, who remained seated in his chair but whose tremendous tadger had now risen up and was standing stiffly between his thighs. He was working his hand up and down his shaft and I thought to myself that letting him toss himself off would be a dreadful waste of a thick prick, so I threw off my robe and rushed over to him. I straddled myself over him and reached down to trail my fingers from the bottom of his ballsack, upwards along his hot, pulsing shaft to the smooth, domed crown of his cock.

Now it was time to grasp hold of this monster and ease the purple knob between the pouting lips of my juicy pussy, propelling it in, inch by inch, until his dark and my blonde pubic hairs were matted together. With a deep cry, the lad threw his hands round my waist and pulled me up and plunged me down so that his thrilling tool speared me deliciously every time I bounced down upon it. Oh, what simply divine sparks shot out from my cunney as I rode this wonderful monster which was crashing with increasing speed in and out of my squelchy slit.

Nikolai lunged and lunged again, and I responded by rocking in rhythm to his thrusts. My climax came on so swiftly that I had to make the youth finish the fuck as soon as possible. Like Tanya, Nikolai spoke no English, but actions speak louder than words so I let my hand go down and squeeze his balls to signal him to shoot his load. Happily, this stratagem had the desired effect and he unleashed a flood of hot sperm into my cunney and I shuddered with ecstatic delight as a mixture of Nikolai's spunk and my own love juices overflowed in rivulets down my thighs.

I kept his still semi-stiff shaft inside me as I relaxed and lay forward on Nikolai's shoulder, but then a high squeal from behind me interrupted my reverie. I straightened up and turned my head to see that Tanya and Laura were now busy with Philip and Robert. Philip was engaged in licking Tanya's tawny titties, lapping at one engorged nipple whilst playfully rubbing the other hard teat against the palm of his hand whilst she wriggled her way across him and took up a similar position as myself upon Nikolai, sliding on top of his prick, ramming herself up and down on his quivering stiffstander, squeezing her cunney muscles to grip and release his shaft so beautifully that Philip groaned deeply, lost in a haze of erotic abandon.

At the same time, Laura was proving herself no slouch as she slurped vigorously on Robert's pulsating pole. I thought she was going to bring him off herself in this way, but suddenly she opened her lips to release his twitching tool, and taking it in her hand she brought his cock up to behind Tanya who, sensing what Laura was about, without missing a beat of her rhythm as she slid up and down Philip's throbbing shaft, leaned forward so that Laura could place the tip of Robert's knob against the entrance to the puckered little brown rosette of her bum-hole.

Robert took hold of Tanya's plump, firm bum cheeks and opened them wide as he pushed his prick between them. As it was well moistened by Laura's tonguing, it took only a moment to cork Tanya to the full. She let out a yelp of discomfort at first, but quickly wriggled her bum so that she could fully enjoy the two men jointly ramming their tools inside her. When they pushed in together they must have felt their cocks rubbing together, being separated only by the thin divisional membrane, and it was all too exciting for

111

the lusty couple who soon pumped jets of frothy white spunk into Tanya's cunney and bum simultaneously as the Russian girl also reached the summit of the mountain of sensual pleasures, and they fell back in a rather undignified heap of entangled limbs on the bed.

This fired us all and we formed a novel fucking chain with Robert fucking Laura whilst he diddled Tanya's cunney with the dildo as Philip worked his noble cock inside her now juicy little arse, and I sucked his big balls as at the same time I opened my legs wide to let Nikolai slide home his magnificent meaty prick inside me.

We changed around in various similarly exciting positions until we tired and then we left Nikolai and Tanya asleep on the bed and took small, bandy-legged steps back to the other guests in Countess Marussia's bedroom. We found them all sprawled out together, deep in the arms of Morpheus, but neither Laura nor I wanted to stay the night, so along with Philip and Robert, our two sturdy escorts, we roused the Countess and Prince Adrian and thanked them warmly for their hospitality.

'We can find our way out by ourselves,' said Robert, and we waved goodbye to our new friends and I glanced at the clock in the hallway to see that it was now almost three o'clock in the morning. Topping and Mellor, our faithful chauffeurs, were ready and waiting and Philip and I made an arrangement to meet Robert and Laura at Lord's to see the annual cricket match between Oxford and Cambridge Universities.

'Let's meet at half past three in the main stand,' said Philip to Robert. 'I promised cousin Quentin that I would be there to cheer him on, but there's no need to get there at the start of play. Frankly, I'm not a great cricket buff, although I know that you are quite keen on the game.'

'Yes, I do play a little,' said Robert modestly, not mentioning the fact that he turned out quite often for Kent's second team, and occasionally even for the county's first eleven.

Mellor drove back to Aunt Elizabeth's and Philip opened

the door for me before handing back the keys. 'Goodnight, Rosie,' he said. 'Shall I pick you up at about a quarter to three?'

'That would be fine, darling,' I replied, kissing his cheek. 'I'm glad Mellor is driving you home as you look quite tired. You don't have to get up early, do you?'

'No, I have no engagements until luncheon when I'm meeting my Uncle Patrick at the Travellers' Club,' he said. 'You too sleep late, Rosie, it's been a wonderful but exhausting evening.'

3

Sports Report

I had no problem in taking Philip's sound advice and slept soundly until almost eleven o'clock. I rang the bell after I woke up and Elaine came bustling in and tossed a newspaper on my bed before going to the window and opening the curtains.

'Good morning, Miss Rosie, did you have a good time with Lord Philip?' she asked as I stretched my arms out and yawned.

'I certainly did, Elaine,' I replied, and then I recalled that she, too, had been out on the town. 'And tell me, how did your tryst turn out with Humphrey Allingham-Jones? Did you manage to sneak into his hotel without being discovered?'

'Oh yes, Miss Rosie, and thank you again for letting me stay out last night. Thanks to your kindness I had a marvellous time. If you remember Humphrey signed me in as the second occupant of his colleague, Miss Murdoch's, suite so there was no problem. First we had a lovely supper at an Italian restaurant in Charlotte Street, and then we caught a bus to Piccadilly Circus and he bought seats for the second house at the Empire music hall. Harry Tate was top of the bill and did he make us laugh! [*Harry Tate was one of the greatest popular comedians of the Edwardian era. A wonderful droll, his best-known material usually involved perplexed and irritated self-important sportsmen in a world,*

114

to quote J. B. Priestley which drifted away from sense and logic, cause and effect. Sketches like Tate's Feasts of Unreason offered off-beat, surrealist and even black humour to the rest of society from the hard-driven industrial working class – Editor]

'Humphrey really pushed the boat out, and I remonstrated with him when he insisted on flagging down a motor-cab to take us back to Bedford Square. "You must have already spent almost ten shillings [*fifty pence! – Editor*] tonight. We could have taken a bus back to the hotel." But Humphrey would have none of it. "It's sweet of you to think of my pocket," he said as we snuggled up together in the cab, "but I'm not short of a bob or two. Although being a vicar, Dad is perpetually hard-up, my maternal grandfather gives me a generous allowance, so please don't worry your pretty little head about such things." '

'Humphrey was absolutely right, it was very nice of you to be concerned about how much he was spending on you,' I commented. 'I do hope that afterwards you reaped your reward.'

She gave a warm smile and said: 'That I did, Miss Rosie, as he fucked me beautifully when we got back to the hotel. No-one saw me go into his room and we kissed as we took off our hats and coats. We sat on the bed and he put his tongue in my mouth, which always drives me wild. He cupped his hands round my breasts and I ran my fingers along his lap, feeling the swollen rod throb under my touch. As we continued the embrace, our mouths seemed locked together, I unbuttoned his trousers and out sprang his wonderful thick cock. It was diamond-hard and yet when I stroked it, the skin was blissfully warm and smooth to my touch.

'We drew apart momentarily whilst we tore off our clothes, and then I lay backwards on the bed with Humphrey bending over me as I worked his shaft up and down. I was ready to take the pink, round knob in my mouth when he spread my thighs and plunged his face between them. Well, my juices had already started to flow even before he took each cunney lip in turn and sucked it gently, before carefully smoothing back the pussy hairs and holding open the red chink of my love channel. He pressed his half-open mouth to it, probing my lubricated cunney wickedly with his tongue, at first toying with it and then, like a javelin, darting into the depths. I almost fainted clean away from the sheer force of this gorgeous tongue-fuck.

'Dear Humphrey is one of the few men who knows how to eat pussy — he slid a hand underneath my bum and lifted my pussy to his mouth so that he could slide his tongue into my juicy crack, pushing it in as far as possible, and I gasped with ecstasy as he found my clitty and rolled it about his mouth. His clever tongue jabbed and jabbed again at my excited cunt as I rotated my hips as, with my eyes closed and my head turned to one side, I thrilled beneath his skilled lips and tongue. I soon went off in a crackling series of tiny, electric climaxes and there was no doubt that Humphrey loved licking me out, for a few moments later I wet his lips with a liberal flow of love juice which he carefully lapped up and swallowed, and I ground my crotch into his face as I felt the rush of the incoming orgasm. I seized his tousled hair and rubbed my curly bush all over his face, feeling his nose against my bum cheeks and then against my cunt as I heaved myself against him, smearing his mouth and chin with love juice as I spent in a superb series of powerful, thrusting quivers.

'When we had quietened down I drew myself up and made him change places with me. "I want to taste your lovely cock, darling," I said and he gave me a wolfish smile. "Please be my guest," he replied as he settled his head on the pillow.

'I must be careful not to let him spend too soon, I thought to myself as my fingers closed around his pulsating prick. I popped my lips over the mushroom pink bulb and curled my tongue around his knob, licking and teasing as with one hand I cupped the taut weight of his hairy ballsack and with the other I gripped the rock-hard shaft at the base.

'I bobbed my head up and down in my favourite rhythm

116

— three short licks followed by one long, fierce suck deep into the back of my throat, and then repeated at a faster pace. "Whew, steady on, Elaine," he gasped as his prick began to shudder violently as I held it lightly between my teeth. "I won't be able to stop myself spunking in your mouth if you do much more of that."

'So I drew it out of my mouth slowly and distracted him by tonguing just the very tip of his knob, and I caught my breath as his prick began to twitch even more convulsively in my hand. With a huge effort of concentration, the darling lad managed to hold back as I lay down and he knelt in front of me. He gave his cock a few encouraging rubs and then placed it squarely between my pouting pussy lips. "Go right in, Humphrey!" I whispered and he pulled out a fraction before driving home, and I threw my arms about him, wrapping my thighs around his waist as he started pumping his smooth white prick in and out of my eager cunt.

'I could feel the love juices fairly pouring out of me now, clinging in drops in my pussy hair as his cock crashed through my clinging cunney, and he kept ramming his well-greased weapon to and fro until we were both crying out in unison as we came together and he filled me to the brim with a tremendous outpouring of hot, sticky sperm. He pumped away as I threshed around beneath him and his wonderful penis stayed hard in me for so long that I just lay there, moaning for joy as I felt trickles of our combined love fluids run down my thighs.

'Humphrey rolled off me and lay gasping for breath as he recovered his senses. But what a fiery nature the dear boy possesses, Miss Rosie! In no time at all he took my hand and gently laid it on his flat, muscular stomach. I moved my fingers downwards into the curly mass of pubic hair and then curled them around his burgeoning shaft which was not quite fully erect but had that lovely full look about it. I gently squeezed this swelling staff and very soon it was standing stiffly upwards, as hard as a rock as I slid my hand up and down the blue-veined pole. I moved myself forward and leaned across to kiss and lick the smooth-skinned

117

monster with the tip of my tongue. Then I started to suck greedily on this appetising sweetmeat, dwelling around the ridge, up along the underside and sucking as much of his cock as I could into my mouth.

'I pumped his prick as firmly as possible, keeping my lips taut on his length as I took him fully into my mouth in long, rolling sucks. I continued to palate his penis furiously until I sensed the juices boiling up inside his balls. So I opened my lips and took out his throbbing tool and transferred my attention to his hairy ballsack which I licked all over before returning to his cock. I sucked in his shaft between my lips and rolled my tongue gently around the knob.

'This caused Humphrey to spend almost immediately in fierce, powerful jets of jism which I swallowed to the final sticky drops, smacking my lips with total abandon as at last, his cockstand began to wilt and his prick started to shrink down to its normal, not inconsiderable size.'

'What splendid fun,' I said, sitting up and scanning through the pages of *The Daily News* (like Papa, Aunt Elizabeth is a staunch devotee of Mr Asquith and so subscribes to this Liberal newspaper, much to the disgust of Uncle Sidney who is a rabid Tory). 'I'm sure you slept like a log after such a super bout of fucking.'

Elaine giggled and said: 'Well, I don't mind admitting that I was a little tired by now and I had it in mind that we should doze off for an hour or two and then resume our love-making. But then there was a knock on the door and I dived under the bed-clothes as Humphrey called out: "Who's there?"

' "It's only me — Edwina Murdoch," came the reply, and he sighed with relief as he slipped on a dressing-gown and padded across to the door which he unlocked and opened to reveal his colleague, also clad in a night-robe, who at his invitation stepped into the room. Humphrey closed the door behind her and I rose up from beneath the sheet where I had been hiding.

' "Hello there, you must be Elaine," she said, coming across to shake hands with me. "I've heard a great deal about you from Humphrey and I must say that you are every bit as pretty as he said you were.''

' ''Thank you very much,'' I said, trying not to blush, and I noticed the gleam in her eyes as she gazed over my naked body. ''But you too are a very attractive young woman.'' This was said not merely for the sake of politeness but was quite true. Edwina Murdoch's hair was deep brown and the silky locks tumbled down almost to her shoulders. Her cheeks were rosy pink and her full lips were cherry red and I saw that her snow-white teeth were even and firm when she smiled and said: ''From your state of nudity I would guess that I have interrupted your pleasures. Do forgive me, but it was so lonely in my suite that I thought I would come to your room to see if you would allow me to join your frolics.''

' ''Of course you can . . . well, as far as I'm concerned, that is,'' I replied promptly and we both turned round to Humphrey who smiled broadly and said: ''I'm still a little pooped out, Edwina, and unless Elaine has any objection to the idea, what I'd really love to see is her going down on you. Would you both be prepared to humour my fancy?''

'Edwina and I chorused our approval and the tall, graceful girl slipped off her gown and slid into bed with me. I was more than willing to oblige Humphrey, though it felt a wee bit strange at first, for though I've had many lovely romps with other girls, I've never made love to one in the presence of a man. Anyhow, this initial shyness soon wore off and I felt no embarrassment as we slipped straight into each other's arms and I admired Edwina's beautiful slender legs and marble thighs; her slender waist and the rounded cheeks of her bottom; her full, firm breasts with their cute, red raspberry nipples; and above all, one of the most beautiful cunts I have ever seen in my life.

'It was a truly ravishing affair, Miss Rosie, a bushy hill of silky brown curls and her cunney lips were really luscious, pouting outwards, and she purred like a kitten when I smoothed my hand across her lovely long crack. But I began my seduction of this glorious girl by reaching out and rubbing up one of her nipples to a rubbery hardness. Humphrey then moved over and pressed my head down onto her soft breasts and Edwina sighed with delight as I moved my head from one bosom to another, twirling my tongue all the while around her erect red nipples.

'At first she lay passively, but then with a cry she held me close to her, holding her soft torso close to mine as I relentlessly teased up her stalky titties to new heights. I followed this by letting my tongue travel the full length of her velvety body, and her skin smelled so clean and fresh that I was trembling all over with anticipation as I finally reached the perfumed hairs of her pussy. My tongue ran the length of her parted love lips and a tremor ran through her when I found her clitty, which had by now hardened into a little ball. I gave it my fullest attention, nibbling from side to side, up and down as Edwina jerked and writhed as I reached up and let my hands play with her titties which excited her even more.

'She arched her back and Humphrey cleverly slid a pillow underneath her bum to allow her to press her pussy even harder against my face. Her cunney seemed to open even wider as she lifted her bottom and I flashed my tongue through the pink lips, licking between the grooves of her clitty in long, thrusting strokes. I was now completely lost in Edwina's delicious cunt, licking and lapping the sweet juices that were pouring so freely from her honeypot.

' "Oooh! Oooh! Push your tongue further up my cunt! Further! Harder! Aah, that's the ticket! Oh, Elaine, I think I'm going to spend!" she cried, as my tongue revelled in her sopping muff, out of which her clitty was now protruding like a tiny cock. I took her clitty in my mouth, relishing the aromatic flavour of the delicate morsel as she tightened her thighs about my neck. Then with a great scream she yelled out: "Yes! Yes! I've come, you darling girl! What a wonderful spend!"

'I worked my tongue until my jaw ached, sucking up her

flood of love juice as Edwina heaved violently once more in the throes of her tremendous orgasm.'

'I'm sure that excited Humphrey and that he was soon ready to fuck you again,' I commented, and Elaine's eyes sparkled as she gleefully answered: 'I should say so, Miss Rosie! Why, he fucked me twice more that evening, once in the cunney and once up my bum whilst in between Edwina gave him a good sucking-off.'

'Didn't she want to be threaded too?' I wondered, but Elaine shook her head and said: 'It was a bad time of the month and she didn't want to take any chances, you know, so I frigged her pussy whilst she gobbled Humphrey's cock.'

I quite understood how frustrated poor Edwina must have been, as even the most skilled tongue or pliant fingers can only be but mere substitutes for the genuine article — viz, a big stiff cock. Our family physician, the famous Doctor Cecil Aigin of Harley Street, recently told me that the day will come when all that will be required for ladies to prevent unwanted fertilisation is the swallowing of a little pill every evening. However, Mama believes that the good doctor is guilty of wish-fulfilment and is, alas, wandering into the realms of fantasy. [*Lady d'Argosse's scepticism was more than understandable almost ninety years ago, although of course the birth control pill did finally appear some fifty years after this narrative was written — Editor*]

After I had bathed and taken my usual light breakfast (much to the horror of old Simpson who, like Sayers, our own old retainer at Argosse Towers, thought that two slices of toast, a cup of tea and an apple was totally insufficient for a growing girl) I settled down to read the newspaper in earnest.

A front page advertisement for Mr Selfridge's new Oxford Street premises caught my eye and I decided to pay a visit to this new-fangled 'store' which, according to the advertisement, boasted more than one hundred and twenty-five departments and was only about eight minutes' walk away. Then, just as I was about to call Mrs Godfrey, Aunt Elizabeth's cook-housekeeper, to order luncheon, the telephone rang and Simpson came in and announced that Countess Marussia of Samarkand was on the line for me.

'Hello, Rosie, how are you?' said the Countess gaily when I picked up the receiver. 'I do hope you enjoyed yourself at our *soirée* last night. Actually, Adrian and I were wondering whether you and your friends had made any arrangements for today.'

I explained that Philip and Robert were taking Laura and myself to Lord's later in the afternoon and that I was about to go out and look round Selfridges. 'Ah, what a good idea,' she exclaimed. 'You've reminded me that I need to make one or two purchases before we leave for France on Thursday. Perhaps you would like to meet me there in about half an hour? We could take luncheon together in one of the restaurants.'

We arranged to meet by the Hanseatic-American steamship ticket office on the third floor, and I told Simpson that I would not be in for luncheon but would return home by half past two when Lord Philip Pelham would call for me. 'I'm pretty certain we're dining out, so unless I call you by teatime, you may assume that I won't come home until late,' I informed the butler, who then asked if I needed the services of Randall the chauffeur who was at my service if required.

I considered his suggestion but then rejected the idea of sitting in a traffic jam as, in the West End, even the side streets were clogged with motor cars, carts and omnibuses. 'No, I don't think so, Simpson, I think I'd prefer to take a short constitutional for, although it's rather cloudy, I think the rain will hold off, and if I'm tired or it does begin to rain, I'm sure that Countess Marussia will offer to take me home or at worst, I'll flag down a taxi-cab.'

Not forgetting to take my cheque book, for Mama only had accounts at Harrods and the General Trading Company, I walked out into the hustle and bustle of the London streets. I'd better tell Randall he can spend the day making any repairs or washing down Aunt Elizabeth's vehicles, I thought, so I walked through the mews to the motor-house

[the word 'garage', from the French garer, *was not widely used until the second decade of the century — Editor]*

So I strolled down the narrow side street and saw Aunt Elizabeth's superb new Rolls Royce parked by the kerb, but there was no sign of Randall. Where in heaven's name could he be? The door of the motor-house was closed but I went up to it and peered through the window and, to my great amusement, I saw a most interesting scene. The broad-shouldered chauffeur was standing with his back up against the wall, his trousers and drawers round his ankles and his sturdy shaft in the hands of a petite, stunningly beautiful Indian girl dressed in a rich red sari who was sitting on a low stool as she lustily sucked his shining stiffie.

Her huge, liquid eyes fluttered upwards as she palated his prick with all the delicate artistry one would expect, and the assured way her soft tongue rolled over the wide, rounded knob of Randall's cock reminded me of some of the positions shown in *An Introduction To The Eastern Art Of Fucking* by Mustapha Pharte and An English Country Gentleman which my brother and I discovered one rainy day on a top shelf in our Uncle Gordon's library. She slid her hands under his hanging ballsack and I guessed she tickled his arse-hole with the tip of her finger because within a few seconds the chauffeur groaned and called out: 'I'm coming, Ayisha, brace yourself, my little dark beauty!'

She began swallowing in anticipation as he jerked his cock deep inside her mouth and shot his sticky jism there, although as he withdrew a few drops of his creamy ejaculation dripped down onto her sari. 'Oh blimey, I hope that won't stain,' he said anxiously, and the girl gave his meaty prick a final friendly squeeze. 'Don't worry, Michael, it will wash out very easily,' she said. 'Anyway, it serves me right for frigging your bottom. I knew that I would make you spend, and it would have been better to have waited for you to finish in your own time.'

'Don't worry, it's just as well because I'd better find out from Mr Simpson whether Miss Rosie needs me this morning,' he said, bending down to pull up his trousers.

123

The girl looked puzzled. 'Miss Rosie? Who is this Miss Rosie, Michael?' she queried. 'Have I seen her anywhere?'

'I don't think you have, Ayisha,' said the saucy chauffeur as he cupped his hands round her breasts and lifted his lover back up on her feet. 'Miss Rosie is the mistress's niece and lives down in Sussex. But she is staying here for a few days' holiday.'

'Is she a pretty girl?'

Randall nodded as he buttoned his trousers. 'Miss Rosie's a real cracker, quite tall and really pretty with a lovely curvy figure and long, silky blonde hair. She's being courted by some lucky young toff, what's his name now, Lord Philip Pelham. And I hear she didn't get back home till three o'clock this morning so I'll bet a pound to a penny that she's being well fucked by his noble lordship.

'But she's not as pretty as you, sweetheart,' he added hastily, giving his colonial paramour a big hug. Ayisha smiled and said: 'I'm glad to hear it as I don't want to share your nice cock with anyone else. Go on, you'd better be off — will you be able to take me out tonight, do you think?'

'Well, I can't say for sure,' he sighed. 'I'm on duty and it all depends if Miss Rosie wants me to drive her anywhere. But this Lord Philip, her boyfriend, has his own car so I doubt if I'll be needed.'

Ayisha kissed him and said: 'I must be going too or my father will wonder where I've been. Leave a message for me with Sabu and hopefully I'll see you this evening.'

I hastily drew back from the window and placed myself by Aunt Elizabeth's motor as the garage door opened and Ayisha came out. She walked briskly round the corner and Randall emerged a few moments later. He saw me and came smartly to attention.

'Good morning, Miss, can I be of service?' he asked.

'No thank you, Randall, I shan't need the car this morning. In fact, I won't need you at all today as Lord Philip Pelham is meeting me this afternoon and we won't be back until late tonight. However, I'm sure you can find things to do, can't you?'

I could not resist adding: 'By the way, who was that lovely young girl dressed in Indian clothes who I saw coming out of the motor-house just a minute ago?'

Randall's face coloured as red as Ayisha's sari as he answered: 'Oh dear, you saw her, did you, Miss? Her name's Ayisha and she's the daughter of the Rajah of Tantzerstan. She's very interested in motors, but I'd be obliged if you didn't tell anyone you saw her because her father's terribly strict and I'd get into all sorts of trouble if he knew that she'd been speaking to me.'

'I won't say a word about it,' I promised with a smile. 'But what were you doing in there when the car was parked out in the street?'

He thought quickly and then replied: 'I was showing her my equipment, Miss. I keep quite a few bits and pieces handy in case I ever break down.'

Well, that was one way of putting it! I chuckled and said carelessly: 'And was she impressed by what you showed her?'

The chauffeur looked sharply at me and I wondered if he guessed that I'd seen Ayisha sucking his cock. But wisely he decided not to risk saying any more and simply said: 'I think she liked what she saw, Miss. Er, I can't take you anywhere this morning then?'

I looked up at the sky just as the edges of a thick grey cloud covered the sun and I decided to change my mind and avail myself of Randall's offer. 'Well, I was going to walk to Selfridges but as the sun's gone in I think I'll be lazy and let you take me there.'

In fact the traffic was relatively light and it only took a few minutes for him to deposit me at the front entrance of the new department store. When the uniformed porter opened the car door for me I leaned forward, pulled open the dividing glass and said to Randall: 'No need to wait, I'm meeting somebody who will take me home after luncheon.'

'Very good, Miss Rosie,' he said and just before I moved to get out I added: 'And you can tell Ayisha that I will keep

125

secret not only her visit to our motor-house but also, more importantly, the fact that she appears to be a most accomplished fellatrice! Next time, though, take more care when fornicating and ensure that you cannot be spied upon whilst enjoying yourselves. Honestly, I would hate to think what her father would do to you if one of his servants ever reports seeing Ayisha sucking your prick. These Indian potentates are noted for exacting terrible revenge in such circumstances and you would be in very real danger of losing more than your job, my good man, if you follow my drift.'

He gulped and said: 'Yes, Miss, I understand, and thank you again for being so understanding about the situation,' and I gave him a brief nod before alighting from the car. I must record here the fact that no more was ever said about this incident, so I presume that the randy couple took my advice to heart. Now some readers may wonder why I did not take the matter further, but my credo has always been 'live and let live' and as the Bard of Avon puts it, there are none who can separate young limbs from lechery.

Anyway, I looked at the festooned windows of this new giant emporium based upon the American department store idea. Mr Selfridge [*Harry Gordon Selfridge (1858–1947) was a partner in the famous Marshall Field store in Chicago – Editor*] had built an imposing new edifice which was decorated with festoons and flags. In the many windows there were costumes of many nations displayed against colourful painted panels and the spacious interior presented the appearance of a fair rather than a shop. There were small orchestras playing on every floor and I was most impressed by the glittering array of wares to be seen to good advantage in every department that I visited. There seemed a plentiful supply of courteous, cheerful assistants on hand everywhere and I spent some time studying the pictures in the superbly stocked art gallery. I was especially pleased to see on the walls three landscapes by the Canadian-born water-colourist Clarissa Clements who now resides in West London and whose work I had so admired after seeing her pictures at last year's summer exhibition at the Royal Academy. Indeed,

I was so taken by her stylish depiction of the spring display of flowers in Richmond Park that I purchased the painting as a gift for Aunt Elizabeth and Uncle Philip, and arranged for it to be delivered on Saturday when they returned from their holiday.

I hurried through to the railway and steamship offices where I had arranged to meet Countess Marussia and, as arranged, I stood by the offices of the Hanseatic-American line. I had only to wait two or three minutes before the Countess arrived and, after greeting me, she asked if I minded coming in with her whilst she made a booking on the S.S. *Amerika* for next month.

'We're going to New York for a month and I usually travel on ships of this line of which my friend, Johnny Gewirtz, is a major shareholder. If I inform him of our arrangements, he will send a message to the captain to ensure that the slightest of our personal whims are carefully attended to by the officers and crew.'

This unusual name rang a bell in my memory and, after we sat down in the most exclusive of the restaurants on the top floor, I suddenly remembered that when Philip introduced me to the Countess at Zaines last night, she mentioned that she had met my roguish old uncle, Lord MacChesney, at Count Gewirtz's Tuscan villa.

'Yes, Johnny is a good friend of ours,' mused Marussia. 'You really must meet him one day. He doesn't have the biggest prick in the world but he's very controlled in his fucking and always manages to hold on until one has spent.'

'One of nature's gentlemen,' I said gravely, and she nodded her head in agreement. 'Yes, far more of a gentleman that certain others whom I have entertained. As a lover, he is consideration personified — which is more than I could say of your King Edward, with whom I spent a weekend in Biarritz nine years ago when he was the Prince of Wales and waiting, with barely concealed impatience, for his mama to be joined again with her beloved Albert. But that is another, albeit fascinating story which I plan to keep until I publish my memoirs. [*All copies of Countess*

127

Marussia of Samarkand's scandalous autobiography, Naughty Days and Naughtier Nights, *published privately in Paris in 1923, unfortunately appear to have been lost —* Editor]

'In actual fact, His Excellency Graf Johann Gewirtz of Galicia, to give him his full title, is not entirely a stranger to you, Rosie, for I heard a most exciting report from Tanya about the wonderful love-making you enjoyed with her and Nikolai last night.

'No, don't blush, my dear girl, I heartily approve of spreading happiness throughout the social scale. You will agree, I am sure, that members of the lower orders have every right to enjoy a good fuck just as much as us.'

'Certainly Nikolai's member deserves every consideration,' I murmured, and we both giggled. 'But I am at a loss to understand where the Gewirtz prick comes into the reckoning.'

My companion smiled and said: 'Ah, well, that's easy to explain. Do you remember the dildo with which you fucked Tanya? That hand-made instrument was modelled on a plaster cast of Johnny Gewirtz's cock and was painted in his racing colours which you will see, incidentally, on his horse, Silver Salver, at Goodwood this summer. Johnny gave the dildo to me last autumn as a memento of an exquisite night of fucking in Paris. Interestingly enough, he invited me to see it being fashioned by the famous Zwaig manufactory in Drancy where all the ladies' comforters are hand-modelled from life.'

'I didn't realise at the time that we were playing with such a valuable piece,' I said. 'Truthfully, I did not notice the Zwaigian hallmark on the dildo.'

'Just as well, perhaps, for otherwise you might have felt inhibited about sliding it up Tanya's juicy cunney,' said the Countess. 'Though I must say I found it fascinating to see how these artefacts are produced.'

'Do tell me more,' I urged her. 'I've heard about these special dildoes based upon the prick of a particularly good lover, and I've often wondered about how they were made.'

A waitress came up to take our order and, as we ate a delicious and most reasonably priced luncheon, I learned about the unique process by which Monsieur Zwaig creates his masterpieces. 'To begin with,' the Countess informed me as we sipped our glasses of excellent fresh orange juice, 'as instructed by Monsieur Zwaig, Johnny Gewirtz sat on a high chair clad in only his shirt and underclothes. The process started when a ravishingly beautiful girl came in with a jar and a metal container on a tray which she put down by his feet. She curtsied and said: *"Bonjour, Monsieur le Comte — je m'appelle Babette et je suis votre masseusse privée,"* and then without any warning, reached out and tugged down his drawers and clasped his shaft in her fist as she planted a great big kiss on his lips.

'She pulled open her blouse and brought out her proud, young naked breasts for Johnny to squeeze as she stroked his swelling tool up to its highest erection. When she was satisfied that his straining shaft was at its peak strength, Babette bent her head and let her tongue swirl tantalisingly over his knob for just a few seconds. The little minx giggled as Johnny sighed with delight and she dipped her long fingers into the jar of oil on the tray and carefully rubbed the perfumed ointment along every inch of his throbbing tool, and then she reached downwards to smooth a liberal amount over his dangling, hairy ballsack.

'After making sure that he was well coated with this special unguent, she plunged his cock and balls inside a small container of freshly mixed liquid plaster and commanded him to stay as still as he could. As I said, Johnny can be very calm and controlled in his fucking so he did not find it too difficult to keep his cock quite still, enjoying the cool, wet sensation of the plaster around his rigid rod as Monsieur Zwaig entered the room. He checked his pocket watch and exactly three minutes later he instructed Babette to pull Johnny's prick out of the now-hardening plaster.

'She did so and then cleaned his cock with a soft towel and a bowl of warm soapy water. To Johnny's delight, she then washed his shaft once more with her tongue and, whilst she was busy palating his prick, I asked Monsieur Zwaig when the dildo would be ready, and he told me that we would have to wait until the end of the week for the plaster to harden. What then happens is that the mould is filled with liquid wax and, when that is set, the cast is broken open and *voilà*, we have a perfect, life-size replica of the famed Gewirtz penis. This mould is then coated with clay and placed in a kiln where, of course, the wax inside melts away. The pottery can reproduce any number of copies from the mould, and painted decoration can be added either before or after glazing, which follows a second firing at a much higher temperature.

'Babette brought Johnny off most skilfully and, after she had finished gulping down his spicy jism, he thanked her for her expert services and pressed a twenty franc note into her hand. This was a generous gratuity and when she warmly thanked him, he patted her pert bottom and told her to call at his house at six, rue de la Paix whenever she wanted. "Bring a friend with you as well," I heard him say as Monsieur Zwaig proudly showed me his unique display of dildoes modelled upon the pricks of scions of several European royal houses, and there and then I made an appointment to bring Prince Adrian and have a mould made of his regal rod for my use whilst he is away for eight weeks early next year on some tiresome state visit to the East Indies. Indeed, Rosie, this is the sole reason why we are going to Paris on Thursday morning.'

I looked up at the clock on the wall facing me and told Countess Marussia that, alas, it was time for me to be getting back to Chandos Street. 'Yes, I too must be on my way,' she said, motioning to the *maître d'hôtel* to bring us our bill. 'Now, my telephone number is Gerrard 47. Do call if you and Philip have any free time in the next few days. It would be lovely to spend some more time together.' She insisted on paying for our luncheon and, as the weather had brightened up considerably, I refused her kind offer of a lift in her car and instead walked back home.

Philip was as usual punctual to the very minute and we

arrived at Lord's, the famous cricket ground in St John's Wood, shortly before three o'clock. The match had not attracted a large attendance and we had no problem in finding Laura Matthews and Robert Bacon who had arrived earlier. Oxford had scored only sixty runs for the loss of five wickets and, as Robert explained to me, the two batsmen now at the wicket were concerned more to keep their wickets intact rather than venture out and score some runs. This made for rather dull viewing and, in any case, I must admit that cricket is not a game which I really enjoy watching for more than half an hour at a time — not unless the sun is shining and I am with a group of friends picnicking on some village green and the match itself is secondary to having a jolly time, even if others we know who are playing fail to score centuries or bowl out the opposition.

But here in this hallowed ground, the game was taken seriously and scattered groups of spectators who all fancied themselves as keen and knowledgable critics, analysed performances and tactics and crusty, older gentlemen compared the players on the field (unfavourably, of course!) to Varsity teams from ten, twenty and thirty years ago. I am sure that since time immemorial, according to the lights of a well-known type of stuffy old codger, cricketers, like youth, have been going to the dogs!

A few desultory claps greeted a hit by the Oxford batsman which produced two runs, and I borrowed Philip's binoculars to take a closer look at the young man who (according to Robert) had produced a fine cover drive. If you will forgive the pun, dear reader, I was bowled over myself when I took a closer look at this attractive young man.

Through the powerful lenses of Philip's binoculars I could see that he was an auburn-haired, strapping youth with a handsome face, clear blue eyes and a wide, generous mouth. I noted his broad shoulders and lean, masculine frame, though when I saw a certain swell between his legs I thought the lens might be distorting my vision. 'Who is that good-looking boy about to face the bowling?' I asked.

131

Robert shaded his eyes from the sunlight and replied: 'Do you mean the red-haired chap? Why, that's young Richard Savory, Rosie, and he represents Oxford's best chance of knocking up a respectable score. We played together for Brasenose College when he was a fresher and I was in my final year at Oxford. Incidentally, you may be interested to know that we used to call him Donkey Dick on account of the prodigious dimensions of his prick.'

'His prick? Ah, that explains the protuberance I could see in his groin,' I exclaimed, a remark which caused great merriment. 'No, no, Rosie, even Richard's wedding tackle wouldn't show like that,' laughed Robert. 'What you could see was the outline of the "box" which batsmen wear to protect themselves from a delivery hitting them in the balls. It doesn't provide total protection from pain but does cut down the chance of serious injury.'

Laura was now looking through the binoculars and she said: 'I think the other batsman looks rather sweet, and his face is somehow familiar. Have we met him somewhere, Robert?'

'Indeed we have, my love,' he replied promptly. 'We were introduced at Sir Baker Taylor's Empire Day ball last spring. The name of the young chap is Gary Wright from Cape Town, South Africa and while we were chatting we discovered that your Papa was an old friend of Gary's father, who is the deputy governor of Cape Province. Gary's a fine all-round sportsman who played a great deal of cricket back home before coming to England to complete his education. He's probably more proficient with the ball than the bat as he loses patience against steady bowling and would score more runs if he wouldn't try to drive every other ball to the boundary.' And bless me, as if to confirm Robert's judgement, only three deliveries later, the wiry young Springbok swung his bat wildly and skied the ball high in the air to give a waiting fieldsman the easiest of catches.

'There you are, what did I tell you?' said Robert triumphantly as Gary Wright walked off the field and up the pavilion steps to a languid round of applause, which was well deserved as, despite the aberration which had cost him his wicket, he had still scored a very valuable thirty-five runs.

'Would you all excuse me for a moment?' asked Laura, rising to her feet. 'I do remember meeting Gary now and would like to see him again. I'll see if he's free to come and talk to us whilst his side finishes its innings.'

Twenty minutes later when the players trooped off for tea, Laura had still not returned. 'Where on earth can Laura be?' asked Philip with a worried expression on his face. 'Perhaps we should go and look for her.' But Robert shook his head and said: 'Don't be concerned about Laura, I noticed a gleam in her eye when I mentioned Gary's name and I think she wanted to see if he were capable of bowling a maiden over!'

'But where could they find anywhere to fuck at Lord's?' I said and Robert stroked his chin with his fingers as he looked round the ground before answering me. 'Let me see now, yes, look over there, just to the right of the scoreboard. Do you see those five small private hospitality tents? It wouldn't surprise me one little bit if Laura and Gary were canoodling in one of them.'

'Well, I still think we should make sure you're right and let Laura know where we are,' demurred Philip. 'Rosie, would you mind very much going across to the tents and seeing if Laura is indeed busy as Robert has suggested. It would be less embarrassing for her if you interrupted anything. We'll order tea in the members' café and meet you there.'

'Very well, I'll go straightaway and come back with her,' I agreed, and strolled round to where Robert had directed. All the tents had the ends of their flaps tied so that those inside could enjoy total privacy from prying eyes, and all had 'strictly private' notices plastered on the canvas. No-one else was outside as the sparse crowd had drifted off during the tea interval, so I listened carefully and sure enough, from a tent on my right, I heard a throaty feminine groan which sounded very much like Laura engaged in her favourite occupation.

I went up to the opening and shouted through the gap: 'Laura, that is you, isn't it? It's me, Rosie, I'm sorry to disturb you but the boys and I were a little worried about where you had gone off to.'

There was a brief silence and then, sure enough, Laura called back: 'Come inside, Rosie, just undo the flaps and quickly do them up again immediately afterwards.' I did as she instructed and then turned to see for myself what was making Laura moan so sensuously. Well, Robert Bacon had certainly known what he was talking about for there was Laura, sitting up on the edge of a table wearing only a chemise which had ridden up to expose her frilly French knickers as she dangled her legs over the side. Her dress had been carefully laid out on a chair along with Gary Wright's white flannels, for he stood with his shirt flapping around his thighs as Laura formally introduced us. 'Gary, this is Miss Rosie d'Argosse from Sussex — Rosie, meet Mr Gary Wright from Cape Town, South Africa.' It felt rather strange accepting a handshake from a gentleman clad only in a shirt and whose naked prick poked stiffly upwards out of his drawers whilst he said: 'A pleasure to meet you, Miss d'Argosse. Would you mind if Laura and I complete some unfinished business?'

'Not at all,' I said, and sat down on a second chair next to them as Gary turned his attentions back to Laura. She lifted her bottom so that he could pull down her panties which he tossed over to me. Then he placed his hands on her knees and lovingly looked down on the pouting pink lips of her open cunney. 'What a lovely-looking cunt. Let me pay my homage to Miss Pussy with a big, big, kiss,' he said and he lowered his head between her thighs and started nuzzling his lips against her hardened clitty which popped out as he gave it his full attention, licking from side to side, up and down and around it.

In no time at all she was clutching his curly head and moaning: 'Aaah! Aaah! Gary, Gary, more, more, I'm almost there!' as he came up for breath and instead began rubbing and pinching her clitty with his thumb and forefinger. This had the effect of making Laura twist from side to side as her love juices started to flow and she slipped down the straps of her chemise so that she could play with her breasts, massaging her elongated strawberry nipples as she cried out: 'Rub harder, Gary, that's the way!' as her gyrations increased and she twisted and writhed, heaved and humped until with a shriek she achieved her climax and she imprisoned his hand between her legs, wrapping it tightly between her jerking thighs as the force of her spend slowly subsided.

Gary Wright stood before her, the red uncapped knob of his cock still peeping though his drawers, and Laura looked mischievously down at his erect shaft and took the twitching tool in her hand.

'You had better go now, or won't you miss being presented to the Duchess of Hampshire after the tea interval?' she enquired, but the gallant Gary looked her straight in the eyes and said: 'Frankly, my dear, I don't give a damn. I'd forgo the honour any time of shaking hands even with King Edward himself for the pleasure of feeling your lips slide over my knob.'

'Thank you, Gary, it is always nice for a girl to know how much she is appreciated,' said Laura as she slipped down from the table and rested on her knees in front of the lusty young South African sportsman. She clenched his shaft in her fingers and kissed his uncapped helmet. Then she opened her mouth and took the smooth purple crown of his luscious cock inside it, enclosing her lips around it as firmly as she could, working on the so-sensitive tip with her tongue. She eased her lips around his throbbing shaft, cramming in more and more as her hands circled the base and she worked the loose skin up and down his staff as, at the same time, she began to bob her head up and down and his hands went straight to the back of Laura's head, pushing his pulsing prick even further down her throat.

Somehow she managed to swallow even more of his veiny pole and the erotic squelchy sound must have floated out into the open air as she sucked with gusto on his thick prick.

Laura had learned the art of fellatio from her friend, Ada Langtry, a niece of the famous courtesan [*Rosie is referring here to Lily Langtry, one of King Edward VII's earliest mistresses — Editor*] and proved herself to be an adept pupil. Certainly Gary Wright could contain himself for only a short time before he thrust his hips forward and spurted his spunk inside her mouth in a great gush. Laura tried as hard as possible to swallow all of his creamy emission, but some of the precious liquid dripped from her lips and onto the rug.

I heard the sound of applause from outside and thought for a wild moment that the flaps of the tent had opened and that spectators were clapping this splendid sucking-off. But in fact the cheers were for the two sides who were sauntering out of the pavilion ready to be presented to the Duchess of Hampshire. Gary threw on his clothes in record time and raced towards the centre of the pitch, buttoning his fly as he took his place in the Oxford team just as his captain stepped forward to be introduced to the noble guest of honour. Later, Gary told us that the Duchess was certainly a game old girl, for just then his hands were still smeared with the spunk which had clung to his cock and had transferred itself to his fingers as he popped his prick back inside his drawers. After shaking hands with him, Gary told us, the Duchess had murmured: 'Unless I am much mistaken, young man, you've been up to something naughty during tea — well, a certain part of your anatomy has, that's for sure.'

Gary blushed, but the Duchess had gone on to put him at ease by saying: 'No, dear boy, please don't apologise, I quite understand. The Duke always tosses himself off before going out with the local fox hunt. He tells me that playing with himself relieves the tension and he prefers to wank rather than fuck one of the maids. As he once remarked, when taking oneself in hand, one meets such a nice class of girl. But then Bertie is a terrible snob, I sometimes wonder why he married me as my Papa was only a poor country baronet.'

Anyway, I waited for Laura to dress and then we

136

sauntered back to our seats. Philip greeted us with a cheery wave. 'Hello, you two, would you like some tea now?' he asked. 'Yes, please, but it seems a pity to take you away from the game,' said Laura and, as she spoke, Cambridge's fast bowler raised his arms in triumph as Richard Savory's stumps went flying. 'Your cousin Quentin is the next man in, you'd better stay and watch him bat.'

'I'll take you ladies in to tea,' said Robert, but Laura told him to stay and keep Philip company. 'We'll go to the ladies' room first and we'll see you back here after we've refreshed ourselves.'

However, after we had finished in the rest-room, when we went inside the tea-tent who should be waiting for us but Gary Wright and Richard Savory. Gary introduced his friend to us and (though strictly against the silly Lord's rules about where ladies may or may not go) the boys smuggled Laura and myself and a bottle of chilled white wine into the Oxford dressing room. There was a great cheer outside and Richard looked through the high window and said: 'Good heavens, Quentin Parsifal has hit a six! If he and Billy Daniels can knock up another fifty or so between them, we'll still be in with a chance of winning this match.'

'And let's pray that he and his partner keep at the crease so we won't be needed to play for some time yet,' added Gary with a grin, pulling down Laura to sit next to him on one of two rather battered old sofas. 'Phew, Richard, hadn't you better take a shower? You must be very sweaty after being out at the crease for so long.'

Richard looked at me apologetically and said: 'Do forgive me, Miss d'Argosse, but would you mind very much if I left you temporarily to clean myself up?'

'Of course not,' I said and he took off his cricket shoes and socks and then pulled his sweater over his head. Then he unbuttoned his shirt and stood bare-chested in front of me. I looked at the prominent bulge between his legs for a second time that afternoon and exclaimed: 'I would very much like to see the protective box about which our mutual friend Robert Bacon has been telling me.'

137

He gave me a tiny smile and then nonchalantly replied: 'I'm awfully sorry, Miss d'Argosse, but actually I left mine behind in rooms back at college and I played today without one.'

Good grief! I trembled with excitement as a sensuous tingle started to make itself felt in my pussy and we sat down next to each other. What would be revealed when Richard Savory took down his trousers? The cheeky young man must have been reading my mind for he took hold of my soft hand and placed it firmly against the massive tube of flesh in his crotch. I opened the buttons of his trousers and out sprang his swollen cock, rising sturdily upwards, slightly curved but of what length and thickness! I took hold of this satin-smooth monster and gently rubbed it up and down, making the warm, red knob swell and bound in my hand.

The sight of Richard's succulent shaft sent my cunt on fire and I resolved there and then to have it inside my cunney. He assisted me by deftly unhooking the buttons at the back of my dress and, before you could say Jack Robinson, I stood stark naked in front of him and I looked across to see a marvellous picture of myself in a full-length mirror frigging Richard's enormous affair, and I know that the others were also enjoying this lewd tableau.

My blonde hair, now undone and hanging down in long tresses, veiled yet somehow highlighted my thrusting, uptilted breasts and the swell of my bosoms acted as a magnet for Richard's hands and he cupped the soft spheres, rubbing the tawny nipples up against his palms until they were as firm as tiny bullets.

Gary and Laura now undressed and it was most stimulating for us to see each other nude in the mirror. There was I, first kneeling on the floor, then rising up to sit on Richard's lap, now kissing him violently on the lips whilst my hand stole up and down his huge cock, whilst his hands roamed all over my curvaceous body. Then, shaking clear a fringe of wispy hair from my face, I bent downwards to take his rock-hard shaft in my mouth. I sucked slowly, tickling and working round the tiny 'eye' on top of the bulbous dome,

138

whilst Richard parted my unresisting thighs and inserted one, two and then three fingers into my moistening cunney.

'Aaaah . . .' he breathed as with one hand I caressed his giant prick with feathery little licks whilst I cuddled his hairy ballsack in my hand. His twitching tool jerked wildly as I washed the smooth mushroom helmet before putting my entire open mouth around the shaft as far as it would go, sucking hard for just an instant before letting it out of my mouth.

I looked up and saw that Richard was in the seventh heaven of delight, lying back with his eyes closed, his body totally relaxed as he revelled in the luxurious warmth of this unhurried sucking-off. Behind us I heard Gary politely ask Laura how she preferred to be fucked. She replied: 'I'm agreeable to most positions, kind sir, but just now I have a fancy to be fucked from behind so that I can watch Rosie and Richard at the same time.'

'Your wish is my command,' said Gary gallantly as Laura lay on her tummy with her head and shoulders over the arm of the sofa. He piled two cushions under her belly so that her hips and the beautifully rounded cheeks of her bottom were raised high in the air. He moved between these luscious globes and nudged her knees a little further apart, before taking his throbbing stiffstander in his hand and sliding it firmly in the crevice of her bum and into her sopping slit.

Gary was an athletic young man and he fucked Laura in a steady, fast-paced rhythm, achieving maximum penetration by bending forward and taking hold of her hanging breasts and rubbing her titties up to new peaks of hardness as the hairs on his broad chest brushed against her back as he continued to pump his prick in and out of her juicy cunt.

I continued to suck Richard's tremendous truncheon as I relished Gary's polished performance, watching his gleaming shaft slewing so easily in and out between the cheeks of Laura's glorious bum. Her soft cheeks slapped against his muscular thighs as she fitted herself into his rhythm, and I could see her tiny rear dimple quiver with every thrust of Gary's sizeable staff as I lapped Richard's shaft in time with Gary's pumping strokes. She felt behind her until she found his tight, wrinkled ballsack which she gently cradled in her hand as they fucked happily away in perfect unison.

Now I turned my eyes up towards Richard to see if he was still happy with the proceedings, but his eyes were still closed and he moaned with pleasure as I gently squeezed his balls. I now changed this teasing titillation by rolling my tongue up into a warm little arrow which circled around his swollen knob, and then I raised my head slightly and powered my mouth down on this huge helmet, first just holding it lightly between my teeth and then taking in as much of the pulsating shaft inside my mouth as I could on top of my now-flattened tongue. I sucked slowly and his enormous organ tasted as sweet as the most delicious lollipop. I tickled and worked my way around his helmet as to my side I heard a cry from Laura. She yelled out: 'More! I must have more! Empty your balls, Gary, I'm coming! Yes, I'm coming!'

Gary smiled and duly obliged, quickening his tempo and panting hard as his cock slithered in and out of Laura's cunney at breathtaking pace until, with a final tremble, he shot a torrent of sticky white jism inside her willing cunt. He panted hard as Laura contracted her cunney muscles to milk him of the last drops of spunk as she herself now climaxed gloriously, letting out a whoop of delight as the frenzy of the orgasm spread like wildfire through every fibre of her quivering body.

This made my own cunney throb even more and I wanted more inside my love channel than Richard's fingers, however cleverly he manipulated them. So I gave his monstrous pole a final lubricious kiss and slid upwards on top of him, placing a knee on each side of his body.

Richard understood at once what was required of him and he teased my dripping crack with the tip of his knob, rubbing it along the length of my slit, smearing the juices all round my pussy hair. Then I lowered myself slowly down on top of his thighs — though I was genuinely concerned that my little chink would be unable to accommodate what was surely the biggest cock I had ever seen. Yet somehow my cunney stretched to receive his glistening, rigid rod and he managed to embed it all in my engorged cunt. I moved up and down slowly at first on his pulsing pole, but then I quickened the pace until I was riding Richard like a jockey in sight of the winning post, savagely thrusting myself down on his thick shaft, eluding his grasping hands which tried to slow me down, for the dear boy was worried that he might spend too quickly.

But then he caught the rhythm and thrust upwards in time with my downward plunges so well that his cock caressed my clitty beautifully, as madly we rocked together until, in a splendidly powerful release, he drenched my pussy with a deluge of frothy sperm, just as I too climbed the highest pinnacle of pleasure, and we gasped out our delight as my cunney released its own flood of love juice which flowed down my thighs and into the auburn curls of Richard's pubic hair.

However, to my amazement, my new young lover was immediately ready for a further joust. Without taking his hard prick out of my dripping crack, he pulled me down on my back and began pumping that astonishingly big cock in and out of my willing cunt, whose velvet lips opened and closed over his still rock-hard weapon. Our mouths met in the sweetest of kisses and I wriggled my bum to better absorb his mighty prick as Richard pushed forward and, to my surprise, managed to bury his entire shaft inside me so that our pubic hairs matted together as his balls banged against my bum cheeks.

We stayed motionless for magic moments of pure, unadulterated lust, enlaced in an aura of wonder at the delights afforded by our bodies, and our lusty coupling had urged on Laura and Gary to start their own second session of love-making with Laura lying down on her back with her legs wide, giving Gary a close, full frontal view of her pouting pussy lips which peeked through her dark pubic hair. He sat astride her and brought his knees up to either side of her hips and then sat back on his heels. This had the desired effect of opening up her cunney and changed the angle of his cock's penetration as he slid his shaft inside her willing crack. She gasped as Gary moved his cock as he reached behind and took her ankles in his hands. This kept Laura's legs stiff and gave her something to push against, which made the fucking even more pleasurable for them both.

He began to pump faster and Richard and I could hear the squelching sounds of Gary's prick pistoning its way in and out of Laura's clinging cunney. They climaxed together fairly quickly, and Gary grunted hoarsely as he squirted his jets of jism, shuddering with each jerk of his cock until his swiftly deflating shaft was milked dry.

Meanwhile I now felt Richard moving his throbbing shaft against the walls of my cunney and he whispered: 'Rosie, how lusciously tight your love sheath holds my cock. What a wonderful girl you are!'

'And you have such a gorgeous big prick, Richard,' I replied, stroking his silky hair with my fingers. 'Oh yes, that's the way, darling, keep working your shaft to and fro. Go faster now, faster, I want to feel all your hot, spunky cream inside my cunney.'

He willingly complied with my request and the sofa shook as we fucked away frantically. I raised my legs high to wrap them round his lean torso, which helped him bury his shaft fully inside my cunt as his heavy balls slapped against my bum. Waves of ecstasy rolled out from between my legs as Richard's thrusting prick slid effortlessly in a sensual rhythm, moving faster now as my bottom arched up to meet it. He clasped my bum cheeks as we fucked like a couple possessed, his long, thick cock working backwards and forwards in my sopping cunney, and I tightened my legs round his waist and squeezed as hard as I could to feel every ridge of his wonderful cock. My cunney was now on fire as a raging orgasm shuddered a path through my body and Richard's climax followed almost at once. 'I'm coming,

Rosie, I'm coming!' he cried joyously. 'Work your hips, make me spend! Yes, yes, yes, I can feel the spunk rising up from my balls. A-h-r-e! There it goes!'

The dear boy shuddered as he spent copiously inside me and I delighted in the spasms of liquid fire which shot into my willing honeypot. When we had recovered we sat together with the other couple, with Laura and myself perched upon the boys' knees.

Laura bent down and took their two limp cocks in her hand and sighed: 'Oh my, would you look at these two sorry specimens, Rosie. How are the mighty fallen! Still, we can't really grumble at their performances, can we?'

'No, I have no complaints whatsoever,' I said, patting the thick, dangling shaft which had just reamed out the furthest nooks and crannies inside my cunt. 'But I see now why you are known as "Donkey Dick", Richard. You must have been the object of much envy by your friends at school.'

'Not really,' he said glumly. 'At first it was alright and I was one of the most popular chaps in the Lower Fifth. I used to be cheered when I came into the shower after games, and I won every cock-measuring session in the changing-rooms or at night in the dormitory after lights-out. One of my friends, who was keen on algebra, even calculated the cubic size of my cock!'

'Really?' said Laura with interest, being a clever mathematician herself. 'Presumably he used a formula of $\pi r^2 1$, where r is the radius and 1 the length of the shaft.'

Richard shrugged his shoulders and said: 'I'm pretty sure you're right. But anyway, the novelty soon palled and having a thick prick didn't make me confident as far as girls were concerned. My birthday is just after Christmas and Sally, our parlourmaid, agreed to give me a birthday kiss under the mistletoe. One afternoon, when we were alone upstairs, I took her into my bedroom and produced a sprig and held it up over head. She kissed me and let me feel her breasts, which of course made my cock swell up against her.

' "My, what have you got in your pocket, Master

Richard?'' she asked, and when I unbuttoned my fly and brought out my stiffie to show her — for I thought she would be as impressed as my friends back at school — she took one look at my cock and said in a horrified tone: ''That's far too big a tadger for a young boy like you, Master Richard. It's even bigger than your Papa's prick (funnily enough, at the time, I actually wondered how on earth she could know *that*!). I don't think I could take it in my pussy now. Coo, I wonder what size it might grow to by the time you're sixteen.'' So, as I've told anyone who has envied me those extra inches — stick to what you've got for believe me, a bigger cock is no guarantee for getting girls to drop their drawers.'

'So Sally wouldn't go further than a kiss and a feel of her tits?' asked Gary. 'Gosh, I would have thought she would have liked to have taken your cherry, old man, despite the outrageous size of your cock.'

'Well, after much persuasion she did,' admitted Richard, but a burst of applause from ouside sent Laura scurrying to the window. 'Your innings has ended and the players are coming off the field,' she announced and, snapping her fingers she added: 'Quick, someone, lock the door whilst we get dressed.' Gary sprang forward and smartly turned the key whilst we hastily threw on our clothes. Laura and I managed to slip out through a side door and rejoin Philip and Robert, and though they complained about how they had missed our company, Laura made up for our absence by recounting in graphic, uncensored detail just what we had been doing to the middle wickets of the two good-looking young cricketers in the dressing-room!

'I do hope that mid-match fucking will not have adversely affected Gary Wright's bowling,' remarked Robert with a frown. 'I've wagered a hundred pounds with Captain Archer that Oxford will bowl out Cambridge for less than their own total of one hundred and seventy-five runs.'

'That's a very substantial bet, Robert, aren't you going in a bit steep?' said Philip doubtfully. 'Captain Archer has pots and pots of money but your Papa will want a better reason than a foolish gamble if you have to ask him to increase your allowance.'

Well, the moral of this little conversation is that one should never bet money that you can't afford to lose. At first Gary Wright was Robert's hero, taking three Cambridge wickets in two overs. However, dogged resistance and aggressive batting by the partnership of Lord Cheetham and the Hon. Nicholas Austin smartly pushed Cambridge's score up to one hundred and one for the loss of only the three wickets taken by Gary Wright. They seemed invincible and Robert roundly cursed the wretched Oxford wicketkeeper, who muffed the easiest of opportunities to dismiss Lord Cheetham when he mistimed a big hit and the ball spun up invitingly high in the sir, only for a slip fieldsman and the wicketkeeper to collide as they both went for the catch, and the chance was lost. But luckily for Robert, the wheel of fortune turned again and Lord Cheetham was run out after a misunderstanding with his partner. The remaining batsmen faltered and at one stage Cambridge had nine out of their ten wickets down for just one hundred and forty-eight.

Now it seemed that Robert would win his bet, but the last Cambridge batsmen held out until they had actually equalled Oxford's total of one hundred and seventy-five runs and the bet was therefore cancelled, which perhaps was as well for Robert was so relieved not to have lost such a substantial amount of money as one hundred pounds that he swore never to wager more than a fiver on any horse or any sporting event ever again.

I cannot say I was totally displeased at the outcome, or indeed that a bank of dark clouds now covered the sun and threatened us with the kind of heavy shower for which April is so noted. 'Why don't we all go back to my place for some bubbly? Cooney's have just delivered two cases of '03 Bollinger that should be well worth tasting,' suggested Robert. 'I'm staying at the house my parents have rented, just round the corner in Avenue Road, but I'm all alone as Mama and Papa are away taking the cure at Marienbad [*one of the fashionable European health spas — Editor*] and both my sisters have left England to spend the summer in Paris and the South of France with young Lady Shackleton's set. But all the servants are there and Mrs Kenton's a jolly good cook, so I will ask a few other people round for supper as well and we'll have a jolly party.'

This sounded like a good idea, but first Philip trotted off to say a few words to his cousin Quentin and wish him the best of luck if the rain allowed the match to be finished. He returned from the players' lounge and, as we walked back to our motor cars, he passed an envelope to me. 'Richard Savory asked me to pass this letter to you, Rosie,' he said and I stuffed it in my handbag to read later in the privacy of my own home.

In the end we decided to forgo temporarily Robert's kind offer to try out his newly delivered champagne, but were delighted to take up his invitation to dine at Avenue Road. But we all needed to change our clothes, so Robert went home in a taxi-cab and put Topping, his chauffeur, at Laura's disposal. As she lived in Knightsbridge, I said that if Topping would drop me off at Chandos Street, this would save Philip a journey for he could then go straight home and pick me up after he had changed, whilst Topping would wait at Laura's until she was ready to be brought back to Robert's house.

This plan was swiftly agreed and Laura and I waved goodbye to the boys as Topping swung Robert's Mercedes-Benz into Wellington Road. 'I didn't just suggest these transport arrangements for pure convenience,' I confessed to Laura as we settled down in the luxurious leather seats. 'I wanted to read this letter that Richard Savory has written to me without Philip and Robert looking over my shoulder.'

'You naughty girl,' giggled Laura, placing her arm round my waist and cuddling up to me. 'But you don't mind my reading it, though, do you?'

'No, of course not, I'd like you to see it as I would be surprised if you weren't mentioned in it,' I replied and rummaged in my bag for the letter. I opened it and read it out to Laura:

'Dearest Rosie,

I have just time to write a few short words of thanks from Gary and myself to you and Laura for our delightful little get-together this afternoon, which we assure you both will remain locked in our memories for many a year. As you may not know, I dabble a little in poetry and at present I am choosing verses for an anthology of my work to be published later this year. Last month I penned the following lines which in the book will be dedicated to 'Rosie and Laura':

Let us with prudence, skill and nerve
Our side not selfish interest serve.
Nor be cast down though fortune frown, whatever
    class our ticket.
For Life's a pitch which plays too fast,
The best long hops are quickly past,
The strongest player, the greatest player will
    sometimes lose his wicket.
When work and sport alike are o'er,
And all our deeds are in the score,
May we have won, not vainly done
Our lifetime game of cricket.

We do hope that you and Laura will write to us c/o Brasenose College, Oxford. We would love to see you both again as soon as possible.

Yours ever,
Richard

'What a charming letter! I must keep it safely locked away in my private drawer,' I said and Laura snuggled even closer to me. 'It must have been wonderful to be fucked by such a big cock as Richard Savory's,' she murmured as she slipped her hand under my skirt and I squeezed my thighs

147

together, trapping her hand as her fingers petted my pussy through the fine linen of my knickers.

'It was certainly quite an experience,' I quietly replied. 'Do be careful, Laura, Topping can see us in his driving mirror and if we stop, a bicyclist or passing pedestrian might glance through the window and see more of us than they should.'

'Quite right, one should never exhibit oneself in public,' said Laura, throwing a good-size travelling rug over our legs which neatly concealed her hand, which I now released to enable her to tug down my drawers and slide her fingers across my furry blonde bush.

'M'mmm, that's very nice,' I said as the tip of a finger slid between my yielding cunney lips. I lay my head back and purred: 'Oooh yes, that's very nice indeed!'

Her hand continued its journey and now she slipped a second long, probing finger inside my fast-dampening cunt. I turned my head and kissed her warmly and she softly sighed: 'How I would love to set your pert titties free here and now — oh, Rosie, how marvellous it would be to see them spill out of your bodice and fall into my hands. I would like nothing better in the whole wide world than to kiss and nibble at those two delightful little cherries right this minute!'

A flush of desire seeped through my body and I could feel my nipples swell against their light covering as I answered: 'And nothing would give me greater pleasure, Laura, but I am sure we will be able to pleasure ourselves together at some point later this evening.'

Meanwhile, I eased my thighs apart to allow a third of Laura's fingers to join its fellows inside my juicy love channel. Suddenly she touched upon my eager clitty and I almost jumped up in my seat at the thrill which shot through me as Laura giggled happily and continued to rub it firmly. I almost screamed with delight as her wicked fingers made me gasp and tremble as she eased them deeper and deeper inside my cunt and very soon I felt the first stirrings of an orgasm. As I felt myself beginning to climax, I writhed wildly against Laura, holding her hand firmly against my pussy with my legs as I uninhibitedly squeezed my breasts with my hands. This fabulous pressure kept me at a delicious peak of sensual pleasure for what seemed a wonderfully long time, and even when my orgasm eventually subsided, my pussy still tingled and I continued to feel very aroused and desperately needed to be finished off.

However, the car was now turning into Chandos Street and I called out to our driver to pull up outside Aunt Elizabeth's house. I must say that Topping, who probably saw more than he should in his driving mirror, was the very model of discretion and he did not give me even the slightest knowing look, nor did he betray any unwanted leer in his voice as he respectfully wished me a pleasant 'good afternoon, ma'am'. So I was not surprised when later that evening Robert confided to me that he had with some success pressed Topping's tool into active service when, as occasionally happened at one of his 'fast' dinner parties, a male guest succumbed to the miseries of 'brewers' droop' and was unable to produce a stiff cock for a waiting pussy. Indeed, after being fucked by Robert's chauffeur, Lady Fuster roundly declared that Topping was one of the best-endowed lovers in London, along with the talented amateur musician Sir Peter Stockman, the Australian athlete John Clarke who is rumoured to have the biggest balls in Melbourne and, of course, Robert Bacon himself.

Be that as it may, as soon as Simpson opened the door I rushed upstairs and was about to call Elaine to run my bath when I distinctly heard a girl let out a yelp, followed by a muffled giggling from Aunt Elizabeth and Uncle Sidney's bedroom. Now, although, as I have already made abundantly clear in this narrative, I have absolutely no objection to the lower classes fucking whenever they like, there was no excuse for servants to use their employers' bedroom whilst they were away. Therefore I resolved to investigate without delay just who were taking advantage of their situation in Aunt Elizabeth's bedroom — but I was temporarily thwarted, for I soon discovered that the door had been bolted from the inside.

However, there was no key in the lock so I looked through the keyhole and to my astonishment saw my Uncle Sidney rolling about naked on his four poster bed with Janette, the pert little chambermaid, who was wearing only a pair of crisp, white cotton knickers. As I watched the two of them playfully wrestling with each other, Janette rolled over on to her tummy and Uncle Sidney pulled down her panties to expose her bouncing bum cheeks, which he slapped playfully with his left hand as he cupped his right hand round his thick prick and coaxed up his shaft to a rock-hard erection.

What was it about my uncles that made them behave so naughtily with the staff? In my previous book [*Rosie Vol One: The Intimate Diaries*] I chronicled the many sexual encounters of my Mama's brother, Lord Gordon MacChesney. Uncle Gordon, though, was a gay old bachelor and so was therefore quite entitled to fuck whoever he wished. And frankly, it also crossed my mind that it was rather *infra dig* for Uncle Sidney to use his marital bed for extra-mural fucking.

Not that fucking Janette on his own bed seemed to bother Uncle Sidney, whose head was now between Janette's legs with his mouth glued to her hairy pussy. I could see his hand come up to part the folds of her cunney lips and I could hear him slurp his tongue along her dampening crack as the girl scrunched her thighs together as he tasted her oozing juices, noisily lapping up her tangy spend as she panted: 'Alright, sir, that's made me sopping wet — I'm ready for your nice fat pork sword now!'

Janette spread her legs wide open and bent her knees as Uncle Sidney fondled his cock and raised his body up prior to plunging his prick inside her waiting pussy. Now Uncle Sidney was a shortish man of just about my height, yet one good look at his cock was all I needed to see the truth of the old racing adage that the smallest jockeys carry the biggest whips! He took hold of his enormous tool and stroked his shaft along Janette's soaking quim, making his huge knob slippery with her love juices. She arched her back to receive it in her honeypot and Uncle Sidney buried the full length in her clinging cunney as he gasped: 'Aaah! What a lovely feeling – I'm right up your gorgeous cunt, you naughty little minx!'

They then fucked away in great style, his hard, stiff staff pistoning up and down in and out of her squelchy cunt as she responded eagerly, wrapping her legs around him and clawing at his back with her fingernails. 'I'm coming,' gasped Uncle Sidney, whose parents arrived in England from Italy more than sixty years ago, but Sidney had discovered that occasionally dropping into his mother tongue pleased many women who enjoyed being wooed in the flowery, melodious tones of that delightful language. 'I'm coming – I'm spunking – right up your delicious little notch, *la bella donna della mia miente*!'

Janette began to grind her bottom round in a circular movement as Uncle Sidney thrust downwards and his cock spurted its offering of sticky white cream, whilst his hips jerked violently as he creamed her eager cunney with his copious emission.

The sight of this lascivious scene, together with the stimulation my cunney had been receiving just beforehand from Laura in the back of the car, was driving my poor pussy wild. I rubbed myself between my legs as I watched the cheeky young girl now lay Uncle Sidney on his back and grasp his glistening shaft in her hand. She slid her fingers up and down his sinewy staff which, surprisingly soon, was as hard and stiff as a flagpole. She knelt down beside him and thoroughly wet the smooth, uncapped crown of his cock with her tongue. Then, opening her mouth as wide as possible, she slid the purple knob inside, closing her lips around it, easing her lips forward to take in as much of his thick cock as she could. She circled the base with her hand and sucked lustily, gulping in as much as possible until his knob must have been touching the back of her throat.

Then, just as I saw her cup his hairy bollocks in her hand, my concentrated stare through the keyhole was broken by

151

a discreet cough behind me. I whirled round and to my great embarrassment found out that Smith, the young footman, was standing not three feet behind me. 'I'm sorry if I startled you, ma'am,' he said apologetically. 'But Mr Simpson asked me to come upstairs and help your maid run your bath. The hot tap was jammed and she could not open it. But I've managed to unlock the tap and the water's running freely now.'

'Oh, that's good,' I said, not quite knowing what to say to this good-looking lad who could not have been more than eighteen. After sampling Richard Savory's wonderful prick, though, my appetite had been whetted for youthful if inexperienced lovers and I freely confess that the lewd idea did cross my mind as to whether Smith possessed a prick which would be able to satisfy my seething cunney.

Little did I dream, however, that this idle thought might actually transfer itself into actuality — but as it so happened, my perky little maid Elaine now came bustling up to us and announced that my bath was now ready for me to use. The footman moved away to go back downstairs, but Elaine said to him: 'Can you stay up here for a minute, Dudley, I think Miss Rosie might need your services in a minute?'

She pulled me to one side and whispered: 'Smith fucked me after lunch, Miss Rosie. He has a nice thick prick and what is even better news is that he really knows how to use it. Now I saw you frigging yourself watching your Uncle and Janette, and it's obvious that it has made you feel very randy. So how would you like to try out Dudley Smith's cock before your bath? He'll be happy to oblige if asked.'

In other circumstances I may well have reprimanded Elaine for her impertinence, but my blood was up and I replied: 'Give me five minutes then send him into my room.'

'Very good, Miss Rosie, I know that you won't be disappointed,' she giggled as I marched to my room and undressed completely. Then I stretched myself out totally naked on my bed, waiting for the young footman to come and show me his mettle. The expected knock on the door soon followed and I called Smith in. I let my finger stray sensuously over my breasts, flicking up my nipples to two little red peaks of hardness as the young footman stood awkwardly by the door — though I could see from the large swelling in the front of his trousers that his cock was not suffering from any shyness!

I smiled encouragingly to him and said: 'Come here, Dudley — it is Dudley, isn't it? — come over here and you'll get a better look at my sweet little pussy. Don't you think it's pretty with its fringe of silky blonde hair? And aren't my cunney lips nice and pink? You know, they can hardly wait for you to slide your thick prick between them.'

He smiled but said nothing as he walked nervously towards me. When he reached the side of the bed I stretched out my arm and rubbed the palm of my hand against the stiff bulge in his groin. This had the desired effect of setting a match to the tinder and he ripped open the buttons of his trousers and pulled out his straining shaft which sprang out like a Jack-in-the-Box. I encircled his rigid rod with my hand and planted a luscious wet kiss on top of the uncapped red knob.

'Steady, Miss! I haven't locked the door. Suppose someone comes in?' he gasped.

'Elaine will make sure no-one comes in, you silly boy,' I laughed, making a fist round his throbbing tool and gently frigging his stiff prick which bounded and jerked in my grasp. Actually, the idea of illicit, covert intercourse does give me an added thrill and the very notion that someone might come in and discover us somehow gave the whole proceedings an additional spice. There was no real danger of young Dudley Smith losing his courage and fleeing from me — especially when I pressed his hand to my breasts. At first this startled him, but very quickly he responded by rubbing my nipples and squeezing my bosoms as we engaged in the most delicious kiss, our tongues fluttering away in each other's mouths, and his hands were now running all over me. I grasped his naked cock and I dived down and wrapped my lips around the swollen helmet of his rigid prick. My warm breath and moist mouth sent chills racing up and down his spine, and my tongue slithering round his veiny pole soon brought him to the brink of a spend. I was enjoying sucking his thick shaft and now I gripped the firm, muscular cheeks of his bottom, moving him backwards and forwards until with a final, juddering throb he spurted a creamy stream of tangy jism into my willing mouth. I swallowed his copious emission, smacking my lips with unfeigned gusto, and his body quivered with convulsions of delight as we finished by hugging each other and sealing our pleasure with a loving kiss.

Now of course, even for a well-hung young man like Dudley Smith, there are physical limits of stamina to which even the most sensuous must accept. Dudley had just fucked Elaine and now I had sucked him off, so naturally his poor prick lay dangling forlornly over his thigh. So, though I was impatient to be fucked, I forced myself to relax and snuggle down beside him as he girded his loins for the *pièce de résistance*, and when I judged that he had had sufficient time to recover, I lay back and spread my legs invitingly as I cupped my hands under my breasts and pushed them out towards him as I let my fingers twiddle my hardening titties. Then I started to stroke my pussy through the fine growth of silky blonde hair, between which my pink cunney lips coyly peeped out. I slipped a finger into my moist slit and began to rub myself off. Dudley looked on with great interest and I was delighted to see his prick begin to stiffen as I continued the show by kissing his nipples and then working my way down to his rising cock. With one sudden gulp I took his balls in my mouth whilst I massaged his member up to its previous rock-hard state.

This time, I wanted his smooth ivory shaft in my cunt so I wriggled my way round until my pussy was above his face and, as I lowered myself down on him, he lapped eagerly all around my juicy crack. His lips closed in on my cunt as I continued to suck his throbbing tool. His soft tongue ran along my slit in wet, teasing strokes and I moved my cunney up and down as Dudley rolled his hips to slide his tasty cock in and out of my yearning mouth. I would

154

have loved to have felt more of his dextrous tongue but I did not want to chance his spending before he fucked me properly, so I moved off his face and instead sat astride him, taking hold of his proud prick and pressing down the yielding lips of my aching cunney to the tip of his glowing knob. Slowly, I spitted myself upon his cock, bathing his shaft with my love juices, and I wriggled around to work the hard, fleshy shaft inside me as far up within my love channel as possible.

Once I had fully embedded his cock, I began to bounce merrily up and down on it. Dudley asked if I was comfortable and I gasped: 'Yes, oh, yes, I enjoy occasionally being on top during fucking. It's quite an exhausting position as it leaves the girl to do most of the work, but you need the rest and honestly, I rather like a change of diet now and then. Anyhow, a thick prick like yours works well this way as it gives my cunney a really hard pounding. Ooooh, that's lovely, Dudley, there's a good boy, work your bum round when I sit down on you as this gives my clitty a good rub as well!'

Now some men enjoy this kind of fuck and simply lie back and watch, but as I worked my own bottom from side to side, Dudley threshed wildly beneath me and he caught my rhythm, arching his back upwards to meet my downward thrusts. I moved my hips faster and faster and the feel of my clinging, wet honeypot now brought off the dear lad and, with a hoarse groan, he grabbed my bum cheeks and pulled me down on his pulsating cock as he jetted a hot stream of sticky spunk up into my waiting love cunney. My cunt throbbed and rubbed itself against his gorgeous prick until I felt it begin to shrink, and I moved off him as he lay panting with fatigue, his chest heaving up and down as he slowly recovered his senses.

It was time to say farewell to my young hero but I was faced with a ticklish problem — would the dear lad be offended if I gave him a present for services rendered? I decided immediately that a monetary gift would be inappropriate — it would surely smack too much of a

155

commercial transaction, but surely, a small token of my appreciation would not come amiss. So I resolved to go back to Oxford Street the next morning and purchase a small gift for Dudley — a good book, perhaps, though even a wonderful store like Selfridges would not stock Mr David Pickering's classic work *An Illustrated Guide to The Eastern Art of Fucking* with photographs by Dr Marmaduke Bell and Sir Antony Hammond. Alas, this splendid book is available only in a few educational bookshops and is then only offered to selected customers.

There was time to soak myself in a nice, warm bath and then change into one of my favourite evening dresses, a low-cut blue gown my Mama bought for me when we went to Paris last month, and I was in the drawing room listening to Uncle Sidney explain that he had to leave my Aunt at the country house party they were attending as he had received a telegram from his sister-in-law that his brother, Albert, had been badly injured in an accident on his estate down in Devon. My uncle was unable to give me a plain answer when I enquired what exactly had befallen the unfortunate gentleman, but from his convoluted explanation I gathered that Albert and a milkmaid had been examining the loft of an old barn which collapsed under their weight. Luckily, the pair had landed on thick bales of hay, but Albert had suffered a broken leg, though happily the girl escaped with only heavy bruising. However, even from Uncle Sidney's delicate bowdlerisation of the incident, I soon gathered that the pair had been found naked in each other's arms and indeed, Albert's cock was still ensconced inside the unfortunate girl's cunt when they were discovered by an alert passing horseman.

Uncle Sidney was doubtless pleased to be saved from any further questioning by the ringing of the front door bell. Simpson came in and announced: 'Miss d'Argosse, Lord Philip Pelham is here to see you.'

'Show him in, please,' I said and I introduced Philip to Uncle Sidney who said: 'We've met before, haven't we, my Lord, at an Old Harrovians cricket match?'

156

'You know, I distinctly recall that after Countess Marussia's party you said you weren't too keen on cricket, and you have told me many times how boring you found your schooldays,' I remarked to Philip as we sat in the back of his Rolls Royce and Mellor negotiated his way through the heavy West End traffic. 'So I'm rather surprised to hear that you bothered to go to a game just to meet former pupils of your old school.'

Philip shrugged his shoulders and said: 'Well, you're quite right, Rosie, for unless I had a compelling reason to be there, you wouldn't have got me back to Harrow to play cricket for a thousand pounds. But my young brother Edwin is still at the school and is captain of the first eleven. So I agreed to take part in the Goose Match last September.'

'The Goose Match? That's nothing to do with goosing, I suppose?'

'Unfortunately not, my love, it's just the name given to the last game of the cricket season between the School and an Old Boys Eleven. The match goes on till the light fades and then players and spectators sit down to a slap-up-dinner. You can imagine what's on the menu, of course!

'After disposing of the goose, the older set go to the King's Head and reminisce over all the past matches — it's all part of the school tradition, you see:

> Games to play out, whether earnest or fun,
> Fights for the fearless and goals for the eager,
> Twenty and thirty and forty years on.

'To be fair to the School, although I felt that far too much time was spent in the classroom studying the classics, there were several motivated masters who thought that instead of writing Latin elegiacs, the young members of the future governing class ought to be reading the daily newspapers, not just for the sporting pages but to find out about the condition of the country.

'But in fact I had a very jolly time at the Goose Match last autumn, which is when I met your Uncle Sidney, because

157

I'd rather rashly promised young Edwin that if he scored at least fifty runs or took more than two wickets, I would take some positive action about relieving him of the virginity which I knew Edwin had been desperately keen to lose. Although he was more than ready to cross the Rubicon, he has always been a shy chap and hadn't been able to find a willing girl for himself even by the time he was seventeen.'

'*Seventeen?* My goodness, you already had notches on your gun by the time you were fifteen, Philip, although you were always forward for your age,' I said lightly, running my hand across his lap and rubbing my palm against his shaft. 'Your cousin Stephen once told me that no young maid was safe in your house once you had spunked for the first time after taking yourself in hand one day just after your thirteenth birthday!'

Philip grinned and shook his head. 'The female staff at Pelham House were as safe as they wanted to be! Surely you could not think I would be as caddish as those brutal louts about who, being unable to win favour by fair means resort to foul, and take advantage of their social position to force themselves upon defenceless servants. My Papa would have rightly thrashed me to within an inch of my life if any of the girls had complained about being pestered by me, and naturally that deterrent also applied to my two brothers as well.

'True enough, Rosie, I was indeed an early starter, but that was only due to the kindly attention of Mrs Colchester, our cook. I haven't time to go into the details of my first ever fuck just now, but I can state without fear of contradiction that there is no finer experience for a young boy than that imparted in bed by a wise and sensitive older woman.'

'I wouldn't argue with that,' I said, giving his balls a squeeze as we approached Marble Arch. 'And it conversely applies to a young girl with an older man. But to come back to your poor brother Edwin, how did you manage to help him in his rite of passage?'

'Very easily, Rosie,' he said simply. 'I had taken Polly

Prestwich to the game in anticipation of Edwin claiming his prize.'

'I don't think I have had the pleasure of meeting this young lady,' I said thoughtfully and Philip gave a wry smile. 'I would not have thought it likely that your paths would have crossed, Rosie. Miss Prestwich is a fulltime consultant at the special clinic set up by the progressive medical physician, Dr Jonathan Letchmore. [*The suitably named Dr Letchmore was later to become a devoted admirer of Rosie d'Argosse with whom he spent a month in Biarritz in the summer of 1911 — Editor*] Now you probably haven't heard of him either, have you? Well, he has dared to suggest that sexual problems such as impotence can cause grievous mental damage to many gentlemen. So he employs pretty, friendly girls like Polly to stay for a few days at the patient's house or in an understanding seaside hotel if more convenient. They go out for walks, to restaurants and the theatre and nature soon takes its course!'

'Fascinating! Does the girl always have sexual congress with the patient for a cure to be effected?'

'Yes, in the vast majority of cases where the simple treatment of being with an attractive, sympathetic girl who soothes away all anxieties and fears does the trick. And in these cases, where applicable, the men go back to their wives or mistresses refreshed and invigorated, so both partners will have benefited.'

I thought about this for a moment and said: 'But isn't there a risk of some men falling in love with their instructors?'

'This has happened,' admitted Philip. 'But usually a patient simply continues to use the services of his lover once he has returned home. The liaison is not encouraged, however, and more often than not dies a natural death, especially as the treatment is far from cheap and this extra service is even more expensive, though Dr Letchmore does take on some patients *pro bono publico*, which is very decent of him.'

'And Polly Prestwich is on Dr Letchmore's staff?' I

asked. 'It sounds most interesting work, not to be lightly undertaken.'

Philip nodded and said: 'Absolutely so, which is why the girls are very well-paid and chosen with great discretion, for I hardly have to tell you what headlines would be made if one of Dr Letchmore's girls spilled the beans about her clients, for they move in the very highest circles. Why, I've even heard it rumoured that members of the Royal Family have availed themselves of the girls' services. Actually, I met Polly a few weeks ago at a party given by Lord Finchley and that's how I found out about her work. She thoroughly enjoys fucking and I knew she would love to take my young brother's cherry.'

I am sure it is because Lord Philip and I have such an open and honest relationship, free from all petty jealousies, that such a close, firm friendship exists between us. I did not even think of remonstrating with him about the obvious fact that he had fucked this girl Polly Prestwich, who I was sure equally enjoyed being threaded by Philip's noble tool. On the other hand, it is fair to record that neither would Philip have been too upset about my little excursion below stairs with the cuddly Dudley, my handsome young footman who I had seduced only a couple of hours before.

'So were you able to grant Edwin's dearest wish?' I murmured.

'I certainly did,' said Philip with just a hint of complacency in his voice. 'And I was justly rewarded myself in the process. It so happened that it was a glorious September day, one of the warmest I can ever remember. I drove Polly down myself in my Wolsley open tourer, and once the match began she suggested that we find a nice spot to have our picnic luncheon which I'd picked up at Fortnum's. The school side had been put in and Edwin, being an all-rounder, was batting at number six, so unless there was a shocking collapse of his team against some very ordinary bowling, there was no need for Polly and I to stay and watch a game in which I frankly had little interest.

'We found a secluded spot through a patch of woodland

and the sun was beating down so hard that Polly said: "Blow fashion! Whilst milky white skin might be favoured by some, I'm going to take Dr Letchmore's advice and let the sun get to my skin for an hour or so."

'I helped her step out of her dress, which I carefully placed on a blanket, and she then unbuttoned her bodice and her full breasts jumped out. My heart started pounding and my cock began to thicken as she produced a bottle of lotion from her bag and said: "Philip, please do me the kindness of rubbing some of Miss Thomson's Essence du Soleil on my back — it makes lying in the sun so much more comfortable."

'As I massaged her back with the perfumed liquid I said: "I'd better put some on your milky white bottom, hadn't I?" and Polly said nothing but pulled down her cream silk knickers for my inspection. What delightful round bum cheeks Polly possessed! I gazed at them rapturously with my eyes glistening and my cock as stiff as a poker as I passed my hand over the alabaster-white, smooth skin. I massaged these delicious *rondeurs* and she moved her long, slender legs slightly apart as my fingers rubbed the cool lotion onto the back of her thighs. My hands trembled as I let my fingertips lightly graze the lips of her pussy, but Polly then closed her legs saying with a smile: "Don't be impatient now, Philip, you naughty boy. Remember, I'm here to help the needy, not the greedy!"

'She must have been moved by the look of desperate frustration on my face for with a sigh she unbuttoned my trousers and took out my straining, naked cock. Then she swooped down and her tousled dark tresses were between my legs and her lips were upon my cock as she kissed the uncapped helmet. She opened her lips wide enough to encircle my knob and I gasped with excitement as she let her tongue swirl all over the smooth dome. She took my shaft in her hand and worked the skin up and down, bobbing her head in rhythm with her frigging as she sucked away lustily on my throbbing tool.

'Polly was such an experienced *fellatrice* that I climaxed

161

almost immediately, shooting a great gush of spunky jism down her throat as a delightful orgasm shuddered through my body. She licked me dry and then said: "There, that should keep you quiet for a moment. We'd better get back and see how the game is going."

'I stuffed my prick back inside my trousers whilst Polly dressed herself and then we walked slowly back to the car which we had left on a hillock not far from the boundary rope. We had only twenty minutes to wait before Edwin came out to bat and, perhaps buoyed by the prospect of getting laid (to use the fashionable American colloquialism now popular with the 'fast' London set), my young brother promptly hit three fours in succession as he raced towards his target of fifty runs for which he would be rewarded in the manner I have already described.

'He was then forced to play with care when faced with an over from Eric Minor, the Old Boys' star bowler who captained the Essex county second eleven, but Edwin survived the fierce onslaught and soon began to pile on the runs. However, as soon as he had passed the magic figure, he deliberately skied a ball high in the air which was easily caught by a waiting fieldsman, and he almost ran back to the pavilion to divest himself of his bat and pads. He came out of the dressing room and hurried across to where Polly and I were sitting to be introduced to Polly Prestwich and to receive our congratulations on his splendid knock.

' "Thank you, Philip, er, may I join you for luncheon?" asked Edwin. "As it's already twenty past twelve, the umpires have decided to take the luncheon interval as soon as our innings finishes, and I shouldn't think that will take very long now. We won't restart play until two o'cock, I mean clock." '

'This slip of the tongue showed what was on your brother's mind!' I commented and Philip gave a short chuckle. 'And how!' he snorted. 'And it did not go unnoticed by Polly who gave me a sly wink before suggesting that as it was a little early for luncheon, we should return to the seclusion of our place in the woods. Edwin was trembling with anticipation when we reached the clearing and I noticed that his hands were positively shaking as he helped me lay the blankets down upon the ground whilst Polly went behind a clump of trees for a minute before returning to join us.

'Immediately she began to undress for the second time, saying to Edwin as she stood clad only in her knickers: "I was sun-bathing, as the Germans call it, earlier. It is so lovely to feel the warm sun on your bare body that I'm sure it does one good." And with those words she pulled down her knickers to reveal her wonderfully hairy pussy, and I saw Edwin colour a deep shade of puce as he gazed in awe at this veritable forest of silky black curls between Polly's slender thighs and the pink, pouting cunney lips which peeped through so invitingly.

' "Why don't you come and join me, Edwin?" smiled Polly and she took hold of his hand to draw him closer to her as he stood transfixed with his eyes still riveted upon Polly's silken triangle of black hair which graced the base of her smooth, flat belly. "Now don't be shy, young man. I know you must be nervous as this will be your first fuck, but don't worry, my dear boy, just let nature take its course and all will be well. Virginity can be a tiresome state but it is most easily cured between the ages of sixteen and twenty-four, after which it can be somewhat more bothersome."

'Expertly, she unbuckled his belt as he slowly began to undo the buttons of his shirt. To make him feel more at ease I called out cheerfully: "Bye, bye, you two, I'm off for a stroll and I'll see you back at the car." But I must confess that I fibbed because I actually stayed to watch my brother's initiation into manhood, hiding myself behind an oak tree at the very edge of the clearing.

'By now, Edwin was naked except for his drawers and he appeared to hesitate about taking them down. Polly waited for a few moments and then took the matter into her own hands and pulled them off. Poor Edwin was so frightened by her boldness that he covered his cock and balls with his hands. "Oh dear," said Polly reproachfully. "What

163

is the matter with your nice prick? Is it because you haven't managed a cockstand? Edwin, that is only to be expected, I assure you.''

' "Really?" I heard him whisper quietly, and she gave him a warm kiss on his lips. "Come and lie down here beside me, Edwin, and I promise you that all will be well very shortly," she assured him.

' "Now stop thinking about it and just let your mind and body relax," she added as they scrambled down together and Polly placed his hand on her hand. "Rub your palm against my nipple and watch it shoot up, just like your cock will when I get my hands on it!"

'Naturally the clever girl's prophecy was absolutely spot-on — Edwin only had to feel the soft, warm touch of her fingers on his shaft to make his prick swell up to a fine, youthful exuberance. "There you are," exclaimed Polly as she gently frigged his pulsing stiffstander. "I told you that all you had to do was let nature take its course. My, what a thick, meaty whopper! Are you sure it's never found its way into a cunt before?"

'He cleared his throat and in a more confident voice my brother replied: "No, I'm afraid the chance has never presented itself." He closed his eyes and let out a heartfelt, blissful sigh as Polly drew back his foreskin and made his purple knob bound in her hand.

'Well, Edwin's time had now come and he clambered up on top of Polly, who spread her legs and reached down to guide his yearning cock between the gate of her cunney lips and into the slippery depths of her love channel. She pulled him further inside her by wrapping her legs round his waist as he lay motionless, savouring to the full the emotion of the moment.

' "There, that wasn't so difficult, was it?" said Polly with a smile. "Isn't that nice?"

' "It's wonderful, simply wonderful," he replied and she now instructed him on how best to continue. "Push your prick inside me as far as you can, my love, and then pull it out — not too fast now, that's good, that's very good!"

'My young scamp of a brother needed no further urging as his pelvis jabbed down and Polly eagerly lifted her hips to welcome his thrusting, virgin prick which slid squelchily inside her juicy honeypot. She clutched at his jerking arse as she heaved herself upwards, doing her best to pull him even further inside her. His pumping became more and more frenzied as he plunged his penis deeper and deeper, feeling for the first time the joy of having his shaft caressed by the slippery membranes of the walls of a warm, wet cunt. His hands raced across her soft, stiff-tipped rosy nipples and Polly panted: "Slow down, Edwin, slow down, there's a good boy. A considerate lover always waits for his lady."

' "Waits for his lady?" gasped Edwin.

' "Yes, you must try to wait so that your partner can spend too," she told him, but this set him off again and she clung to him as best she could, bucking her hips urgently so as not to be left behind and lifting her bum from the ground to achieve the maximum contact with his pulsating young prick. He groaned and I could see his whole body go rigid as his cock popped out of her cunney and slid crazily across her belly, spilling a fountain of sticky spunk all over Polly's snow-white belly. Desperately she grabbed hold of his still-stiff penis and pushed it back inside her pussy to milk the last drops of sperm out of him.

'Edwin sank down for a moment, his eyes closed in sheer bliss, but then he lifted his head and enquired anxiously: "Was that alright, Polly? Did I do everything properly?"

' "Certainly you did," she replied kindly, although it was obvious to me that she had not managed to reach the heights. "It was most thoughtful of you not to spunk in my cunt, although I would have been happy for you to do so as not only is it a good day according to my monthly rhythm but I also popped a tiny piece of sponge soaked in linseed oil up my crack before we began to fuck. [*This was a popular if crude method of birth control much favoured around the turn of the century and was probably used by Rosie and her friends, although this is the only mention of it in the d'Argosse diaries. Linseed oil is an effective spermicide, but*

165

the method could hardly be guaranteed! The first modern
intrauterine devices (I.U.D.s) were only available from the
early 1930s — Editor]

' "However, at your age your cock will recover very
quickly and you can fuck me again. You'd like me to suck
your prick, wouldn't you, Edwin?"

' "Oh yes, please, Polly, I've been tossed off by one of
the laundry maids back home and I've often wondered what
it would be like to have my cock sucked," said Edwin
eagerly.

'Polly could not resist a smile as she said: "I don't think
you will be disappointed," and she leaned across him and
let her head rest on his thigh. She took his limp shaft in her
hand, snapped back his foreskin and began to tease his shiny
knob by running the tip of her tongue around the edges of
the springy cap, whilst at the same time she cupped his balls
in her hand and squeezed them gently through their bag of
soft, wrinkly skin.

' "Oooh! Oooh! That's marvellous! Oooh! Oooh!"
groaned the lucky young rascal as he clutched at Polly's hair
whilst she drew her hot, wet tongue from his balls right up
the length of his fast-swelling shaft. She pulled his now rock-
hard truncheon from between her lips and lapped up the
pre-spend juice which had already oozed out of his cock.
She flicked her tongue delicately all along his helmet before
opening her mouth wide and taking in his entire prick right
down to the root. She kept up a regular rhythm as she sucked
lustily on his rigid rod and, every so often, she took her lips
off his glistening shaft, giving his knob a swirling lick before
plunging his thick shaft inside her mouth whilst she brought
herself off by diddling her hairy cunney with her fingers.

'She was sucking his cock so hard that I knew she would
very soon be swallowing all the spunk from his tightening
ballsack. Indeed, as I had guessed, barely ten seconds later
Edwin let out a strangled cry and Polly jammed her mouth
over his knob, swishing her tongue over the bulbous dome
as the thick sticky sperm began to flow. She swallowed
quickly to be rewarded by another spasm and then a third

as she gulped down every last drain of jism until she was sated, and she lifted her head up and let his shrinking shaft flop back limply on to his thigh.

' "Well done, Edwin, well done, I came as well that time," exclaimed Polly, giving him a loving kiss on his lips. I think he would have liked to have stayed longer, but Polly said with a sigh: "I'm afraid that it's time we were making tracks, though I'd much rather stay here and let you fuck me again instead — but we'd better get dressed and go back and have some luncheon. You have to finish your game and all that fucking must have made you hungry."

'I left them to it and walked back briskly to the car from which I pulled out the hamper, and by the time Polly and Edwin returned, looking just a tiny bit dishevelled they both exuded a healthy glow.'

I stopped him at this juncture and placed my finger on his lips as I said: 'Philip, you can tell me the end of the story later in the evening. Do you realise that we've been parked outside Robert Bacon's house for at least the last five minutes!'

'Good grief, have we really,' laughed Philip, giving me a big cuddle. 'Well, I'm not surprised. Look, I forgot to close the window between us and the driver!' He leaned forward and called out sarcastically to the driver: 'Did you enjoy my little anecdote, Mellor?'

'Very much, my Lord, very much indeed,' replied his chauffeur perkily. 'Miss Rosie's quite right, we have been parked here for about five minutes, but I didn't say anything as I didn't think you particularly wanted to be interrupted. And to be truthful, I had such a horn on through listening to you I would have done my tadger a nasty injury trying to slide out under the steering wheel!'

I burst out laughing, though Philip glared at the cheeky driver who nipped out smartly to open the door for us. 'You can go and have something to eat, but be back here not later than half past ten. If that's not too much trouble,' he said heavily as he took my arm and we walked up the drive of the large house Robert had rented for the summer from Sir

Louis Segal, the noted merchant banker and philanthropist. [*Renting one's home for several months was the usual practice in late Victorian and Edwardian times by those going to spend a season out of town or abroad. The actual rental was relatively small, but many owners preferred not to leave their properties empty as ninety years ago there were plenty of burglars on the prowl — Editor*]

'St John's Wood is a nice area of London,' I said to Philip as he rang the bell. 'But I suppose the actual wood is long gone.'

'For more than a hundred years, I would imagine. It was once a royal forest and was named after the Priors of St John who lost the land during the Reformation. There are some elegant Regency villas nearby and, over the last fifty years especially, some handsome houses have been built around here and ever further north, up towards Hampstead Village.'

A manservant opened the door and showed us in. I could hear the chatter of voices from the drawing room and I said to Philip: 'I thought this was just going to be a cosy little party, but it sounds as though Robert has invited quite a large number of people to help finish the last cases of his Papa's '03 Bollinger champagne.'

Robert came out of the drawing room to greet us. 'Hello, folks!' he called out. 'Come on in, Laura arrived five minutes ago and I've a nice unexpected surprise to tell you about — you remember that I came home from Lord's this afternoon by taxi? Well, as I was paying off my driver, who should walk by but Richard Tucker, the famous theatrical impresario.'

'Richard Tucker? I've met the great man several times as he's a close friend of our family,' I said excitedly. 'But surely he's supposed to be in America with Harley Granville-Barker on some business or other.' [*Harley Granville-Barker (1877–1946) was a close friend of George Bernard Shaw and was one of the most important men in the Edwardian Theatre. His liaison with Vedrenne, manager of the Court Theatre, Sloane Square was especially productive and included the premieres of eleven of Shaw's plays — Editor]*

'He was in New York until last week, but he came back on that new fast French liner, *La Normandie*, and arrived back in London yesterday,' explained Robert. 'I know him through my cousin Claude who has invested a small fortune in his proposed New York season of British plays. So I invited him to dine with us tonight along with some members of the troupe he hopes to take to New York in September. Do come inside and say hello, Rosie. I am sure that Mr Tucker will be delighted to make your acquaintance again.'

He ushered us into the lounge where a group of about a dozen people were avidly engaged in a babble of conversation, much of it centred around the elegant figure of Richard Tucker, who was standing with his back against the fireplace, holding forth on the state of the British theatre to an eager group of his thespians. The impresario was a handsome, well-built man in his prime, perhaps just the wrong side of forty, of medium height and with an open, friendly face and soft, brown eyes. His gleaming hair was stylishly shaped, cleverly cut to mask as much as possible the bald patch on the crown of his head.

'Ah-ha, who have we here?' he asked as Robert brought Philip and myself into the circle of people around him. 'Why, it's Rosie d'Argosse, isn't it? How are you keeping, my dear girl? And how are your lovely parents? When I saw them a couple of months ago at one of Pierre Gottlieb's new productions in Paris, your Papa told me that they would be spending much of the summer on the Continent.'

'They're in England until the end of the month, but just now they're staying for a few day with the Countess of Warwick at her country house in Essex.' [*The Countess of Warwick was a lavish hostess and one of Edward VII's favourite mistresses — "my own darling Daisy" — who later shocked Society by converting to Socialism — Editor]*

'So you're in town all on your own and making hay whilst the sun shines, eh? Or is this stalwart young gentleman your chaperone in this wicked city?' he chuckled.

I introduced him to Philip and added that I could make

hay, as he put it, just as easily in the country as in the great Metropolis, and not just because of the greater availability of grass! 'Yes, I'm sure you can, Rosie,' he said with a huge grin as he swivelled round to take the arm of a very pretty girl dressed in a daringly low-cut green silk gown. 'Hazel Corbett here is, like you, a country girl born and bred and she is always telling me that there is just as much social intercourse taking place in rural society as there is in town. Mind you, Hazel won't be seeing much of the country now that she has joined my company which will play for three months in New York from early September.'

'You're an actress, then?' I asked the girl, who smiled at me and said: 'Yes, I've played the provinces in repertory and I was lucky enough to have Mr Tucker in the first night audience when I gained my first West End role last month, even though the play was a bit of a stinker.'

Before she could continue, Philip snapped his fingers and said: 'Of course! That's where I've seen you, Miss Corbett. Didn't you play the parlourmaid in *The Trottsberry Hall Scandal* at the Criterion? You were jolly good, although I must admit I didn't think much of the play, either. In fact, I think my friend and I left after the second interval and spent the rest of the evening at the Jim Jam Club.'

'I don't blame you,' said Richard Tucker. 'And your view was shared by the critics who gave it such a pasting that the management was forced to close the production after only ten days, and poor Hazel thought that her hard-won chance of fame and fortune had gone for ever.

'But you were right, my Lord, Hazel's talents shone through, even in such a poorly written piece, and she will star in my production of a wonderful new comedy, *Strangers At Home* by Charles Divine, which in five months time I shall stage at the Century Theatre on Broadway to open the British Festival of Drama in New York.'

'What's the play about, Mr Tucker?' asked Philip.

'Oh, it's a very warm and witty drama about what happens when two young women, Kay and Jean, find that their mother and aunt have joined forces to dispel boredom by throwing open their large country house to the "bed and breakfast" tourist trade. The invasion of guests force the girls out of their home to seek fresh pasture for their own private lives, and they have quite a few adventures on the way. Hazel will take the major role of Kay, and Kate Radcliffe, the pretty blonde girl over in the corner talking to our host, will play the part of Jean.

'Although it's a British play, I'm having to open it in New York because of the damned Lord Chamberlain's office [*the British theatre was rigidly censored by this office until it was abolished in 1967 – Editor*] which won't allow any play to be staged that might possibly offend a Victorian maiden aunt.'

'Yes, official censorship can be most frustrating,' agreed Philip. 'Though one can always use a theatre club to put on uncut plays and at least once a production has been passed, you can't get busybodies trying to bring in the police and taking out court orders to have it banned. This happens frequently in some Amercan states, I believe.'

'It certainly does,' growled Richard Tucker. 'But the present administration in New York takes a liberal view in such matters, and I don't anticipate any trouble. But I do so yearn for the day when people will be able to see and read what they want, unfettered by agents of the State making the choice for them.'

'So you are against all censorship?' someone ventured, and Richard Tucker grinned. 'Put it like this, if you can make me believe in being just a little pregnant, then you can make me believe in just a little censorship.'

A rap of a gavel on a table quietened this and all other conversation as Robert announced: 'Ladies and gentlemen, I'm sure you'll appreciate that as I gave Mrs Kenton no real notice about dinner, I can only offer you a light supper. But if you will make your way to the dining room, my staff will serve your from the buffet table.'

Robert had no need to apologise for the fare, as Mrs Kenton had cooked two large turkeys and, together with hot vegetables and a selection of salads, these made a more than adequate meal, especially as every mouthful was washed down with a seemingly inexhaustible supply of chilled champagne!

After dinner, Laura and some other guests took up Robert's invitation to try their hands at billiards upstairs in the games room, whilst Philip and Kate Radcliffe were deep in some earnest discussion in the far corner of the drawing room. Hazel Corbett came up to me and said in a friendly, light manner: 'Oh dear, has Lord Philip deserted you for Kate? Perhaps I should introduce you to Archie Webster, one of the leading men in our company.'

I laughed and said, 'It would serve him right, wouldn't it? But I'd be more interested in talking to you. A close girl friend of mine is a talented amateur actress and she would like to make a career on the stage, though her parents would be horrified if they ever knew she was even harbouring such thoughts. How would you advise her to begin?'

'I wouldn't,' Hazel promptly replied. 'Unless your friend is passionately keen about the theatre and willing to undergo many privations, public and personal, then the best advice I could give her is to keep her amateur status. Believe me, Rosie, the stage might appear to offer a girl a glamorous and exciting life, but I have sometimes wondered whether it is worth all the effort. If Mr Tucker had not offered me a contract to join his troupe going to New York, I think I might have retired from the profession.'

'You surprise me, Hazel, don't you enjoy your work?'

The pretty girl nodded her head and replied: 'Of course I do, but there is so little work for so many actors and actresses. We must be the only trade with at least seventy-five per cent of our members always out of work! And can you imagine what producers and managers expect, even to let you audition for a good part!'

'I'm not altogether surprised,' I murmured as we walked through into the library and sat ourselves down in two comfortable armchairs. 'Actresses have always been regarded as fair game by lecherous clubmen like my old Uncle Gordon, who comes down to London from

Manchester for a week every so often to see his old friends at the Travellers and the Jim Jam. Whilst in town he always books a seat for the talked-about new plays and visits the Gaiety or the Empire music halls. I overheard him tell my Papa that he always sends his card round backstage afterwards and usually ends up dining at Romanos or Jacksons with a pretty chorus girl.'

Hazel slapped her hand against the soft leather of the chair as she leaned forward and said to me: 'Don't tell me that your uncle is Lord Gordon MacChesney?'

'The very same,' I replied with a frown, for I was now concerned that I might have let slip an indiscretion, but my worries were immediately dispelled when Hazel chuckled and said: 'He's a game old boy, isn't he? I would imagine that practically all of the pretty soubrettes in London have been dated by your uncle. But Gordon is a perfect gentleman who wines and dines girls in great style, and expects nothing in exchange except sharing a jolly supper after the show and hearing about the latest gossip.'

Her remarks surprised me because I know Uncle Gordon's proclivities only too well [*see* Rosie Vol 1: Intimate Diaries *for a graphic account of Lord — Editor*] and I had to say that this didn't sound like my uncle, who was always ready for a more physical amorous engagement.

'Oh, I didn't mean to imply that Gordon doesn't enjoy a good fuck,' corrected Hazel. 'And he is an ardent practitioner in *l'arte de faire l'amour* as I know from my own experience. But he is much liked and respected because he accepts without question that if a girl says "no" she means what she says, and he would never attempt to force a girl into even a kiss let alone anything more torrid. Gordon shows the same gentlemanly traits between the sheets as well. For example, he bedded my friend Sophie recently and, though Sophie adores being fucked and having her pussy eaten, she simply cannot bring herself to suck her lover's cock.'

'Really?' I said with interest, for I also have some friends who eschew this highly pleasurable activity, including several who, despite my urgings, have not even attempted to try it for themselves. 'What a shame, the poor girl doesn't know what she's missing. It amazes me how many girls are kept unaware of the delights of gobbling or having their pussies licked out. Even an oblique mention of such ideas horrifies them.'

'I do so agree with you, Rosie. I love sucking a thick meaty prick myself, but there is no accounting for taste. Perhaps her strict upbringing in a convent school has something to do with it, and certainly I would agree that Sophie would benefit by being schooled in the grand art of *fellatio*. But the point here is that Gordon was very patient with her, even though I know he loves nothing better than lying back and being sucked off. He did not whine or moan but simply accepted her wishes not to proceed down that path just as, without demur, he accepted my own *caveat* of not poking his noble prick up my bottom.'

'Ah, then you yourself have been fucked by my Uncle Gordon?'

'Only the once, when I was playing Princess Katherine of France in *Henry V* with the Peter Lucas Shakespearean players at the Theatre Royal in Nottingham. Gordon came down to see the play and the wicked old rogue said that he was so entranced by my performance that he stayed overnight and booked a box for the next night. He sent a huge bouquet of red roses backstage with a letter requesting the pleasure of taking me out to supper after the show. Well, I was born and bred in Kent and perhaps you know the little verse about the young lady from Kent — no? Oh, well, it goes:

> *There was a young lady of Kent,*
> *Who said that she knew what it meant,*
> *When men asked her to dine,*
> *And poured out the wine,*
> *She knew what it meant — but she went!*

'Anyhow, I accepted his invitation and though given no encouragement except for a chaste good-night kiss, he sent round an even bigger bouquet the next night with an invitation to take luncheon and a walk round Northenden Manor, a country house only some fifteen miles outside Nottingham, where he was staying for a fortnight whilst the owner, Colonel Hellen, was up in Scotland for a fishing holiday.'

'Yes, Uncle Gordon is a great house-minder,' I chuckled softly. 'He often comes down to Argosse Towers to stay when my parents are away.'

'Well, he certainly knows how to make himself comfortable! He called at my lodgings in Colonel Hellen's carriage and we had a splendid lunch, home-made country pâté, baked trout and a dessert of delicious profiteroles which he had asked the cook to prepare especially for me as I had mentioned how fond I was of chocolate!

'We went for a short walk round the grounds but by three o'clock we were in his bed, rolling around naked in each other's arms. It turned out to be a very interesting fuck for us both. When I took hold of Gordon's cock in my hand — he's very well-endowed, by the way — he began to lick and lap my titties which greeted his tongue by rising up like two rubbery red bullets — '

But just as she was about to tell me more, there was a sudden commotion from outside the library. We jumped up from our chairs and went to investigate . . .

VOLUME THREE

Reckless Raptures

INTRODUCTION

From the earliest times to the present day, the upper and middle classes in societies all over the world have taken upon themselves the self-imposed duty to protect the lower orders from their own 'base' instincts, and many readers will be aware that when puritanical prudery was at its height during the mid-Victorian era, the sexual act was considered at best a necessary evil and the very idea of ordinary people actually enjoying copulation — even within marriage — was anathema to many worthy citizens.

Indeed, the slightest thought of young, unmarried men and women indulging in the Sins of the Flesh sent shivers of horror down the spines of all but an enlightened minority. As Dr Steve Humphries remarks in his fascinating social history *A Secret World of Sex*: 'the concern with the moral control of young people was of paramount importance and this control was frequently used for religious, political or ideological motives,' though in fairness he adds that there was still much ignorance about contraception, and genuine dangers from several epidemics of venereal diseases at a time when syphilis was incurable and gonorrhea and other sexually transmitted diseases were difficult to treat.

So although some of the suffocating restrictions of the Victorian age may have been eased by the time the *Rosie* novels appeared midway through Edward VII's brief reign, there were still overwhelmingly powerful (if sometimes hypocritical) Establishment voices preaching sexual restraint. One channel of resistance to the smug and often hypocritical doctrines of abstinence was found in the growth of totally uninhibited underground magazines such as *The Pearl*, *The Oyster* and *The Cremorne* which flourished during the 1880s and enjoyed a wide popularity until the outbreak of the First World War.

Many of these were written by journalists working on the fledgling popular newspapers and the *Rosie* novels were written by two young radical feminist scribes, Geraldine Newman and Anna Barnes-Cooney. The first novel, *Her Intimate Diaries*, first appeared in 1907, in twelve monthly instalments of *The Ram*, a spectacularly rude and illicit scandal sheet produced by 'The Friends of Venus and Priapus', a *sub rosa* group of upper-middle-class men and women which held wild parties in London, New York and the South of France. Some four years later, they were published privately in book form by the Scottish racing driver Grahame Johnstone under the false imprimatur of The Edinburgh University Press!

Little is known of this clandestine club except that several characters who appear in Rosie's narrative — the theatrical impresario Richard Tucker; two notorious *roués*, Lord Philip Pelham and Colonel Piers Rankin; and one of King Edward VII's favourite young mistresses, Mrs Sally Cambridge — actually existed and all contributed to *The Ram*, if the recently discovered diaries of the famed Society beauty, Lady Erica Boleyn, are to be believed.

This devil-may-care openness led Professor Barry Barr to comment in his foreword to *Her Intimate Diaries* that the very fact that the authors' friends allowed their names to be used with impunity in the saucy text indicated 'that they believed themselves to be part of a loosely organised, like-minded group and that ordinary members of the general public would always be excluded from this close, private fraternity.

'And it is true that the circulation of this clandestine book was probably so exclusive that the use of real names became a daring indulgence, a kind of curious in-joke amongst the *cognoscenti*.'

This chronicling of sexual adventures in these Edwardian 'horn' books served a useful educational purpose at a time when so many people were racked with unnecessary guilt about their sexuality and even more were lost in total ignorance. However, I am certain that Geraldine Newman and Anna Barnes-Cooney would readily admit that the primary reason for the publication of the *Rosie* novels was financial, for although both girls came from wealthy backgrounds, neither of their families would support their work for Mrs Pankhurst's Women's Social and Political Union, which campaigned for female suffrage or for other radical organisations.

Indeed, when asked by Anna for an increase in her allowance, Lady Marcella Barnes-Cooney not only refused point-blank but added: 'My earnest hope is that the political franchise will not be given to any woman. To give it may be "progress", but in my view it is a progress in the wrong direction. The only possible benefit of admitting women to the franchise might be to show the fallacy of modern democratic doctrines and weaken the belief in purely popular government. As your dear father has often told you, the people will be best served when they realise that government must be conducted solely by the enlightened and the capable — the aristocracy in the strict sense of the word — for the benefit of the masses.'

This drew forth a trenchant reply from Anna, who at the time was in the throes of a passionate affair with Robert Bacon, the handsome young man-about-town, noted sportsman and dilettante of whom Mrs Patrick Campbell once acidly remarked that 'large blue eyes like his might be found in many a stately nursery'.

In *His Mighty Engine*, perhaps the seminal work on turn-of-the-century erotica, the American social historian Dr Alexander Raspie makes the interesting suggestion that Geraldine Newman and Anna Barnes-Cooney based Rosie's adventures in *Reckless Raptures* upon the real-life frolics of Louise Burrell-Jones, the youngest daughter of a brigadier in the Indian Army who for reasons of health was forced to take early retirement and return to London with his family at the turn of the century.

For the record, Louise Burrell-Jones was presented at Court shortly after her eighteenth birthday in September 1902 and she enjoyed an extremely hectic social life with her name often to be seen in guest lists in *The Tatler* but also in more popular periodicals such as *The Harmsworth Magazine* which published her photograph regularly in their *Monthly Gallery of Womanly Beauty* series, a precursor of the modern Page Three pin-up, although all Louise bared was her shoulders!

A few months later, she met King Edward VII in less formal circumstances at one of Lady Bristow's famous country house parties in Worcestershire and by 1905 was rumoured to have been seduced by him at a wild orgy thrown by the King at his house in Biarritz where he stayed every year for at least a month with his favourite mistress, Mrs Alice Keppel. However, a prurient commentator in *The Ram* informs us that His Majesty knew full well that 'his Louise was skilled in the execution of *l'art de faire l'amour*', having already enjoyed several torrid liaisons with the aforementioned Robert Bacon, Lord Philip Pelham (whose raffish sexual appetites were gleefully detailed in *Rosie 2: Young, Wild and Willing*) and one of Edward's famous band of Jewish friends, the merchant banker and noted philanthropist, Sir Ronnie Dunn.

By all contemporary accounts, Louise was a bright and independent girl, and in 1907 she dropped out of the charmed upper-class social circle and joined the small group of radical suffragettes who perpetrated acts of violence (though against property as opposed to people) in their fight to obtain the vote, and in that year went to prison for seven days after refusing to pay a fine for breaking the windows of a jeweller's shop in Bond Street. Like Anna Barnes-Cooney, she was disowned by her family and was forced to live in a small Bloomsbury apartment, although in 1908 her parents paid for her and a friend to spend the summer in Italy, perhaps in an attempt to bring Louise 'back to her senses'. Whether or not this trip had any effect on her is debatable (especially if the narrative of *Reckless Raptures* is based on her Italian adventures) but no doubt to Brigadier Burrell-Jones' great relief, Louise fell in love with Teddy Godfrey, an American architect she met in London, shortly before her twenty-seventh birthday. After their marriage in 1911 she left London for Norfolk, Virginia where she settled happily with her husband and Louise never returned to Europe, although she continued to write to her old friends until the mid 1920s.

Whether she collaborated with Anna Barnes-Cooney in the actual writing of *Reckless Raptures* will never be known, but there is a fresh, robust vitality in the lusty narrative which contains some very frank evocations and descriptions of a wide variety of sexual activity, and there are some stylistic differences to previous *Rosie* novels which suggest that a fresh hand might have produced this particular book.

In any case, whoever the author may have been, it is undeniable that these memoirs clearly show that however repressive the climate of opinion may be, the interest and enjoyment of sexuality will never change, and however much the official culture may try to suppress its importance, there

11

will always be an influential minority opinion which will argue to the contrary and insist that sexuality is one of the most important factors in our lives.

For certain, this jolly romp, published now for the first time in its original unexpurgated form, will amuse and intrigue a new generation of readers of gallant literature.

Simon Galloway
Leeds
July, 1993

I never travel without my diary. One should always have something sensational to read on the train.

Oscar Wilde

CHAPTER ONE

Packing My Bags

I will never forget the beautiful afternoon of the twenty-third of June, nineteen hundred and eight, which I spent in the heart of the Welsh countryside. After a picnic luncheon, Lord Philip Pelham and I climbed to the top of a steep hill and we had looked down at the fresh, deep green of the valley below us, watching the silver stream glisten in the summer sunshine as a warm breeze caressed the backs of our necks.

I turned round to speak to Philip who was standing a few yards away but I tripped over a small mound of earth and stumbled into his arms. He held me and wordlessly pressed the length of his body to me, kissing my lips, my face, my throat and I clung to him as we sank to the ground . . .

But before I continue, I must retrace the events which led me to this beautiful, unspoiled part of the Principality and begin the story five weeks earlier when a letter arrived for me from Susannah Meverson, an old school friend from St Hilda's Academy for Young Ladies, inviting me to spend a long weekend at her parents' country home in the wilds of rural Pembrokeshire.

Susannah had written that in the absence of her parents in France, she was holding a lawn tennis weekend and amongst the guests would be Anthony Wilding, the Cambridge University champion and Gabrielle Renaud, the winner of the French and Italian tournaments and, knowing my enjoyment of the sport, she hoped that I would be able to come to her family's house deep in the Welsh countryside near the little town of Cardigan.

It had been an especially pleasant duty to write back to Susannah and tell her that I would be accepting her kind invitation for, frankly, I had not thought that my parents would allow me to attend this gathering. Besides having to undertake a long journey to South West Wales from the Sussex coast with only a servant to escort me, I would have to stay overnight in London at an hotel, for our town house in St John's Wood was undergoing extensive renovation and would be out of use for another four weeks. Also, when Mama read in Susannah's letter that Lord Philip Pelham was planning to join the party, I assumed she would ensure that I stayed at least a hundred miles from Pembrokeshire for she nursed a shrewd suspicion that, behind her back, Philip and I were carrying on a clandestine love affair. However, when she read that Susannah's aunt, the formidable Mrs Augusta Sheringham who had written several articles in the society papers about the need for strict etiquette to be observed between young people, had consented to act as chaperone [*an older or married woman who supervises young, unmarried girls on social occasions — Editor*], I finally managed to persuade Mama to give her consent to my plea to be allowed to spend a few days at Meverson Hall on the condition that Dennison, our footman, accompanied me there. I had no objection to this arrangement as I needed a strong pair of hands to look after my luggage and his accommodation at Meverson Hall would cause no problem for my hostess as Susannah would expect most of her guests to bring a servant with them.

Of course, readers of my earlier reminiscences [*see 'Rosie 1: Her Intimate Diaries'* and *'Rosie 2: Young, Wild and Willing', New English Library — Editor*] will know that my

Mama's misgivings about Lord Philip Pelham were not without foundation. I must confess that the young scamp had been fucking me for some six months now and the cheeky rascal had even used my name under a lightly disguised pseudonym in his essay for the literary competition for a prize of one hundred guineas offered by *The Oyster* [*perhaps the most spectacularly rude of all the many underground magazines of late Victorian/Edwardian times – Editor*]. Contestants had been asked to compose between fifteen hundred and two thousand words about their most enjoyable sexual escapade in 1907 and Philip had penned a racy account of my eighteenth birthday party when he and I (and later Miss Fiona Brookchester) had threshed around naked in my bed after the other guests had left Argosse Towers for their own homes. But that is another story best left untold, especially now that Miss Brookchester is engaged to be married to Lieutenant Harold Elton-Potts of the Grenadier Guards.

By happy chance, the day before I was due to leave home to begin the long trek to Pembrokeshire, my parents also left the house to go to Edinburgh to attend the wedding of my mother's niece to the Duke of Midlothian. After waving goodbye to Papa and Mama outside our front door, I went back inside to supervise the packing of my luggage for the journey. I was going to entrust the packing of my clothes to my personal maid, Elaine, who was by far the most proficient at this tiresome chore than anyone I have ever met, but Sayers, our old butler who had been in service at Argosse Towers since before I was born, informed me that Elaine was nowhere to be found.

'Very well, Sayers, but ask her to come up to my bedroom when you do see her,' I told him, but I speculated that I would discover Elaine's whereabouts well before the faithful old retainer. I slipped out of the house through the back door and made my way to the motor-house [*the word*

17

'garage' did not come into general use until after World War One — *Editor*].

Elaine and I had few secrets [*see 'Rosie 2: Young, Wild and Willing — Editor*] and I knew full well where Elaine disappeared to — and why — during the day. She was conducting a torrid liaison with Jack Dennison, the footman who was to accompany me to Wales, and I rightly guessed that she had taken him out to the motor-house to enjoy a quick spooning session before going upstairs to pack my cases.

As I quietly approached the empty building (my parents were being driven to Euston Station in North London by Haines, our chauffeur, in our new Rolls Royce where they would catch the night sleeper to Edinburgh, and my young brother Jonathan had taken out the Mercedes for a spin with his best friend, Charles, the dashing young son of Colonel Nettleton who lived some two miles down the road towards Midhurst) I could hear faint sounds of panting and sighing which confirmed my conjecture that Elaine and Dennison were engaged in a spot of rumpy-pumpy.

I walked softly towards the door which the randy couple had carelessly left slightly ajar and peeped through the gap, and saw my maid and footman entwined in the most amorous of caresses, both stark naked on an old mattress that Haines used to lie on when inspecting the undercarriage of our motor-cars, upon which they had thrown an old blanket and a couple of pillows, doubtless filched from the housekeeper's cupboards. This was not the first time I had seen Jack Dennison fuck one of our female servants in the motor-house. A few months ago I had come across him coupling with Kathie, a scullery maid who had also entertained my naughty old Uncle Lord MacChesney and, in consequence, had subsequently gained a position as housemaid in his bachelor apartments in Curzon Street, Mayfair.

Elaine was a prettier girl than Kathie, full-bodied though

18

not run to fat, firm and curvaceous everywhere with large, rounded breasts and a smooth white skin which set off to good effect the mass of dark curly hair that nestled at the base of her belly. To be fair, I should also note that Jack was a good-looking young fellow, broad-shouldered and wide-chested and, as they kissed and canoodled together, I saw his hand cup one of Elaine's soft breasts whilst she slid her fingers round the thick shaft which was standing up between his thighs, and Elaine's nipples seemed to grow before my eyes and they appeared to almost stab at Dennison's palm as he fondled each delicious bared breast in turn.

Then suddenly he scrambled to his knees and Elaine lay down with her head on the pillows as he knelt between her parted legs. She then pulled his head down to her bosom and turned his face from side to side, kissing each engorged, stalky tittie in turn whilst his right arm reached down so that his hand was set between her legs and his fingers played inside the silky forest of hair which covered her prominent mound.

My hand stole down to rub my own moistening pussey as I watched them kiss, and I saw Jack Dennison's hand cup one of Elaine's large, bare breasts whilst she grasped his thick, erect shaft which had risen up between his muscular thighs and rubbed his truncheon up and down, capping and uncapping the wide mushroom knob. Her raised-up red nipples seemed to grow before my eyes as they appeared to stab at his palm as he fondled each beautiful bosom in turn and she continued to slide her hand up and down his blue-veined boner.

Then, suddenly, she was forced to release his huge cock as he scrambled to his knees and knelt between her parted legs whilst Elaine lay on her back with her head resting on one pillow as she slid the second under her bottom. Then she pulled his head to her breasts and he turned his lips from

19

side to side, kissing each engorged, rubbery nipple. Now he reached down so that his right hand was between her thighs and I could see his fingers play around inside the silky bush of dark curls which covered her mound.

He parted the pale pink lips of her cunney which protruded through the nest of pubic hair and her body twisted and turned as she rolled her belly on his stiff, throbbing tool whilst he sucked her tingling titties. Elaine threw back her pretty head and moaned with passion as he brought her up to the very peak of unfulfilled desire. However, I was delighted to note that Dennison was a skilled and considerate lover for, instead of simply ramming his rigid rod inside her honeypot, he first ensured that Elaine was ready to receive his pulsating prick.

Quickly, he pressed his fingertips against the open, sodden slit of her cunt, flicking at the erect little clitty that had already peeked out, and only then did he take hold of his huge, erect cock and thrust his helmet between the yielding lips of her juicy cunt, and Elaine gurgled with joy as he propelled inch after inch of hot, pulsing prick inside her love channel until their pubic hairs were matted together.

For a few moments he stayed still with his shaft totally embedded inside her but then he pulled back slowly and drove back down again, pushing his full length inside the gorgeous girl, repeating the movement again and again, faster and faster as she urged him on, closing her feet together at the small of his back to force very last millimetre of cock inside her soaking cunney. She drummed her heels upon the base of his spine as he pistoned his prick in and out of her clinging sheath, but such passion brought matters to a swift conclusion and with a gutteral cry of 'I'm coming, Elaine, I can't stop!', Dennison jerked up and down in a frantic rhythm before withdrawing his glistening, wet cock for one final plunge and he crashed home, spurting his seed inside Elaine's willing womb as he sank down upon her.

20

'Wow! You must have shot a pint of spunk inside me,' said Elaine as she ruffled his hair with her long fingers. 'But you don't have to worry, I made sure to douche my pussey with a good dollop of linseed oil [*a crude but relatively effective contraceptive used widely at this time, although not as good, of course, as modern birth-control methods – Editor*] before we began. Not that I'm really bothered as I've only just finished my monthlies, but it's better to be safe than sorry, isn't it?'

'I should say,' panted the lucky lad. 'Oh God, that was a wonderful fuck, Elaine, but I'm sure I came too quickly for you. No, don't try to fool me, I know you didn't spend.'

'Don't worry, I still enjoyed myself,' she assured him with a loving kiss. 'And anyhow, we had to finish quickly or Miss Rosie will come looking for me. I should have started to pack her cases at least fifteen minutes ago. Gosh, I wish I were going with you, Jack, you lucky devil. I'll miss you, you know, I really will.

'And I'll miss you too,' she added, bending down to plant a smacking great kiss on his still semi-erect shaft which was dangling over his thigh. 'Promise me that you won't be dipping into any strange pussies whilst you're away.'

Dennison looked down briefly at the tousled head resting in his lap, but then he sighed and he reached across for his clothes. 'Chance would be a fine thing! Look here, much as I'd love to have my cock sucked, we'd better get ourselves dressed pronto and get back to the house, for it would be wrong for you to take any liberties with Miss Rosie, she's a real toff. Why, I bet that if you told her why you were late and that you hurried our love-making, she would have told you not to have been so silly and to have waited till you had spent.'

I smiled at this compliment and left them to dress as I strolled back to my bedroom. Five minutes later Elaine knocked at my door and apologised for her absence. I did not wish to embarrass her but I could not resist saying: 'Are you feeling well, Elaine? I hope you're not letting anything get on top of you?'

'No, Miss Rosie, everything in the garden's lovely, thank you,' she replied pertly as she opened the door of my wardrobe.

Yes, and things aren't too bad in the motor-house either, are they? I thought, but I refrained from mentioning what I had just witnessed and simply showed Elaine which of my clothes I wished to take to Meverson Hall. I had purchased a compressed cane dress trunk from the Army and Navy Stores on my last visit to London. This new case was rather an extravagant purchase, as Papa commented when he wrote a cheque to settle the account, for it cost ninety shillings and sixpence [£4.52! – Editor]. But as I pointed out to Papa, it was fitted with a tray for accessories, and had straps all round with a double action lock, very necessary to foil the growing number of sneak thieves on the railways and elsewhere.

This reminded me to make sure that the present for Susannah I had ordered from Mr Selfridge's new store in Oxford Street was securely packed in my best valise, a large Imperial with two lever locks and two keys. I hoped she would like my gift, a Picnic Compact gramophone with a Swiss motor that played two twelve-inch records with just one wind of the handle, and I left Elaine to her work and went downstairs to ensure that the machine had not been taken out of the wooden box in which it had been delivered by Selfridge's carrier.

Looking back with hindsight, I suppose I should have rung for Sayers or Dennison, one of whom would have come up to my room but I needed to write an important letter before leaving for Wales. This was to Antoine Delvoie, a young Swiss gentleman of my own age with whom I had enjoyed a brief if fervent relationship during my stay at a finishing school on the beautiful banks of Lake Lucerne some two years before.

Antoine and I wrote to each other regularly, not only because we wanted to keep up our friendship, but because from the start of the correspondence we agreed to keep up our familiarity of each other's language. Antoine would write in English and I would reply in French! Dear Antoine always gallantly insisted that my French was better than his English. Alas this was not the case, although I possess enough knowledge of the language to read Monsieur Zola or Victor Hugo in the original, a great benefit, for much is lost even in the most sympathetic translation.

Before going to the library to write to Antoine, I decided to seek out Sayers and find out whether Susannah's gramophone had been securely packed as I had instructed − but what a shock I got when I entered the butler's pantry! For there standing stark naked against the wall was the plump figure of Lizzie, the vicar's youngest daughter and old Sayers, who was still in uniform except for his trousers and underpants which were lying over his ankles, was busy slewing his prick in and out of her hairy pussey.

At first I stood unseen as the butler's lean bottom cheeks jerked to and fro as the couple rocked in time as they pursued this amorous exertion. Then Lizzie let out a scream when she saw me looking on at this lewd scene. Sayers spun round and I was surprised to note the prodigious size of his prick which was definitely longer than Dennison's although perhaps not quite so wide in girth.

The old retainer's face went white and he clapped his hand over his mouth, but I was irritated rather than offended, and that only because all the servants seemed to be enjoying a good fuck today whilst it had been a full fortnight since I had enjoyed the sensation of a nice, thick prick inside my pussey, and that only a brief hour snatched with my brother's friend Michael Beecham in his rooms in Great Titchfield Street.

Meanwhile, Lizzie and Sayers stood transfixed until I said: 'Don't mind me, you two, I'll happily wait until you've finished.

'Yes, you mustn't keep a lady waiting, Sayers,' I added, rather enjoying the butler's discomfiture. 'Her need is greater than mine.'

I winked at Lizzie who giggled and said: 'Come on then, Sayers, you heard what Miss Rosie said, let's not waste any more time.' And to encourage him, she turned round with her feet apart and stuck out her rump so that her chubby buttocks were pushed out saucily towards him. Sayers cleared his throat as he shuffled between her legs and nudged her knees apart, taking his sizeable shaft in his hand.

'Are you ready, Miss Lizzie?' he asked and, after receiving a quick nod of assent, he guided his gleaming member into the crevice between her bum cheeks, before sliding through into the warm, welcoming wetness of her cunt.

Then Sayers showed the truth of the old saw about many a good tune being played on an old fiddle, because as soon as his prick was safely ensheathed in Lizzie's cunney, he started to fuck her in a slowish but regular rhythm. He reached round to fiddle with her large, tawny nipples, tweaking them between his fingers as he continued to slide his cock in and out of her sopping slit. Her backside slapped enticingly against his thighs as he increased the pace, and she wiggled her bottom from side to side as she cried out: 'Harder, fuck me harder, you randy old goat!'

He obliged by increasing the pace, withdrawing his tool almost completely before pushing home and sheathing his shaft so fully at each stroke that his balls banged against her bum cheeks.

'I'm coming, oh, I'm coming, yes, yes, YES!' screamed the uninhibited girl and she shuddered to her climax with a screech of pure ecstasy. Seconds later Sayers' torso went rigid and his sturdy old tool expelled its emission of frothy jism into her seething crack. She yelped with glee as the glorious sensations of her own orgasm swept like magic through her body and she twisted her bum lasciviously to draw out the last drains of sperm from Sayers' twitching todger.

'Oh, that was wonderful, let's do it again,' beamed Lizzie brightly, turning round to show us her shining face.

'I'm sorry, but I'm not up to it, Miss Lizzie. Besides, I mustn't neglect my duties,' said the butler as he pulled up his trousers. 'What can I do for you, Miss Rosie?'

I explained my concern about Susannah's gramophone, but he assured me that the machine had been packed in its original case and would come to no harm on the journey to Pembrokeshire.

'Very good, that's all I wanted to know,' I said and turned on my heel and walked away, but Lizzie called me back. 'Rosie, have you a moment to spare?' she asked with a worried expression in her voice.

'Of course I have,' I replied. 'When you're ready, meet me in the library and perhaps Sayers would ask Mrs Moser to prepare a pot of tea for us.'

Ten minutes later we were sipping tea together and, after exchanging some idle trivialities, Lizzie leaned forward and took my hands in hers. 'Rosie, I am so embarrassed being caught *in flagrante delicto* with your butler,' she said, blushing furiously as she added: 'I just don't know what came over me. It isn't that we haven't indulged before. You may as well know that Sayers has been fucking me regularly for the last three months.'

'This is a matter solely between you and him,' I said gently. 'It does not concern me or, come to think of it, anyone else in any way whatsoever, and of course you may completely rely on me to keep my silence about what I saw just before in my butler's pantry.'

25

'You are as kind as a sister,' said Lizzie, rising up to kiss my cheek, 'and if I can ever repay you, be assured I will never hesitate to do so.'

'Well, thank you, Lizzie, I appreciate what you say,' I replied and the girl looked at me with a mischievous smile. 'Oh, come on, Rosie, surely you're dying to know how I became intimately involved with one of your servants. You certainly have a right to know.'

I returned her smile and said: 'I can't deny that this question did cross my mind, but as I just said, this matter concerns only the two of you.'

'Oh, I don't mind telling you about it,' she said, settling herself into her armchair. 'It all began when I heard a sermon from Mr Kavanagh, Papa's new curate. You've not met him, have you?'

I shook my head, for, like both my parents, my brother and I are firm agnostics and attend Church only for baptisms, weddings and funerals.

'Well, Mr Kavanagh is a Christian socialist and when Papa was unwell one Sunday, he asked Mr Kavanagh to preach and he delivered a rousing address on the iniquities of the present political system,' she went on, leaning forward with her knees pressed tightly together. 'He took as his theme the Sermon on the Mount, and he captured my attention in a way which frankly my father has never managed to do.'

'What did he have to say?' I enquired, for I was curious to know how a young curate could so affect Lizzie.

'Well, pretty much what I have heard him since repeat at political meetings in Midhurst and Crawley,' she said. 'He explained how there has been an unparalleled increase in our powers of production which has resulted in huge accumulations of wealth. But only the owners of capital have benefited, while for the great mass of people there has only been an increase in misery and insecurity. He argued that the working classes will no longer endure this unfair division of society and he contrasted the lazy, luxurious lifestyle of the well-off with the hard labour of factory workers and the humiliating subservience demanded by the wealthy from the vast army of domestic servants.'

'I say, that's a bit strong,' I commented with a frown. 'I wouldn't have thought that our staff believe they are being exploited at Argosse Towers.'

'That's exactly what Sayers said after the service, but after Mr Kavanagh finished his discourse, one of Farmer Searle's labourers muttered loudly: "Well, if Socialism means fair shares of pussey for all working men, then I'm all in favour!". Fortunately, Mr Kavanagh did not hear this *sotto voce* comment and I congratulated him on his sermon. However, I'm afraid that Sayers was not convinced and we engaged in a long discussion as we walked through the village together. I invited Sayers into our home for some refreshment and we continued our argument. My mama and my sisters were visiting her cousin in Pulborough and I had stayed behind to minister to my sick papa who was suffering from a severe feverish chill. I went upstairs and saw that he was sleeping peacefully and then returned to continue my debate with Sayers.

'I opened a bottle of claret and I really couldn't tell you just how it happened, but after a while I found myself sitting on the sofa (for by now we were on first name terms) and my sensual appetite would not be denied.

'He played with my breasts, cupping them in his hands through the thin material of my dress and underslip, and I moved my hand to the front of his trousers and felt the hard stalk that threatened to tear the material which covered it. His thighs moved as he tried in vain to ease his erection, but I had already decided to offer a helping hand. So great was my desire to hold and play with his stiffstander that I unbuttoned his fly and grasped his thick shaft which showed out of his trousers, quivering like an arrow. Nothing

27

loath, Cuthbert unbuttoned the top of my dress and caressed my naked breasts as I rubbed his hot, hard cock up to peak condition.'

Lizzie paused and sipped her tea before continuing: 'When I judged that he was on the point of spending, I took my hand away and we locked ourselves into a lingering, erotic kiss with our tongues probing inside each other's mouths. I kissed him all over until my lips found their way to the purple, uncapped crown and I popped the pulsating knob between my lips, jamming down his foreskin and lashing my tongue around his fleshy staff. I sucked hard, drawing at least half of his extraordinarily long cock into my mouth whilst I toyed with his hairy ballsack. Then I started to lick this lovely lollipop, drawing my wet tongue all the way from his balls right up his shaft and I ended by washing his helmet with saliva and lapping it up with the edge of my tongue which made him moan out loud with pleasure.

'His cock tasted like nectar and I took all of his knob back inside my mouth and eased in the rest of his throbbing tool. I bobbed my head up and down on his shaft and three short licks and one long fierce sucking was enough to send him off. He released a torrent of hot, salty spunk which cascaded down my throat. Cuthbert has quite enormous balls, by the way, and only by swallowing convulsively could I gulp down all of his copious emission. Of course, I was now dying to be fucked, but unfortunately my papa chose this time to wake up and bang down on the ceiling with his stick to demand my attention.

'However, we were not to be denied and we arranged to meet on his next afternoon off, which happily was only two days away, and we consummated our relationship in Farmer Searle's meadow on the banks of the little stream which runs round the south side. And from then on, we have made love regularly, Rosie, and very nice it has been, too. There is much to be said for a more mature lover. Cuthbert might not be able to fuck with the vigour of an eighteen-year-old, but he doesn't shoot off before I'm ready, and he knows a trick or two about lovemaking that comes only with experience.'

'Or by reading my papa's copy of *The Oyster*!' I grinned, and Lizzie burst out laughing. 'More than likely,' she agreed. 'Does your Papa receive *The Oyster* regularly? I've only seen the magazine once, but it was far more interesting to read than *Hymns Ancient and Modern*!'

We finished our tea and I escorted Lizzie to the front door. 'Good-bye, and do come again for a chat,' I said as we shook hands, and then I dropped my voice as I went on: 'My parents are away for a few days and I've been invited down to Wales to spend a long weekend with an old friend. Only my brother Jonathan will be here and he is out most of the day with Charles Nettleton, so I am sure that Sayers will have plenty of time on his hands.'

Her eyes lit up as she heard this welcome information and she gave me a warm hug before turning away and walking briskly down our carriage drive. I chuckled as I sauntered back to the library. Since my sixteenth birthday I have had my own private drawer in the large desk there (the study boasts a beautiful, late-Georgian mahogany desk but, as Government papers are occasionally stored there, the study tends to be out-of-bounds to all except my father). [*On the very first page of her diaries, we are informed that Rosie's father is a senior Civil Servant in the Foreign Office – Editor*]

But first I wanted to read Antoine's last letter to me in detail before I dashed off my reply, for I had only previously scanned through the first couple of pages. He had written about how he had met up again in Paris with one of my contemporaries at the finishing school in Lucerne, a Scottish girl named Belinda Briskin from Inverness. As I took the sheets out of the envelope, I remarked out loud how I would

29

wager a pound to a penny that Antoine spent at least one
night in her bed, for Belinda was one of the friskiest fillies
at Madame Dupont's establishment.

I was soon proved right as this extract from his letter
shows:

*So, my dear Rosie, on the second evening of her stay,
Belinda managed to slip away from her wealthy aunt and
uncle who were accompanying her on the trip to Paris to
which they had treated their niece as a present to celebrate
her nineteenth birthday. When Sir Ronald and Lady Jennifer
Briskin suggested a post-prandial walk down the Champs
Elysées, Belinda pleaded a slight headache and retired to
her rooms.*

*I was waiting in the hotel lobby and once I saw Sir Ronald
and Lady Jennifer disappear out of the hotel, I sent a
message up to Belinda's suite and five minutes later we were
sitting on her bed, drinking iced champagne. We chatted
about the fine times we enjoyed whilst Belinda was studying
at Madame Dupont's and when I mentioned your name,
Rosie, saying that I wrote to you regularly, she asked me
for your address as she would also like to correspond with
you. She also asked me to send you her very best wishes
(which I now do) and inform you that she is now residing
at Gibson House, Chester Street, Edinburgh should you wish
to write to her.*

*Then, as I remembered how Belinda always enjoyed a
good joke, I told her the story of the Englishman who went
to a club privé in Berlin and spent the night with one of the
girls there. In the morning, he got up whilst the girl was still
asleep and dressed himself as he had arranged an early-
morning business appointment, so he put a five pound note
on the bedside table and shook the girl's shoulder to wake
her up.*

'What's all this?' said the girl sleepily and he replied: 'Just

a little payment for your services, Fraulein,' but the girl looked at the note and said: 'Mr Smith, I'd rather have marks.' So he coolly put the note back in his wallet and said: 'Very well, my dear, eight out of ten!'

This made Belinda laugh so heartily that she spilt some champagne down her skirt. I took out a handkerchief to help mop up the damp patch, but she was not unduly distressed and said: 'It will dry out soon enough if I hang up the dress now. In fact, why don't we both undress now because I can hardly wait for you to make love to me and I far prefer to fuck naked.'

So, without further ado we stood up and I took off my jacket whilst Belinda threw her dress over her head, an action which revealed that the naughty girl had already dispensed with her underclothes. Her beautiful bare breasts with their jutting pink nipples and the abundant thatch of fluffy blonde hair between her thighs fired me with great desire, and my penis instantly swelled up to an almost painful hardness as I struggled to rid myself of the remainder of my clothes.

Once we were both naked, I covered her mouth with passionate kisses and then, suddenly, Belinda dropped to her knees and her pretty flaxen ringlets were between my legs as she kissed my rampant rod which was standing up as stiffly as a guardsman outside your Buckingham Palace. The tip of her tongue flicked and licked all around the ridge of my unhooded helmet and, when she opened her lips and encircled my knob, instinctively I jerked my hips forward to push my prick further inside her sweet mouth.

Belinda looked up at me with a wicked smile as her tongue washed all over my stiff cock and her teeth scraped the tender flesh as she drew me in between those luscious red lips, sucking in almost all my shaft which sent shivers of delight coursing through my whole body. Now she circled the base of my truncheon with one hand whilst with the other she gently squeezed my balls, and she started to bob her head back and forth, sucking my prick with gusto in the most sensuous of rhythms. Then she let my twitching cock fall from her mouth as she changed her ministrations to down below, nibbling upon the soft, wrinkled skin of my ballsack which sent me into fresh paroxysms of the purest pleasure.

Finally she switched her attentions back to my penis and she palated my prick wonderfully as I plunged my quivering chopper down her willing throat. I let out a great shout and spent copiously, filling her mouth with a hot gush of sticky seed that gushed out of my throbbing cock. She gulped down my ejaculation with great enjoyment, smacking her lips as she swallowed all my spunk, licking and lapping until my sated shaft started to shrink and I lifted her to her feet and led her to the bed where we lay down together on the soft eiderdown.

'Oh dear, I feel so randy, Antoine, though I suppose your poor little dickie needs a little rest,' she sighed, flicking my flaccid shaft with her finger.

'I'm afraid so, but I'm sure I can pleasure you in other ways,' I replied with as much gallantry as I could summon, and I hauled myself up to kneel between her creamy thighs. 'M'mm, are you planning to lick me out?' she enquired eagerly. 'I do hope so, Antoine darling, because the British are so backward when it comes to the noble art of eating pussey that I can't remember the last time I was brought off this way. And I do have a pretty pussey, don't I, darling?'

'It's beautiful,' I said in a low voice and Belinda smiled contentedly as she thrust her hips upward as I dipped my head down and imprinted a kiss on her cute little cunt, pressing my mouth to her cunney lips in a long, clinging embrace.

But I wanted to assist Belinda to climb the highest peaks of erotic delight so, to her surprise, I pulled my head up and moved back a few paces on my knees. 'What are you doing?' she asked with some anxiety, but I assured her that she would enjoy what I had in mind.

'Relax, ma chérie,' I whispered and I bent down and began to titillate the big toe of her right foot with the tip of my tongue. It astonishes me that so few men know that this celebrated Continental recipe for arousing passion is well-nigh infallible, and almost immediately I started this sensuous stimulation, Belinda began to fling herself from side to side, her hands clutching at the eiderdown as she moaned with excitement. Her lovely face was flushed and her body was heaving up and down as I lowered my lips to her ankles and travelled up her legs as she continued to quiver from side to side.

Rapidly moving upwards, I kissed her knees and her inner thighs and when I reached her groin, I buried my face in her crotch, sliding my tongue between the pouting pussey lips which made her scream out with joy. She clamped my head between her thighs as my tongue inserted itself inside the warm, wet crevice of her quim and within seconds her body began to shake and tremble. With a few wild heaves she soon approached her climax and I assisted by licking and lapping around her dripping treasure-trove. I could feel her clitty swell as I slipped my tongue inside her sweet pussey and I probed deeper and deeper until with a few more moans and violent twists and turns she reached her orgasm.

'I want you inside me,' she whispered, releasing my head from its prison between her thighs and she took hold of my shoulders to roll me across on my back. I let myself be so moved and Belinda moved over me brushing her perky pink titties across the tip of my prick which had by now almost fully recovered, and the feel of her rubbery nips over my knob had the desired effect of making my member stand up to a rock-hard stiffness. She grasped my slippery shaft in her fist and rubbed it up and down until I was more than *ready for the fray. Then she squatted over my straining knob and guided it between her squishy cunney lips, and my cock slid all the way up her sopping slit as I reached up with my hands to squeeze her proud young breasts.*

Belinda rode me with powerful movements of her supple thighs. I began to move with her and played with her luscious, red-stalked nipples, rubbing them to bullet hardness whilst she rode me at an ever faster pace. Ma foi, Rosie, this was no slow, lingering fuck — we were both so urgent in our needs that with every thrust downwards upon my prick, I rose up to meet her with equal vigour.

We enjoyed this superb fuck for as long as I could hold out, but then the tingling in my cock became stronger and I could feel the first gush of sperm forcing its way up inexorably from my bollocks. My prick twitched uncontrollably and I thrust my hips upwards and jetted a fountain of sperm inside Belinda's cunt as her love channel quivered all round my shaft and she started to spend herself in a glorious mutual climax. The muscular contractions of her cunney increased my pleasure even more and I shot a second, tremendous spurt of spunk into her juicy honeypot and she fell forwards into my arms, shaking and yelping in delight as her cunney poured out its own liquid tribute, and the mix of our joint spends dribbled out of her crack and soaked the eiderdown.

We lay exhausted for some minutes, still coupled together, sucking in great gulps of air, and for a while neither of us could speak. Then Belinda smiled at me and puckered up her lips to blow me a tiny kiss. I lifted her gently off my hips and looked sadly down at my now shrunken organ. 'I regret that for some time I shall be hors de combat,*' I remarked sadly, but Belinda gave my prick an encouraging rub and said: 'Your dickie has worked very hard and deserves a rest. Anyhow, I'm not sure that I can carry on for a while. My poor pussey also needs time to recover.'*

Suffice it to say that I spent the rest of the night with Belinda, licking and lapping, fucking and sucking in all sorts of ways. We were not interrupted by her uncle and aunt who thoughtfully decided not to disturb their niece when they returned from their evening walk, and instead played bridge with Colonel Piers Rankin and Mrs Sally Cambridge who also happened to be staying at the same hotel. Is it true what the more salacious French magazines are writing about Mrs Cambridge? They say she is rivalling Mrs Keppel for your King's attentions these days, but then as you English say, one must never believe what one reads in the newspapers.

Write back to me soon, Rosie, and be sure to be as frank as I have been with you. The encounter I described above took place ten days ago and since then, alas, I have lived like a monk. Well, not like some monks who are notorious 'arse-bandits'. Is that not the correct English colloquialism? I have been called many things, but never one of those!

Finally, I must convey best wishes from Mademoiselle Justine de Villeneuve [see 'Rosie 1: Her Intimate Diaries — Editor] *who wishes to be remembered to you.*

All my love,
Antoine

I took a deep breath as I put down Antoine's lovely letter. Truth to tell, his erotic epistle had made me so randy that I needed some instant relief. I rushed upstairs to one of the spare bedrooms and locked the door behind me. I swiftly undressed and stood naked in front of the long wardrobe mirror, letting my gaze run down to the flaxen pubic hairs which curl over my crack, and slowly but surely I rubbed my finger all along my moist slit. Then I reached up and took out a small box which I had prepared for such occasions, in which I had placed a hand mirror and the divine ivory dildo Countess Marussia of Samarkand had kindly sent me from Cairo as a birthday gift a few months before.

Then I placed the mirror on the carpet between my legs and, by crouching down, I had a marvellous view of my love lips which I separated with my fingertips until I could see to the very depths of my now wet, tight cunney. As I closed my eyes and pictured Belinda's lithe, gleaming body rocking up and down upon Antoine's stalwart shaft, I pushed two fingers inside my honeypot to get the juices flowing and sure enough, in no time at all, my pussey was dripping wet.

I picked up the dildo and eased its smooth ivory head between my yielding cunney lips, slowly manoeuvring it round and round, touching my little clitty which spread wonderful waves of sheer ecstasy out from my pussey all over my body as I watched myself in the mirror. Then I rushed over to lie down on the bed and, opening my legs, started to slide the artefact in and out of my cunt, ever faster and deeper until, whoosh! A genuine orgasm shuddered its path through me as my cunt exploded and my love juices flowed unabated. I stayed still for a minute or so and then ambled into the bathroom where I sponged myself dry and washed the dildo with soap and warm water, feeling much rejuvenated by this solo gratification.

Perhaps I should add at this juncture that unlike so many young people, I have never had any qualms about masturbation. On my thirteenth birthday, my dear mama left by my bedside a copy of *Human Procreation Explained for Boys and Girls* by the noted Harley Street specialist, Dr Iain MacGregor. Therefore, unlike so many of my unhappy contemporaries, I have never felt unnecessary guilt about this practice, for although Dr MacGregor assures his young readers that self-stimulation is a quite natural and completely harmless pursuit, several misguided physicians still insist that it can lead to the most fearful illnesses such as blindness and softening of the brain. What absolute bunkum! How can there be any harm in it? Certainly, no boy ever caught an unwanted infection from tossing-off, and no girl ever found herself *enceinte* through finger-fucking.

Be that as it may, whilst I was slipping back into my clothes, my reverie was interrupted by the sound of raised voices from below and I hastily buttoned up my dress and went downstairs to investigate. The commotion was coming from the servants hall and when I arrived there, I was startled to see our cook-housekeeper, Mrs Moser and the village schoolmaster, Mr Whiteman, standing there in their coats which were literally covered with mud and a foul-smelling substance which looked suspiciously like manure. Our usually placid cook was red-faced with anger and was loudly cursing Mr Jerbutt, one of our neighbours, whilst Elaine, Dennison and Sayers were attempting to brush off the dirt from her clothes.

'What's going on here?' I demanded loudly. 'Mrs Moser, what on earth has happened to you? Have you been involved in an accident?'

'No accident, Miss Rosie, because three sacks of horse manure were quite deliberately thrown all over Len and me,' replied our cook hotly.

I looked at her in astonishment. 'Who was responsible for this outrage? We should report the incident immediately to the police.'

The mild-mannered Mr Whiteman coughed and said: 'I'm afraid that wouldn't do much good Miss d'Argosse. You see, the perpetrators were none other than your neighbour Mr Jerbutt and his men, Davies and Muttley.'

'Does that matter? Surely they can be charged with assault,' I remonstrated, but the schoolmaster shook his head and went on: 'Mr Jerbutt is Master of the local hunt and all the local magistrates are members. In any case, the matter would never be brought to court because he is also friendly with the senior officers of the Mid-Sussex police force through his Masonic connections.'

'Nevertheless, I want you to tell me exactly what happened,' I insisted, sitting down on a chair as I waited to hear his story.

He shrugged his shoulders and said: 'Very well, but I still don't think there is anything that can be done.

'Mrs Moser and I were walking back from the school (it was a half-holiday today) and we had planned to spend an hour or so on the Downs finishing off our water colour paintings.'

'Really, I didn't know that you had any artistic leanings, Mrs Moser, although perhaps I should have guessed from the exquisite pictures of the countryside on the walls of the kitchen. Were you responsible for them?'

'She certainly was,' intoned Mr Whiteman. 'As you may know, I hold a painting class on Sunday afternoons and Mrs Moser is without doubt my most talented pupil.'

His words cooled our cook's anger and she said rather coyly: 'Now then, Len, don't embarrass me like that. Take no notice of him, Miss Rosie.'

Mr Whiteman smiled and continued: 'We were walking along the Midhurst Road when one of the hunt followers, whom I recognised as James Davies, rode up and began questioning a young girl in a cart which was standing on the side of the road. After many loud enquiries as to the whereabouts of the hounds and how far he was behind them, he spurred up his horse and galloped past us, bespattering us both with mud from his horse's hooves. I shouted my anger but he spurred up, acknowledging my words with a rude gesture which there is no need for me to repeat in front of you.

'A minute or so later, Mr Jerbutt and Herbert Muttley rode up and brusquely enquired as to whether we had seen Davies. "Yes, and he is responsible for coating us with mud," I said sharply but Mr Jerbutt, whose demeanour and breath plainly showed that he had been drinking heavily,

38

simply laughed out loud, calling out to Muttley: "Haw! Haw! Haw! Look at this pair, they would hardly need any make-up to play in one of those nigger minstrel shows!"

'For sheer boorishness and absolute disregard for people's feelings, I have never seen anything to equal his behaviour. Naturally, Susan, Mrs Moser that is, was very angry at this caddish behaviour and she said as much. But then Muttley peered down at us and said to his master: "Don't worry about these two, sir, I've heard this fellow speak out against hunting in the pub." He may have been referring to a discussion there last week when I quoted the late Oscar Wilde who categorised fox-hunting as "The unspeakable in pursuit of the uneatable".

'Well, they rode off in a swaggering way but as Mrs Moser and I were making our way back here, the three of them came charging back, each holding a sack of manure, dismounted and tipped the contents of their sacks over us before riding off.'

'If my papa were here, he'd make them pay you damages,' I said angrily, looking across at Mrs Moser's new coat which Elaine was doing her best to clean, a tailor-made double-breasted Cheviot serge garment with velvet trimmings and lined to the waist with silk, for which she had paid fifty-seven and sixpence [£2.88! – *Editor*], a huge sum for even a well-paid servant such as our cook.

Elaine looked up and said with a giggle: 'I've just thought of a good idea of how we could get our own back, Miss Rosie, but I think I'd better tell you about it in private.'

I did not question her as to why she should want to speak to me secretly, for Elaine was a bright girl and I trusted her judgement. 'Very well,' I said and motioned for her to join me in the hall.

When we were alone, she looked round to make sure that no-one could hear and said: 'Miss Rosie, you know that I'm friendly with Millie Fosberry who works at Colonel

39

Nettleton's house. Well, Millie has been carrying on with Mr Jerbutt for the last two or three months. She's a very naughty girl because she doesn't like him all that much but her dad's been out of a job since he broke his leg at work last November, and her mum's doing her best to try and keep the family out of the workhouse.'

'Oh yes, Fosberry was quite a hero, wasn't he? I remember reading about the incident in the local newspaper. Didn't the poor man get injured trying to stop a runaway horse?'

'That's right, Miss Rosie, only as it happened on his way to work, his employer gave him the sack, and even though she's taking in washing, Millie's mum is finding it a struggle with three young children, though Millie gives her as much as she can,' Rosie explained. 'So Millie was tempted when Mr Jerbutt offered her a sovereign [*one pound — Editor*] to come round to his house and be nice to him, as he put it, whilst his wife was away.'

A frown settled on my brow because, although I am a true libertarian when it comes to enjoying a good fuck, I do not approve of married men straying from the straight and narrow, although as will shortly be seen, I was forced to bend my rule in Wales with none other than — well, dear reader, you must wait and see.

Meanwhile, Elaine was about to tell me more about Mr Jerbutt's sexual peccadillos when Sayers came out of the kitchen and said: 'Excuse me interrupting, Miss Rosie, but Mrs Moser wants to know if Coq Au Vin will suit you tonight for she needs to begin work on dinner as soon as possible. Oh, Elaine, your friend Millie Fosberry has come to see you.'

What a happy coincidence! I told Sayers that Coq Au Vin would be lovely and that he should send Millie out to us immediately. 'My goodness, I quite forgot that it's her afternoon off and that she was coming to sit with me this

40

evening,' said Elaine. 'She'll tell you all about Mr Jerbutt herself.'

Millie Fosberry was a slim young girl of no more than eighteen years of age who sported a mane of long, dark hair, large blue eyes and a pretty *retroussé* nose, and I could see why Mr Jerbutt had been attracted to her. At first, Millie was reticent to talk about her experiences with him, but after a little persuasion she confided in me that the first time she had gone round to his house, Mr Jerbutt had been very civil to her and plied her with all kinds of delicacies, and together they had drunk a bottle of the best French champagne.

'Then we went up the stairs to his bedroom,' she confided as we moved into the drawing room and sat down on the sofa. 'And as I knew what I was expected to do for my sovereign, I started to take off my clothes and I heard him groan when I slid my slip down and let him see my bare breasts. He seemed shy so I cupped them in my hands, stroking the nipples till they stood up and I said: "Well, aren't you also going to undress?" and he replied: "That's capital, capital!" and he came forward and squeezed my bum before sitting on the bed and taking off his shoes and socks. But he seemed to hesitate so, to put him at his ease, I tugged down my knickers and stood stark naked in front of him, and then he unbuttoned his shirt and pulled down his trousers and stood up wearing only a pair of white linen drawers.

'I yanked them down and looked down at a mass of wiry black hair from which dangled a thick, well-formed prick. Of course, I just could not understand why that juicy looking cock wasn't already as stiff as a poker, jutting upwards ready and waiting for me! I sank to my knees and kissed the tip and drew back the foreskin to uncover his knob, but I simply couldn't make his cock swell up, despite taking his helmet inside my mouth and licking it all over.

' "Why, Mr Jerbutt, don't you fancy me?" I asked with

41

a genuine note of reproach in my voice, for although I was only there because I desperately needed the money for my poor family, frankly, I felt rather sorry for him.

'I allowed his soft shaft to fall from my mouth and he said in a strained voice as he pulled me to my feet: "Ah, Millie, there is something you can do to help me to a cockstand if you are willing." I nodded guardedly and silently he bent down and from under the bed he produced a stout black Malacca cane. He led me by the hand to the bed and for a moment I was frightened in case he wanted to beat me with it, but I soon found out that the opposite was the case because he placed the cane in my hand and bent over the bed with his face pressed against a pillow, his legs spread wide and his feet firmly on the floor.

' "Go on, Millie," he said, his voice muffled in the pillow. "Crack away!"

' "Where?" I asked hesitantly.

' "On the arse, you silly girl," he replied sharply. "Give me six of the best and you'll see my cock stand to attention."

'This was all new to me, but I grasped the cane and still with some reluctance brought it smartly down across his dimpled bottom.

' "Harder, Millie, harder!" he called out, waggling his bum cheeks, so I laid on three more strokes, raising long red weals all over the surface of his backside. He wriggled and writhed as the stinging cuts of the cane fell with a swishing sound on his firm white buttocks, striping the skin in all directions, and I felt the beginnings of a warm glow all over my body as I laid on a fifth cut to the deep crease of his arse. He arched his naked rump to me and I struck the final stroke across both cheeks which made him yell out: "Ow! Ow! Ow! That'll do, that'll do!"

'I laid down the cane as I felt this warm glow spread out from my pussey to my breasts and the back of my neck. Mr Jerbutt stood up and faced me and, my goodness, what a difference the beating had made! His cock was now rock hard, standing up as straight as a die against his belly and he drew back his foreskin himself, making the pink knob swell and bound in his hand.

'What a magnificent stiffstander he could muster once he was aroused! I could hardly grasp it in my fist, even though my fingers aren't particularly stubby. But Mr Jerbutt was so urgent to insert his rampant weapon that I simply lay down on the bed and opened my legs and let him enter me. And I must confess that I enjoyed the fuck as he pushed his massive member slowly between my cunney lips until I could feel the full length of his shaft inside my love channel. He pumped away enthusiastically, stroking in, holding himself in place and then slipping out in a quickening rhythm as his balls slapped against the back of my thighs.

' "You fuck like a lady rather than a mere servant," he said breathlessly, a cack-handed compliment but I said: "And how does a lady make love?"

' "Oh, she gives and takes with equal gusto," and I laughed at this, saying: "Then you must fuck me like a gentleman would," as I wrapped my legs around his back. He moved up slightly so that his prick slid in and out at a higher angle and tickled the edge of my clitty. I wriggled my hips wildly as Mr Jerbutt increased the pace and I soon spent and my love juice coated his cock as it ploughed in and out of my well-oiled cunney until he let out a hoarse yell and shot a stream of hot seed into me.'

'Did he give you the sovereign he promised?' I enquired, and Millie nodded. 'Yes, eventually, but I had to wallop his bottom again and then suck his cock before he would give it to me.'

She turned to Elaine and added: 'As it happens, I walked over to tell you that Mr Jerbutt has told me to be at his house at five o'clock if I want to earn another gold coin. So I'll go there now and come back here afterwards if that's convenient.'

43

'I've an even better idea,' said Elaine excitedly. 'I'll come with you if it's all right with you, Miss Rosie. Don't worry, I'll be back in plenty of time to finish the packing for your trip tomorrow.'

I was puzzled by her words. 'Why on earth do you want to go with Millie to Mr Jerbutt's house?' I asked, and she replied with a sly smile: 'Well, if you would let me take along your brother, Mr Jonathan's, Secret Waistcoat Camera, I would photograph Mr Jerbutt fucking Millie and then we could warn the old bugger that if he didn't pay for a new coat for Mrs Moser and for the cleaning of Mr Whiteman's clothes, we would show the photographs to his wife.'

Now whilst I could appreciate the rough justice in such a scheme, I could not agree to my maid's plan. 'No, I don't think so, Elaine,' I said with some reluctance. 'Because in my experience the end rarely justifies the means and Mrs Jerbutt would be hugely embarrassed even though she is innocent of any wrong-doing.

'However, the scheme is not totally without merit. What you could do is to photograph Mr Jerbutt in a ridiculous rather than a compromising position. Millie, perhaps you could persuade him to wear something silly whilst you are whopping him. Then we could warn him that if he did not make suitable redress, we would release the photographs and he would be a laughing stock around the county. To be honest, I still have grave reservations for, despite our good intentions, the idea is still blackmail by any other name, but at least we would not be greatly hurting Mrs Jerbutt by exposing her husband as an adulterer.'

'Oh yes, Miss Rosie. Why, Mr Jerbutt said he was going to dress up as a schoolboy this afternoon and I should pretend to be his housemaster and cane him for being a naughty boy,' said Millie, her eyes shining with excitement at the thought of Mr Jerbutt being humbled. 'But I don't know how he would feel about letting Elaine watch.'

44

Elaine smiled at this and said: 'Leave that to me, Millie, you would be surprised how when their pricks are stiff, most men lose any common sense they possess, especially if they believe that they are going to get their cocks sucked!'

I could not help but agree with these sentiments and I said; 'Very true, and so long as you confine yourself to snapping shots of Mr Jerbutt being caned on his bare bottom, then you may have Jonathan's camera and proceed with your plan. I don't think it necessary to inform him unless he returns before you, Elaine, though in the circumstances I'm sure that Jonathan won't mind our borrowing his property without his permission.'

'I know where he keeps it, Miss Rosie, shall I bring it down?' asked Elaine with a wicked grin spreading all over her pretty face.

'Very well, you naughty girl,' I sighed and she rushed off upstairs to fetch the camera, a small circular affair which could be attached to one's clothing and was ideal for sneaking a quick snapshot, for all the wearer had to do was pull a short string that opened the shutter and hey presto, a photograph was taken on the glass plate inside it.

Elaine returned with the apparatus and said with satisfaction: 'There is space for four more photographs on the plate, which will be enough for us.'

'All right, off you go, girls, and good luck,' I said, although I still felt a little doubtful as to whether I was right to give my consent to what was afoot. 'Elaine, please try not to be too late as you still have to finish packing my clothes.'

'I'll be back in good time,' she promised, and the girls scuttled out to keep their assignation whilst I informed Mr Whiteman and the other servants that I had set in hand a plan to compensate them financially, even if an apology from the awful Mr Jerbutt was probably too much to ask.

'In the meantime, give me your measurements and I will

write to my tailor, Mr Rabinowitz, who will make you up a nice new summer coat,' I said to Mrs Moser. 'Only last week he sent me some sketches from a French magazine which I'll give to you and you're bound to find something that you'll like in it. There was one design with a tight-fitting back and a pouched front, lined to the waist with silk that I thought would suit you down to the ground. Don't worry about the cost, Mr Jerbutt will cough up, I assure you.'

Mrs Moser thanked me profusely, but she was still a trifle nervous and she said: 'It's very kind of you to trouble yourself, Miss Rosie, but just suppose you're wrong and he doesn't pay up. I can't afford five pounds for one of Mr Rabinowitz's coats.'

I thought about Elaine snapping away with her secret camera and said grimly: 'I am so confident that I will tell him to put the garment on my account if I am proved wrong and Mr Jerbutt does not pay handsomely for his disgraceful behaviour.'

Having sorted out this dispute, I went back to the library to compose my reply to Antoine whilst Elaine and Millie were busying themselves on their righteous mission, for there would be little time in Wales for me to write back to my dear old friend and I knew how much he enjoyed reading my letters, especially when they were nice and spicy! Before I sat down at the desk, I searched for a French dictionary, for remember, dear reader, that I had to reply to Antoine in his own language. I decided to take out the large new Larousse I had purchased at Mr Blow's bookshop in the Charing Cross Road, but to my great surprise, as I pulled it from the shelf, an envelope slipped out from between the pages and landed on the carpet. I picked up the envelope which was addressed personally to Mr Blow. My only excuse for what followed was that the envelope was already open . . .

I took both the book and the envelope back to the desk

46

and took out the perfumed pages of expensive writing paper. I opened them up and immediately recognised the address printed in raised letters on the first sheet: *Stomson House, Hurstpierpoint, East Sussex*. Only yesterday I had been glancing through the pages of *The Tatler* in which there were photographs taken at the ball given by Lord and Lady Stomson to celebrate the twenty-first birthday of their eldest daughter, Pamela.

Mea culpa, I succumbed to temptation and read the letter which turned out to be not from Lady Stomson or Pamela but Angela, their seventeen-year-old younger daughter. She began her epistle by thanking him for sending her the twelve volumes of the complete Shakespeare she had ordered, and then she commented roundly upon the letter he must have sent her with the books:

You indicate some surprise that Mama queried the price of five pounds plus postage for my books. Well, yes, they may be printed in clear, bold type with numerous illustrations and bound in best, half-polished calf with gilt top edges, but I do not believe that you are in a good position to judge whether this price is expensive. I have always understood that booksellers are deluged with advance gratis copies by publishers' representatives hoping to solicit orders. True, a new book is cheaper than dinner at a good restaurant or a seat at the Opera, but in these fast times, I regret to say than many people would rather enjoy a decent meal at Baum's Chop House [a fashionable establishment in Bloomsbury patronised by the fast young set − Editor] *or patronise the Empire Music Hall, Leicester Square rather than sit for hours and hours wading through a heavy novel by Sir Walter Scott, Charles Dickens or Robert Louis Stevenson. So the book trade cannot afford to sit on its laurels and must offer a wide selection of new, exciting young writers at popular prices.*

Anyhow, talking of books, I had the most extraordinary experience the other day. My young fifteen-year-old cousin Toby was staying with us for the weekend with his parents and on Saturday afternoon, everyone except me went out for a constitutional after luncheon. At least, I thought everyone had gone out when I wandered upstairs to my bedroom where I had left a magazine which I had been reading. However, as I was crossing the landing, I heard a sound like a creaking bedspring coming from Toby's bedroom. The door was closed and normally I would have probably ignored it for one of the maids might have been up there, but recently, according to the local newspapers, there has been a spate of housebreaking around this neighbourhood, and so I put my eye to the keyhole to see if anything was amiss.

My goodness, what a shock I got! For there was Toby lying naked on his bed holding a book in one hand and massaging his stiff, swollen shaft with the other! And this was no boyish little tool that Toby had between his legs but a splendid specimen of a fully grown cock, large and strong, in the full flush of youthful power and beauty. He had drawn down the white skinned cover from his knob which gleamed redly as his hand slicked up and down his proud pole. Oh, but Toby looked so sweet lying there and I gazed upon his slim, lithe torso with wonder and admiration, but naturally it was his erect prick and surprisingly big balls which most attracted my eyes.

A warm glow spread all over my body and as I watched him rub his meaty tool I felt a moistness between my own thighs and, pulling up my dress, I started to finger my cunney through the thin material of my knickers. Indeed, I felt randier and randier until I just could not bear it any longer and, after giving my damp pussey a final fingering, without further ado I opened the door and marched straight in!

Goodness me, Toby's face was a picture! In an instant,

all the colour drained from his cheeks and he dropped the book and released his shaft as he tried somewhat ineffectually to cover his cock and balls with his hands.

'Jesus Christ! What are you doing here, Angela? I thought you were all going out for a walk!' he blurted out wildly. 'Oh God, what shall I do!'

For reply, I said quietly: 'Do? Why, Toby dear, you do not have to do anything at all,' as I closed the door behind me and turned the key in the lock, an elementary precaution which poor Toby had failed to take. 'Now it's nice to play with yourself, but I know an even better game,' I continued smoothly, opening the buttons of my blouse and sliding the garment off my shoulders. He looked on open-mouthed as I continued undressing and giving my young cousin his first view of the naked female form.

I did not bother wasting time in preliminary foreplay but immediately reached for his cock, which was no longer fully erect but still thick with unslaked passion. His shaft sprang back to life in my grasp, swelling up to its previous proud, hard state. For a young lad, it was surprisingly large, for Toby isn't particularly big for his age. Yet believe me, I am not exaggerating when I tell you that his erect prick must have been at least seven inches long and his pubic thatch was quite dense, with the hair lying in a sweeping wave over the base of his cock. However, I then remembered listening outside the door at a dinner party after the ladies had retired and the men were passing the port and dear old Dr Macdougall was telling Papa that Edward confronted Lily Langtry [one of Edward VII's most notorious mistresses when he was Prince of Wales — Editor] *about the fact that her pubic hair was much darker than the hair on her head. According to Dr Macdougall, this is by no means unusual, and many a blonde woman has been wrongfully accused of dyeing her hair after an intimate encounter has revealed a dark pubic bush.*

Slowly at first, I ran my fingers up and down the length of Toby's tool and then I tightened my grip and began to slide my fist up and down and then delicately encircled the uncapped, bulbous crown and lowered my head to implant a kiss on it. This excited my poor cousin so much that I only had time to lick his rounded knob once more before his boner began to twitch and he reached his climax with sperm shooting out from his cock and trickling down my fingers. As the sticky white froth came bubbling out of his knob, I jammed my mouth over his helmet and slurped up his jism which I found very pleasant to taste, being less tangy than yours, dare I say, and juicier than that of Lieutenant George Lucas of the Household Cavalry who fucked me last month at Annabel Blumer's coming out party. I gulped down every drop of Toby's copious emission until his tadger shrank back, not to a complete flaccidity, but to a sensuous semi-erectness.

I lay down on the bed and gave Toby the chance to explore my body. 'Oh, Angela,' he said, his voice cracking with emotion. 'You are such a beautiful girl and I've dreamed so often of fucking you whilst I've been wanking. Just looking at your breasts, God, those lovely red titties . . .' and his voice trailed off as I gently pulled him to me and I took his hand and encouraged him to roll my nipple against his fingers until it was as hard as a pebble.

He kissed my neck and throat with great fervour and then moved down to my breasts and sucked hard on my pointy titties whilst he rolled himself over on top of me and brought the crown of his erect-again prick to my waiting pussey lips.

Without hesitation I grabbed his cock and with my own hands guided it to its destination, and the sensation of his throbbing, virgin prick squeezing into my quim made me tingle all over with excitement. A deliciously ecstatic feeling spread all over my body and I went off into a little series of delirious spends which oiled my cunney so nicely that

Toby was able to squeeze every inch of his iron-hard boner inside me, and I revelled in the sensations afforded by his young, meaty cock within the soft, luscious folds of my love sheath.

My cunt was now on fire and as a marvellous climax shuddered through my veins I felt Toby's body go rigid and he shot a glorious flood of jism inside me. His spunk spurted with such intensity that I could imagine it splashing off the rear wall of my cunney and, indeed, so abundant was his spermy ejaculation that my pussey and thighs were well lathered by our love juices. Then he pulled out his shrunken penis, rubbing his shaft amorously in a last salute against my sticky cunney lips.

I looked at my bracelet watch and told the young scamp we had better dress ourselves and go downstairs to await the return of our parents. This we did, which was just as well, for not ten minutes later they came back to find Toby reading a newspaper and me playing the piano in the drawing room.

I do feel somewhat ashamed at fucking my young cousin, but he wanted it even more than I, for unwanted virginity is a most troublesome complaint. So where can there be any harm in this dalliance, especially as I do not intend to repeat the performance now that Toby has lost his cherry, to coin the expressive if rather vulgar American phrase.

As always, dear David, I would welcome your honest opinion on the matter, for you are one of the few people I can rely upon to give me an unbiased view on personal matters.

With all my love,
Angela

I did not have to wait long to find out what advice had been given to Angela Stomson for, as I folded the sheets of this letter and stuffed them back inside the envelope, I

51

noticed another crumpled sheet of paper in the dictionary. With a smile of satisfaction, I opened it out and discovered that it turned out to be a carbon copy of the bookseller's typewritten reply to her *cri de coeur*, and it was with interest that I perused his reply which was as follows:

Dearest Angela,

My thanks for your letter and I take it as the greatest of compliments that you entrust me with your intimate thoughts. As you have stated, your cousin was delighted to have crossed the Rubicon into manhood and you will have earned his undying gratitude by guiding him on this occasionally perilous journey.

First love can be idyllic or quite disastrous and in later years, Toby will consider himself extremely fortunate to have been initiated into the pleasures of love-making. It is a time-honoured tradition that older women make the best partners for shy young virgin boys, although fifteen is not that young (after all, there is only two years difference in your ages) and he was obviously sexually competent and you were each turned on by the other, so all in all, I am sure that the experience will have been of mutual benefit, although I am equally certain that you are very wise not to continue the relationship.

I well recall the gossip a few years ago over a very similar state of affairs which involved Briony, Lord McBain's daughter and Oliver, the son of Sir Jonathan and Lady Abigail Letchmore. She was twenty-seven and he was sixteen. Whilst Oliver was a handsome boy and well-built for his age, the affair was doomed by infatuation. Whilst Briony felt more in control of the relationship with a younger man after a passionate sexual involvement with Colonel Bronzite (who, as you may know, is well-known in and around Mayfair for his robust sexual proclivities), alas, her entanglement with young Oliver also ended in mutual recrimination.

The draft ended at this point and I decided to destroy the letter, a fair copy of which I assumed had been posted in reply to Angela Stomson. I tore it up into little pieces and dropped them into the waste-paper basket and then wrote a short note to Mr Blow, enclosing Angela's letter to him, explaining how it had arrived in my hands and, after a pause for thought, I must confess that I decided to tell a white lie. Crossing the fingers of my left hand, I went on to assure him that although the envelope had been opened, to the best of my knowledge the letter had not been read! I salved my conscience by telling myself that if one of Mr Blow's assistants had not been so careless, this incriminating material would never have fallen into my hands and that it was fortunate that only I had seen the letters and not someone caddish enough to ask either party for money to restore the correspondence to its rightful owner.

At the same time, to soften the blow (please pardon the pun!) I ordered a copy of *Modern Daughters* by Miss Anne Fox-Smythe, the daring new book of conversations with girls of all classes on the foolish restrictions bound upon them by Society. Profusely illustrated with photographs and elegantly bound in silk cloth, the book will make an ideal present for Lord Gordon MacChesney, my old rogue of an uncle, who still has old-fashioned ideas about the place of women, a subject about which he is solely concerned in that every night there should be an attractive female between himself and the mattress!

CHAPTER TWO

Some Forbidden Escapades

What a difference the railway and the internal combustion engine have made to our social habits! Journeys which took my grandparents a fortnight can now be easily accomplished in a day. How much more pleasant it is to relax in the luxury of a first class carriage on a Southern Railways express where one can stretch one's legs, partake of refreshments, read a book or simply stare out of the window than to be jolted up and down inside a cold, cramped coach! And now even most minor roads are metalled, if not tarred, so that travelling by motor-car is so much nicer than bumping along rutted roads.

Nevertheless, although I could have travelled to Meverson Hall in one day, I decided to break my journey in London and, in the morning, Dennison and myself caught the early train to London and, as arranged, the Savoy had a motor car and driver waiting to meet us at Victoria Station.

By a happy coincidence, in the lobby of the hotel, whom should I meet but Mademoiselle Nicole Coulandre, another old friend from Madame Dupont's Academy in Lucerne.

'Rosie! How wonderful to see you!' she cried out in her sensually accented English. 'Normally I would have written to you to say I am coming to England, but we are staying only two days before journeying up to Newcastle where we will take a ship to Copenhagen to visit my sister Françoise who, as you may remember, married a Danish boy.'

Nicole was the daughter of a wealthy and well-connected family of wine-growers from the Bordeaux region and on my birthday, without fail she would send a case of chateau-bottled claret to Argosse Towers. In return, on her birthday (which was only six weeks before this chance meeting) I would reciprocate by ordering from Selfridge's their best Irish table linen of which she was very fond, and this year I had sent her a hemstitched and hand-embroidered bedspread which, according to her letter of thanks, she had adored.

I must mention here that she was perhaps the most beautiful of all the girls attending Madame Dupont's establishment. She was stunningly pretty with waist-length, liquorice-black hair and ice-blue eyes, an aristocratic, aquiline nose and full, sensuous lips. Nicole spoke impeccable English (her maternal grandmother hailed from Devon) and she and I had become close friends almost from the moment we first met, recognising a shared sense of humour and a taste for adventure not immediately apparent in many of our fellow students.

We fell into each other's arms and Nicole asked me what my plans were for the day. 'My parents have gone to the British Museum for the day,' explained the lovely girl, 'but I have arranged to meet Sir David Pickering after luncheon and he has promised to take me to the famous Jim Jam Club to see one of their naughty Victor Pudendum exhibitions.'

[*The Jim Jam Club in Great Windmill Street was a raffish establishment for upper crust Society gentlemen where all kinds of erotic entertainment took place during its heyday between the mid-1890s and 1914. Many underground magazines, including* The Oyster *and* The Rupert Mountjoy Diaries *make mention of the club which was secretly*

'I'm sure your parents don't know about *that* arrangement,' I laughed and Nicole nodded and went on: 'No, they think he is taking me to an afternoon concert at the Queen's Hall!

'Oh Rosie, it is good to see you again! Can you join me for luncheon? And of course, if you are free, you are very welcome to join Sir David and myself at the Jim Jam Club.'

'I don't know about that, Nicole,' I replied doubtfully as we strode arm-in-arm down the corridor, 'but I'll happily join you for luncheon.'

We ate a light meal of consommé, lamb steak marinated in lemon and garlic and a fresh fruit salad which was quite delicious and gave the lie to the old canard about our restaurants only being able to offer solid English fare, although I had to admit to Nicole that the Savoy chef was in all probability a Frenchman!

'I'm really looking forward to seeing this Victor Pudendum exhibition of fucking,' Nicole confided to me as we walked into the lounge to have our coffee. Alas, we had only sat down for a moment when a page-boy came up to her with a message from Sir David Pickering, apologising profusely for the short notice but regretting that he would be unable to take her to the Jim Jam Club that afternoon as his Aunt Maud had been taken ill and he felt it necessary to rush down to Bournemouth to be at her bedside.

'Damn, that puts paid to my afternoon,' she said crossly. 'I would suggest that we went together, but I understand that only members are allowed to attend, and they can only bring two guests to a Victor Pudendum show.'

'Never mind;' I said, squeezing her arm, 'there'll always be another opportunity. Look, after you have visited your sister in Denmark, are you going home via London? If you are, I am sure that Lord Philip Pelham is a member of the

Jim Jam Club and he will be pleased to escort us both to next month's Victor Pudendum contest.'

'What a splendid idea, Rosie! Yes, we will be back in London for three whole days from the seventeenth of July, but won't you be out of town during the summer?'

'Yes, but we shall not be travelling to France until the last week of July and the building work on our London house will be finished by then, so I can stay there,' I replied and Nicole leaned over and gave me a little kiss on the cheek.

Then she rummaged unsuccessfully in her bag for a notebook and said: '*Zut*, I have left my diary in my bedroom. I tell you what, though, come up to my room and I will write in our arrangement. Also, I would like you to taste some of the delicious cognac Gerard gave me as a leaving present before we left Bordeaux.'

'Who is Gerard?' I queried, and Nicole smiled as we rose and walked out towards the staircase. 'Gerard Leclerc is a nephew of one of our neighbours,' she explained. 'He is a very nice boy who has declared his undying love for me, but such are the strange ways of the heart, I cannot reciprocate his affections and whilst I have been tempted to surrender myself to him, I am sure you will agree, Rosie, that it is wrong to let a man fuck you simply out of pity for him. However, Gerard showers me with gifts and he insisted that I take a bottle of cognac with me on my travels, for medicinal purposes as well as for pleasure.'

Once in her room, Nicole made a note in her diary of our arrangement and then she opened her trunk and passed me a copy of *La Vie Folâtre* which I browsed through whilst she poured out two glasses of her boyfriend's cognac for us.

This very naughty magazine was full of the most lascivious photographs imaginable taken by 'Monsieur Jean-Paul, the well-known photographic artist whose work is reputedly collected by both His Majesty King Edward VII and the up-and-coming Mr Lloyd-George. The photographs showed naked young men and women with their cocks, pussies and bottoms freely displayed as they frigged, sucked and fucked each other in all kinds of ways and my blood began to warm as I looked at these sensual works of art.

Perhaps my favourite photograph was of a beautiful, dark-skinned African girl seated on the lap of her lover — but she had lifted her bottom just enough so that one could see that his thick, stiff shaft was already half embedded inside her cunt. Her arms were around his neck and her face was turned up, beaming with the satisfaction she was experiencing in her well-filled cunney.

Another showed two pretty nude girls in a clinch, their bodies pressed tightly together with their arms round their partner's waist and pressing the other's soft, rounded bottom. Each had a little finger slipped inside the cleft between the other's chubby bum cheeks.

'Does that picture excite you? Look at her luscious lips, her aroused nipples, she is lost in those first exquisite moments of a lovely fuck,' said Nicole softly as she handed me a glass of cognac. I sipped at the fiery liquid and then watched the lovely French lass toss her drink down in one gulp.

'I like the look of her as well,' I said hoarsely, and before I could say any more, the sweet girl nimbly unbuttoned my blouse and as if in a trance I unbuttoned my cuffs to allow her to slide the garment from my shoulders. We gazed at each other in silence for a moment and she whispered quietly: 'Shall we continue?'

I nodded my head and then we began to tear off all our clothes until we both stood naked. I placed my hands on Nicole's shoulders as she wriggled towards me and looked with delight at her elegant, slim body. We slid into an embrace and staggered drunkenly towards the bed, onto which we threw ourselves and began to kiss and cuddle. Brushing my palm against her stalky red nipples, I saw them swell and stand up proudly as I traced the slight curve of Nicole's stomach until my fingers became entangled in the thick dark curls of her bush. As our tongues waggled inside each other's mouths we sinuously rubbed our bodies together.

'You be the gentleman, *ma chérie*,' gasped Nicole as she lay on her back with her legs wide apart, and I gave my assent to her request by running my hand through the glossy pussey curls one more time before bending forward to flick my tongue against her large, erect, strawberry-coloured nipples which made her moan with delight. She pushed my head downwards until my face was buried between her thighs, and I kissed her moistening slit, licking and lapping at her sopping muff. Now, from the serrated vermilion lips, out popped Nicole's stiff, rubbery clitty, as big as a thumb. I opened her love lips further with my fingers and passed the tip of my tongue lasciviously up and down her juicy crack before taking her clitty in my mouth and playfully nipping it with my teeth. She wriggled deliciously and with a cry of: 'Oooh! Aaah! You are making me come, darling Rosie!' she spent profusely all over my mouth and chin.

We changed places and Nicole lay on top of me and, running her wet, pink tongue over her lips, she gently took one of my breasts in each hand and lowered her face to my nipples whilst with her clever fingers she opened my crack as wide as possible and then, directing her clitty at the pouting opening of my cunt, she somehow managed to stuff the hard, erectile flesh between my cunney lips, holding them tightly together with her hand. This kind of intra-feminine fucking was quite novel to me and I found it tremendously stimulating to have her clitty inside me.

In no time at all my cuntal juices were flowing freely as Nicole continued remorselessly to fuck my pussey, adding one, two and then three fingers until I felt the first faint waves of orgasm start deep inside me. These soon began to spread, setting every nerve on fire with intense pleasure, and I cried out with joy as I discharged a flood of love juice over her hand and over my thighs.

I stayed with Nicole until three o'clock and then we decided to dress and attend an afternoon concert arranged by the generous philanthropist, Sir Ronnie Dunn, in aid of the East End Milk Fund just a short taxi ride away at the Connaught Rooms. The Mayfair String Quartet which provided the entertainment was made up of four of the most gifted amateur musicians in London. The Quartet was led by the Honourable Jonathan Crawford, younger son of Viscount Sevenoaks and included Mr Peter Lucas, a popular young man-about-town, on second violin whilst the viola was in the capable hands of Miss Caroline Connor, the talented young niece of the Canadian High Commissioner and the group was completed by Dr Jonathan Abigaille, the popular Society physician whom gossip has involved with Lady Gaiman and Fiona Davidson, the prettiest of this year's crop of débutantes presented at Court. His mastery of the 'cello is less well-known although, as I later found out from Miss Connor, for the last three years he has been studying with the maestro Ludwig Seligsohn in Paris.

The large room was packed with the cream of Society and amongst the guests I recognised from the pages of *The Illustrated London News* were Mrs Michael Reynolds, Lady Shella de Souza and Mr Andrew Edwards, the immensely wealthy Kentish landowner reputed to possess one of the most enormous penises in all Europe, if one may believe his biographical details which were published in the latest scurrilous edition of *The Oyster*.

Nicole and I took our seats and after a few introductory words from Sir Ronnie Dunn, the musicians took the stage. The first piece of music on the programme was Haydn's gravely thoughtful String Quartet in F Sharp minor, an emotive and unusual key little used by the classical composers. Indeed, so little is composed in F Sharp minor that in more than six hundred works, Mozart only wrote one movement in it. However, as any of my musical readers will know, the stern opening to the Quartet soon modulates to a warmer A major before reverting back to the original key at the end of the first movement. I closed my eyes and enjoyed the music which was followed by Schubert's 'Death and the Maiden' Quartet and, after the interval for tea, the musicians were joined by the professional clarinettist Simon Kunowski for Brahms' heavenly Quintet in B Minor for Clarinet and Strings.

After the concert I was approached by Mr Edwards, a handsome gentleman in his early thirties, who bowed as he said: 'You are Miss Rosie d'Argosse, are you not? Perhaps you don't remember me but my name is Andrew Edwards and we were introduced by Lady Beckmann at the Marquis de Soveral's banquet at the Portuguese Embassy last October.'

Truthfully, I did not remember the introduction at which my father represented the Foreign Office, but I had no desire to hurt his feelings, so I flashed him a smile and said: 'Of course I remember you, Mr Edwards. And may I present you to my friend Mademoiselle Nicole Coulandre from Bordeaux.'

'*Enchanté, mademoiselle,*' he said, taking Nicole's hand and kissing her fingers in Continental style as he added shyly: 'But I'm ashamed to say that my French will not take me much further.'

Nicole fluttered her long eyelashes at Andrew Edwards' merry brown eyes and wide, generous lips and I could see that there was an instant attraction between the pair. She replied in her throaty Continental voice: 'That will be of no importance, Mr Edwards, because I wish to practise my English whilst I am in London.'

I will not bother to record the full details of what happened during the next hour but as soon as we could, we left the Connaught Rooms with Andrew who guided us towards his Rolls-Royce motor car which was standing just a few yards from the entrance. His chauffeur opened the doors for us and we drove back to the Savoy in style.

We went into the bar where he insisted on ordering a bottle of champagne. 'After all, it is my birthday tomorrow,' he said with a grin as we toasted his birthday in a superb Moet et Chandon '02 vintage. Then we toasted the *Entente Cordiale* [*the friendly treaty between Britain and France reached in April, 1904 which settled all outstanding colonial disputes between the two countries − Editor*], Nicole, myself, the Savoy Hotel and others which frankly I cannot remember!

However, I do remember that we adjourned to Nicole's suite after she had invited Andrew to taste the cognac which we girls had already downed before we left the hotel for the concert. After we had again toasted Andrew's birthday, Nicole's eyes lit up and she said: 'Rosie, come inside the dressing room for a moment. Andrew, please excuse us for a minute but I have just thought of a lovely birthday present for you. Would you like to take off your jacket, shoes and socks and turn and face the door.'

Slightly puzzled, I followed her into the small ante-room and she whispered to me: 'I know exactly the kind of gift that Andrew would appreciate,' as she kicked off her shoes. 'Come on, take off your clothes!'

She then told me of her plan and at first I demurred, but Nicole did not find it too difficult to make me change my mind! We both stripped to the buff and we peeked through the slightly open door to make sure that Andrew was following Nicole's instructions. Then we crept up on tip-toe behind him and Nicole reached up and covered his eyes with her hands.

'Are you ready for your surprise?' she asked with a giggle.

'Just about,' he said with a mixture of amusement and trepidation in his voice.

Nicole removed her hands and spun Andrew round so that he was treated to the sight of two beautiful girls, both stark naked, singing:

> *Happy birthday to you,*
> *Happy birthday to you,*
> *Happy birthday dear Andrew,*
> *Happy birthday to you*!

Andrew's jaw slackened and he blinked in disbelief at the sight of our glorious nude bodies. His chest heaved as his breathing quickened as his eyes darted from Nicole to me and back again, and his senses were obviously stirred by the sight of our pert, jiggling breasts, our peachy bottoms and hairy pussies as we danced gaily around him.

'Well now, Rosie informed me earlier this afternoon at the concert that in *The Oyster* it was reported you were given a five-star rating for fucking by the ladies at the Jim Jam Club,' said Nicole boldly, letting her hand brush across the front of Andrew's trousers where a noticeable swell had swiftly appeared. 'The point is, we want to give you something very special on your birthday, but we would not want to upset you by our little gift. Perhaps you can guess what it is, so if you would prefer not to receive it, do speak out now and I promise we will not be offended.'

'Oh, there's not the slightest danger of my being anything but delighted by whatever you have in mind,' said Andrew with a wolfish grin as I began to unbutton his shirt and Nicole unbuckled the smart leather belt around the waist of his trousers.

It took only a minute to divest our companion of all his clothing except for his drawers, and Nicole dropped to her knees and tugged them down to his feet. As she did so, his released thick shaft sprang up as if on a spring to stand up erect against his flat belly, rising majestically out of a mossy nest of crinkly hair under which dangled a pair of heavy-looking balls in their wrinkled, pink sack.

'*Alors*, this is a truly magnificent cock,' said Nicole with admiration as she grasped this twitching love truncheon in both hands. 'Does it taste as good as it looks?'

'This I cannot tell you,' replied Andrew as he pulled her head towards him. 'You will have to find out the answer for yourself.'

She wet her lips with her tongue as she cupped his hairy ballsack in her left hand whilst lightly running the fingers of her right hand up and down the muscular, ivory shaft of his massive penis.

'Is that nice, Andrew?' she asked rhetorically and when he gasped out his affirmation the naughty minx added mischievously: 'Well, if the wrapping paper is to your liking, come and see what's inside the box,' and Nicole pulled him by his prick towards the bed. They lay down together and their two faces moved closer until, closing their eyes, their lips met in a frenetic kiss, the moisture spreading as if they were eating a soft fruit which melted and dissolved as their tongues swished around in each other's mouths.

Andrew broke away from this embrace to move his lips down towards her thrusting nipple, running the tip of his tongue with surprising delicacy around the sensitive, encircling areole before cupping her breast in his hand and taking the erect tittie between his teeth and playfully nipping it, which caused the hot-blooded girl to squirm with new-found passion.

In the meantime, Nicole continued to massage his hot, smooth cock as Andrew's hand now glided across her dark pubic bush and spread the lips of her cunney.

'Nicole, your pussey is sopping wet — are you ready to

take my tadger inside your cunney?' he grunted, and she panted: 'Yes, oh yes, Andrew, slide that fat staff inside my cunt, you big-cocked boy!'

It did cross my mind as to whether Nicole would be able to accommodate such a thick pole as Andrew grinned and rolled the sweet girl onto her back, his hands slipping under her to grasp hold of her gorgeous bum cheeks as he lowered himself slowly upon her. The tip of his knob just touched her pouting pink cunney lips and he hesitated to plunge forward until Nicole repeated her demand to be fucked. Then he pressed home, inserting the domed helmet inside her honeypot, and her love tunnel miraculously expanded to take in his giant boner and he continued to push forward, inch by inch, until their pubic hairs were intermingled.

Nicole rotated her pretty backside around the fulcrum of his throbbing tool and she whimpered in appreciation as Andrew withdrew some three inches of his meaty shaft and then plunged forward again to the hilt. He continued this delicious movement until the length of his prick was glistening with the lubrication of Nicole's cuntal juices.

'Oooh! Oooh! *C'est magnifique!*!' she cried out as he increased the pace, his balls banging against her bottom with each lunging thrust, and as he lunged forward he gasped in a voice husky with lust: '*There*, can you feel my cock reaming out your pussey?'

'Yes, yes, YES!' she screamed as he added his fingers to rub her clitty whilst he continued to pound his enormous rampant rod in and out of her squelchy slit. Nicole trembled as she twisted and turned until her body stiffened and she screamed out: 'I'm coming! I'm coming! Quick, flood my cunt with spunk! Now!'

Andrew's cock fairly vibrated as it slid in and out of her juicy crack faster and faster until, with a hoarse cry, he jetted a torrent of frothy white spunk inside her love sheath which mingled with her own flood of tangy spend, and Nicole sighed with sheer bliss as they dissolved into the mutual glow which accompanies such a fervent fuck.

'Now, what else would you like for your birthday?' cooed Nicole and as he pondered the question I joined the lewd couple on the bed. He thought for a moment and then replied: 'Well now, Nicole, what would be very nice is to see you kiss Rosie's blonde-haired pussey. Would you humour my fancy, assuming of course that Rosie has no objection.'

'Far from it,' I replied, not offering the information that Nicole and I had already explored each other's bodies earlier in the afternoon. 'I adore being sucked off so much that I hardly care who is doing it. Indeed, for what it is worth, girls are far more adept at eating pussey than men.'

Andrew had ejaculated so violently into Nicole's willing womb that his prick was at half-mast (though even in this state it was bigger than many fully erect organs I have seen in my three years of active fucking), but his member twitched as, in a flash, Nicole and I began to cuddle up together and her hand snaked out to insert itself between my legs. I returned the embrace and she snuggled up even closer to me, brushing her face against mine as her other hand slid round my shoulder.

'M'mm, what lovely silky yellow hair you have, Rosie, and such beautiful pink cunney lips too! I'm sure they are wider than mine,' sighed Nicole as she rubbed her palm against the entrance to my pussey. I lay back to savour the exquisite feeling as she murmured: 'Part your legs a little wider, my darling, and bend your knees and then you can rub yourself off on my hand.'

I followed her instructions and I saw Andrew Edwards' cock twitch again as I worked my furry love lips upon the heel of her palm, forward and back again, increasing the speed as my excitement grew steadily and the love juices began to drip down onto my thighs.

With a low growl, Nicole now raised her thumb, causing it to caress my clitty with each forward bumping of my hips, so that my head began to swirl and I moaned and worked my bottom faster whilst Nicole increased the pace of the circling with her thumb. This wonderful frigging brought down a flood of cuntal juices and I swam in a sea of lubricosity as deep quivers of ecstasy charged through my body and I spurted my spend on Nicole's hand whilst Andrew scrambled to his knees and presented the uncapped knob of his huge cock to my mouth. I lapped at the glowing helmet with my tongue, tasting his salty 'pre-cum' as my warm fingers tried to encircle his tremendous tool, but I needed both hands to do so. I moved my head downwards to lick his balls and my nostrils were filled with his distinctive musky maleness. Lightly, I ran my tongue from the base to the tip of his cock and back again as he groaned with delight. Then, in one sinuous movement, I opened my mouth as wide as possible and took in as much of his stupendous shaft as possible between my lips. I could only manage to suck in about half the length of his big boner but I enjoyed the experience and I sucked strongly and rhythmically whilst my gentle fingers stroked and tickled his wrinkly ballsack.

Then, seeing that try as I may I was having some difficulty with his over-large member, he withdrew and whispered to me to get up on my knees and face the wall. I did as I was told and held on to the head-board and I bent forward with my legs slightly apart and my bum cheeks stuck out provocatively, waiting for Andrew to split them with his immense cock. I did not have long to wait and I felt the lusty man guide his pulsing prick into my cunt from behind. He slewed his shaft in and out forcefully, whilst Nicole ducked her head between his legs and sucked one of his balls inside her mouth whilst she frigged her own pussey in time with Andrew's shaft as it moved backwards and forwards in the narrow crevice between my buttocks. He wrapped his arms tightly around me and his hands cupped my breasts, and this proved such a stimulating experience that very soon we spent almost simultaneously, and I thrilled to the power of the electric shocks that crackled out from my cunney as Andrew spunked copiously inside my tingling love tunnel.

The three of us fell back exhausted onto the pillows, but when we had recovered, Andrew invited us to dine at his rooms that evening (he kept a small suite in one of the new blocks of apartments in Park Lane). 'My sister Gwendolen will be there and if you ladies play bridge, after dinner we could play a few rubbers.'

We accepted his offer with genuine pleasure for we were both keen bridge players. Nicole played with great flair although she was wont to over-value her hand, and I remember once reminding her of the anecdote told by my parents who were playing against His Majesty and Mrs Keppel. Our Monarch bid outrageously and when as dummy he put down his hand for his partner to play the round, Mrs Keppel blanched and said: 'Sire, all I can say about this contract is God save the King because the cards won't!'

As it happened, the cards favoured me and I won every rubber with whoever partnered me. 'Lucky in cards, unlucky in love,' I sighed, but Andrew rebuked me and said robustly: 'Nonsense, Rosie, a girl like you can have her pick of all the most handsome bachelors in town.'

The next morning I bade farewell to Nicole and the hotel motor-car took Dennison and me to Paddington where we caught the express train to Cardiff. I have always enjoyed travelling on the railway. Even when I was a little girl I never used to draw back from the edge of the platform when the engine came huffing and puffing into Midhurst station. Also, as my diary will show, I have enjoyed some marvellous fucking in railway carriages (although it is preferable to have a private compartment for privacy). [*see 'Rosie 2 — Young Wild and Willing — Editor*]

Yet I can truthfully say that sensuous adventures were far from my mind as Dennison opened the door of the first class ladies-only carriage. 'Are all the bags safely on board?' I asked and after he assured me that he had personally seen the porter stow our cases in the guard's van, he shut the door and made his way to his reserved seat in the second-class section of the train. Unlike most of our neighbours who book their servants third class, we always allow our staff to relax in the more comfortable second-class seats.

'We're stopping at Bath and Bristol, Miss Rosie. Shall I come by at Bristol to see if there's anything you need?' said my footman.

'Thank you, that won't be necessary, Dennison,' I answered, handing him my morning paper which had little news that was of interest to me. 'I have a bell to call for an attendant if necessary. Enjoy the trip and I'll see you in Cardiff.'

'Very good, Miss,' he said as he retired and I sat down alone in the compartment. But as I settled into my seat I noticed that opposite me, two of the other seats had 'reserved' labels attached to them. I looked at my watch — the ladies who had booked these seats had better hurry because the train would leave in less than five minutes.

I opened the novel which I had purchased from the W. H. Smith station bookstall and had just started to read the first page, when the door from the corridor burst open and in came the two late arrivals.

'Rosie d'Argosse! Fancy seeing you here,' said a familiar voice, and I looked up to see that one of the two young ladies who had entered the compartment was none other than an attractive girl of my own age whom I had met at Lord Philip Pelham's birthday party some six or seven weeks before.

70

Frantically I searched the recesses of my brain for her name and fortunately I recalled it in time to spare any blush of embarrassment. 'Hello there, it's Vicky Clipstone, isn't it? How are you keeping?'

'Very well, thank you,' said Vicky and she turned to her companion and said: 'Sheila, this is Miss Rosie d'Argosse. Rosie, meet my cousin Miss Sheila Collingham.'

We shook hands and as the station-master blew his whistle and the train lurched forward, I said to Vicky: 'How nice to see you again. I don't suppose we are travelling to the same destination by any chance.'

'We've been invited for a few days' tennis in the wilds of rural Wales by a girl Sheila and I have known since we were very young,' she replied, and I said with a smile: 'Not Susannah Meverson by any chance?'

'Yes, that's right. Why, don't tell me you have been invited, too? How jolly! But if I remember rightly, you live in Sussex, don't you Rosie? How do you come to know the Meversons?'

I explained that Susannah and I were old friends and Vicky said: 'Of course! When we met at Phil Pelham's party you told me that you spent four years at St Hilda's and that's where you first came across that handsome young man Robert Bacon who was chatting to us before dinner.'

At the mention of Robert's name, Vicky's cousin blushed a bright crimson and I looked more closely at the pretty young girl who could have been little more than sweet seventeen. She was extremely pretty, being of a light complexion, rather slender of figure but with well-proportioned breasts and hazel eyes.

Vicky was of my age, some two or three years older and she was a lovely rosy-cheeked girl with a merry twinkle in her blue eyes, which were of a similar shade to mine, although her strawberry blonde hair was two or three shades lighter than mine (I don't believe I have mentioned before

71

that my colouring comes from my maternal Swedish grandmother).

Anyway, Vicky also noticed the change of colour in her cousin's face and she winked at me as she said: 'Now, now, Sheila, you don't have to worry. Even as we speak, Robert is boarding the *S.S. Mauretania* and will be in New York for the next three months. Did you know that, Rosie?'

With a nod, I replied: 'Yes, Robert telephoned me to tell me about it last week. He was only given a week's notice but his uncle, Lord Richmond, is indisposed and so Robert will represent the Bacon and Wright merchant bank at some important business meetings. It will be his first visit to America and he sounded very excited about the trip.'

'There, so you see there is no call for you to be concerned,' said Vicky to her young cousin. She could see that I was curious to know why Robert's presence might embarrass Sheila and she said: 'It's all too ridiculous for words, Rosie, but the fact of the matter is that after dinner at Phil Pelham's, Sheila and Robert went upstairs to the music room.'

I raised my eyebrows at this remark because only a day or so before the party, Philip was chuckling about the fact that he had arranged for a few honoured guests who required privacy to be given keys to any of the several unused rooms in his imposing town house in Belgrave Square.

'I can't believe that Robert acted in a caddish way towards you,' I remarked with some feeling. 'In my experience [*see 'Rosie 2: Young Wild and Willing'* — *Editor*] he is a perfect gentleman.'

'Quite so, and that evening Robert did nothing underhand,' said Vicky robustly. 'Look, Rosie, I know that you can be trusted to keep a secret. What concerns my dear cousin is the fact that — well, Sheila, you tell Rosie yourself about what happened between you and Robert. Don't be shy, I know that you may speak to her in complete confidence and if she confirms what I have told you, then perhaps you'll stop worrying about it.'

The young girl's cheeks coloured up again and she wriggled uncomfortably in her seat, but she decided to take this advice for she said: 'Yes, I trust you, Miss d'Argosse, as Robert mentioned to me at the party that you and he were acquainted and he said some very nice things about you.'

'How nice! And I am only too happy to return his compliments,' I said with an easy smile. 'Now then, tell me how I can help you.'

She lowered her eyes and said: 'Well, the very moment that I set eyes on Robert Bacon, my heart began pounding. Perhaps it was his handsome face, the set of his muscular shoulders or the clearness of his deep blue eyes that raked the gathering with a predatory gaze as he cut through the crowd of girls who flocked around him with the cool assurance of a panther stalking its prey. I could hardly believe my luck when I was placed next to Robert at dinner and I found him a most agreeable companion, so easy to talk to and during the course of our conversation, we discovered that we had several interests in common. One of these interests was sport and Robert was rather taken with the fact that I was keen on cricket.'

Sheila paused and I said encouragingly, 'Yes, of course, Robert was captain of cricket at St Trippett's school and won his cricket blue at Oxford. He now plays for *I Zingari* and whenever time allows, turns out for the Kent county side.'

'He is a talented all-round sportsman,' she agreed with an animated expression on her face. 'And did you know that he also won his University colours for soccer and hockey as well?'

Oh-ho, it was becoming very clear that Sheila had been

smitten by Robert Bacon, which was hardly surprising for he was after all a noted Lothario, but I said nothing and waited for her to continue.

'I don't deny that I was very attracted to Robert and when after dinner he suggested that we went to look at Lord Pelham's sporting prints in the music room, I knew what he meant — but I went! Well, of course, we didn't waste too much time looking at Phil Pelham's pictures and in minutes we were locked together in a passionate embrace on a sofa. I was wearing a low-cut evening dress and oh my, I felt so frisky when Robert moved his hands from my back to rove over my scantily covered bosom, and I made no objection when he unhooked the top of my dress and pulled out my bare breasts. I nearly swooned with delight.

'He kissed and sucked my titties, making them stand up like little red soldiers and even though I knew I should have protested, I made no attempt to stop him when he placed his hand on my knee and started to work it up my leg. I even let him slip his fingers inside my knickers and allowed them to toy with my dampening bush.

'We continued to kiss and cuddle in this way and when Robert placed my hand on the huge bulge in his lap, I eagerly squeezed the fat, stiff pole inside his trousers. He quickly unbuttoned his trousers and I plunged my hand inside and felt for his naked prick which sprang out like a Jack-in-the-box. I grasped hold of his hot, velvet-skinned shaft and began to slide my hand up and down it, capping and uncapping his big, wide knob. Now I had never taken a boy's cock in my mouth before but my lips were drawn as if by some invisible magnet to the mushroom-like helmet of Robert's lovely tadger. I kissed the smooth crown and then, after licking all round it, I opened my mouth and sucked his knob into my mouth.

'Ah, it tasted wonderful with a fine, masculine tang as I closed my lips round his shaft as firmly as possible and continued to work on his knob, washing it all over with my tongue. I tried to cram more of his throbbing tool inside my mouth and I almost choked in the attempt. "Don't try too hard," he whispered lovingly. "Here, let me rub your titties whilst you suck my prick," and he began to flick at my rock-hard nipples, exciting me even more as I sucked away with my hands cupping his hairy balls which I massaged gently, lifting and separating each from the other as I gobbled furiously on my fleshy sweetmeat, savouring the salty taste and he jerked his hips upwards, thrusting more of his slippery shaft deeper between my lips. "Oh my God, I'm coming!" he gasped and before I could even think of pulling away he shot his sticky cream down my throat and I swallowed his spunk in great gulps, sucking on his pulsating prick until I had milked it of all the contents of his big balls, and his shaft started to shrink back to its normal size.

'We went no further, which was just as well because there was a rattle at the door as some other couple tried to come in, but afterwards I could hardly look Robert in the eye when we rejoined the main group of guests. What would Robert think of my being so forward on the very first time of our meeting? And would he tell his friends about what I did, earning me an unwanted reputation as a hussy?'

The girl looked piteously at me and I took her hands in mine and gently squeezed them. 'Oh, Sheila, you are a silly billy!' I cried with total sincerity. 'Now I don't know what Vicky has said to you about the incident, but in my opinion Robert won't mention a word of what happened between the two of you to a living soul.

'To begin with, he is a gentleman and as such would never disclose the names of his lovers to a living soul. And frankly, as he would tell you himself, to find an English girl who obviously enjoys cock-sucking as much as you is a real joy. So many are led to believe that there is nothing more to fucking than lying back and letting the man do the familiar

75

old in-and-out. Why, I can hardly begin to tell you how many of the gay blades around town would be on their bended knees if you would give them a — now what do the Americans call it — a "blow job" such as you have just described. Robert will want to keep you to himself, that's for sure, and so you have absolutely nothing in the world to worry about.'

'Do you really mean it, Rosie?' said Sheila hopefully, and I looked straight into her eyes as I answered: 'Yes, of course I do,' and Vicky added triumphantly: 'See, Sheila, what did I say? Rosie has confirmed exactly what I told you. Now will you stop worrying and enjoy yourself?'

She nodded and said gratefully: 'Oh, thank you both so much for listening to me. Now I can enjoy the next few days without a care in the world.' But then she clapped her hand over her mouth and said: 'Oh dear, there is something else I'm worried about — I don't think I reminded Elsie to pack my new tennis racquet!'

'You were far too busy thinking about Robert Bacon,' laughed Vicky. 'I guessed that you might forget something so I supervised the packing whilst you were writing a letter to your sister, Maud.'

Vicky turned to me and said: 'Have you brought any servants with you? We just have Elsie, one of our housemaids, accompanying us.'

I told them that Dennison was in one of the second-class carriages and then a conductor came into the compartment to clip our tickets and to see if we required any refreshments before luncheon. The three of us decided not to eat anything before the mid-day meal, which would be served at twelve-thirty, for we were due in Cardiff a little more than an hour and a half later.

'Would you like something saucy to read before luncheon, Rosie?' enquired Vicky as she opened her travelling bag. 'I have this month's copy of *The Oyster* if it is of interest.

76

Sheila is going to finish *The Rupert Mountjoy Memoirs* whilst I would like a little nap.'

'I did buy a book at the station, but I'd much rather read your naughty magazine,' I confessed, holding out my hand for the elegantly bound publication which, since being printed on art paper in Paris, could be taken for a learned journal with its plain dark blue cover.

I opened the latest edition of the best of our *sub rosa* periodicals at a fascinating letter by Colonel Piers Rankin of the Sixth Punjab Rifles on *The Beauties of the Bare Behind* in which he chided the editor of *The Oyster* for not showing more photographs of girls' backsides. For those readers who have not had the good fortune to read Colonel Rankin's essay, here is an abridged copy of what he had to say:

Sir,
In my opinion, the female backside has sadly been neglected in your selection of photographs for the monthly picture gallery. Several of the girls featured are the most admirable specimens of female pulchritude and I especially commend those of Misses Paxford, Robson and Walshaw in the January issue. Yet whilst admitting that pictures of face, breasts, thighs and pussey are to be commended, why ignore the twin voluptuous orbs of the buttocks which are so firm and yet so tender, so resilient and so inviting?

A girl's bum cheeks, perhaps more than any other part of her anatomy, transmit the results of a good fucking. In the heat of passion, these pneumatic spheres tremble and twitch with each thrust of the prick in a lusty language of sensuality which should be studied by all men who aspire to be great lovers.

So in your next issue, Mr Editor, let us see a girl with a nice rounded bottom. For preference, dress her up in a pair of stockings, because these accentuate the luxuriant curves of the bum very nicely. Perhaps she could be wearing a dress, but no knickers, and bend over with her dress pulled up showing her delicious behind and looking saucily over her shoulder as if to say: 'If you like what you see, come and get it!'

Another good pose would be to have the wench lying face down on the bed, pushing out her snowy white buttocks towards the camera with her thighs open just enough so that we might catch a look at her hairy crack.

Of course, I do not want you to omit any photographs which show the glories of the female form from the front! Your excellent magazine shows us many beauties that make my old pego almost burst out from my trousers. But do not forget confirmed lovers of the bum like myself who frequently search through the pages of The Oyster *for our most favoured poses with little or no success.*

I am, Sir, your honourable servant,
(Colonel) Piers Rankin M.C.
New Delhi, India

Underneath his letter was a short reply from the Editor:

I sincerely hope that the next two pages of photographs showing Miss Fiona Feltham-Hardie of East Croydon and Mr George Lucas of Bloomsbury will be of especial interest to the gallant Colonel, whose criticisms have been noted.

With a trembling hand I turned the page and drew a sharp breath as I looked at the superb photograph of young George Lucas, a popular guest at many a country house weekend, fucking a tall blonde girl from behind, sliding his thick prick between her pert bum cheeks as she stood upright with her hands against a wall with her bottom thrust out. In the next picture, taken from a side angle, dear Lucas was seen rubbing his fingers over her high tilted breasts whilst

78

her own hand was placed between her legs, tweaking her clitty and in a final photograph, taken after the actual fuck, George was shown on his knees licking out her spunk-filled cunney whilst Fiona stood with her head thrown back and her body arched back in ecstasy.

My pussey began to tingle as I studied the photographs, which I noticed had been taken by Count Gewirtz of Galicia, who was described quite recently in *The Times* as by far the most talented amateur photographer in all Europe. How I would have enjoyed being fucked by George Lucas, I thought to myself, but my reverie was broken by a knock on the door from the conductor who called out to us that luncheon would be served in five minutes.

With a heavy sigh, I tapped Vicky on the arm and gave the magazine back to her and then the three of us trooped out and went to the luncheon car where we ate a very good mayonnaise of salmon, and I chose an equally good roast chicken as my main course whilst my travelling companions opted for braised ox tongue. Although the roast potatoes were delicious, as usual in England, both the green vegetables were slightly overcooked and we were somewhat disappointed with the raspberry and currant tart, the pastry of which should have been lighter. But the bottle of claret we shared was very drinkable and all in all we could not grumble at the bill which worked out at exactly half a crown [*12½p! – Editor*] a head.

The large locomotive thundered into Cardiff dead on time and Dennison supervised the loading of Vicky's and Sheila's luggage along with my valises onto the local train for Carmarthen. We left at half past two and after leaving the grimy industrial heartland of South Wales, we trundled through the beautiful countryside at a gentle pace until we reached Carmarthen where Owen, the Meverson's chauffeur, was waiting with the family's splendid Mercedes motor car to transport us in fine style on the final stretch of our long journey to Meverson Hall some eight and a half miles away in the heart of the verdant Pembrokeshire countryside. A local van driver had been hired to bring on our servants and the luggage, which I am sure was not nearly as comfortable as the luxurious leather seats of the Mercedes Simplex, not one of the newest automobiles but certainly one of the most reliable. [*Rosie was a good judge of a motor car – in 1991 a Mercedes Simplex was bought at auction for more than two million dollars! – Editor*]

It was almost six o'clock when we reached the gates of Meverson Hall and Susannah was out in the drive with a young man whose face was vaguely familiar to me but whom at first I did not recognise.

'Hello, everyone, welcome to Wales!' she cried as she kissed all three of us in turn. 'How lovely to see you all! Now before we go any further, let me introduce Michael Harper to you.'

Susannah's mention of the name of her companion was enough to make further introduction unnecessary, for of course this good-looking fellow was none other than the famous tennis champion who is so popular at the Hurlingham Club, not only for his feats on court but also for his prowess in the bedroom. It is an open secret that he and Helena, the daughter of Lord Oxford, have long conducted a passionate if clandestine affair, whilst his name has also been linked to two older women, Mrs Charles Arbuthnot and Mrs Rayleigh de Berri, both of whom are supposed to have showered gifts upon the muscular young sportsman for his favours.

It was easy to see why women were so attracted to Michael Harper. He was slim and tall with a shock of curly chestnut hair, deep brown eyes with a straight nose and full, sensual lips. He was also fortunate enough to possess the most beautifully even set of white teeth and these were set off so well by his bronzed complexion, which he doubtless owed to the fact that his mother was of Italian ancestry, being the sister of the Duke of Padua.

We shook hands and, was it my imagination, but did Michael Harper hold my hand just a little longer than was necessary, and could I have misjudged the lingering caress of his fingers against mine as our eyes locked together?

'You three girls must be exhausted after your travels,' declared our kind hostess, escorting us up the steps of the impressively large mansion. 'Do come inside and have some refreshment. Your luggage should be here shortly and the staff will put your cases in your respective rooms.

'Our party is now complete,' Susannah informed us as I took a glass of white wine from the tray being offered round by a footman. 'The other three gentlemen arrived at noon and they went for a walk this afternoon.'

'Might I know any of them?' enquired Vicky, and Susannah shook her head. 'Probably not, although I am sure you will find them all quite charming. The first is one of Michael's friends from Oxford, Rodney Bakewell-Fisher, whose great passion in life is ornithology.'

'Oh, what a fortunate coincidence, did you know that I have taken up bird-watching since we last saw each other?' said Sheila shyly, and our hostess smiled and said: 'Certainly I knew, my love, your cousin told me and this was one of the reasons why I invited Mr Bakewell-Fisher to join us this weekend. Now the other two guests are Herr Oskar Gottlieb, a frightfully nice Jewish lawyer from Switzerland who works for old Tum-Tum's friend, Sir Ernest Cassel. [*'Tum-Tum' was the nickname given to the increasingly portly Edward VII by his cronies in the Marlborough House set, and Sir Ernest Cassel was the King's foremost financial adviser and close friend — Editor*] And the guest list will be completed by Lieutenant Christopher Cooney of the Household Cavalry. Lord Philip Pelham had planned to join us but, alas, he had a prior engagement.'

Vicky frowned and said: 'I think I have met Lieutenant Cooney, Susannah, but I can't quite recall the time and place. Wait a moment, could it have been at Lady Heather Dewsnap's coming-out ball in Cheltenham last summer?'

'Yes, you probably did — Christopher is a Dewsnap on his mother's side. Did you dance together by any chance?'

A rather odd little smile appeared on Vicky's lips but she shook her head and said mysteriously: 'Not exactly, but Christopher and I did engage in some intimate conversation.'

I resolved to ask her to explain this cryptic remark as Palmer the butler arrived to inform us that our luggage had arrived. I stood up but Susannah said: 'There's no rush, Rosie, we won't dine until half past eight tonight. Wouldn't you like to wait and meet Oskar and Christopher before you go upstairs? Oh, and there's something else I must say. You all remember that in my invitation I mentioned that my aunt, Lady Sheringham, was to be here to act as a chaperone in the absence of my parents. Well, unfortunately, dear Aunt Augusta has been laid low by an attack of influenza and is unable to move from her home.

'What a terrible shame,' she added ironically. 'If any of you ladies feel unsafe without Aunt Augusta prowling around the landing at night to make sure that there is no flitting between the rooms, of course I will understand if you want to return home tomorrow!'

We all laughed heartily as I made for the door. I wanted to take a bath before dinner, so I excused myself and Palmer showed me to my room where a maid had already opened my trunks and was busy hanging out my clothes. She bobbed a curtsy to me as I entered and said in a pleasing Welsh lilt: 'Good evening, ma'am, my name is Jenny, and I'll be looking after you whilst you are at Meverson Hall. There's a bell by the side of your bed if you need to call me or whoever is on duty.'

'Thank you, Jenny,' I said to the attractive slip of a girl, who was of about my own age with cornflower hair, light blue eyes, a tiny nose and lovely heart-shaped lips.

She stood there silently for a moment, fidgeting from side to side, and so I added: 'Don't let me disturb you, Jenny, I'll run my own bath whilst you finish unpacking,' but the girl still stood there looking flustered and tongue-tied as she fumbled with her apron.

'Is there something you want to ask me?' I said patiently, and finally she screwed up her courage and said: 'Excuse me, ma'am, I hope you don't mind my asking but did I catch a glimpse of Jack Dennison down in the servants' hall a few minutes ago?'

'Yes, he's my footman. Why do you ask? Have you two met before?'

Jenny nodded and said: 'Jack, I mean, Mr Dennison and I were in service together at Mr Duntocher's house in Gloucestershire before I left to come here and he took up service with you.

'I haven't seen him since,' she added, and from the tone of her voice I deduced that she was not exactly over-pleased to see my servant again.

I took her arm and pushed Jenny gently down on the bed. Then I sat myself down next to her and said softly: 'I think there's something bothering you about Dennison, isn't there? You can tell me about it if you like. I promise I won't repeat anything to Miss Meverson or any of the other guests.'

The petite little filly wriggled uncomfortably and murmured: 'You're ever so kind, ma'am, but it's such a rude story.'

'That doesn't matter at all,' I said in a cheerful tone, and I took her hand and went on: 'Jenny, you might have heard of Mrs Patrick Campbell, she's a very famous actress and a friend of the highest in the land. Well, she once remarked that she didn't care a damn how people wanted to fuck, just

83

so long as they didn't do it in the street and frighten the horses!'

My words brought a smile to her face and she said: 'Did she really? Oh go on, she never did, did she?'

'She did,' I assured her, noting that Jenny had not turned a hair at my deliberately down-to-earth language. 'So don't be bashful, I'm a country girl myself and where I come from, we call a spade a spade.'

This gave the attractive girl more confidence and she told me how on one of her weekly half holidays, the rain was tumbling down outside so she spent the afternoon lying on her bed reading a copy of *The Oyster* which she had filched from the waste-bin in Mr Duntocher's study. She was reading about one of Sir Ronnie Dunn's horny adventures and as she put it: 'I became very excited when he wrote how he tore off Laura Bayswater's satin nightgown, leaving her naked and trembling on the bed and how, after ripping off his own clothes, he jumped on top of her and she grabbed his thick prick and pressed his knob between the damp lips of her juicy cunney . . .

'Almost unconsciously I allowed my hand to slip inside my blouse and I soon lowered my chemise and found my nipple and began to roll it between my fingers as my own pussey began to moisten. I continued to read, quite glued to the page as Sir Ronnie described how he kissed Laura's large red titties and then let his lips travel down to the neat little triangle of crisp brown hair which covered her mount.

'I shivered all over as I unbuttoned my skirt and pushed my hand into my knickers. My fingertips strayed towards my pussey and soon I started to slide them in and out of my love hole. Oooh, I felt so randy as I read on, with one set of fingers tweaking my tittie and with the other dipping my fingers in and out of my wet honeypot, rubbing my thumb against my clitty which always drives me wild.

'I was just building up to a spend when, I just don't know why, I almost jumped out of my skin when I looked up and saw that I was not alone! Jack Dennison was at the doorway, leaning against the wall and looking at me with a lust-laden expression on his face. I gasped and pulled down my skirt but he begged me to carry on. "Don't stop now, Jenny," he growled hoarsely. "I've seen so much already that it would be torture not to let me see you finish yourself off."

'All sorts of ideas now crossed my mind. I'd never played with myself in front of a man before and part of me felt terribly embarrassed — yet there was something weirdly exciting about knowing that Jack was there watching me, and from the bulge in his trousers I could see that his prick was hardening as he looked down at me. This very thought made me decide to continue, so I murmured: "Lock the door," which he did as I slowly began to undress, opening my blouse and pulling out one of my breasts from my chemise, letting it jut out proudly as I pulled down my knickers, threw up my skirt and spread my legs wide apart so that he could see the red chink of my cunt as I let my fingers stray through my bush.

'I closed my eyes and began to finger-fuck myself, taking my clitty and pressing its pink, shell-like firmness and I squeezed my legs together — oooh, I'm sorry, Miss, just thinking about it is making my knickers wet again!

'Then I heard a grunt coming from Jack's direction and I opened my eyes to see him standing there with his trousers down, rubbing his big stiff dick for all he was worth and each time he slid his fist up and down his shaft it made a squelchy sort of sound which made me even more excited.'

Jenny lowered her voice and went on: 'Jack's very well-made, if you know what I mean, ma'am. He's been blessed with the thickest prick I've ever seen and when he walked towards me and presented me with this shiny monster, I simply couldn't resist giving his knob a little kiss. He shuddered all over when I did this and moved even closer. I took his hot, hard cock in one hand as I continued to lick his helmet and with the other, I weighed his balls in my palm and then gently scraped them with my fingernails.

'This sent Jack wild and his prick bucked inside my mouth as I sucked in his knob between my lips. This made his shaft swell even more, especially when I grabbed his bum cheeks in my hands and pulled him even closer and took another three inches of his tool inside my mouth. I massaged the underside of his pole with my tongue, keeping my head still as Jack jerked his cock in and out until he went rigid and, with a groan, he spurted jets of sticky spunk which I gulped down as his shaft softened and he took it out of my mouth.

'Naturally, after he had recovered he begged to be allowed to fuck me. But I explained that it was too risky a time for that unless he had a Frenchie [a condom — Editor]. "I don't, but I swear that I won't spend inside you," he promised, but I'd known too many accidents playing that game and I shook my head. "I'll go through the tradesmen's entrance," he urged, but I have to be in the mood for bum-fucking and I didn't fancy it just then.

' "You'll just have to settle for a mutual sucking-off," I told him and to give him credit, he didn't try to force the issue. I positioned him on his knees in front of me between my legs and I parted them so that he could have a good look at my pouting pussey lips. Then I took his hand and placed it in the silky wet clump of cunney hair. His fingers splayed my love lips whilst the knuckles of his other hand ran down the full length of my gash. Then he pushed his fingertip inside my cunt and, as he penetrated my squishy slit, my hips rose to meet this miniature imitation cock.

'Oh, I really wanted his big, meaty prick there, but I knew I had to resist the temptation so slipped my fingers round his glistening wet shaft and lapped up the sticky jism which was already oozing from the tiny little hole in his knob.

'Then I tugged off my skirt and moved myself up over Jack until my pussey was over his nose, and he pulled me down and buried his face in my soaking bush, licking my cunney so beautifully that my love juice was soon dripping onto his lips and chin. My own lips were now as busy as his and I swirled my tongue all around his knob before cramming as much of his throbbing tool as I could into my mouth. I wrapped one hand round his hot shaft and sucked the smooth purple helmet, flicking the tip of my tongue over the slitted end whilst I cradled his balls through their crinkly covering of pink skin.

'It was all so exciting that we soon climaxed together, and my cum streamed out all over his face as he shot a frothy stream of creamy seed between my lips, so fiercely that the first jet hit the back of my throat. Honestly, ma'am, he spent so copiously that I could not swallow all his spunk and some of the jism dripped out of my mouth into the rough, wiry hair around the base of his cock.'

A smile of fond remembrance spread over the face of the young maid and I commented. 'Well, that all sounds very nice to me. Many people actually prefer a *soixante neuf* to a fuck. So why does Dennison's appearance in the servants' hall now distress you?'

She pouted prettily and said: 'He lost me my position, ma'am, because he peached upon me and the master to Mr Duntocher's aunt, Lady Clydebank.'

I looked at her questioningly and she explained: 'A few days after what I have just described took place, I was serving breakfast to Mr Duntocher. Unfortunately, I had overslept and had to be woken up by Mrs Cheatham, the housekeeper, and I was in such a hurry that I rushed downstairs to begin work without putting on any underclothes, and just before I served the master I looked in the mirror and I could see my nipples straining against the thin white cotton of my blouse. "Hurry up, Jenny, take in the bowl of fresh fruit to the dining room,'' called Mrs Cheatham, so there was no time to rush back upstairs and change. I took a deep breath and marched in, hoping that Mr Duntocher wouldn't take exception to looking at my titties.'

'I'm sure your master was far from displeased to catch even a glimpse of such a fine pair as yours, my dear,' I commented, running my hand across her high, uptilted breasts.

'Thank you, ma'am, and yes, in fact Mr Duntocher was so taken aback by the sight of my titties pressing against the almost transparent white material of my blouse that he dropped the toast-rack and its contents. When I bent down to help him pick up the toast he pinched my bottom and we ended up having a grand morning fuck on the dining-room table.

'From that morning on, I was being fucked every morning by Mr Duntocher and every evening by Jack Dennison. And that's where that fearful old cow Lady Clydebank, on whom Mr Duntocher depends for his annual allowance, comes into the picture. She disapproves of any familiarity, as she calls it, "with members of the lower orders", the cheeky old cow. Well, when she arrived at the house on an unexpected visit, Jack deliberately showed her into the dining room, knowing full well that at the time I was in there, down on my knees, gobbling the master's cock, and later that day I was told to pack my bags.'

This puzzled me and I asked: 'But why would Dennison want you to be sacked? After all, he was fucking you every night, wasn't he?'

Jenny shrugged her shoulders and replied: 'He was jealous about sharing my favours with the master, I suppose. Mr Duntocher didn't really want me to leave, but his aunt was adamant that unless I was out of the house in twenty-four hours she would stop his allowance. He wrote me a wonderful letter of reference, though, and gave me a ten pound note (that's six months' money) as a leaving present. Luckily, I was engaged at Meverson Hall a week later and I far prefer working here, so everything's turned out well. And the funny thing is, Lady Clydebank insisted that Mr Duntocher give all the servants notice as she decided they must all be infected with the same disease of immorality, and Dennison had to look for a new position. Now I know they say you must forgive people who trespass against you, but at the time I swore that I never wanted to see Jack Dennison again, and that still holds good.'

I sat down on the bed and said slowly: 'To be honest, Dennison has given my family excellent service since he has been in our employ, but if what you say is true, I shall have to look on him in a new light. Still, I'm glad you've informed me of your feelings.'

She continued to unpack my clothes whilst I went into the bathroom and switched off the taps. Whilst I lay in the bath I resolved that I would broach what I had heard with Dennison, because although we are of a more liberal persuasion than Lady Clydebank, I wouldn't be able to trust Dennison again until I heard his side of the story.

After my bath I decided to wear one of my favourite evening gowns, a daring, close-cut blue dress with a *décolleté* line which fully exposed the tops of my creamy breasts. I met Vicky Clipstone on the landing and we went down to the drawing room together where the other guests were already gathered. Sheila was already chatting happily away to Rodney Bakewell-Fisher, the ornithologist, and after Michael Harper, who was obviously Susannah's partner for the evening, had greeted us, our hostess brought over to Vicky and myself the other two gentlemen whom we had yet to meet.

The first of these was the Swiss lawyer, Oskar Gottlieb, a good-looking, slightly thickset man in his early thirties with friendly, laughing eyes who kissed my hand in the Continental manner and said: 'How delightful to meet you, Miss d'Argosse. Your face is very familiar, though I can't quite remember where we could have seen each other before. Ah, I have it, did I not see you dancing with Sir Mark Nathan at Count Gewirtz's *Quartorze Juillet* ball in Paris last year?'

I said: 'Yes, my parents and I were there, but I must confess that I don't remember us being introduced.'

He smiled roguishly and replied: 'We weren't introduced, but I could never forget such a pretty face as yours. I must confess that I tried to find out who you were, but the Count disappeared upstairs to a private room with Viscountess Allendale and Countess Marussia, and by the time he returned you were about to leave.'

'Oskar, you are incorrigible!' scolded Susannah, who had overheard our conversation. 'Take no notice of him, Rosie, Oskar can charm the birds from the trees. Now let me introduce Lieutenant Christopher Cooney to you.'

I turned round and shook hands with the handsome young soldier. He was at least five or six years younger than Oskar Gottlieb, being no more than twenty-five, clean-shaven, with a clear white skin and short straight hair. He looked very nice in his evening suit yet I must record that in my admittedly limited experience, military men rarely live up to their boasts or the expectations of their ladies. They tend to strut and brag at their clubs and in the mess, but all too often they cannot match words with deeds. Perhaps the tightness of their uniforms has something to do with it, because this is especially true of the cavalry officers, although in all fairness the boyish Lieutenant Cooney looked likely to be an exception to the rule.

Anyhow, as it happened, any interest of mine in the gallant lieutenant would have been purely academic for I could see that a bond of mutual attraction had immediately formed between him and Vicky, in the same way as Oskar had immediately appealed to me.

Indeed, Oskar and I soon found that we had an interest, that of furniture, in common and he informed me that he had spent several days in London trying to track down some genuine Chippendale chairs. [*Thomas Chippendale (1718–1779) was one of the great English master cabinet-makers of the eighteenth century – Editor*] 'There are many fine copies and it takes a good eye to distinguish true and "in-the-style-of" Chippendales. There are so many mahogany chairs with squarish backs and cabriole legs that look right until you look very closely at them,' said Oskar.

'He never stinted on the carving, though, for he had access to the best mahogany,' I remarked, taking a glass of champagne from Dennison, for my footman had been pressed into service that evening. 'His chair splats have a delicacy that often escapes the work of the copier.'

Oskar nodded his head. 'Indeed, those abroad who worked from his book would miss some of the niceties,' he agreed. 'I was recommended to a Mr Laurie in Islington who had two Chippendale-style chairs for sale and I purchased them because although not by the Master himself, they were beautifully made with interlaced ribbon backs and finely carved legs.'

We chatted away happily and Oskar escorted me into dinner whilst I noted that Sheila was taken in by Rodney Bakewell-Fisher, Vicky was on the arm of Christopher Cooney and so the ladies and gentlemen had paired up very nicely.

The repast was lavish with oysters, sole cooked in Chablis, followed (naturally) by Welsh lamb so that by the time the dessert course was due, I was feeling totally replete and I was pleased that there seemed to be a somewhat longer delay than might have been expected in the bringing in of what

I imagined would be a selection of fruits, puddings and ice creams.

Then just as I thought there may have been a problem in the kitchen, the old butler, Palmer, came in and whispered something to Michael Harper who leaned across the table and, with a wide grin on his face, asked Rodney Bakewell-Fisher if he would assist him in wheeling in the desserts trolley. 'Of course,' said the puzzled ornithologist, and he rose from the table and walked to the door, which he opened, and I could see a large table set on castors covered completely by a dazzling white cloth which reached down almost to the floor.

'Thank you, Palmer, we'll serve ourselves,' said Susannah lightly and Dennison and two maids who were acting as waitresses cleared the table and retired as Michael Harper called for silence.

'Ladies and gentlemen, we have a special surprise for one of our guests who celebrates his twenty-fourth birthday tomorrow,' he announced, and he turned to Christopher Cooney and said: 'Happy birthday, Chris, from us all, and perhaps you would now uncover this special dish which has been prepared in your honour.'

We all cheered and sang 'Happy Birthday' as Christopher got to his feet and, with a fine flourish, swept off the cloth to reveal beautifully arranged mounds of fresh hothouse fruits such as oranges, pineapples and strawberries, but the *pièce de résistance* was a living tableau in the middle of the table where, posed as still as for a photograph, were the delicious nude bodies of Jenny, my pert little chambermaid, and a dark-complexioned, shortish youth (whom I later discovered was a stable-lad on the Meverson estate). This lucky young chap was lying on his back, his skin shining from the fruit juices Jenny had rubbed onto his skin whilst Jenny herself was crouched between his legs, her lips just touching the tip of his semi-erect prick which, even as I looked, was rising perceptibly from the mass of dark curls at its root, whilst she frigged his shaft with both her hands.

At first we were too shocked to do anything but gape in silence at the erotic spectacle, but then Oskar led the well-merited applause and we watched intently as Jenny jammed down the foreskin of the youth's shaft and started to lick and lap around the purple, uncovered helmet. Simultaneously, she wriggled her glistening, naked body round so that her pussey was above the boy's mouth and then she sat down on his face and he noisily nuzzled his lips into her thatch of silky pussey hair, embedding his nose into her cunney as he flicked his tongue through her yielding love lips and, as I imagined from her grunt of contentment as she sucked his big, shiny shaft, immediately finding her clitty as he lapped her juicy honeypot.

'M'mm, what a fat young tadger, I wouldn't mind gobbling that myself,' murmured Vicky, and Susannah overheard her guest and said: 'Well, don't feel shy, darling. After all, Lewis's cock is available to any of my female guests whilst Jenny's pussey is really Christopher's birthday present.'

I turned to my left and saw that Michael Harper must have already informed the dashing cavalry officer of his good fortune, for Christopher Cooney was already tearing off his clothes and Susannah and Michael thoughtfully took the cloth which had covered Lewis and Jenny and placed it over a large Chesterfield [*a large, tightly stuffed couch upholstered in leather — Editor*].

They beckoned Christopher to the sofa and he sat there alone for just a moment, for Jenny now left off tonguing her erstwhile partner's prick to leap nimbly off the trolley and, to a roar of laughter, she padded over to the Chesterfield and plastered the best part of a jug of cream over his boner. Then she proceeded to lick it off in long, sweeping strokes whilst he lay back and groaned in ecstasy.

Even with the coating of cream, Jenny must have sensed that Christopher was in danger of spunking, because she brought her head up sharply and lay back herself to let him kiss her large, erect nipples. *Apropos* of my earlier complaint about the inability of many Englishmen to eat pussey properly, in fairness I must record that Christopher Cooney showed himself to be an exception to the rule, for he slowly kissed his way down Jenny's flat, snow-white belly to the cushion of pussey hair. I moved my chair closer and saw him lick his lips in anticipation and his tongue shot out to move slowly round her pink, pouting cunney lips and he parted them with the very tip of his tongue which sought the moist cleft where already, I was sure, Jenny's clitty was swelling. Her rounded bottom cheeks squirmed around on the cloth as Christopher sucked on her pussey and I could see the rivulets of love juice trickling down her thighs.

Jenny tossed back her head and muttered fiercely: 'Oh fuck me, sir! Please fuck me! I want your cock so much!'

This caused him to lift his head and he hauled himself over her and covered her petite frame with his broad-shouldered trunk. Jenny felt with her hand for his throbbing tool which had been sandwiched between their bellies and guided it between her thighs where it sank straight into her sopping cunt. But then, after he had begun to fuck Jenny in earnest, Christopher whispered a few words into her ear and he withdrew his prick as she hauled herself up on her knees, and they changed positions so that Christopher was now flat on his back on the wide sofa.

'What in heaven's name is he up to?' Sheila wondered with some concern in her voice, for as the youngest participant in the revels she was not as experienced as the other members of the company in the many variations of *l'art de faire l'amour*.

'Ah, well that is because Christopher went out for a long walk this afternoon and he is very probably too tired to perform in an over-energetic fashion,' explained Michael Harper, who during the evening was to prove himself a fount of wisdom on matters of an intimate nature.

'I would imagine that he has asked Jenny to do most of the work,' he went on, and in seconds was proved absolutely right as Jenny sat herself astride her partner's body. She took hold of Christopher's cock, which was waving like a flagpole in a high wind, and then lifted herself upwards over his knob and spread her cunney lips apart with her own fingers. Then she directed the tip of his knob to her gateway of delight and slowly but surely pressed herself down upon the glowing purple dome, letting him savour the glorious feeling of his shaft being enclosed by her clinging wet cunney sheath.

Christopher's hands slid under her luscious bum cheeks and Jenny wriggled around to work his iron-hard boner inside her cunt as far up as possible, and she began to bounce merrily up and down on his pulsating prick as the young officer released her buttocks to reach up and tweak her titties.

'Some men think it is demeaning to let the girl be on top, but I enjoy this lazy way of fucking occasionally,' confessed Rodney Bakewell-Fisher, and Susannah agreed with him, saying: 'I do too, sliding up and down on a nice thick prick gives the walls of my cunney a good pounding, especially if the man is well-endowed and I can grind my arse round at the same time − it gives my clitty a good rub as well.'

As she spoke, as if to prove her mistress's point, Jenny now rolled her bottom from side to side as Christopher jerked his hips, lifting himself to meet her downward thrusts. She reached between his legs and took his balls in her hand, scraping the sensitive skin with her fingernails, and Christopher began jamming his shaft upwards, so powerfully that Jenny lifted herself off him slightly, letting her pussey hover over his prancing prick as the tides of approaching orgasm overtook them. She slammed herself down again and felt the full length of his weapon twitch and contract, and then he sent a torrent of frothy spunk shooting up her love channel as she, too, climaxed and soaked his pulsing prick with her pungent cuntal juice.

'Rosie, I do hope you enjoyed that erotic show as much as I did,' remarked Oskar softly as we watched Jenny lever herself off Christopher's now softened shaft. 'It's always a pleasure to see such uninhibited fucking, is it not?'

I agreed with the sophisticated Swiss as Jenny gave Christopher's cock a final kiss before leaving the room, and he slipped on his undershorts and rejoined us at the table. After we did justice to the delectable desserts, the girls retired to the richly furnished drawing room and left the men to their vintage port and Havana cigars.

'Honestly, I do find it irritating to be excluded from the table just so the men can smoke and tell each other smutty stories,' grumbled Vicky, who like myself was an active member of Mrs Pankhurst's Women's Social and Political Union. 'After we get the vote, I think we must campaign for the reform of dinner parties!'

Susannah agreed with her and said: 'You're quite right, Vicky, why should we be treated like second-class citizens at the end of a meal? I'm sure that this silly fashion will die out in time. Meanwhile, can I offer coffee to anyone? And we must try some of this liqueur which Oskar has given to me. It is called kümmel, and he says it is very popular in Central Europe.'

She poured out tiny glasses of this drink which was new to us all. I found the delicate aroma very pleasant and Susannah added: 'Oskar says it is distilled from caraway seeds and so has a positive digestive quality as well as a delightful taste.'

After we had all downed two glasses, Vicky smacked her lips and said: 'It *is* very nice, Susannah. But I wonder if it tastes as tangy as Christopher's spunk?'

'Vicky Clipstone! You naughty girl, how could you say such a thing!' scolded Sheila, who was greatly shocked to hear her cousin speak so rudely.

'Quite easily,' said Vicky, whose tongue had been loosened by the lavish amount of wine we had all indulged in during dinner. 'I adore sucking cocks and I don't mind admitting that I'm very partial to the taste of jism, and I've always found it highly arousing when the first squirt of sticky seed shoots down my throat. What about you, Rosie?'

'Well, I must say that I like sucking cocks as well,' I said carefully. 'But perhaps more as an *hors d'oeuvres* rather than as a main course, if you follow my drift. Susannah and Sheila, what are your views on the subject?'

'Oh, I'm as keen as you are, Rosie,' replied our hostess instantly. 'I do get a thrill out of sucking a fine stiffstander but all the boys I know spend so quickly. I would prefer to suck for at least ten minutes, licking and lapping, nibbling it with my teeth and swirling my tongue over the knob. Mind sometimes I stop before the boy spends, so that his cock is rock-hard before I slip it inside my pussey.'

Sheila said timidly: 'I've only sucked Robert Bacon's cock so I don't have enough experience to offer an opinion, but although I enjoyed it, I was always slightly afraid that his prick would choke me.'

'Well, we all know about Robert Bacon of Bloomsbury, don't we, girls?' I said with a chuckle. 'And there's no doubt that he is a big boy, and I'm not surprised that you were worried about trying to cram all of his colossal cock between your lips. But with any man, so long as you remain in control, there should be no problem.

'The solution is for your man to lie still whilst you move your head. Now that way there can be no possibility of his thrusting his tool deep into your throat and making you gag — and if you're still worried, you can also grip the base of his prick in your hand to limit penetration. Then you'll find you are more relaxed and you'll want to let him slide his cock in and out of your mouth for a while. However, don't feel pressured to rush things. The best way is to take your time and vary your movements and I know that you'll thoroughly enjoy bringing off your lover with your lips.'

Vicky said: 'That's good advice, Sheila, and I've just remembered that I have a little book in one of my cases which you must remind me to lend to you. It's called *Fucking For Beginners* by Dr Ian Hughes and I can recommend it to all of you.

'Now all this talk has made me feel terribly randy. Why don't we bring in the gentlemen and let's play Blind Girl's Cock.'

Susannah corrected her: 'Surely you mean Blind Man's Buff,' but Vicky's eyes gleamed as she shook her head and said: 'No, Blind Girl's Cock, it's much more fun. The game is quite simple − we bring in the four men and they undress. Then in turn I give each of their pricks a little suck before one of you blindfolds me and I finish them all off. I win a guinea for each cock I correctly identify, but I lose five guineas to each man who manages not to spunk for three minutes after I've identified his shaft.'

'Sounds fun and a good way of relieving the boys of their cash!' I remarked with a laugh. 'And I suppose one of us can take a turn afterwards, but after you've milked their pricks it would be easier for them to hold back, so we might lose our money.'

'Ah, but the second girl gets five minutes to suck them dry and, if there's a third, she gets seven minutes and so on and so on,' Vicky explained. 'However, as we were saying earlier, very few men can raise a stiffie after one sucking off, let alone two.'

'Well, this should be very interesting, but suppose the gentlemen don't want to play,' said Sheila, but Susannah, Vicky and I were quick to reassure her that this was most unlikely because none of us had ever fucked a fellow who didn't want his cock sucked. 'Men like nothing better than being gobbled,' I told her with complete confidence. 'They find it even more heavenly than we do when we have our pussies eaten. No, the boys in the dining room will be only too glad to play this lewd game.'

'Exactly so,' said Susannah as she stood up and walked to the door. 'I'll go and tell them what we have in mind and I wager they will sink their drinks, put out their cigars and be back here within ninety seconds.'

In fact, they were so eager to play that Susannah returned in under a minute and as soon as the door was closed they began undressing, throwing off their clothes until they all stood stark naked in front of us, their pricks already full and heavy-looking in anticipation of what was to come.

At Vicky's request, they stood shoulder to shoulder in a line and then she dropped to her knees and gave each of the pricks a lovely lick, lapping each cock from the tip all the way down to the balls and back up again along the sensitive underside.

By now, all four shafts were standing majestically to attention and I called out: 'Very well, gentlemen, Susannah is now going to blindfold Vicky and she will suck you off one at a time. Remember, she wins a guinea if she correctly identifies your cock, but you have a chance to win five guineas if you can hold on for three minutes after she has taken off the blindfold.'

Susannah lifted up an antimacassar from an armchair and tied the cloth round Vicky's head, turning her round to face the wall whilst I called out to the men: 'You can change places as much as you like.'

When they had settled into a line, Vicky turned round and we led her to stand immediately in front of Rodney Bakewell-Fisher. She dropped to her knees and felt for his red-domed love truncheon. She pertly stuck out her tongue and teased his knob, lazily running the tip of her pink tongue all around the edges of the springy crown whilst at the same time she manipulated his bollocks through the soft, wrinkled skin of his ballsack. Then she opened her mouth and enveloped his helmet between her lips and lustily sucked for some ten seconds on the throbbing lollipop before she pulled back her head and said! 'I'm almost certain I know who is the owner of this noble instrument.

'Yes, a little bird told me,' she giggled as she stroked his glistening shaft and we burst into applause, for of course she was referring to Rodney's ornithological interest. 'It is Rodney's prick, isn't it?'

Well, Vicky had won her guinea, but would Rodney be able to refrain from spunking in three minutes. I acted as timekeeper, using Oskar's gold hunter, and as soon as I said: 'Go!' Vicky took off her blindfold and jammed down Rodney's foreskin with her hands, bobbing her head to and fro as she sucked greedily on her meaty lollipop. Rodney's eyes were screwed up tightly and he threw back his head whilst she clasped his bum cheeks in her hands as she gobbled furiously on his pole. I could see that Rodney would be unable to last the course and sure enough before a full minute was up he spurted his frothy jism, which Vicky gulped down with evident glee. She rubbed his twitching tool in her hands until she had swallowed his complete emission and his shaft began to droop pitifully downwards.

We blindfolded Vicky again and she put out her hand, this time round the stiff, thick prick of Michael Harper. Her soft hands caressed his hairy balls as she slowly licked up and down the length of his sizeable shaft, taking her time to reach the wide, purple knob. Then she lashed her tongue around his big boner and noisily slurped away whilst her hands encircled the root and began a sliding up-and-down rhythm. This was too much for Michael to bear and before she could even guess whose cock was slewing its way in and out of her mouth, with a groan he shot a flood of hot, sticky seed down her throat.

She licked her lips as a sympathetic murmur ran round the room and the pretty girl said: 'I've never tasted this cock before but I just know that it belongs to Michael Harper.'

To a round of applause she went straight to her last task, which was to show us that she could differentiate between the two remaining pricks of Christopher and Oskar. Cleverly, she took a shaft in each hand and frigged them both and at this stage, dear reader, I realised that she could hardly go wrong for, remember, Oskar Gottlieb was of the Jewish persuasion and thus possessed the only circumcised cock on view. So once Vicky established which prick was minus its foreskin, she no longer had to guess the identity of the proud owner!

But the dear girl was nothing if not a sport and she first licked the pre-cum from the straining pink knob of Christopher's cock before gradually working his shaft inch by inch into her mouth whilst continuing to slick her left hand up and down Oskar's throbbing tool. She washed her tongue over Christopher's uncapped helmet and chirped: 'I'm glad that your fine tadger has fully recovered from its bout with Jenny,' and Christopher generously led the applause as Vicky went back to sucking his stiff prick, clasping his buttocks and squeezing him close up to her mouth until his balls were slapping against her chin.

We had no need of my timekeeping services for within seconds he shouted hoarsely: 'My God! I'm going to spend! Oh yes, that's it! I can feel my fuck juice coming! Brace yourself, Vicky!'

And with a few short, convulsive jerks of his dimpled bum cheeks, he expelled his copious emission into Vicky's willing mouth. She swallowed his jism joyfully as he quivered in convulsions of delight, sinking to his knees to join her as they wrapped their arms around each other and sealed the game with a passionate kiss.

Thus the sport ended and left poor Oskar looking very forlorn as he pulled on his clothes, but he cheered up considerably when I went across and whispered to him that I would minister to his disappointed cock later in the evening.

We spent the rest of the evening playing charades, but whilst we were being served tea before we retired to bed, Michael Harper discovered a book of verse lying underneath his chair. He showed the book to Susannah who said: 'This belongs to my Mama, she loves poetry and she must have been reading it before my parents left for London on Wednesday. Well, as you've found it, Michael, how about reading a poem to us whilst we have our tea?'

At first he demurred, but Susannah persuaded him with a kiss and after thumbing through the pages he looked up and read out:

> *When as in silks Susannah goes*
> *'Tis then methinks how sweetly flows*
> *That liquefaction of her clothes.*
>
> *Next, when I cast mine eyes and see*
> *That brave vibration each way free;*
> *O how that glittering taketh me!*

I recognised Michael's adroit adaptation of Robert Herrick's love poem, but then Christopher stepped forward to deliver some doggerel straight out of the officers' mess:

> *Oh 'give me a damsel of blooming sixteen,*
> *With two luscious thighs and a crack in between,*
> *With a fringe on the edge and two red lips I say,*
> *In her cunt I'd be diving by night and by day.*

So here's to the female who yields to the man,
And here's to the man who'll fuck when he can,
For fucking creates our best joys on this earth
And from fucking, you know, we all date our birth.

This lowered the level of verse and from memory Vicky recited one of the naughty limericks which are all the rage amongst the fast set:

There was a young lady of Harrow,
Who complained that her cunt was too narrow,
For times without number
She'd fuck a cucumber
But could not accomplish a marrow.

I had no objections to these naughty rhymes but I caught a glimpse of Oskar trying to stifle a yawn — after all, although his English was excellent, he was not fully conversant with the common *argot*, so I sidled over to him when Susannah adopted a Cockney accent and began:

My name is Kate, my hair is brown
And I live in a house in Kentish Town.
My pussey is smooth, not a hair in sight,
I lather and shave it every night —

Oskar smiled politely as she continued her comic monologue, but his eyes lit up when I whispered: 'Come on, let's take two glasses and the bottle of that lovely kümmel and go up to my room.'

'I would like nothing better, but wouldn't our hostess be upset if we slipped away?' he asked anxiously.

'Not in the slightest, all country house parties end with couples going off together,' I told him. 'But the usual form is to visit each other's bedrooms after lights out. However,

103

as Susannah's aunt, who was supposed to have acted as a chaperone this weekend, is indisposed and cannot be present, we can dispense with all that hypocrisy.

'Of course you needn't come upstairs with me if you don't want to,' I added wickedly, and Oskar chuckled: 'Does a starving man refuse food, Rosie? If you would like to make your exit now, I will follow you in just a minute.'

Oskar was as good as his word and very soon afterwards we were sitting on my bed sipping this delicious liqueur. One glass led to another and in no time at all Oskar and I were travelling down a familiar road on a journey towards ecstasy — a journey that began when he tenderly took my hand in his and bestowed a burning kiss on my lips.

I returned his kiss with ardour, clasping him to me as our bodies pressed together. I moaned with delight as I felt the palm of his hand caress my bosom and my nipples hardened into hard little rubbery points against his hand. Our tongues washed against each other as with commendable dexterity he unfastened my low-cut bodice and exposed my rounded, bare breasts. His ardent lips roamed over my rosy titties, flicking them with the tip of his tongue until they stood out like two tiny red thimbles.

Now he pulled down my dress and a low, throaty growl escaped from his lips when he saw that I was wearing a garter belt, suspenders and a pair of lacy French knickers which were almost transparent. I unsnapped the belt myself, rolled down my stockings and finally wriggled out of my knickers whilst Oskar wrenched off his shirt. I unbuckled his belt and he tore off his trousers so quickly that I was concerned that he might lose a button from his flies.

My hand stole its way into the slit of his drawers and I pulled out his stiff, naked shaft which sprang out of its unwilling confinement as if on a spring, and his prick leaped and bounded between my fingers. I grasped his thick, upstanding shaft and looked with interest at his circumcised cock, for it was the first time I had actually had such an organ in my hand, although I had seen the awesome member of Mr Baum, the concert pianist, at one of Lord Philip Pelham's wild gatherings in London. Therefore it was with interest that I studied Oskar's tool and I must record that I found it quite pleasing to the eye and would imagine that for the proud possessor of such a prick, it must give extra pleasure to be fucked or sucked without any additional covering over one's cock.

I tugged down his drawers and we rolled across the bed and, as our lips met in another sensuous kiss, Oskar separated my thighs and let his fingers twirl around the silky blonde hair of my pubic bush. I lay on my back as his hand continued to tease my pussey and he kissed my breasts before lowering his head between my legs. He looked up and with the lust shining from his dark, liquid eyes he declared: 'Rosie, you must have the prettiest pussey in England. It is so lovely that I will pay homage to its beauty by licking you out.'

Oskar was as good as his word and I shivered with pure bliss when he lovingly kissed my fast-moistening slit and ran his long tongue down the full length of my rolled, parted love lips. Up and down his clever tongue moved as I clasped his head between my legs and grasped at the headboard as I lost myself in the excitement of this amorous encounter.

My new Swiss lover proved himself to be one of the most adept eaters of pussey it has ever been my good fortune to meet. First, he gently parted my cunney lips with the utmost care before running his tongue very lightly along the edges of my crack, which made me almost swoon with sheer delight. I wriggled madly as Oskar quickened the pace and his tongue darted in and out of my dripping slit so quickly that I thought that I was actually being fucked! Then he found the swollen little button of my clitty and started to nip at it playfully with his teeth, rolling his tongue all around it whilst he slid two of his fingers into my open wetness.

I ran my fingers through his dark, curly hair as I felt myself getting wetter and wetter and I cried out: 'Now fuck me, Oskar, darling! I want your fat cock inside me this very instant!'

He lifted his head and in a trice he was on top of me, clutching the firm cheeks of my bottom as he guided his knob towards my tingling honeypot, and I reached down with my hands to part the pouting red love lips as Oskar manoeuvred the wide crown of his helmet between them and felt fresh flames of lust crackle through me.

'A-a-a-a-h!' he panted as he felt his shaft slide into its desired haven, and every last nerve in my entire body thrilled in exquisite rapture as I heaved up to meet his thrusts, winding my legs around him so that his heavy, hairy ballsack banged against my bum as he buried his marvellous cock in my cunt to the very hilt with deep, strong plunges that almost mashed my clitty against his pubic bone. My cuntal juices were flowing so freely that when he suddenly stopped moving and held his prick quite still inside my love channel, it sent a series of little electric shocks speeding through my trembling frame.

When my spasms stopped and I lay gasping for breath he began to stroke into me again, moving with lightning speed for perhaps a minute until I screamed out my orgasm, and only some seconds later he himself spent copiously and I gloried in the rush of liquid fire as with every throb of his quivering cock, spasm after spasm of creamy spunk, as white as liquid starch, shot into my sated pussey.

My blood was on fire as Oskar rolled off me so I slithered down the bed to kiss his pendulous balls. I kissed and sucked each one in turn and then took hold of his slippery wet length, fondling it in my hands until it stiffened up again to its former powerful solidity. Delicately, I fingered the crown of his bulbous cock and then twirled my tongue all around the ruby knob before drawing in some six inches of his majestic, velvet shaft, which seemed to grow even harder in my mouth. I sucked up and down, varying the intensity and the timing before I released the sweet tube from between my lips and looked up at Oskar's face.

His eyes were closed and he was breathing heavily as I returned to my labours and I gave his cock a long, swirling lick before plunging my lips downwards and giving the ridge around his knob a teasing little brush with my teeth. Oskar put his hands on my hips and eased me up and over him so that my dripping cunney was positioned over his face and then the dear man buried his face again in my blonde bush as he pulled me down on top of him, and I felt his tongue tracking through my pussey hair to seek out my cunney lips which were already open and welcoming, and next my clitty, engorged, erect and so sensitive to the magic touch of the tip of his tongue.

My own mouth was still busy, working its way over his knob whilst my hands cradled his lovely big balls. Soon I felt them pulsate in my palms and I guessed that he was on the verge of a climax and would be unable to hold back for much longer. Sure enough, within seconds a stream of sticky, warm seed spurted into my mouth and his prick throbbed as I held it lightly between my teeth. I sucked out all the creamy jism which poured out of his magnificent, circumcised cock and my own love juices flowed freely over Oskar's face as he gallantly continued to lap at my cunney whilst he spent.

At last I felt the spongy-testured helmet soften as I rolled my lips and nibbled away at the rounded bulb of his knob until his shaft shrivelled up into an exhausted limpness. To be absolutely honest, I was more than ready for a final fuck, but this was asking too much of Oskar — after all, the poor man had risen at six o'clock that morning to catch his train, had made the five-hour journey from London after which he had enjoyed a three-hour afternoon walk with Rodney and eaten a large dinner into the bargain.

So it was no wonder that he fell asleep in my arms. I decided to stay the night in his room and snuggled myself up against him. Although, as I say, I would have welcomed one more joust, I was far from unhappy — and, after all, there was always the morning to which I could look forward with gleeful anticipation!

CHAPTER THREE

Anyone for Tennis?

I was the first to stir after a good night's sleep and I dived down the bed to check the state of Oskar's prick. Although flaccid, it had a nice, bulky feel to it and when I rubbed my palms gently along his shaft, his turgid penis responded immediately and as soon as it had regained its full stiffness I planted a wet 'wake-up' kiss on the top of his knob.

He opened his eyes and said drowsily: 'Hello, Rosie, a very good morning to you.' Then he passed his hand over his mouth and added with a sleepy chuckle: 'I was having a wonderful dream. Some pretty girl was kissing my *schmeckle* and . . . Oh, I say, it was no dream!'

His voice trailed off as I swirled my tongue round his knob one final time and then without further ado lay back on the bed with my thighs spread widely apart. Oskar paused for a moment to admire my pouting cunney lips which protruded through my flaxen-haired pussey, and then he heaved himself over me and placed himself between my legs. With a twinkle in his dark, sensuous eyes, he took hold of his throbbing tool and cosily rubbed his knob against my crack whilst he kissed my neck and throat, and then he guided his cock between the yielding love lips directly into my cunt. I purred with pleasure as his thick tadger slid home divinely and my cunney was soon engorged by Oskar's circumcised cock. We lay still for a moment or two, enjoying the mutual sensations of repletion and possession which are so delightful to each of the participants of a loving fuck, before commencing in earnest the soul-stirring movements that would soon lead to us climbing the highest peaks of pleasure.

Oskar slowly began to move his cock backwards and forwards inside my honeypot and the feel of his hot, thick shaft squeezing its way through my wet cunney made me squeal with excited desire. My whole body started to tingle and soon I was coming off in a series of fierce little spends as he now increased the pace and pumped his prick gaily in and out of my love channel, burying his pulsating prick up to the hilt, his balls banging against my bottom. Ah, how I revelled in the joy afforded by his noble tool as it enveloped itself within the soft folds of my pussey!

'Oh God! How wonderful! Do come, Oskar! Drive on, you big-cocked boy!' I cried out as I felt the first stirrings of an exquisite climax.

Nothing loath, Oskar now fucked me in an even faster rhythm, pistoning his prick into me with swinging thrusts as my bottom arched up and down to receive his powerful strokes and we continued the fuck at a full tempo, his rampant cock plunging deeper and deeper, and my legs left the bed to wrap themselves around his back. My hands clutched at his shoulders as his body suddenly went rigid, signalling that the build-up to his spunking had already begun.

'*Gott in Himmel,*' he bellowed as his orgasm juddered to boiling point, and I felt his prick throb wildly in my honeypot as his creamy jism crashed out of his cock and coated the walls of my cunney, and my own spend came on in a rush as my saturated clitty sent waves of sheer bliss coursing through my entire body.

Dear reader, my pussey is all of a tingle at the thought of these sweet recollections of lying naked with dear Oskar on those crushed and rumpled sheets, watching the early morning sunlight and listening to the muted sounds beyond the bedroom as the Welsh countryside woke to another morn.

But there was little time to lose if we were going to take part in the lawn tennis tournament that Michael Harper had arranged for us. So I bolted back into my room and within forty-five minutes I was downstairs taking breakfast with the other guests. From the healthy, glowing cheeks of Rodney Bakewell-Fisher, I speculated that the ornithologist had spent at least part of the night in young Sheila's room, whilst Christopher Cooney and Vicky were looking adoringly into each other's eyes whilst of course Michael Harper and Susannah, our kind hostess, made little effort to conceal the fact that they were sleeping together.

'Everyone must take a hearty breakfast,' commanded Susannah gaily. 'After all, we'll need all our strength to take part in the strenuous games Michael has arranged for us this morning.'

I helped myself to some scrambled eggs, toast, marmalade and tea. 'Is that all you are having, Rosie?' asked Rodney as he sat down next to me, putting down a heaped plate of bacon, sausages, devilled kidneys and eggs.

'I was never one for a big breakfast,' I explained as he proceeded to tuck in as Oskar came and sat on my other side. He, too, was eating sparingly with just a piece of poached haddock on his plate, and I was about to comment upon this when Palmer the butler entered with an envelope on a silver salver and announced: 'Miss Susannah, a telegram has been delivered for one of your guests, Miss Rosie d'Argosse.'

My heart began to pound and the colour drained swiftly from my face — for instinctively I thought the missive would be of bad news. With trembling hands I tore open the

111

envelope, but happily the message contained no news of illness or worse.

The telegram was from none other than my dearest friend, Lord Philip Pelham [see 'Rosie 2: Young, Wild and Willing' — Editor] and read: MUST SEE YOU. VERY URGENT. WILL BE ARRIVING AT MEVERSON HALL BY MID-AFTERNOON WITH TERENCE WHITER, PLEASE TELL SUSANNAH — PHILIP.

What could this cryptic communication mean? Susannah said that to the best of her knowledge, Philip was spending a few days in Sussex at a sporting party given by Count Gewirtz of Galicia at the large country house he rented near Broadbridge Heath. This was no surprise, for Philip was in constant demand at such gatherings for he was a first-class shot, and a bold man across country. He had a good eye for a cricket ball. Furthermore, he was a popular visitor who would amuse the women at dinner and his prick could also be relied on to perform when called upon to make some illicit nocturnal liaisons with any lonely ladies amongst the guests.

But who was Terence Whiter? I showed the telegram to Michael Harper and asked if he knew who this mysterious man might be. He thought hard for a moment and then remarked: 'It's only a guess, Rosie, but do you know Harry Whiter who owns a couple of thousand acres down in Kent? Well, I think Phil must be referring to Harry's brother, a young scamp of sixteen who, if my memory serves me right, has just been expelled from Eton.'

I thanked Michael, but his words made the whole affair even more curious. One thing was for sure, it would have to be something serious to drag Philip away from one of Count Gewirtz's lavish parties. However, all would doubtless be revealed when he arrived with young Terence Whiter. So I informed Susannah who laughed and said: 'Just like Phil, he does like to make an entrance. There are plenty of bedrooms so there's no problem accommodating them unless — but no, I simply can't believe that of Philip Pelham . . .'

'What's that?' I asked and she went on: 'He wouldn't be *involved* with this lad, would he? I mean, you say the boy was expelled from Eton, and we all know why so many young men leave public schools under a cloud. But no, whatever one has heard about Philip one has never heard a whisper of his being that way inclined!'

'Certainly not,' I said warmly. 'Let's be frank, Susannah, we've both been fucked by Philip and we are but two of his many conquests. Charming and sophisticated he may be, but Lord Philip Pelham is also a one hundred per cent, red-blooded heterosexual.'

'Yes, of course he is, how silly for the thought to even cross my mind,' said Susannah. 'I am quite ashamed of myself, but I just can't imagine why Phil should leave Count Gewirtz's shindig with a sixteen-year-old boy in tow. I can't wait to find out, I really can't!'

'Oh well, we'll all know soon enough,' said Christopher airily. 'In the meantime, don't forget that we are supposed to take part in a tennis tournament. We might not be up to Michael Harper's expertise at the game, but I for one am determined to give him a good run for his money.'

Two courts had been laid out in the gardens and the ladies were dressed in white blouses and white skirts which we wore daringly high, about six inches from the ground. My first match was against Sheila, which I lost four six, three six. My second opponent was Susannah, whom I beat six three, six two, and then I was matched against Vicky. I won the first set easily but Vicky took the second and, although we had been on court for almost an hour, we decided to play a deciding third set.

'Ready,' I called and Vicky served a rather poor shot high over the net. The ball bounced invitingly high and I drew back my arm to send back a forehand drive. Alas, perhaps through tiredness, I mistimed my return, slicing my shot badly, and the ball flew off at a tangent off the corner of my racquet at an acute angle to my right where Sheila, who had already vanquished Susannah, had been watching our match with interest. As the ball flew towards her, the sweet young girl instinctively turned her head away, but the ball thumped against her left temple and she dropped to the ground.

We rushed over to the stricken spectator and fortunately Sheila was dazed rather than hurt. 'I'm all right,' she said, struggling to her feet. 'Do carry on, I'll just go back and take a shower before changing for luncheon.'

'Are you sure?' I asked anxiously. 'Oh, Sheila, I am so sorry.'

She smiled groggily and said: 'Don't worry, Rosie dear, it was a complete accident. I dare say you couldn't repeat that shot if you were playing for a month of Sundays.'

And she insisted that we finished the set whilst she walked slowly back through the gardens to the house. I found it hard to concentrate after this interruption and I lost the final set by two games to six.

I ran up to the net and shook hands with my conqueror. 'I think I'd better go back and make sure that Sheila is all right. Would you like to come with me?' I said to Vicky, but she declined, saying that Sheila would make a full recovery, and suggested instead that we saunter over to the other court and see how the men's tournament was progressing, although it was an academic question as to who would win, for Michael Harper had only lost one singles match in the previous eighteen months and that was in New York against the American champion, Arnold Friedlander.

So I waved goodbye to Vicky and strolled back to the house. I went straight upstairs and changed out of my tennis outfit and wrapped a silk robe round my naked body before

114

walking across the landing to Sheila's suite. I knocked on the door and thought I heard an answer from inside so I opened the door and entered the bedroom.

There was no sign of Sheila so I called out: 'Is anyone at home?' and Sheila's shouted reply came from behind the closed door of the bathroom.

'Sheila, it's me, Rosie d'Argosse,' I said loudly as I stepped up to the bathroom door. 'I came up to see if you were feeling better.'

'Oh, thank you, Rosie, how nice of you. Do come in, the door's not locked.'

I went in and Sheila gave me a friendly wave from the large, round bathtub in which she was sitting in a pool of warm water. She said: 'There was no need for you to have come back, Rosie, I was only suffering from shock. See for yourself, the ball didn't leave a bruise.'

Leaning forward, I put my hands on her cheeks and carefully examined the pretty girl's head, thinking to myself how stunning she looked with her small but proudly jutting snowy white breasts, which were well separated with each tawny tittie looking a little away from the other, two rosebud points that were made to kiss and caress. Her belly was broad and flat, dimpled in the centre with a sweet little button and was like a smooth white plain which appeared more dazzling from the thick growth of russet pussey hair that curled in rich locks at the base between her thighs.

'No, I'm glad to say there's no sign of any mark,' I said softly and as I moved slightly to the side to check round behind her ear, one of my breasts slipped out of my robe. 'Ooh, Rosie, what big bosoms you have,' said Sheila admiringly. 'I wish mine were as big as yours.'

I looked at her slender young body and smiled as she lifted herself up out of the bath, and I spread open an enormous bath towel as I said: 'You're a very pretty girl, Sheila. I'm sure you're never short of male admirers.'

She pouted sensuously as I wrapped her up in the folds of the big towel and murmured: 'Oh, don't talk to me about men. I'm right off the male sex just at the moment.'

'Why, Sheila, you surprise me, I thought you spent the night with Rodney Bakewell-Fisher,' I exclaimed in surprise.

'I did, and he is a nice enough chap,' she answered as she snuggled herself into the towel, 'and he fucked me three times last night, but just because he is hung like a donkey Rodney thinks all he has to do is ram in his prick like a steam-hammer.'

'Oh dear,' I sighed in genuine sympathy. 'I have also come across this problem. I'm afraid that certain well-endowed gentlemen think that the mere display of their cocks send us girls into deliriums of ecstasy. Well, I'm not denying that the sight of a goodly-sized thick, stiff prick is certainly stimulating, but as the Americans say, it's not the size of the ship that counts, it's the motion of the ocean. Why, one of the best lovers I have ever entertained in my bed was a lad named Horace Bent. Poor Horace can only boast five inches at most, but he is such a considerate and imaginative partner that I always spend profusely when he fucks me.

'I never tire of telling my men that technique is far, far more important than the mere size of the instrument,' I added.

Sheila reached up and cupped my breast which was still hanging out of my robe. 'I often find that I can spend without the aid of any cock, can't you, Rosie?' she asked brazenly. 'Oh, I do hope I'm not offending you by squeezing your nice big tittie.'

'Not at all, my dear,' I replied huskily and I shucked off my robe and stood naked in front of her, and she let her hand move down and brushed her fingers through my already dampening blonde bush.

'My, your pussey's getting wet,' she giggled as she drew

her forefinger all along the length of my crack, and she clung to me whilst I rubbed her all over with the towel till she was dry, and then I dusted her gorgeous, lithe body all over with talcum powder, letting my hands linger on her breasts, bum and titties.

Then we moved to the bed and, lying naked together, we dissolved into a passionate embrace. Without further ado I spread her legs and sank my head into her fluffy little muff, flicking my tongue back and forth across her already swollen clitty. She purred with pleasure as I nibbled at the juicy morsel and gasped: 'Oh yes, how delicious. Suck my pussey, Rosie, it needs tender loving care after Rodney's big cock came crashing through it last night.

'Oooh, that's lovely,' she breathed, clutching the back of my head as I continued to lick remorselessly at her soaking slit until I felt her tremble at the approach of a climax. She writhed and twisted as her orgasm came quickly, and when it had passed I raised my head and climbed on top of her so that our two nude bodies were rubbing together cheek by jowl, or in this case, nipple to nipple and pussey to pussey.

'Now let me be the gentleman,' she whispered as she fondled my waiting breasts and swirled the hardened nipples into her mouth, sending chills of unslaked desire up and down my spine, and as her knowing fingers inched towards my cunney I felt my thighs stiffen and my hips involuntarily thrust forward in tantalising anticipation of what was to come.

Sheila traced her finger daintily through my golden pussey hair and settled on my cunt, around which she drew hard little circles until I was squirming with delight. Then, as she slid two fingers between my yielding love lips into my soaking cunney, she breathed into my ear: 'Oh, Rosie, touching you like this is making my pussey tingle. Feel my cunt, it's as wet as yours.'

117

I had not expected such passion from the demure seventeen-year-old, but with a firm hand she guided my hand between her silky, warm thighs as she kissed my titties again with unbridled lust. Then she suddenly stopped and I opened my eyes wide in shocked disappointment, but before I could say anything she murmured: 'Just lie back, darling Rosie, and I'll give you a wonderful surprise.'

What could this be, I wondered, as Sheila reached over to the bedside table and picked up an exquisite silver box which she placed on the bed between us. 'An old school friend sent me this for my birthday,' she explained as she opened the box to reveal a beautifully carved wooden two-headed dildo from Monsieur Zwaig's famous Parisian manufactory, sitting on a bed of plush purple velvet.

'This wonderful instrument has been moulded from casts taken from the magnificent pricks of His Royal Highness Prince Adrian of the Netherlands [*the consort of Countess Marussia of Samarkand and an old friend of Rosie's, whose exploits are chronicled in 'Rosie 2: Young Wild and Willing – Editor*] and Dr Jonathan Letchmore of Hertfordshire,' Sheila continued as she also took out of the box a small jar of strawberry-flavoured oil which she poured liberally over both knobs of the dildo, shaking the last drops all over my pussey.

I lay back and Sheila went to work on my cunney with her mouth, but now she added the dildo, pressing it gently to my pink love lips, using the head modelled on Prince Adrian's prick, working it in slowly but surely until it filled me as completely as the gallant Prince's prick which as readers of my earlier diaries will know, was not exactly unknown to my love channel. Then, when the godemiche was fully embedded, she lifted herself up until she was sitting astride my thighs and our eyes locked as I watched her finger herself with one hand whilst with the other she vibrated the wooden cock in my tingling cunt.

When her own pussey was ready she raised herself up and inserted the other, opposite head of the dildo into her pussey. Then she reached for me and pulled me forward until we were pressed tightly together, separated only by the stem of the splendidly carved mahogany prick.

I wrapped my arms as tightly as I could around her and Sheila wrapped hers around me and, as we rocked back and forth, we achieved a wonderful rhythm which allowed the dildo to slide thrillingly in and out of our juicy honeypots, sending pulses of sheer ecstasy to every nerve-centre in our bodies and, as our excitement grew, our fucking became even more frenzied.

'A-h-r-e, Rosie, this is divine, please don't stop!' screamed Sheila.

'I won't! I won't! How scrumptious! More! Do it more!' I gasped wildly as Sheila slid her fingers down my back with gentle, titillating strokes, sending chills of desire all along my spine whilst we continued to fuck ourselves up to the highest peaks of pleasure as this marvellous dildo prodded through our pussies, nipping its way along the grooved walls of our cunnies as we arched our bodies in absolute bliss. We fucked each other so perfectly that simultaneously we began to shudder and writhe in a veritable sea of lubricity, yelping with joy and pleasure as love juices flooded out from our cunts as we climaxed together.

We lay there quietly for some moments, our pussies still pressed together, enjoying the sensation of the dildo inside our cunts, when we were startled by a knock at the door.

'Who's there?' Sheila called out, and a continental voice replied: 'It's me, Oskar Gottlieb. May I come in?'

Sheila giggled as she looked at me and I winked back at her. 'Why not?' I said, for after all, it would be fun to see the reaction of the urbane Swiss lawyer to the sight of two naked girls lying on the bed with a double-headed dildo stuck up their noonies!

Oskar came in wearing only a dressing gown over his drawers, and how his jaw dropped when he saw Sheila and me in our happy state! However, Oskar was a true gentleman and he quickly recovered his composure and said: 'Ah, I am glad to see that you have made a complete recovery from the unfortunate accident about which Vicky informed us after Christopher and I had finished our game.'

'Did you win the match, Oskar?' I enquired, and he nodded his head absent-mindedly, for his attention was drawn to the sight of Sheila's peachy bum cheeks which she had stuck out provocatively towards him. He walked over to the bed and squatted down beside us, and when I asked him to remove the dildo, he smiled and used his long, tapering fingers to prise out the wooden knobs from our cunts.

I placed my hand on his lap and slipped my fingers through his gown to stroke his stiffening tool. 'H'mm, I suppose we should reward you for freeing us,' I said reflectively as I pulled out his prick from his drawers and started to rub my hand up and down his shaft. Sheila looked at his circumcised cock with interest and said: 'Oooh, I've never seen a dickie like this before, have you, Rosie? What's happened to your foreskin, Oskar, did you have to have it surgically removed? I hope this was not the result of catching a nasty disease!'

'No, of course he hasn't suffered from any disease, Sheila,' I said, wishing to save Oskar from any embarrassment. 'Have you never seen a circumcised cock before? All Jewish and Mohammedan boys have their foreskins chopped off in infancy.'

'Heavens, how painful!' Sheila shuddered, but Oskar chuckled as I helped to disengage his arms from his dressing-gown and replied: 'It might have been but I don't remember anything about it, being only eight days old when the operation was performed.'

I eyed his swollen phallus which was now almost at its full, majestic height before licking my lips and jamming them over his rubicund helmet whilst Sheila tugged down his drawers. 'Does it taste as good as it looks?' she enquired, and she cupped his dangling, wrinkled ballsack in her hand as she continued: 'Rosie, perhaps you would be kind enough to coat Oskar's cock with the peach-flavoured oil you'll find in the box.'

Then she turned round to present us with a close-up view of her deliciously soft rounded bottom cheeks as I placed the dildo back in its receptacle and took out the second small bottle inside the embossed silver container and, as requested, I started to pour the cool, sticky liquid over Oskar's pulsating prick.

'H'mm, how beautiful,' murmured Oskar as my fist slicked up and down his veiny shaft.

'What's so beautiful, my frigging or Sheila's bum?' I demanded, and he gave a throaty little laugh. 'Both, *mein leibchen*, though actually I was admiring that outstanding silver box,' he admitted. 'I would have to check the hallmarks but I would judge it to be English, made perhaps at the Barnard family factory about thirty years ago.'

'Well now, Oskar, my botty is also English and is only seventeen years old. Doesn't that take pride of place?' demanded Sheila as she wriggled herself up on her knees and pushed out her glorious backside towards him.

He hesitated for an instant but I pulled his thickly erect prick forward and placed it in the cleft between Sheila's bum cheeks and said: 'Do your duty, Oskar, this pretty girl wants to be bum-fucked.'

'That's right,' said Sheila, turning her face round and upwards to the surprised lawyer. 'I want a nice big pressing of juice up my arse.'

At this, Oskar went to work with a will and, parting her buttocks with his hands, jerked his hips forward so that the

121

tip of his helmet was pushing against the puckered entrance of Sheila's rear-dimple.

'Ouch!' she ejaculated as he pushed on and soon his cock was ensconced in her tight little back passage. Soon she was responding gaily to every shove and I could see and hear Oskar's heavy balls bouncing against Sheila's bum as her buttocks were drawn irresistibly tight against his commendably flat tummy. He bottom-fucked her at a regular pace in a slowish, shunting movement, snaking his right hand round her back to let his fingers tweak her cunney, giving the girl the double pleasure of being fucked both in front and behind at the same time.

Oskar came to the boil quite quickly and with an almighty thrust he spurted his seed inside her, working his cock to and fro to warm and lubricate her back passage, though his shaft was still stiff when with an audible 'pop' he uncorked it from her well-lathered bum-hole.

I lapped up and swallowed Sheila's love juices until she climaxed and then I lay back on the bed and spread my legs open wide. Now it was Sheila's turn to grasp Oskar's cock in both hands and frig his shaft whilst she said: 'I hope you still have enough spunk in your balls to satisfy my dear friend,' as I spread open my pussey lips, revealing the glistening interior of my cunney. Oskar knelt between my thighs and aimed the knob of his throbbing tool at the mark. He began by rubbing my clitty with the tip of his cock, which made me jerk up and down quite crazily and almost took me to the brink of spending at once.

'I'm going to fuck you, Rosie,' he announced as he rolled me over onto my tummy and I felt his hand on my buttocks, parting them to let his shaft sink between them. But whilst I enjoy being taken from behind, I did not fancy a bottom-fuck so I called out: 'Don't go through the tradesmen's entrance, Oskar, I'd prefer you to proceed through the front gate.'

'Your wish is my command,' he panted and he eased his knob between the lips of my pussey and wrapped his arms around me with his hands busy squeezing and caressing my breasts. I pushed myself back onto his rigid rod as he slewed his sturdy shaft to and fro, and the quicker he pistoned his prick in and out of my juicy love-box, the wilder became my responses.

'Faster!' I yelled out shamelessly. 'Fuck me faster!' and Oskar duly obliged, quickening his pace appreciably and his prick pulsed and twitched as the honey poured from me and, as he swung forward, his prick made little sucking sounds as it entered my cunney. I thought he was going to drive on to the end of the road but instead he lay back on the bed, legs apart with his glistening wet cock raised high in the air and I sat on it, swallowing it up to the hilt inside my cunt, and I wriggled around on his sinewy shaft, dancing circles around his throbbing tool. I raised myself a little so that I kept only his knob jammed between my pussey lips which clasped his purple helmet like a mouth. My ears picked up tiny gasping sounds and I turned my head towards their source and saw Sheila standing by the side of the bed, finger-fucking herself furiously as she watched me ride Oskar's rigid rod.

Then he gripped me round the waist and pressed me down on my back again, and his circumcised shaft slicked in and out of my sopping slit as I felt my inner depths exploding into waves of pure bliss which bathed me in a truly wonderful release which flowed through every fibre of my body. I screamed with joy as Oskar's cock twitched and, with a final tremble, he shot a torrent of hot, frothy spunk inside my love channel. He pumped out his sticky libation, panting hard as my cunney milked him of the last dribbles of jism and he collapsed on top of me before rolling to one side.

Sheila stretched herself between us and Oskar turned

123

himself towards her and said with concern: 'You haven't spent, have you?'

'No, not yet,' she admitted. 'But it doesn't matter.'

'Oh yes it does,' he said sternly, and despite his exhaustion he heaved himself between her legs and began kissing her damp love lips. Quickly inserting his tongue between her cunney lips, he soon found her swollen clitty and simultaneously he frigged her with two fingers with his face pressed up against Sheila's crack. She writhed from side to side as he licked her out, making her scream with delight as she reached the apogee of erotic delight and a flood of love juices exploded out of her pussey which splattered over Oskar's fingers as well as his nose and lips as he sucked on her pussey and gulped down her girlish jism.

After a while Oskar and I left Sheila to dress for the picnic luncheon which Susannah's cook, Mrs Hartfield, had prepared for us in the gardens. Along with the other guests we tucked into mulligatawny soup, ragout, roast chicken, roast beef, apple dumplings and a fruit compôte.

It was almost half past two and Dennison was helping one of the maids serve coffee when we heard the familiar chug-chugging sound of a motor car being driven up the drive.

I rose from my chair and said excitedly: 'That must be Phil Pelham — I can hardly wait to find out what he meant by sending that mysterious telegram.'

Susannah and I walked back briskly to the house to greet the unexpected new guest, if indeed the car did herald the arrival of my old friend. Sure enough, as we reached the french doors of the conservatory, Palmer met us and informed us that Lord Pelham and Mr Whiter were in the hall. We hurried through and there waiting for us was the handsome scallywag himself, accompanied by a good-looking lad whom Michael Harper had speculated was the young brother of Harry Whiter, a Kentish country gentleman with whom both Susannah and I were acquainted.

'Susannah! Rosie! How lovely to see you both!' he cried, kissing us both on the cheek. 'Susannah, darling, you must forgive me for trespassing on your hospitality in this extraordinary way. I was so flustered at the time that I couldn't even find the time to use a telephone and then, in error, my man Topping sent the wire to Rosie instead of you.'

'Don't worry, Philip dear, let's get you both unpacked and then you can tell us all about it,' said Susannah with a welcoming smile as she turned to his companion. 'But first, do introduce this nice young man to us.'

'Yes, of course. Terence Whiter, meet our kind hostess, Miss Susannah Meverson, and this lady next to her is Miss Rosie d'Argosse.'

'How do you do?' said the handsome youth politely, and I could see immediately that Susannah was struck by Terence's boyish good looks. But all I was interested in was why Philip had brought the boy all the way across country from Sussex to the wilds of Pembrokeshire, probably driving through much of the night.

'You must be very tired. Come outside and have some coffee and you can meet the others,' I urged and Susannah said, 'Yes, please do, whilst I confer with Palmer about which rooms to place you in.'

So the two new arrivals followed me out to the garden and I made the necessary introductions. 'Would you two like to rest?' enquired Susannah when she came back from the house. 'Your rooms are ready.'

'That would be spiffing, Miss Meverson,' said Terence Whiter, rising to his feet. 'We only managed about three hours sleep last night in the car and I could do with some shut-eye.'

'How about you, Philip?' I asked, but he shook his head. 'No, I'd rather not, if you don't mind. I am tired but before settling down for a snooze, I'd rather like to stretch my legs for a bit as we've been cooped up in the car since we left Count Gewirtz's party yesterday.'

'I'll come for a walk with you, if you'll all excuse us,' I said promptly and Christopher called out: 'Fine, but don't be too long, Rosie, as we're starting the mixed doubles tournament at four o'clock and you and I have been drawn against Oskar and Vicky.'

I promised I would be back in good time and Philip and I strolled out through the back gate and took the track up the hill. The stone hedgebanks along the pathway were ablaze with flowers — stitchwort, foxglove and red campion — and when we reached the crest some ten minutes later we sat down on the warm grass and I said: 'Look down there at those standing stones, Phil, did you know that stones like those were transported all the way to Salisbury Plain three thousand years ago to form the inner circle of Stonehenge? And there were no roads let alone any railways to help get them there! It's a real puzzle as to how and why the stones were moved — as mysterious as the journey you and young Terence have just completed.'

Philip grinned as he rolled his jacket up into a pillow and lay his head down upon it. 'It's a strange story, Rosie, and no mistake, though if I tell you the circumstances you must promise to keep quiet about them as the tale involves the highest in the land. Honestly, it would be better if I didn't say any more about what happened at Broadbridge Heath.'

Oh-ho, I said to myself, I'll lay a pound to a penny that this involves His Majesty, the King, who was sixty-seven years old but still, according to London gossip, very active between the sheets with Mrs Keppel and, when in France, with a variety of saucy chorus girls.

'Come on, Phil, I won't spill the beans,' I coaxed, curling myself up to him. 'You know I can keep a secret.'

My old friend sighed and then gave a little chuckle. 'Yes,

I know you can, Rosie. What the heck, why should I deprive you of a good laugh?'

And then he proceeded to relate what had happened at Count Gewirtz's get-together, and the only reason that I am recounting the tale is that later His Majesty saw the funny side of the incident and repeated it to Mrs Greville at a sporting weekend only a few weeks later, although of course it is still hardly common knowledge.

Philip and I settled down and he began: 'Well, we all arrived in good time for luncheon on Wednesday afternoon and, knowing His Majesty's fondness for good food, Count Gewirtz had engaged the famed Mrs Bickler as cook for the four days he planned to stay at Allendale Priory, the country mansion he had rented from Colonel Horrocks. So, as you may imagine, every meal was a feast and that first luncheon was more of a banquet designed especially for the King. We had poussin stuffed with quails' eggs, fillet of lemon sole, a splendid sirloin of beef, a cream pudding, a savoury and cheeses all accompanied by the very finest of clarets and champagne from Colonel Horrocks's extensive cellars.

'After luncheon, I asked young Terence if he would care to accompany me for a constitutional for I needed to walk off the substantial meal we had consumed. He gratefully accepted, for I am sure he had not really wanted to come, but his parents, Sir Roger and Lady Elizabeth Whiter, had insisted that he joined them, for they were not prepared to leave him to his own devices after his unfortunate exit from Eton College. I should add here that Sir Roger and Lady Elizabeth Whiter themselves had been invited to Allendale Priory by the Count on the express wish of the King, who I am sure was keen on a midnight dalliance with Lady Elizabeth.

'Anyhow, Terence and I sauntered down past the croquet lawn and through the orchard and I carried a bag of pastries which Johnny Gewirtz had insisted we take with us in case

127

we fancied an early tea-time snack. As we strolled along I said to Terence that it was rotten luck having to spend four days here with no-one of his own age to keep him company. "It must be very boring for you," I said to him with genuine sympathy.

' "Yes, it's not been a good year for me," answered Terence as he moodily kicked at a pebble on the path. "I suppose you know that I was chucked out of Eton earlier this year?"

' "Yes, I had heard about that unfortunate incident, old chap," I replied consolingly. "May I ask why, or perhaps this is a matter you would prefer not to discuss?"

' "No, I don't mind talking about it, Lord Philip, for I still don't believe that I did anything terribly wrong. It all began one afternoon when I had just come into my study after a grand game of footer, feeling very pleased with life in general, for we had just beaten Charterhouse by three goals to two and I had scored the winner three minutes from time. I had showered with the fellows in the changing room and when I looked in the mirror in my study, I could see my cheeks were glowing and as I said, I was feeling on top of the world. Perhaps it was this very sense of well-being that caused my prick to suddenly begin to swell, as I had not been thinking any sensual thoughts whatsoever, but my member often springs to life as if it had a will of its own."

' "Don't worry, this happens to all young men," I advised him and he nodded. "Thank you, but I did know this could be expected because my Uncle Edmund had given me a copy of Dr Billy Bucknall's *Human Sexuality Explained For Young People* for my sixteenth birthday. I tried to adjust my trousers but my cock simply would not go down, so I lightly stroked my shaft until there was a sudden cough behind me and I whirled round to see Patricia, one of the housemaids, behind me. 'I've come to do your bed, Master

128

Terence,' she said with a leer. 'Though from the look of you I'm sure that's not the only thing I could do for you.'

' "I blushed and the bold girl moved forward and muttered: 'I can see your tadger trying to poke its way out of your trousers, the poor thing. Why don't we put it out of its misery?' And with that she came over to where I was standing, knelt down in front of me and, after unbuckling my belt, began to undo my fly buttons! When she pulled down my trousers and pants, my cock sprang up to greet her and I almost fainted with delight when she took my prick in her soft, warm hands. No girl had ever tossed me off before and I thought I was going to come then and there when she said: 'Aren't you well-developed, Master Terence! My, what a thick cock you've got for a boy of sixteen. I'll bet it's the biggest in the whole of the Upper Fifth.'

' "As it happened, she was quite correct and false modesty not being one of my vices, I told her so. She smiled as with one hand she continued to rub her hand up and down my stiffie and with the other she swiftly undid the buttons of her blouse and uncovered her breasts for me to see. I'd only seen photographs of bare breasts in a copy of *Cremorne* which Bolsover Major smuggled in during the previous term, but here in front of my eyes were two gorgeous, snowy white globes topped with cherry-red nipples. I could scarcely believe my eyes as she tweaked her titties with the tip of my knob and I let out a hoarse little cry of delight.

' " 'Do you like that, Master Terence?' Patricia whispered with a gleam in her eye, and all I could do was nod my head as I was far too excited to reply coherently.

' " 'Well, if you like that, see what you think of this,' she hissed, and to my astonishment she took my prick between her lips and began sucking my cock, teasing my knob against the roof of her mouth. Her darting tongue washed all round my helmet and I thrust my quivering prick forward as her hot, wet tongue lashed against my throbbing

129

tool. The exquisite washing of her tongue on my shaft caused me to come almost straight away and she sensed this and let go of my twitching tool for a brief moment. Then she returned to the attack, licking the underside and squeezing her hand around the base of my cock whilst she licked and lapped so wonderfully that I simply could not prolong this delicious feeling any longer.

' "I'm coming," I gasped and as the spunk rushed up from my balls, she clamped her lips round my cock and sucked away lustily, and in seconds I had flooded her mouth out with my sticky seed. My jism filled her mouth and gushed out from her lips and after she had gulped down my foamy emission, she smacked her lips and said: 'Goodness me, not only have you got the largest cock in Eton but I've never known any boy spunk like that. I was nearly drowning in it!'

' "Oh, I'm sorry, I didn't mean to make you swallow my cum," I said falteringly, but she laughed and said: 'Don't apologise, my dear. I love the taste of spunk, it's nicer than almost anything I know. Do you know that your form master, Mr Cowen, once told me that there was an Empress of Russia called Catherine the Great who used to suck off three men every morning before breakfast because she liked the taste so much!'

' "You've sucked Mr Cowen's cock?" I gasped in astonishment and she nodded gaily and replied: 'Oh, yes, Jimmy's a game old boy and enjoys nothing better than a good sucking off.'

' "I could hardly believe my ears, but Patricia gave me a quick kiss and said she had to go, saying: 'I'll come back here at this time on Thursday, and then you can fuck me if you like. You've never fucked a girl before, have you? You'll love it, Master Terence, it's great fun!' "

' "You lucky young pup," I said enviously to young Terence. "I would have given everything I had for an afternoon with a girl like Patricia when I was your age.''

'He shrugged his shoulders and said nothing for a while as we decided not to continue our walk because it was now very warm, so we turned round and began to tramp back to the house. Then Terence said: "What happened next was most unfortunate. After lights out in the dormitory, I could not sleep for thinking about Patricia's bare white breasts with their jutting strawberry titties and I let myself drool about how I would let my hands rove across those soft spheres and then down to her curly bush where her pouting pussey would be waiting for my sturdy shaft.

' "Naturally, these lewd thoughts made my prick swell up to a capital stiffstander and when I judged that everyone else was asleep, I began to give myself some much-needed relief, capping and uncapping the bulging red helmet in my fist. I was so engrossed in this erotic reverie that I did not even see the door open and Patricia steal in and stand by my bed, dressed only in a light robe.

' " 'Oooh, have you started without me, you naughty boy?' she hissed as she slid out of her robe and slipped into my bed and added: 'I don't see why we should wait till Thursday for our fuck.'

' " 'Neither do I,' I whispered back and our naked bodies pressed together as our lips met in a lusty wet kiss. Patricia turned sideways so that I could insert my hand between her legs and explore her pussey which was thatched with a light covering of curly hair. 'Kiss my titties, Terry, they love being suckled,' she panted and I wasted no time licking and nipping those jutting rubbery strawberries and then, just as she grasped hold of my throbbing cock, disaster struck.''

' "What happened?" I asked and Terence grimaced: "I was just about to roll on top of her and plunge my prick in her waiting pussey when the door of the dorm opened and Mr Cowen came in to make sure we were all in our own beds. It was not regarded as such a great crime if you were found having a mutual wank and the standard punishment was a short lecture and six of the best, on your bum. But because I was found in bed with a girl instead of another boy, I was expelled for gross misbehaviour! And of course Patricia was also dismissed the very next morning. Luckily, though, I telephoned my Aunt Gwendolen who I knew had a vacancy for a willing parlourmaid and on my recommendation she engaged Patricia there and then, so at least the poor girl didn't find herself penniless on the streets.''

'We were now in sight of the house and Terence went on: "Although my parents were very angry with me, and I now have to work very hard for my Oxford University examinations with a private tutor at home, at least I can look forward to my next visit to London and take tea with Auntie Gwen in Bedford Square!

' "I say, I think I have a photograph of Patricia she sent me the other day — would you like to see it, Phil?''

' "Very much so,'' I said, adding: "If Patricia has a friend of a similar nature, perhaps we could make up a foursome and take the girls out on their day off — and I don't have any tenants in my town house this year, so we could have some real fun together!''

' "That would be jolly,'' said Terence as we walked into the house and went upstairs to his bedroom, where he rummaged in his case for a photograph of his beloved. Meanwhile, I took out the pastries that Mrs Bickler had given me and put them on a plate by the open window. Terence found the photograph, but as he handed it to me we heard the sound of a high-pitched squawk followed by a burst of girlish giggling float up from below. We craned our heads out of the window and saw none other than His Majesty with Lady Chigleigh who was wagging her finger at the grinning monarch.

' "Oooh, you naughty King,'' she squealed in mock

132

anger. "Can't a lady bend down to pluck a flower without having her bottom assaulted. How would you like it if I pinched your cock, sire?"

' "I would have no objection whatsoever, m'dear," he rejoined, taking her hand in his own and planting it directly upon the royal rod, and the lusty Lady Sheena Chigleigh giggled saucily as the King cupped the firm swell of her proud young bosoms in his hands before pulling open her blouse to uncover her bare breasts.

' "That's nice, very nice indeed," she purred as he tweaked her titties between his fingers, and she swiftly unbuttoned his trousers and took out the royal cock, and her silky stroking soon had his sizeable shaft hard and erect as it twitched in her grip.

'With a throaty growl the King ripped off her blouse along with his jacket and began to pull down her skirt, but she wriggled out of his grasp and said: "We can't fuck here, sire, not out in the open air."

' "Kings can do as they please, Sheena," he retorted warmly. "And anyhow, there's no-one about, everyone else has gone off bicycling down to Southwater — except for Phil Pelham and young Terence Whiter who are out walking and our genial host, Johnny Gewirtz, who informed me at luncheon that he planned to spend the afternoon fucking Miss Rosamund Fortescue. Still, if you prefer the privacy of the bedroom, so be it. But at least suck me off before we go indoors."

' "It will be my pleasure," she cooed and dropped to her knees, opening her mouth wide, she slipped in his bulbous knob whilst sliding her fist up and down his thick, gnarled shaft. Terence leaned forward to obtain a better view but his sleeve caught the plate of pastries and sent it toppling out of the window. Fortunately, the plate only caught the King a glancing blow on the shoulder, but two of the pastries landed smack on top of His Majesty's head and an angry bellow of rage escaped from his lips as Terence and I both pulled back immediately from the window.

' "Oh crumbs, that's torn it," gasped Terence, his face as white as a sheet. I popped my head out again quickly and saw the King dancing wildly about, howling with wrath and clawing at a sticky mess of jam and cream which was plastered over his head and shoulders. "Quick now, Terence, we'd better make ourselves scarce," I said to him and we rushed out onto the landing and ran upstairs to the billiards room.'

Philip paused for breath and I chuckled as I made myself more comfortable as I laid my head inside the crook of his shoulder. 'What a hoot,' I said. 'Still, you weren't caught so I don't quite understand why you had to leave the gathering in disgrace.'

'Fair comment, my love,' he grunted as I cuddled up to him. 'The trouble was that Lady Sheena had been so startled when the plate come whizzing down that she closed her teeth far too sharply round the King's shaft and the scream we heard was one of agony rather than anger.

'Well, to cut a long story short, Count Gewirtz insisted on calling in a doctor, who we knew would be sworn to silence by virtue of his Hippocratic oath and thankfully, although the royal prick was painfully sore, the doctor pronounced it undamaged. However, Lady Sheena was now in such disgrace that Terence and I felt it necessary to shoulder the blame and later that evening we confessed our guilt, stressing of course the purely accidental character of the incident. I expected an explosion for His Majesty has been short-tempered of late, but he simply glowered at us and muttered: "The whole affair is best forgotten," and he marched out of the room without saying another word, slamming the door shut behind him.

'But Johnny Gewirtz, whom I had asked to be present during this painful conversation, asked us to wait on and said to us: "Philip, I would strongly advise you and this young man to leave the house first thing tomorrow morning. Incidents like this somehow soon find their way into scurrilous gossip and the wisest course of action for you and Terence is to take a holiday abroad for at least a week or two, somewhere far from the madding crowd where you will not be questioned. Furthermore, I suggest that you travel separately, to avoid any possible identification.

' "Terence, I have an errand you could perform for me. I need someone to take some papers to a business associate of mine in Rome. If you would care to undertake this task, I will pay all expenses for yourself and a slightly older person to go to Rome, and I'll also give you fifty pounds for your trouble. I will speak to your parents and tell them how such a visit would be most educational. If you leave before breakfast, of course, it will be a *fait accompli*, but I am sure I can talk them round.

' "Now how about you, Philip? Will you heed my advice?"

'I nodded miserably, for I trusted the judgement of the sophisticated Count Gewirtz who was a true and trusted friend. "I'll book myself a passage to Barcelona. Your agent in Catalonia, Senor Ribalta, wrote to me only last month that I should find time to visit him this summer. Do you need any documents to be taken out to him?"

'He declined my offer with thanks and well, that's it, Rosie. I'm travelling back to London tomorrow and then on to Spain.'

Philip finished with a sigh and I mulled over his long tale. 'I'm sorry to hear that you've had such troubles, but all will be well,' I said with as much reassurance as I could muster. 'A trip abroad can be such fun. Gosh, I really envy Terence his task because Italy is my favourite country, and I would love to have taken the Count's papers over for him.'

'Would you really, Rosie? To be honest, I decided to come

here to see you because it's so far out in the wilds and also because I wondered if you could suggest any fellow of about our age who might like to go to Rome with young Terence.'

I shook my head but then I had an idea. 'Can't I go with him, Phil? If I can persuade my Papa, I'm sure he'll agree for he's in the Foreign Office and if you tell him, which you can in all honesty, that my journey is to be kept secret as it involves a very sensitive matter, I'm sure he won't object — especially if you tell him that Count Gewirtz will back your request.'

He stared at me and said: 'Are you joking, Rosie?'

'No, honestly, I'm not,' I said firmly, tapping him on the nose. 'We don't have a telephone here but Susannah mentioned in our letters of invitation that in an emergency we could motor down to Cardigan and use the Post Office telegraph there. Do it this afternoon — you've plenty of time, the Post Office doesn't close till six o'clock. My parents are away, incidentally, so you must send the wire to the Caledonian Hotel in Edinburgh.'

Poor Philip could hardly believe it but when he finally saw that I was in earnest, he gave a short laugh and said: 'Well, one thing's for sure. Young Terence will be delighted as he's one of your secret admirers! When I told him that you would be here he said: "Will I really meet Miss d'Argosse? I've seen her photograph in the papers and she is the prettiest girl I've ever seen."'

'Oh stop it, Philip,' I chuckled as he squeezed me even closer to him. 'You're making that up.'

'I promise you that I'm not,' he protested, his merry blue eyes now sparkling with bright mischief and, as ever, the sensual energy that he generated was beginning to affect me. I was helpless as Philip mentally undressed me with his usual panache which, whilst making me feel naked under his gaze, in no way offended me.

'Would you care to be fucked, Rosie?' he enquired with

136

the utmost tenderness in his voice, 'as I'm off to Spain tomorrow and you may be on your way to Rome, heaven knows when we'll have another chance to make love.'

'What a splendid idea, Phil, I thought you'd never ask!' I replied and lay back to enjoy the sweetest of kisses whilst he unbuttoned my blouse and started to caress my breasts. As we embraced I felt his noble cock stiffen against my tummy as I kicked off my shoes and helped Philip take off the rest of my clothes until I was naked. Then he shrugged off his own garments, spreading out his shirt so we could lie upon it, and I slid my hand across his manly chest and then lowered my wrist until I had his rock-hard swollen shaft in my fist. How stiff and hot it was in my grasp and I let out a tiny 'wow!' as Philip reciprocated by dipping his own hand between my thighs, running his fingertips through my silky muff of golden pussey hair, and then he gently penetrated my cunney with his forefinger and my honeypot began to moisten under his experienced touch.

The soft light made the ripples of Philip's body glow and I could hardly wait for him to fill me with his thick prick as the musky aroma of maleness filled my nostrils. He kissed me passionately, starting on my neck and throat before moving down to my high-tipped breasts. His full lips enveloped my engorged red nipples and he sucked hungrily upon them as his tongue teased the erect rubbery titties, making me quiver all over with carnal excitement. Then I pulled his head down to my fluffy bush and he licked and lapped at my tingling pussey, his tongue sliding through a smooth passageway between my love lips to wash around my pulsating clitty.

'Oooh, oooh, oooh!' I moaned as I climaxed delightfully, whilst he continued to kiss and suck my sopping slit until he raised himself on his knees and took his throbbing tadger in his hand. He gave it a quick rub and then without further ado he pushed the rounded helmet against my yielding

137

pussey lips which opened like magic to receive him. How I relished the feel of Philip's broad boner inside my love-box! He began to thrust hard and fast, his wrinkled pink ballsack slapping my bum cheeks as he swung his cock in and out of my cunt whilst his hands played with my breasts.

Oh, how we enjoyed this passionate fuck on the brow of that Welsh hill that warm midsummer afternoon! I will never forget how with every thrust of his superb shaft my own hips thrust back, kissing his cock with all the muscles of my cunney. We rocked to and fro as I waggled my bum to obtain every inch of his marvellous member inside me and I shuddered with delight as its fat, gleaming head stretched my cunt which had somehow expanded to receive his pulsating organ.

Again and again he pounded his prick into my pussey, faster and faster at a tremendous rate of knots which I could no longer even attempt to match. Oh how I loved each powerful stroke as my cuntal juices coated his cock, making it slide in and out even more freely.

'God, I'm going to spend again!' I yelled out as my moment of truth rapidly approached. 'Shoot your spunk, Phil, fill my cunt with your creamy jism, you lovely fucker!'

His slim body went rigid and his face contorted as his own orgasm was also very near. He cried out hoarsely as he shot a thrilling torrent of gushing seed into my crack before his body relaxed and he pressed his lithe frame slowly down on top of me, careful to keep his cock inside my cunney as we calmed down.

'Alpha plus, my lord, that was truly magnificent,' I said, kissing him on the lips. 'As they say in America, you fuck like a rattlesnake.'

'Thank you, Rosie, we always have a good time together, don't we?' he said, rising up to pull on his drawers. 'Alas, I wish we had more time but I must go to Cardigan and send the telegram to your Papa, and I dare say you had better rejoin the others on the tennis courts or they might send out a search party for you!'

So we dressed ourselves and sauntered back to Meverson Hall. I changed back into a tennis dress and waved good-bye to Philip as he made his way to the motor house.

When I arrived at the tennis courts, a game of mixed doubles was taking place between Sheila and Christopher against Susannah and Michael. 'What's the score?' I asked Oskar, who was the sole spectator. 'And come to think of it, where have Vicky and Rodney disappeared to? I hope you haven't been waiting for me to show up.'

'No, not at all, I've only been here for five minutes myself, and the last I saw of Vicky and Rodney they were disappearing into Rodney's bedroom after luncheon,' said Oskar as he applauded Christopher's athleticism in reaching a surprisingly fast serve from Susannah which hit the ground in front of him and broke sharply to the right. It looked a winner but the cavalry officer caught the ball with a superb half volley and lifted it low across the net.

'Well played, sir!' I called out and Christopher acknowledged my applause with a wave of his racquet. Oskar and I sat down to watch a thrilling game, for although Michael Harper was far and away the most talented player on court, Susannah was probably the weakest and this evened up the contest to give Christopher and Sheila a fighting chance to steal some points. When Michael served, retreat to the back line was the only possible recourse, but both Christopher and Sheila managed to return Susannah's serves with comparative ease. Every game was hotly contested and every point was fought for but in the end, after almost three quarters of an hour, Michael and Susannah finally triumphed by six games to four.

With perfect timing, Palmer, Dennison and my pert little chambermaid, Jenny, now arrived on the scene trundling

139

tea trolleys in front of them and they were soon followed by Vicky and Rodney whose flushed faces betrayed the fact that they had been engaging in some strenuous indoor exercises!

I first sat down next to Susannah and told her that I would have to leave Meverson Hall in the morning. I begged her to excuse my early departure and said that although I was not at liberty at this time to clarify the circumstances to her, I had been asked to assist Philip Pelham resolve a delicate situation and that it would be churlish to refuse him.

'I quite understand, Rosie,' said Susannah scratching her head in puzzlement. 'Well, actually I don't, but I'm sure it must be a very important affair because you were enjoying yourself here, weren't you?'

'When the matter is finally resolved, I'll be happy to explain everything in full detail,' I promised, and happily this satisfied Susannah who gave orders to Jenny to help me pack my cases this evening, and to Palmer to have Owen the chauffeur on call early tomorrow morning with the Mercedes in good time to transport me to Carmarthen Station.

After tea I had a quick word with Dennison and instructed him to be ready to leave tomorrow morning, and then I played what was to be my final game of tennis — a hard-fought doubles match with Oskar against Rodney and Vicky which we won by six games to three. Oskar and Rodney stayed on court to be coached on the finer points of the game by Michael, but Vicky and I decided to call it a day and sauntered back to the house.

'You must be very fit, Rosie, as you were scampering around the court during our game, even though you'd been playing tennis all afternoon whilst I was fagged by the middle of the set,' said Vicky as we reached the open French doors to the lounge.

'Not really, in fact I was only watching the others before

you came, as I'd been canoodling with Lord Pelham till nearly half past three,' I confessed.

Her face brightened as we sank ourselves into two comfortable armchairs and she went on: 'Oh, so then I wasn't the only one to enjoy a post-prandial fuck, though poor Rodney needed some extra help to get a cock-stand after our first joust.'

Her words added weight to my long-held argument that the prick is the most treacherous of all the male organs. So often, and at times without any reasonable cause, it wilfully insists on countermanding the orders of its owner. And I do not refer just to its disloyal refusal to do its duty in bed but also to its contrary habit of erecting itself at the wrong time and in the wrong place. Many young men in particular are afflicted by this strange contrariness, being embarrassed by a sudden bulge in their trousers in a public place, only to find their weapons flaccidly uncocked whilst spooning with the object of their affections just a few hours later!

So it was with interest that I urged Vicky to tell me more about poor Rodney's recalcitrant rod and she was happy to comply, saying: 'I knew that Rodney was keen on some rumpy-pumpy because although during luncheon he was across the table from me and had no opportunity to say so directly, he sent me unmistakable messages under the tablecloth. He had taken off his right shoe and during the meal he was busy rubbing his toes up and down my legs. I said nothing but slipped off my own shoes and reciprocated so that he would know that his attentions were not unwelcome.

'So after luncheon we quietly left you all down here and went upstairs to Rodney's bedroom. We wasted little time in preliminaries and after a passionate embrace, I said to Rodney: "Let's take off all our clothes now so as not to get them crumpled." So we undressed and I carefully hung

141

my dress on a hanger and carefully folded my underclothes in a neat pile. I turned round to see that Rodney had already stripped off and was standing naked in front of me, his cock standing up high and mighty as we engaged in a delicious wet kiss, our tongues flicking away in each other's mouths and our hands running all over each other's bodies as we staggered to the bed and lay entwined upon the eiderdown.

'I grasped his hard cock and slid my hand up and down the hot, stiff shaft, but to my distress his prick began to twitch wildly in my hand and before we had really even started to enjoy ourselves, he groaned and he discharged a sticky fountain of jism all over my fingers.'

'Oh dear, so Rodney suffers from a hair-trigger,' I commented and Vicky sighed and said: 'I thought he was just over-excited but let me first finish telling you what happened.

'I gave his cock a little kiss and said cheerfully: "Don't worry, Rodney, I'll soon make you splendid again." I slid out of bed and stood in front of him and then opened my legs wide and began to stroke my moist pussey through my curly bush. I slipped my finger inside my slit and began to frig myself as he looked on with wide-eyed interest. I was sure this would do the trick but his prick obstinately refused to rise up except for a slight thickening of the shaft. So I tried licking and sucking his soft staff, tonguing his knob whilst his hands played laconically in my hair, but this, too, failed to produce any response.

'Rodney cleared his throat and said: "Um, I must apologise for my silly refusal to play the game. I'm a very naughty boy and richly deserve to be punished. Vicky, would you please chastise me? I need a good spanking."

'He rolled over onto his tummy and stuck his bum in the air. "Are you sure this is what you want?" I asked and he replied in a small voice: "Slap one cheek at a time," so I straddled his legs and prepared to administer the punishment. He wasn't the first man I've met who needed a whacking before being able to fuck, and I'm sure you have come across the same phenomenon.'

'*Le vice anglais*, I said, shaking my head thoughtfully. 'Dr Letchmore once took me to a lecture by the noted Professor Hammond who propounded the theory that the anxiety and guilt drummed into young boys at school has much to do with this matter.'

'The public schools certainly have much to answer for,' she agreed and went on: 'Anyway, I did what he asked and began to spank him, laying the slaps only on the right cheek of his bum, not touching the left one at all. "Ow, Ow, Ow!" he cried out as the smacks sounded loudly as they fell in slow succession on his plump, firm backside. After a dozen smart slaps I inspected his bottom which looked rather odd with the bright scarlet colour of the spanked cheek contrasting strongly with the snow-like whiteness of the untouched buttock. So I set to work on the virgin cheek and he winced and wriggled his bum the whole time whilst I gave him twelve sharp smacks.

'Now his posterior was red all over but my face fell as he hauled himself on to his side and I saw that his prick was still at best only semi-erect. "Well, what now, Rodney?" I asked in desperation and in reply he opened his bedside table and took out – '

'Not a dildo, surely,' I interrupted, thinking back to the double-headed godemiche that her cousin Sheila had produced during our all-girl romp before luncheon.

'Well, yes, in a manner of speaking,' said Vicky, who no doubt wondered how I could have guessed what she was about to say. 'Not one of the wonderful ladies' comforters like those produced by Monsieur Zwaig of Paris, but a long, rather thin affair coloured pink and shaped more like a candle than a cock. He anointed it with some oil from a tiny bottle and I rolled onto my back, thinking that he was going to finish me off with it — but I was wrong.

'Instead, he gave me the instrument and he scrambled onto his knees and pulled apart his still smarting bum cheeks. "Shove this up my arse, Vicky, and you'll see how quickly I'll get a capital stiffstander," he muttered.

'This was a new game to me, Rosie, but I'll try almost anything once, so I grasped the imitation member as Rodney raised his knees and pulled them back till they touched his chest, and his nether region was now completely exposed to me. Gingerly, I took hold of his limp shaft and looked underneath his dangling ballsack where his wrinkled little arsehole was staring up at me whilst Rodney panted: "Yes, go on, dear girl, gently does it."

'I placed the tip of the dildo against the tiny puckered entrance and pressed it lightly inwards and the slippery mock phallus slipped a full inch into its tight sheath. Frankly, I found the experience somewhat unnerving but Rodney didn't seem to be too uncomfortable.

' "Aaah! That's just the ticket, Vicky," he grunted hoarsely and as I pressed forward another few inches Rodney groaned and quite suddenly his orifice relaxed and I inserted fully half the candle up his bum.

' "Now fuck me with it," he commanded and so I pulled the greasy pole out a couple of inches, before pushing it back up again. "Yow-ow-ow!" hissed Rodney through clenched teeth as I drove the dildo in and out, rotating it in small tight circles as he grabbed his own cock and began to frig himself vigorously and, to my delight, his prick was now rampant, its mushroom uncapped helmet standing proudly on top of a thick, pulsing shaft.

'I was in no mood to waste this fine erection so I hastily clambered up on top of him and guided his knob between my pouting pussey lips and I bounced up and down on his juicy cock as I continued to hold the dildo steady whilst

Rodney fucked himself on it with powerful, thrusting hip movements, levering himself up and down exactly as I was doing on his own throbbing tool. With my free hand I reached down to my sopping cunt and lightly flicked at my clitty which was by now popping out from between my love lips.

'We were now both so fired up that my cuntal juices began to flow and Rodney grabbed my bum cheeks in his hands as he gloried in the sensations of fucking and being fucked at the same time. He came with a huge rush of frothy jism which flooded my cunney and I went off shortly afterwards so all was well. But isn't it quite weird what has to be done to coax some cocks to stand up and be counted!'

'How very true! But tell me, has Rodney any idea what has caused this strange pattern of behaviour?'

Vicky spread out her hands and said: 'Oh yes, his story fits in with your earlier comment. It seems that when Rodney was in the second form at St Birchemalls, there was one sadistic master who used to frig the boys whilst he caned them and he also suffered at the hands of the captain of cricket who used to bugger the prettier boys whenever he had the chance.'

As I mulled over her answer, we heard the unmistakable noise of Philip's car drawing up and I excused myself and ran out to greet him. He climbed out of the car as I approached and gave the thumbs-up sign. 'Good news, Rosie, I sent a wire using a special code word used by the Foreign Office to denote an emergency. Go back to the Savoy Hotel in London and I'll wager a thousand pounds that you'll have a telegram delivered to you from your Papa giving you his blessing to spend ten days in Rome with Count Gewirtz's associate, Signor Carlo Nettlotone. Now, has young Terence woken up yet? We must hurry and give him the good news.'

Dear reader, I can hardly find the words to describe the excitement! I thought of the words of Dr Johnson who once declaimed that a man who has not been to Italy is always conscious of an inferiority. We rushed up to tell Terence about all the arrangements, and after dinner I retired early for we had to leave Meverson Hall early to make the necessary connections for the London express. Nevertheless, Philip came to my room at half past ten and I need hardly record how we spent the next three hours!

CHAPTER FOUR

Roman Scandals

For the sake of brevity I will just briefly sketch the details of how, just a little more than four days after returning to London, I came to be sitting in the cool, marble-floored drawing room of Carlo Nettolone's beautiful villa off the Via Tiburtina on the outskirts of the Eternal City.

As Lord Philip Pelham had correctly surmised, my father readily gave his approval for my new trip. Philip made all the travel arrangements at breakneck speed via the excellent offices of Thomas Cook and the following afternoon, he and Dennison (who returned home to Argosse Towers) saw Terence Whiter and myself off at Victoria Station. Although all this hectic travelling was very tiring, young Terence proved himself an amiable companion and we were able to rest in comfort on the luxurious Blue Train which, whilst we slept, sped us through France all the way to Genoa.

There we changed trains for Rome and here I must relate an incident that took place as we journeyed in our private compartment on the Milan to Rome express. I was reading a copy of *The Times* I had purchased at the station bookstall in Milan and Terence was gazing out of the window at the rolling Tuscan hills.

'I can hardly believe what has happened to me over the last few days,' said the handsome youth with a small, pensive sigh. 'Do you know, now and then I've been pinching myself to see if I'll wake up and find out that all this is merely an amazing dream.'

Putting down my newspaper I looked hard at the lad, whose head must be whirling after all that had happened to him since the fateful moment when he sent a plate of cream cakes crashing down upon the portly figure of His Royal Majesty King Edward VII. 'This is no dream, though I am sure that you must be rather homesick,' I assured him kindly. 'But don't worry, all being well, we'll be back in England within a month.'

'Oh, I'm not homesick at all,' he replied robustly. 'This is all great fun and far better than cramming for my exams with my tutor.'

'You must be fed up with all these train journeys, though,' I said. 'I know that I feel that I've been living for the last week in a railway carriage and I can't wait to get to Rome.'

Terence shrugged his shoulders. 'Railway journeys don't bother me at all. In fact I really enjoy travelling by train far more than by horse or motor car. I must have inherited this attribute from my great-great-uncle, Major Terence Whetstone, one of the first pioneers of the steam engine. I was named after him, as a matter of fact.'

'How interesting, Terence. Was your uncle a friend of George Stephenson?'

'Absolutely so, and when he began building the first railway lines in the Midlands he became very wealthy,' said Terence and, with a grin, he added: 'However, the poor old major came to a sad end in the Headingley railway disaster of 1864.'

I looked at him with a frown. 'Terence Whiter, you should be ashamed of yourself,' I said severely. 'How can the demise of your relative be a subject of levity?'

He threw up his hands in surrender at my rebuke. 'Sorry, Miss Rosie, I suppose I shouldn't laugh about it but when I found out the way he departed this mortal coil I simply

148

couldn't keep a straight face, when I read the letter of condolence to our family from his great chum the social historian, Professor William Bucknall. You see, it appears that although the old boy was seventy-three at the time of the crash, my old namesake was still very interested in the ladies and in his private carriage he was entertaining a music hall artiste named Nellie Clifton, a lady whose name might not be unfamiliar to you. [*Nellie Clifton was the vivacious young actress who in 1861 relieved the future Edward VII of his virginity when, as the Prince of Wales, he was attached to a battalion of the Grenadier Guards at the Curragh Camp in Ireland — Editor*]

'Due to the collision the carriage was thrown off the track and it careered down an embankment. When rescuers reached Major Terence and his lady friend, they were startled to find the pair of them coupled together and totally naked! He was crying out: "Help me! Help me!" but Nellie, who was sitting on the Major's lap with his prick up her love channel, was screaming: "Fuck me! Fuck me!"

'Afterwards Nellie confided to Professor Bucknall that at first she believed the jolting motion she had just experienced was caused by the major's massive member (he was supposed to have been particularly well-endowed) and it took a good few seconds for her to realise that the earth had indeed moved!'

'But your poor great-great-uncle had been killed in the crash?'

Terence laughed out loud and said: 'Not at all, the major was unhurt. Oh, they were both very shaken of course and Nellie suffered some slight bruising, but otherwise they were quite fit to continue their journey. No, Miss Rosie, what did for the old boy was that he caught influenza after being brought out naked from the carriage into the chill Yorkshire air, and he popped his clogs about three weeks later.'

In spite of my earlier scolding, I could not help letting a wry smile form on my lips. 'Nevertheless, a sad way to go,' I observed with a twinkle in my eye and Terence sighed: 'Well, one could argue that it was rough justice for he was a notorious womaniser, although he was careful to keep his paramours well away from his home life. His wife never suspected anything of his goings-on and was quite shocked when a floral tribute, in the shape of an erect penis, from a group of his lady friends arrived at the church on the day of his funeral. However, a quick-thinking friend consoled her by stating that the arrangement had been sent by local horticulturalists as a tribute to the major's success in the raising of giant marrows.'

This was stretching my credulity to the limits and I looked hard at the young man, but he returned my stern stare totally straight-faced so I did not further question his story, for my parents had always firmly dinned into my brother and myself that it is the height of bad manners to doubt the veracity of another person's story, especially if it is entertaining.

The train slowed to a halt and we both gazed out of the window. My eyes swivelled over the landscape when Terence caught his breath. 'Good heavens, Miss Rosie, can you see what that couple are up to under the large tree where the black horse is standing? Oh, I say, just look at that!'

I am a tiny bit short-sighted so I opened my bag and took out a pair of opera glasses and peered through them. When I focused them upon the spot he had mentioned, I could see why Terence was gawping through the window with such total concentration! For on the grass behind a hedge were a naughty couple engaged in a most energetic bout of fucking. Through my binoculars I could see the dark-haired girl pulling up her dress and undoing her blouse and I could see her voluptuous bare breasts spilling out of her unloosed bodice. Her lover nuzzled greedily away at her big tawny

150

titties, sucking at her engorged nipples as she pressed him to her. His trousers were down to his knees and the sun flashed across his white bottom as he raised himself up before plunging his prick inside her cunney. She raised her well-made thighs and her strong legs clasped themselves around his waist in a vice-like grip. The rise and fall of his arse now increased to a frenzied pace and I saw the girl's hips lifting clear off the grass as she forced his cock even deeper inside her honeypot.

'Have a closer look,' I said as I passed the glasses over to my young fellow traveller, and I could hardly help noticing the huge bulge which had formed in Terence's trousers.

The engine whistle blew and we began to move slowly forward. Terence kept the binoculars trained on the fornicating pair until they were out of vision and then he dropped them from his eyes and said hoarsely: 'By God, I wish that it were me under that tree! But with my luck I'll be as old as the major on his last fuck with Nellie Clifton.'

'Now what makes you say that, Terence? You are a good-looking young chap and I am certain that when the time is right there will be no shortage of girls ready to initiate you into the joys of *l'art de faire l'amour*.'

'I very much doubt it,' he replied gloomily. 'It's true that Patricia, the maid who was involved in my expulsion from Eton, is now in service at my Aunt Gwen's, but if I know anything about my Uncle Eric, he'll be fucking her at every opportunity and I won't find it easy to win back her favours.'

'That would be most unfortunate,' I said, laying my hand on Terence's knee. 'Lord Philip Pelham told me of the circumstances which led to your plight and I must say that in my opinion you did nothing to warrant such a severe punishment.'

'Thank you, but I do seem to have had my share of bad

151

luck. I did think that I was going to cross the Rubicon only a few nights after I was sent down from Eton, but although I almost achieved my goal, at the very last Dame Fortune refused to smile upon me.'

'You poor boy! Why, what happened?' I enquired with genuine solicitude in my voice, for I did feel sorry for him, although I readily confess that I was equally keen to hear what promised to be an interesting erotic anecdote! 'Don't be bashful, Terence, you can share any intimate secret with me,' I said, letting my fingertips run lightly down his leg.

His face coloured slightly at this but he did continue, saying: 'It was on a Saturday evening and my parents had invited several members of the family to dine with us. I was sitting next to my cousin Molly, a pretty, fair-haired girl who had only the previous week celebrated her eighteenth birthday. She was wearing a low-cut gown and during dinner I could hardly keep my eyes from the swell of her luscious breasts which sat so temptingly inside her soft silk dress.

'After dinner I asked Molly if she would care to play table-tennis with me and, with our parents' approval, we left the lounge and scuttled upstairs to the games room. Once we were alone she looked mischievously at me and said with a little giggle: "Oh, Terry, you really are a naughty boy."

' "Me? Naughty? Why do you say that?" I asked and she answered boldly: "Well, for a start, during the meal you made it very obvious how interested you were in my bosoms."

'I was taken aback by her forthright reply and blushed deeply as I mumbled a few words of apology.

' "No, you really don't have to apologise, you silly thing," Molly breathed as she pulled me closer to her. "At least, so long as you can prove to me that it was my looks which were making such a bulge in your lap and not anyone else's."

'I could hardly believe my ears, but when she pressed

152

herself against me and kissed me full on the lips I decided that further words were not needed and I returned her kiss, taking the lovely creature into my arms.

'Our lips opened and we wiggled our tongues inside each other's mouths, and then Molly stepped back a pace and unhooked the catch at the back of her dress. She stepped out of the garment which fell to the floor and my shaft pressed against my trousers so forcefully that it threatened to tear through the material. Then she pulled her white chemise over her head and my heart began to pound as she bared her beautiful, rounded breasts with their erect, quivering nipples, and I had to steady myself by leaning against the wall when she stepped out of her shoes and stood naked before me except for her stocking belt and frilly lace panties.

'With a sensual smile she tugged down the front of her drawers just an inch or two to let me catch a glimpse of her golden pussey bush and she whispered: "Would you like to see more, Terry?"

'All I could do was to nod my head, for I was now far too excited to give a coherent reply. Molly gave me another wicked grin and went on: "Very well, you may in a minute then, but let's first make ourselves comfortable."

'We sat ourselves down on the sofa and resumed our embrace and now Molly let her fingers fall directly on my throbbing tool and rubbed it with the palm of her hand. I tore off my jacket and unbuckled the belt of my trousers whilst she nimbly unfastened the buttons of my flies. I lifted my hips and she pulled them down together with my drawers so that my naked prick and balls were exposed to her view.

' "Oh, my God!" I gasped as she grasped hold of my swollen shaft and moved her body across and downwards to kneel in front of me. Then she leaned forward and licked all around my knob before opening her mouth and sucking

153

in my tool between her soft, wet lips. She sucked and sucked, slowly and skilfully, teasing my balls with her fingernails, twirling her tongue round my knob, biting, lapping, kissing. This was so stimulating that she only had time to bob her head a couple of times up and down my rigid rod before I was ready to shoot my seed down her throat.

'Molly understood my urgent need to spunk and she gave my balls a gentle queeze and this made me explode immediately, sending a rush of seed through my twitching tadger gushing into her willing mouth. My cock pulsed wildly as she happily swallowed my sticky emission, milking my trembling tool of every last drop of jism, and then she licked her lips and said: "Gracious, you *are* a big boy, Terry. Why, your dickie is still almost as hard as before I sucked it. Let me see if I can make it rise up again to its full height."

'I stood there dazed as she added: "Oh dear, my pussey is so wet that I must take off my knickers or my skin will become chapped." And with that she slowly pulled down her panties, and at the sight of her damp thatch of blonde pussey hair, my prick swelled back up to a bursting erection and Molly scrambled to her feet and threw herself back on the sofa with her legs wide apart.'

Terence wiped his brow and I exclaimed: 'For heaven's sake, Terence Whiter, what further invitation could you have wanted? So what did you do then? Ask her if she wanted to play ping-pong?'

'No I did not!' he snapped at me. 'But just as I was about to climb on top of her I heard footsteps on the stairs and I sprang across the room to switch off the electric light and we hid behind the sofa. The door opened and my father came in and called: "Hello there, anyone in?"

'We waited with bated breath until he closed the door and then dressed ourselves in record speed. We managed to creep downstairs and when asked where we had been, we made

154

some excuse about teasing my father by playing hide-and-seek with him.

'So there you are, Miss Rosie,' he concluded unhappily. 'My best chance of becoming a man was stymied by a cruel twist of fate. I feel so despondent thinking about it that I wonder if I am doomed to remain celibate for the rest of my life!'

'Stuff and nonsense!' I replied robustly. 'Mark my words, I'll wager you a pound to a penny that you'll lose your unwanted virginity in the Eternal City. Sit at a pavement café and watch the world go by in the *passegiata*, the ritual evening parade, and I guarantee that you will soon need an extra pillow for a bed-mate.'

Terence lapsed into a sulky silence for he thought that I was merely humouring him, though it is a fact that many young people of both sexes whom I count as close friends have enjoyed intimate, forbidden escapades in this lovely country. However, he cheered up as we approached the environs of the city and Signor Nettolone was on the station platform to welcome us, holding up a placard with our names above his head so that we would be able to recognise him.

Carlo Nettolone was a handsome, swarthy gentleman of about thirty years of age with curly black hair, deep dark eyes and when he smiled a greeting to me he showed a perfect set of gleaming white teeth that were set off so strikingly against his olive complexion.

'*Buon giorno, Signorina d'Argosse, Signor Whiter, benvenuto a Roma,*' he beamed, shaking our hands. 'I have Dino, my servant here to attend to your luggage. Leave everything to him and follow me.'

Obediently we followed him and we travelled in a convoy of three motor cars directly to his villa where he lived with Fiona Robson, a charming American lady and a noted photographer from New York who had been commissioned by a publisher to produce work for a new illustrated

155

guidebook to Italy. Carlo Nettolone was a bachelor but to my relief he made no attempt to conceal his relationship with Fiona, perhaps knowing that anyone with any connections to either King Edward VII or Count Gewirtz of Galicia would have to be of a broadminded and tolerant disposition.

After Terence and I were shown to our bedrooms and given the chance to refresh ourselves, I hastened to pass a heavy brown envelope to Carlo from the Count, thus fulfilling our part of the arrangement with Johnny Gewirtz who, as he had promised, had not only given young Terence fifty pounds spending money but had in addition wired me the same amount to the Savoy in London before we set off. And he had also paid all our travelling expenses, and Carlo was quick to inform me when I asked to be allowed to contribute to the expenses of the household that he had taken it upon himself to reimburse Carlo for entertaining Terence and myself.

We dined simply on *Zuppa Pavese* (a clear soup with eggs poached in it), *Gnocchi* (poached dumplings made from flour, cheese and eggs), followed by *Trotelle all'Italiana* (trout baked with fennel and wine). We drank the famous Est! Est! Est! white wine from Montefioscone and we finished our repast with ice cream and fresh fruit.

'Thank you for a delicious meal,' I said to Fiona as Carlo and Terence rose from the table to take a post-prandial stroll in the gardens.

'Ah, for that you have to thank Angelica. She is a superb cook and I don't know what we would do without her, although employing her does have a strange drawback.'

However, just as I was about to ask what that might be, an ear-piercing yell made me nearly jump out of my skin. It had floated up from the kitchen and I was concerned that mayhem was being committed down there, but Fiona put her hand on my arm and said with a smile: 'Don't be alarmed, Rosie, there is nothing to worry about. You must forgive me, for I should have warned you before we sat down at the table that we might hear such noises after dinner.'

Another tremendous shriek rent the air and I gasped: 'But for heaven's sake, who is responsible for that din?' and Fiona chuckled as she replied in a surprisingly casual fashion: 'I'm afraid that it's Angelica enjoying her regular Wednesday evening fuck with Father Lionel.'

This shocked me to the core. 'With a priest?' I echoed in amazement, but Fiona explained herself further: 'Ah, I realise that this may sound somewhat scandalous to you, but then Father Lionel is a rather unusual man of the cloth. He is the chief pastor in Rome of the Worldwide Epicurean Church to which Angelica belongs.'

She saw the blank look on my face and kindly continued: 'The Epicureans follow the teachings of their mentor, the Greek philosopher Epicurus who held that the pursuit of pleasure is the highest good. In the case of our cook, this is being fucked doggie-style by Father Lionel who spends much of his time making himself available for such pastoral duties.'

'Quite a screamer, isn't she?' I remarked whilst I digested Fiona's information about this unusual organisation, and then I added hastily. 'Not that I mind the noise, for the sounds of a lusty couple enjoying themselves can be quite exciting. I don't suppose we could have a look, could we?'

'Certainly we could,' said Fiona, rising to her feet as another yell assaulted our ears. 'Come downstairs with me. Angelica won't mind at all, although at this stage I would imagine she will be far too busy with Father Lionel's prick to notice us.'

We descended the stairs into the kitchen where Angelica, a well-made girl of not more than twenty-five, was standing nude in front of the kitchen table, bending forward with her arms outstretched and her fingers curled round the edges of the table. The quivering white globes of her bottom stuck out saucily whilst behind her was a slight gentleman who was pistoning his glistening boner in and out of the cleft between the cheeks of her luscious arse and, with every vigorous thrust, he buried his cock to the hilt, his heavy balls banging against her heaving, rounded buttocks.

The girl's plump backside slapped nicely against his thighs as she fitted easily into the rhythm of Father Lionel's fucking. Again she shrieked with pleasure as his gleaming shaft see-sawed in and out of her dripping crack. Reaching behind her, Angelica caressed his wrinkled pink ballsack as she rocked to and fro, her head thrown back and her hair whipping from side to side as she called out: '*Dio mio, mio caro Lionel, più, più, per favore*!'

She wriggled her bottom in a wild frenzy, her hips rotating to achieve the maximum penetration and then she threw back her head in total abandon as she let out a final, uninhibited whoop of passion as she climaxed. Seconds later, Father Lionel's wiry torso stiffened and with an anguished cry he made one final, gigantic thrust forwards, his balls slapping against the back of Angelica's thighs before he pulled out his prick and spurted spasm after spasm of hot, frothy spunk over her bum cheeks.

'Note how the good padre ensures that he does not spend inside her cunney, as the silly girl hasn't taken any precautions,' commented Fiona as Angelica handed her ecclesiastical paramour a dishcloth to wipe his seed from her buttocks, and Father Lionel turned to us and said in a broad American twang: 'Yeah, I'm always telling girls to follow that maxim of the Boy Scouts, *be prepared*, Fiona, if they don't want to be put in the family way.'

So this athletic young man of the cloth hailed from the United States and I wondered how he came to be in Rome. In the meantime, Fiona introduced him to me and, after accepting our invitation to join us upstairs, he gave Angelica a farewell kiss and a friendly pat on the rump as the sultry girl dressed herself.

Back on the verandah, Fiona poured out cognac for Lionel whilst she and I sipped *strega* and I made so bold as to ask my question aloud and asked where he had been ordained.

'Well now, I guess ordination isn't quite the right word,' he drawled as we sat ourselves down in the comfortable easy chairs. 'To be absolutely honest, the Worldwide Epicurean Church is hardly a religious organisation in the strict sense of the word. It's more of a fraternity, but by making the club a church, our subscriptions, or donations, as we prefer to call them, can be set against income tax.'

'So people of all faiths may join the Epicureans without compromising their religion?' I said and Father Lionel nodded. 'Certainly they may, Miss d'Argosse. I happen to be a Methodist, but back in the States we have in our ranks Protestants of all denominations, Catholics and Jews. We refuse to operate any restriction on the grounds of race, colour or creed and in the East, for example, we can boast of many Muslims, Sikhs and Hindus within our ranks. The Maharajah of Lockshenstan is an honoured member, as is Prince Mumsahbedanida of Mesopotamia.

'In England, we also have a number of *sub rosa* adherents including the entire committee of the Jim Jam Club [*a notorious high class salle privée in Great Windmill Street patronised by, amongst others, Edward VII and Mr Lloyd-George — Editor*] and we have just opened a chapter of the organisation here in Rome. In fact, the reason you find me here is because as one of the few full-time officials of the order, I am supervising the opening party which will be held next week.'

'I suppose that the Epicureans is only for men,' I remarked, but Father Lionel shook his head and said: 'Certainly not, my dear, we welcome women, and if you

159

are interested I will enrol you here and now as a member of our British branch. Fiona joined us last month and I think I may safely say she has already received good value for her annual subscription of one hundred dollars. It's a great deal of money, I know, but those less well-off like Angelica are charged only a nominal sum.'

At this point I saw Carlo and Terence sauntering back through the garden and I said hastily: 'That young lad walking beside Signor Nettolone would benefit from membership for he is quite desperate to lose his virginity, but circumstances have militated against his achieving this ambition.'

'Well now, Miss d'Argosse, you must understand that the Epicurean Church is much more than a glorified house of pleasure,' said Father Lionel stiffly. 'We organise concerts, conversaziones, and many cultural activities and we donate thousands of dollars to charitable institutions around the globe. On the other hand, we do pride ourselves on lending a hand whenever possible — but to the needy, not the greedy.'

'Oh, Terence falls very much in the former category,' I said with a twinkle in my eye. 'It would do him the world of good to relieve his frustrations with a young lady who could instruct him in the sensual arts.'

Father Lionel stroked his chin and then said quietly to me: 'After I leave this evening, tell the boy to come to forty-seven, Via Trippetto, at noon tomorrow and tell the maid he has an appointment with Signorina Sophia.'

Carlo and Terence now joined us and I should have mentioned before that my fascinating new acquaintance was wearing a cassock and, whilst we sat chatting of this and that, Terence respectfully addressed him as Father until the Epicurean said: 'There's no need to call me Father, my boy, as actually I'm not even a Christian clergyman let alone a Catholic priest.'

Naturally Terence was very surprised and so Lionel continued: 'I rather enjoy dressing in clerical garb as, generally speaking, I've found that I've been treated far more politely by everyone from shopkeepers to the police.'

'That may well be, but I'm not certain that your practice is legal,' mused Carlo, who as I later discovered was one of the most distinguished lawyers in Rome, which is how he came to be recommended to Count Gewirtz.

'Probably not, said Lionel cheerfully, 'but then so many of life's pleasures are similarly frowned upon by society. However, I suspect I do far less harm than many in Holy Orders, my philosophy being that of enjoying oneself to the full — though at the same time always taking the utmost care to ensure that no-one is ever harmed by one's behaviour.'

He rose up to leave but Fiona placed her hand on his arm and said: 'Oh, don't go, Lionel, it's only half past ten. Perhaps you would stay for a few hands of bridge.'

'It is a little late for a game, isn't it?' he said, but after I noticed Fiona wink at him, he changed his mind and sat down again.

'If you are going to play bridge, may I be excused?' said Terence politely. 'It's been a long day and I can hardly keep my eyes open.'

We wished him good night and I walked into the lounge with Terence and whispered Father Lionel's message to him. He looked puzzled, so I told him that I would explain everything to him at breakfast the following morning. When I returned to the others on the verandah I expected Fiona to be searching for some playing cards, but instead the others were standing up as if ready to come back inside the villa.

In all innocence I asked: 'Aren't we playing outside? It's a very warm evening and we could set up a card table on the verandah.'

Fiona laughed and took me to one side. 'Rosie, I didn't

have cards in mind when I asked Lionel to stay. The truth of the matter is that I'm really in the mood for a little dancing. I'll put on the gramophone as I'm dying to hear the new ragtime records my sister has sent me from New York. Would you like to partner Carlo whilst I take the floor with Lionel?'

'It will be my pleasure,' I said and it really was delightful dancing with Carlo who whirled me elegantly round the room to the lively music. Then we took a breather and sat on the sofa watching Fiona and Lionel holding each other very tightly and swaying to a tune in a far slower tempo. I felt somewhat ill at ease looking at them but when I glanced across at Carlo, he put a finger to his mouth and slipped his arms round my waist as he said: 'Don't be concerned, Lionel is one of our best friends and Fiona has my permission to enjoy herself as she pleases.'

This was just as well, for Lionel had guided Fiona onto the sofa opposite us and his hands were busily running over her breasts whilst her own hands had raised his cassock and were hauling down his drawers. He gave a gasp which I assumed signalled that Fiona had grabbed hold of his thick prick and he then pulled the cassock over his head to reveal that this was indeed the case.

He helped Fiona tear off her clothes until she, too, was naked and then she rolled Lionel over onto his back. Her mop of beautiful chestnut hair disappeared between his legs, lightly touching his balls as she kissed and sucked his enormous erection. He groaned with delight as she stayed on her knees, licking and lapping the uncapped ruby helmet of his pulsating prick, and as she leaned over to take more of the blue-veined shaft between her lips, her luscious backside moved sensuously from side to side.

'Rosie, how would you like to join them?' whispered Carlo. 'Fiona adores being licked out, and I would love to see you eat her pussey.'

162

The sight of the young couple had fired my senses and I needed no second bidding. Carlo helped me strip off my clothes and I carefully positioned myself behind Fiona. She wriggled with pleasure as I squeezed her deliciously soft bum cheeks and then I turned myself round to lie on my back in the same direction as Lionel and slid my head underneath her and, without further ado, I began to lick the silky thatch of pussey hair which lightly covered the pouting lips of her cunney.

Fiona sucked lustily on Lionel's cock whilst I now slipped my tongue inside her cunt and, avoiding her clitty, I lapped steadily away on her vaginal walls and tasted the mushy wetness of her love juice. I heard Lionel moan: 'Christ, I'm coming, I'm coming, I can't stop now!' and as she swallowed his jets of salty jism I nipped her clitty gently with my teeth and, as spasms of pure ecstasy shot through her body, I continued to fuck her sopping pussey with my tongue, lapping up her cuntal juices which were now pouring out of her dripping crack.

Meanwhile Carlo had now undressed and had padded over to join us. Stripped, Carlo looked even more attractive — his torso was quite hairy and his cock looked very exciting, not perhaps the biggest I have ever seen but certainly of a fine length, sticking upwards at an angle with the foreskin slipped back to reveal a well-formed, purple helmet. I had no time to notice any more for immediately he positioned himself carefully between my open legs. He began by kneading my breasts and almost before I could catch my breath, his head was between my legs, nestling in my blonde bush. His tongue was soon at work on my moist honeypot, flicking and licking, lapping and slurping against my pouting pussey lips which swiftly opened to allow him to suck on my clitty.

My excitement grew stronger as I lovingly clutched his head, murmuring my approval as his lips pressed against my cunt. He slid his tongue up and around, sucking my clitty as I ground my slit against his mouth, feeling my love button emerge from its protective sheath and rise up in size like a miniature penis. He flicked it so expertly with his tongue that I came very quickly, my juices dousing his face as he eagerly lapped up the sweet flow.

'I'm ready for your prick now, Carlo,' I whimpered and seconds later I thrilled to the feel of his fat knob parting my pussey lips. I lifted my thighs and Carlo's cock slid straight into my love channel, deeper and deeper until his balls slapped against my bum and I worked my legs upwards, wrapping them around his back as, slowly and with great deliberation, he fucked me with his gorgeous, stiff truncheon.

'*Bello! Bello! Bello!*' Carlo cried as he upped the tempo, pumping furiously into my juicy cunt as his heavy balls banged away on my bum until his tool trembled inside my cunt and we melted away in a sea of sperm, his sticky seed mingling with my own love liquids which flowed freely from my tingling cunney.

We lay still in what would have been a superb *pose plastique* with Lionel flat on his back, his flaccid prick still jammed inside Fiona's mouth as the pretty girl knelt between his legs, her own thighs open to accommodate me, whilst Carlo lay on top of me, his throbbing tool still semi-erect even after spewing out such a copious spunky emission.

As is not unusual in these situations, the so-called superior males were *hors de combat* and needed time to recover, although Fiona and I were more than ready for a further helping of cock and Fiona looked reproachfully at our gallants as she slid her fingers around their limp shafts and squeezed them. But both pricks stayed soft and with a disdainful look at the two crestfallen cocks, she sighed: 'Rosie, I'm afraid that we shall just have to amuse ourselves

164

until these two gentlemen recover,' and I replied lustfully: 'No matter, I'm happy to lie back and enjoy whatever might come my way.'

'We'd all be a lot more comfortable in bed,' observed Lionel as he slid himself out from under Fiona and rolled onto the carpet, and we took up this sensible suggestion and crept upstairs into Carlo and Fiona's bedroom.

'Lie down, Rosie,' instructed my hostess and so I placed a pillow under my head and reclined on the soft mattress, lewdly raising and parting my thighs so that my pussey was open and inviting to all who wished to see it. Fiona jumped on the bed and sat on her knees in front of me as she eased her hands under the firm, resilient cheeks of my bottom as I raised my hips towards her pretty face.

Without hesitation she buried her mouth in my silky thatch of golden hair before sliding the tip of her tongue between my cunney lips. Licking and sucking with a delicate touch, she brought me to the very edge of a spend in no time at all. But then she withdrew her tongue and ran her long forefinger down the length of my puffy crack.

'Look at the parting of Rosie's love lips,' she said to Carlo and Lionel. 'They proclaim her need for a thick, stiff prick to slide in between them. Surely one of you is ready to give this young girl what she wants?'

I was pleased that Lionel's prick was the first to stand stiffly to attention, for whilst Carlo's cock did a fine job, variety is the spice of life and I doubted if I would be given another chance to sample the member of the Epicurean minister which had already performed sterling service, not only with Fiona, but also in the servants' quarters with the cook.

Anyway, Lionel gave his thick prick a shake and then clambered on top of me. He placed his knob against my blonde muff and rubbed it up and down against my cunney lips, which I found extremely stimulating. I reached down and guided his shaft inside my honeypot and, once he was fully embedded, I wrapped my legs around his waist and urged him onwards.

We struck up a good rhythm from the beginning and as his lusty cock slewed in and out of my juicy pussey, his fingers worked in unison over my engorged raspberry nipples. Oh how superbly Father Lionel fucked me, his whole body moving with such easy grace, sending thrills of delight inside my tingling cunt again and again as he pistoned his marvellous prick inside the innermost depths of my cunt.

He moved his hands to my bottom, holding my bum cheeks and massaging them with each stroke of his marvellous cock, and steadily the pace of this wonderful joust increased as we thrust against each other, our hearts and minds joined together in the intensity of these magnificent moments.

Suddenly I felt the first, long-drawn-out shudder of my approaching spend sweep over me. And now Lionel's prick began to tremble and, when I realised that he too was approaching his climax, I reached down and cradled his balls. This caused his body to go rigid and he exploded into me in a rush of liquid fire. It was my turn to shiver all over as I felt the first surge of frothy seed flood into my cunt and then my entire body was bathed in a glorious, warm sensation as Lionel's creamy injection filled my love channel. Gripping him with my thighs, I forced his throbbing tool even deeper inside my cunt and with every throb of his majestic penis, wonderful waves of utter bliss rippled through my body.

'More! More! More!' I cried out, desperate to prolong this blissful feeling and, gamely, Lionel drove on as I milked his prick of the last spurts of his copious emission. One last joint spasm racked our bodies until he collapsed on top of me and I could feel his proud shaft now deflating inside my drenched cunney.

I rolled him off me and he lay on his back, his chest still heaving from the physical efforts of our love-making (Dr Letchmore once informed me that in terms of exercising the body, a good fuck is the equivalent of a brisk, two-mile run). I hauled myself up and bent over to lick the remaining drops of jism from the tip of his now-shrivelled cock as his knob disappeared under the cover of his foreskin, like a rabbit fleeing into its warren. I ran my hands over his hairy balls and rubbed them in the stickiness of his crinkly pubic hair. At first he was puzzled by my action, but then he understood my intentions when I held his wrists lightly and pressed his hands to my own pubic thatch. Taking this cue from me, Lionel rubbed and fondled my pussey until I raised his fingers to my lips and I licked my own love fluids from him.

Fiona was now eager for further frolics, but alas poor Carlo was still unable to maintain a rock-hard stiffie. So shucking off her robe, she threw herself down beside me and, twisting me upon my hip, the pretty girl whispered for me to relax whilst her soft, nude body cuddled closer to mine.

I lay shimmering with pleasure whilst she sucked my tongue into her mouth and we clung together, our hands roaming over each other's breasts, our nipples flaring up into hard little bullets against our hands. We revelled in our kissing and hugging and then Fiona moved her lips downwards to lick my titties, and then even lower to glide her tongue inside my sopping cleft, prodding my clitty as she brought me off in a little series of electric shivers which ran up and down my spine.

Then she raised herself on top of me, pressing her nubile young body hard against me and our hands were now everywhere, pinching, grabbing, squeezing as our bodies melted together, demanding an early release. The adorable girl jerked her thick, curly-fleeced cunt savagely against my own moist muff and our pussies rubbed lubriciously together until Fiona looked up and saw that her partner had climbed onto his knees beside us and from the state of his shaft, which was standing smartly to attention almost vertically up against his flat belly, Carlo was at last ready for the fray.

However, having waited so long for the arrival of Carlo's cock, Fiona was determined to extract the maximum pleasure from his love truncheon. She hauled herself off me and swung round to present herself on all fours, with her lovely bottom just inches away from my face. She turned her pretty head round and said to me: 'Rosie, as you probably agree, it's even nicer when the prick follows the tongue. Would you prepare my cunt for Carlo's cock by licking me out before he fucks me?'

'With the greatest of pleasure, dear Fiona,' I replied and I parted the soft cheeks of her glorious backside and slid my tongue inside the cleft between them. The tip of my tongue tickled the lips of her dripping crack whilst I stabbed my forefinger in and out of her cunney with a fierce intensity which caused her to cry out with delight.

I moved my tongue along the rolled grooves of her pussey and she moved slightly backwards to sit upon my face whilst I sucked her tangy cuntal juices which were now cascading out of her cunney.

It would not have been too difficult to finish her off, but Carlo was waiting impatiently to stake his claim so I lifted Fiona's bum from my lips and rolled over to the side to let him continue this lascivious spooning.

They lay on their sides facing each other and I sat up to see Carlo's hand cup one of her jutting bosoms and Fiona take her partner's glistening stiffstander between her fingers, her hand working up and down the swollen shaft. Her nipples seemed to grow before my very eyes as Carlo fondled each of her proud, naked breasts. Now he moved his head from side to side, kissing each luscious tittie whilst his right arm reached down to let his fingers toy in the silky chestnut mass of hair at the base of her belly or slide directly into the crimson chink buried in its folds.

Fiona rolled her head from side to side on the pillow and groaned with joy as he continued to suck on her raised-up raspberry nipples, whilst ever so lightly his fingers traced the open wet slit of her cunney, flicking the tiny, erect clitty which was now peeping out.

'Fuck me, Carlo! Ram your Roman rod inside my juicy pussey,' she cried out, and being ever-ready to give a helping hand, I leaned forward, grasped Carlo's cock in my hand and inserted the wide, purple helmet between her pink, pouting pussey lips. He pressed forward slowly, propelling in inch after inch until their pubic hairs were matted together, and then he pulled back before quickly driving forward the full length of his pulsating prick inside her delectable honeypot again and again.

She urged him on, closing her feet together at the small of his back to force even more of his throbbing tool inside her clinging cunney, and Lionel moved over to sit next to me to watch Carlo's quivering cock work in and out of Fiona's sopping sheath, her love lips opening and closing over the fleshy lollipop which was pleasuring her cunney so exquisitely.

Carlo was now panting with exertion as he rammed home his gleaming shaft, which pistoned at speed in and out of Fiona's drenched crack, his muscular body rocking backwards and forwards between her thighs. Fiona shuddered into a glorious spend whilst Carlo fucked her at an ever-increasing rate of knots. She raked her fingernails down his back as she thrilled to the voluptuous sensations of his big cock pumping in and out of her cunt until, with a hoarse roar, he spurted a fierce flow of hot, sticky seed into her welcoming womb.

Father Lionel stayed the night with me in the Nettolone bedroom with Fiona and Carlo and we spent the small hours in various whoresome foursomes, my favourite perhaps being that of being bum-fucked by Carlo whilst on my knees sucking Lionel's balls as he lay flat on his back with Fiona bouncing up and down on his rigid, upright cock. Also to my taste was the arrangement of our bodies when we woke up the next morning. This finished up with me lying on top of and slightly across Fiona, our hairy pussies grinding together as I sucked her horny titties whilst using both my hands to toss off Carlo's cock, slicking my hands up and down his veiny shaft, and Fiona gobbled on Lionel's knob which he had inserted between her rich, red lips as he knelt by her side.

Surprisingly, I was not tired after I left my fellow revellers and, after taking a refreshing warm shower, I dressed myself and on the landing I saw a servant girl, carrying a tray of croissants and coffee, about to knock on young Terence Whiter's door. This reminded me to speak to the young scamp about his appointment at noon with Signorina Sophia.

'Here, I'll carry that into his bedroom,' I said to the maid, lifting the tray out of her hands. '*Bene, Signorina*,' she replied with a curtsy and I knocked on the door and strode straight in.

Of course it was inexcusable not to wait for Terence to shout 'come in' and he had every right to be angry about my unwarranted interruption. For as he did not immediately realise I had come in, he continued to play with his prick unaware that I was watching him finish himself off in the final stage of his early-morning masturbation. He was lying naked on the bed, pumping his fist up and down his erect shaft and, with a little grunt, he climaxed in front of me, and I looked on with interest as the gummy essence spurted out from his knob onto his belly and curly pubic hair which surrounded the base of his prick.

'Oh, damn and blast!' he cried out when he suddenly

realised that I was standing in front of the bed, and he covered himself with the eiderdown.

'Good morning, Terence, did you sleep well?' I said in as neutral a voice as I could muster. 'I just thought I would remind you of your appointment at noon with Signorina Sophia. Would you like to take a walk through the city with me this morning? It so happens that it would be most convenient for me to go with you to Via Trippetto, as Fiona has recommended a fashion house in the Piazza de Souza which is only round the corner from where you are bound.'

'Yes, thank you, Miss Rosie, thank you very much,' he stammered out as I turned on my heel and went out, taking care to close the door behind me.

An hour or so later, the Nettolone's chauffeur drove us through to the centre of the city and Terence and I wandered happily through the bustling streets towards the Piazza di Spagna. In my humble opinion, there is no other city in Europe which can rival the unique attractions of Rome — such an intensely alive city where people live, work and enjoy themselves in and among colour-washed medieval tenements, Renaissance palazzi and the marble columns of ancient times.

We made our way up the Spanish Steps through the Borghese Gardens to the Villa Borghese, built in the early seventeenth century by Cardinal Scipione Borghese, which houses his fine collection of paintings and sculpture as well as the best pieces sold by Camillo Borghese to his brother-in-law, Napoleon, in 1807.

There was not time to visit the Villa this morning but I said to Terence: 'One day you must spend a day there. There is one particular statue by Canova which I know you would find especially interesting. I am referring to a most provocative nude study of Napoleon's beautiful sister, Pauline, who was married to Prince Borghese, but she was reputed to have had a string of lovers and was the cause of much scandalous gossip.'

He grinned as he pulled out his pocket watch and said: 'I'll certainly bear that in mind, Miss Rosie — but I think we had better walk back to Via Trippetto as I don't want to be late for my appointment with this mysterious Signorina Sophia.'

So we returned to the Spanish Steps and at the bottom turned into the Via della Croce and a hundred yards further along we found ourselves at the junction with Via Trippetto.

'I'll leave you here,' I said brightly. 'And let's rendezvous over there at Otello's restaurant between half past one and two o'clock.'

This would give him enough time to enter the gates of Elysium, I thought to myself as I waved goodbye and strolled round the corner into the elegant Piazza de Souza and soon found *Di Sylvana*, the exclusive shop which Fiona had insisted I visit adding, rather oddly I thought, that I would be certain to enjoy the experience.

The small shopfront was richly dressed with what appeared to be the latest in fashionable apparel, and as I entered the shop I was welcomed by an extremely attractive girl of about my own age with a finely formed face on which was perched a mass of shiny brown hair which fell down in ringlets upon her shoulders. Her eyes were also a deep shade of brown and her tight blouse accentuated a pair of high, thrusting bosoms which I noticed with a tad of envy were probably slightly larger than my own.

She was wearing a beige linen skirt which further accentuated her tanned complexion and she greeted me with a pleasant smile. *'Buon giorno, Signorina,'* she said and I returned her smile: ' *'Parliamo inglese, per favore?'* I asked and she nodded and said in perfect, if slightly accented, English: 'Yes, I can speak English, though not as well as I would like. But I am happy to say that many British and

172

American ladies come to this shop and I have many opportunities to practise the language. May I ask, did one of these ladies recommend that you visited me?'

'Yes, Signorina Fiona Robson told me that I was certain to find something I would like in your shop,' I answered as I looked around the crowded room which was stocked with racks of gowns as well as many bolts of material. 'I presume that this is your shop, signorina?'

'It is indeed. I am Sylvana Vitelli, the prioprietor of this establishment,' she said with a sweep of her hand. 'And whom do I have the honour of serving this afternoon?'

I introduced myself and Sylvana put her hand to her mouth as her brow furrowed. 'D'Argosse . . . d'Argosse . . . this name is very familiar to me. Ah, I think I have it. May I ask, have you ever made the acquaintance of Countess Marussia of Samarkand?'

Had I ever made the acquaintance of Countess Marussia of Samarkand?! Readers of my previous set of recollections [*Rosie 2: 'Young, Wild And Willing* – *Editor*] will surely need no reminder of the uninhibited orgy Lord Philip Pelham and I attended at the Countess's house in Mayfair, and I wondered just how well Signorina Sylvana knew the sensuous Countess and her escort, the charming Prince Adrian of the Netherlands.

My unasked question was soon answered by this dark, voluptuous girl who smiled at me and, as she looked directly into my eyes, said: 'On my last visit to London, the Marquis de Soveral [*the suave Portuguese chargé d'affaires in London and a great favourite in London Society* – *Editor*] escorted me to a secret party at the Countess's house in Grosvenor Square. Perhaps you have been to such a gathering, Miss d'Argosse?'

'Yes, I have had that pleasure,' I said carefully and she added boldly: 'May I take it, then, that like myself you were also fucked by either Prince Adrian or the Countess?'

173

'To be honest, I cannot exactly remember who was had by whom,' I confessed with a giggle. 'But obviously we both attended the same sort of party, even if the guests were different.'

'In that case, I know just the sort of clothes that will interest you, Signorina Rosie,' said Sylvana as she skipped to the door of the shop and turned the key in the lock. Then she pulled down the window blind, which still let plenty of light through into the shop, and went on: 'There, that will give us some privacy. Now would you excuse me a moment, I must change my dress.'

I looked blankly at her and she explained: 'I model our creations myself for my favourite clients so they can see what my clothes look like from all angles before deciding whether or not to place an order for my staff to make up the garments especially for them.'

With that she disappeared behind a red curtain into the rear of the shop. 'Please stay where you are, Signorina Rosie,' she called out brightly. 'I will ask you to join me in just a few moments.'

There was a rustling sound behind the curtain and after only a minute or so, Sylvana's hand came round the side of the curtain and beckoned me into the inner sanctum. I pulled the curtain to one side and caught my breath. She was wearing a silk *robe de nuit*, a wide sweeping garment with ruffles which was held together only by a sash around her waist. She stepped towards me and from her luscious body I could smell the exquisite aroma of an expensive perfume which she must have dabbed upon her swelling, white breasts.

'This is a nightgown I made for Fiona Robson — although she says she usually goes to bed in the nude, for Carlo is a very passionate gentleman!

'But this is such a charming robe, so sensual is it not?' she said swivelling round coquettishly.

174

'Both the robe and the model are stunning,' I replied softly and at once Sylvana tugged at the sash and untied the simple knot. The gown opened, it fell to the ground, and Sylvana stepped forward towards me in all her naked glory. I caught my breath as she stood before me, like a statue crafted by a master sculptor come magically to life. Below the mass of sultry dark hair and her pouting pretty face, beautiful full breasts stood out proudly, whilst between her perfectly proportioned thighs lay a lustrous veil of dark, silky hair which contrasted so delightfully with the snowy whiteness of her belly.

Sylvana turned on her heel and went over to bend over a small ice-box which gave me the opportunity to admire the pert, spherical *rondeurs* of her delicious bum cheeks. From the ice-box she took out a tray upon which stood a bottle of Asti Spumante and two tall glasses.

'Good heavens, do you always stop work for a drink in the middle of the day? What a splendid custom!' I said as Sylvana opened the bottle and the cork flew out with a 'pop'.

'Only on special occasions, like when entertaining new friends,' she murmured as she passed me a glass of the sparkling, fizzy wine which we clinked together before sipping at our refreshingly cold drinks. 'Now, would you like to undress and try on this robe?'

Well, to cut short this story, we finished the bottle before I undressed, but as I stood in front of the mirror I twisted round to view my bottom.

'Oh dear, I'm afraid that my backside is getting just the tiniest bit flabby,' I declared but Sylvana stepped behind me and ran her hands over my dimpled cheeks as she breathed: 'No, no, not at all, Rosie, you have a superb *derrière*. You have a gorgeous bottom which is begging to be squeezed. Oh, how smooth and so firm it is!

'There, isn't that nice?' she asked as she gently caressed my buttocks in her hands.

'Very nice indeed,' I said softly as I turned round and we stood silently for a moment facing each other, so close that our nipples were touching and then, wordlessly, we slipped into each other's arms and exchanged a huge, wet kiss. We fell back upon a small sofa and as our tongues swirled around inside the other's mouth, we each had our hand over each other's pussies, rubbing our palms against our glossy bushes.

I was particularly aroused by Sylvana's thrilling young body. She was like a sleek, pampered kitten as she arched her back in delight as I explored further between her legs and a warm, tingling feeling swept through me as the yielding lips of her cunney opened out under my gentle probes. Now I slid my hand under the firm cheeks of her delectable bum and for a short while I frigged her wrinkled little rear dimple which made her wriggle from side to side. Then I switched back to her pussey which she obviously preferred for she began to coo contentedly as I transferred my hand to her cunt, rubbing my knuckles against her sopping slit until she was breathless with excitement. I inserted one and then two fingers inside her sopping cunt and spread the lips out wide as she gurgled with delight. I rubbed harder and harder against her clitty which very soon swelled up like a little, stiff cock.

Her cuntal juices flowed like honey as I started to kiss her hard, pointed titties, licking and sucking them until they stood out like two little red bullets. I kissed her flat tummy and moved my mouth downwards to the firm curves of her pubis, slithering my lips over her dripping quim, and I tasted her tangy juices as I sucked hard on her big clitty that was projecting from between the pouting lips of her cunt, prodding it to great effect as Sylvana gasped with pleasure.

'A-h-r-e! *Magnifico, cara Rosie!*' she cried and I buried my mouth in the lavish succulent padding of pussey hair, and her love juice came gushing out as I worked my lips until my jaw ached, teasing my tongue inside the rubbery grooves of her love channel.

My hands were busy tweaking her rubbery red nipples as I placed my lips over her clitty and nibbled daintily at it before sucking up the erectile flesh into my mouth where the tip of my tongue started to explore it from all directions. Then I found the little joy button under the fold at the base of her clitty and began twirling my tongue around it. As I moved it up and down she became more and more excited and I was forced to let go of her titties and grasp her bum cheeks to maintain my oral suction. The faster I vibrated her clitty, the quicker she began to gyrate, moaning loudly and rocking her head from side to side as the juices cascaded out from between her pouting pussey lips.

Oh how wet she was! Her head was thrown back, her shoulders shaking as little quakes ran through her body whilst I lapped even quicker along the ribbed grooves of her cunney, licking up her tangy cuntal fluids which ran down like a stream and mixed with my saliva. Her pussey was now gushing love juice and each time I flicked at her clitty I felt it stiffen perceptibly, ever more eager and pulsating until with a piercing scream she exploded into a marvellous, all-embracing orgasm.

Now it was my turn to lie back, spread my legs and wait to be pleasured by Sylvana's darting tongue. She placed her pretty head against my soft blonde mount and without further ado started to lick my pussey lips which she parted with her long fingers.

She looked up at me and leaned back, her lips sticky from where she had been kissing my cunney lips and said: 'What a sweet-smelling cunt you have, Rosie. I shall give you the most exquisite licking out you have ever experienced, my dear girl.'

'I want action, not words! Finish me off with your tongue,' I pleaded and Sylvana bent forward again, her lips nuzzled against my juicy crack, teasing her tongue inside my pussey. She found my clitty and kept up a blissful rhythm of the most salacious sucking until I was so wet that I could feel my own cuntal juices dribbling down my thighs. She jabbed one, two and then three fingers inside my cunt, sliding them in and out of my pussey at breakneck speed whilst her wicked tongue lapped around my clitty.

I squeezed her head between my thighs, urging her on as I felt myself on the brink of the ultimate pleasure as waves of lust ran up and down my spine.

'Aaaah! Aaaah! You've made me come,' I panted as I spent profusely, soaking Sylvana's mouth with love juice which she greedily slurped and swallowed as I writhed from side to side into the most wonderful orgasm. However, despite the undoubted fact, as I have mentioned before in these recollections, that on the whole (please pardon the pun!) girls are far more adept at eating pussey than boys, I still prefer a thick, meaty cock in my cunt than anything else!

Be that as it may, I spent a very pleasant time with Sylvana and although I did not purchase the *robe de nuit*, I did buy a beautifully styled linen blouse and before I left, I promised to come again to Sylvana's shop for one of the exclusive fashion shows which she gave every Thursday afternoon.

I walked slowly to Otello's restaurant and looked around for young Terence. At first I thought he had not yet arrived, but then I heard him call from a table placed out on the pavement under the restaurant awning.

'Hello there, Rosie, here I am,' he cried and immediately I noticed an extraordinary change in the young man's bearing. His eyes were sparkling, his face was slightly flushed and he was possessed of a *joie de vivre* which made it plain that Father Lionel's friend had provided him with a tonic which no doctor could have prescribed!

I sat down and, after ordering a light meal of pasta and

a bottle of white wine, I prompted Terence into telling me what had happened to him inside Sophia's apartment. All must have gone well with him, for he did not demur and launched directly into an account of his visit and said: 'Oh, everything went swimmingly, Miss Rosie — and do you know, after you left me I walked up and down the Via Trippetto outside number sixty-nine for at least five minutes, very much in two minds as to whether I should keep this appointment. Luckily, I finally plucked up enough courage to ring the bell and a beautiful young blonde girl answered the door.

' "Good afternoon," I stammered hesitantly. "My name is Terence Whiter and I have an appointment with Signorina Sophia at noon."

' "Ah yes," she said in perfect English as she beckoned me inside. "Do come in, Terence, Father Lionel telephoned earlier and told me to expect you."

'I followed her into the hall and into a beautifully furnished drawing room and she asked me to sit down and make myself at home. She went on: "I'm afraid that Sophia will not be here until tonight as she is spending the day sitting for the talented American artist, Mr Jason Kelvin, who has been living in Rome since March.

' "My name is Kitty Glanville and I am also spending the summer in this wonderful city. I'm living with Sophia, who is an old friend from my days at finishing school." '

'Wait a moment, Terence,' I interrupted excitedly. 'You did say that this girl's name was Kitty Glanville?' He nodded and I clicked my fingers together and exclaimed: 'What an amazing coincidence! This shows how modern travel is making the world such a small place these days — why, I know Kitty Glanville and, come to that, her friend Sophia Visconti very well. They were both contemporaries of mine at Madame Dupont's Finishing School in Lucerne. If you are planning to see them again, you must give them my kindest regards. In fact, I'll write a letter to Kitty. She is a blonde girl, petite but very pretty and hails, if I remember rightly, from Edinburgh.'

'Yes, you've described her perfectly, and she does have a very pleasant light Scottish accent,' gasped Terence. 'As well as a wonderfully generous nature, as I found out an hour or so ago.'

The waiter brought us our wine and Terence continued his story which I was now certain would have a happy ending, for whilst at Madame Dupont's establishment, both Kitty and Sophia were known as two randy girls who enjoyed nothing better than bedroom romps with Pierre, Madame Dupont's handsome young son [see 'Rosie 1: Her Intimate Diaries' – Editor]. So I listened avidly as he continued:

' "Yes, Father Lionel telephoned this morning and informed us of your problem," she said sweetly, and I must have blushed because she added hastily: "Oh, do not be ashamed, Terence. Virginity is a condition easily cured between the ages of sixteen and twenty-five. After that, it can be a little more difficult to cure."

'I smiled glassily at this remark and she returned my smile, showing pearly white teeth which sparkled in the bright, midday sunlight that poured through the large windows. Kitty was dressed in a loose white gown with short sleeves and I noticed that her feet were bare as she walked towards me. She took hold of my hand and said softly: "I was upstairs having a siesta when you called – would you like to join me?"

' "Yes please," I croaked as she took my hand and guided me upstairs into her bedroom.

'By the window of her bedroom stood an artist's easel and she said to me as she cast a critical eye over my body: "I also paint, although I doubt if I'll ever be as famous as Jason Kelvin. Would you mind modelling for me, Terence, whilst I make a quick charcoal sketch?"

' "Not in the slightest," I replied and honestly, Rosie, I had no idea what Kitty was about to suggest. "Where would you like me to stand?"

'She considered this question for a few moments and then replied: "I think you'd look best lying down on the bed."

' "Very well," I said, and took off my jacket and was about to take up a position when she said with a coy giggle: "Oh, but you'll have to take off all your clothes for me to make a proper sketch."

' "All my clothes?" I echoed, and Kitty must have sensed my modesty because she added encouragingly: "Look, if it makes you feel any easier, I'll take my clothes off, too. It's so warm today that I'll be far more comfortable working in the nude."

'Like in a dream, I sat down on a chair and took off my shoes and socks. Then I took off my trousers and my shirt, but my hands trembled as I turned around to face the wall and tugged down my drawers. "What a nice bum you have, Terence," she said with what sounded like genuine admiration in her voice. "Now turn round, there's absolutely no need for such a handsome boy like you to be shy."

'I obeyed and she told me to lie on the bed with my hands behind my head and my legs slightly apart. Then she gave me a luscious smile and ran the tip of her tongue over her top lip as she unhooked the buttons on her dress and, in one quick movement, pulled it over her head. My heart began to beat nineteen to the dozen as I looked at her beautiful body silhouetted against the light. Kitty's uptilted bare breasts bounced invitingly as she walked towards me, though I could hardly tear my eyes away from the thick fleece of blonde pussey hair at the base of her flat tummy. My cock swelled up straight away and by the time she had taken the three steps necessary to reach me, my shaft was sticking high up in the air, although my hands were still

181

locked together behind my head. She ruffled my hair with her fingers and murmured: "Before we begin work, let's get to know each other a little more. I need to capture your very essence before I can produce anything on canvas." '

'I can imagine what essence she captured and I'll wager it didn't take very long for you to produce it,' I said roguishly, and Terence gave a little chuckle as he said: 'It didn't take very long at all. Kitty kissed me and in an instant her tongue was in my mouth, probing and rousing as my hands caressed her taut nipples, squeezing the succulent globes of her breasts whilst she clasped my pulsating prick and jerked her hand up and down my throbbing shaft. Seconds later a shuddering orgasm of pleasure ran through my body and a miniature fountain of spunk gushed out of my cock and ran down over her fingers.

' "Oh dear, we can't have you finishing before we've really begun, can we now?" she murmured and she pushed me down on the bed and began to stroke my still quivering cock with her skilful fingers. Surprisingly quickly, my shaft soon regained its former thickness and then Kitty dipped her tousled blonde head between my legs and kissed my knob. Instinctively, I heaved my hips upwards to slide my cock between her lips.

'Oh, how wonderful it was when her tongue circled my shaft and swirled around my helmet. I felt my balls hardening and shouted that I was going to come again, and so she opened her mouth and climbed on top of me with her knees on either side of my hips. She pulled open her pussey lips with her fingers and rubbed her cunney back and forth across the tip of my knob, which really drove me wild for I knew the moment of truth was finally at hand. Then, sure enough, I crossed the Rubicon as Kitty sat down on my thick prick, and somehow she managed to tighten her cunney to hold my cock in place whilst she rocked backwards and forwards upon it. She rode me hard, sliding her juicy love channel up and down my delighted prick and then she screamed out as now she began to climax. This excited me so much that I soon felt the white froth spurting upwards from my balls.

' "Yes, yes, shoot your spunk!" she yelled with joy as the hot, creamy jism flooded into her, and I pumped out my sticky seed into her dark, wet cunney as her own love juices flowed over my twitching tool. We lay there for a while, panting with exhaustion and I was in the very seventh heaven of delight, though it grieved me to think of what I had been missing!'

Terence's voice trailed off as the waiter bustled up to our table with two large bowls of *Pasta con cacio pepe*. I twirled the twists of spaghetti round my fork and said: 'May I offer my congratulations, Terence. Most people would agree that one's first fuck is a traumatic experience and I am truly delighted that your first adventure went so well. First love can be idyllic or, frankly, an absolute disaster. I hope you won't mind my saying so, but you were fortunate to be accompanied on your first journey along the highway of sensuous pleasures by an uncomplicated yet sophisticated girl who was happy to allay any fears you may have entertained about making love to her.'

Terence nodded his head vigorously. 'If truth be told, it would be more accurate to state that Kitty made love to me,' he agreed as he took a large mouthful of spaghetti. 'M'mm, this is very good, Rosie. What herbs have been mixed in with the pasta?'

'Only black pepper and cheese,' I said, and we both tucked in with relish and finished our tasty meal. 'But tell me, now, do I presume we have now come to the end of your first sexual foray?'

'Actually, no. After we had rested for a while, I was surprised to discover that my cock could still rise to the occasion when Kitty squeezed my limp shaft inside her fist.

"I don't think I can do any more," I whispered to her, but she winked at me and said gaily: "What, a strapping young lad like you! I'll bet you can still get a hard-on!"

'Sure enough, I soon felt the first stirrings of an erection as she slowly rubbed my stiffening shaft. Gently, she stroked the underside, allowing her fingers to trace a path around and underneath my balls which made my shaft as hard as rock, and she leaned forward and gave my knob a loving suck whilst she diddled her own pussey, slicking her finger between her sticky love lips.

' "I think you're more than ready for a final fling," she said huskily as she rolled over onto her back and motioned for me to scramble up in front of her. I was on my knees in double quick time, my knob just inches away from the gaping lips of Kitty's cunt which were pouting redly through the moist, silky hairs of her pussey bush. I brought my straining shaft and fairly ran it through the sopping depths of her juicy cunney until my ballsack swished against Kitty's bottom.

' "Lie still for a moment," she commanded, and her cuntal muscles squeezed my cock so deliciously that I almost swooned with ecstasy. Then she heaved up her bum and I responded with a mighty shove of my own and we began heaving to and fro. It crossed my mind that the waves of blissful pleasure which were coursing through my veins were those of an exciting fuck, and I knew that nothing I had ever known or would experience in the future could ever match these unique delights.

'I looked down and saw my prick working in and out of her sopping love sheath and our movements were now locked into a furious rhythm. With a choking cry Kitty panted: "Come on, Terry, give my cunt a good fucking with that luscious young cock! Faster, faster, keep thrusting! I know you have lots of lovely jism boiling in your balls!" and she clawed my back as she writhed under me with the force of her approaching orgasm. We fucked at an even greater speed, until, with a tiny wail, she slumped backwards, her thighs clenched around my waist as her body shook in a rapidly drawn-out series of spasms. Her cunney squeezed my cock even more tightly and I exploded into her, shooting off a further flood of hot spunk into her saturated love channel and draining my prick so completely that it shrivelled into limpness even before I had taken it out of her love-hole.'

He sighed and closed his eyes and a slow smile creased its way across his face as he relived these marvellous, heart-stopping moments. Then as an after-thought he added: 'Of course, there was not time for Kitty to begin sketching me, but I have promised to go to her apartment tomorrow morning and she will begin work then.'

Terence's tale had stirred my own imagination, although I said nothing until we had finished our meal with some fresh fruit and coffee. I gave him some money to pay the bill and he left a lavish gratuity for the waiter, who bowed us out of the restaurant. Then we strolled back to where Carlo Nettolone's chauffeur was waiting for us — and in the car, I leaned over and whispered in his ear: 'Terence, I thoroughly enjoyed hearing the stirring story of your first fuck. Now, unless you have any objection, I want you to come back to my room here and now and let us see whether your next fuck will be just as ecstatic as your first!'

No-one appeared to be at home, except a manservant who opened the front door for us so, without further ado, we raced upstairs and once safely in my bedroom I hoisted up my skirt to take off my suspenders. Terence must also have been fired by the prospect of further erotic adventures because before I knew it the cheeky young scamp's hands had beaten mine and my suspenders were unhooked and my knickers were being pulled down.

We tumbled crazily onto the bed, tearing at each other's clothes in a lustful frenzy. I ripped open his trousers and grabbed hold of his thick, naked cock which sprang up to greet me. I delicately fingered the bulbous helmet and found out that it was already wet with jism. So, smacking my lips, I lapped up his sweet love juice whilst we continued to throw off our clothes and we were both stark naked.

Terence groaned with delight as I worked on his grand, hard cock, running my teeth gently against the ribbed nodules of his prick. Then I sucked in his ruby-mushroomed knob and swirled my tongue over the dome, washing the sensitive, uncapped crown whilst my hands fondled his heavy balls. This excited me so much that I opened my mouth and whispered fiercely: 'I must have this lovely cock inside me!' and I leaped on top of him and jammed his thick prick inside my juicy honeypot as I sat with my bare bum facing him.

Young Terence may have been inexperienced but his instincts led him firmly on the right road, for now he grasped my bum cheeks with both hands and started to squeeze them rhythmically as I pushed up and down, contracting my powerful pussey muscles with every movement so as to grip every inch of his gorgeous truncheon inside my cunt. I reached between his legs and toyed with his bollocks as I ran my fingers back along to his hairy arse and forward again to his balls, scraping the pink, wrinkled sack with my fingernails as he writhed in ecstasy underneath me.

He began to jerk his hips up and down so fast as I continued to ride him that I soon felt the tide of an approaching orgasm approach me. We moved together in perfect unison as the hard ball of his knob rubbed against my clitty and the first ripples of orgasm crackled through my veins. Flames of fire lashed through me as my clitty now throbbed with excitement, and I shrieked out loud as my cunney went into wild spasms and Terence's slim, youthful frame went rigid and his prick twitched madly before sending a torrent of warm, creamy spunk right up inside me, just as my own climax exploded into a mass of shooting stars and I ascended the highest peaks of pleasure. Our mutual emissions were so copious that my cunney overflowed with jism, and our love liquids ran down his cock and over his balls whilst we lay quivering with passion until the end of this glorious mutual spend.

Oblivious to everything but each other, we lay naked in each other's arms and fell into a light but refreshing sleep, from which we were woken by an insistent knocking on the door. I scrambled inside the covers whilst Terence leaped out of bed and slipped on his dressing gown before calling out: 'Come in.'

The door opened and the lithe figure of Fiona Robson stood framed in the doorway. 'Hello there, you lovebirds,' she drawled with a wide smile upon her attractive face. 'I am truly sorry to interrupt your canoodling, but a telegraph message has just arrived for Rosie from London.'

I sat up in bed and Fiona came up and passed the telegram to me. I dislike telegrams as I always have awful forebodings that they will contain bad news. However, in this case my fears were quite unfounded as the cable came from none other than Count Gewirtz, Terence's erstwhile host at Broadbridge Heath, where the incidents which caused Terence and Lord Philip Pelham to go into temporary voluntary exile took place.

The message read: DELIGHTED TO REPORT THAT H.M. HAS FORGIVEN AND FORGOTTEN WHAT HAPPENED AT BROADBRIDGE AND INSISTS WE ALL JOIN HIM AND MRS K IN BIARRITZ. DETAILED LETTER TO FOLLOW.

'Well, I'm glad to know that your randy old King doesn't bear grudges,' commented Fiona when I showed her the message.

187

'So am I,' chipped in Terence. 'But who the heck is Mrs K?'

Fiona and I exchanged glances and I cleared my throat and explained: 'The Count is referring to Alice Keppel. She's been the King's favourite mistress for some ten years now, and even goes to stay with him for a month or so every Easter in Biarritz.'

This little revelation shocked Terence. 'Good grief, doesn't her husband mind?' he said, and I shook my head and replied: 'He makes his own arrangements elsewhere, no doubt, and I don't believe that the Queen is too bothered by her, for Mrs Keppel is one of the few people who can deal with His Majesty's temper, which is becoming shorter by the day, as you yourself can testify.'

Fiona winked at me and said: 'Well now, Terence, I'm sure your prick is not suffering from that malady, especially since your visit to Father Lionel's friend, and now your little recreation with Rosie.'

Her hands deftly unknotted the sash of his robe and she pulled the garment off his shoulders. The handsome youth stood naked before her and Fiona weighed his heavy, semi-erect shaft in her hand and added: 'What a fine, meaty cock! Tell me, have you two been engaged in a game that only two can play, or may I join in?'

Terence didn't know how to reply, but I said cheerfully to our pretty hostess: 'Oh, I'm sure we can fit you in somehow!'

Fiona swiftly undressed and first bared her rounded white breasts, but Terence's cock swelled up and stood proudly erect when she divested herself of her knickers and exposed her luxuriant thatch of jet black pussey hair and superbly chiselled crack with its pouting red lips. She dropped to her knees and cupped his balls in her hand as she gulped his uncapped helmet into her mouth, softly biting it and tickling it with the tip of her tongue. Then she thrust the whole of the throbbing shaft between her lips and by her palating and sucking soon brought him to the brink of a spend.

Then she eased his pulsing prick from her mouth and turned her face to me and said: 'Ah, Rosie, would you diddle my pussey whilst I suck off young Terence? And then I'll get my dildo and we can play some more jolly games.'

TO BE CONTINUED